"THE GODFATHER OF HISTORICAL NOVELISTS."
—*Los Angeles Times*

John Jakes
HEAVEN AND HELL

"WONDERFUL . . . HIS BENT FOR HISTORICAL ACCURACY IS UNMATCHED IN COMMERCIAL FICTION. . . . WE FEEL TRANSFERRED INTO ANOTHER PERIOD OF AMERICAN HISTORY. . . . IT CAN BE READ ALONE, BUT IF YOU'VE READ *NORTH AND SOUTH* AND *LOVE AND WAR*, YOU'RE GOING TO LOVE *HEAVEN AND HELL*."
—*San Francisco Chronicle*

"HE SHOWS YOU GEORGE ARMSTRONG CUSTER, ANDREW JOHNSON, BUFFALO BILL CODY, AND A VAST ARRAY OF OTHER HISTORICAL FIGURES WHOSE CONTENDING AMBITIONS CONTROL THE EVENTS . . . BUT HE ALSO SHOWS YOU WHAT PEOPLE WORE, WHAT THEY READ, AND WHAT THEY DRANK AND ATE. . . . WHAT YOU GET IS THE FEELING THAT THIS IS *LIFE*. THAT'S ART."
—*Sun Times* (Chicago)

"HIS PORTRAIT OF A DIVIDED, DEMORALIZED NATION, INFLAMED WITH HATRED . . . EMERGES AS AN ENJOYABLE WORK."
—*The New York Times*

"THOSE WHO CHERISH THE MAINS OF SOUTH CAROLINA AND THE HAZARDS OF PENNSYLVANIA WILL REJOICE . . . THERE'S ENOUGH ACTION, ROMANCE AND EXCITEMENT IN THESE PAGES TO BRING THE TRILOGY TO A WONDERFUL CONCLUSION, ONE THAT CERTIFIES JAKES'S POSITION AS A POPULAR STORYTELLER OF THE FIRST RANK."
—*The Chattanooga Times*

"AN ENGROSSING STUDY . . . WEAVING FACT AND FICTION TOGETHER INTO AN ENTERTAINING LESSON IN AMERICAN HISTORY."
—*The Houston Post*

"SPLENDID READING . . . IDEALISM AND CORRUPTION, TENDERNESS AND BRUTALITY, INNOCENCE AND INSANITY all figure in the narrative, a highly colored amalgam of heaven and hell."
—*Publishers Weekly*

"A HEARTWARMING CONCLUSION TO A STORY THAT YOU DON'T WANT TO SEE END."
—*The State* (Columbia, SC)

Historical Novels by John Jakes

Under the pseudonym Jay Scotland

I, Barbarian (1959)
Strike the Black Flag (1961)
Sir Scoundrel (1962)
The Veils of Salome (1962)
Arena (1963)
Traitor's Legion (1963)

The Kent Family Chronicles

The Bastard (1974)
The Rebels (1975)
The Seekers (1975)
The Furies (1976)
The Titans (1976)
The Warriors (1977)
The Lawless (1978)
The Americans (1980)

The North and South Trilogy

North and South (1982)
Love and War (1984)
Heaven and Hell (1987)

HEAVEN
AND
HELL

John Jakes

A DELL BOOK

Published by
Dell Publishing
a division of
The Bantam Doubleday Dell
Publishing Group, Inc.
666 Fifth Avenue
New York, New York 10103

The musical theme attributed to one of the characters in this novel was
composed by Bill Conti for the main title of the David L. Wolper
television production of *North and South*. © 1985 by Warner Bros.
Music. It is reproduced by permission of the composer and the copyright
owner, whose generous cooperation is hereby acknowledged with thanks.

For information address: Harcourt Brace Jovanovich, Publishers,
Orlando, Florida.

The trademark Dell ® is registered in the U.S. Patent and Trademark
Office.

ISBN: 0-440-20170-5

Reprinted by arrangement with Harcourt Brace Jovanovich, Publishers
Printed in the United States of America
Published simultaneously in Canada

October 1988

10 9 8 7 6 5 4 3 2 1

KRI

For
all my friends
at HBJ

With the exception of historical figures, all characters in this novel are fictitious, and any resemblance to living persons, present or past, is coincidental.

*The loss of heaven
is the greatest
pain in hell.*

CALDERÓN DE LA BARCA

HEAVEN
AND
HELL

PROLOGUE:
THE GRAND REVIEW
1865

. . . saying, Peace, peace; when there is no peace.

JEREMIAH 6:14, 8:11

Rain fell on Washington through the night. Shortly before daybreak on May twenty-third, a Tuesday, George Hazard woke in his suite at Willard's Hotel. He rested a hand on the warm shoulder of his wife, Constance. He listened.

No more rain.

That absence of sound was a good omen for this day of celebration. A new era began this morning, an era of peace, with the Union saved.

Why, then, did he feel a sense of impending misfortune?

George slipped out of bed. His flannel nightshirt bobbed around his hairy calves as he stole from the room. George was forty-one now, a stocky, strong-shouldered man whose West Point classmates had nicknamed him Stump because of his build and his less-than-average height. Gray slashed his dark hair and the neat beard he'd kept, as many had, to show he had served in the army.

He padded into the parlor, which was strewn with newspapers and periodicals he'd been too tired to pick up last night. He began to gather them and put them in a pile, taking care to be as quiet as possible. In the second and third bedrooms, his children were asleep. William Hazard III had turned sixteen in January. Patricia would be that age by the end of the year. George's younger brother, Billy, and his wife, Brett, occupied a fourth bedroom. Billy would march in today's parade, but he'd gotten permission to spend the night away from the engineers' camp at Fort Berry.

The papers and periodicals seemed to taunt George for his sense of foreboding. The *New York Times,* the *Tribune,* the *Washington Star,* the most recent issue of the *Army and Navy Journal* all sounded the same triumphant note. As he created the neat pile on a side table, the phrases leaped up:

> *Though our gigantic war is but a few days over, we have already begun the disbandment of the great Army of the Union . . .*
>
> *They crushed the Rebellion, saved the Union, and won for themselves, and for us, a country . . .*
>
> *The War Department has ordered to be printed six hundred thousand blank discharges on parchment paper . . .*
>
> *Our self-reliant republic disbands its armies, sends home its faithful soldiers, closes its recruiting tents, stops its contracts for material, and prepares to abandon the gloomy path of war for the broad and shining highway of peace . . .*

Today and tomorrow were to be celebrations of that: a Grand Review of Grant's Army of the Potomac and Uncle Billy Sherman's roughneck Army of the West. Grant's men would march today; Sherman's coarser, tougher troops, tomorrow. Sherman's Westerners sneered at Grant's Easterners as "paper collars." Perhaps the Westerners would parade the cows and goats, mules and fighting cocks they'd brought to their camps along the Potomac.

Not all of the men who went to war would march. Some would lie forever hidden from loved ones, like George's dearest friend, Orry. George and Orry had met as plebes at West Point in 1842. They had soldiered together in Mexico, and had preserved their friendship even after Fort Sumter surrendered and their separate loyalties took them to different sides in the conflict. But then, in the closing days, Orry met death at Petersburg. Not in battle; he fell victim to the stupid, needless, vengeful bullet of a wounded Union soldier he was trying to help.

Some of the young men made old by the war still tramped the roads of the South, going home to poverty and a land wasted by hunger and the fires of conquering battalions. Some still rode northbound trains, maimed in body and spirit by their time in the sinks that passed for rebel prisons. Some from the Confederacy had vanished into Mexico, into the army of the khedive of Egypt, or to the West, trying to forget the invisible wounds they bore. Orry's young cousin Charles had chosen the third path.

Others had ended the war steeped in ignominy. Chief among them was Jeff Davis, run to earth near Irwinville, Georgia. Many Northern papers said he'd tried to elude capture by wearing a dress. Whatever the truth, for certain elements in the North prison wasn't enough for Davis. They wanted a hang rope.

George lit one of his expensive Cuban cigars and crossed to the windows overlooking Pennsylvania Avenue. The suite offered a fine view of the day's parade route, but he had special tickets for a reviewing stand directly across from the President's. With care, he raised a window.

The sky was cloudless. He leaned out to let the cigar smoke blow away and noticed all the patriotic bunting on the three- and four-story buildings fronting the avenue. Brighter decorations were at last replacing the funeral crepe that had hung everywhere after Lincoln's murder.

A scarlet band of light above the Potomac River basin marked the horizon. Vehicles, horsemen, and pedestrians were beginning to move on the muddy avenue below. George watched a black family—parents, five children—hurry in the direction of President's Park. They had more than the end of the war to celebrate. They had the Thirteenth Amendment, forever abolishing slavery; the states had only to ratify it to make it law.

A clearing sky, a display of red, white, and blue, no more rain—with such favorable portents, why did his feeling of foreboding persist?

It was the families, he decided, the Mains and the Hazards. They had survived the war, but they were mangled. Virgilia, his sister, was lost to the rest of the family, self-exiled by her own extremism. It was particularly saddening because Virgilia was right here in Washington, although George didn't know where she lived.

Then there was his older brother, Stanley, an incompetent man who had piled up an unconscionable amount of money through war profiteering. Despite his success—or perhaps because of it—Stanley was a drunkard.

Matters were no better for the Mains. Orry's sister Ashton had vanished out in the West after being involved in an unsuccessful plot to overthrow and replace the Davis government with one that was more extreme. Orry's brother, Cooper, who had worked in Liverpool for the Confederate Navy Department, had lost his only son, Judah, when their homebound ship was sunk off Fort Fisher by a Union blockade squadron.

And there was his best friend's widow, Madeline, facing the struggle to rebuild her life and her burned-out plantation on the Ashley River, near Charleston. George had given her a letter of credit for forty thousand dollars, drawn on the bank in which he owned a majority interest. He'd hoped she would ask for more; most of the initial sum was needed for interest on two mortgages and to pay federal taxes and prevent confiscation of the property by Treasury agents already invading the South. But Madeline had not asked, and it worried him.

Even at this early hour, the horse-and-wagon traffic on the avenue was heavy. It was a momentous day and, if he could believe the sky and the soft breeze, it would be a beautiful one. Then why, even after isolating his anxieties about the two families, could he not banish the feeling of impending trouble?

The Hazards ate a quick breakfast. Brett looked particularly happy and excited, George thought with a certain envy. In a few weeks, Billy planned to resign his commission. Then the two of them would board a ship for San Francisco. They'd never seen California, but descriptions of the climate, the country, and its opportunities attracted them. Billy wanted to start his own civil engineering firm. Like his friend Charles Main, with whom he'd attended West Point—both inspired by the example of George and Orry—he wanted to go far from the scarred fields where American had fought American.

The couple needed to travel soon. Brett was carrying their first child. Billy had told this to George privately; decency dictated that a pregnancy never be discussed, even by family members. When a woman neared her term and her stomach bulged, people pretended not to notice. If a second child arrived, parents often told their firstborn that the doctor brought the baby in a bottle. George and Constance observed most of the proprieties, even many that were silly, but they had never stooped to the bottle story.

The family reached the special reviewing section by eight-fifteen. They took seats among reporters, congressmen, Supreme Court justices, senior army and navy officers. To their left, the avenue jogged around the Treasury Building at Fifteenth Street; the jog hid the long rise of the street up to the Capitol.

To their right, for blocks into the distance, people jammed behind barricades, hung from windows and roof peaks, sat on sagging tree limbs. Directly opposite stood the covered pavilion for President Johnson's party, which would include Generals Grant and Sheridan and Stanley Hazard's employer, Secretary of War Stanton. Along the pavilion's front roof line, among bunting swags and evergreen sprays, hung banners painted with the names of Union victories: ATLANTA and ANTIETAM, GETTYSBURG and SPOTSYLVANIA, and more.

By quarter to nine there was still no sign of the President. The blunt-featured Chief Executive sailed in a sea of gossip these days. People said he lacked tact, drank heavily. And he was common—well, that was true. Johnson, a tailor, later senator, was the self-educated son of a Tennessee tavern porter, but he did not have the skills that had enabled Lincoln to turn his rustic background into a personal advantage. George had met Johnson. He found him a brusque, opinionated man with an almost religious reverence for the Constitution. That alone would put him at odds with the Radical Republicans, who wanted to expand interpretation of the Constitution to suit their vision of society.

George agreed with many Radical positions, including equal rights and the franchise for eligible males of both races. But frequently he found Radical motives and tactics repugnant. Many of the Radicals made no secret of their intent to use black voters to make the Republicans the majority party, upsetting the traditional Democratic dominance of the country. The Radicals displayed a vicious animosity toward those they had conquered, as well as any others they deemed ideologically impure.

President Johnson and the Radicals were locked in an increasingly vindictive struggle for control of reconstruction of the Union. It was not a new quarrel. In 1862, Lincoln had proposed his Louisiana Plan, later amplifying it to allow for readmission of any seceded state in which a "tangible nucleus" of voters—only ten percent of those qualified to vote in 1860—took a loyalty oath and organized a pro-Union government.

In July of 1864, the Radical Republicans had retaliated with a bill written by Senator Ben Wade, of Ohio, and Representative Henry Davis, of Maryland. It outlined a much harsher reconstruction plan, which included a provision for military rule of the defeated Confederacy. The bill fixed control of reconstruction in the Congress. Early in 1865, Tennessee had formed a government under the Lincoln plan, headed by a Whig Unionist named Brownlow. The Radicals in Congress refused to seat elected representatives of that government.

Andrew Johnson had accused Jefferson Davis of acting to "inspire" and "procure" the assassination at Ford's Theatre. He made the obligatory harsh statements about the South, but he also insisted that he would carry out Lincoln's moderate program. Lately, George had heard that Johnson intended to implement the program by means of executive orders during the summer and fall. Since Congress had adjourned and was not scheduled to reconvene until late in the year, and since Johnson certainly wouldn't call a special session, the Radicals would be thwarted.

So the political wind carried word of coming Radical reprisals. One of George's missions in Washington was to speak to a powerful Pennsylvania politician, to state his views on the situation. He donated enough to the party each year to feel entitled to do so. He might even do some good.

"Papa, there's Aunt Isabel," said Patricia from behind him.

George saw Stanley's wife waving from the presidential stand. He grimaced and returned the wave. "She wanted us to be sure and see her."

Brett smiled. Constance patted his hand. "Now, George, don't be spiteful. You wouldn't trade places with Stanley."

George shrugged and continued scanning the crowd on his side of the street, searching for the congressman from his state whom he wanted to corner. While he was occupied, Constance reached into her reticule for a piece of hard candy. Her red hair shone where it curled from beneath a fashionable straw bonnet. She still possessed a pale Irish loveliness, but she'd gained thirty pounds since her marriage, at the end of the Mexican War. George said he didn't mind; he considered the weight a sign of contentment.

Promptly at nine, a cannon boomed, off by the Capitol. In a few minutes, the Hazards heard a distant brass band playing "When Johnny Comes Marching Home." Then they heard unseen thousands cheering parade units beyond the jog in the avenue. Soon the first marchers rounded the corner by the Treasury, and everyone leaped up to clap and hurrah.

Scholarly General George Meade led the parade, riding to the presidential pavilion amid an ovation. Small boys hanging from the trees behind it leaned out to clap and nearly fell. Meade saluted the dignitaries with his saber—neither Grant nor Johnson had yet arrived—then handed his horse to a corporal and went to sit with them.

Women cheered, men wept openly, a chorus of young schoolgirls sang and showered the street with bouquets and nose-gays. The sun struck white fire from the alabaster of the Capitol dome as General Wesley Merritt led the Third Division into sight. The regular commander, Little Phil Sheridan, was already en route to duty on the Gulf of Mexico. When the Third appeared, even William, who was afflicted with adolescent disdain for nearly everything, jumped up and whistled and clapped.

Sixteen abreast in a column of platoons, sabers flashing in the sunshine, Sheridan's cavalry passed. The troopers had a trim, freshly barbered look and showed few signs of war-weariness. Many of them had stuck small bunches of daisies or violets into the muzzles of the carbines carried behind them on shoulder slings.

Each rank dipped its steel to the Chief Executive, who had finally entered the pavilion with General Grant, looking apologetic. George heard a woman several rows behind wonder aloud whether Johnson was already drunk.

Dust clouds rose. The smell of horse droppings ripened. Then, from Fifteenth Street, George heard a chant. "Custer! Custer! *Custer! . . .*"

And there he came, on his fine high-stepping bay, Don Juan: the "Boy General"—shoulder-length ringlets, yellow with a reddish patina, flushed face, scarlet neckerchief, golden spurs, broad-brimmed hat doffed to acknowledge the chanting of his name. Few Union officers had so captured the fancy of public and press. George Armstrong Custer had been last in his class at West Point, a brigadier at twenty-three, a major general at twenty-four. Twelve horses had been shot from under him. He was fearless or reckless, depending on your view. It was said that he wanted to be president after Ulysses Grant ran for the office. If he did want that—if the famed "Custer's luck" stayed with him and the public didn't forget him—he'd probably get what he wanted.

The Boy General led his troop of red-scarfed cavalrymen while his regimental band blared "Garry Owen." The schoolgirls surged up, ready to sing again. They threw flowers. Near the presidential stand, Custer stretched out his gauntlet to catch one. The sudden move spooked the bay. It bolted.

George glimpsed Custer's furious face as the bay raced toward Seventeenth. When Custer regained control of Don Juan, it was impossible for him to turn back against the tide of men and horses to salute Johnson. Enraged, he rode on.

No Custer's luck this morning, George thought, lighting a cigar. The road of ambition was not smooth. Thank God he himself had no designs on high office.

According to his engraved program, it would be a while before the engineers appeared. He excused himself to search again for the politician he hoped to find in the crowd.

He did find him, holding forth among the trees behind the special stand. Congressman Thaddeus Stevens, Republican of Lancaster and perhaps the foremost of the Radicals, was over seventy but still had an aura of craggy power. Neither a clubfoot nor an obvious and ugly dark-brown wig could diminish it. He wore neither beard nor mustache, letting his stern features show clearly.

He finished his conversation, and his two admirers tipped their hats and walked away. George stepped up, extending his hand. "Hello, Thad."

"George. Splendid to see you. I'd heard you were out of uniform."

"And back at Lehigh Station, managing the Hazard works. Do you have a moment? I'd like to speak to you as one Republican to another."

"Surely," Stevens said. A curtain dropped over his dark blue eyes. George had seen this happen before with the eyes of politicians put on guard.

"I just want to say that I'm in favor of giving Mr. Johnson's program a chance."

Stevens pursed his lips. "I understand the reason for your concern. I know you have friends down in Carolina."

God, the man had a way of setting you off with his righteousness. George wished he was five inches taller, so he wouldn't have to look up. "Yes, that's right. My best friend's people; my friend didn't survive the war. I must say in defense of the family that I don't consider them aristocrats. Or criminals—"

"They are both if they held blacks in bondage."

"Thad, please let me finish."

"Yes, certainly." Stevens was no longer friendly.

"A few years ago, I believed that overzealous politicians on both sides had provoked the war, unnecessarily. Year after year, I rethought the question, and I decided I was wrong. Terrible as it was, the war had to be fought. Gradual peaceful emancipation would never have worked. Those with vested interests in slavery would have kept it going."

"Quite right. With their cooperation and encouragement, the blackbirders imported and sold slaves from Cuba and the Indies long after Congress outlawed the trade in 1807."

"I'm more interested in this moment. The war's over, and there must never be another one. The cost to life and property is too high. War defeats every attempt at material progress."

"Ah, there it is," Stevens said with a frosty smile. "The businessman's new creed. I am well aware of this tide of economic pacifism in the North. I'll have nothing to do with it."

George bristled. "Why not? Aren't you supposed to represent your Republican constituents?"

"Represent, yes. Obey, no. My conscience is my sole guide." He laid a hand on George's shoulder and gazed down; the mere act of inclining his head was somehow condescending. "I don't want to be rude, George. I know you donate heavily to the state and national organizations. I'm aware of your fine war record. Unfortunately, none of that changes my view about the Southern slavocracy. Those who belong to that class, and all who support them, are traitors to our nation. They presently reside not in sovereign states, but in conquered provinces. They deserve full punishment."

In the eyes beneath the overhanging brows, George saw the light of true belief, holy war.

Cynics often cited sordid reasons for that fanaticism. They linked Stevens's championship of Negro rights with his housekeeper in Lancaster and Washington, Mrs. Lydia Smith, a handsome widow, and a mulatto. They linked the burning of his iron works in Chambersburg by Jubal Early's soldiers with his hatred of all things Southern. George didn't entirely believe the explanations; he considered Stevens an honest idealist, though an extreme one. It had never surprised him that Stevens and his sister Virgilia Hazard were close friends.

Still, the congressman by no means represented all of Republican opinion. Again sharply, George said, "I thought the executive branch was in charge of reconstructing the South."

"No, sir. That's the prerogative of the Congress. Mr. Johnson was a fool to announce his intention to issue executive orders. Doing so has generated great enmity among my colleagues, and you may be assured that when we reconvene, we will undo his mischief. Congress will not have its rights usurped." Stevens rapped the ferrule of his cane on the ground. "I will not have it."

"But Johnson is only doing what Abraham Lincoln—"

"Mr. Lincoln is dead," Stevens said before he could finish.

Reddening, George said, "All right, then. What program would you enact?"

"A complete reconstruction of Southern institutions and manners by means of occupation, confiscation, and the purging fire of law. Such a program may startle feeble minds and shake weak nerves but it is necessary and justified." George grew even redder. "To be more specific, I want harsh penalties for traitors who held high office. I'm not content that Jeff Davis be held in irons at Fortress Monroe. I want him executed. I want amnesty denied to any man who left the Army or Navy to serve the rebellion." Unhappily, George thought of Charles. "And I insist on equal rights, full citizenship for all Negroes. I demand the franchise for every eligible black male."

"For that, they'll throw rocks at you even in Pennsylvania. White people just don't believe blacks are their equals. That may be wrong—and I think it is—but it's also reality. Your scheme won't work."

"Justice won't work, George? Equality won't work? I don't care. Those are my beliefs, I'll fight for them. In matters of moral principle, there can be no compromise."

"Damn it, I refuse to accept that. And a lot of other Northerners feel the same way about—"

But the congressman was gone, to see three new admirers.

The battalion from the Corps of Engineers, Army of the Potomac, swung down Pennsylvania Avenue toward the presidential pavilion. Eight companies marched, smartly outfitted in new uniforms, which had replaced the soiled, ragged ones worn during the last days of the Virginia campaign. On the belts of half the marchers swung short spades, emblems of their dangerous field duty—bridge building, road repair—often done under enemy fire they were too busy to return.

Marching with them in the hot sun, neatly bearded, the pain of his healing chest wound almost gone, Billy Hazard strode along with pride and vigor. He glanced toward the stand where his family should be sitting. Yes, he saw his wife's lovely, luminous face as she waved. Then he noticed his brother and nearly lost the cadence. George looked abstracted, grim.

The brass band blared, sweeping the engineers past the special stands through a rain of flowers.

Constance, too, saw something amiss. After Billy went by, she asked George about it.

"Oh, I finally found Thad Stevens. That's all."

"That isn't all. I can see it. Tell me."

George gazed at his wife, weighed down again by that feeling of hovering disaster. The premonition was not directly related to Stevens, yet he was a part of the tapestry.

A similar feeling had come over George in April of 1861, when he watched a house in Lehigh Station burn to the ground. He had stared at the flames and visualized the nation afire, and he had feared the future. It had not been an idle fear. He'd lost Orry, and the Mains had lost the great house at Mont Royal, and the war had cost hundreds of thousands of lives and nearly destroyed the bonds between the families. This foreboding was much like that earlier one.

He tried to minimize it to Constance, shrugging. "I expressed my views, and he put them down, pretty viciously. He wants congressional control of reconstruction and he wants blood from the South." George didn't mean to grow emotional, but he did. "Stevens is willing to go to war with Mr. Johnson to get what he wants. And I thought it was time to bind up the Union. God knows our family's suffered and bled enough. Orry's, too."

Constance sighed, searching for some way to ease his unhappiness. With a forced smile on her plump face, she said, "Dearest, it's only politics, after all—"

"No. It's much more than that. I was under the impression that we were celebrating because the war is over. Stevens set me straight. It's only starting."

And George did not know whether the two families, already wounded by four years of one sort of war, could survive another.

BOOK ONE

LOST CAUSES

We all agree that the seceded states, so called, are out of their proper practical relation with the Union, and that the sole object of the government, civil and military, in regard to those states, is to again get them into that proper, practical relation. I believe that it is not only possible, but in fact easier, to do this without deciding or even considering whether these states have ever been out of the Union, than with it. Finding themselves safely at home, it would be utterly immaterial whether they had ever been abroad.

Last public speech of ABRAHAM LINCOLN,
from a White House balcony,
APRIL 11, 1865

Grind down the traitors. Grind the traitors in the dust.

CONGRESSMAN THADDEUS STEVENS, after
Lincoln's assassination, 1865

1

All around him, pillars of fire shot skyward. The fighting had
ignited the dry underbrush, then the trees. Smoke brought tears
to his eyes and made it hard to see the enemy skirmishers.

Charles Main bent low over the neck of his gray, Sport, and
waved his straw hat, shouting "Hah! Hah!" Ahead, at the gallop,
manes streaming out, the twenty splendid cavalry horses veered
one way, then another, seeking escape from the heat and the
scarlet glare.

"Don't let them turn," Charles shouted to Ab Woolner,
whom he couldn't see in the thick smoke. Rifle fire crackled. A
dim figure to his left toppled from the saddle.

Could they get out? They *had* to get out. The army desperately needed these stolen mounts.

A burly sergeant in Union blue jumped up from behind a
log. He aimed and put a rifle ball into the head of the mare at the
front of the herd. She bellowed and fell. A chestnut behind her
stumbled and went down. Charles heard bone snap as he galloped
on. The sergeant's sooty face broke into a smile. He blew a hole
in the head of the chestnut.

The heat seared Charles's face. The smoke all but blinded
him. He'd completely lost sight of Ab and the others in the gray-
clad raiding party. Only the need to get the animals to General
Hampton pushed him on through the inferno that mingled sunlight with fire.

His lungs began to hurt, strangled for air. He thought he saw
a gap ahead that marked the end of the burning wood. He applied spurs; Sport responded gallantly. "Ab, straight ahead. Do
you see it?"

There was no response except more rifle fire, more outcries, more sounds of horses and men tumbling into the burning leaves that carpeted the ground. Charles jammed his hat on his head and yanked out his .44-caliber Army Colt and thumbed the hammer back. In front of him, strung across the escape lane, three Union soldiers raised bayonets. They turned sideways to the stampeding horses. One soldier rammed his bayonet into the belly of a piebald. A geyser of blood splashed him. With a great agonized whinny, the piebald went down.

Such vicious brutality to an animal drove Charles past all reason. He fired two rounds, but Sport was racing over such rough ground he couldn't hope for a hit. With the herd flowing around them, the three Union boys took aim. One ball tore right between Sport's eyes and splattered blood on Charles's face. He let out a demented scream as the gray's forelegs buckled, tossing him forward.

He landed hard and came up on hands and knees, groggy. Another smiling Union boy dodged in with his bayonet. Charles had an impression of orange light too bright to stare at, heat so intense he could almost feel it broil his skin. The Union boy stepped past Sport, down and dying, and rammed the bayonet into Charles's belly and ripped upward, tearing him open from navel to breastbone.

A second soldier put his rifle to Charles's head. Charles heard the roar, felt the impact—then the wood went dark.

"Mr. Charles—"

"Straight on, Ab! It's the only way out."

"Mr. Charles, sir, wake up."

He opened his eyes, saw a woman's silhouette bathed in deep red light. He swallowed air, thrashed. Red light. *The forest was burning—*

No. The light came from the red bowls of the gas mantles around the parlor. There was no fire, no heat. Still dazed, he said, "Augusta?"

"Oh, no, sir," she said sadly. "It's Maureen. You made such an outcry, I thought you'd had a seizure of some kind."

Charles sat up and pushed his dark hair off his sweaty forehead. The hair hadn't been cut in a while. It curled over the collar of his faded blue shirt. Though he was only twenty-nine, a lot of his handsomeness had been worn away by privation and despair.

Across the parlor of the suite in the Grand Prairie Hotel, Chicago, he saw his gun belt lying on a chair cushion. The holster held his 1848 Colt, engraved with a scene of Indians fighting Army dragoons. Over the back of the same chair lay his gypsy cloak, a patchwork of squares from butternut trousers, fur robes, Union greatcoats, yellow and scarlet comforters. He'd sewn it, piece by piece, during the war, for warmth. The war—

"Bad dream," he said. "Did I wake Gus?"

"No, sir. Your son's sleeping soundly. I'm sorry about the nightmare."

"I should have known it for what it was. Ab Woolner was in it. And my horse Sport. They're both dead." He rubbed his eyes. "I'll be all right, Maureen. Thank you."

Doubtfully, she said, "Yes, sir," and tiptoed out.

All right? he thought. How could he ever be all right? He'd lost everything in the war, because he'd lost Augusta Barclay, who had died giving birth to the son he never knew about until she was gone.

The spell of the dream still gripped him. He could see and smell the forest burning, just as the Wilderness had burned. He could feel the heat boiling his blood. It was a fitting dream. He was a burned-out man, his waking hours haunted by two conflicting questions: Where could he find peace for himself? Where did he fit in a country no longer at war? His only answer to both was "Nowhere."

He shoved his hair back again and staggered to the sideboard, where he poured a stiff drink. Ruddy sunset light tinted the roofs of Randolph Street visible from the corner window. He was just finishing the drink, still trying to shake off the nightmare, when Augusta's uncle, Brigadier Jack Duncan, came through the foyer.

The first thing he said was "Charlie, I have bad news."

Brevet Brigadier Duncan was a thickly built man with crinkly gray hair and ruddy cheeks. He looked splendid in full dress: tail coat, sword belt, baldric, sash with gauntlets folded over it, chapeau with black silk cockade tucked under his arm. His actual rank in his new post at the Military Division of the Mississippi, headquartered in Chicago, was captain. Most wartime brevets had been reduced, but like all the others, Duncan was entitled to be addressed by his higher rank. He wore the single silver star of a brigadier on his epaulets, but he complained about the confusion of ranks, titles, insignia, and uniforms in the postwar army.

Charles, waiting for him to say more, relighted the stub of a cigar. Duncan laid his chapeau aside and poured a drink. "I've been at Division all afternoon, Charlie. Bill Sherman's to replace John Pope as commander."

"Is that your bad news?"

Duncan shook his head. "We have a million men still under arms, but by this time next year we'll be lucky to have twenty-five thousand. As part of that reduction, the First through the Sixth Volunteer Infantry Regiments are to be mustered out."

"All the Galvanized Yankees?" They were Confederate prisoners who had been put into the Union Army during the war in lieu of going to prison.

"Every last one. They acquitted themselves well, too. They kept the Sioux from slaughtering settlers in Minnesota, rebuilt telegraph lines the hostiles destroyed, garrisoned forts, guarded the stage and mail service. But it's all over."

Charles strode to the window. "Damn it, Jack, I came all the way out here to join one of those regiments."

"I know. But the doors are closed."

Charles turned, his face so forlorn Duncan was deeply moved. This South Carolinian who'd fathered his niece's child was a fine man. But like so many others, he'd been cast adrift in pain and confusion by the end of the war that had occupied him wholly for four years.

"Well, then," Charles said, "I suppose I'll have to swamp floors. Dig ditches—"

"There's another avenue, if you care to try it." Charles waited. "The regular cavalry."

"Hell, that's impossible. The amnesty proclamation excludes West Point men who changed sides."

"You can get around that." Before Charles could ask how, he continued. "There's a surplus of officers left from the war but a shortage of qualified enlisted men. You're a fine horseman and a topnotch soldier—you should be, coming from the Point. They'll take you ahead of all the Irish immigrants and one-armed wonders and escaped jailbirds."

Charles chewed on the cigar, thinking. "What about my boy?"

"Why, we'd just follow the same arrangement we agreed on previously. Maureen and I will keep Gus until you're through with training and posted somewhere. With luck—if you're at Fort Leavenworth or Fort Riley, for instance—you can hire a noncom's wife to nursemaid him. If not, he can stay on with us indefinitely. I love that boy. I'd shoot any man who looked cross-eyed at him."

"So would I." Charles pondered further. "Not much of a choice, is it? Muster with the regulars or go home, live on Cousin Madeline's charity, and sit on a cracker barrel telling war stories for the rest of my life." He chewed the cigar again, fiercely. Casting a quizzical look at Duncan, he asked. "You sure they'd have me in the regulars?"

"Charlie, hundreds of former reb—ah, Confederates are entering the Army. You just have to do what they do."

"What's that?"

"When you enlist, lie like hell."

"Next," said the recruiting sergeant.

Charles walked to the stained table, which had a reeking spittoon underneath. Next door, a man screamed as a barber yanked his tooth.

The noncom smelled of gin, looked twenty years past retirement age, and did everything slowly. Charles had already sat for an hour while the sergeant processed two wild-eyed young men, neither of whom spoke English. One answered every question by thumping his chest and exclaiming, "Budapest, Budapest." The other thumped his chest and exclaimed, "United States Merica." God save the Plains Army.

The sergeant pinched his veined nose. " 'fore we go on, do me a favor. Take that God-awful collection of rags or whatever it is and drop it outside. It looks disgusting and it smells like sheep shit."

Simmering, Charles folded the gypsy robe and put it neatly on the plank walk outside the door. Back at the table, he watched the sergeant ink his pen.

"You know the enlistment's five years—"

Charles nodded.

"Infantry or cavalry?"

"Cavalry."

That one word gave him away. Hostile, the sergeant said, "Southron?"

"South Carolina."

The sergeant reached for a pile of sheets held together by a metal ring. "Name?"

Charles had thought about that carefully. He wanted a name close to his real one, so he'd react naturally when addressed. "Charles May."

"May, May—" The sergeant leafed through the sheets, finally set them aside. In response to Charles's quizzical stare, he said, "Roster of West Point graduates. Division headquarters got it up." He eyed Charles's shabby clothes. "You don't have to worry about being mistook for one of those boys, I guess. Now, any former military service?"

"Wade Hampton Mounted Legion. Later—"

"Wade Hampton is enough." The sergeant wrote. "Highest rank?"

Taking Duncan's advice made him uncomfortable, but he did it. "Corporal."

"Can you prove that?"

"I can't prove anything. My records burned in Richmond."

The sergeant sniffed. "That's damned convenient for you rebs. Well, we can't be choosy. Ever since Chivington settled up with Black Kettle's Cheyennes last year, the damn plains tribes have gone wild."

The sergeant's "settled up" didn't fit the facts as Charles knew them. Near Denver, an emigrant party had been slain by Indians. An ex-preacher, Colonel J. M. Chivington, had mustered Colorado volunteer troops to retaliate against a Cheyenne village at Sand Creek, though there was no evidence that the village chief, Black Kettle, or his people were responsible for the killings. Of the three hundred or so that Chivington's men slew at Sand Creek, all but about seventy-five were women and children. The raid had outraged many people in the country, but the sergeant wasn't one of them.

The dentist's patient shrieked again. "No, sir," the sergeant mused, his pen scratching, "we can't be choosy at all. Got to take pretty near whoever shows up." Another glance at Charles. "Traitors included."

Charles struggled with his anger. He supposed that if he went ahead—and he had to go ahead; what else did he know besides soldiering?—he'd hear plenty of variations on the tune of traitor. He'd better get used to listening without complaint.

"Can you read or write?"

"Both."

The recruiter actually smiled. "That's good, though it don't make a damn bit of difference. You got the essentials. Minimum of one arm, one leg, and you're breathing. Sign here."

The locomotive's bell rang. Maureen dithered. "Sir—Brigadier—all passengers on board."

In the steam blowing along the platform, Charles hugged his bundled-up son. Little Gus, six months old now, wriggled and fretted with a case of colic. Maureen was still wet-nursing the baby, and this was his first bad reaction.

"I don't want him to forget me, Jack."

"That's why I had you sit for that daguerreotype. When he's a little older, I'll start showing it to him and saying Pa."

Gently, Charles transferred his son to the arms of the housekeeper, who was also, he suspected, the older man's wife-without-marriage-certificate. "Take good care of that youngster."

"It's almost an insult that you think we might not," Maureen said, rocking the child.

Duncan clasped Charles's hand. "Godspeed—and remember to hold your tongue and your temper. You have some hard months ahead of you."

"I'll make it, Jack. I can soldier for anyone, even Yankees."

The whistle blew. From the rear car, the conductor signaled and shouted to the engineer. "Go ahead! Go ahead!" Charles jumped up to the steps of the second-class car and waved as the train lurched forward. He was glad for the steam rising around him, so they couldn't see his eyes as the train pulled out.

Charles slouched in his seat. No one had sat next to him, because of his sinister appearance: worn straw hat pulled down to his eyebrows, the gypsy robe beside him. On his knee, unread, lay a *National Police Gazette*.

Dark rain-streaks crawled diagonally down the window. The storm and the night hid everything beyond. He chewed on a stale roll he'd bought from a vendor working the aisles, and felt the old forlorn emptiness.

He turned the pages of a *New York Times* left by a passenger who'd gotten off at the last stop. The advertising columns caught his eye: fantastic claims for eyeglasses, corsets, the comforts of coastal steamers. One item offered a tonic for suffering. He tossed the paper away. Damn shame it wasn't that easy.

Unconsciously, he began to whistle a little tune that had come into his head a few weeks ago and refused to leave. The whistling roused a stout woman across the aisle. Her pudgy daughter rested her head in her mother's lap. The woman overcame her hesitation and spoke to Charles.

"Sir, that's a lovely melody. Is it perchance one of Miss Jenny Lind's numbers?"

Charles pushed his hat back. "No. Just something I made up."

"Oh, I thought it might be hers. We collect her famous numbers in sheet music. Ursula plays them beautifully."

"I'm sure she does." Despite good intentions, it sounded curt.

"Sir, if you will permit me to say so"— she indicated the *Gazette* on his knee—"what you are reading is not Christian literature. Please, take this. You'll find it more uplifting."

She handed him a small pamphlet of a kind he recognized from wartime camps. One of the little religious exhortations published by the American Tract Society.

"Thank you," he said, and started to read:

Verily, verily, I say unto you, Hereafter ye shall see heaven open, and the angels of God ascending . . .

Bitter, Charles faced the window again. He saw no angels, no heaven, nothing but the boundless dark of the Illinois prairie, and the rain—probably a harbinger of a future as bleak as the past. Duncan was undoubtedly right about hard times ahead. He sank farther down on the seat, resting on the bony base of his spine and watching the darkness pass by.

Softly, he began to hum the little tune, which conjured lovely pastel images of Mont Royal—cleaner, prettier, larger than it had ever been before it burned. The little tune sang to him of that lost home, and his lost love, and everything lost in the four bloody years of the Confederacy's purple dream. It sang of emotions and a happiness that he was sure he would never know again.

MADELINE'S JOURNAL

*June, 1865. My dearest Orry, I begin this account in an old
copybook because I need to talk to you. To say I am adrift
without you, that I live with pain, does not begin to convey my
state. I will strive to keep self-pity from these pages but I know
I will not be entirely successful.*

*One tiny part of me rejoices that you are not here to see
the ruin of your beloved homeland. The extent of the ruin is
only emerging slowly. South Carolina offered some 70,000
men to the misbegotten war and over a quarter were killed,
the highest of any state, it's said.*

*Freed Negroes to the number of 200,000 now roam at
large. This is half the state's population, or more. On the river
road last week I met Maum Ruth, who formerly belonged to
the late Francis LaMotte. She clutched an old flour sack so
protectively, I was moved to ask what it contained. "Got the
freedom in here, and I won't let it go." I walked away full of
sadness and anger. How wrong we were not to educate our
blacks. They are helpless in the new world into which this
strange peace has hurled them.*

*"Our" blacks—I have paused over that chance wording.
It is condescending, and I am forgetful. I am one of them—in
Carolina one-eighth black is all black.*

*What your sister Ashton spitefully revealed about me in
Richmond is now known all over the district. No mention has*

*been made of it in recent weeks. For that, I have you to thank.
You are held in high esteem, and mourned. . . .*

*We planted four rice squares. We should have a good
small crop to sell, if there is anyone to buy. Andy, Jane, and I
work the squares each day.*

*A pastor of the African Methodist Church married Andy
and Jane last month. They took a new last name. Andy
wanted Lincoln, but Jane refused; too many former slaves
choose it. Instead, they are the Shermans, a selection not exactly certain to endear them to the white population! But they
are free people. It is their right to have any name they want.*

*The pine house, built to replace the great house burned
by Cuffey and Jones and their rabble, has a new coat of whitewash. Jane comes up in the evening while Andy works on the
tabby walls of their new cottage; we talk or mend the rags that
substitute for decent clothing—and sometimes we dip into our
"library." It consists of one* Godey's Lady's Book *from 1863,
and the last ten pages of a* Southern Literary Messenger.

*Jane speaks often of starting a school, even of asking the
new Freedmen's Bureau to help us locate a teacher. I went to
do it—I think I must, in spite of the bad feeling it will surely
generate. In the bitterness of defeat, few white people are inclined to help those liberated by Lincoln's pen and Sherman's
sword.*

*Before thinking of a school, however, we must think of
survival. The rice will not be enough to support us. I know
dear George Hazard would grant us unlimited credit, but I
perceive it as a weakness to ask him. In that regard I surely
am a Southerner—full of stiff-necked pride.*

*We may be able to sell off lumber from the stands of pine
and cypress so abundant on Mont Royal. I know nothing of
operating a sawmill, but I can learn. We would need equipment, which would mean another mortgage. The banks in
Charleston may soon open again—both Geo. Williams and
Leverett Dawkins, our old Whig friend, speculated in British
sterling during the war, kept it in a foreign bank, and will
now use it to start the commercial blood of the Low Country
flowing again. If Leverett's bank does open, I will apply to
him.*

*Shall also have to hire workers, and wonder if I can.
There is wide concern that the Negroes prefer to revel in their*

freedom rather than labor for their old owners, however be-
nevolent. A vexing problem for all the South.

But, my sweetest Orry, I must tell you of my most un-
likely dream—and the one I have promised myself to realize
above all others. It was born some days ago, out of my love for
you, and my longing, and my eternal pride in being your
wife. . . .

After midnight of that day, unable to sleep, Madeline left the
whitewashed house that now had a wing with two bedrooms.
Nearing forty, Orry Main's widow was still as full-bosomed and
small-waisted as she had been the day he rescued her on the river
road, although age and stress were beginning to mark and
roughen her face.

She'd been crying for an hour, ashamed of it, yet powerless
to stop. Now she rushed down the broad lawn under a moon that
shone, blinding white, above the trees bordering the Ashley
River. At the bank where the pier once jutted out, she disturbed a
great white heron. The bird rose and sailed past the full moon.

She turned and gazed back up the lawn at the house among
the live oaks bearded with Spanish moss. A vision filled her mind,
a vision of the great house in which she and Orry had lived as
man and wife. She saw its graceful pillars, lighted windows. She
saw carriages drawn up, gentlemen and ladies visiting, laughing.

The idea came then. It made her heart beat so fast it almost
hurt. Where the poor whitewashed place stood now, she would
build another Mont Royal. A fine great house to endure forever
as a memorial to her husband and his goodness, and all that was
good about the Main family and its collective past.

In a rush of thought, it came to her that the house must not
be an exact replica of the burned mansion. That beauty had represented—hidden—too much that was evil. Although the Mains
had been kind to their slaves, they had indisputably kept them as
property, thereby endorsing a system that embraced shackles and
floggings and death or castration for those rash enough to run
away. By war's end, Orry had all but disavowed the system;
Cooper, in his younger days, had condemned it openly. Even so,
the new Mont Royal must be truly new, for it was a new time. A
new age.

Tears welled. Madeline clasped her hands and raised them in
the moonlight. "I'll do it somehow. In your honor—"

She saw it clearly, standing again, the phoenix risen from the ashes. Like some pagan priestess, she lifted her head and hands to whatever gods watched from the starry arch of the Carolina night. She spoke to her husband there amid the far stars.

"I swear before heaven, Orry. I will build it, for you."

> *A surprise visitor today. Gen. Wade Hampton, on his way home from Charleston. Because of his rank, and his ferocity as a soldier, they say it will be years before any amnesty reaches high enough to include him.*
>
> *His strength and good disposition astound me. He lost so much—his brother Frank and his son Preston dead in battle, 3,000 slaves gone, and both Millwood and Sand Hills burned by the enemy. He is living in an overseer's shack at Sand Hills, and cannot escape the accusation that he, not Sherman, burned Columbia by firing cotton bales to keep them from the Yankee looters.*
>
> *Yet he showed no dismay over any of this, expressing, instead, concern for others . . .*

Outside the pine house, Wade Hampton sat on an upright log that served as a chair. Lee's oldest cavalry commander, forty-seven now, carried himself with a certain stiffness. He'd been wounded in battle five times. Since coming home, he'd shaved his huge beard, leaving only a tuft beneath his mouth, though he still wore his great curving mustaches and side whiskers. Under an old broadcloth coat, he carried an ivory-handled revolver in a holster.

"Laced coffee, General," Madeline said as she emerged into the dappled sunlight with two steaming tin cups. "Sugar and a little corn whiskey—though I'm afraid the coffee is just a brew from parched acorns."

"Welcome all the same." Smiling, Hampton took his cup. Madeline sat down on a crate near a cluster of the trumpet-shaped yellow jasmine she loved.

"I came to inquire about your welfare," he said to her. "Mont Royal is yours now—"

"In a sense, yes. I don't own it."

Hampton raised an eyebrow, and she explained that Tillet Main had left the plantation to his sons, Orry and Cooper, jointly. He had done so despite his long-standing quarrel with

Cooper over slavery; at the end, blood ties and tradition had proved stronger in Tillet than anger or ideology. Like a majority of men of his age and time, Tillet looked to his sons because he prized his property and had a less than generous view of the business and financial abilities of women. When he wrote his will, he didn't worry about anything more than a token bequest of cash to each of his daughters, Ashton and Brett, presuming they would be provided for by their spouses. The will further stipulated that when one son predeceased the other, that son's title in the estate passed directly to the surviving brother.

"So Cooper is the sole owner of record now. But he's generously allowed me to stay on here out of regard for Orry. I have the management of the plantation, and the income from it, for as long as he remains the owner, and so long as I pay the mortgage debt. I'm responsible for all of the operating expenses too, but those conditions are certainly reasonable."

"You're secure in this arrangement? I mean to say, it's legal and binding?"

"Completely. Only weeks after we got word of Orry's death, Cooper formalized the arrangement in writing. The document makes it irrevocable."

"Well, knowing how Carolinians value family ties and family property, I should think Mont Royal would stay with the Mains forever, then."

"Yes, I'm confident of that." It was her single firm hold on security. "Unfortunately, there's no income at all right now, and no great prospect of any. About the best I can say in answer to your question about our welfare is that we're managing."

"I suppose that's the best any of us can expect at present. My daughter Sally's marrying Colonel Johnny Haskell later this month. That lightens the clouds a little." He sipped from the cup. "Delicious. What do you hear from Charles?"

"I had a letter two months ago. He said he hoped to go back in the army, out West."

"I understand a great many Confederates are doing that. I hope they treat him decently. He was one of my best scouts. Iron Scouts, we called them. He lived up to the name, although, toward the end, I confess that I noticed him behaving strangely on occasion."

Madeline nodded. "I noticed it when he came home this spring. The war hurt him. He fell in love with a woman in Virginia and she died bearing his son. He has the boy with him now."

"Family is one of the few balms for pain," Hampton murmured. He drank again. "Now tell me how you really are."

"As I said, General, surviving. No one's raised the issue of my parentage, so I'm spared having to deal with that."

She looked at him as she spoke, wanting to test him. Hampton's ruddy outdoorsman's face remained calm. "Of course I heard about it. It makes no difference."

"Thank you."

"Madeline, in addition to asking about Charles, I called to make an offer. We all face difficult circumstances, but you face them alone. There are unscrupulous men of both races wandering the roads of this state. Should you need refuge from that at any time, or if the struggle grows too hard for any reason and you want a short respite, come to Columbia. My home and Mary's is yours always."

"That's very kind," she said. "Don't you think the chaos in South Carolina will end soon?"

"No, not soon. But we can hasten the day by taking a stand for what's right."

She sighed. "What is that?"

He gazed at the sun-flecked river. "In Charleston, some gentlemen offered me command of an expedition to found a colony in Brazil. A slaveholding colony. I refused it. I said this was my home and I would no longer think of North and South; only of America. We fought, we lost, the issue of a separate nation on the continent is resolved. Nevertheless, in South Carolina we confront the very large problem of the Negro. His status is changed. How should we behave? Well, he was faithful to us as a slave, so I believe we ought to treat him fairly as a free man. Guarantee him justice in our courts. Give him the franchise if he's qualified, exactly as we give it to white men. If we do that, the wandering crowds will disband and the Negro will again take up Carolina as his home, and the white man as his friend."

"Do you really believe that, General?"

A slight frown appeared, perhaps of annoyance. "I do. Only full justice and compassion will alleviate the plight of this state."

"I must say you're more generous to the blacks than most."

"Well, they present us with a practical issue as well as a moral one. Our lands are destroyed, our homes are burned, our money and bonds are worthless, and soldiers are quartered on our doorsteps. Should we make matters worse by pretending that our cause is not lost? That it somehow might prevail even yet? I think it was lost from the start. I stayed away from the 1860 special convention because I thought secession an impossible folly. Are we to start living our illusions all over again? Are we to invite reprisal by resisting an honorable effort to restore the Union?"

"A great many people want to resist," she said.

"And if gentlemen such as Mr. Stevens and Mr. Sumner try to force me into social equality with Negroes, I will resist. Beyond that, however, if Washington is reasonable, and we are reasonable, we can rebuild. If our people cling to their old follies, they'll only start a new kind of war."

Again she sighed. "I hope common sense prevails. I'm not certain it will."

Hampton rose and clasped her hands between his. "Don't forget my offer. Sanctuary, if you ever need it."

Impulsively, she kissed his cheek: "You're a kind man, General. God bless you."

Away he went on his fine stallion, disappearing where the half-mile lane of splendid trees joined the river road.

At sunset, Madeline walked through the fallow rice square, pondering Hampton's remarks. For a proud and defeated man, he had a remarkably generous outlook. He was also right about the plight of South Carolina. If the state, and the South, returned to old ways, the Radical Republicans would surely be goaded to retaliate.

Something on the ground jabbed the sandal she'd fashioned from scrap leather and rope. Digging down in the sandy soil, she uncovered a rock about the size of her two hands. She and the Shermans had found many similar ones while cultivating the four planted squares, and had puzzled about it. Rocks weren't common in the Low Country.

She brushed soil from it. It was yellowish, with tan streaks, and looked porous. With a little effort, she broke it in half. Rock didn't shatter so easily. But if it wasn't rock, what was it?

She brought both halves up to her face. As she grew older, her eyes were increasingly failing. Since she'd never broken open one of the peculiar rocks, she was unprepared for the fetid odor.

It made her gag. She threw the broken pieces away and hurried back to the pine house, her shadow flying ahead of her over ground as deeply red as spilled blood.

> *I wish I could believe with Gen. H. that our people will recognize the wisdom and practical importance of fair play toward the freed blacks. I wish I could believe that Carolinians will be reasonable about the defeat and its consequences. I cannot. Some kind of dark mood is on me again.*
>
> *It came this evening when I cracked open one of those strange rocks you pointed out once before the war. The stench—! Even our land is sour and rotten. I took it as a sign. I saw a future flowing with bile and poison.*
>
> *Forgive me, Orry; I must write no more of this.*

2

At twilight on the day of Hampton's visit to Mont Royal, a young woman dashed around a corner into Chambers Street, in New York City. One hand held her bonnet in place. The other held sheets of paper covered with signatures.

A misty rain was beginning to fall. She hastily tucked the papers under her arm to protect them. Ahead loomed the marquee of Wood's New Knickerbocker Theater, her destination. The theater was temporarily closed, between productions, and she was late for a special rehearsal called by the owner for half after seven o'clock.

Late in a good cause, though. She always had a cause, and it was always as important as her profession. Her father had raised her that way. She'd been an active worker for abolition since she was fifteen; she was nineteen now. She proselytized for equal rights for women, and the vote, and for fairer divorce laws, although she had never been married. Her current cause, for which she'd been collecting signatures from the theatrical community all afternoon, was the Indian—specifically the Cheyenne nation, victimized last year by the Sand Creek massacre. The petition, a memorial to be sent to Congress and the Indian Bureau of the Interior Department, demanded reparations for Sand Creek and permanent repudiation of "the Chivington process."

She turned left into the dim passage leading to the stage door. She had worked for Claudius Wood only a week and a half, but she'd already found that he had a fearful temper. And he drank. She smelled it on him at nearly every rehearsal.

Wood had seen her play Rosalind at the Arch Street Theater in Philadelphia and had offered her a great deal of money. He was about thirty-five, and he'd charmed her with his fine manners

and marvelous voice and raffish, worldly air. Still, she was beginning to regret her decision to leave Mrs. Drew's company and
sign with Wood for a full season.

Louisa Drew had urged her to accept, saying it would be a
great step forward. "You're a mature and capable young woman,
Willa. But remember that New York is full of rough men. Do you
have any friends there? Someone you could turn to if necessary?"

She thought a moment. "Eddie Booth."

"You know Edwin Booth?"

"Oh, yes. He and my father trouped together in the gold
fields when I was little and we lived in St. Louis. I've seen Eddie
several times over the years. But he's been in seclusion ever since
his brother Johnny killed the President. I would never bother
him with anything trivial."

"No, but he's there in an emergency." Mrs. Drew hesitated.
"Do mind yourself with Mr. Wood, Willa."

Questioned, the older woman would not elaborate beyond
saying, "You'll discover what I mean. I don't like to speak ill of
anyone in the profession. But some actresses—the prettier ones—
have trouble with Wood. You shouldn't pass up this chance because of that. Just be cautious."

The young woman going down the passage in a rush was
Willa Parker. She was a tall, leggy girl, slim enough for trouser
roles, yet with a soft, full bosom ideal for Juliet. She had wide-set,
slightly slanted blue eyes that lent her an exotic quality, and hair
so pale blond it shone silvery when she was onstage in the lime-
light. Mrs. Drew, with affection, called Willa a gamine. Her
charming Irish husband, John, called her "my fair sprite."

Her skin was smooth, her mouth wide, her face given an air
of strength by the line of her chin. Sometimes she felt forty years
old, because her mother had died when she was three, her father
when she was fourteen, and she'd played theatrical roles since age
six. She was the only child of a woman she couldn't remember
and a free-thinking, hard-working father she loved with total de-
votion until a heart seizure felled him in the storm scene of *Lear*.

Peter Parker had been one of those actors who worked at his
profession with ardor and enthusiasm even though he had realized as a young man that his talent would provide only a subsis-
tence, never let him shine with his name above the title of a play.
He'd begun playing child parts in his native England, growing

into older roles done in the dignified classical style of the Kemble family and Mrs. Siddons. In his twenties, he'd performed with the flamboyant Kean, who won him away from classicism to Kean's own naturalism, which encouraged an actor to do whatever the part demanded, even scream or crawl on the floor.

It was after his first engagement with Kean that he forever abandoned the last name he'd inherited at birth, Potts. Too many unfunny uses of it by fellow actors—Flower Potts, Chamber Potts—convinced him to adopt Parker as more practical and more likely to inspire favorable recognition. Willa knew the family name, which amused her, although from her earliest years she'd thought of herself as a Parker.

To his daughter, Parker had passed on various technical tricks of different acting styles and some other characteristics. These included the energy and idealism typical of actors, an encyclopedic knowledge of theatrical superstition, and the defensive optimism so necessary to survive in the profession. Now, going through the stage door, Willa called on that optimism and assured herself that her employer wouldn't be angry.

In the shadows just inside, the elderly janitor was struggling into a rubber rain slicker. "He's in the office, Miss Parker. Shouting for you every five minutes, too."

"Thank you, Joe." So much for optimism. The janitor jingled his keys, preparing to lock up. He was leaving early. Perhaps Wood had given him the night off.

Willa dashed through the backstage area, dodging between bundles of unpainted prop tree branches—Birnam Wood, which would come to Dunsinane in the next production. The vast fly space smelled of new lumber, old make-up, dust. Light spilled from a half-open door ahead. Willa heard Wood's deep voice:

"I go, and it is done—the bell invites me. Hear it not, Duncan; for it is a knell—that summons thee to heaven or to hell." Then he repeated *"or to hell,"* changing the inflection.

Willa stood motionless outside the office, a shiver running down her back. Her employer was rehearsing one of the leading character's speeches somewhere other than the stage. This play of Shakespeare's was a bad-luck piece, most actors believed, although some noted that it contained a great deal of onstage fighting, and thus the causes of a gashed head, a bad fall, a broken arm or leg were in the text, not the stars. Still, the legend persisted. Like many other actors and actresses, Willa laughed at it while respecting it. She never repeated any of the lines backstage, or in dressing rooms or green rooms. She always referred to it as "the Scottish play"; saying the title in the theater guaranteed misfortune.

She glanced behind her into the darkness. Where were the other company members she'd assumed would be here for the rehearsal? In the stillness she heard only the tiniest creak—perhaps the playhouse cat prowling. She had an impulse to run.

"Who's there?"

Claudius Wood's shadow preceded him to the door. He yanked it fully open, and the rectangle of gaslight widened to reveal Willa with the petition in her hand.

Wood's cravat was untied, his waistcoat unbuttoned, his sleeves rolled up. He scowled at her. "The call was half past the hour. You're forty minutes late."

"Mr. Wood, I apologize. I fell behind."

"With what?" He noticed the papers with signatures. "Another of your radical crusades?" He startled her by snatching the petition. "Oh, Christ. The poor wretched Indian. Not on my time, if you please. I'll dock your wages. Come in, so we can get to work."

Something undefined but alarming warned her then— warned her to run from the silent theater and this burly man, whose handsome face was already giving way to patterns of veins in his cheeks and a bulbous, spongy look to his nose. But she desperately wanted to play the difficult role he'd offered her. It called for an older actress, and an accomplished one. If she could bring it off, it would promote her career.

And yet—

"Isn't there anyone else coming?"

"Not tonight. I felt our scenes together needed special attention."

"Could we do them onstage, please? This is the Scottish play, after all."

His bellow of laughter made her feel small and stupid. "Surely you don't believe that nonsense, Willa. You who are so intelligent, conversant with so many advanced ideas." He flicked the papers with his nail, then handed them back. "The play is *Macbeth,* and I'll speak the lines anywhere I choose. Now get in here and let's begin."

He turned and went back in the office. Willa followed, a part of her saying he was right, that she was infantile to worry about the superstitions. Peter Parker would have worried, though.

Overhead, a rumbling sounded—the storm growing worse. The actor-child in Willa was convinced that baleful forces were gathering above Chambers Street. Her hands turned cold as she followed her employer.

"Take off your shawl and bonnet." Wood moved chairs to clear a space on the shabby carpet. The office was a junkshop of period furniture and imitation green plants in urns of all sizes and designs. Handbills for New Knickerbocker productions covered the walls. Goldsmith, Molière, Boucicault, Sophocles. The huge desk was a litter of bills, playscripts, contracts, career mementos. Wood pushed aside Macbeth's enameled dagger, a metal prop with a blunted point, and poured two inches of whiskey from a decanter. Green glass bowls on the gas jets seemed to darken rather than lighten the room.

Nervous, Willa put the signed petitions on a velvet chair. She laid her velvet gloves on top, then her shawl and bonnet. All in a pile in case she needed to snatch them quickly. She had started to mature at twelve, and men who worked around the theater soon began responding to her beauty. She'd learned to stand them off with good humor, even a little physical force when necessary. She was expert at running away.

Wood strolled to the door and closed it. "All right, my dear. First act, seventh scene."

"But we rehearsed that most of yesterday."

"I'm not satisfied." He walked back to her. "Macbeth's castle." Grinning, he reached out and ran his palm slowly down the silk of her sleeve. "Begin in the middle of Lady Macbeth's speech, where she says *'I have given suck.'*"

He relished the last word. The gas put a highlight on his wet lower lip. Willa struggled to suppress fear and a sad despair. It was so obvious now, so obvious what he'd wanted all along, and why he'd engaged her when there were scores of older actresses available. Mrs. Drew had done everything but tell her in explicit language. She wasn't flattered, only upset. If this was the price for her New York debut, damn him, she wouldn't pay.

"Begin," he repeated, with a harshness that alarmed her. He caressed her arm again. She tried to draw away. He simply moved and kept at it, blowing his bourbon breath on her.

"I have given suck, and know—" She faltered. *"How tender 'tis to love the babe that milks me."*

"Do you, now?" He bent and kissed her throat.

"Mr. Wood—"

"Go on with it." He seized her shoulders and shook her, and that was when freezing terror took hold. In his black eyes she saw something beyond anger. She saw a willingness to hurt.

"I would—while it was smiling in my face, have plucked my nipple from his boneless gums—"

Wood's hand slid from her arm to her left breast, closing on it. "You wouldn't pluck it from mine, would you?"

She stamped her high laced shoe. "Look here, I'm an actress. I won't be treated like a street harlot."

He grabbed her arm. "I pay your salary. You're anything I say you are—including my whore."

"No," she snarled, yanking away. He drew his hand back and drove his fist against her face. The blow knocked her down.

"You blonde bitch. You'll give me what I want." He caught her hair in his left hand, making her cry out when he pulled her head up. His right fist pounded down on her shoulder, and again. "Does that convince you?"

"Let go of me. You're drunk—crazy—"

"Shut up!" He slapped her so hard, she flew back and cracked her head on the front of his desk. "Pull up your skirts." Lights danced behind her eyes. Pain pounded. She reached up, fingers searching for some heavy object on the desk. He stood astride her right leg, working at his fly buttons. "Pull them up, God damn you, or I'll beat you till you can't walk."

Out of her mind with fright, she found something on the desk—the prop dagger. He reached for her wrist, but before he could stop her she swung it down. Although the point was blunt, it tore through the plaid fabric of his trousers because she struck so hard. She felt the dagger meet flesh, stop a second, then sink on through.

"Jesus," Wood said, groping with both hands for the prop weapon buried two inches in his left thigh. He struggled with it, bloodying his fingers. "Jesus Christ. I'll kill you!"

Wild-eyed, Willa pushed him with both hands, toppling him sideways. He shouted and cursed as he overturned a fake palmetto plant. She crawled to the chair, snatched her things, and ran from the office and through the dark. At the door she struggled with the bolt, shot it open, and half fell into the rainy passage, expecting to hear him in pursuit.

———

I,———, do solemnly swear in the presence of Almighty God, that I will henceforth faithfully support, protect and defend the constitution of the United States and the Union of the states thereunder, and that I will in like manner abide by and faithfully support all laws and proclamations which have been made during the existing rebellion with reference to the emancipation of slaves. So help me God.

> Oath required of all Confederates
> seeking presidential pardon, 1865

3

"I must take this oath?" Cooper Main asked. He'd ridden all the way to Columbia to see about the matter, and suddenly had doubts.

"If you want a pardon," said lawyer Trezevant, from the other side of the flimsy table serving as a desk. His regular offices had burned in the great fire of February 17, so he'd rented an upstairs room at Reverdy Bird's Mortuary on the east side of town, which the flames had spared. Mr. Bird had converted his main parlor to a shop selling cork feet, wooden limbs, and glass eyes to maimed veterans. A buzz of voices indicated good business this morning.

Cooper stared at the handwritten oath. He was lanky man and had a lot of gray in his untrimmed hair, though he was only forty-five. The scarcity of food had reduced him to gauntness. Workdays lasting sixteen hours had put fatigue shadows under his deep-set brown eyes. He was laboring to rebuild the warehouses, the docks, and the trade of his Carolina Shipping Company in Charleston.

"See here, I understand your resentment," Trezevant said. "But if General Lee can humble himself and apply, as he did in Richmond last week, you can, too."

"A pardon implies wrongdoing. I did nothing wrong."

"I agree, Cooper. Unfortunately, the federal government does not. If you want to rebuild your business, you have to free yourself of the onus of having served the Confederate Navy Department." Cooper glowered. Trezevant continued. "I went to Washington personally, and, within limits, I trust this pardon broker, even though he's a lawyer, and a Yankee on top of it." The bitter humor was lost. "His name is Jasper Dills. He's greedy, so I know he'll get your application to the clerk of pardons, and to Mr. Johnson's desk, ahead of many others."

"For how much?"

"Two hundred dollars, U.S., or the equivalent in sterling. My fee is fifty dollars."

Cooper thought a while.

"All right, give me the papers."

They talked for another half hour. Trezevant was full of Washington gossip. He said Johnson planned to appoint a provisional governor in South Carolina. The governor would call a constitutional convention and reconvene the state legislature as it was constituted before Sumter fell. Johnson's choice was not unexpected. It was Judge Benjamin Franklin Perry, of Greenville, an avowed Unionist before the war. Like Lee, Perry had proclaimed his loyalty to his state, despite his hatred of secession, saying: *"You are all going to the devil—and I will go with you."*

"The legislature will have to fulfill Mr. Johnson's requirements for readmission," Trezevant said. "Officially abolish slavery, for example." A sly expression alerted Cooper to something new. "At the same time, the legislature may be able to, ah, regulate the nigras so that we'll have a labor force again, instead of a shiftless rabble."

"Regulate them how?"

"By means of—let's call it a code of behavior. I'm told Mississippi is thinking of the same thing."

"Would such a code apply to whites, too?"

"Freedmen only."

Cooper recognized danger in such a provocative step, but the morality of it didn't concern him. The end of the war had brought him, his family, and his state a full measure of humiliation and ruin. He no longer cared about the condition of the people responsible—the people the war had set free.

By noon, Cooper's slow old horse was plodding southeast on the homeward journey. The route carried him back through central Columbia. He could hardly stand the sight. Nearly one hundred and twenty blocks had been burned down. The smell of charred wood still lay heavy in the air of the hot June day.

The dirt streets were littered with trash and broken furniture. A wagon belonging to the Bureau of Freedmen, Refugees and Abandoned Lands dispensed packets of rice and flour to a

large crowd, mostly Negro. Other blacks crowded the few
stretches of wooden sidewalk still in place. Cooper saw military
uniforms and some civilian gentlemen, but well-dressed white
women were notably absent. It was the same everywhere. Such
women stayed indoors, because they hated the soldiers and feared
the freed Negroes. Cooper's wife, Judith, was an exception,
which irritated him.

General Sherman had destroyed the wooden bridge span-
ning the Congaree River. Only the stone abutments remained,
standing in the stream like smoke-stained gravestones. The slow
crossing on the ferry barge gave Cooper an excellent view of one
of the few buildings the fire had spared, the unfinished statehouse
near the east shore. In one granite wall, like periods on paper,
three Union cannonballs testified to Sherman's fury.

The sight of them raised Cooper's anger. So did the burned
district, which he reached soon after leaving the ferry. He rode
along the edge of a lane of scorched earth three-quarters of a mile
wide. Here, between flaming pines, Kilpatrick's cavalry had pil-
laged, leaving a black waste marked by lonely chimneys—Sherman's Sentinels, all that remained of homes in the path of the
barbaric march.

He stayed the night at a seedy inn outside the city. In the
taproom he avoided conversation but listened closely to the impoverished yeomen drinking around him. To hear them, you'd
think the South had won, or at least was able to continue fighting
for its cause.

Next morning, he rode on, through heat and haze promising
another fierce summer in the Low Country. He traveled on dirt
roads left unrepaired after Union supply trains tore them up. A
farmer would need a strong new wagon to get through the eight-
inch ruts in the sandy soil and reach market with his crop—if he
had a crop. Probably the farmer couldn't find a new wagon to
buy, or the money for it, either. Cooper seethed.

Riding on toward Charleston and the coast, he crossed a
roadbed; all the rails were gone and only a few ties were left. He
met no white people, though twice he saw bands of Negroes moving through fields. Just past the hamlet of Chicora, on his way to
the Cooper River, he came upon a dozen black men and women
gathering wild herbs at the roadside. He reached into the pocket
of his old coat and took hold of the little pocket pistol he'd
bought for the trip.

The blacks watched Cooper approach. One of the women wore a red velvet dress and an oval cameo pin, probably, Cooper thought, stolen from a white mistress. The rest were raggedy. Cooper sweated and clutched the hidden pistol, but they let him ride through.

A big man with a red bandanna tied into a cap stepped into the road behind him. "You ain't the boss 'round here any more, Captain."

Cooper turned and glared. "Who the hell said I was? Why don't you get to work and do something useful?"

"Don't have to work," said the woman in red velvet. "You can't force us and you can't whip us. Not no more. We're free."

"Free to squander your lives in sloth. Free to forget your friends."

"Friends? The likes of you, who kept us locked up?" The bandanna man snickered. "Ride on, Captain, 'fore we drag you off that nag and give you the kind of hidin' *we* used to get."

Cooper's jaw clenched. He pulled out the pocket pistol and pointed it. The woman in velvet screamed and dived into the ditch. The others scattered, except for the bandanna man, who strode toward Cooper's horse. Suddenly, good sense prevailed; Cooper booted the nag and got out of there.

He didn't stop shaking for almost ten minutes. Trezevant was right. The legislature must do something to regularize the behavior of the freedmen. Liberty had become anarchy. And without hands to labor in the heat and damp, South Carolina would slip from critical illness to death.

Later, when he calmed down, he began to consider the work to be done at the shipping company. Fortunately, he didn't have the extra burden of worrying about Mont Royal. Decency and propriety had prompted him to make his arrangement with Orry's widow, and she now bore all the responsibility for the plantation to which he held title. Madeline was of mixed blood, and everyone knew it, because Ashton had blurted it to the world. But no one made anything of her ancestry. Nor would they so long as she behaved like a proper white woman.

Melancholy visions of his younger sisters diverted him from thoughts of work. He saw Brett, married to that Yankee, Billy Hazard, and bound for California, according to her last letter. He saw Ashton, who'd involved herself in some grotesque plot to unseat Davis's government and replace it with a crowd of hot-spurs. She'd disappeared into the West, and he suspected she was dead. He couldn't summon much sorrow over it, and he didn't feel guilty. Ashton was a tormented girl, with all the personal difficulties that seemed to afflict women of great beauty and great ambition. Her morals had always been despicable.

The sun dropped down toward the sand hills behind him, and he began to wind through glinting salt marshes, close to home. How he loved South Carolina, and especially the Low Country. His son's tragic death had transformed him to a loyalist, although he still perceived himself to be a moderate on every issue but one: the inherent superiority of the white race and its fitness to govern society. Cooper was at this moment about ten minutes away from an encounter with a man who carried Southern loyalty far beyond anything he ever imagined.

His name was Desmond LaMotte. He was a great scarecrow of a man, with outlandishly long legs, which hung almost to the ground as he rode his mule through the marshes near the Cooper River. His arms were equivalently long. He had curly carrot-colored hair with a startling streak of white running back from his forehead; the war had given him that. He wore a neat imperial the color of his hair.

He came from the old Huguenot stock that dominated the state's town and plantation aristocracy. His late mother was a Huger, a Huguenot name pronounced You-gee. The war had cut down most of the young men in both families.

Des was a native Charlestonian, born in 1834. By the time he was fifteen he'd reached his adult height of six feet four inches. His hands measured ten inches from the tip of the little finger to the tip of the thumb when the fingers were spread. His feet measured thirteen inches from heel to big toe. So naturally, like any strong-willed, contrary, and defiant young man with those physical characteristics, he decided to become a dancing master.

People scoffed. But he was determined, and he made a success of it. It was an old and honorable profession, particularly in the South. Up among the hypocrites of New England, preachers always railed against mixed dancing, along with dancing in taverns, Maypole dancing (it smacked of pagan ritual), or any dancing with food and drink nearby. Southerners had a more enlightened view, because of their higher culture, their spiritual kinship with the English gentry, and their economic system; slavery gave them the leisure time for learning how to dance. Both Washington and Jefferson—great men; great Southerners, in Des's view—had been partial to dancing.

Early in life, whether riding or thrusting with a foil or idly tossing a horseshoe with some of the children of Charleston's free Negro population, Des LaMotte demonstrated an agility unusual in any boy, and remarkable in someone growing so large so quickly. His parents recognized his ability, and because they believed in the benefits of dance instruction for young gentlemen, they started his lessons at age eleven. Des never forgot the first stern words of his own dancing master. He'd committed them to memory and later used them with his own pupils:

> The dancing school is not a place of amusement, but a place of education. And the end of a good education is not that you become accomplished dancers, but that you become good sons and daughters, good husbands and wives, good citizens and good Christians.

In the five years preceding the war, well and happily married to Miss Sally Sue Means, of Charleston, Des had established a school in rooms on King Street, and developed a thriving trade among the Low Country plantations, through which he made a circuit three times annually, always advertising in local papers in advance of his visit. He never lacked for pupils. He taught a little fencing to the boys, but mostly he taught dances: the traditional quadrilles and Yorks and reels, with the dancers in a set or a line that would not compromise their morals through too much physical contact. He also taught the newer, more daring importations from Europe, the waltz and polka, closed dances with the couples facing one another in what some considered a dangerous intimacy. An Episcopal divine in Charleston had preached against "the abomination of permitting a man who is neither your fiancé nor your husband to encircle you with his arms and slightly press the contour of your waist." Des laughed at that. He considered all dancing moral, because he considered himself, and every one of his pupils, the same.

The five years in which he taught from the standard text, Rambeau's *Dancing Master*— his worn copy was in his saddlebag this moment—were magical ones. Despite the abolitionists and the threat of war, he presided at opulent balls and plantation assemblies, watching with delight as attractive white men and women danced by candlelight from seven at night until three or four in the morning, hardly out of breath. It was all capped by the glorious winter social season in Charleston, and the grand ball of the prestigious St. Cecilia Society.

Des's knowledge of dancing was wide and eclectic. He had seen frontier plank dancing, in which two men jigged on a board between barrels until one fell off. On plantations he'd observed slave dancing, rooted in Africa, consisting of elaborate heel-and-toe steps done to the beat of clappers made of animal bone or blacksmith's rasps scraped together. Generally, the planters prohibited drums among their slaves, deeming them a means of transmitting secret messages about rebellions or arson plots.

He had dreamed long hours over an engraved portrait of Thomas D. Rice, the great white dancer who'd enthralled audiences early in the century with his blackface character Jim Crow. From Carolinians who'd traveled in the North, he'd heard descriptions of the Shaking Quakers, notorious nigger lovers whose dances gave form to religious doctrine. A single slow-moving file of dancers, each placing one careful foot ahead of the other, represented the narrow path to salvation; three or more concentric rings of dancers turning in alternate directions were the wheel-within-a-wheel, the Shaker vision of the cosmos. Des knew the whole universe of American dance, though to those who paid him he admitted to liking only those kinds of dancing that he taught.

His universe was shattered with the first cannon fire on Fort Sumter. He mustered at once with the Palmetto Rifles, a unit organized by his best friend, Captain Ferris Brixham. Out of the original eighty men, only three were left in April of this year, when General Joe Johnston surrendered the Confederacy's last field army at Durham Station, North Carolina. The night before the surrender, a beastly yankee sergeant and four of his men caught Des and Ferris foraging for food and beat them unconscious. Des survived; Ferris died in his arms an hour after officers announced the surrender. Ferris left a wife and five young children.

Embittered, Des trudged back to Charleston, where an eighty-five-year-old uncle told him Sally Sue had died in January of pneumonia and complications of malnutrition. As if that wasn't enough, throughout the war the whole LaMotte family had been shamed by members of another family in the Ashley River district. It was more than Des could bear. His mind had turned white. There was a month of which he remembered nothing. Aging relatives had cared for him.

Now he rode his mule through the marshes, looking for plantation clients from the past or people who could afford lessons for their children. He'd found neither. Behind him, barefoot, walked his fifty-year-old servant, an arthritic black called Juba; it was a slave name meaning musician. After his return home, Des had signed Juba to a lifetime contract of personal service. Juba was frightened by the new freedom bestowed by the legendary Linkum. He readily made his mark on the paper he couldn't read.

Juba walked in the sunshine with one hand resting on the hindquarters of the mule ridden by a man with only two ambitions: to practice again the profession he loved in a world the Yankees had made unfit for it, and to extract retribution from any of those who had contributed to his misery and that of his family and his homeland.

This was the man who confronted Cooper Main.

A yellow-pine plank thirty inches wide lay across the low spot in the salt marsh, a place otherwise impassable. Cooper reached the inland end of the plank a step or two before the ungainly fellow on the mule reached the other end with his mournful Negro.

On a dry hillock twenty feet from the crossing, an alligator lay sunning. They were common in the coastal marshes. This one was mature: twelve feet long, probably five hundred pounds. Disturbed by the interlopers, it slid into the water and submerged. Only its unhooded eyes, above the water, showed its slow movement toward the plank. Sometimes 'gators were dangerous if too hungry, or if they perceived a man or an animal as a threat.

Cooper noticed the 'gator. Although he'd seen them since he was small, they terrified him. Nightmares of their tooth-lined jaws still tormented him occasionally. He shivered as he watched the eyes glide closer. Abruptly, the eyes submerged, and the alligator swam away.

Cooper thought the young man with the imperial was familiar, but couldn't place him. He heard him say, from the other end of the plank, "Give way."

Hot and irritable, Cooper began, "I see no reason—"

"I say again, sir, give way."

"No, sir. You're impertinent and presumptuous, and I don't know you."

"But I know you, sir." The young man's glance conveyed suppressed rage, yet he spoke in a conversational, even pleasant, way. The contradiction set Cooper's nerves to twitching.

"You're Mr. Cooper Main, from Charleston. The Carolina Shipping Company. Mont Royal Plantation. Desmond LaMotte, sir."

"Oh, yes. The dancing teacher." With that resolved, Cooper started his horse over the plank.

It had the effect of a match thrown in dry grass. Des kicked his mule forward. Hooves rapped the plank. The mule frightened Cooper's horse, causing it to sidestep and fall. Cooper twisted in the air to keep from being crushed, and landed in the shallows next to the horse. He thrashed and came up unhurt but covered with slimy mud.

"What the hell is wrong with you, LaMotte?"

"Dishonor, sir. Dishonor is what's wrong. Or does your family no longer understand the meaning of honor? It may be insubstantial as the sunlight, but it's no less important to life."

Dripping and chilled despite the heat, Cooper wondered if he'd met someone unbalanced by the war. "I don't know what in the name of God you mean."

"I refer, sir, to the tragedies visited upon members of my family by members of yours."

"I've done nothing to any LaMotte."

"Others with your name have done sinful things. You all smeared the honor of the LaMotte family by allowing Colonel Main to cuckold my first cousin Justin. Before I came home, your runaway slave Cuffey slew my first cousin Francis."

"But I tell you I had nothing to do—"

"We have held family councils, those of us who have survived," Des broke in. "I am glad I met you now, because it saves me from seeking you out in Charleston."

"For what?"

"To inform you that the LaMottes have agreed to settle our debt of honor."

"You're talking nonsense. Dueling's against the law."

"I am not referring to dueling. We'll use other means—at a time and place of our choosing. But we'll settle the debt."

Cooper reached for his horse's bridle. Water dripped from the animal and from Cooper's elbows, plopping in the silence. He wanted to scoff at this deranged young man, but was deterred by what he saw in LaMotte's eyes.

"We'll settle it with you, Mr. Main, or we'll settle it with your brother's nigger widow, or we'll settle it with both of you. Be assured of it."

And on he rode, mule shoes loud as pistol fire on the plank. After he reached solid ground, his hunched serving man followed, never once meeting Cooper's eye.

Cooper shivered again and led his horse from the water.

Late that night, at his house on Tradd Street, near the Battery, Cooper told his wife of the incident. Judith laughed.

That angered him. "He meant it. You didn't see him. I did. Not every man who goes to war comes back sane." He didn't notice her mournful glance, or recall his own mental disarray in the weeks following their son's drowning.

"I'm going to warn Madeline in a letter," he said.

WINTER GARDEN

Broadway, between Bleecker and Amity sts.

THIS EVENING,

commencing at 7½ o'clock,

RICHELIEU; THE CONSPIRACY.

Characters by Edwin Booth,

Charles Barron, J. H. Taylor, John Dyott,

W. A. Donaldson, C. Kemble Mason,

Miss Rose Eytange, Mrs. Marie Wilkins, &c. . . .

4

Willa woke suddenly. She heard a noise and a voice, neither of which she could identify.

Memory flooded back. Claudius Wood—the *Macbeth* dagger. She'd fled along Chambers Street in the rain and almost been run down by the horse of a fast hansom when she slipped and fell at an intersection. Only after four blocks had she dared look back at the dim lamplit street.

No sign of Wood. No pursuit of any kind. She had turned and run on.

The noise was a fist pounding the door. The unfamiliar voice belonged to a man.

"Miss Parker, the landlady saw you come in. Open the door, or I'll force it."

"Ruin a good door? I won't permit it."

That was the voice of the harpy who ran the lodging house. Earlier, when Willa had come dashing in from the rainy street, the woman had peered at her from the dining room, where she presided over bad food and the four shabby gentlemen who occupied the other rooms.

Willa had raced away from those hostile eyes and up the stairs to her sleeping room, with its tiny alcove crowded with her books, theater mementos, and two trunks of clothing. Safe inside the room, she'd thrown the bolt over and fallen on the bed, trembling. There she had lain listening for nearly an hour. At last, exhaustion had pulled her into sleep.

Now she heard the man in the hall tell the landlady, "You've got nothing to say about it. The girl's wanted for questioning about an assault on her employer." He pounded again. "Miss Parker!"

Willa hugged herself, not breathing.

The man shouted: "It's a police matter. I ask you one last time to open the door."

She was already dressed. A swift look into the dark alcove was her brief farewell to her few possessions. She snatched her shawl and raised the window. The man heard and started to break the door with his shoulder.

Fighting for breath, fighting terror, Willa climbed over the sill, lowered herself, holding on with both hands, then let go. She plunged downward through rainy blackness. An anguished cry went unheard as the door splintered and caved in.

"God—my God—I've never been through anything like this in my life, Eddie."

"There, there." He pulled her close to his shoulder. His velvet smoking coat had a nubby, comforting feel. While her clothes dried, she wore one of his robes, golden silk and quite snug; he was a small man. A strand of pale blond hair straggled across her forehead. Her bare legs rested on a stool in front of her. He'd wrapped her left ankle in a tight bandage. She had twisted it when she dropped to the alley, and she had been in pain as she hobbled all the way to his brownstone townhouse, Number 28 East Nineteenth Street.

"The policeman nearly caught me. Wood sent him, didn't he?"

"Undoubtedly," Booth said. He was thirty-two, slim and handsome, and had a rich voice critics called "a glorious instrument." His expressive eyes held a look of abiding pain.

Rain poured down on the townhouse and streaked its tall windows. It was half after one in the morning. Willa shivered in the silk robe as Booth continued. "Wood's a foul man. A discredit to our profession. He drinks far too much—on that habit I am an expert. Combine that with his temper and the result is catastrophic. Last year, he nearly crippled a gas-table operator who didn't light the stage precisely as he wanted it. Then there was his late wife—"

"I didn't know he was ever married."

"He doesn't talk about it, with reason. On a crossing for a London engagement, in heavy weather, she slipped and fell into the sea and disappeared. Wood was the sole witness, although a cabin steward later testified that on the morning of the mishap,

Helen Wood had bruises on her cheek and arm, which she'd attempted to cover with powder. In other words, he beat her."

"He can be such a charming man . . ." Willa's words trailed off into a sigh of self-recrimination. "How stupid I was to be taken in!"

"Not at all. His charm fools a great many people." Booth patted her shoulder, then stood up. He wore black trousers and tiny slippers; his feet were smaller than hers. "You feel chilly. Let me bring you some cognac. I keep it, though I never touch it."

Nor did he take any other spirits, she knew. When Booth's wife, Mary, lay dying in 1863, he'd been too drunk to respond to pleas from friends that he go to her. That part of the past burdened him almost as much as the fatal night at Ford's Theater.

Willa stared at the rain while Booth poured cognac into a snifter and warmed it in his hands. "I'll slip out tomorrow and try to discover what Wood's doing now that you have eluded the police." He handed her the snifter. The cognac went down with pleasing warmth and quickly calmed her churning stomach. "Meanwhile, I wouldn't count on his letting matters rest. Among his other wonderful traits is his talent for being vindictive. He has many friends among the local managers. He'll keep you from working in New York, at the very least."

Willa wiggled her bare toes. Her ankle hurt less now. In the fireplace, apple-wood logs crackled and filled the sitting room with a sweet aroma. While she sipped the cognac, Booth stared in melancholy fashion at a large framed photograph standing on a marble-topped table: three men wearing Roman togas. It was from the famous performance of November 1864, when he'd played Brutus to the Cassius and Antony of his brothers, Johnny and June, for one night.

She set the snifter aside. "I can't go back to Arch Street, Eddie. Mrs. Drew has a full company. She replaced me as soon as I gave notice."

"Louisa should have warned you about Wood."

"She did, indirectly. I wasn't alert to what she was trying to say. I have a lot of faults, and one of the worst is thinking well of everyone. Like John Evelyn's knight, I am 'not a little given to romance.' It's a dangerous shortcoming."

"No, no, a virtue. Never think otherwise." He patted her hand. "Supposing New York is closed to you, is there somewhere else you can work?"

"Somewhere I can run to? Running is always the remedy that comes easiest to me. And I'm always sorry afterward. I hate cowardice."

"Caution is not cowardice. I remind you again, this is something more than a schoolyard quarrel. Think a moment. Where can you go?"

Forlorn, she shook her head. "There isn't a single—well, yes. There's St. Louis. I have a standing offer from one of Papa's old colleagues. You know him. You and Papa trouped with him in California."

"Sam Trump?" Finally Booth smiled. "America's Ace of Players? I didn't know Sam was in St. Louis."

"Yes, he's running his own theater, in competition with Dan DeBar. He wrote me about it last Christmas. I gather things aren't going well."

Booth walked to the windows. "His drinking, probably. It seems to be the curse of the profession." He turned. "St. Louis might be an ideal sanctuary, though. It's quite far away, but it's a good show town. It has been ever since Ludlow and Drake set up shop there in the twenties. You have the whole Mississippi valley for touring, and no competing playhouses until you reach Salt Lake City. I liked playing St. Louis. So did my father."

He stared out the dark window, smiling again. "Whenever he appeared there, he could always save a few pennies by hiring bit players from the Thespians, a fine amateur company. Unfortunately, he just spent the pennies for one more bottle." He shook off the memory. "More to the point, Sam Trump's a decent man. He'd be a successful actor if he hadn't gone overboard for Forrest's physical technique. Sam turned the heroic style into a religion. He doesn't tear a passion to a tatter; he shatters it beyond repair—"

Another thoughtful pause, then a nod. "Yes, Sam's theater would do nicely. Who knows? You might even straighten him out."

Exhausted and unhappy, Willa said, "Must I decide right now?"

"No. Only when we find out what Wood's up to. Come." He extended his hand in a smooth, flowing move worthy of a performance. "I'll show you to your room. A long sleep will help immensely."

On the way out, he glanced at Johnny's picture again. Poor

Eddie, she thought, still hiding from the world because so many bayed for revenge, even though Johnny had been tracked down and shot to death near Bowling Green, Virginia, almost two months ago. Thinking of Booth's plight instead of hers helped her fall asleep.

She woke at two the next afternoon to find her friend gone. The skies outside were still stormy. A light meal of fruit, floury Scotch baps, and jam was set out downstairs. She was eating hungrily when his key rattled and he walked in, looking rakish in his slouch hat and opera cloak, and carrying an ebony cane.

"Bad news, I'm afraid. Wood swore out a warrant. I'll buy your ticket and advance you some traveling money. You don't dare visit your bank. Or your lodgings."

"Eddie, I can't leave my things. My collection of Mr. Dickens. The sides from all the parts I've played since I first started acting—every side is signed by all the actors in the play."

Booth flung his hat aside. "They may be precious to you, but they aren't worth imprisonment."

"Oh, dear God. Did he really—?"

"Yes. The charge is attempted murder."

A day later, after dark, he spirited her out of the townhouse and into a cab, which rattled swiftly over cobbles and through mud to a Hudson River pier. He handed her a valise containing some clothing he'd bought for her, kissed her cheek long and affectionately, and murmured a wish for God to guard her. She boarded the ferry for New Jersey and on the crossing didn't look back at him or at the city. She knew that if she did, she'd break down, cry, and take the return boat—and that could lead to disaster.

When she left the train in Chicago, she telegraphed Sam Trump. She stayed in an inexpensive hotel and waited for his reply, which came to the telegraph office the following morning. The message said he would happily provide board, lodging, and a premier place in his small permanent company. For a man in the throes of alcoholic failure, he certainly sounded confident. She was under such stress that she overlooked the obvious: He was an actor.

Like Willa's father, Mr. Samuel Horatio Trump had been born in England, at Stoke-Newington. He'd lived in the United States since the age of ten, but he diligently maintained his native accent, believing it contributed to his considerable and fully merited fame. Self-christened America's Ace of Players, he was also known in the profession, less kindly, as Sobbing Sam, not only because he could cry on cue, but because he inevitably did so to excess.

He was sixty-four years old and admitted to fifty. Without the special boots to which a cobbler had added inserts to lift the heels an inch and a half, he stood five feet six inches. He was a round, avuncular man with warm dark eyes and a rolling gait that jiggled his paunch. His wardrobe was large but twenty years out of date. Managers who flung plagiarized adaptations of Dickens on the stage always wanted to cast him as Micawber. Trump, however, saw himself as a Charlemagne, a Tamerlane, or, truly straining the credulity of his audiences, a Romeo.

In his lifetime Trump had known many women. When sober or even slightly tipsy, he was a blithe and winning man. To anyone who would listen, he confessed to many cases of a broken heart, but the secret truth was that Trump himself had ended every romantic affair in which he'd been involved. As a young man he had decided that the responsibilities of wedlock would only impede a career that was certain to end in international acclaim. So far it hadn't.

Although Willa and many others in the profession practiced the craft of theatrical superstition, Trump raised it to a high art. He refused to tie a rope around a trunk or hire a cross-eyed player. He never wore yellow, never rehearsed on Sunday, and ordered his doorkeeper to throw rocks at any stray dog that approached the stage door during a performance. He always rang down the curtain if he spied a red-headed spectator in the first five rows. He wore a blue-white moonstone mounted in gold for a cravat pin and kept a chrysanthemum—never yellow—in his lapel; he always had both somewhere on his person when onstage. He wouldn't even consider producing or appearing in the Scottish play.

The one superstition he violated was that about discussing the future and thereby jinxing it. Some of his favorite words were "next week" and "tomorrow" and "the next performance," invariably linked with phrases such as "important producer in the audience" or "telegraphed message" or "wanting a full year's engagement."

His theater, Trump's St. Louis Playhouse, had been built by another manager at the northwest corner of Third and Olive Streets; Trump called the latter Rue des Granges. He thought it more elegant to use the town's original French names. The theater held three hundred people, in individual seats rather than the more typical benches.

On the long trip to St. Louis, Willa made peace with herself over what had happened at the New Knickerbocker. Perhaps in a few years the manager would drop the charges, and she could go back. Meanwhile, in case Wood's spite reached beyond New York, she would bill herself as Mrs. Parker. Perhaps that would confuse anyone searching for a single woman, and also deter undesirable men. She refused to go so far as to call herself Willa Potts.

She was in reasonably good spirits by the time the river ferry deposited her on the St. Louis levee. She found Sam Trump painting a forest backdrop at the theater. He cried while they hugged and kissed dramatically, then opened a bottle of champagne, which he proceeded to drink all by himself. Near the bottom of the bottle, he made a startling admission:

"I falsified the tone of my telegraph message, dear girl. You have chosen to inhabit a house in ruin."

"St. Louis looks prosperous to me, Sam."

"My theater, child, my theater. We are months in arrears to all of our creditors. Our audiences are satisfactory. There is even an occasional full house. Yet, for reasons entirely beyond my ken, I can't keep a shilling in the till."

Willa could see one of the reasons, made of green glass and reposing, empty, in a silver bucket from the property loft.

Sam astonished her a second time when he said, with a hangdog look, "It wants a clearer head than mine. A better head than this gray and battered one." Only gray around the ears. He dyed the rest a hideous boot-polish brown.

He seized her hand. "Along with your acting duties, would you perchance consider managing the house? You are young, but you have a great deal of experience in the profession. I can't pay you extra for the work, but I can offer the compensation of billing equivalent to mine." With great solemnity, he added, "That of a star."

She laughed as she hadn't in days. It was the sort of work she had never done before, but, as far as she could see, it needed mostly common sense, diligence, and attention to where the pennies went.

"That's a heady inducement, Sam. Let me think about it overnight."

Next morning, she went to the playhouse office, a room with all the spaciousness and charm of a chicken coop. It also had the inevitable horseshoe nailed over the lintel. She found Trump disconsolately holding his head with one hand and stroking the black theater cat, Prosperity, with the other.

"Sam, I accept your offer—conditionally."

He overlooked the last word, crying, "Splendid!"

"This is the condition. My first act as manager is to put you on an allowance. The theater will pay your living expenses, but nothing for whiskey, beer, champagne, or strong drink of any kind."

He smote his bosom with his fist. "Oh! How sharper than a serpent's tooth—"

"Sam, I just took over this theater. Do you want me to quit?"

"No, no!"

"Then you are on an allowance."

"Dear lady—" His chin fell, covering the moonstone cravat pin. "I hear and I obey."

MADELINE'S JOURNAL

July, 1865. The dark mood has passed. Hard work is a strong antidote for melancholy.

The state remains in turmoil. Judge Perry is now the provisional governor. He has pledged to implement Johnson's program, and set Sept. 13 for a constitutional convention for that purpose.

From Hilton Head, Gen. Gillmore commands the nine military districts, each with a Union garrison whose primary purpose is to forestall violence between the races. In our district some of the soldiers are Negroes, and many of my neigh-

*bors angrily say we are being "niggered to death." So we shall
be, I think, until we resolve differences and live in harmony.
It is my heart, Orry, not my ancestry, leading me to believe
that if Almighty God ever set a single test by which to judge
the republic's ability to fulfill its promise of liberty for all
men, that test is race.*

*Freedmen's Bureau of the War Dept. now operating.
Gen. Saxton at Beaufort the assistant commissioner for the
state. Needed food is beginning to find its way to the destitute . . .*

*A strange letter from Cooper. C. met a certain Desmond
LaMotte of Charleston, whom I do not know. This D. L.,
whose profession is dancing master, said the LaMottes believe
I cuckolded Justin, and they want reprisal. After so much
bloodshed and privation, how can anyone find energy for such
hatred? I would consider it ludicrous but for Cooper's warning that I must take it seriously. He thought this D. L. quite
fanatic, therefore possibly a threat. Could he be one of those
tragic young men whose nerves and reason were destroyed by
the war? I shall exercise caution with strangers . . .*

*Brutal heat. But we have harvested our rice crop and got
a little money for it. Few Negroes want to work as yet. Many
on abandoned plantations in the neighborhood are busy tearing down the old quarters where they lived as slaves in order
to put up new homes, however small and primitive, as emblems of their freedom.*

*Andy and Jane continue to press me about a school for
the local freedmen. Will decide soon. There are risks to be
weighed.*

*Yesterday, in need of lamp oil, walked to the old store at
the Summerton crossroads. I went the shorter way, through
the lovely bright marshes, whose hidden paths you taught me
so well. At the crossroads, a sad spectacle. The Gettys Bros.
store is open but surely will not be for long—shelves are bare.
The place is little more than a shelter for members of that
large family, one of whom, an oafish old man with a squirrel
rifle, keeps watch on the property . . .*

The noon sun shone on the Summerton crossroads. Three
great live oaks spread shade over the store and its broken stoop.
Near them, clusters of dark green yucca with spear-sharp fronds

grew low to the ground. Madeline stood looking at the old man with the rifle on the edge of the porch. He wore filthy pants; his long underwear served as his shirt.

"Ain't nothin' here for you or anybody else," he said.

Sweat darkened the back of Madeline's faded dress. The hem showed dampness and mud left by her trek through the salt marshes. "There's water in the well," she said. "Might I have a drink before I start back?"

"No," said the nameless member of the Gettys clan. "Go get it from the wells of your own kind." He gestured to the empty tawny road winding away toward Mont Royal.

"Thank you so much for your kindness," she said, picking up her skirts and stepping into the blaze of light.

A half-mile down the road, she came upon a detachment of six black soldiers and a white lieutenant with a downy, innocent face. The men lay at rest in the hot shade, their collars unfastened, their rifles and canteens put aside.

"Good day, ma'am," the young officer said, jumping up and giving a little salute of respect.

"Good day. It's a hot day for travel."

"Yes, but we must march back to Charleston all the same. I wish I could offer you water, but our canteens are empty. I asked that fellow at the store to let us fill up, and he wouldn't."

"He isn't a very generous sort, I'm afraid. If you'll come along to my plantation—it's about two miles and right on your way—you're welcome to use its well."

So it has risen to haunt me again. "Your own kind," the old man said. Cooper's letter said the dancing master made reference to my ancestry, too.

Went last night on foot along the river road to the Church of St. Joseph of Arimathea, where we worshiped together. Have not been there since shortly after the great house burned. Father Lovewell greeted me and welcomed me to meditation in the family pew for as long as I wished.

I sat for an hour, and my heart spoke. As soon as possible I must travel to the city on three errands, one of which is sure to provoke people such as the dancing master and that old Mr. Gettys. Let it. If I am to be hanged regardless of what I do, why should I hesitate to commit a hanging offense? Orry, my love, I draw courage from thoughts of you, and of my dear father. Neither of you ever let fear put chains on your conscience.

5

Ashton let out a long wailing cry. The customer writhing on top of her responded with a bleary smile of bliss. Downstairs, Ashton's employer, Señora Vasquez-Reilly, heard the outcry and saluted the ceiling with her glass of tequila.

Ashton hated what she was doing. That is, she hated the act when she had to do it to survive. Being stuck in this flyblown frontier town—Santa Fe, in New Mexico Territory—was unspeakable. To be reduced to whoring was unbelievable. Moaning and yelling let her express her feelings.

The middle-aged gentleman, a widower who raised cattle, withdrew, shyly averting his eyes. Having already paid her, he dressed quickly, then bowed and kissed her hand. She smiled and said in halting Spanish, "You come back soon, Don Alfredo."

"Next week, Señorita Brett. Happily."

God, I hate greasers, she thought as she sorted the coins after he left. Three of the four went to Señora Vasquez-Reilly, a widow whose burly brother-in-law made sure the señora's three girls didn't cheat. Ashton had gone to work for the señora early in the summer, when her funds ran out. She'd given her name as Señorita Brett, thinking it a fine joke. It would have been an even better one if her sweet, prissy sister knew about it.

Ashton Main—she no longer thought of herself as Mrs. Huntoon—had decided to stay in Santa Fe because of the treasure. Somewhere in the Apache-infested wasteland, two wagons had vanished, and the men bringing them from Virginia City had been massacred. One man, her husband, James Huntoon, was no loss. Another, her lover, Lamar Powell, had planned to create a second confederacy in the Southwest, with Ashton as his consort. To finance it, he'd loaded a false bottom in one of the wagons with three hundred thousand dollars in gold refined from ore out of the Nevada mine originally owned by his late brother.

The massacre had been reported by a wagon driver who reached a trading station shortly before he died of his wounds. In his pain-racked, disjointed telling, he never revealed the site of the killings. Only one person might have that information now: the guide Powell had hired in Virginia City, Collins. Rumor said he'd survived, but God knew where he was.

When she first heard of the massacre, Ashton had tried to find a wealthy patron in Santa Fe. Candidates were few. Most were married, and if they philandered at the señora's, they also showed no desire to get rid of their wives. As for finding a man at Fort Marcy, the idea was a joke. The officers and men who garrisoned the run-down post near the old Palace of Governors weren't paid enough to support their own lusts, let alone a mistress. They had all the prospects of a hog headed for a Low Country barbecue.

Of course she could have avoided working for the señora if she'd written an appeal to her sanctimonious brother Cooper, or to the sister whose name she delighted in muddying, or even to the slutty octoroon Orry had married. But she was damned if she'd stoop to asking any of them for charity. She didn't want to see them or communicate with them until she could do so on her own terms.

Ashton put on her working clothes—a yellow silk dress with wide lace-trimmed shoulder straps, meant to be worn over a blouse with dolman sleeves. The señora had denied her the blouse as well as a corset, so that the bulge of her partly exposed breast would tempt the customers. The dress had been fashionable about the time her damn brother Orry went to West Point. She hated it, along with the coy black mantilla the señora insisted she wear, and the shoes, too—leather dyed a garish yellow, with laces, and thin high heels.

She adjusted the mantilla in front of a small scrap of mirror and ran her palm down her left cheek. The three parallel scratches barely showed, thank heaven. Another of the girls, Rosa, had attacked her in a dispute over a customer. Before the señora pulled them apart, Rosa had scratched Ashton's face badly. Ashton had wept for hours over the bloody nail marks. Her body and her face were her chief assets, the weapons she used to get whatever she wanted.

For weeks after the fight, she'd plastered salve on the slow-healing wounds, and rushed to the mirror seven or eight times a day to examine them. At last she was sure there would be no permanent damage. Nor would Rosa trouble her again. Ashton now carried a small sharpened file in her right shoe.

Occasional thoughts of the mine in Nevada only sharpened her greed. Wasn't that mine hers, too? She'd practically been married to Lamar Powell. Of course, if she wanted to get possession of the mine, she faced two gigantic obstacles: She'd have to convince the authorities that she was Mrs. Powell, and, before she could do that, she had to reach Virginia City. Ashton considered herself a strong and resourceful young woman, but she wasn't crazy. Cross hundreds and hundreds of miles of dangerous wasteland by herself? Not likely. She focused instead on the nearer dream, the wagons.

If she could just *find* them! She was convinced the Apaches had not stolen the gold. It had been cleverly concealed. Moreover, they were ignorant savages; they wouldn't know its value. With the gold she could buy much more than material comfort. She could buy position, and power. The power to travel back to South Carolina, descend on Mont Royal, and, in some way yet to be devised, rub dirt in the faces of those in the family who'd rejected her. Her consuming desire was to ruin every last one of them.

Meanwhile, it had come down to a choice of starving or whoring. So she whored. And waited. And hoped.

Most of the señora's customers loved Ashton's white Anglo skin and her Southern speech and mannerisms, which she exaggerated for effect. Tonight, when she descended to the cantina with her grand airs, her performance was wasted. No one was there but three elderly vaqueros playing cards.

The cantina looked particularly dismal after dark. Lamplight yellowed everything, and revealed the bullet holes, knife marks, whiskey spills, and general filth on the furniture, floor, and adobe walls. The señora sat reading an old Mexico City newspaper. Ashton handed her the coins.

The señora favored her with a smile that showed her gold front tooth. *"Gracias, querida.* Are you hungry?"

Ashton pouted. "Hungry for some fun in this dreary old place. I miss hearing a little music."

The señora's upper lip and faint mustache dropped down to hide the gold tooth. "Too bad. I can't afford a mariachi."

The brother-in-law, a stupid hulk named Luis, walked in through the half-doors. The only piece of free goods the señora allowed him was Rosa, who had stringy hair and had had the pox. Soon after Ashton started to work, Luis had tried to fondle her. She couldn't stand his smell or his swinish manners, and she already knew the señora held him in low regard, so she slapped him. He was about to hit back when the señora stepped in and cowed him with shouted profanity. Ever since, Luis never got close to Ashton without letting her see his sullen fury. Tonight was no different. He stared at her while he grabbed Rosa's wrist. He dragged the girl past the door leading to the office and store-room and pulled her up the stairs. Ashton rubbed her left cheek. I hope he works her like a field hand, she thought. I hope she gives him a good case, too.

A hot wind swept dust under the half-doors. No customers showed up. At half past ten, the señora said Ashton could go to bed. She lay in the dark in her tiny room listening to the wind bang shutters and again entertaining the idea of robbing the señora. Now and then customers spent a lot at the cantina, and cash sometimes accumulated for over a week. She couldn't think of how to commit the robbery, though. And there was a great risk. Luis had a fast horse and some bad friends. If they captured her, they might kill her or, just as bad, disfigure her.

Anger and hopelessness kept her from sleep. Finally she re-lighted the lamp and reached under the bed for her lacquered Oriental box. On the lid, bits of inlaid pearl formed a scene: a Japanese couple, fully clothed and in repose, contemplating cups of tea. Raising the lid and holding it against the light revealed the couple, with kimonos up, copulating. The woman's happy face showed her response to the gentleman's mammoth shaft, half inside her.

The box always lifted Ashton's spirits. It held forty-seven buttons she'd collected over the years—West Point uniform buttons, trouser-fly buttons. Each button represented a man she'd enjoyed, or at least used. Only two partners didn't have a button in the box: the first boy who took her, before she started her collection, and her weakling husband, Huntoon. The collection was growing rapidly in Santa Fe.

For a few minutes, she examined one button and then another, trying to put a face with each. Presently, she put the box away, and examined her perspiring body in the mirror. Still soft where it should be, firm where it should be, and the nail marks on her face hardly showed. Gazing at herself, she felt her hope renewed. Somehow, she would use her beauty to escape this damnable place.

She went to sleep then, enjoying a dream of repeatedly pricking Brett's skin with her little file, till it bled.

Three nights later, a coarsely dressed Anglo walked into the cantina. He had mustaches with long points and a revolver on his hip. He downed two fast double whiskeys at the bar, then wobbled over to the hard chairs where Ashton and Rosa waited for customers. The third girl was at work upstairs.

"Hello, Miss Yellow Shoes. How are you this evening?"

"I'm just fine."

"What's your name?"

"Brett."

He grinned. "Do I hear the accent of a fallen blossom from the South?"

She tossed her head, flirted with her eyes. "I never fall unless I'm paid first. Since you know my name, what's yours?"

"You might find my first name a bit peculiar. It's Banquo, from Mr. Shakespeare's tragedy *Macbeth*. Last name's Collins. I may be back to see you after I have a couple more drinks."

He ambled back to the bar, while Ashton gripped her chair to keep from toppling off.

Banquo Collins pounded a fist on the bar. "I'll buy for everybody. I can spend ten times that much and never worry."

The señora closed in. "Bold words, my dear sir."

"But they're true, lass. I know where to mine some treasure."

"Ah, I knew you were fooling. There are no mines around here."

Collins swallowed all of a glass of popskull. "I don't mine dirt; I mine wagons."

"Wagons? That makes no sense."

"Does to me."

He extended his arms and began to shuffle his booted feet. "Ought to have music in this place, so a man could dance."

Because everyone was watching him, they missed the wild look
on Ashton's face. This was the man—Powell's guide!

"Gonna be rich as Midas," he declared, rubbing his crotch.
Rosa primped furiously. Ashton slid the file from her shoe and
beneath her left arm. Rosa gasped when the point jabbed her.

"This one's mine," Ashton whispered. "If you take him, I'll
put your eye out tomorrow."

Rosa was white. "Take him. Take him."

"Gonna have plenty of music when I see the world. Rome,
the Japans—" Collins belched. "But not here. Guess I can get
pleasured here, though."

He lurched to the girls. Ashton stood. He grinned again,
took her hand, and headed upstairs.

After latching the door, she helped him undress. She was so
excited she pulled one trouser button too hard. It flew and ticked
against the wall. He sat on the bed while she worked his pants off.
"That was interesting talk downstairs," she said.

He blinked, as if he hadn't heard. "Where'd you come from,
Yellow Shoes? You're sure no greaser."

"I'm a Carolina girl, stranded here by misfortune." A deep
breath, and then the leap. "A misfortune I think we both know
something about."

Despite all he'd drunk, and his aroused state, what she said
put him on guard. "Are we gonna talk or fuck?"

She bent forward, ministering to him a moment to curb his
irritation. "I just want to ask about those wagons—" He grabbed
her hair. "Collins, I'm your friend. I know what was in those
wagons."

"How come?" Furious, he yanked her hair. "I said *how
come?*"

"Please. Not so hard! That's better." She leaned back, frightened. Suppose he really felt threatened? Suppose he decided to
kill her? Then she thought, *If you stay here you're as good as dead
anyway.*

She collected herself and said carefully, "I know because I'm
related to the man who owned the wagons. He was a Southerner,
wasn't he?"

His eyes admitted it before he could deny it. She clapped her
hands. "Sure he was. Both of them were. And you guided them
from Virginia City."

She dragged the shoulder straps down to show off her

breasts, red and firm already. Lord, she was all worked up over the mere thought of the gold. "Do you know where those wagons are, Collins?"

He just smirked.

"You do. I know what was in them. What's more, I know where it came from—and how to get hundreds, why maybe a thousand times, more of the same."

She detected a gleam of interest and pushed the advantage. "I'm talking about the mine in Virginia City. It belongs to me, because one of the men who died, Mr. Powell, owned it, and I'm related to him."

"You mean you can prove it's yours?"

Without hesitation or change of expression she said, "Absolutely. You share what's in those wagons, then help me get to Nevada, and I'll split an even bigger fortune with you."

"Sure—an even bigger fortune. And there's seven cities of gold waiting to be found round here, too—never mind that nobody's turned them up since the Spanish started searching hundreds of years ago."

"Collins, don't sneer at me. I'm telling the truth. We need to pool our information. If we do, we'll be so rich you'll get dizzy. We can go all over the world together. Wouldn't that be exciting, lover?" Her tongue gave a moist demonstration of her excitement.

Seconds passed without a response. Her fear crept back.

Suddenly he laughed. "By the Lord, you're a canny lass. Canny as you are hot."

"Say we're partners and I'll treat you to some special loving. Things I won't do for anybody else, no matter how much they pay." She whispered salacious words in his ear.

He laughed again. "All right. Partners."

"Here I come," she cried, dropping her dress and pantaloons and falling on him on the bed.

She kept her word, but after ten minutes his age and his drinking caught up with him, and he began to snore.

Ashton pulled up the covers, toweled herself and slipped in next to him, her heart thumping. Finally, patience had been rewarded. No more whoring. She had the man who had the gold.

Imagination painted pictures of a new Worth gown. The

grandest hotel suite in New York City. Madeline cringing while Ashton slashed her across the face with a fan.

Delicious visions. They'd soon be real. She fell asleep.

She woke murmuring his name. She heard no answer.

Daylight showed through slits in the shutter. She felt the bed beside her.

Empty. Cold.

"Collins?"

He'd left a penciled note on the old bureau.

Dear Little Miss Yellow Shoes,

Keep shining up the story of the V. City "mine." Maybe somebody will swallow it. Meantime I already know what was in the wagons because I've got it and I don't figure to share it. But thanks for the special stuff anyway.

Goodbye,
BC

Ashton screamed. She screamed until she woke the whole place—Rosa, the third whore, the señora, who stormed in and shouted at her. Ashton spit in her face. The señora slapped her. She kept on sobbing and screaming.

Two days later, she found the button that had popped from Banquo Collins's pants. After examining it, and crying all over again, she put it in her box.

Hellish heat settled on Santa Fe. People moved as little as possible. Every evening she sat on the hard chair, not knowing what to do, how to escape.

She didn't smile. No customers wanted her. Señora Vasquez-Reilly began to complain and threaten her with eviction. She didn't care.

MADELINE'S JOURNAL

July, 1865. To the city yesterday. Shermans insisted Andy drive the wagon, to protect me. Strange to ride that way, like a white mistress with her slave. For a few moments on the trip it was easy to imagine nothing had changed.

Impossible to imagine that in Charleston. Cooper's firm on Concord Street overlooks vast empty warehouses where tur-

*key buzzards roost. He was absent, so left a message asking to
see him later. Could not guess how he would receive the news.*

*Little has been rebuilt from the great fire of '61. The
burned zone looks as though Gen'l. Sherman visited it. Rats
and wild dogs roam amid the ruined chimneys and weed-
choked foundations. Many homes near the Battery show shell
damage. The house of Mr. Leverett Dawkins on East Bay
untouched, however. . . .*

If there was a fatter man than the old Whig Unionist
Dawkins, Madeline had never met him. Fiftyish, with impeccable
clothes specially tailored for him, Dawkins had thighs big as wa-
termelons and a stomach round as that of an expectant mother of
triplets. On the parlor wall behind him hung the inevitable array
of ancestral portraits. When Madeline entered, Dawkins was already seated in his huge custom-made chair, gazing across the
harbor at the rubble of Fort Sumter. He disliked having anyone
see him walk or sit down.

She asked about the Mont Royal mortgages. There were
two, totaling six hundred thousand dollars and held by Atlanta
banks. Dawkins said his own Palmetto Bank would open soon,
and he would ask his board to buy and consolidate the mortgages. "Mont Royal is fine collateral. I'd like to hold the paper on
it."

She described the sawmill idea. He was less encouraging.

"We won't have much to lend on schemes like that. Perhaps
the board can find a thousand or two for a shed, some saw pits,
and a year's wages for a gang of nigras. If you can find the
nigras."

"I had thought of installing steam machinery—"

"Out of the question if you must borrow to buy it. There are
so many wanting to rebuild, begging for help. This is a wounded
land, Madeline. Just look around the city."

"Yes, I have. Well, you're very generous to help with the
mortgages, Leverett."

"Please don't consider it charity. The plantation is valuable
—one of the finest in the district. The owner, your brother-in-
law, is an esteemed member of the community. And you, as the
manager, are an excellent risk as well. An eminently responsible
citizen."

He means, she thought sadly, I am not a troublemaker. How

responsible would he think her if he knew the nature of her next call?

> . . . *So we will not proceed as fast as I hoped.*
>
> *Took myself next to the Freedmen's Bureau, on Meeting. A pugnacious little man with a harsh accent met me, calling himself Brevet Colonel Orpha C. Munro, of "Vuh-mont." His official title—hardly less grand than "caliph" or "pasha"—is sub-assistant commissioner, Charleston District.*
>
> *I made my request. He said he felt sure the bureau could obtain a teacher. He will notify me. I left with the feeling of having done some criminal deed.*
>
> *Noting the time, I sent Andy off by himself and walked to Tradd Street to call on Judith before my meeting with Cooper. Judith surprised me by saying he was home, and had been since returning to dine at noon.*

"Instead of going back to the company, I stayed here to work on these," Cooper said. At his feet on the dry brown grass of the walled garden lay pencil sketches of a pier for the Carolina Shipping Company. From the house came a hesitant version of the central theme from Mozart's Twenty-first Concerto, in C, played on a piano badly out of tune.

Cooper turned to his wife. "May we have some tea, or a reasonable substitute?" Judith smiled and retired. "Now, Madeline, what prompts this unexpected and pleasant visit?"

She sat down on a rusting bench of black-painted iron. "I want to start a school at Mont Royal."

In the act of bending to gather the penciled sheets, Cooper jerked his head up and stared. His dark hair hung over his pale forehead. His sunken eyes were wary. "What kind of school, pray?"

"One to teach reading and arithmetic to anyone who wants to learn. The freed Negroes in the district desperately need a few basic skills if they're to survive."

"No." Cooper crushed all the sketches and threw the ball under an azalea bush. His color was high. "No. I can't allow you to do it."

Equally emotional, she said, "I am not asking your permission, merely doing you the courtesy of telling you my intentions."

A flat-bosomed young girl poked her head from a tall window on the piazza one story above. "Papa, why are you shouting? Why, Aunt Madeline, good afternoon."

"Good afternoon, Marie-Louise."

Cooper's daughter was thirteen. She would never be a beauty, and indeed might be homely in maturity. She seemed aware of her deficiencies and worked hard to overcome them with tomboy energy and a great deal of smiling. People liked her; Madeline adored her.

"Go inside and keep practicing," Cooper snapped.

Marie-Louise gulped and retreated. The Mozart began again, with nearly as many wrong notes as right ones.

"Madeline, allow me to remind you that feelings against the nigras, and anyone who champions them, are running high. It would be folly to exacerbate those feelings. You must not open a school."

"Cooper, again, it isn't your decision." She tried to be gentle with him, but the message was unavoidably harsh. "You gave me management of the plantation, in writing. So I intend to go ahead. I will have a school."

He paced, glowering. This was a new, distinctly unfriendly Cooper Main, a side of him she'd never seen. The silence lengthened. Madeline tried to patch over the difficulty. "I had hoped you'd be on my side. Education of black people is no longer against the law, after all."

"But it's unpopular . . ." He hesitated, then burst out, "If you goad people, they'll no longer exercise any restraint."

"Restraint in regard to what?"

"You! Everyone looks the other way now, pretending you're not—Well, you understand. If you start a school, they won't be so tolerant."

Madeline's face was white. She had expected someone, someday, to threaten her about her parentage, but she'd never expected it would be her brother-in-law.

"Here's the tea."

Curls bobbing, Judith brought a tray of chipped cups and saucers down the stairs. On the last iron step she halted, aware of the storm on her husband's face.

"I'm afraid Madeline is leaving," he said. "She only stopped by to tell me something about Mont Royal. Thank you for your courtesy, Madeline. For your own sake, I urge you to change your mind. Good day."

He turned his back and hunted under the azalea for the crushed drawings. Judith remained on the step, stunned by the rudeness. Madeline, concealing her hurt, patted Judith's arm, hurried up the noisy iron stairs, and ran from the house.

> . . . *There it rests for the moment. I fear I've made him my enemy. If so, my sweet Orry, then at least I have lost his friendship in a worthy cause.*
>
> *A message came! And only two weeks after my visit to Col. Munro. The Freedmen's Aid Society of the Methodist Episcopal church, Cincinnati, will send us a teacher. Her name is Prudence Chaffee.*
>
> *Cooper silent. No sign of retaliation yet.*

6

The U.S. Army trained cavalry recruits at Jefferson Barracks, Missouri. The camp of instruction was located on the west bank of the Mississippi, a few miles south of St. Louis.

When Charles arrived there, a contract surgeon examined him for false teeth, visible tumors, and signs of venereal disease and alcoholism. Pronounced fit, he was marched away, along with a former corset salesman from Hartford who said he craved adventure, a New York City roughneck who said little and probably was running away from a lot, an Indiana carpenter who said he'd awakened one morning to discover he hated his wife, a chatterbox boy who said he'd lied about his age, and a handsome man who said nothing. When the recruits reached a ramshackle barracks, the white-haired corporal pointed to the silent man.

"French Foreign Legion. Can't hardly speak no English. Jesus an' Mary, don't we get 'em all? And for a rotten thirteen dollars a month." He studied Charles. "I seen your papers. Reb, wasn't you?"

Charles was edgy about that. He'd already drawn some sharp looks because of his accent, and had heard "Goddamn traitor" behind his back once. He wanted to snap at the corporal, but he remembered Jack Duncan's caution and just said, "Yes."

"Well, it don't matter to me. My first cousin Fielding, he was a Reb, too. If you're as good a soldier as him, you'll be more use to Uncle Sam than the rest of this flotsam. Good luck." He stepped back and yelled, "All right, you people. Through that door and find a bunk. Hurry it up! This ain't a goddamn hotel you're checkin' into."

Charles took the oath to support and defend the Constitution. He had no problem with that; he'd already taken it once, at West Point. And when the war ended, he'd made up his mind to raise his son as an American, not a Southerner.

It did seem strange to be issued so much blue again. The light blue kersey trousers with the yellow stripes and the dull gray fatigue shirts reminded him of the Second Cavalry. So did the barracks, with its poor ventilation, smoky lamps, narrow slot windows at each end, and sounds of scurrying rodents at night. So did his Army cot, an iron-framed torture device with wood slats and stringers and a mattress shell filled with smelly straw. So did the Army food, especially the hardtack and the beef served up in tough slices at noon mess, then submerged in a sludgy gravy for supper; the meat tasted better with the gravy, which masked the faint odor of spoilage.

Jefferson Barracks proved to be not so much a training center as a holding pen. Recruits were sent out as soon as a regiment's required number of replacements could be gathered. So training could last two months or two days. That didn't speak well for the postwar Army, Charles thought.

Most of the instructors were older noncoms putting in time until they retired. Charles worked hard to look inexperienced and awkward in front of them. During a bareback equitation class, he deliberately fell of his pathetic sway-backed training horse. He fumbled through the manual of arms, and at target practice never hit the bull, only the edge of the card. He got away with it until one trainer got sick and a new one took over, a runty corporal named Hans Hazen. He was a mean sort; one of the men said he'd been busted from top sergeant three times.

After a saber drill, Hazen drew Charles aside.

"Private May, I got a queer feeling you ain't no Carolina militiaman. You try to look clumsy, but I saw some of your moves when you thought I was watchin' somebody else." He thrust his chin out and shouted. "Where were you trained? West Point?"

Charles looked down at him. "Wade Hampton Legion. Sir."

Hazen shook a finger. "I catch you lyin', it'll go hard. I hate liars near as much as I hate snobs from the Point—or you Southron boys."

"Yes, sir," Charles said loudly. He kept staring. Hazen looked away first, which shamed him to anger.

"I want to see what you're made of. A hundred laps of the riding ring, quick time. Right now. March!"

After that, Corporal Hazen stayed on him, yelling, criticizing, questioning him daily about his past and forcing him to lie. Despite Hazen—maybe, in a strange way, because of him; because Hazen recognized an experienced soldier—Charles felt happy to be back in the Army. He'd always liked the dependable routine of trumpet calls, assemblies, drills. He still felt a shiver up his backbone when the trumpeters blew "Boots and Saddles."

He kept to himself and didn't find a bunky, a partner. Most soldiers paired up to ease their work load and share their miseries, but he avoided it. He survived three weeks that way, although not without some sudden bouts of despondency. Thoughts of the past would return suddenly, the burned-out feeling would grip him, and he'd call himself a prize fool for donning Army blue again. He was in that kind of mood one Saturday night when he left the post and crossed the main approach road to the nameless town of tents and shanties on the other side.

Here a lot of noncoms lived with their wives, who took in post laundry to supplement Army pay. Here civilians hawked questionable whiskey in big tents, docile Osage Indians sold beans and squash from their farms nearby, and elegant gentlemen ran all-night poker and faro games. Charles had even seen a few earnestly stupid recruits betting on three-card monte or the pea and shells.

Other amenities were available in any tent with a red lantern hung in front. Charles called at one of these and spent a half hour with a homely young woman anxious to please. He walked out physically relieved but depressed by memories of Gus Barclay and a feeling that he'd dishonored her.

Two young boys ran after him as he walked through the tent town. They taunted him with a chant:

> "Soldier, soldier, will you work?
> No indeed, I'll sell my shirt . . ."

The public certainly held the Army in high esteem. As soon as the war ended, soldiers had again become the unwashed, the unwanted. Nothing ever changed.

He'd been at Jefferson Barracks four weeks when orders came through: He and seven other recruits were given twelve hours to prepare to leave on a steamer bound up the Missouri River to Fort Leavenworth, Kansas, all the way across the state of Missouri. Established in 1827 by Colonel Henry Leavenworth, the great cantonment on the right bank of the river was the most important post in the West. It was headquarters for the Department of the Missouri and the supply depot for all the forts between Kansas and the Continental Divide. At Leavenworth they would find transportation, they were told, to carry them to duty with the Sixth Cavalry, down on the northern Texas frontier. The prospect pleased Charles. He'd loved the natural beauty of Texas when he was stationed at Camp Cooper before the war.

While a thunderstorm flashed and roared above the barracks, he packed his carpetbag and a small wooden footlocker in which he kept his Army-issue clothing. He put on his blue blouse, which had a roll collar, and his kepi with the enlisted man's version of the cavalry's crossed sabers. The storm quickly diminished, and he walked through light rain to the tent town, whistling a jaunty march version of the little tune that reminded him of home.

The storm had toppled some of the smaller tents and muddied the dirt lanes. Charles headed for the largest and brightest of the drinking tents, the Egyptian Palace, whose owner came from Cairo, Illinois. The tent was shabby. A piece of canvas divided an area for officers from the one for enlisted men and civilians. The whiskey was cheap and raw, but Charles felt a rare contentment as he sipped it.

Right after he'd ordered a second drink, a trio of noisy noncoms stumbled in. One was Corporal Hazen, wobbling. Evidently he'd been drinking for some time. He spied Charles at the end of the plank bar and made a remark about a foul smell.

Charles stared at him until he looked away and shrilly ordered a round for his friends. Charles was thankful Hazen didn't feel like pushing it. He felt too good.

That lasted ten minutes.

Passing by on his way to the officers' entrance, a small, slight man saw a familiar face among the enlisted men inside. He looked away, took three more steps, then halted, his mouth open. He about-faced and peered into the smoky tent—

There was no mistake.

Color rose in his face as he went in. The men noticed his look and stopped talking.

The officer walked toward the end of the bar with an aggressive swagger—probably to make up for standing only five feet six. His shoulders were pulled back with the stiffness of someone preoccupied with Army formality. Everything about him suggested fussiness: the waxy points of his mustache, the impeccable trim of his goatee.

Yellow facings and trouser stripes identified him as cavalry. A lieutenant colonel's silver-embroidery oak leaf decorated his shoulder straps. He marched down the bar and, as he passed a burly, bearded civilian wearing a notched turkey feather in his hair and a buckskin coat decorated with porcupine quills and gaudy diamond-shaped pony beads, he accidentally bumped the man's arm, spilling whiskey.

"Hey, you jackass," the man said. As he turned, the beads on his coat shot darts of reflected light through the tent. A brindle dog at his feet responded to his tone and growled at the officer, who strode on without apology, tightly clutching the hilt of his dress sword.

"Cap'n Venable, sir," Charles heard Hazen say as the officer reached the three noncoms. The silver oak leaf was from a wartime brevet, then.

"Hazen," the man said, striding on. Charles watched him, and the back of his neck started to itch. He didn't recognize the officer. Yet something about the man bothered him.

Venable halted two feet from Charles. "I saw you from the street, Private. What's your name?"

Charles tried to place the accent. Not truly Southern, but similar. One of the border states? He said, "Charles May. Sir."

"That's a damn lie." The officer snatched the whiskey glass from Charles's hand and threw the contents in his face.

A sudden uproar of talk; then, just as suddenly, silence. Whiskey dripped from Charles's chin and ran off the edge of the plank bar. Charles wanted to hit the little rooster but held back because he didn't understand what was happening. He was certain there was some mistake.

"Captain—" he began.

"You'll address me as colonel. And don't bother to keep on lying. Your name isn't May; it's Charles Main. You graduated from West Point in 1857, two years before I did. You and that damn reb Fitz Lee were thick as this." The officer held up two fingers. Instantly, the bearded face acquired a past that Charles remembered.

He bluffed. "Sir, you're mistaken."

"The hell. You remember me, and I remember you. Harry Venable. Kentucky. You put me on report four times for a messy room. Twenty skins each time. I damn near accumulated two hundred and took the Canterberry Road because of you."

Even in a stupor, Hazen caught on. He wiped his nose and exclaimed to his friends, "Didn't I tell you? Didn't I spot it?" He stepped away from the bar, in case Charles tried a dash to the entrance.

Charles didn't know how to extricate himself peacefully. More memories came back, including Venable's cadet nickname. It was Handsome, usually spoken sarcastically. No one liked the little bastard. He was too correct, a fanatic perfectionist.

"You had to lie to get in the cavalry again," Venable said. "West Point graduates are excluded from the amnesty."

"Colonel, I have to earn a living. Soldiering's all I know. I'd be in your debt if you could overlook—"

"Overlook treason? Let me tell you something. It was men from your side—John Hunt Morgan's men—who overran my mother's farm while I was serving on General Sherman's staff. Those men ran off our stock, burned the house and outbuildings, cut my mother down with sabers, and committed—" he reddened and lowered his voice—"sexual atrocities on my twelve-year-old sister, God knows how many times. Then they killed her with three minié balls."

"Colonel, I'm sorry, but I'm not responsible for every Confederate partisan, any more than you're responsible for all of Sherman's bummers. I am truly sorry about your family, but—"

Venable slammed Charles's shoulder with the palm of his hand. "Stop saying sorry like some damn parrot. Sorry doesn't begin to pay the bill."

Charles wiped whiskey from his cheek. The tent was very still. "Don't push me again."

Venable quickly surveyed the crowd, saw Hazen and his friends ready to help. He flexed his fingers at his sides, closing them in a fist. "I'll push you whenever I please, you fucking traitor." He gut-punched Charles.

Charles wasn't expecting the blow. It doubled him. He grabbed his middle, choking. Venable pounded his jaw, spinning him sideways. Hazen and the other two noncoms jumped forward to seize Charles as he flailed, off balance.

Venable signaled toward the tent entrance. The noncoms dragged Charles the length of the bar and threw him outside. Still off balance, he landed in the mud.

Venable by then had removed his dress sword. He unfastened his brightly polished buttons and stripped off his dress coat. To the crowd he said, "Before that lying reb gets a bad-character discharge, he's going to get a little something from me. Come help out if you want."

Most of the soldiers and civilians grinned and clapped, although the burly man in the beaded coat said, " 'Pears to me those odds are kind of unfair, Colonel."

Venable turned on him. "If you don't want to join in, keep quiet. Else you'll get what he gets."

The burly man stared and restrained his growling dog as Venable strode out.

In the light rain, Charles struggled to rise from the mud. Hazen darted past Venable, yanked Charles's head up by the hair, and smashed his nose with his other hand. Blood spurted. Charles flopped on his back. Hazen stamped on his belly.

"I want him," Venable said, pushing the corporal away. He gazed down at Charles, who was clutching his middle and trying to sit up. Venable's mouth wrenched as he drew his right boot back. He kicked Charles in the ribs.

Charles cried out and fell on his side. Venable kicked him in the small of the back. Flushed, he said, "A couple of you get him up."

Hazen and a companion grabbed Charles under his arms and pulled. Charles's head rang. His ribs ached. Usually he could take care of himself, but, taken by surprise, he'd lost the advantage.

On his feet, he wrenched away from the noncoms hanging

on him. He was slimy with mud. It glistened in the lamplight and dripped from his hair and mingled with the blood running from his nose. He swayed in the circle of rain-slicked faces, most of them laughing; few took this with the unsmiling ferocity Venable displayed. Charles knew his second chance in the Army was lost. All he could do now was extract some punishment. Like a bull, he lowered his head.

He charged Venable, who leaped back. Charles pivoted and caught the startled Hazen, as he'd planned. Teeth clenched, he pulled Hazen's head down with both hands while raising his knee. Hazen's jawbone cracked like a firecracker going off.

The corporal reeled away, shrieking. One of the other non-coms flung himself at Charles from behind, battering Charles's neck with the side of his hand. Charles staggered. Venable punched his head twice, kicked his groin. Charles flew backward into the crowd. They pushed him forward again, laughing, jeering.

"What happened to that ol' fighting spirit, reb?"

"Got no more rebel yells left, reb?"

"Pass him around the circle, boys. We'll get a yell out of him."

So they began, one man holding him while the man on the right punched him. Then the holder passed him to the next man and became the one who punched. When Charles sagged, they pulled him back up. They were about to pass him to a fourth man when someone said, "Leave him be."

Venable started to swear. Something hard and cool slipped across his throat and, from nowhere, a hand shot under his left arm and up to his neck. He was caught between a calloused palm pushing on the back of his neck and a hand holding the cutting edge of a huge Bowie against his throat.

It was the man in the beaded coat. He smelled of wet buck-skin and horses. A civilian snarled, "Another goddamn Southron."

"No. And I don't even know this fella. But you wouldn't treat a four-legged cur that bad. Drop him."

The men holding Charles watched Venable. With the knife at his throat, he blinked rapidly and whispered, "Do it." The men released Charles. He toppled facedown, sending up splatters of mud. With a contemptuous shove, the bearded man let go of Venable, who started to swear again. The bearded man stopped him by laying the point of the Bowie against the tip of Venable's nose.

"Anytime, little man. Just anytime, one to one, 'thout a platoon to help you."

Venable shook his finger at Charles, sprawled in the mud. "That son of a bitch is through in the U.S. Army. Done!"

The bearded man twisted the knife. A little ruby of blood appeared on Venable's nose. "Light outa here, you slime. I mean right now."

Venable blinked and blinked and somehow managed a sneery smile. He turned and limped into the Egyptian Palace. "Follow me, lads. I'm buying this round."

They gave him three cheers and a tiger, carried Hazen inside, and didn't look back.

The rain fell harder. The man in the beaded coat sheathed his knife and watched Charles struggle to rise, fail, and flop back in the mud face first.

The man, who looked to be fifty or so, walked toward the lee of the tent. The dog, trotting after him, was good-sized, gray with white and black markings. A circle of black ringed its left eye, a piratical touch. It shook itself twice, showering water. Then it whined. Its owner merely said, "Shut up, Fen."

Standing in the shadows by the tent was a large, fat boy of fifteen, pale and beardless. He wore an old wool coat and jeans pants, heavily mended. His limpid dark eyes had a slight slant, and above his eyebrows and ears his head was much larger, round and almost flat on top, resembling a section of fence post.

The youngster looked frightened. The man laid a hand on his shoulder. "You're all right, Boy. The fightin's over. There won't be no more. You don't need to be scairt."

The boy reached out with both hands and clasped the right hand of the older man, a pathetic look of gratitude on his face. The man reached over with his left hand and patted the boy's, reassuringly. "I'm sorry I gave in to my thirst and made you wait out here. But you can stop bein' scairt."

The boy watched him, eager to understand. In the lane, Charles groaned and jammed his fists in the mud. He raised his head and chest two feet off the ground and blearily looked toward the speaker. The man in the pony-bead coat knew the soldier didn't see him.

"Determined cuss," he said. "Plenty of sand. And he sure

can't go back in the Army now. Maybe we found our man. If we didn't, we can at least do the Christian thing and shelter him in our tipi."

He pushed the youngster's hands down and gently took hold of one, squeezing it. "Come on, Boy. Help me pick him up." Hand in hand, they walked forward.

MADELINE'S JOURNAL

July, 1865. Three more freedmen hired, bringing the number to six. Palmetto Bank approved $900 for timber operation. Digging of first saw pit began yesterday. Andy S. supervises work till noon, then cuts in the big stand of cypress with two other men until four, then tills his own plot while daylight lasts. Each new worker receives five acres, his wage, and a small share of whatever crop or timber we eventually sell.

Nemo's wife, Cassandra, expected more than five acres. Weeping, she showed me a bundle of stakes painted red, white, and blue in slapdash fashion. The poor guileless woman gave her last dollar for them. The white peddler who played the trick is long gone. Sad and astonishing, how privation brings out the best in some, the worst in others. . . .

"Painted stakes?" Johnson fumed.

"Yes, Mr. President. Sold to colored men in South Carolina for as much as two dollars."

Andrew Johnson flung the ribbon-tied report on his desk. "Mr. Hazard, it's disgraceful."

The seventeenth president of the United States was a swarthy man of forty-eight. He was in a choleric mood. His visitor, Stanley Hazard, thought him canaille. What else could one expect of a backwoods tailor barely able to read or write until his wife taught him? Johnson wasn't even a Republican. He'd run with Lincoln in '64 as a National Union Party candidate, to create a bipartisan wartime ticket.

Canaille and a Democrat he might be, but Andrew Johnson still meant to have an explanation. His black eyes simmered as Stanley picked up the report with hands that trembled slightly. Stanley was one of Edwin Stanton's several Assistant Secretaries at the War Department. His particular responsibility was liaison with the Freedmen's Bureau, an administrative branch of the department.

"Yes, sir, it is disgraceful," he said. "I can assure you the Bureau had no hand in it. Neither Secretary Stanton nor General Howard would tolerate such a cruel hoax."

"What about the rumor that inspired the swindle? Every free nigra down there to be given a mule and forty acres by Christmas? Forty acres—his to stake out in patriotic colors. Who spread that story?"

Sweat shone on Stanley's pale, jowly face. Why did Howard, chief of the Bureau, have to be away from Washington, leaving him to answer the summons to the President's office? Why couldn't he speak forcefully, or at least recall some of Howard's religious platitudes? He wanted a drink.

"Well, Mr. Secretary?"

"Sir"—Stanley's voice quavered—"General Saxton assured me that Bureau agents in South Carolina did nothing to inflame the Negroes, create false hope, or spread the rumor."

"Then where did it come from?"

"So far as we know, sir, from a chance remark by—" He cleared his throat. He hated to criticize an important member of his own party, but he had to think of his job, much as he loathed it. "A remark by Congressman Stevens."

That scored a point. Johnson sniffed as though smelling bad fish. Stanley went on. "He said something about confiscating and redistributing three hundred million acres of rebel land. Perhaps that is Mr. Stevens's wish, but there is no such program at the Bureau, nor any intent to begin one."

"Yet the story spread to South Carolina, didn't it? And it enabled unprincipled sharps to sell those painted stakes far and wide, didn't it? I don't think you understand the extent of the mischief, Hazard. Not only is the rumor of forty acres and a mule a cruel deception of the Negroes, but it also affronts and alienates the very white people we must draw back as working partners. I dislike the planter class as much as you—" More, Stanley thought. Johnson's hatred of aristocrats was legendary. "But the Constitution tells me they were never out of the Union, because the Constitution makes the very act of secession impossible."

He leaned forward, like a truculent schoolmaster. "That is why my program for the South consists of three simple points only. The defeated states must repudiate the Confederate war debt. They must overturn their secession ordinances. And they must abolish slavery by ratifying the Thirteenth Amendment. They are not required to do more because the federal government cannot, constitutionally, ask more. General Sherman failed to understand that when he confiscated coastal and river lands with his illegal Field Order 15, now rescinded, thank the Almighty. Your Bureau doesn't understand. You talk widely and blithely of the franchise, when qualifying a voter is a matter for the individual states. And no one at all seems to understand that if we threaten to give away their land, we will further harden the hearts of the very Southerners we want back in the fold. Do you blame me for being exercised? I am signing pardons at the rate of a hundred a day, and then I receive *that* report."

"Mr. President, I must respectfully repeat, the Bureau is not in any way responsible for—"

"Who else spread the promise of forty acres? In lieu of any evident culprit, I hold the Bureau responsible. Kindly convey that to Mr. Stanton and General Howard. Now be so good as to excuse me."

These days Stanley Hazard's life was unremitting misery. To try to make it bearable, he regularly took his first drink before eight o'clock in the morning. He kept various wines and brandies locked in his desk in the old office building temporarily housing the Freedmen's Bureau. If he drank too much during the day, and so misunderstood a question or stumbled or dropped something, he always muttered the same excuse, that he was feeling faint. But he fooled few.

Stanley did have reasons for being wretched. Years ago, his younger brother George had denied him any control of the family ironworks. Deep down, Stanley knew why. He was incompetent.

His wife, Isabel, two years older, was an ambitious harpy. She'd borne him twin sons, Laban and Levi, who were in trouble so often Stanley kept a special bank fund for bribing magistrates and jailers and paying off pregnant girls. The twins were eighteen, and Stanley was desperately shoveling bribe money—Isabel referred to it as "philanthropic donation"—to Yale and to Dartmouth, hoping to get the boys admitted and out of his house. He couldn't stand them.

Nor, paradoxically, could he understand or deal with the enormous wealth generated by his shoe business during the war.

The factory up in Lynn was now on the market. Isabel insisted they get out of the trade, because normal competition was returning. Stanley knew he didn't deserve his success.

Then, too, his former mistress, a music-hall artiste named Jeannie Canary, had deserted him after Isabel discovered the relationship. Jeannie was bound to leave him anyway, Stanley had decided. Many other suitors had as much money as he did, and he was not a good lover; stress and whiskey made it impossible for him to get it up often enough to satisfy her. Miss Canary was rumored to be the mistress of some Republican politician, thus far nameless.

All Stanley had to show for a life of struggle and suffering was more of the same, and a horsy, pretentious wife he faced every night in the huge, beautiful, desolate dining room in their mansion on I Street. So he drank. It kept him going when he was awake. And, mercifully, it put him to sleep.

"Johnson is after the Bureau, is that it, Stanley?"

"Yes. He'd like to see it dismantled. He believes that by acting in accordance with Radical objectives, we're tampering with states' rights."

"I suppose it isn't surprising," Isabel mused. "He's a Democrat and essentially a Southerner. I'm curious about land in the South. Why should it be fought over? Is it that valuable?"

Stanley swallowed the rest of his third glass of champagne. "Not at the moment. Some confiscated by the Treasury can be bought for almost nothing. Of course, long term, it's very valuable. Property is always valuable. And cash crops are the whole basis of the Southern economy. They have no industrial economy and never did."

Isabel's eyes gleamed above the candles. "Then perhaps we should look into investments in the South, to replace the factory."

He sat back, astounded as always by her audacity, and the way her mind leaped to sink fangs into some prey he hadn't even spotted. "Are you saying you'd like me to make inquiries at the Treasury?"

"No, sweet. I'll make them. In person. I am going to leave you for a week or so—I'm sure that grieves you terribly," she added with venom. He silently called her a witch, smiled a sickly smile, and poured more champagne.

Old Mr. Marvin, our long-time friend at Green Pond,
called to say good-bye. He is embittered, angry—bankrupt.
Treasury men seized $15,000 in Sea Island cotton, marking it
"Confederate" right at his gin and hauling it off while he
watched. It happened because he refused to pay the bribe the
Treasury man demanded. The Yankee would have let M.
keep the cotton and sell it, but he would have had to surren-
der half the profits to the agent.

Land and crops are being stolen everywhere by these two-
legged vultures. Marvin's neighbor lost a fine farm, Pride's
Haven, when unable to pay $150 of back taxes. We have our
share of sinners down here, but all the saints and seraphims
do not reside in the North . . .

Philo Trout, a cheerful, muscular young Treasury agent, met
Isabel's steamer in Charleston. Their inland journey was delayed
twenty-four hours because a tropical storm came onshore, ripping the city with gale winds and pouring out more than six
inches of rain before moving inland.

Once they set out, Trout's covered buggy labored along
muddy roads, and Isabel surveyed submerged fields on either
side. She asked about the standing water. Trout said, "Storm
surge from the tidal rivers. The salt will poison those fields for a
few seasons."

This immediately banished the idea that had brought Isabel
south: absentee ownership of Carolina farmland. The storms,
which came regularly, created too great a risk for her taste, or her
money, although she didn't say this to Trout.

On the river road along the Ashley, he pointed out various
plantations including Mont Royal. Isabel reacted with silent disgust, but she never so much as hinted that she knew the owners.

A few miles farther on, Trout stopped the buggy at a crossroads store, whose crookedly hung sign said GETTYS BROS.
Nailed over the front door was a board painted with one word:

CLOSED.

Trout pushed back his straw planter's hat and put his boot
on the footboard. "Now here's an interesting proposition, though
it isn't what you said you wanted. Still, someone could make

money on this little store and never have to worry about the salt in the rivers."

Isabel wrinkled her nose. "How could such a sorry place be profitable?"

"Three ways, ma'am, all predicated on having the capital to stock it properly. Real money, not Confederate paper. The local planters need goods. Implements, staples, seed. First, the store could charge plenty at the time of the sale. But the planters and the freedmen don't have real money to pay. So the store could treat each sale as a loan—the cost, at any price you set, plus interest, at any rate you determine. Fifty percent? Ninety? They'd have to take it or starve."

Just then, despite the cloying heat of the marshy country, and the insects, and the stench of decay, Isabel decided that the discomforts of the trip were worth it.

"You mentioned a third way, Mr. Trout."

"Yes indeed. To secure every loan with goods, you also demand a fixed percent of the next rice or cotton crop." He grinned. "Ingenious?"

"I couldn't think of anything more ingenious myself." She dabbed her moist lip. "Who could run a store like this?"

"Well, ma'am, if *you* bought it, you'd undoubtedly want a new manager, your husband being with the Bureau and all. The fellow who ran it before it closed, Randall Gettys, is pretty much of a secesh. I know him. If he stayed on, and assuming he'd even consider selling to nig—uh, the colored, he'd charge them eight or ten times what he charged whites, just for spite."

Isabel beamed. "Why, dear Mr. Trout, what of that? It's true that my husband and I are Republicans, but I really don't care about the prejudices or operating policies of a store manager if he makes money."

"Oh, Randall Gettys could do that, definitely. He knows everybody around here. Used to print a little newspaper for the district. Wants to start it again."

"He may charge the nigras ten times what he charges white people, so long as no one in Washington finds out, and my husband and I are never connected with the business. That point would have to be impressed on him."

"Randall and his kinfolk are so desperate, they'd sign a contract to sell ice in hell."

Isabel could hardly contain her excitement. As usual, it was she who prospected and struck gold, while Stanley stayed behind.

"Everything could be arranged," Trout assured her. He picked up the reins and turned the buggy around. "I can buy the property for you at tax auction next month."

The horse plodded back toward Mont Royal. Shadows of Spanish moss drifted across Isabel's perspiring face.

"We have one more consideration to discuss, ma'am."

"Your fee for services—and silence?"

"Yes, ma'am." Trout's sunny face shone. "You know, I worked as a telegraph operator in Dayton, Ohio, before my uncle got me this job. I've made more in six months than I'd make in a lifetime up North."

"The South is proving a land of opportunity for all, isn't it?" said Isabel with another smugly charming smile.

> *Gettys Bros. open again. New whitewash inside and out, new goods crowding the shelves and floor. Young Randall G. is enthroned as manager amidst this new affluence. He has put up a gaudy sign on the roof. It features a painted flag— the Confed. battle ensign—and a new name,* THE DIXIE STORE.
>
> *He refuses to discuss the sudden reversal in his fortunes, so we have a mystery now. I cannot solve it, but neither will I give much time to it. You know my feelings about the bigoted Mr. Gettys.*

7

"Too short a visit," George said, raising his voice above the racket of baggage being loaded two cars ahead. He hugged Brett. Despite her voluminous skirts, he was conscious of her stomach. "Take care of that youngster I'm not supposed to mention—and get to San Francisco in plenty of time."

Steam blew around them. Brett's lavender-scented cheek felt damp against his. "Don't worry. He'll be born a Californian."

"You're certain it's he?" Constance said.

"Positive," Billy answered. He looked spruce in his new sack-style coat of dark gray and trousers and cravat of lighter gray. He and Constance embraced, then the ladies hugged. George shook his brother's hand.

"I can't hide it, Billy. I wish you'd stay in Pennsylvania."

"Too many memories on this side of the Mississippi. I'll always love West Point, but, like you, I've had my bellyful of armies." *And what armies are sent out to do.* George heard that unspoken conclusion.

"God protect you and everyone, George," Billy said.

"And you and Brett and your new son. Since Constance is the religious one in the family, I'll ask her to pray for calm seas while you sail down South America and around the Cape."

"It's winter there, but we'll manage."

Better than I'm managing, George thought, with a deep melancholy. It had held him in its grip, making him unreasonably pensive and lethargic, ever since his confrontation with Stevens in Washington.

Constance said, "If your ship calls at the port of Los Angeles for more than a few hours, please visit my father's law office, and give him my love."

"By all means," Billy said, nodding.

The conductor called, "All aboard." From a few steps away, Patricia waved at the departing travelers. William had his eye on an attractive girl hurrying into a rear car. Through her smile, Patricia hissed, "Wave, you rude beast!" William stuck out his tongue at her, then waved.

The Lehigh Valley local began to move. George rushed along the platform beside Billy and Brett's car, calling out, "Do press Madeline about another loan if she needs it."

"We will," Brett called back.

"Billy, send a message when you're safely settled."

"Promise," his brother shouted. The whistle shrilled. "You let me know if the War Department finds Charles."

George replied with an emphatic nod; the car was drawing away. So far the Department had failed to answer two letters from Billy asking the whereabouts of his best friend, who was supposed to be serving in the cavalry out West.

George ran faster, waving his shiny plug hat and shouting other things, which no one heard. Constance called to him to come back. The train chugged past the end of the platform and gained speed, following the riverbank and the old canal bed. Billy and Brett disappeared.

How George envied their youth, their independence. He admired their bravery, too, in setting out for a state they'd only read about in unreliable Gold Rush guidebooks. Americans were prospering in California, though. Four businessmen were blasting and tunneling through the Sierras to build part of a transcontinental rail line, and in a few years the Pacific coast would be linked with the rest of the country. Billy was determined to start a civil engineering firm, and no promise from George of a secure and lucrative future with Hazard's would deter him.

"Damn," George said, stopping at the end of the platform. He wiped his eyes before turning back to his family. He knew what his brother meant about memories east of the Mississippi. They had discussed it for hours one night, after everyone else was asleep. The war had touched both of them—changed them, perhaps damaged them, in ways that were deep, fundamental, and, in some cases, beyond understanding.

George described a meeting with two ex-soldiers before he left Washington. In the saloon bar at Willard's Hotel, the men had been drinking heavily; they were blearily candid. One and then the other admitted that he felt bereft now that the highly charged excitement of the war was but a memory.

As the night grew older, each of the brothers told of his own ghosts. Billy would forever be haunted by memories of his comrade, old Lije Farmer, who'd died in battle despite his unshakable belief in God's goodness. Nor could he forget his internment in Libby Prison, or the mistreatment there; he still had nightmares about it. He probably would have died there but for his wild, desperate escape, planned and carried out by Charles and Orry Main. And, from the end of the war, he remembered the ruthless, bleak look of his best friend, Charles, the last time they met.

George couldn't forget the moment he learned of Orry's death, or the half hour he'd knelt by Orry's empty grave at Mont Royal, burying there a letter of friendship written in 1861 but never sent. The letter expressed his hope that the ties of affection between the Mains and the Hazards would survive the war, and that each of the family members would survive, too. For Orry, it had been a vain wish.

Sunk in despondency, George walked back to his family. Constance saw his condition. She took his arm as they returned to the lacquered phaeton, its hinged top section folded down in the August heat. The driver held the door for the Hazards, then took his seat and popped the whip over the heads of the fine matched bays.

My town, George thought as the phaeton proceeded toward the hill road. He owned a majority interest in the Bank of Lehigh Station, one square over, and he owned the Station House Hotel, on his left, and about a third of the real estate within the town limits. Most of it was in the commercial section along the river, but he also owned fourteen substantial brick homes on the higher, terraced streets. These were rented by foremen at Hazard's and by some of the wealthier merchants.

As the carriage rolled along, George searched the streets for the town's three war casualties. He saw the blind boy begging on the crowded sidewalk near Pinckney Herbert's general store. He didn't see the peg-legged boy, but in the next block he spied Tom Hassler.

"Stop, Jerome. Just for a moment."

He jumped from the carriage; Patricia and William sighed with impatience. George's short legs carried him to the boy he'd given a job at Hazard's. But Tom couldn't manage even the simplest task, so he shambled through Lehigh Station every day, rattling a tin cup in which his mother put pebbles to suggest that others had already given. George stuffed a ten-dollar note in the cup. The sight of Tom's slack mouth and dead brown eyes always destroyed him. Like the town's other two maimed veterans, Tom Hassler was not yet twenty.

"How are you today, Tommy?"

The boy's vacant eyes drifted across the hazy river to the laurel-covered slopes on the far side. "Fine, sir. Waiting for orders from General Meade. We'll charge those rebs over there on Seminary Ridge before dark."

"That's right, Tom. You'll carry the day, too."

He turned away. How shameful, this urge to weep that came upon him so often of late. He climbed into the phaeton and slammed the half-door, avoiding his wife's eye. *How shameful! What is happening to me?*

What was happening, he sometimes understood, was exactly what had happened to his brother and to thousands of other men. Powerful and unfamiliar emotions in the wake of the surrender. Bad dreams. Thoughts of friendships formed in the strange giddy atmosphere of ever-present death. Memories of good men slain in pointless skirmishes, and of fools and pale trembling cowards who survived by accident or by means of a feigned illness the night before a battle . . .

What had happened to George, and to America, was a four-year struggle of a kind never before experienced in the world. Not only had cousin slain cousin, brother slain brother—that was not new—but mechanized weapons, the railroad, the telegraph, had brought a new efficiency to the art of slaughter. In meadows and creek bottoms and pretty, rustic glens, innocents had fought the first modern war.

It was a war that refused to release George now. Constance saw that in her husband's pained, lost eyes as the phaeton followed the winding road up toward Belvedere, their mansion on the summit. She wanted to touch him, but she felt that his pain was beyond her reach—perhaps beyond anyone's.

George spent the afternoon at Hazard's. The firm was almost completely converted from war production to the fabrication of wrought iron for architectural embellishment, cast-iron parts for other products, and, perhaps most important, rails. Nearly all of the South's railroads were in ruins. And in the West, two lines had created another huge new market. The Union Pacific, along the Platte route, and the Union Pacific, Eastern Division, in Kansas—no connection despite similar names—were racing each other to the hundredth meridian. The first to lay track to the meridian would win the right to go the rest of the way and link up with the Central Pacific, building east from California.

George didn't arrive home until the family members had dined and were gathered around their new treasure, a grand piano, sent as a gift by Henry Steinweg and his sons in New York. Hazard's provided much of the iron plate for the firm's pianos, which were called Steinways, because Steinweg thought that name more euphonious, commercial, and American. Steinweg had come a long way from the red field of Waterloo, where he'd soldiered against Napoleon. George liked him.

He greeted the family and in the kitchen found some slices of cold roast, all he needed for supper. On the veranda, he sat down, put a foot on the rail, and penciled comments on an architect's site plan for a new foundry he wanted to build in Pittsburgh. The city, situated on two rivers that flowed into the Ohio, would almost certainly become the iron and steel center of the nation in the next ten years. George wanted to be in early, with Bessemer-process converters modified for greater dependability by a technique from Sweden.

Inside, Constance and Patricia sang while Patricia played. "Listen to the Mocking Bird" and "Dixie's Land"—Brett's favorite—and "Hail, Columbia!", which many considered the national anthem; Congress and the public couldn't decide on an official one.

Presently the singing stopped. George kept working until the August daylight failed. He saw the caretaker's lantern moving through the sheet-shrouded rooms of Stanley and Isabel's house next door. The owners were seldom in residence. George didn't miss them.

He tried some mathematical calculations involving a piece of land he was considering for the new plant. He got the wrong answer four times and finally threw the papers aside. The melancholia, formless yet consuming, came on him again. He wandered inside, feeling old and spent.

In the empty library, he stopped beside a polished table and studied the two objects he kept there. One was a fragment of a meteorite—star-iron, it was called in the trade in ancient times. To him, it represented metal's incredible power to improve life or, forged into weapons, eradicate it. Beside the meteorite lay a sprig of mountain laurel, so abundant in the valley. In the Hazard family, by tradition, the laurel was an emblem of resilience, survival, the certain triumph of hope and goodness made possible by love and by family. The sprig was dead, its leaves brown. George flung it into the cold hearth.

Behind him, the door rolled open. "I thought I heard you in here." When Constance kissed his cheek, he smelled the pleasant sweetness of chocolates. Her red hair was pinned up, her plump face shiny from a scrubbing.

She studied him. "What's wrong, dearest?"

"I don't know. I feel so damn miserable. I can't explain why."

"I can guess some of the reasons. Your brother's on his way to the other side of the continent, and you're probably feeling like those two men you told me about. The men at Willard's who admitted they missed the excitement of the war."

"I'd be ashamed to admit I missed killing human beings."

"Not killing. A heightened sense of life, like walking on the edge of a precipice. There's no shame in admitting that if it's the truth. The feelings will pass."

He nodded, though he didn't believe it. The near-despair seemed overwhelmingly potent.

"It will be even emptier here in a few weeks," he said. "William off to start at Yale, Patricia back in Bethlehem at the Moravian Seminary."

She stroked his bearded face with the cool back of her hand. "Parents always feel sad when the fledglings leave for the first time." She took his arm. "Come, let's walk a while. It will do you good."

In the hot night wind, they climbed the hill behind Belvedere. Away to the left below them spread the furnaces and sheds and warehouses of Hazard's, casting a red glare on the sky.

Unexpectedly, their path brought them to a place Constance would have preferred to avoid, because it symbolized despair. They were at the large crater produced by a meteorite that fell in the spring of '61, right at the time the war started.

George leaned over the edge and peered down. "Not a blade

of grass. Not even a weed yet. Did it poison the earth?" He glanced at the path running on up the hill. "I suppose Virgilia passed this way the night she stole all that silver from the house."

"George, it doesn't help to recall only bad things."

"What else is there, goddamn it? Orry's dead. Tom Hassler wanders the streets with a mind that will never be right. We didn't strive hard enough to prevent war, and now we've inherited the whole rotten mess. They talk about the South's cause being lost. Well, so is America's. So is our family's. So is mine."

The chimneys of Hazard's shot spark showers into the night sky. Constance held him tightly. "Oh, I wish I could banish those feelings. I wish you didn't hurt so terribly."

"I'm sorry. I'm ashamed of how I feel. It isn't manly." He muffled an oath by burying his face in the warm curve of her throat. She heard him say, "Somehow I can't help it."

Silently, she prayed to the God in whom she devoutly believed. She asked Him to uncloud her husband's mind and lift his burdens. She begged Him not to add so much as one new burden, however small. She feared for George if that happened.

Silent in each other's arms, they stood a long time on the empty hill beside the dead crater.

MADELINE'S JOURNAL

August, 1865. She is here!—Miss Prudence Chaffee of Ohio.

She is twenty-three, very robust—she is the child of a farm family—and calls herself, without self-pity, a plain person. It is true. Her face is round and she is stout. But every word, every expression shines with a miraculous glow. Not of impossible perfection, but of dedication—the glow of those rare and decent people who will leave this earth better than they found it.

Her father must have been a special man, for he did not subscribe to the popular notion that education for young girls is a waste—even dangerous, because higher mathematics is too taxing for the female brain, science too indelicate, studies such as geography too threatening to the teachings of Genesis. She has faith and good training as well, the latter received at the Western College for Women.

She arrived with a valise of clothing, her Bible, a Pilgrim's Progress and a half-dozen of McGuffey's Eclectic

Readers. *The first evening, over a poor meal of rice, I tried to be honest about the obstacles we face, especially ill will from neighbors.*

To that she said, "Mrs. Main, I prayed for this kind of situation. No reverses will defeat me. I am one of those lucky few St. Paul described in his Epistle to the Romans—'Who against all hope believed in hope.' I am here to teach, and teach I shall."

Orry, I think I have found a confidante—and a friend.

. . . Prudence continues to astonish me. Took her this morning to the schoolhouse, already under construction halfway down the road to the abandoned slave quarters. Lincoln, our newest freedman, is roofing it with cypress shakes split by hand. Prudence said it was her school, so she should share the toil. Whereupon she hoisted her skirts between her legs and knotted them and scampered up the ladder. Lincoln looked stunned and embarrassed, though he quickly got over it when she began to drive nails as if born to it. I asked later about her skill.

"Papa taught me. He felt I must be prepared to provide for myself in every circumstance. I believe he felt—never saying it, mind—that no man would wed an ugly duckling with abolitionist views. I may marry someday. I told you I have hope. But whether that's true or not, carpentry is good to know. Learning anything useful is good. That's why I teach."

. . . To the Dixie Store this morning, which I had not seen since it reopened. The plump and white Mr. Randall Gettys, himself, greeted me from behind the counter.

Evidence of his literary pretension was prominently in view in an old woodbox on the floor. Secondhand copies of Poe, Coleridge, the novels of Gilmore Simms, doubtless bargained away by some impoverished landowner. Who will buy them, even at five cents each, I cannot imagine.

Evidence of Mr. Gettys's political views reposed even more prominently upon the counter—a neat stack of issues of The Land We Love, *one of several publications pandering to the sad belief that the South's cause is not lost. . . .*

Gettys affected an exaggerated politeness, hovering uncomfortably close to Madeline. His small round wire-rimmed spectacles shone. A huge white handkerchief billowed from the breast pocket of his greasy coat. Even closely shaved, his dark beard lent him a vaguely soiled look.

Madeline noted the profusion of goods on the shelves. "I didn't know you were so well stocked. Nor that you had the capital for it."

"A relative in Greenville furnished the money," Gettys said at once. She saw him glance at her breasts while he wiped his chin with his handkerchief. "It's a decided pleasure to see you, Mrs. Main. What may I sell you this morning?"

"Nothing just yet. I'd like to know your prices." She pointed to a barrel. "That seed corn, for instance."

"One dollar per bushel. And one-quarter of the crop produced, or the cash equivalent. For the colored, the price is double."

"Randall, I'm happy to have the store open, but I don't believe we can stand that kind of price-gouging in the district."

She said it without rancor. Even so, it enraged him. He shed his smarmy politeness. "What we can't stand is that infernal school you're putting up. A school for niggers!"

"And any white person who cares to better himself."

Gettys ignored the remark. "It's an outrage. Furthermore, it's a waste. A darky can't learn. His brain's too small. He's only fit to be our hewer of wood, our drawer of water, exactly as Scripture says. If a nigger does have a scintilla of intelligence, education just inflames his base passions and foments hatred of his betters."

"Dear God, Randall, spare me that old cant."

"No, ma'am," he exclaimed, "I will not. We lost the war but we haven't lost our senses. The white citizens of this district will not permit it to be Africanized."

Wearily, she turned and walked to the door.

"You'd better listen," he shouted. "You've been given fair warning."

Her back was toward him; he couldn't see her face, and the startled emotion evident there. She thought unhappily of Cooper's letter about Desmond LaMotte. How many would turn against her?

Saturday. Sawmill shed finished, on the bank of the river, so that lumber may be shipped by steam packet if service ever resumes. With considerable pride, I watched our two

*mules drag the first cypress log to the site. With Lincoln at
ground level and Fred below in the pit, the log was split with
the long two-handed saw. The method is antiquated, back-
breaking, but until we have steam power there is no other way.
It is a beginning.*

   *Prudence wants to attend church tomorrow. Will take
her. . . .*

   *To the Church of St. Joseph of Arimathea this morning. I
wish we had not. . . .*

Parking the wagon and tethering the horses, Madeline saw
two men from the congregation throw away their cigars and dart
inside the small tabby church where Episcopalian families from
the district had worshiped for generations.

Both Madeline and Prudence wore their best bonnets. They
approached the double doors. Music from the church's tiny
pump organ squealed to silence as the avuncular priest, Father
Lovewell, stepped into the entrance. Beyond him, in sunlit pews,
members of the congregation turned to stare at the women. Madeline saw many people she knew. They didn't look friendly.

"Mrs. Main—" The priest's pink cheeks shone with sweat
that steamed his spectacles. He pitched his voice low. "This is
most regrettable. I am asked to remind you that, ah, colored are
not permitted to worship here."

"Colored?" she repeated, as if he'd hit her.

"That's right. We have no separate balcony to accommodate
you, and I can no longer allow you into the family pew." She saw
it, second from the front on the left, empty. Her self-control dis-
integrated.

"Are you in earnest, Father?"

"Yes, I am. I wish it could be otherwise, but—"

"Then you're a vicious man, with no right to claim that you
practice Christianity."

He put his face close to hers, wheezing. "I have Christian
compassion for my own race. I have none for a mongrelized race
that promotes unrest, plots arson, advocates hatred, and wor-
ships the devilish doctrines of black Republicanism."

Prudence looked baffled and angry. Madeline managed a ra-
diant smile. "God smite you where you stand, Father. Before I
creep off to hide like some—some leper, I'll see you in hell."

"Hell?" The smug, sweating face drew back. Soft white hands gripped the doors. "I doubt that."

"Oh, yes. You just reserved your place."

The congregation broke into angry conversation. The doors slammed.

"Come along," Madeline said, kicking her skirt out of the way as she whirled and marched to the wagon. Prudence hurried after her, confused.

"What did all that mean? Why did he call you a colored woman?"

Madeline sighed. "I should have told you when you arrived. I'll tell you as we drive home. If you wish, you can leave. As to what else Father Lovewell meant, I'm afraid it was a declaration of war. On Mont Royal, on the school, and on me."

. . . Prudence knows all. She will stay. I pray God she will not regret the choice, or come to any harm because of it.

8

Charles opened his eyes, braced his hands, pushed upward. An invisible sledge slammed his forehead and dropped him. "Godamighty."

He tried again. This time, despite the pain, he succeeded.

He stared across a small fire built in a shallow hole in the ground. Beyond the fire, a bearded man weather-burned to a dark brown bent a flexible stick back and forth, trying to break it. The man wore a coat so heavily beaded he might have come from a traveling medicine show. Near him a brindle dog lay gnawing a bone. Behind the man, cross-legged, sat a youth with slanted eyes and a malformed head.

Charles smelled something vile. "What in hell's that stink?"

"Bunch of herbs mashed in a paste of buffla brains," the man said. "I rubbed it on where they banged you the worst."

Charles began to perceive his surroundings. He was inside a tipi of hides stretched over a dozen eighteen-foot poles to form a cone, with a smoke hole at the top. He heard rain falling.

"That's right, this yere's our tipi," the bearded man said. "In the tongue of the Dakota Sioux, tipi means place-where-a-man-lives." He broke the stick and handed half across the fire. "Jerky. Do you good."

Charles bit off a chew of the smoked buffalo meat. "Thanks. I've had it before."

"Oh," said the man, pleased. "This ain't your first time in the West, then."

"Before the war, I served with Bob Lee's Second Cavalry in Texas."

The stranger's grin revealed stained teeth. "Better 'n' better." Charles changed position; the sledge struck again. "Listen, I wouldn't move too quick. You got more purple on you than a side of bad beef. While you was knocked out, I scouted around some. That little rooster who beat you up, he charged you with takin: the Grand Bounce."

"Deserting?"

"Yep. You better not go back on the post."

Charles sat up, fighting dizziness. "I have things there." The stranger pointed. Behind him, Charles discovered his carpetbag.

"I went in and picked it up. Nobody said boo 'cept for the boy on sentry duty. For a dollar, he looked the other way. What's your name?"

"Charles Main."

The man shot a hand over the fire. "Pleased to know you. I'm Adolphus O. Jackson. Wooden Foot to friends."

He lifted the leg of his hide pants and whacked his right boot, producing a hard sound. "Solid oak. Necessitated by a meet-up with some Utes when I was fourteen. My pa was alive then. We trapped beaver in the east foothills of the Rocky Mountains. One day, I was out alone and I got my foot in another man's trap by accident. Then the three Utes chanced by, in a bad mood. It was either get kilt or get outa that trap. I took my knife and got out. Well, part way. Then I fainted. Lucky for me, Pa come along. He drove off the Utes and got me out and took my foot off. He saved me from bleedin' to death." It was all said as if he were discussing the jerky he was chewing.

Charles waited till the dizziness passed. "I'm grateful to you, Mr. Jackson. I was in the cavalry till that little son of a bitch spotted me."

"Yes, sir, he's still fightin' you Southron boys, that's plain."

"I appreciate your taking me in and patching me up. I'll move along and find some other—"

"Stay right there," Jackson interrupted. "You ain't in no shape." He picked his teeth. " 'Sides, I didn't pull you out of the mud just because the fight was one-sided, with you on the wrong side. I got a proposition."

"What kind?"

"Business." Jackson discovered a speck of jerky in the tangle of white and brown hairs in his big fan beard. He flicked it away and said, "This yere group's the Jackson Trading Company. You met me already. This fine lad behind me is my nephew, Herschel. I call him Boy. It's easier. When his pa died of the influenzy back in Louisville, he didn't have no one else to look after him. He tries hard, but he needs carin' for."

Wooden Foot regarded the youngster with affection and sadness. That one glance made Charles like the man. Jackson made him think of Orry; he, too, had taken in a relative, and given him love and purpose to replace bitterness and hell-raising.

"And this here—" Jackson indicated the dog chewing the bone—"his name's Fenimore Cooper. Fen for short. Don't look like much. Border collies never do. But you'd be surprised how much weight on a travois he can pull."

Jackson finished the jerky. "Y'see, we go on reg'lar trips out among the *Tsis-tsis-tas.*" He stressed the second syllable.

"What the devil's that?"

"All depends on who you ask. Some say it means our people, or the people, or the folks that belong here, to give it a loose translation. The Sioux translation's *Sha-hi-e-la,* which means red talk. Foreign talk. Other words, people the Sioux can't understand." Jackson watched his guest with a cheerfully superior smile. When he'd had enough fun, he said, "We trade with the Southern Cheyennes. You say their name this way, everybody understands." He executed a series of fast, smooth gestures, fist rotating, fingers jutting out or bending.

"I know that's sign language," Charles said. "Comanches in Texas used it."

"Yes, sir, the universal tongue of the tribes. What I just said was: We trade with Cheyennes in the Indian Territory. We take trade goods; we bring back Indian horses. It's a good livin', though not as rich as it could be. I won't deal in guns, or fermented spirits."

By then, Charles had a general fix on the nature of the proposition. "A good living, maybe, but pretty dangerous."

"Only now and then. They's two, three hundred thousand red men out this way, but way less than a third of 'em ornery, and those not always. You can get along all right if they know you ain't scairt."

He plucked the turkey feather from his hair and ran his index finger into the broad V cut in the vane. "They can read a coup feather notched this partic'lar way. It says I met a bad Indian once and took his scalp, so he wouldn't have no afterlife, and then I cut his throat."

"The feather says that?"

Jackson nodded.

"Did you do it?"

Jackson's mild eyes stayed on his. "Twice."

Charles shivered. Boy laid a soft hand on his uncle's shoulder, his face showing pride. Fen lazily licked his forepaws. The rain pattered on the tipi. "You mentioned a proposition."

"I need a partner to watch my back. I can teach him the country, and all that goes with it, but I got to trust him, and he's got to shoot straight. The first time."

"I'm a fair shot. I practiced a few years with General Wade Hampton's scouts."

Wooden Foot responded with an enthusiastic nod. "Southron cavalry. That's a tip-top recommendation."

"Are you adding a man or replacing one?"

Again the trader squished his tongue around his teeth. "No sense lyin' if we're to ride together, I guess. I lost one last trip. My partner, Dean. He laid hands on a woman. Her husband and some of his Red Shield friends carved Dean up for stew meat."

The jerky seemed to perform a leap in Charles's belly. "What's a Red Shield?"

"Cheyenne soldier society. They's several of 'em. The shields, the Bow Strings, the Dog Men—Dog Soldiers, they's sometimes called. 'Bout half the braves in the tribe belong to that one. When a young man gets to be fifteen or sixteen winters, he joins a society, and it's just about the most important thing in his whole life. All the societies started a long time ago. The way the legends tell it, a young Cheyenne brave named Sweet Medicine wandered way up north to the Sacred Mountain, which may be in the Black Hills—nobody's real sure. They say Sweet Medicine met the Great Spirit on the mountain and they powwowed a while. The Spirit told Sweet Medicine to go back and set up the societies to protect the tribe. Then the Spirit gave him all the society names, the special songs for each one, how each one oughta dress—the entire shebang. The societies are still run the way Sweet Medicine told the people to run 'em. They rule the roost, and you better not forget it. Even the forty-four chiefs in the tribal council don't fart in the wind 'thout the society men sayin' all right, go ahead."

"What exactly do these society men do besides boss the tribe?"

"Biggest job's to police the camp when it's time for a buffla hunt. They keep the young fellas in line, so nobody jumps sud-denlike and scares off a prime herd."

"And I'd be replacing a man who got butchered by these people?"

"Yes, sir, Mr. Main. I wouldn't pretend they's no risk. They's rewards, though. The sight of some of the cleanest, sweetest country God ever made—and some of the fairest maidens. I get along fine with most of the Cheyennes. They like old Wooden Foot."

With a gurgle and a coo, Boy knelt beside his uncle and patted his beard. Jackson took Boy's hand between his and held it. The youth was calm and happy.

"Here's the cut of the cards," the trader said. "First year, I give you twenty percent of whatever we get for the horses we bring back. You prove out, I raise you ten percent a year till you're in for a full half-share. Till that time, I own all the goods and stand all the risks. Oh"— he grinned—"I mean excludin' the risks to your hair and your life. What do you say?"

Charles sat quietly, unable to say anything just yet. The trader proposed a change both large and profound. The presence of Boy made him think of his son. If he joined Jackson, he wouldn't see little Gus for months at a time. He didn't like that. But he needed work; he needed an income. And before the war, serving in Texas, he'd vowed that he would return and settle there. He'd loved the beauty of the West.

"Well, Mr. Main?"

"I'd like to sleep on it." He smiled. "I don't honestly know if I could get used to calling a man Wooden Foot."

"I don't give a damn about that if you shoot straight."

Shortly after, Charles rolled up in a warm buffalo robe by the dying fire. He squirmed until he found the position in which his bruises hurt him least, and fell asleep.

Instead of enormous prairie vistas or fierce Indians, he dreamed of Augusta Barclay. In the gray and featureless land-scapes of sleep he had his hands on her warm bare body. Then other women slipped in, taking her place. He woke to stiffness, and guilt, then the burned-out feeling of homelessness, made all the more painful because of his aborted Army career.

He still had doubts about Jackson's offer. It was better than some dull, monotonous job, but it was also plainly dangerous.

Thinking on it, he turned over. His ribs ached; he groaned. The sound produced another, which he identified as Fen waking up and padding across the tipi to stand beside his head. Charles lay rigid. Would the dog bite him?

Fen's head bobbed down. His raspy warm tongue licked Charles's bruised face three times.

On such small affections do large decisions turn.

"Fine, damn fine," Wooden Foot exclaimed when Charles said yes in the morning. The trader rummaged in a heap of blankets and canvas-wrapped bales, found two supple objects that he pressed into his new partner's hands.

"What are these?"

"Buffla-hide moccasins. From a winter kill. You get the thickest coat on the buffla then. You turn it inside, see? These'll keep you warm where we're goin'."

The tipi filled with the rich smells of coffee boiling and sowbelly frying in a cast-iron skillet. With a mitten on his right hand, Boy squatted and held the skillet over the fire, an almost demented concentration on his face.

"I'll need a horse," Charles said.

"I got an extra I brought back from the Indian Territory. A four-legged jug-headed whelp of Satan nobody would buy. If you can ride him, you can have him."

"I have to qualify to be your partner?"

The trader squinted at him. "That's the size of it."

"I'm still pretty sore. Riding some wild horse won't help that any."

Wooden Foot shrugged to acknowledge the point. "I s'pose we could wait a day or so—"

Charles rubbed his aching ribs and thought about it. "No. Let's get it over with."

Heavy fog hid most of the ground around Wooden Foot's tipi, which he'd erected west of the tent town near Jefferson Barracks. The trader led Charles to the horse, tethered some distance from his other saddle animals and pack mules. The small, rangy piebald was black and white, with a broad face blaze.

"I think he's a killer," Wooden Foot said, reaching for the low tree branch to which he'd tied a rope fastened to the headstall. "I prob'ly oughta shoot him."

"Watch out," Charles yelled, pushing Jackson as the horse reared. Front hooves slashed the mist where the trader had stood a moment before.

"See?" he said, from where the push had spilled him. "I broke him, but nobody can ride him. I come close to puttin' a bullet in him twice already."

Charles felt tense, uneasy. He was remembering his last, and fatal, ride on Sport in Virginia. Sport, an enemy bullet in him, had carried Charles to safety with speed and great heart while his lifeblood pumped away behind, splashing the snow. Sport had been a horse nobody had wanted.

"Don't try killing him in front of me," he said. "I lost a fine gray charger in the war. I can't tolerate anyone hurting a horse."

Still, he understood the trader's apprehension. The piebald had murder in his eye. Charles saw some virtues, though. Lightness—he estimated the horse at about a thousand pounds—a fine neck, and the smaller hooves and head typical of a Southern saddler.

"Indian pony, you said?"

"Yep. The Army ruins 'em. Chokes 'em with grain so they forget livin' on grass. Makes 'em weak and slow. Won't happen to this one. He won't live that long."

"Let's find out. Where's that blanket and saddle?"

The mist rolled thick around them. Wooden Foot tied the rope to the tree again. With a listing gait, Charles walked to the piebald. "It's all right," he said, putting the blanket on. "It's all right."

The piebald lifted his right foreleg. Charles's belly tightened up. Down went the hoof again, plop, and the piebald exhaled. Charles saddled him with care, tossing Wooden Foot a surprised look when the saddle's weight caused no problem. He didn't understand. Maybe there was some unfathomable streak of madness in that beautiful head.

He dropped the stirrups down and mounted slowly, as much from pain as caution. The piebald stayed still, though he turned his head, trying to see his rider. The mist rolled, the centaur figure rising from it. On the distant Army post, bugles sounded a morning call.

Quietly, Charles said, "Untie the rope."

Wooden Foot darted in and did it fast. Charles took the rope, wrapped it around one hand, gave an easy tug.

Shooting skyward, his left leg wrenched by jerking out of the stirrup, Charles thought, *Jackson will have to kill him.* He struck the piebald's croup as he came down, then hit the dirt, while the horse bellowed and kicked. The impact made him feel like torches had been lit in his body. A hoof gashed his forehead before he rolled clear and snatched out his Army Colt. Kneeling, in excruciating pain, he steadied the revolver with both hands, waiting for the horse to come after him.

The piebald snorted, stamped, but stood still. Boy hugged his uncle's waist from behind, peeking at the horse and the man aiming the gun.

"Better do it, Main."

"No, not unless—wait. I didn't notice before. Do you see that red bubble on his mouth?"

Peevish, Jackson said he surely didn't. Charles knew that men the trader's age often had trouble with their eyes. He shoved the Colt away and approached the horse cautiously. "Let me see," he said in a soothing voice. "Just keep quiet and let me see." His heart hammered; the piebald's eyes held that raging look again.

But he let Charles gently pry his jaws apart, revealing the blood-slimed bit. Charles exploded with laughter born of relief. "Come see this. Not too fast." Wooden Foot sidled in behind him. "There's your killer streak. An abscessed molar. Leave the reins alone, and he's fine. Pull them, he goes crazy."

"I missed it," Wooden Foot said. "Just damn completely missed it."

"Easy enough to do." Charles shrugged, unwilling to tell the older man he should buy a pair of spectacles. He reached under to rub the piebald's chest. "Soon as we find a horse doctor to nick that tooth and drain and poultice it, he'll be fine."

"You'll keep him?"

"That was the deal, wasn't it? You want to pat him, Boy? It's all right."

Wooden Foot's nephew scuttled forward, a heartbreaking elation on his white face. He touched the piebald and smiled. The trader sighed, his tension gone.

"Then he's yours to name, Charlie."

Charles thought a bit, joining Boy in patting the horse. "Let's see. It should be a name to make people respect him, and not fool with him. They don't need to know he's gentle." He patted the horse again. "You said the devil whelped him. I'll name him for his papa. Satan."

"Hot damn," the trader cried, starting a little jig, bouncing from his good foot to the artificial one with amazing agility. "Hot damn, oh, hot damn. This here outfit's back in business."

———————

TRUMP'S
ST. LOUIS PLAYHOUSE
Opening Soon in Repertory!
MR. SAMUEL HORATIO TRUMP, Esq.
"America's Ace of Players"
—and—
Direct from Triumphant New York Appearances
The Divine MRS. PARKER
starring in
"STREETS OF SHAME"
an ENTIRELY NEW Melo-Drama of
New York HIGH and LOW Life
by H. T. Samuels
from a conception by
MR. TRUMP
—alternating with—
S. H. TRUMP's
Monumental & Internationally Famed Personation of
"The Life & Death of
KING RICHARD III"

———————

Numerous Seats at 50¢
NONE HIGHER THAN $1.50 ! ! !

9

The day after Charles said yes to Wooden Foot Jackson's proposition, the trader took the piebald to a veterinarian. Leaving Boy with the horse doctor, he and Charles set off for the city. To avoid soldiers from Jefferson Barracks who might recognize Charles, they circled around and rode in from the west. The border collie ran along behind them.

Early Creole settlers had nicknamed the place Pain Court—Short of Bread—because so little of its commerce had anything to do with agriculture; it was then the fur-trade center.

Times had changed. On the road bordered by sycamores and lindens, milkweed and climbing bittersweet, they passed farm wagons piled with apples or sacks of grain. They rode around two farmers driving pigs that filled the air with squealing and a characteristic stink.

Presently, rooftops appeared down the road and, above them, a hovering gray cloud. "Don't breathe too much in St. Lou," Wooden Foot advised. "They's buildin' more foundries and tanneries and flour mills and sheet-lead works than I can rightly keep track of. I guess 'Mericans don't care if they choke to death on fact'ry smoke so long as they go out rich."

The day was bright and nippy. Charles felt good. The effects of the beating were wearing off, and the gypsy robe kept him warm. His first impression of Wooden Foot had been right; the trader was a man to like and trust. Maybe his spirits would lighten in the weeks ahead, even if he did have to ride all the way to the Indian Territory to make it happen.

They rode toward the busy heart of town, passing old Creole homes of stone, frontier cabins of hand-hewn logs, and newer, half-timbered houses with Dutch doors built by members of the

large German population. Around one hundred fifty thousand
people lived in St. Louis, Wooden Foot said.

Reaching Third Street, they could already hear the wagon
traffic and shouting stevedores on the mile-and-a-half-long levee
ahead of them. A riverboat's whistle blew as Wooden Foot
handed Charles a roll of notes.

"I'll stock up on trade goods while you buy some winter
clothes. Also a knife. Also a rifle that satisfies you, and plenty of
ammunition. Don't go scant or cheap. They ain't no general
stores out where we're goin', and you'd be pretty unhappy to
have a dozen hoppin'-mad Cheyennes on your neck and no more
cartridges in your pouch 'cause you saved a penny. Oh"—he
grinned—"buy some of them cigars you fancy. Man needs a little
civilized pleasure on the plains. The winter nights are mighty
long."

He waved, turned left at the corner in front of an oxcart, and
disappeared.

Ten minutes later, Charles walked out of a tobacco shop on
Olive Street with three wooden boxes under his arm. He slipped
them in an old saddlebag Wooden Foot had given him.

He'd kept one cigar out to smoke. As he lit it, he noticed an
Army officer striding along the walk on the other side of the
street. He didn't know the officer's name, but he recognized his
face from Jefferson Barracks. He held absolutely still. The match
burned down, scorching his fingers.

The officer went around the corner without seeing him.

Charles exhaled, flicked the dead match away, and rubbed
his stinging fingers on his leg. He relit the cigar as a wagon pulled
up at the Olive Street side of a large two-story building on the
corner. A second-floor signboard mounted to be readable from
both streets said TRUMP'S ST. LOUIS PLAYHOUSE in showy red
letters.

The wagon carried a load of unpainted boards. The teamster, a pot-gut with the front brim of his black hat pinned up, tied
the rein to a hitching post and smacked the hip of the old dray
horse as he got down—an unnecessary unkindness that made
Charles frown. The teamster looked grumpy, but that was no
excuse.

The man entered a door marked STAGE. He shouted something, then came out and began pulling boards from the wagon. He looked like he hated the work, and the world.

A black cat strolled out of the theater and approached the dray horse. The horse began to whinny and sidestep. The cat arched its back and hissed. The horse reared, whinnying wildly and lunging toward the street, almost causing a collision with a green-and-white hotel omnibus bringing passengers and luggage from the levee. One of the passengers leaned out to swat the wagon horse away. The horse reared again.

As the omnibus rattled on, the teamster dropped three boards on the walk and slapped the horse's hind quarter with his black hat. "Goddamn miserable nag." He hit again, and again.

Charles's face changed as he watched. The horse tried to nip his tormentor. The teamster reached under the seat and came up with a quirt. He laid it on the old plug's neck, withers, haunch.

Charles dashed around his mount's head and into the street, jumping to avoid being run down by a horseman. The teamster kept striking with the quirt. "Teach you to bite me, you fucking jughead."

A gentleman passing with a lady objected to the language. The teamster whirled and threatened him with the bloodied quirt. The man hurried the woman away.

The feeble prancing of the old horse amused the teamster. He struck the animal again.

"Hit him once more and I'll put one between your eyes."

The teamster glanced up to see Charles on the sidewalk, both hands extended in front of him, clasping the Army Colt. Charles's cheeks were deep red. The sight of the quirt marks enraged him. His heart beat at great speed, roaring in his ears. He drew the hammer back.

"He's my horse, for Christ's sake," the teamster protested.

"He's a dumb animal. Take your misery out on a human being."

To Charles's left, in the theater doorway, a woman said, "What is all this about?" Charles mistakenly looked at her, and the teamster laid the quirt across his shoulder.

Charles staggered back. The teamster knocked the Colt from his hand. Something exploded in Charles's head.

He tore the upraised quirt away from the teamster and flung it. Then he jumped the man and bore him down to the wooden walk. His right arm pistoned back and forth. Someone from a gathering crowd grabbed his shoulders. "Get up. Stop it."

Charles kept pounding.

"Get up! You're killing him."

Two men succeeded in pulling him away. The red haze cleared from his mind, and he saw the pulped, dripping face of the teamster, who lay on his back. One of the men from the crowd said to the teamster, "You better unload and get out of here."

Charles tossed the teamster a blue bandanna from his back pocket. The man batted it away and called Charles a filthy name. Charles flexed his aching right hand as the teamster struggled up and began to pull boards from the wagon, watching Charles from an eye already showing a purple bruise.

"Pretty severe punishment for horsewhipping," one of the onlookers said to Charles.

"The man jumped me." He stared until the onlooker muttered something and turned away.

To someone inside the theater, the woman said, "Arthur, please come help unload the lumber." Charles turned to her, completely unprepared for what he saw: a woman perhaps twenty years old, a picture-pretty thing, slim but well formed, with blue eyes and blond hair so pale it had silver glints. Her dress was a plain yellow lawn, dusty in places. She held the black cat in her arms.

"That stray cat spooked the horse. That's what started everything." Charles remembered his manners and dragged off his old straw hat.

"Prosperity isn't a stray. She belongs to the theater." The young woman indicated the signboard on the building. "I'm Mrs. Parker."

"Charles Main, ma'am. Believe me, I don't always blow up like that, though it does happen if I catch somebody mistreating a horse."

A broad-shouldered black man helped the teamster carry the boards inside. It was hard to say whether the teamster was more sullen over the beating or working with a Negro.

Mrs. Parker said, "Well, if that's a failing, it's in a good cause."

Charles acknowledged the remark with a nod and put on his

hat, ready to go. The young woman added, "There's water in our green room if you'd like to clean your hands."

Reaching down to pick up his revolver, he saw that they were bloodstained. Something in him shied from accepting even casual kindness from any woman, but in spite of it he said, "All right. Thanks."

They stepped into a gloomy area backstage. From the stage, brilliant under calcium lights, a portly man approached with a queer sidestep gait. He walked bent over, a large pillow roped to his back like a hump. His tongue lolled from the corner of his mouth. His dangling hands swung to and fro, pendulumlike. All at once he straightened up.

"Willa, how can I concentrate on the winter of my discontent when a hundred idlers are rioting on my doorstep?"

"It wasn't a riot, Sam, just a small dispute. Mr. Main, my partner, Mr. Samuel Trump." She pointed to the pillow. "We're rehearsing *Richard the Third.*" Charles thought that was Shakespeare but didn't want to show his ignorance by asking.

Trump said, "Have I the honor of addressing a fellow thespian, sir?"

"No, sir, afraid not. I'm a trader." It surprised him a little to say it for the first time.

"Do you trade with the Indians?" the young woman asked. He said yes. "You sound Southern," she continued. "Did you serve in what they call 'the late unpleasantness'?"

"I did. I'm from South Carolina. I rode with General Wade Hampton's cavalry all four years."

"Lucky you came out unscathed," Trump declared. Charles thought it pointless to contradict so foolish a statement.

Mrs. Parker told Trump what had happened outside, in words that flattered Charles and minimized his brutal rage. "I invited Mr. Main to clean up in the green room."

"By all means," Trump said. "If you wish to view a performance of our new production, sir, I recommend booking a seat early. I anticipate capacity business, perhaps even an offer to transfer to New York."

Willa gave him a rueful smile. "Sam, you know that's bad luck."

Trump paid no attention. "Adieu, good friends. My art summons me." Dangling his hands again, he sidled toward the stage, bellowing, *"Grim-visaged war has smooth'd his wrinkled front . . ."*

"This way," Willa said to Charles.

She closed the door of the spacious, untidy green room to confine Prosperity for a while. On a love seat with one leg missing, a gentleman snored, his handwritten part covering his face. Prosperity jumped on his stomach and began to wash herself. The actor didn't stir.

Willa showed Charles to a basin of clean water on a table strewn with make-up pots, brushes, jars of powder. She found a clean towel for him.

"Thank you." He was conscious of great awkwardness. After Gus Barclay's death, he'd withdrawn from the company of women. His visit to the tent-town whore had passed with almost no conversation.

Using the damp towel, he cleaned the blood from his hands. Willa folded her arms, taking his measure. "What do you call that garment you're wearing? A cape? A poncho?"

"I call it my gypsy robe. I sewed it together a piece at a time when uniforms started to wear out and Richmond couldn't send any new ones.

"I know little about the war except what I've read. I was only fifteen when the fighting began."

That young. He dropped the towel beside the basin; the water had turned red. "Before you ask, I'll tell you. I wasn't fighting for slavery and I didn't give a hang for secession. I left the U.S. Army to fight for my state and my family's home."

"Yes, Mr. Main, but the war's over. There's no need to be belligerent."

He apologized; he hadn't realized he sounded angry. There was a certain irony there. To how many men had *he* said the war was over?

"It was a bad time, Mrs. Parker. Hard to forget."

"Perhaps something pleasant would help. You performed a humane deed outside. You deserve a reward. I should like to buy you supper, if I may."

His jaw dropped. She laughed. "I shocked you. I didn't intend it. You must understand the theater, Mr. Main. It's a lonely business. So theater people cling to one another for company. And there's very little conventional formality. If an actress wants an hour's friendly conversation, there's no shame in her asking a fellow actor. I suppose it doesn't look so innocent from outside. No wonder preachers think us loose and dangerous people. I assure you"— she kept it light but it was pointed—"I'm neither."

"No, I wouldn't imagine so, you being married."

"Ah—Mrs. Parker. That's only a convenience. It keeps some of the stage door crowd at bay. I'm not married. I just like to choose my friends." Her smile was warm and winning. "I repeat my offer. Can you join me for supper? Say, tomorrow evening? We're rehearsing tonight."

He almost said no. Yet something prompted him the other way. "That would be very enjoyable."

"And no quibbling over a mere female paying the bill?"

He smiled. "No quibbling."

"Seven o'clock, then? The New Planter's House on Fourth Street?"

"Fine. I'll try to look more respectable."

"You look splendid. The very picture of a gallant cavalryman." She shocked him with that easy frankness, and then again with the forthright way she shook hands. "Until tomorrow."

"Yes, ma'am."

"Oh, no, please. Let it be Willa and Charles."

He nodded and got out of there.

As he went from store to store, buying what he needed, he tried to figure out why he'd entangled himself with the supper engagement. Was it simple hunger for a woman's company? Or the way she had approached him, with unexpected candor and a reversal of the usual roles? He didn't know. He did know the young actress fascinated him, and that bothered him on two counts. He felt guilty because of Gus Barclay, and he was wary of the potential for pain that existed even in a friendship.

"She did the askin'?" Wooden Foot exclaimed when Charles told him about it.

"Yes. She isn't, well, conventional. She's an actress."

"Oh, I get it now. Well, take advantage, Charlie. They say actresses are always good for a fast romp on the sheets."

"Not this one," he said. It was one of the few things about Willa Parker he could state with any certainty.

10

To say the blue cutaway was old was to say the Atlantic was a
pond. The coat had cost Charles four dollars, secondhand. "This
yere's strictly a loan," Wooden Foot had said. "I approve of romance but it ain't my habit to finance it." The haberdasher threw
in a used cravat, and with another dollar borrowed from his new
partner, Charles bought some Macassar oil. Dressed up and with
his long hair slicked down, he felt foolish and foppish.

That opinion seemed to be shared by two black men in green
velvet livery who received guests at the entrance of the elegant
New Planter's House, the second hotel in St. Louis to bear that
name. Charles handed his saddle horse to a groom and stalked
between the doormen. His sharp stare and vaguely sinister appearance forestalled any comment about his looks.

Willa rose from one of the plush seats in the spacious lobby.
Her quick smile relieved his nervousness a little. "My," she said,
"for an Indian trader you're certainly elegant."

"Special occasion. I don't have many. I'd say you're the
elegant one."

"Thank you, sir." She took his arm and guided him toward
the dining room. By some feminine magic he didn't begin to
understand, she fairly sparkled with youthful prettiness, even
though her outfit was nearly all black: her hooped skirt, her trim
silk sacque, her small hat with a single black-dyed feather. White
lace spilled at her throat and fringed her cuffs—just enough for
dramatic contrast.

The haughty headwaiter tried to seat them behind a potted
fern next to the kitchen entrance. "No, thank you," Willa said
pleasantly. "I'm Mrs. Parker, of Trump's Playhouse. I send many

of our patrons here to enjoy your cuisine, and I won't take your worst table. That one in the center, please."

It was a table for four, but the man was defeated by her charm. He thanked her effusively.

Soft gaslight and candles on the tables combined to create a civilized, intimate atmosphere in the busy room. Several gentlemen interrupted conversations to cast admiring looks at Willa. The black dress and her vivid blue eyes produced a lovely effect as she sat across from Charles, a swath of pink tablecloth between them. Napkins in the wine goblets resembled pink flowers.

"I'm out of place here—" he began.

"Nonsense. You're the handsomest chap in sight. No more begging for compliments, if you please."

He started to protest and saw she was teasing. The waiter delivered leatherbound menus. Charles blanched when he opened the one for wine.

"It's in French. I think it's French."

"It is. Shall I order for us?"

"You'd better. Do they serve any grits or corn bread?"

It made her giggle, as he'd intended. He began to enjoy himself. She said, "I doubt it. The veal medallions are always fine. And *escargots* first, I think." Charles examined his silver to conceal his ignorance about the nature of *escargots*.

"Do you like red wine?" she asked. "They have a Bordeaux from the little village of Pomerol, and it's reasonable."

"Fine." The waiter retired. "You know a lot about food and wine."

"Actors spend a great deal of time in hotels. Ask me to plant a garden or catch a fish, I'd be helpless." Her smile put him wonderfully at ease. He warned himself to be careful, remembering Gus and how it felt when he lost her.

"So you're ready to leave for the Indian Territory. Perhaps this year it will be peaceful out there." He pulled a cigar halfway out of his pocket; put it back. "No, go ahead. I don't mind cigars."

He lit it, then said, "You keep up on the Indians?"

He meant it facetiously. Her reply, "Oh, yes," was serious. "In New York I belonged to a group called the Indian Friendship Society. We circulated memorials to be sent to Congress asking the government to repudiate the massacre at Sand Creek. You're familiar with that?" He said he was. "Well, the blame for it lies entirely with the white man. We steal land belonging to the Indians, then slaughter them if they resist or object. The white man's relationship with the native tribes is a shameful history of deceit, injustice, broken promises, violated treaties, and unspeakable cruelty."

Charles found himself in awe of her crusader's passion. "My partner would agree with you," he said. "He likes the Southern Cheyennes. Most of them, anyway."

"And you?"

"I've only had experience with a few Comanches, in Texas—all of them mad enough to shoot at me."

"I know it's impossible to stop westward expansion. But it mustn't come at the price of extermination of the original inhabitants of this country. Thank heaven there are signs of a movement toward peace. That bloodthirsty General Dodge wanted to unleash a thousand men to kill any Indians found along the Santa Fe wagon road, but he was blocked. And yesterday I read in the *Missouri Gazette* that Colonel Jesse Leavenworth, the Indian agent, has managed to get a truce with some of the Indians he oversees through his Upper Arkansas Agency. Do you realize what that means?"

She leaned forward, vivid color in her cheeks. "It means that William Bent and Kit Carson and Senator Doolittle of Wisconsin have a real chance to arrange a peace conference soon. Perhaps for once we'll have a treaty both sides will honor."

The waiter brought small silver forks and curious shell-like things arranged in a semicircle on each plate. Charles lifted the little fork, baffled.

"*Escargots,*" she said. "Snails."

He coughed and groped for his cigar, resting in a crystal dish. Several deep puffs pulled him through his first encounter with snails that were eaten rather than observed in a motionless journey across a rock or a leaf.

After the waiter decanted the rich, heavy Pomerol, and Charles drank some, conversation became easier. He told Willa something of his war experiences, and of his closest friend, Billy Hazard, whom he'd rescued from Libby Prison. He described the officer named Bent who held an inexplicable grudge against both his family and Billy's. "He disappeared in the war. A casualty, I suppose. I can't say I'm sorry."

More wine, then the veal, appealingly garnished with bright

yellow rounds of squash and large whole pea pods. He spoke of other matters with obvious emotion. He described his abiding love for Mont Royal—burned, but rebuilding—and his affection for his cousin Orry, who'd saved him from self-destruction.

Presently he said, "What about you? Is this your home?"

She concentrated on lifting a bit of veal with the fork in her left hand, something Charles had seen only among people of great refinement. "No. I answered an appeal from Sam Trump to help him put his theater on a profitable basis. He's an old friend of my father. Whose name was not Parker, by the way. It was Potts." She crossed her eyes and made a face, and he laughed.

They talked on, Charles forgetting how bizarre his slicked-down hair must look, or how ill at ease he felt in the frayed cutaway. The wine slipped down quickly, muting the candlelight, enhancing her prettiness. A violinist and cellist, solemn whiskered fellows in white ties and tail coats, began to play semi-classical airs from seats in a corner.

"What brought you to St. Louis as a trader, Charles?"

"Actually—" Did he dare trust her? He searched her blue eyes. Yes. "I've never gone out before. I graduated from West Point, you see. After the war I went back in the Army, but someone at Jefferson Barracks—a man who went to the Academy when I did—recognized me. They booted me out. Literally. Well, I needed a way to support my son—"

She dropped her spoon. It hit the edge of her dish of blueberries in cream and fell to the floor. Charles saw her anger. "Oh, no, wait." Without a thought, he shot his hand over to clasp hers. "I didn't trick you. I do have a son, eight months old. His mother died in Virginia when he was born."

"Oh. I'm truly sorry." Relaxed again, she picked up the new spoon the waiter had silently laid beside her gold-rimmed dish. With her eyes on the dessert, she murmured, "We both have a past out of the ordinary, it would seem."

He wondered about the undertone of pain in those words. A man tipped the musicians to play "Lorena." Charles and Willa exchanged looks, letting the sweet sad music speak for them.

The night smelled of wood smoke and approaching autumn. Willa suggested they walk on the levee, and they linked arms. This time she wasn't quite so careful; the silken thrust of her bosom rested easily, moved lightly against his sleeve. He experienced a strong physical reaction.

They turned right on the levee, a wide esplanade between the piers and a row of wood and stone warehouses and commercial buildings. A sickle moon hid the dirt and litter, and softened the silhouettes of great crates and casks piled up awaiting shipment. A cargo watchman resting on a keg took his cob pipe from his mouth. "Evening." His left hand remained on his shotgun.

"It's been a delicious evening," Willa said, sighing. "Since you already know I'm forward, I might as well tell you that I'd love to repeat it."

Now, Charles thought. *Cut it off. Leave it there.* But he'd drunk too much of the rich red fruit of the village of Pomerol.

"So would I."

"Good. How long must I wait?"

"Till spring, I suppose. That's when Jackson comes back with the horses he gathers during the winter."

"All right." The black feather bobbed on her hat as she nodded. "Starting the first of next April, I'll leave a standing order at the ticket window. You'll have a box seat for any performance. When I see you in the audience, I'll know it's time for another supper."

"That's a bargain. You're very confident the theater will prosper."

"I'll make it prosper." She wasn't bragging, merely stating what she believed. "Like so many actors, Sam's a lovely, charming man, vanity and all. But he has a weakness for drink. If I can keep him away from it, and we can mount three or four new shows in repertory, a Molière comedy, perhaps, and another of those melodramas Sam writes under the name Samuels—they're dreadful, really, but audiences love them, because he does know how to write stirring lines for himself—if we can accomplish that much by the time you return, we'll make it. Time then to think of adding actors for a touring troupe."

"For someone so young, you're very determined."

She watched the river. A great white side-wheeler churned upriver toward the Missouri, a necklace of amber lights gleaming along her cabin deck. From the channel drifted the slushing of her paddles and the bleating and squawking of sheep and chickens in crates stacked among new farm wagons lashed to the decks.

"Isn't she a pretty sight, Charles?"

"Yes, but the cabin lights make me feel lonesome."

"I know. I've felt that way ever since I was small and passed through strange towns with my father, wishing one of the lamps was lighted to welcome us— It's late," she said abruptly. "We should go back. I always check to be sure Sam's tucked in, and sober. We're running through *Streets of Shame* in the morning."

They walked in silence, comfortably, amid the night sounds of St. Louis: a man and woman quarreling; a banjo doing "Old Folks at Home"; street mongrels yapping and snarling over scraps. "That's a lovely tune," she said as they approached the theater. "What is it?"

"What do you mean?"

"The tune you were humming." She repeated a few notes.

"I didn't realize I was—it's just something I made up to remind me of home."

"That's something I've never had, a real home." They stopped by the stage door. She found a key in her silk reticule. "Sam sleeps in the office, and I have a pallet in the scene loft. It saves the cost of lodgings, though I hope I can move to better quarters if we're successful this season." She raised her head, waiting. Charles leaned down and gave her a brotherly kiss, barely touching one corner of her lips with his. Her left hand darted up to press the back of his neck a moment. They separated.

"Take proper care of yourself out West. I want to see you again in the spring."

"Willa—" He struggled; this had to be said. "You're forthright. Let me be the same. I live a solitary life, especially now that my son's mother is gone. I don't want—attachments."

Without emotion, she asked, "Does that include friendships?"

He was put off; could only repeat, "Attachments."

"Why don't you want attachments?"

"They hurt people. Something happens to one person, and afterward it's bad for the other. I don't mean to suggest that you and I—that is—" He cleared his throat. "I like you, Willa. We should leave it at that."

"Perfectly fine with me, Charles. Good night."

She unlocked the door and disappeared. He remained outside, gazing at the moon-washed building and congratulating himself on speaking at the right moment.

But if he'd done such a fine job of it, why was he so filled with delight, even a surprising yearning, as he thought of her face, the feel of her breast brushing his sleeve, things she'd said, the little graces that seemed to come so naturally to her?

Something was astir in him, something dangerous.

You'll have a lot of time for getting over that, he said to himself as he turned and strode off toward the hotel stable.

Inside Trump's Playhouse, Willa leaned against the street door. "Well," she said, "it was only a small hope."

She'd learned long ago that, in this world, hopes were easily and frequently dashed. She straightened up, touched her eyes briefly, then moved toward the band of light showing under the office door. The sound of Sam's snoring rescued her from the spell of the night and the tall Southerner, and the evening's foolish fancies.

Lesson XIII.

The Good Girl.

MOTH-ER, may I sew to-day?

Yes, my child; what do you wish to sew?

I wish to hem a frill for your cap. Is not this a new cap? I see it has no frill.

You may make a frill for me; I shall like to wear a frill that you have made. . . .

Jane sat down upon her stool and sew-ed like a lit-tle la-dy. In a short time she said, Moth-er, I have done as far as you told me; will you look at it?

Yes, my child, it is well done; and if you take pains, as you have done to-day, you will soon sew well.

I wish to sew well, Moth-er, for then I can help you make caps and frocks, and I hope to be of some use to you.

McGuffey's Eclectic
First and Second Readers
1836–1879

MADELINE'S JOURNAL

September, 1865. Cooper is pardoned.

This from Judith. She drove from Charleston with Marie-Louise to see to our welfare. I showed them the school-house, nearly complete, and introduced Prudence, who charmed them. Cooper will no longer come here because of the school. Judith says he insists that the only acceptable social order puts the colored forever beneath the white. He grants them freedom but not equality. It saddens Judith.

Knowing of our growing isolation, J. left certain Charleston papers describing the momentous work of the constitutional convention meeting at Columbia's Baptist church. The secession ordinance is overturned, the Thirteenth Amendment ratified. Provisional Governor Perry rebuked a minority who tried to amend the motion to abolish slavery by compensating former slaveowners and forbidding Negroes from all but manual work. Perry: "No; it is gone—dead forever—never to be revived."

So two of Johnson's conditions are met. The third, repudiation of the war debt, is not. Perry: "It will be a reproach to South Carolina that her constitution is less republican than that of any other state."

Delegates recommended that James Orr be elected governor. A moderate man, opponent of the hotspurs and once Speaker of the House in Washington; I remember you respected him. While in the Confederate Senate he pleaded for a negotiated peace, predicting certain military defeat. None would listen.

Inflammatory language was struck from an appeal for clemency for Mr. Davis. Delegate Pickens was blunt: "It does not become us to vapor, swell and strut—bluster, threaten and swagger. Our state, and world opinion, bid us bind up Carolina's wounds and pour on the oil of peace."

Some hooted him down. Are we forever prisoners of old ways, old passions, old errors? . . .

A strange parcel found at dusk at the entrance to our lane. Do not know how it came there. . . .

The mule recognized the hunched black man and nuzzled him. Juba dragged his tired, arthritic body across the porch of the Dixie Store. In pain, he clutched the door frame. The two white men didn't acknowledge his presence for almost a minute.

Finally LaMotte said, "You left it where I told you?" His height reduced the spectacled storekeeper, Gettys, to the size of a boy.

"Yessir, Mist' Desmond. Nobody seen me, neither."

Gettys laughed. "It's a fine jest. Choice."

"Only the opening salvo," Des said. "Wait outside, Juba."

"I was wonderin', sir—I ain't et since mornin'—"

"We'll be back in Charleston in a few hours. You can eat then."

Miserable, Juba knew better than to object. He moved slowly outside to the lowering dark.

Des said, "When I stopped here to wait while my nigger did the errand, I never supposed I'd meet someone like you. Gettys."

"It does appear that we share the same convictions, Mr. LaMotte."

"What you said about Mont Royal stupefies me. I had no idea that black bitch would be so audacious. She must be stopped. If you are equally strong about that, we should join forces."

"Yes, sir, I am strong about that."

Out in the dark, Juba leaned his aching body against a live oak. His head was full of sad thoughts of the heartlessness of which some men were capable.

Madeline held the mysterious package at arm's length, to sharpen the letters crudely inked on the wrapping, which was old wallpaper. She couldn't afford the glasses she needed.

MADELINE MAIN. She saw that clearly. Seated in a rocker on the other side of the lamp, Prudence said, "What on earth can it be?"

"Let's find out."

She opened the flat, square package. She discovered an old browned daguerreotype about ten inches high, mounted on a piece of cardboard. The subject was one of the ugliest black women she had ever seen, a woman with a long jaw and jutting upper teeth. Although the woman was smiling, it was a peculiar smile, full of malice. Everything the woman wore—frilly dress, lace mittens, feathered hat—was white. So was the open parasol she held over her shoulder.

Madeline shook her head. "It must be some reference to my background, but I don't know this woman."

She put the daguerreotype on a little shelf. Both women studied it. The longer they looked, the more sinister the smiling face became. Madeline saw it in her dreams that night.

Next day, a matter at the saw pit brought Lincoln to the house. As he began to speak, he noticed the daguerreotype and went silent. Madeline caught her breath.

"Lincoln, do you recognize that woman?"

"No, I—yes." He avoided her eye. "I worked for her once, for two weeks. Couldn't stand her meanness, so I just picked up an' ran." He shook his head. "How'd that awful thing come into this house?"

"Someone left it in the lane last night. Do you know why?"

Again he evaded her eye.

"Lincoln, you're my friend. You've got to tell me. Who is that woman?"

"She goes by the name Nell Whitebird. Please, Miss Madeline—"

"Go on."

"Well, the place I worked, her place, there was a lot of fine white gentlemen coming and going at all hours."

He hadn't the heart to say more. Madeline put her hand on her lips, angry, sorrowful, frightened too. Whoever her anonymous tormentors might be, they knew not only that she was an octoroon, but also that her mother had been a prostitute.

There have been no further "gifts" or incidents of any kind. Prudence urges me to burn the picture. I insist we keep it, a reminder that we must be vigilant . . .

. . . A full week—all quiet. Governor Orr has con-

*vened the legislature, and there is spirited debate over a new
set of laws purporting to aid and benefit the freed blacks as
well as improve economic conditions generally. I do not think
well of the regulations proposed thus far. They are the old
system tricked out in new clothes. If those who need field
labor have their way and these regulations become law, we
will surely reap a harvest of Northern anger.*

*. . . A day of rejoicing. At least it began as such. Pru-
dence enrolled her first pupils, Pride, who is twelve, and
Grant, fourteen. They are sons of our freedman Sim and his
wife, Lydie. When Francis LaMotte owned the boys, they were
called by affected classical names—Jason, Ulysses. The latter
boy turned the tables and named himself after a less popular
Ulysses!*

*Even more heartening, we have a white pupil. Dorrie Otis
is fifteen. She came shyly, at the insistence of her mother, and
quickly showed a hunger to know the meaning of the curious
marks printed in books. Her father is a poor farmer, never a
slaveowner but in sympathy with the system. How glad I am
that his wife won the battle over schooling for the girl.*

A single day of rejoicing—that was all granted to us . . .

"Wake up, Madeline." Prudence shook her again. Madeline
heard a man shouting. "Nemo's outside. There's a fire."

"Oh my God."

Madeline hastily rose from the rocking chair, rubbing her
eyes. With clumsy fingers she fastened the four top buttons of her
stained dress. She'd opened them for a little relief from the humid
heat, and fallen asleep where she sat.

She ran to the open door. The lamplight revealed Nemo
outside, his face tearful. She saw light in the sky. "Is it the
school?" He couldn't speak, only nod.

She dashed from the whitewashed house and ran barefoot
along the sandy road to the old slave quarters. Prudence kept up
with her, dampness plastering her cotton nightgown to her broad
bosom and wide hips. The bright glare through the trees lighted
their way.

Just as they reached the schoolhouse, the last wall fell inward, a brilliant waterfall of fire and sparks. The heat was fierce.

Prudence didn't seem to think of that. "All my books are in
there. And my Bible," she cried.

"You can't go in," Madeline said, dragging her back.

Prudence struggled a moment before she gave up. She stood watching the fire with pain and disbelief in her eyes.

Behind the two women, some of the blacks gathered: Andy and Nemo and Sim and their wives. Pride and Grant looked confused and lost.

"Did anyone see strangers around here?" Madeline asked. No one had. Sim said the fire's glare had wakened him; he was a light sleeper.

Madeline paced, almost dancing on her tiptoes, so angry was she, so overwhelmed with a sense of violation of her self, of her property, of simple and reasonable principles of decency and practicality.

She flung a damp strand of hair off her forehead. "Randall Gettys warned me not to open the school. I suspect he had a hand in this. He wouldn't set a fire by himself, I think. He strikes me as a perfect coward. He would need accomplices."

She watched the nearby trees, in case the fire spread. It didn't; the cleared area around the burned building contained it. The flames receded but the heat remained intense.

"The worst part is not knowing who your enemies are. Well, no help for that. Will one of you go up to the house and bring me that picture of the black woman?"

Lincoln stepped forward. "I will."

He hurried off. Madeline kept pacing. She couldn't control her nervous excitement. Prudence spoke softly to the blacks, shaking her head and shrugging because she couldn't answer their questions.

Lincoln brought back the daguerreotype of Nell Whitebird. Madeline took it and stalked toward the glowing ruins. "This fire was the work of men so despicable, they have to hide their deeds under cover of darkness. I'm sure the same men sent me this." She thrust her arm out, showing them the face of the prostitute. "This is a black woman of bad character. The men who burned the school are saying blackness equals evil, evil equals blackness. God curse them. Do you know why they sent me this particular picture? My mother was a quadroon." They were astonished. "What's more, during a certain period in her life she sold herself to men. Yet my father adored her. Married her. I honor her memory. I'm proud to have her blood. Your blood. They want us to think it's a taint. Inferior to theirs. We're supposed to cringe in a corner and bless them when they deign to throw us scraps, or thank them if they choose to whip us. Well, to hell with them. This is what I think of them, and their tactics, and their threats."

She ripped the daguerreotype in half and flung the pieces on the coals. They smoked, curled, burned, vanished.

Madeline's face glowed red in the firelight. It ran with sweat from the heat, and her anger. "In case all of you are wondering, yes, this upsets me terribly, but, no, it doesn't change anything. When the ashes are cold, we'll clear them out and we'll start building a new schoolhouse."

> One of the "Negro laws" foolishly enacted by the new legislature defines a person of color as one with more than one-eighth Negro blood. So I am exempt. Somehow, my dearest, I think that will have no effect on those who are against me.
>
> I am convinced Mr. Gettys is one of them. Could another be that dancing master? I don't know, nor care much. They have declared war, we need to know nothing else.
>
> I can tell you, my dearest, that I am badly frightened. I am a person of no special courage. Yet I was brought up to understand right and wrong, and the need to persevere for the former.
>
> The school is right. The dream of a new Mont Royal is right. I will not submit. To thwart me they will have to kill me.

> A Negro is allowed to buy and hold property.
>
> A Negro is allowed to seek justice in the courts, to sue and be sued, and to be a witness in any case involving Negroes only.
>
> A Negro is allowed to marry, and the state will recognize that marriage and the legitimacy of children of that marriage.
>
> A Negro is not allowed to marry a person of a different race.
>
> A Negro is not allowed to work at any trade except that of a farmer or servant without a special license costing $10 to $100 per annum.
>
> A Negro is to be whipped by authority of a judicial officer and returned if he runs away from a master to whom he has

attached himself as a servant; if under 18, he is to be
whipped moderately.
A Negro is not to join any militia unit or keep any weapon
except a fowling piece.
A Negro is to be hired out for field labor if found guilty of
vagrancy by a judicial officer.
A Negro is to be transported out of state or put to hard labor for
all crimes not demanding the death penalty.
A Negro is to be put to death for inciting rebellion, for breaking
and entering a home, for carnal attack upon a white
woman, or for stealing a horse, a mule, or baled cotton.

Some provisions of
South Carolina's "Black Code," 1865

11

Dear Jack, Charles wrote, I am going west with a trading company for 6 mos. to a year. My partner says leave any messages at Ft. Riley, Kans. I will be in touch as soon as I come back. I hope my son will stay well & will remember me & won't be too much trouble for you & Maureen. Give him an extra big hug from his "Pa."

I have to do this because I'm not in the Army after all. I had some trouble at Jefferson Barracks. . . .

A slit of brilliant light lay between the land and solid gray clouds pushing down through the western sky. The calendar still said summer, September, but the rain-freshened vegetation and the chilly air tricked the senses into thinking autumn.

Out of the woods rode the entire Jackson Trading Company, leading a dozen mules heavily loaded with trade goods. Canvas parcels held bags of glass beads in both pony and smaller seed sizes; Wooden Foot Jackson favored diamond and triangle shapes, like those that glittered and flashed on the bosom of his coat.

The trader had explained to Charles that Cheyenne women wanted beads to decorate the apparel they made. White men had introduced beads to the West, so it was an acquired liking. An older, traditional, one was that for porcupine quills, which were abundant among the Mississippi but scarce on the dry plains, where they were going. The mules were carrying bundles of quills, too.

Jackson had also stocked up on some relatively bulky items. Iron hoe blades, which lasted longer than those made of a buffalo's scapula tied with rawhide to a stick. Durability was a virtue of another item he carried in quantity—a small iron rectangle with one long edge sharpened by a file. The tool replaced a similar one of bone used to scrape hair from buffalo hide and render it ready to sew into garments or a tipi cover.

The trader said there were plenty of other things he could sell, but he preferred to carry just a few that had proved popular year after year. All the merchandise was for women, but it would be paid for by men, using the most common form of Indian wealth, horses.

Charles absorbed this along with Wooden Foot's explanation of his success.

"They's fort traders who sell the exact same goods I do, only the Cheyennes won't go near 'em. And vice versey. I been haulin' goods into the villages near twenty years."

"Don't the Indian agents regulate trading?"

Wooden Foot spat out some plug tobacco, thus expressing his opinion of the Interior Department's Indian Bureau employees. "They sure would like to, because they're mostly greedy nogoods who want the trade all to themselves. I keep an eye peeled for 'em. If they don't find me they can't stop me. The Cheyennes won't turn me in, for the same reason I still got my hair. I'm a friend."

"Who might turn into something else if you were crossed?" Charles pointed to the notched feather.

"Well, yes, they's that, too."

A cigar curled smoke up past the brim of Charles's brand-new flat-crowned wool hat. He sat comfortably on Satan, having sewn strips of scraped buffalo hide to the inner thighs of his jeans pants. The piebald was again in good fettle, though Charles took care to rein him lightly and guide him with knee and hand pressure whenever possible. Satan was responsive; he was smart. Charles hadn't picked wrong.

In the saddle scabbard he carried a shiny new lever-action Spencer that fired seven rounds from a tube magazine in the stock. His gypsy robe hid a foot-long bowie knife and a keen hatchet with Pawnee decorations, feathers, and beaded wrappings on the shaft. He was better equipped than the U.S. Cavalry, which had to put up with war surplus arms, no matter what.

The autumnal landscape, the chilly temperature, and the lowering night cast a melancholy spell over him. Wooden Foot attempted to counter it with lively conversation.

"How's that little actress? Pinin' away?"

"I doubt it."

"Plan to see her again?"

"Maybe in the spring."

"Charlie, you got a funny look. I seen it on men before. Did you lose some other woman?"

"Yes. Back in Virginia. I don't like to talk about it."

"Then we don't. Still, it's nice you got the actress, for comfort."

"She's only an acquaintance. Besides, one woman can't replace another. Can we drop it?"

"Sure. You'll soon forget about it anyway. They's lots of other things to command your attention where we're goin'." His tone said he meant perils, not amusements.

Charles wished he could forget Gus Barclay for even a little while, but he couldn't. And in the privacy of his heart he wished that his conscience would let him think in a more personal way about Willa Parker. She did capture his fancy with her striking combination of youth and worldliness, idealism and cheerful tolerance. He supposed it wouldn't hurt to accept her offer of a ticket to a performance when he got back.

If he got back.

Wooden Foot seemed confident. Still, there was a vast country lying ahead of them. And no denying that some of the tribes were angry about the presence of the Army and the steady westward waves of migration.

Fenimore Cooper switched his tail and frisked back and forth ahead of the riders, bolting now to the left, now to the right but always loping back with joyous barks. Charles wondered if the dog was happy about not being hitched to a travois just yet.

Boy saw a blue jay bickering in a shrub and clapped his hands in delight. Charles puffed his cigar and patted Satan. Growing smaller and smaller in the immense wooded landscape, the Jackson Trading Company passed out of sight and into darkness.

12

HEAVEN AND HELL

A thunderstorm roared over the city of Richmond. Rain poured from the eaves of the City Almshouse and splashed the gravestones of Shockoe Cemetery immediately to the south. The noise of the storm kept patients awake in the charity wards this bleak September night.

One patient lay on his side, knees drawn up to his chest, arms clasped tightly around them. His cot was on the end of the row, so he was able to face the bare wall and hide with his thoughts.

In the dark high-ceilinged room men turned and groaned and rustled their bedding. A matron's lamp floated through like a firefly. A young man with a completely white beard sat up suddenly. "Union Cavalry. Sheridan's cavalry on the left flank!"

The matron rushed to his bedside. Her voice soothed him to silence. Then her lamp floated away again.

The Almshouse had been a Confederate hospital at the height of the war. Toward the end, it became temporary headquarters for the Virginia Military Institute, which had been forced out of the Shenandoah by the ferocity of Phil Sheridan's horse. Since the surrender, several wings had reopened on a temporary basis to care for mentally disturbed veterans, the human debris cast up by the tide of war and left to lie on the shore of peace, abandoned, forgotten. At present the Almshouse sheltered about fifty such men. Hundreds more, perhaps thousands, huddled in the South's ravaged cities and wandered its ruined roads, without help.

The patient on the end cot tossed and writhed. A familiar awl of pain pierced his forehead and turned, boring deeper and

deeper. He'd suffered with the pain, and a broken, almost deformed body, ever since he took a near-fatal fall into . . .

Into . . .

God, they'd destroyed his mind, too. It took him minutes
just to finish the thought.

Into the James River.

Yes. The James. He and fellow conspirators had planned to
rid the Confederacy of the inept Jefferson Davis. They'd been
discovered by an Army officer named . . .

Named . . .

No matter how he tried, it wouldn't come back, though he
knew he had reason to hate the man. In the struggle that ensued
after the discovery of the plot, the man had pushed him through
a window above the river.

He vividly remembered the shocks of the fall. He had never
experienced such pain. Outcrops of rock slammed his head, but-
tocks, legs as he went bouncing downward, finally striking the
water.

He had a recurring nightmare about what had happened
next. Sinking beneath the water, clawing against the current to
reach the surface, and failing. In the dream, he drowned. Reality
was different. Somehow, by effort or by chance, he no longer
remembered which, he'd dragged himself to a bank downstream,
vomited water, and lost consciousness.

Since that night he had been a different man. Pain was a
constant companion. Strange lights frequently filled his head. Lying on the cot in the midst of the storm, he saw them again,
yellow and green pinpoint flashes that blossomed to starry bursts
of scarlet, fiery orange, blinding white. As if all of that wasn't a
sufficient portion of suffering, his memory constantly betrayed
him.

Somehow he had reached Richmond and survived the great
conflagration that leveled so much of the city the night the Confederate government fell. He lived by prowling the night streets,
committing robberies. His most recent had yielded but two dollars and the handsome though old-fashioned beaver hat sitting on
a shelf above his cot. He'd gone without food for long periods—
two, even three days sometimes. Then there was a blank, after
which he awakened in the Almshouse. They said he'd collapsed
in the street.

Why could he remember some things at certain times, and

not at others? Then again, a whole new set of recollections would be clear while the first ones were beyond his mind's grasp for hours, or days. It was all part of the damage done to him by . . .

By . . .

It wouldn't come.

The rain fell harder, a sound like drumming. His hand crawled around under the cot like a blind white spider, seeking something he did remember. He felt it, pulled it up, hugged it tightly to his filthy coarse patient's gown. A torn magazine, given him during one of his lucid periods. *Harper's New Monthly* for July of this year.

He was able to recall paragraphs from the section called "Editor's Easy Chair." The copy described the Grand Review of Grant's and Sherman's armies in Washington, lasting two days in . . .

In . . .

May, that was it.

In the dark, he squeezed his hand into a fist. *I should have marched. People kept me from it. They kept me from playing the role I was born to play.*

He could picture it. He was riding a fine stallion, bowing from the waist to acknowledge the cheers of the mob, saluting President Lincoln with his saber, then riding on, his great steed moving in a high-stepping walk while the mob, sweating, awestruck, chanted as one:

"Bon-a-parte. Bon-a-parte."

He was the American Bonaparte.

No, he *should* have been. They kept him from it, those men named . . .

Named . . .

No use.

But he'd remember them someday. Someday. And when he did, God help them, and all their tribe.

He listened to the drums within the rain most of the night. About four he fell asleep. He awoke at six, clutching the torn *Harper's.* Although free of pain, he was still wretchedly unhappy. He couldn't think of the reason.

He couldn't even remember his own name.

BOOK TWO

A WINTER COUNT

It is to be regretted that the character of the Indian as described in Cooper's interesting novels is not the true one. . . .Stripped of the beautiful romance with which we have been so long willing to envelop him, transferred from the inviting pages of the novelist to the localities where we are compelled to meet with him, in his native village, on the war path, and when raiding upon our frontier settlements and lines of travel, the Indian forfeits his claim to the appellation of the noble red man. *We see him as he is, and . . . as he ever has been, a* savage *in every sense of the word.*

GENERAL G. A. CUSTER,
My Life on the Plains, 1872–74

I was born upon the prairie, where the wind blew free and there was nothing to break the light of the sun. I want to die there and not within walls.

CHIEF TEN BEARS *of the Comanche,*
Medicine Lodge Creek, 1867

13

Silver fans of water rose as they crossed the stream in the dazzling morning. The richly silted valley glistened after rain. Indians working fields of squash and beans and ripening pumpkins waved their man-made hoes and shouted greetings. Upstream, blurs now, stood the solid post-and-beam lodges, covered with grassy sod; the traders had passed the Indian dwellings on their way to this ford.

"Kansa," Wooden Foot said, indicating the workers in the fields. "They're called Kaw, too." He led his companions from the shallows into rippling foot-high bluestem. "They get along with 'most everybody. Guess that was typical of all the tribes a long time ago. Even the Cheyennes, when they lived in Minnesota or wherever. It ain't true no more. You'll soon see the reasons."

Passing almost due west, they did:

Emigrant wagons, westbound, with white tops billowing and snapping in the autumn wind.

A coach of the Butterfield Overland Despatch line bound down the Smoky Hill route with clatter and a cloud of dust.

A railroad work camp, double-story office cars lined up on a spur that ended in the middle of a field of thistles, clover, wilted goldenrod.

"This yere's tribal land, Charlie. The Indians been 'customed to roam anywhere they pleased, like them Arabs way on the other side of the world. Long as anyone can remember, they lived off the land's bounty. Chiefly the game and buffla. The Kansa, f'rinstance, they changed their way. Settled down. But not the Cheyennes. They live the old way. So you can't steal their land or shove 'em on a farm and expect 'em to kiss your foot.

That's why some of 'em's killin' people. Didn't you do the same when the Union boys marched all over your land?"

"Yes, sir," Charles said, understanding.

In Topeka, Wooden Foot bought a load of tin pots. "The women like these better'n rawhide bags or sewn-up buffla stomachs. They can boil water 'thout all the fuss of droppin' in hot rocks."

The new goods required Fen to pick up some of the burden. The collie pulled a travois that held their tipi poles and cover. He went hours at a time, with only his lolling tongue showing his strain.

From a detachment of cavalry they learned that the big peace conclave, the one Willa had mentioned, had started, down on the Little Arkansas. The captain leading the detachment said, "You boys might have a peaceful winter for once."

"Damn fool," Wooden Foot said after the troopers rode on. Red-faced, he showed a surprising amount of sweat in the winy autumn air. "That captain's one more who don't grasp how the tribes work. He thinks that if a peace chief like old Black Kettle, whom we're goin' to see, makes his mark on a treaty, everybody else just puts their feet up and stores their weapons. Mighty few sojers understand that no one Indian speaks for all Indians. Never did. Never will."

"I guess you think pretty highly of the Southern Cheyennes."

"I do, Charlie. They's the finest horsemen in the world. Finest cavalry, if you want to sharpen a point on it. Also, I been out here long enough to see 'em as different people, not just a bunch of copper-color look-alikes. If some Dog Society man rapes a farmer's wife, like as not the cavalry'll shoot some peaceable old chief, 'cause they can't tell the difference. I was lucky. Pa taught me to see each one separate. They's good ones and they's bad ones, quite like the general run of humans. I loved one enough to take her to wife some years back. She died birthin' a little girl. Baby died a week after."

He coughed suddenly; bent his head forward, jaw clenched, as he grasped a handful of his shirt. Charles reined Satan, leaning left to grip Wooden Foot's arm. "What is it? What's hurting you?"

"Nothin' "— the old trader got his breath—"to speak of."

He gulped, eyes watering. "My pa had a bum heart. He passed it along. Don't let it worry you. Let's travel."

The low hills began to flatten; the willows and cottonwoods to thin out. They rode through shorter buffalo and grama grass, empty of habitation except for the mound towns of black-tailed prairie dogs. Autumn light flooded everything, creating a raw beauty from hills sliced open by wind to reveal striations of white and yellow and orange chalk. Charles couldn't exactly say he was happy, but each day he thought of Augusta Barclay a little less.

"All right, Charlie," Wooden Foot said when they'd forded the Smoky Hill. "Time for you to start school."

"You never know when you'll need speed, Charlie. Boy an' me, we practiced till we can put the tipi up in ten minutes and strike it in half that. With your help I figure we can cut it some more. Notice that the round door always faces east? That way you miss most of the big rain and wind storms outa the west, and you catch the mornin' sun. Also, the tribes like to be reminded that way that it's the Great Spirit who sends 'em light and nourishment. Well, let's hop to, Charlie. Up she goes in eight minutes if you want your supper."

Flickering fire shone on the coil of brass wire. Wooden Foot's hair, long to start with, had grown enough to split into braids. He was winding wire round and round the braid hanging over his left shoulder.

Charles munched some pemmican, a chunk of powdered buffalo meat hardened up after the addition of fat and berries. "If you don't want to bother with that, I can cut your hair with my knife."

"Oh, no. You cut off a man's hair, you take away his life in the hereafter. If a Cheyenne ever gets a haircut, his woman burns the cuttings so nobody does mischief with 'em."

Boy jumped up, excited. "Road! Road!"

Charles looked past Boy's pointing finger to the veil of stars unfurled across the heavens. "That's the Milky Way, Boy."

"It's the Hangin' Road, Charlie," Wooden Foot said. "The trail the Cheyennes travel to the spirit world. The road to the place of the dead."

The trader patted his nephew to calm him, then opened his

parfleche, a hide bag decorated with quills and painted designs. From the bag he took a roll of clean, soft animal skin, which he spread by the fire. Next he opened small pots of red and black paint he moistened with spit. He surprised Charles by producing an artist's small brush. With strokes of black he began painting at the upper left corner of the skin. A line of three stick-figure horses and riders. He finished with a smaller four-footed figure out in front.

"What in thunder's that?" Charles asked.

"The start of our winter count. Kind of a picture history of a season in a man's life. Chiefs and braves make 'em." He grinned. "I figure the Jackson Trading Company's important enough to have one this year."

They saw a buffalo herd in seasonal migration southward. By a stream dried to a width of six inches, they waited hours for the herd to pass. It was six or seven miles long, front to back, and a good mile across. Wooden Foot pointed out the old bull leaders.

"One name the tribes got for the buffla is Uncle. Since he provides pretty near everything they eat or use, they figure he's pretty near a relative."

Under an ugly gray sky streaked silver by lightning, Charles held on to his hat and squinted through blowing dust at eight young Indians armed with lances and rifles. They were within hailing distance, so Charles clearly heard them yell, "Sons of bitches. Sons of bitches!"

One brave knelt on his pony's back, thrust out his rear end, and thumbed it with his right hand. Wooden Foot sighed. "They's sure learned all the best we got to teach."

Boy crowded his horse close to his uncle's. Charles rested the Spencer on his right leg, his mouth dry with worry. The lightning streaked east to west, and distant thunder pealed. Behind the braves milled a herd of at least fifty wild stallions, mares, and foals. The white men had stopped when they spied the Indians herding the ponies across some low hills.

"That's money on the hoof, them horses," Wooden Foot said. "Tribal wealth. They won't risk losin' it by comin' after us. They seldom attack 'less they outnumber the other side or they's trapped or provoked. 'Sides, they's near enough to see we got these."

He pumped his rifle up and down over his head a few times. The braves replied with more shaken fists and obscenities. As the wind strengthened and the rain started, they rode away with their herd. It took about ten minutes for Charles to calm down. In wartime combat, he'd never been free of fear, but it seemed sharper and more personal out here. Probably because of the space. All the empty, lonely, beautiful space.

"Dive, Charlie!" Wooden Foot yelled. "Dive and shoot!"

His feet out of the stirrups, Charles threw himself to the left. For a second, falling between the saddle and the grass as Satan galloped, he was sure he'd break his neck.

He didn't. While his legs locked on belly and loin, he shot his left hand under the piebald's neck and hooked it over. Clinging to the piebald's left side in that way, and protected by the horse's body, he tried to forget the prairie flying by beneath him.

"Shoot!" his teacher bellowed. He pulled himself up far enough to snap off a round above the withers of the racing horse. Wooden Foot yelled his approval. "Again!"

After five shots, his arm gave out and he fell off, remembering at the last moment to relax before he hit. The impact left him gasping, half senseless.

Fen ran circles around him, barking. Boy jigged and clapped for him. Wooden Foot pulled him up, slapping his back to help him breathe. "Good, Charlie. Better'n good. Damn fine. You've got a natural talent for plains craft. A real gift, God's truth."

"You think it's important I know how to shoot from behind my horse?" Charles asked with some skepticism.

Wooden Foot shrugged. "The more you know, the better chance you got to save your hair if some wild Cheyenne wants it. They use that little trick in tiltin'. That's a game on horseback, with padded lances. They try to knock each other off. Somebody musta figured out that it's a lot safer shootin' that way, too. How you feel?"

Satan trotted back, dipped his head, and blubbered out breath. Dust-covered, Charles smiled. "Bumped up a good deal. Otherwise I'm fine."

"Good. I think we should try it again. I mean, you did fall off—"

That night, Wooden Foot added a pictograph to the winter count. The stick figure represented Charles shooting while hang-

ing on the side of his running horse. Charles felt a rush of pride
when the trader showed him the finished picture. For the first
time in weeks, he slept without dreams of any kind.

They rode on south, still pupil and teacher.

"This yere says Cheyenne." Wooden Foot drew his right
index finger rapidly across his left one several times. "What it
really says is striped arrow, but it means Cheyenne 'cause they
use striped turkey feathers for fletchin'."

Charles imitated the sign a few times. Wooden Foot then
clenched his hand, extending index and little fingers. "Horse."

And the hands with fingertips touching, an inverted V.
"Tipi."

And a fist at either temple, index fingers raised. "You can
guess this one."

"Buffalo?"

"Good, good. Only a thousand more to learn, give or take a
few."

The lessons covered various subjects. Wooden Foot rode his
horse down a slight slope, back and forth, a continuous Z pattern.

"If an Indian's too far off to see your face or count your
guns, this says you're peaceful."

And, as they watched another wild pony herd stream along
the horizon to the southeast:

"Thing you got to do out here, Charlie, is turn your notions
upside down. White man's rules and ways, they don't operate.
F'rinstance, steal a horse back in Topeka, they'll hang you. Out
here, runnin' off ten or twenty head from another bunch of lodges
is the very bravest of deeds. If we'd learn to parley on Indian
terms 'stead of our own, there might be real peace on the plains."

And, kneeling by some tracks in the steel-colored morning:
"What would you read from this, Charlie?"

He studied the marks, a number of nearly identical sets overlapping and partially obliterating each other. He glanced at Fen,
panting from pulling the travois, then at the flat and empty land.
"Travois. A whole lot of them, according to those pole tracks. A
village."

"Which is what you're s'posed to think. But look back two
miles, to where these tracks started. You won't see any dog droppin's. Just horse turds. No dogs, no village. A few braves made

these, with stone-weighted poles tied to their waists. In a few blinks of an eye, they can conjure up a village big enough to scare you off. Old fear's a powerful medicine. It can trick you into seein' what you expect to be there, 'stead of what is. Look."

He stood in the stirrups to point, his other hand holding his hat in the keen wind. On a rise to the southeast, so far away the figures were miniature, Charles saw horsemen. Four of them.

"There's your whole village. If you just saw the tracks, you'd ride real wide of it, wouldn't you?"

Charles felt stupid and showed it. Wooden Foot slapped his shoulder, to say it was all part of learning. Then he fired a rifle round over his head. The sound boomed away toward the distant riders, who quickly trotted out of sight. Like the other lessons, it burned into Charles's head with the permanence of a white-hot iron.

Old fear's a powerful medicine. It can trick you into seein' what you expect to be there, 'stead of what is.

Over the fire that night, while adding the incident to the winter count with strokes of black and red, Wooden Foot said in a mild voice, "You forgettin' about her some? The one you lost, I mean?"

"Some." These days he occasionally thought of Willa, too. "I'm grateful to you."

Wooden Foot waved the dainty brush. "All in the job. If I wanted a partner worth the name, I knew I had to pull you out of the glooms. They's just too damn many interestin' things and too many kinds of possible trouble out here for a man to stay sunk in a puddle of grief. Man's got to be alert, to keep his hair."

"I believe you," Charles said. He leaned back on his elbows, warmed by the fire and friendship, feeling a new, if fragile, contentment. He was beginning to feel the same kind of affection for this part of the world that he'd felt for Texas.

About an hour before dawn, a familiar pressure woke him. Too damn much coffee again.

As quietly as he could, he rolled out of his buffalo robe. His breath plumed in the dim light from the embers in the center of the tipi floor. He untied the flap thongs and slipped out the round hole without making a noise.

He heard the horses and mules fretting on their picket line

and wondered why. The cold, star-bright night seemed untroubled. One thing sure, if some kind of animal interloper was prowling, Fen would never announce it. He was everything except a watchdog.

Charles walked along the side of a draw, away from the faint glow inside the tipi. He opened his trousers, then his long underwear. Over the stream of water, he heard a voice.

He cut off the water, jerked his clothes back in place, and reached automatically to his hip.

The holstered Colt wasn't there. He slept with it next to his head. He had his Bowie in its belt sheath, though.

He crept back through the draw and saw silhouettes cast by the fire onto the tipi cover. Two people sitting up, a third standing between them with something stubby in his hand.

A gun.

Licking his chapped mouth and furiously blinking sleep away, Charles crept toward the tipi. The intruder, who must have stolen into the tipi right after he left, and not seen him, was speaking to Boy.

"You lie still, you barrel-headed idiot. If you don't, I'll blow this old fool's brainpan to pieces." The shadow man jammed the shadow gun against Wooden Foot's shadow head to demonstrate. "You fucking old geezer, I want some of your trade goods. And whatever money you got."

"Little early in the season for snowbirds, ain't it?" Wooden Foot remarked. Charles suspected he wasn't as calm as he sounded. "I thought fellas like you ate Army food all winter, then lit out in the spring."

"Shut the fuck up, unless you want me to shoot that pruneeyed cretin."

Very quietly, Wooden Foot said, "No, I don't want you to do that."

"Then fetch me the goods."

"They're in travel bags. Outside."

The man pushed the muzzle of the gun into Wooden Foot's shoulder.

"Let's go."

14

Charles drew his Bowie from its sheath. His heart raced as he started for the tipi. Long strides brought him near the round hole a few seconds before Wooden Foot crawled out.

The trader sensed Charles close by, standing against the tipi, but didn't turn his head to give it away. He was followed by the man with the gun. In the starlight, Charles saw a bearded face, then sleeves with yellow corporal's stripes. A deserter, all right.

"Hold it there, old man," the man said, straightening. He was stocky and a head shorter than Wooden Foot, who wasn't all that tall. God knew from which fort he'd bolted. Maybe Larned, or the newer one, Fort Dodge.

Charles shifted his weight for the strike. About to speak, the deserter heard or sensed something. He pivoted, saw Charles, fired.

The ball scorched past Charles's cheek and tore through the tipi cover. Charles rammed the knife into the deserter's blue blouse and turned it, skewering him.

"Oh, no," the soldier said, rising on tiptoe. "No." A second later, he was unconscious on his feet. His hand opened, and the gun dropped. His knees unlocked, and Charles supposed he was dead, or nearly so, as he sprawled on the moonlit ground, boneless as a cloth doll. The stinking excretions of death came quickly.

Charles wiped his knife on the grass. "What do we do with him?"

Wooden Foot was puffing as though he'd run a long way. "Leave him"—more gasps—"for the scavengers. He don't deserve no better."

Fen trotted from the dark, whining; he knew something was

wrong. Wooden Foot patted him. "That was slick work with the knife, Charlie. You're learnin' fast." He grabbed the blue uniform collar, raising the dead man's head. Moonlight on the lifeless eyes made them shine like coins. "Or did you already know how to do that sort of thing?"

Charles finished cleaning the knife with a wad of dead grass. He shot the Bowie back in the sheath and tapped the handle with his palm. The handle hit the sheath with a soft but distinct click. That was answer enough.

In the tipi, Boy crouched with his arms crossed. Hugging himself hard, he cried big tears. By now Charles understood why the youngster reacted that way. It wasn't merely fright. His poor short-weighted mind sometimes understood that his uncle faced a hard task or a rough situation. He always wanted to help but couldn't send the right orders to his hands or feet or any other part of his body. Twice before, Charles had seen him weep in angry frustration.

Wooden Foot took Boy in his arms. He patted and comforted him. Then he plucked at the front of his own shirt. Charles again noticed the deep red of the trader's face. Wooden Foot saw him staring.

"I told you, it ain't anythin'," he said, almost as angry as his nephew.

Charles didn't pursue it.

In early November, the Jackson Trading Company crossed trails with a half-dozen Arapahoes moving north. All wore their hair heavily dressed with grease, but one, more sensitive than the others to the recent summer sunshine, had hair more golden-brown than black. The scalp showing in the part of each man's hair was painted red.

Wooden Foot talked with the Arapahoes in a combination of sign, rudimentary English, and their own tongue. Charles heard "Moketavato" a few times; he recognized the Cheyenne name of Black Kettle, the peace chief Wooden Foot admired and respected.

He needed no special understanding of Indians to recognize the animosity of the Arapahoes. It snapped in every syllable, every sharp gesture and fiery look. Still, they kept talking with Wooden Foot, squatting in a semicircle opposite him, for almost an hour.

"I don't understand," Charles said after the Arapahoes had ridden away. "They hated the sight of us."

"Sure, they did."

"But they talked to you."

"Well, we hadn't done nothin' to stir 'em up, so they was duty-bound to treat us in a civil manner. Most Indians are like that. Not all, though, so don't be lulled."

"You talked to them about Black Kettle."

Wooden Foot nodded. "He and the Arapahoe peace chief Little Raven touched the pen to that treaty on the Little Arkansas not two weeks ago. The treaty stakes out a new reservation, gives a parcel of land on it to every Cheyenne or Arapahoe who's willin' to live there, and sweetens it to a hundred sixty acres if somebody lost a parent or a husband at Sand Creek. The guv'mint came down hard on what happened there, and they's sendin' Bill Bent, a good man, into the villages this winter to see that the sojers don't do the same thing again. Only trouble is, they was only about eighty Cheyenne lodges at the Little Arkansas. They's some two hundred others roamin' loose, and to them the treaty'll be just so much spit in the wind."

Charles scratched his chin; lengthening stubble was turning into a beard. "Did you find out where Black Kettle's camped?"

"Straight ahead, on the Cimarron. Right where I meant to look for him. Let's travel."

Under the rim of the low bluff, Wooden Foot pointed to littered bones. "Buffla jump. They turn the herd and run it over the edge. Pretty soon the buffla are pilin' up and breakin' legs and generally makin' it easy for the braves to kill 'em."

Two days had passed since their meeting with the Arapahoes. Light snowflakes fell in the windless afternoon, melting as they touched the frost-killed grass. Charles relished the warmth of his cigar and wondered how his son would react to his first sight of a snowfall. He surely wished he could be there to see—

"Jumpin' the herd that way ain't quite as glorious as killin' buffla in a reg'lar hunt. But if winter's closin' in and there ain't enough carcasses put by yet, it's a good quick way to—" He broke off, turned his head. "Hold on."

He ran out of the jump and up to the rim. There he knelt, palms pressed to the ground. "What is it?" Charles said.

"Riders. Comin' fast. Damn. They's two dozen or more. I got a hunch we used up all our good luck on that thievin' snow-bird, Charlie."

Charles ran for Satan, jerking his Spencer from the saddle scabbard. Wooden Foot ordered him to put it away.

"Why?"

" 'Cause we need to see who they are. You want to guarantee you'll be kilt, shoot an Indian without tryin' to palaver first."

Wooden Foot walked along the lip of the jump, thumbs in his cartridge belt, his slow slouching gait indicating a lack of worry. Charles saw plenty in his eyes, though. He slid the Spencer back and joined his partner. Wooden Foot motioned Boy to his side as bareback riders in a wide concave line came galloping down on them.

The Indians wore fringed leggings. Some had scarlet blankets tied around their waists. Six wore huge bonnets of eagle feathers. Charles also noted, not happily, three Army-issue garments, two of them short fatigue jackets with the light blue facings of the infantry, the third an old-style tail coat faced with artillery red. The wearer of the tail coat displayed a couple of medals on the front.

Another Indian, a sleek, thin, notably darker man in his mid-twenties, wore a huge silver cross on a chain around his neck. Strands of some wispy material hung from the sleeves and front of his buckskin coat. Almost all of these decorative strands were black, though Charles did notice a few yellow and gray ones. He assumed the cross, like the Army coats, was stolen.

"Oh, God, Cheyennes," Wooden Foot muttered. "And Dog Society men on top of it. They ain't wearin' their regalia, but I recognize the one in front. This couldn't be worse."

"Who is—?"

The rest of the question about the leader went unheard as the Cheyennes reined in, setting the air ajingle with the small round bells braided into the manes of their ponies. Trade bells, from white men, as were the trade carbines they leveled at the Jackson Trading Company. Besides the guns, the Indians carried bows and arrows.

Fen pulled back and forth in his travois harness, growling. Charles bit down on his cigar, now reduced to a stub by rapid puffing. Boy hid behind his uncle.

The darkest Indian, the one wearing the cross, sawed the air and yelled at them in his own tongue. He had a fine, narrow face, though unusually severe. The red paint with which he and the others had decorated their faces and hands was applied to his left cheek with special care. Two broad parallel strokes bracketed a long white scar curving from the outer tip of his eyebrow down along the line of his jaw, where it took a short upward turn beneath the left corner of his mouth—a red-lined fishhook.

The snow fell faster. The Cheyennes eyed Charles and his partner while the leader continued his harangue. Charles understood an occasional word or sign; Wooden Foot's teaching was beginning to sink in. But he didn't need to know any Cheyenne or sign language to understand that almost all of the leader's remarks were angry and nasty.

Persistently, never raising his voice, Wooden Foot kept replying every few seconds. The leader talked at the same time. Charles heard his partner speak of Black Kettle again. The young leader shook his head. He and his friends laughed.

Wooden Foot sighed. His shoulders slumped. He held up his right hand, asking for a respite. Grinning all the more, the leader yelped something Charles took to be assent.

"Charlie, come on." The trader drew him along the lip of the bluff. Carbine muzzles swung to follow them. Wooden Foot looked as depressed as Charles had ever seen him.

"It don't do much good to say it now, but I was wrong. We shouldn't of talked first. These boys are out for blood."

"I thought they didn't attack unless somebody provoked them."

"They's always the exception. I'm afraid that's what we drew in the head man of this bunch." Eyeing the dark Indian unhappily, he went on, "He's a war chief, and a mighty young one at that. His name's Man-Ready-for-War. Whites call him Scar. Chivington's men, they killed his ma at Sand Creek. They cut off her hair. I mean *all* her hair." Back turned to the Indians, he tapped his groin. "Then they hung it out together with a lot of scalps at that Denver theater where Chivington showed off his trophies. Dunno how Scar heard about it—maybe third or fourth hand. They's a number of tame old Indians hangin' around Denver beggin' or stealin' to live. But I know for a fact he did hear about his mama's shame, and he won't forgive or forget that. I guess I wouldn't either. Understandin' his reasons don't help us much, though."

"What about the treaty?"

"You think that counts a pin for him? I told you the treaty chiefs signed for only eighty lodges."

"He did a lot of talking. What does he want?"

"Scar and his friends are gonna take us into the village. Then they'll decide what to do with us."

"Shouldn't that be all right? Isn't it Black Kettle's village?"

Bleakly, Wooden Foot said, "It is, but he ain't come back from the treaty ground yet. He's overdue. Till he gets here, Scar speaks loud. In one way, he's a lot like white folks lookin' at Indians. Can't tell friend from foe, but in his case he don't want to, either."

Charles felt chillier than the falling snow. "What do we do? Grab our guns?"

Wooden Foot turned slightly, enabling him to see his nephew. Boy had his arms wrapped over his chest, clutching; his eyes were huge. "We do that, it's all over. It may be all over at the village, too, but I think I'd rather go there 'fore we dig our heels in. Boy can't defend himself 'gainst a bunch like this. Maybe some of the women'd take pity on him. Keep the men from carvin' him up." He sighed. "Ain't really fair that I ask you to string this out with me. But that's what I'm doin'."

Charles finished the cigar stub and flipped it down on the buffalo bones. The cigar had tasted more savory than usual. He decided it was because it might be the last he'd ever smoke.

"You know I'll go along with you."

"All right. Thanks."

With the trader leading, they walked back to the Cheyennes. Rapidly, Wooden Foot conveyed the decision to accompany the Indians without a fight. The braves smiled, and Scar yipped like a dog, which set Fen dancing in his harness. Scar reached over his shoulder to his arrow quiver and produced a three-foot stick wrapped in red-dyed buckskin decorated with quills. Painted eyes ornamented one end, eagle feathers the other. Dewclaws taken from some animal turned the stick into a rattle, which Scar brandished as he jumped from his pony.

He darted forward, shaking the rattle. Before Charles could sidestep, Scar slashed the rattle against his cheek. Charles swore and brought his fists up. Wooden Foot held him back.

"Don't, Charlie. I said don't. He just counted a coup, a little harder than he ought."

Charles knew about counting a coup by touching a vanquished enemy. It enhanced an Indian's reputation. But again, understanding how things worked didn't help their situation, or lessen his fear.

The dark-eyed Indian threw his head back and yipped and barked. Some of the others took up the cry, driving Fen into a frenzy of jumping and barking. One of the Cheyennes aimed his trade carbine at the dog. Wooden Foot grabbed Fen by the scruff and held him down, getting a nip on his hand for his trouble.

Charles stood rigid, scared and angry at the same time. Boy nuzzled against his side, trying to hide his sad misshapen head in the folds of the gypsy robe. Three of the Cheyennes dismounted and dashed among the pack animals, knifing open the canvas parcels. One Indian crowed over a bunch of porcupine quills. He cut the binding thong and tossed the quills in the air.

Another stabbed into a bag that spilled a diamond waterfall of pony beads. The Indian cupped his hands beneath, filled both, and ran among his friends, distributing some to each. Wooden Foot restrained Fen, clenched his teeth, and said "God damn," over and over.

Scar strutted to the trader and smacked his shoulder with the snake rattle; another coup. He barked louder than ever. The snow accumulated on Charles's hat brim and shoulders and melted in his eyebrows while a strange sense of finality dropped over him. He'd felt something similar on the eve of battle in the war. The premonition was always fulfilled by someone's death.

"Guess you're pretty damn sorry you listened to me," Wooden Foot muttered.

"What do you mean?"

"Well, I kept sayin' they was exceptions to everything, only I guess I didn't learn the lesson good enough myself. I'm some teacher."

With more cheer than he felt, Charles said, "Any teacher can make a mistake."

"Yep, but in this case even one's too many. I'm sorry, Charlie. I sure-God hope we don't travel the Hangin' Road 'fore this day's over."

———

EXECUTION OF WIRZ

Closing Scenes in the Life of the
Andersonville Jailor.

Final Effort of His Counsel to
Obtain Executive Clemency.

Firm Demeanor of the Prisoner on
the Scaffold.

He Asserts His Innocence to the
Last, and Meets His Fate with
Fortitude.

A Remarkable Attempt to Poison
Him Just Brought to Light.

A Bolus of Strychnine Conveyed to
Him by His Wife.

News coverage of the death of
the only American executed for war crimes
November, 1865

MADELINE'S JOURNAL

November, 1865. Cool Carolina winter replaced our smoky
autumn while I slept. The live oaks rise from thick white mist
this morning; the air smells of the salty river tides. When such
beauty abounds, I miss you so terribly.

How I wish reality were as pacific as today's prospect
from my doorstep. Cash very short. Wagon axle broken. Until
Andy repairs it, we can move no timber to Walterboro or
Charleston, hence have no income. Wrote Dawkins pleading

for a few weeks' grace with the quarterly payment. No reply as yet.

Nor have I had any word of Brett from California. She will come to term before Christmas. I pray the confinement is not hard.

School will be rebuilt in 30 days or less. Prudence holds classes on the lawn by the house meanwhile. Another setback: after the fire, Burl Otis, Dorrie's father, forbade her to attend. He is in sympathy with the unknown arsonists, or afraid of them, or both. Went in person to plead. He cursed me and called me a "troublemaking nigger."

A red-haired man has been seen twice at Gettys's store. The Charleston dancing master, I am told. He is said to be without pupils and to be living in reduced circumstances, which enhances his bitterness. Who but a few scoundrels live any differently in Carolina these days?

. . . Gettys, always the dilettante, now fancies himself a journalist. There came to hand a copy of his new, poorly printed little paper called the White Thunderbolt. *Read but a few of the headlines—*THE LOST CAUSE IS NOT LOST; CAUCA-SIAN WIDOW MARRIES NEGRO BARBER, *etc.—before burning it. Vile stuff. Doubly so because Gettys claims to represent Democrats. If he can afford to print such a scurrilous rag, his Dixie Store must be returning usurious profit. A second store named Dixie has opened on the Beaufort-Charleston road, and am told a third is coming to the latter city. Gettys not connected with these. Cannot imagine who in S.C. has the capital to build and finance them . . .*

The exile traveled down from Pennsylvania to Washington, craggy and cynical and confident as ever despite his wartime misfortunes.

Simon Cameron, who had brokered his votes at the 1860 Republican convention in exchange for a cabinet post, was one of those ambitious, ice-hearted rascals who didn't understand the word *defeat*. As Secretary of War, he had caused a scandal with his favoritism in handling supply contracts. Lincoln had got rid of him by exiling him to the post of foreign minister to the court of Russia, and the House of Representatives had censured him for corrupt practices. Yet by 1863 he was back, trying to secure a Senate seat from his home state.

He failed, withdrew to Pennsylvania, and proceeded to strengthen his hold on the state machine. *I will not be kept out of the national government forever,* he wrote to his pupil and campaign contributor Stanley Hazard, when announcing his current visit to Washington.

Stanley invited the Boss to the Concourse Club, to which he had recently been admitted through friendship with Senator Ben Wade and some other high-ranking Republicans. In the club's lavish second-floor rooms, teacher and pupil settled into deep chairs near a marble bust of Socrates. Elderly black men, instructed to be servile, waited on members. One such took Stanley's order and tiptoed away. Immediately, Cameron asked for a donation.

Stanley had expected it. He responded with a pledge of another twenty thousand dollars. Lacking talent, he had to buy friendship and advancement.

Though it was only half past eleven in the morning, Stanley looked puffy about the eyes and dazed. "Feeling faint," he explained.

Cameron said nothing. "How do you find your work with the Freedmen's Bureau?"

"Revolting. Oliver Howard can't forget he's a soldier. The only Bureau men who have his ear are the former generals. I mean to tell Mr. Stanton that I want to be relieved. The trouble is, I don't know where to go if he agrees."

"Have you considered political office?"

Stanley's mouth dropped.

"I'm quite serious. You'd be a great asset in the House." Ah, now he understood. Cameron didn't base the assertion on ability. Stanley would be an asset because he contributed generously and never questioned the orders of party superiors. And obedience was necessary for him, since he didn't have a single original idea about the political process. Still, granting those limits, he found Cameron's suggestion exhilarating.

The stooped black waiter brought their drinks. Stanley's glass contained twice the amount in Cameron's. While his imagination was still soaring, the Boss dashed him down.

"You know, my boy, you'd have a sterling future were it not for one liability."

"You must mean George."

"Oh, no. Your brother's harmless. Idealists are always harmless, because they have scruples. In a tight situation, scruples tame a man, and make his responses completely predictable." Cameron's sly eyes fixed on Stanley as he murmured, "I was referring to Isabel."

Stanley took a few moments to comprehend. "My wife is a—?"

"Major liability. I'm sorry, Stanley. No one denies that Isabel's a clever woman. But she grates on people. She takes too much credit for your success—something most men find offensive." Cameron tactfully ignored his pupil's reddening face; Stanley knew the charges were true.

"She lacks tact," Cameron went on. "A smart politician hides his enmities; he doesn't flaunt them. Worst of all, Isabel no longer has credibility in this town. No one believes her flattery because she is so open about her ambition for social eminence and power."

After a swift look to check on possible eavesdroppers, the Boss lowered his voice. "But if you should ever find yourself— shall we say independent?—and if it should come to pass without any scandal attaching to you personally, I can almost guarantee you eventual nomination to the House seat from your district. Nomination is tantamount to election. We make certain of that."

Astonished and thrilled, Stanley said, "I would love that. I'd work hard, Simon. But I've been married to Isabel for years. I know her. She's a very moral, upright person. You would never find her compromising herself in any, ah, personal scandal."

"Oh, I believe you," Cameron said with sincerity. He thought of Isabel's face; no one would be interested.

"Still, my boy, scandal isn't limited to illicit romance. I've heard rumors about Isabel and a certain factory in Lynn, Massachusetts."

The old pirate. He knew very well that Stanley and his wife had been jointly involved in wartime profiteering through the manufacture of cheap army shoes. Cameron's pointed glance suggested that the truth need not be graven in stone.

The thought of returning to Isabel the kind of scorn and abuse she routinely heaped on him was likewise new, and intoxicating. On her orders, Stanley had abandoned his mistress. He owed Isabel for countless humiliations—and here was the Boss, promising him a prize if he got rid of her.

He didn't want to appear too eager. He exaggerated his sigh. "Boss, I'm sorry, I don't think what you describe will ever happen. However, if by some chance it does, I'll notify you at once."

"I wish you would. Good and loyal party men are hard to find. Women, on the other hand, are available anywhere. Think about it," he murmured, and sipped his drink.

After Cameron left, Stanley could hardly contain his excitement. The Boss had opened a door, and he wanted to leap through. How could he do it?

He refused an invitation to dine with a fellow club member and ate alone, stuffing down huge forkfuls of food, liquefied with great gulps of champagne. As the dessert course arrived—a whole quarter of a blueberry pie, with a creamy sauce—inspiration came, too. He saw a foolproof way to strike at Isabel behind her back, and insure her eventual downfall.

At the same time, the solution would remove him from a situation that, although profitable, bred great anxiety when he considered the possibility of exposure. He could continue collecting his profits for another year, perhaps two. Then, at a time entirely of his choosing—

"Magnificent," he said, and he didn't mean the champagne or the pie.

Before he left the Concourse Club, he set the plan in motion. He was astonished by its simplicity, and pleased by his own ingenuity in devising it. Perhaps he'd sold himself short for too long. Perhaps he wasn't the idiot that George and Billy and Virgilia and axe-faced Isabel thought he was.

He handed a sealed note to the elderly white man at the club's entrance desk. "Please put this in his pigeonhole so that he gets it next time he stops by."

"Is it urgent, Mr. Hazard?"

"Oh, no, not at all," Stanley said with an airy wave of his cane.

The doorkeeper read the envelope as Stanley went down the stairs whistling. *Mr. J. Dills, Esq.* He slipped it into the proper slot, thinking that for the last year or two, he had not seen Mr. Stanley Hazard so high-spirited or so sober in the middle of the day.

A curt letter from the Palmetto Bank. Leverett D. says his board will allow a late payment this once, but not again. In his salutation he addressed me as "Mrs. Main," rather than by my given name, as in the past. I am sure it is the school issue. We are indeed on the eve of winter . . .

15

The sergeant from Fort Marcy left at midnight.

Ashton touched the mussed bed. Still warm. Disgust wrenched her face, then grief. She sat down and held her head while the sadness rolled over her.

She clenched her hands. *You're a spineless ninny. Stop it.*

No use. With each of tonight's customers—a greaser who lacked the manners of Don Alfredo; an oafish teamster from St. Louis; the soldier—she'd come closer and closer to screaming her frustration and outrage. Here it was November and she was ready to run, and never mind the risks of starvation in the wasteland or cruel punishment if the señora's brother-in-law caught her.

She cried for ten minutes. Then, after she blew out the candle, she spoke to Tillet Main, something she hadn't done since visiting his grave a long time ago.

"I wanted to make you proud of me, Papa. Because I'm a woman, it was harder, but I came close with Lamar Powell. Close isn't good enough, is it? I'm sorry, Papa. I'm truly sorry . . ."

Tears again. And waves of hatred. Directed against herself, this place, everything.

That was Tuesday. On Friday, a man walked in and hired her for the entire night.

An old, old man. She'd hit the bottom.

"Close that blasted window, girl. Old wreck like me gets the chilblains this time of year."

He put down a battered sample case with brass corners. "Sure hope you're warmblooded. I want to snuggle up and enjoy a cozy night's sleep."

Lord, what a disgusting specimen, Ashton thought. Age sixty if he was a day. Bland blue eyes, gray hair hanging every which way over his ears and neck, not more than a hundred twenty pounds soaked. At least he looked clean—her only consolation.

Toss, pop, snap, the old man doffed his shabby frock coat, dragged down his galluses, removed pants and shoes. He opened the sample case, revealing a pile of printed sheets, each with an engraving of a fat woman seated at a grand piano. Rummaging among the handbills and items of soiled linen, he found a whiskey bottle.

"For my damn rheumatism." As he sat on the bed, his knee joints snapped like firecrackers. "I'm too old for this traveling all over hell." He swigged whiskey.

Putting on her best professional smile, Ashton said, "What's your name, lover?"

"Willard P. Fenway. Call me Will."

She dimpled. "That's cute. Are you all hot and bothered, Will?"

"No, and I'm not gonna be your lover, either. I hired you for some civilized conversation, a snuggle, and a good long snooze." He peered past the bottle lifted to his lips. "You're a stunner, though. Like that yella dress you got on."

"Will, do you really mean you don't want—?"

"Fucking? No. Don't go all blushy on me, that's a good straightforward word. People who rant and rave about impure speech usually do a lot worse things themselves, only secretly." He stretched out and guzzled some more, admiring her cleavage. "What's your name?"

For some reason she couldn't explain, she didn't lie to him. "It's Ashton. Ashton Main."

"Southron, aren't you?"

"Yes, but don't you dare ask how I got in a place like this. I hear that twenty times a week."

"You do that much fucking? Damn. Wonderful to be young. Been so long for me, I nearly forget the particulars."

Ashton laughed, genuinely amused. She found the old codger likable. Maybe that was why she hadn't lied. Sitting down by him, she said, "I'll tell you this much. I was widowed unexpectedly here in Santa Fe. This hellhole was the only place I could find work."

"And you don't plan to stay forever, huh?"

"No, sir." She eyed the case. "You some kind of salesman?"

"The word's peddler. The kind I am is starving. There's engraved cards in my coat pocket. Willard P. Fenway, Western Territories Representative, Hochstein Piano Works, Chicago."

"Oh, that explains the picture of the fat lady. You sell a wonderful instrument. I saw Hochstein pianos in all the best homes in South Carolina. That's where I grew up. Say, do you mind if I get ready for bed?" He urged her to do it speedily. "Do you want me in a gown, or bare?"

"The latter, if you don't mind. Keeps a man warmer."

Ashton proceeded to undress, unexpectedly enjoying herself. Fenway waved the empty bottle. "Have to correct one of your remarks. I don't sell Hochsteins, I try to sell 'em. This trip I've only unloaded one Artiste—that's the grand model pictured on the sales sheet. Cattle rancher in El Paso bought it, the dumb cluck. His wife couldn't read music, just wanted to put on airs. It's probably the only instrument I'll sell for months. The boss saddled me with a territory consisting of the entire damn nation west of the Mississippi, which means my potential customers consist of crooked gamblers, dead-broke miners, drunk soldiers, red Indians, poor sodbusters, Mexes, whores—no offense—and your occasional half-witted rancher's wife. Say, will you hurry up and lie down and keep me warm?"

She blew out the light and jumped under the coverlet and into the curve of his arm. Old and bony as he was, his flesh felt firm, his hand on her shoulder strong. Travel made him hardy, she supposed. His skin smelled lightly and pleasantly of wintergreen oil.

"You could certainly sell a piano here," she said. "Maybe not a grand, but a spinet. The patrons are always yelling and screaming for music."

"Won't get it from Hochstein's."

"Why not?"

"Old man Hochstein's a Bible-thumper. Strict as sin in public, 'specially in the company of the old mule he married. On the side, a new chippy services him every week. But that's his only relationship with ladies of your profession. Believe me, if I was allowed, I could put a Hochstein in just half of the sporting houses in Illinois, and retire."

"The market's that rich?"

"Throw in Indiana and Iowa, I could live like a damn earl or duke. Hochstein won't touch the cathouse market, though. Competition won't eith—whoa! Where you going?"

"We need some light. We need a discussion."

A match scraped; a flame brightened the room. She grabbed her blue silk robe with peacocks embroidered on it, a present from the señora. It was part of a batch of clothes the señora had taken from a girl she threw out.

Fenway fussed about being cold. Ashton tucked the worn coverlet under his chin, making soothing sounds, then sat down again. "Willard—"

"Will, goddamn it, Will. I hate Willard."

"Excuse me, Will. You just had a wonderful idea and you don't know it. Wouldn't you like to give that old Mr. Hochstein a kick in the seat? And make a lot of money in the bargain?"

"You bet I would. I been his slave twenty-two years now. But—"

"Would you stand some risk to do it?"

He thought about that. "I suppose. Depends on how much risk, for how much reward."

"Well, you just said you could live like a nobleman by selling pianos to parlor houses in three states. What if you sold them all over the West?"

Fenway looked bludgeoned, barely managing to croak, "My God, girl. You're talking about El Dorado."

She clapped her hands. "Thought so. Will, we're going to be partners."

"Partners? I've not been here ten minutes—"

"Yes, you have, and we're partners," she said, giving an emphatic toss of her head. "We're going into the piano business. You *do* know how pianos are made?"

"Sure. The work I don't know how to do myself, I could hire out. But just where would two piano-makers find the forty or fifty thousand dollars it would take to start up? You tell me that."

"We'll find it in Virginia City. Once you help me escape from this damn place."

Ashton leaned forward, the breast of an embroidered peacock bulged by the breast behind it. She smelled Fenway's breath for the first time. Not the usual sewer smell of most customers. He'd sweetened it up by chewing a clove. The clove mingled nicely with the wintergreen. She really liked the old fellow.

"Y'see, Will, my late husband had property in Virginia City. A mine. It belongs to me. All we have to do is get there."

"Why, yes, nothing to it," he said. "It's just a little old hop and a skip to Virginia City. Am I really hearing all this?"

"You surely are. Oh, wait. Have you got any strings on you?"

"You mean wives? Nope. I wore out three, or they wore me out, not sure which." He grinned. Below, someone broke a piece of furniture. Then Ashton heard the culprit yell—Luis. Fenway failed to understand the venomous look that flashed over her face. "You telling me the truth, Miss Ashton? Your husband owned a mine in Nevada?"

"The Mexican Mine."

"Why, I been there. I know that mine. It's a big one."

"I won't lie to you, Will. I don't have a paper to prove I own it. And the marriage license saying I'm Mrs. Lamar Powell got left behind in Richmond."

"If we can reach Frisco, I know a gent who can fix up another paper." Ashton reveled in the way his eyes glowed. He'd begun to see the opportunity. "But that might not be enough—"

She laid his hand on the swelling peacock. "Oh, I've got ways to persuade anybody who's picky."

Fenway was beside himself, turning pink. "Keep talking, keep talking. You may be crazy, but I like it."

"The hardest part—seriously now, Will, no joke—the hardest part will be getting out of here, and out of Santa Fe. The señora, the woman you paid, she's a mean sort. Luis, her brother-in-law, he's worse. Do you have a horse?"

"No. I travel the overland coaches."

"Could you buy two horses over at Fort Marcy, maybe?"

"Yes. I've got enough for that, I think."

"And do you have a gun?"

The color in his face faded fast. "This gonna involve shooting?"

"I can't tell. It might. We need nerve, we need horses, and we need a loaded gun, just in case."

"Well—" A veined hand indicated the sample case. "Root around under those sales sheets. You'll find an Allen pepperbox. She's a good twenty-five years old, but she's popular with traveling men." He cleared his throat. "Afraid mine's for show. No ammunition."

"Then you'll have to buy some."

While he was considering that, the altercation downstairs broke out again. A crashing sound suggested one person breaking furniture on the head of another. Ashton's mouth twisted up meanly when she heard Luis bellow, *"Vete, hijo de la chingada. ¿Gonsalvo, y dónde está el cuchillo? Te voy a cortar los huevos."*

A ululating yell and hammering footfalls signaled the potential victim's retreat. Fenway's eyes bulged.

"Was that the brother-in-law?"

"Never you mind. We can take care of him—if we have a loaded gun."

"But I'm a peaceable man. I can't handle a loaded gun."

Ashton's sweet smile distracted him from her malicious eyes. "I can." She stroked his cheek, stubbled white at day's end. "So I guess it's up to you to decide, sweet. Would you rather keep dragging around the West, safe and poor, or take a little chance and maybe live rich forever?"

Fenway nibbled his lower lip. In the cantina Luis's rumbling, grumbling voice recapitulated his recent brave triumph over the man who'd fled. Fenway gazed at Ashton and thought, This is surely a piece of work. A remarkable piece of work.

He had no illusions about the girl who was petting and cooing over him. Nor did she disguise what she was. Why, she practically wrote it out on a sign, and would bid anyone who didn't like it to kiss her foot. He'd already taken a fancy to the honey-talking she-wolf.

She planted a chaste kiss on his lips. Moist mouth close to his, warm excited breath bathing his face, she touched him with the little tip of her tongue while a finger fiddled in his ear. "Come on, Will, tell me. Poverty or pianos?"

His heart thumped at the prospect of her cleavage, the prospect of riches—and the prospect of losing his life.

"What the hell. Let's try pianos. Partner."

Two nights later, with an early winter storm deluging Santa Fe, Will Fenway returned with his sample case, just as he had the preceding evening, when they'd laid their plans. Slightly wild-eyed, he closed the door and leaned against it while the rain hammered the shutters. Ashton snatched the case from his hands and opened it on the bed. "Did you pay for the whole night?"

"No. Couldn't afford it."

"Will—" she complained, cross and nervous.

"Listen, I'm beginning to think this is a damn-fool idea. I spent every cent I've got on ammunition and those two nags, and now the señora and her nasty-looking relative are playing cards downstairs without another soul in the place, 'cause of this rain. They'll hear every sound."

"We'll wait them out."

Ashton removed the Allen pepperbox from the otherwise empty case. She checked the revolving barrels to be sure they were all loaded, then laid her few meager pieces of clothing in the case. She had no rain cape; she'd have to get soaked.

She felt a tightness in her chest, yet she was composed, in a cool sort of way. She laid the Oriental box in the case. "How long have we got?"

"An hour's all I could pay for."

"It'll have to do. We'll go by the back stairs, and through the storeroom. Did you—?"

"Yes. I did everything," he said, snappish because of his fear. "The horses are in that little shed around back. But—"

"But nothing." Ashton began caressing his forehead with her fingers. His skin was no longer cool or tangy with wintergreen, but slick, clammy. "Sit down, Will. Sit down and we'll wait till it's a little noisier. Luis gets noisy when he drinks. It'll be all right, trust me."

From a pocket of his old frock coat Fenway took a silver watch, which he snapped open. He placed it on the bed. Both of them stared at the black hands. Ten past nine. The bigger hand ticked over a notch. One more minute gone.

Ashton stood behind him, expertly kneading his tight neck and shoulders. "Now just don't worry. We'll pull it off, slick as anything. Partners as smart as we are, no one can stop us."

Except possibly Luis, who helped himself to another drink so noisily that Ashton and Fenway heard the bottle clinking against the glass.

As time ran away from them, their luck appeared to do a miraculous turnabout. Luis began to serenade himself in a loud tuneless baritone. Señora Vasquez-Reilly said, *"No me fastidies,"* but he kept right on. Five minutes later—nine minutes before ten, the hour at which the señora would ascend the stairs and order

Will out—the rainstorm intensified, complete with heavy rolls of thunder.

"We're going to make it, Will. We're going to do it— now." Ashton tied her lacy mantilla under her chin, a wispy scarf, but better than nothing. Pressing the closed case into his hand, she took the loaded Allen and opened the door. She examined the dim, rancid hall, lit by a single stubby candle in a tin sconce.

The hall stretched straight back to the dark rear stairs, empty. Ashton's breath hissed in and out as she edged forward. She whispered, with her mouth against his ear, "Step easy. Parts of the floor squeak if you come down hard."

With almost exaggerated tiptoe steps, they crept along the hall past the first closed door. Ashton heard the girl inside snoring. Then, on the left, they passed the second door, where they heard no sound at all from Rosa.

Ashton risked going faster on the stairs. It worked until she reached the second step from the top, and Fenway put his weight down on the first one, which gave off a sound like a cat with its tail twisted.

The rain had slackened. The sound carried. And their luck reversed completely again.

Rosa's door opened. Naked, she stepped into the hall, carrying her slops jar. Because of the stair noise, she immediately looked to the left—and saw them.

Her scream probably carried all the way to Fort Marcy. *"¡Señora! ¡Señora! ¡La puta Brett, se huye!"*

"That's it," Ashton cried, grabbing Fenway's lapels. "Go fast, lover."

She went plunging down the risers two at a time, and if she had missed one by chance, if she'd fallen, she'd have broken her neck.

As if to tease the fugitives along with a little good fortune now that they'd been discovered, Ashton and her partner made it to the storeroom without so much as a stumble. Rosa, however, kept howling, and the instant Ashton started to slip through the maze of old broken crates, the señora's voice joined in, exhorting Luis to hurry.

The door from the cantina opened. An amber rectangle of light laid itself across the floor, revealing the fugitives near the back door.

Luis charged toward them. Ashton fired the pepperbox.

Through the smoke, she saw Luis fall to one side. Then she saw the señora, in the cantina, wiping blood from her cheek. Blood from flying splinters; Ashton's ball had hit the frame of the door, and Luis had merely taken a dive to save himself.

"Come on, Will," Ashton cried, yanking the back door wide and jumping out into the mud and rain.

Panting, Fenway followed. He pushed her to the left and, in doing so, gave her kneecap a ferocious whack with his sample case. She staggered, almost fell. Fenway caught her elbow and guided her. "Not far. That little shed. Here we are, here."

She smelled and heard the fretful animals. Luis appeared at the back door, pouring out a torrent of profanity. He lunged into the open and darted after them, only to pitch over when his right foot slipped in the mud. The way he yelled as he went down told Ashton he'd broken or torn something.

He sprawled on his side, groping toward the fugitives with his left hand. A faint glare of lightning showed his mud-slimed face. From the door, the señora screamed, *"Levántate, Luis. Maldita seas. Levántate y síguelos."*

"No puedo, puta, me pasa algo a la pierna."

"Mount up, for Lord's sake," Fenway wailed. He was already in the saddle, clutching the handle of his sample case. Ashton seemed to spend an eternity in the few seconds she stared at the tableau behind the cantina: the señora standing there demanding that Luis get up, Luis groping toward them with his outstretched hand while his pained face said he couldn't.

In that momentary eternity, a vivid cavalcade of large and small slurs, insults, unkindnesses passed through Ashton's mind. The señora and Luis were equal offenders, but Luis was the nearer. She stepped two paces toward him, aimed the pepperbox with her arm rigid, and put a ball into his head.

They clattered across the empty central plaza, rain-washed and gleaming. Ashton's horse led. She'd pulled her skirt up between her thighs and rode astride, bent low, watching for obstacles.

From behind, Fenway cried, "Why'd you shoot that man? You didn't have to shoot him, he was down."

"Luis abused me. I hated him," she screamed over her shoulder. Ahead, a pair of soldiers from the fort stepped into her path, rubber ponchos shining in the lightning flashes. One pulled the other back at the last moment; both fell.

As Fenway galloped, the lightning revealed deep dismay on his rain-pelted face. He knew the little Carolina tart was stone-hearted, but he'd never imagined she would go so far as to slay a helpless man. What kind of creature had he hooked up with anyway? Nearly sick from excitement and the motion of the horse, he no longer felt liberated by their escape. Instead, he was gripped by a queasy sense of entrapment.

Accustomed to horses since childhood, Ashton rode expertly, head down over the nag's neck, her only guidance the occasional feeble flare of the lightning. She rode as if hell was behind her and nothing ahead would stop her, and her partner felt dragged along, captured, and pulled by her incredible force of will.

He heard her cry, "We'll make it, honey. We'll outrun those greaser dogs. Keep riding!"

He might indeed outrun any pursuit, he thought as the horse carried him over the slick road like a cork in a typhoon sea, but he doubted he could ever outrun her. It was too late; she'd hooked him.

And she'd committed murder.

With his assistance.

The deputy marshal for the territory and the commandant of Fort Marcy together questioned Señora Vasquez-Reilly, who said to them:

"Of course I can tell you who murdered my sweet, innocent brother-in-law. I can describe her to perfection. I always doubted that she gave me her real name. So whether you ever catch her is up to you."

16

In Richmond, a young doctor made the rounds of the Almshouse wards guided by the matron, Mrs. Pember. The doctor was new, a volunteer, like the others who tended these sad lumps of human refuse.

Here and there a patient gave him a vacant glance, but most paid no attention. One man crouched beside his cot, exploring an invisible wall with the tips of his fingers. Another held a lively silent conversation with unseen listeners. A third sat with his arms crossed and tucked under, straitjacket fashion, weeping without a sound.

The doctor dictated notes to the matron as he proceeded from cot to cot. Near the cot at the end, a man sat hunched on a packing box by an open window. Even this late in the year, smoke still drifted from the burned sections of the city, hazing the thin autumn sunshine.

The man on the packing box was staring out the window, southeast, toward the monuments in the city's Jewish Burying Ground, which was separate from Shockoe Cemetery. His loathing was evident. With her voice lowered, Mrs. Pember said, "Found unconscious in front of the State House, some weeks ago."

Pale and already exhausted by the ordeal of his rounds, the doctor studied the man with mingled disgust and sorrow. Once, the patient might have had a certain physical presence; he was tall enough. Now he looked decayed, shrunken. Skin striations indicated obesity at some past time. Privation had pared away all the fat except for a sizable paunch.

The patient's left shoulder tilted lower than his right. He was barefoot and wore one of the hospital's coarse gowns beneath a filthy old velvet robe donated to the Almshouse. On his head sat a battered plug hat. He glared at Mrs. Pember and the doctor.

Still whispering, the matron said, "He claims he's in constant pain."

"He looks it. Any history?"

"Only what he chooses to tell us. Sometimes he talks about falling from a high bluff into the James River. Then again he says his horse threw him at Five Forks, after the Yankees broke through General Eppa Hunton's lines. He says he was with the reinforcements General Longstreet rushed from Richmond, too late to save—"

"I know all about the fall of Richmond," the doctor interrupted, testy. "Does he have any papers?"

"Sir, how many men have papers since the government burned everything and ran?"

The doctor shrugged to acknowledge the point. He approached the patient. "Well, sir, how are we today?"

"Captain. It's Captain."

"Captain what?"

A long pause. "I can't remember."

Mrs. Pember stepped forward. "Last week, he gave his name as Erasmus Bellingham. The day before yesterday, he said it was Ezra Dayton."

The patient stared at her with strange yellow-brown eyes that held a hint of malice. The doctor said, "Please tell me how you feel this morning, sir."

"Anxious to be out of here."

"In good time. At least do Mrs. Pember the courtesy of taking off that filthy hat when you're indoors." He reached for the plug hat. The matron uttered a warning cry as the patient jumped up and threw the packing box at the doctor with ferocious force.

The box sailed over the doctor's head, thudding in the aisle. The patient lunged. The doctor jumped back, yelling for orderlies. Two country boys in stained smocks raced down the aisle, rushed the man, restrained him, and wrestled him onto his cot. Even with youth and strength in their favor, the patient's flailing fists battered them badly. He hit one orderly so hard, blood oozed from his ear.

Finally, they subdued him, using rope to lash his wrists and ankles to the iron cot frame. The doctor watched from the aisle, shaken. "That man's a lunatic."

"All the other doctors would agree, sir. He's positively the worst case in the Almshouse."

"Violent—" The doctor shuddered. "A man like that will never get any better."

"It's such a pity, the way the war damaged them."

Angered by the attack, he said, "These wards are too crowded to accommodate pity, Mrs. Pember. When he calms down, force laudanum on him, and a strong purgative. Tomorrow put him out on the street. Use the space for someone we can help."

The fire set during the flight of the Confederate government's highest officials on the night of April 3 had swept from Capitol Square to the river, burning away the commercial heart of Richmond—banks, stores, warehouses, printing plants—something like a thousand buildings in twenty square blocks. Even the sprawling Gallego Flour Mill complex was gone, as were the rail trestles over the James.

Few who walked through the burned zone in succeeding months forgot the sight. It was like prowling the surface of some world out among the stars, a world both alien and tantalizingly familiar. Its hills were mounds of brick and broken limestone. Black timbers were the charred bones of strange and mighty beasts. Sections of buildings stood like the grave markers of the alien race.

Two nights after the Almshouse incident, the patient came stumbling through the mammoth Gallego ruins between the mill-race and the Kanawha Canal. He'd been given the shabbiest of used clothing and turned out. He would have paid back those who did it, but for the fact that more important prey demanded his attention.

This evening he was enjoying great lucidity. He recalled in detail his fantasy of parading in the Grand Review. He also remembered the identities of those who had kept him from taking his rightful place in the military history of his country.

Orry Main. George Hazard.

God, how much he owed those two. Ever since they were all cadets at West Point, Hazard and Main had regularly conspired to thwart him. Year after year, one or the other had turned up to interfere with his career. They were responsible for a dizzying succession of falls from grace:

Damage to his reputation in the Mexican War. Charges of cowardice at Shiloh Church. Punitive transfer to New Orleans, and desertion to Washington. Failure in Lafayette Baker's secret police unit, and, finally, desertion to the South, whose people and principles he'd always despised.

All of it could be blamed on Main and Hazard. Their vindictive natures. Their secret campaigns to spread calumnies that had ruined him.

Sometime before he woke in the Almshouse, though exactly how long before, he couldn't remember, he had made inquiries about Main in Richmond. A veteran had recalled Colonel Orry Main's dying on the Petersburg lines. His other enemy, Hazard, was presumably alive. Just as important, each man certainly had a family. He remembered he'd tried to injure one of the Mains in Texas, before the war. Charles—that was his name. Surely there were many other relatives—

He tried to push all that out of mind temporarily and concentrate on the Gallego ruins. After an hour's search he located what he believed to be the right spot. He knelt and dug through the rubble, hearing the sound of swiftly running water. It poured over a giant mill wheel that no longer turned. Like most everything in the South, the wheel was broken.

Sharp fragments of brick hurt his fingers as he dug. Soon the fingers were covered with dust and blood. But he found what he'd buried. His memory hadn't abandoned him altogether.

Clutching the rolled-up oil painting, he moved to a rectangle of brilliant moonlight, there brushing dust from his treasure. The moonlight fell through a window frame high in a jagged section of brick wall. As he brushed the painting, the awl of pain pierced his forehead and began to bore in. Pinpoint lights began to flash—

He remembered his name.

He said it aloud. Beyond three walls standing at right angles to one another, a couple of black squatters by a bonfire turned toward the noise. One ambled over to investigate. After a look at the face of the man in the moonlit rectangle, he left quickly.

With greater power and confidence, the man said it again.

"Elkanah Bent."

Thin, bitter smoke drifted along the spectral walls. The

smoke choked him. He coughed while trying to recall the face in the painting . . . *trying* . . .

Yes. A quadroon whore.

Where had he gotten her portrait?

Yes. A New Orleans sporting house.

That cued an even more important memory—the purpose of his life. He had redefined it, dedicated himself to it, weeks ago, then forgotten it during the bad period in the Almshouse.

His purpose was to make war.

The other war, the war to free the evil nigger and raise him to the level of the superior white man, was over, and lost. His war was not. He had not yet begun to marshal his forces, his strategic cunning, his superior intelligence, to make war on the families of . . .

Of . . .

Main.

Hazard.

To make war, and to make them suffer by killing loved ones —old, young—one by one. A sweet, slow campaign of obliteration, carried out by the American Bonaparte.

"Bonaparte," he cried to the moon and the smoke. "Bonaparte's *masterpiece!*"

The squatters left their wind-tattered fire and melted into the dark.

He tapped his plug hat to seat it firmly on his head and squared his tilted shoulders as best he could. The claw-hammer coat they'd given him shone with age and grease in the moonlight. He executed a perfect military pivot and marched, like a man who had never been ill a moment. He strode into the sharp-edged shadow cast by another great broken wall, and there he temporarily vanished.

17

The Jackson Trading Company rode toward Black Kettle's village surrounded by Scar and his braves. The Indians had relieved the white men of their weapons. Charles had refused to surrender his at first, but he relented when Wooden Foot insisted it was for their own good. "Don't give 'em no excuse to kill us, Charlie."

The day darkened. Wind drove the snow into Charles's face with stinging speed. Suddenly he knew the nature of the wispy fringe on Scar's coat.

"I should have recognized it. I saw scalps in Texas. That's hair," he said to Wooden Foot.

"You're right. A Dog Society man can wear that kind of decoration if he counts enough coup and kills enough enemies."

"Some of the fringe is yellow. There are no blond Indians."

"I told you, Charlie, we bought a load of grief this time."

The trader's attention jumped back and forth between Charles and Fen. Straining in the travois poles, the collie barked and barked. Two braves rode up alongside, raising their lances to throw.

"Don't you do that," Wooden Foot yelled, reddening. The braves laughed and veered away, satisfied with the reaction.

The Cheyennes kept toying with their prisoners: riding close, touching them with their hands and coup sticks. Scar galloped next to the pack mules and with his lance slashed another canvas bag. Triangular pony beads cascaded to the snowy ground.

Charles raised his hand. Wooden Foot grabbed it to restrain him.

"Our hair's worth more'n the goods. We just got to put up with them till we figure some way out."

First they came upon eight boys in fur robes stalking game with blunt arrows. Over the next rise they discovered the horse herd, around a hundred ponies, guarded by more boys. A gentle slope ran down to the Cimarron, where tipis stood along the snowy banks. The wind brought the odor of wood smoke.

Quietly, Wooden Foot said, "No matter what they do, don't get mad. Keep your wits, and if I give you a cue real sudden, take it." Charles nodded, though the trader's meaning wasn't entirely clear.

Riding into the village, they created a stir. Old men, mothers with infants in cradleboards on their back, girls, children, dogs poured from the tipis and crowded around, chattering and pointing, and not in a hostile way, Charles thought. Scar was the hostile one. He jumped from his pony and signed for them to do the same.

Charles dismounted. He noticed buffalo hides pegged to the ground, and others stretched on vertical frames, but because of the bad weather, the outdoor work of the village had stopped.

As he looked around, his eyes made contact with the large, intensely curious ones of a girl in the crowd. She had regular, even delicate features, and shining black hair. She was about fifteen, he judged, starting to look away. She gave him a quick smile to show that not all in the village were his enemies.

Scar's braves crowded around. Wooden Foot took the offensive with a flurry of signs and shouting. "Moketavato! I'll speak to him."

"I told you, Black Kettle is not here," Scar said. "There are no peace chiefs to help you; only war chiefs." He spoke to his men. "Take their goods."

One of the Indians, in a cavalry fatigue blouse, started to slash open Charles's saddlebags. Charles bolted forward to stop him. Wooden Foot yelled a warning, and someone behind him bashed his head with a rifle butt, knocking his hat off. A second blow drove him to his knees. The crowd exclaimed. Fen growled. Scar kicked the collie, making Fen yelp and snap.

The Dog Men swarmed around the pack animals. They cut and tore the bags holding the iron scrapers, hoe blades, tin pots. The crowd pressed forward. Playing to them, Scar ordered his men to distribute the trade goods.

Women and children pushed forward and clamored for this

item or that. The young girl was one of the few who held back, Charles noticed as he picked himself up. Here and there, someone's face reproached the display of greed, but most of the villagers paid no attention. Wooden Foot gazed around him with a peculiar expression, as though he had never seen tipis or Cheyennes before.

Suddenly Scar announced, "These whites are devils, who plan to do us harm. Their goods, and their lives, belong to us." His men made gruff noises to agree.

Wooden Foot lost his bemused look. "Scar, this just isn't right. It isn't the way of the People."

Scar squared his shoulders. "It is mine."

"No-good little shit," Wooden Foot said, loud enough to be heard. Scar understood, too. He gestured.

"Kill them."

Charles's stomach seemed to plummet a half mile. Wooden Foot flashed him a sharp look, snatched Boy's hand, and lunged. The sudden move surprised everyone, allowing the trader and Boy to bowl through between two Dog Men. "Run for it, Charlie. This way."

Charles ran for it.

An iron-bladed trade hatchet, hurled by a Dog Soldier, whisked by his ear. Women and old men screamed. Charles darted between two frightened grandfathers and out of the crowd. He didn't understand Wooden Foot's sudden show of cowardice. What good was running? They'd only be caught again.

Wooden Foot thrust his arm out to indicate a large heavily decorated tipi down a lane to his left. In front of it, snow melting on his gray hair and crossed arms, stood a heavy Indian with a dark, seamed face. Wooden Foot dived past him into the tipi, dragging Boy after him.

Charles kept running. He heard and felt Scar's men close behind. Of all the stupidity, he thought. Cornered in a tipi. Wooden Foot had lost his mind.

He raced toward the old Cheyenne, expecting to be stopped. The gray-haired Indian flicked his eye at the tipi hole and nodded. Feeling hopeless, Charles nevertheless jumped through the oval opening. The Indian immediately stepped in front of it.

A small fire in a shallow pit gave off acrid smoke but little warmth. Crouching in the cold gloom, Charles picked up a stone-headed hatchet lying near him.

"Put that away, Charlie."

"What in hell's wrong with you? They're right outside."

Angry voices verified it. Scar's was loudest. While he snarled, the older Indian spoke in a calm, low voice. The snarls took on a note of frustration. "We don't need weapons now," Wooden Foot said. He pointed over his head.

Hanging there, Charles saw what appeared to be a hat fashioned from the head of a buffalo. A pattern of blue beads decorated it, and the horns were bright with painted designs.

"That's the Buffalo Hat," Wooden Foot said. "Sacred, like the four Medicine Arrows. The hat wards off sickness, and if some fool steals it, the buffalo will go away for good. That old priest outside, he guards it day and night. Anybody who shelters where the hat hangs can't be molested."

"You mean this is a sanctuary, like a church?"

"Yep. Scar can't touch us."

Charles shivered, cooling down as his sweat dried. He felt unexpectedly disgruntled. "Look, the war cured me of inviting fights. But if a fight starts, it galls me to run."

"You mean you think comin' in here's yella."

"Well—"

While the priest continued to argue with Scar, Wooden Foot said, "Didn't I tell you that you got to turn your notions upside down out here? Why do you think Scar's so mad? We just did the biggest thing—I mean the very biggest—any Dog Society man can do. We was about to be beat, murdered, and we got away. That's bigger'n the biggest coup."

The Buffalo Hat priest stooped and entered the tipi. The old Indian smiled in a friendly, admiring way. Charles began to believe what his partner had just said.

The trader and the priest greeted one another with sign. "Half Bear," Wooden Foot said, nodding and smiling. The priest said something in Cheyenne. To Charles the trader explained, "He just said my name. Man-with-Bad-Leg." To Half Bear: "This yere's my partner Charlie, and you remember my nephew, Boy. You know Scar didn't tell it straight, Half Bear. We always come peaceably, just to trade."

Charles understood when Half Bear said, "I know."

"When's Black Kettle gettin' back?"

The old Indian shrugged. "Today. Tomorrow. You stay here. Eat something. Be safe."

"Mighty fine with me, Half Bear." Wooden Foot slapped Boy's shoulder. Boy grinned. Charles did his best to rearrange his notions, the way Wooden Foot had advised.

"My dog's still hitched to the travois, Half Bear."

"I will bring him."

"They took our guns and knives—"

"I will find those, too."

The priest left. Soon Fen lay beside the fire, happily rolling in the dirt.

Charles had a lot of trouble believing that they'd covered themselves with honor by running. He continued to think about it while Half Bear served them berries and strips of smoked buffalo meat. After the meal, the priest arranged fur robes and woven headrests for their comfort.

Early next morning, Black Kettle rode in with a dozen braves. The members of the Jackson Trading Company, having rendered the inside of the tipi very fragrant out of natural necessity, were at last free to step into the open.

In the sunlight that had followed the snow, Cheyennes of all ages again surrounded them, including the pretty girl Charles had noticed. He found himself smiled at, patted, greeted with exclamations of "How!" which he interpreted as a word of approval. Of Scar he saw nothing.

Wooden Foot swelled up like an actor in front of a cheering audience. He grinned all over the place.

"No getting away from it, Charlie. We're heroes."

Better weather brought a resumption of village life outdoors. Bands of boys again stalked rabbits with blunt arrows, training for a tribal hunt when they reached maturity. Women and girls set about their traditional work of scraping hides, stretching them on frames, and then smoke-curing them.

Charles noticed a kind of pupil-and-teacher relationship in an attentive group of girls and mothers addressed by a much older woman. It was instruction by a member of the quilling society, Wooden Foot told him later. Decorative quilling had great religious significance for the Cheyennes, and had to be done in a prescribed way. Only women elected to the society could teach the art.

Black Kettle invited Wooden Foot, Charles, and Boy into his lodge one evening. Charles now knew from conversations with the trader that the Cheyennes had a number of peace chiefs, men of proven bravery and wisdom who advised the tribe when it was not at war. As Wooden Foot stressed, whites always wanted to deal with *the* chief, but he didn't exist. There were peace chiefs and war chiefs, as well as a chief for each camp—Black Kettle also held that position in his village—and there were leaders of the warrior societies. All of them collectively governed the tribe, which had numbered about three thousand people for as long as anyone could remember. If the tribe never increased, neither had it been diminished by disaster, starvation, or its foes. Charles's respect for the Cheyennes went up another notch when he figured that out.

The peace chief Moketavato was a well-built man of about sixty with braids wrapped in strips of otter fur. He had solemn eyes and an animated, intelligent face. He wore the familiar leggings and breechclout and deerskin shirt, all heavily decorated, and, in his hair, a cluster of eagle feathers and three beaten silver coins strung on a thong. He passed a long calumet to the white men after they all sat down. Just a couple of puffs of the smoke made Charles dizzy. His head filled with fanciful shapes and colors, and he wondered what sort of herb or grass was burning in the pipe bowl.

The peace chief's quiet and retiring wife, Medicine Woman Later, served a hearty turtle soup, then bowls of a savory stew. As they ate, Black Kettle apologized for Scar's actions. "The loss of his mother robbed him of reason and warped his nature. We try to curb him, but it is hard. However, your trade goods are safe, and your animals."

As Wooden Foot thanked him, Charles popped another warm morsel of meat into his mouth, following custom by using his fingers. "Delicious stew," he said.

Black Kettle acknowledged that with a smile. "It is my wife's finest, for honored guests."

"Young puppy dog," Wooden Foot said.

Charles almost threw up. He struggled to keep his mouth shut and his face calm while the piece of meat worked its way down his throat against a series of strong spasms. Finally the piece went down, though it didn't settle well. He ate no more, merely made a show of fiddling with the bowl.

"I hope that treaty you signed means peace for a while," Wooden Foot said.

"It is my hope also. Many of the People believe war is better. They believe only war will save our lands." He turned slightly, to include Charles, and spoke more slowly. "I have always thought peace the best path, and I have tried to believe the white man's promises. That is still my way, though fewer and fewer will go with me since Sand Creek. I took the People to Sand Creek because the soldier-chief at Fort Lyon said we would not be harmed if we settled there peacefully. We did, and Chivington came. So now I have no reason to believe promises, no reason but my own burning wish for peace. That is why I touched the pen again. Out of hope, not trust."

"I understand," Charles said. He liked Black Kettle, and saw the liking returned.

Outside the tipi, firelight gleamed, and there was festive music. Boy smiled and marked time in the air with his finger. Charles cocked his head. "Is that a flute?"

"Yes, the courting flute," Black Kettle said. "It is being played at the next tipi. Therefore it is Scar. He does have some interests besides war, which is a boon for the rest of us. Let us look."

They stepped into the twilight and saw Scar, near the adjacent tipi, playing a handmade wooden flute and moving his feet in a shuffling back-and-forth step. Black Kettle spoke a greeting. Scar started to return it, saw the traders and scowled. He blew several sour notes before he got the melody going again.

Tied to Scar's waist thong was a tuft of white fur. Wooden Foot pointed to it. "White-tailed deer. It's a big love charm."

A yellow dog ran by, barking. Fen ran away in pursuit, barking too. From the tipi that Scar was serenading, a young girl emerged—the same girl Charles had noticed the day he arrived. He saw a hand pushing the girl from inside. Evidently parents were forcing her out to acknowledge her suitor.

"It is my sister's child, Green Grass Woman," Black Kettle said to Charles. "She is fifteen winters now. Scar has wooed her for two, and must continue for two more before she can become one of his wives."

The gentle swell of the girl's breast showed that she deserved to be called Woman. She wore leggings and a long ornamented smocklike garment, which was pulled up to her groin and

bunched front and back by a rope between her legs. Strands of
the rope wrapped her body from waist to knee; she hobbled,
rather than walked.

Black Kettle saw Charles's puzzlement. "She's no longer a
child but not yet married. Until she's Scar's wife, her father ties
the rope at night to guard her virtue."

Green Grass Woman tried to smile at Scar, but it was plain
she didn't have much heart for it. Scar looked unhappy and shuffled his moccasined feet faster. Then she noticed the observers.
Her reaction to Charles was sudden and obvious.

So was his. The stiffness startled him. Embarrassed about
being attracted to someone so young, he turned to one side, hoping nothing showed. He eased his conscience by telling himself it
was merely the girl's beauty, the talk of sex, and his relatively
long deprivation that caused the reaction.

Black Kettle observed the exchange of glances and chuckled.
"I heard that Green Grass Woman regarded you with favor,
Charlee."

Scar saw it, too. He glared, stepping between the white men
and the girl and turning his back on them. He spoke to her
rapidly. She replied with equal speed and obvious tartness, irritating him. He deluged her with more pleading. She tossed her head,
grasped the edges of the tipi hole, and stepped over. Before she
disappeared, she cast another lovelorn glance at Charles.

Scar's face wrenched, a mask of black and copper in the
light of a nearby fire. Clutching the flute, he stamped off.

Fen shot into view, chased by the yellow dog. A baby
howled. Wooden Foot sighed.

"Well, I know it ain't your fault. But now that no-good bully's got one more reason to hate us."

Next day they began trading. The weather turned unusually
warm for early winter, enabling Wooden Foot to lead Boy to the
riverbank at dusk. There, out of sight of the tipis, the trader gave
his nephew a much-needed bath, something Boy couldn't do for
himself. Charles stripped, waded out, and washed himself clean.
He felt reborn.

During the trading sessions, Wooden Foot did all the bar-
gaining. Charles fetched and displayed the goods and tended the
horses given in exchange. Along with exposure to the details and
complexities of Cheyenne society came a growing respect for the

tribe. In some ways the Indians remained primitive; sanitation in the village was negligible, with food scraps and night soil carelessly thrown about. In other respects, Charles found the Cheyennes admirable: instruction of the young, for instance.

The Cheyennes considered manhood not merely something inevitable, but a privilege, carrying great responsibility. At night the sides of this or that tipi would be rolled up and tied while members of one of the warrior societies met inside at the fire, fully painted and dressed in society regalia. A large crowd of boys always gathered, as intended, and watched the men speak and dance and perform some of their less secret rituals.

He never saw any of the village children disciplined, but one afternoon all of them were summoned to Black Kettle's lodge, where a man who had stolen another's buffalo robes was to be punished. The young boys and girls watched as the possessions of the thief and his weeping wife were brought forward. Their blankets were torn and cut to shreds with knives. Other families joined in to smash the thief's clay pots and stamp on his woven backrests. Finally his tipi was slashed apart and the poles thrown on the fire. When the punishment was over and the crowd dispersed, the children took with them a vivid impression of what awaited them if they committed a similar crime when they grew up.

Two Contraries lived in Black Kettle's village. They were bachelors because the honored role of contrary required that. Singled out for exceptional bravery and their ability to think deeply about the ways of the tribe, they lived in tipis painted red and carried great long battle lances called thunder-bows. Their special rank demanded special, difficult behavior of them. They walked backwards. If invited to sit, they remained standing. The first contrary to whom Charles spoke said, "When you are finished trading, you will not leave us." Wooden Foot explained that he meant they would leave. The Contraries were a small, strange, mystical order, each member greatly revered.

The trading continued briskly and profitably for eight days. On the ninth morning Charles woke early to find the dawn sky threatening rain. Wooden Foot wanted to get going. They dismantled and packed their tipi in six minutes—beating their own time was a game Charles now thoroughly enjoyed—and after an hour of elaborate farewells to Black Kettle and the village elders, they rode south, herding fourteen new ponies ahead of them.

The wind smelled warm and wet. The tipis on the Cimarron disappeared behind them, and then the thin columns of smoke rising from them. Jogging easily on Satan, Charles thought of Green Grass Woman, whom he'd encountered often in the little village. Each time, her pretty face left no doubt about her feelings. She was smitten. That flattered his vanity but it also made his hermit's life somewhat harder to bear. One night he'd had an erotic dream in which he lay with the girl. But every time he met her he did nothing more than tip his hat, smile, and mutter pleasantries in English. He wondered if, when he returned to St. Louis, Willa Parker might—

"Look sharp, Charlie." Wooden Foot's sudden warning yanked him from the reverie. He pulled out his Colt as a mounted Indian burst from a stand of cottonwoods beside a meandering creek ahead of them. For a moment Charles expected a war party to follow. But no other horsemen charged out of the trees.

The lone brave galloped toward them. Charles recognized Scar.

Gloomy, Wooden Foot said, "He rode mighty fast and mighty far to get ahead of us. Somethin' must be burnin' him bad —as if that's a big surprise, huh?"

Scar trotted his pony up to them. His dark eyes fixed on Charles. "I have words to say."

"Well, we didn't figure you come out here to take the healthful waters," Wooden Foot said, aggrieved. The sarcasm went right by the Indian, who jumped from his pony and took a wide, solid stance.

"Get down, Charlie," Wooden Foot said, dismounting. "Gotta observe the formalities, God damn it."

When the two traders were on the ground, Wooden Foot keeping hold of the rein of Boy's horse, Scar stamped a foot.

"You shamed me before my people."

"Oh, shit." Wooden Foot sighed. "Anybody shamed anybody, it was you shamed yourself, Scar. We did nothin' to warrant killin'. You know it, and Black Kettle knowed it, and if that's your complaint, why—"

Scar grabbed him, furious. "We will meet at the Hanging Road. You will travel it." His eyes jumped to Charles. "And you."

Dark as a plum, Wooden Foot said, "Let go my shirt." Scar

merely twisted it more. The trader shot his hand forward, caught the thong of Scar's breechclout and snapped it. Scar yelled, released him, leaped back as if snake-bit.

"Why, what's this?" Wooden Foot said with exaggerated surprise. He pointed at Scar's exposed genitals. "Sure-God ain't a man."

Inexplicably, Scar screamed and leaped for Wooden Foot's throat. Charles yanked his Colt from the leather. "Hold it!"

The warning brought Scar up short, his fingers inches from Wooden Foot's neck. The trader showed Scar his breechclout. "Gonna have trouble courtin' that girl 'thout this." He tucked the clout under his belt. "Yes, sir, a lot of trouble."

Scar clearly wanted to fight for it, but Charles's Colt, pointed at his head, kept him from doing so. Quietly, Wooden Foot said, "Now you get goin' 'fore my partner puts a bullet where your balls used to be."

Used to be? What the hell was going on?

Scar's departure, for one thing. His disfigured face looked more scarlet than brown. Puffed up as if about to explode, he sprang into the air, caught his pony's mane, flung a leg over, and galloped away.

Charles exhaled as the tension drained. "You're going to have to explain what you did."

Wooden Foot pulled the breechclout from his belt. " 'Member what I said about Cheyennes cuttin' their hair? This is kinda like it. You take a man's clout, he loses his sex. He thinks he ain't a man any more."

Charles watched the Indian galloping fast into the north. "Well, now you and I are even. You gave him a reason to hate us too."

"I did at that," the trader said as the flush left his face. "Pretty dumb, I s'pose." He sniffed. "Enjoyed it, though."

"So did I."

Both men grinned. Wooden Foot clapped Charles on the shoulder, then held his palm to the sky.

"She's gonna be drizzlin' soon. Let's get movin', Boy." As he mounted, he said, with a degree of seriousness, "Guess it's plain we ain't seen the last of that bastard. Hang on to your hair, one and all."

M A D E L I N E ' S   J O U R N A L

December, 1865. No news of Brett. And a murder in the district.

Night before last, Edward Woodville's former slave Tom found on the river road below Summerton with three pistol balls in his body. Col. O. C. Munro of the Bureau and a small detachment marched from Charleston to investigate, without result. If any in the district know the perpetrator, they are hiding it. A tragedy indeed. Tom visited here last week, still overjoyed to be free of Woodville, a bad master.

Munro and his men camped overnight at M. R. Munro inspected the new school and took down what little I could tell him about the fire. He is required to send reports of all such outrages—his term—to superiors in Washington. He will report Tom's murder also. He offered two soldiers to guard the school for a time. I refused but said I would call on him if we are troubled again. . . .

. . . A tourney announced for next Sat. at Six Oaks, where Chas. fought his duel as a young man. I will not go, and dissuaded Prudence after long discussion. Before the war I attended some tourneys with Justin—rather, was dragged to them—and thought them pretentious affairs—the young men on horseback, with plumed hats and satin garments, trying to spear the hanging rings with their polished lances. All gave themselves high-sounding medieval names. Sir This, Lord That. With the pennons and great striped pavilions and gluttonous feasts of barbecued pig or kid, the tourneys seemed too emblematic of the society the war swept away. If slavery was a benevolent institution (so ran the unspoken argument of that society), those practicing it had a need to display themselves as persons above reproach. This soon translated itself into romantic exaggeration—the fondness for Scott's novels, endless disquisition about Southern chivalry, and tourneys.

And where will they find their young knights now, when so many fell as you did, my dearest, in the Virginia woods and fields? . . .

About fifty ladies and gentlemen of the district gathered in the clearing at Six Oaks, by the river. Carriages were parked nearby, and horses tethered. The white spectators ringed two-thirds of the open space, with the low, wet ground nearest the river segregated for black coachmen and servants, all of whom had presumably entered into employment contracts with their masters.

The winter day was warm. Long shafts of dust-moted light patterned the tan ground where three middle-aged riders galloped in a line, their lances leveled at the small wood rings hanging on strings tied to tree limbs.

Hooves pounded. The first rider missed all the rings. So did the second. The third, a graybeard, speared one, then another. An old bugle blared in imitation of a herald's trumpet; the crowd rewarded the victor with desultory applause.

While two more riders prepared, a fat woman who entirely filled one of the seats of a shabby open carriage complained to the gentleman standing beside the vehicle.

"I say to you what I said to Cousin Desmond in my last letter, Randall. It is one word, one query. When?"

Her rouged lips made the question juicy with spite. Mrs. Asia LaMotte, one of the innumerable cousins of Francis and Justin, sweated excessively despite the mild temperature, and badly needed a bath. In the wrinkles and creases of her doughy neck, perspiration had hardened her powder into tiny pellets. Randall Gettys found her a disagreeable old woman but never showed it because of her family's social standing and his friendship for Des. Poor Des, doing stevedore's work, nigger's work, on the Charleston docks to support himself.

Gettys made sure no one was close by and listening before he said, "Asia, we cannot simply march to Mont Royal in broad daylight and take action. The fire failed to frighten her. That mephitic school is open again. Of course we all want it abolished, and the slut punished. We don't want to go to prison for it, though. Those damn Yankees from the Bureau are nosing about because of the murder."

Asia LaMotte wasn't persuaded. "You're all cowards. It wants a man with courage."

"I beg your pardon. We have courage—and I speak for your cousin Des as well as myself. What it wants is a man with nothing to lose. We must find him, enlist him, and let him stand the risks. It only means a delay, not abandonment of the plan. Des is as fiery as ever about getting rid of Mrs. Main."

"Then let him show the family by doing something," Asia said with a sniff.

"I tell you, we need—"

He got no further. A white man had tied his horse near the road and was strolling toward the black spectators. He was a young man, with a ruffian's air. He had a dark beard, which showed even though he was closely shaved, and a scar left by a forehead wound. He looked cocky but very poor in his gray homespun clothes, old cavalry boots, and a broad-brimmed campaign hat. In the waistband of his pants he carried a pair of Leech and Rigdon .36-caliber revolvers.

Smiling, he stopped in front of one of the blacks, Asia LaMotte's driver, Poke. Old Poke wore a cloth cap on his gray head. The stranger drew his revolvers and pointed them at Poke.

"I surely do hate to see a nigger not respecting his betters. Take off that hat, boy."

Others around Poke stepped back, leaving the old man isolated and frightened. The two new contestants restrained their horses, fascinated like everyone else by the little tableau.

Vastly amused, the stranger drew back both hammers. "I said take off the hat."

Trembling, Poke obeyed.

"All right, now prove you're genuinely respectful. Kneel down."

"I am a free man—" Poke began.

The stranger touched one of the revolver muzzles to Poke's forehead. "Yes, sir, free to go to hell after the count of five. One. Two. Three—"

By the time the stranger said four, Poke was on his knees.

The stranger laughed, put up his revolvers, patted Poke's head, and acknowledged applause from a few of the spectators. He strolled toward a white-haired man in shabby clothes. Recognition and surprise popped Randall Gettys's eyes as the young man engaged the older in conversation.

"I'll bet that's him," Gettys whispered. "I'll bet a hundred dollars."

"Who?" said Asia, petulant.

"The roughneck Edward Woodville hired. Look, the two of them are thick as anything." He was right; the stranger, chatting amiably, had one hand on the old farmer's shoulder. Gettys said, "Everybody knew Tom wouldn't sign on to work for Edward any more because the Bureau disapproved of Edward's contract. So Edward swore he'd give fifty dollars to any white man who punished the nigger. I'll be right back." He hurried away. Asia looked befuddled.

Gettys mopped his forehead with the big white handkerchief from his breast pocket. Despite the mild temperature, he was dressed in heavy dark-green velvet. He approached Woodville and the stranger. The latter stopped talking, put his thumb near his right-hand revolver, and gave Gettys a stare that froze his gizzard.

Sweating, fawning, Gettys blurted, "Just wanted to say hello, sir. Welcome to the district. I'm Mr. Gettys. I keep the crossroads store and edit our little paper, *The White Thunderbolt.*"

"You can trust Randall," Woodville said. "He's a good boy."

"I'll take your word," the stranger said. He shook hands, found Gettys's soft and damp, and wiped his palm on his pants. "Captain Jack Jolly. Late of General Forrest's cavalry battalion."

The two mounted men started their horses toward the hanging rings. The crowd hurrahed, but Gettys had eyes only for the stranger. "General Nathan Bedford—?"

"Forrest. Are you hard of hearing or something?"

Gettys flinched away, raising his hands in apology.

Captain Jolly, twenty-four but obviously tough and experienced, chuckled. "That Devil Forrest, as the damnyankees called him. I killed niggers for him at Fort Pillow, and I went the rest of the war riding at his side. Finest soldier in the Confederacy. Joe Johnston said so. He said Forrest would have been number one in the army, except he lacked formal schooling."

Gettys began to experience great excitement. "Do you have kinfolk in these parts, Captain Jolly?"

"No. There's just my brothers and me, traveling and making a profit wherever we can." He smiled at Woodville, who gazed at the ground. The farmer was smiling too.

"Well, this is a fine district," Gettys exclaimed. "Rich in opportunity for men of courage and principle. Perhaps you'd take a drop of corn at my store after the tourney, and let me tell you more. We need residents of your caliber, to help stand off the damn soldiers and the damn Bureau and the damn scalawags among our own people who side with them."

"If you know any of those scalawags," Captain Jack Jolly said, "I'll put them in my gun sights damn quick."

Breathless, Randall Gettys rushed back to Asia LaMotte's carriage. "I must write Des. You see that man with Edward? I've got to persuade him to stay. He's capable of doing what we discussed."

The fat old woman peered at Gettys as if he were speaking Russian. The trumpet blared again. "Don't you understand?" he whispered. "We have the desire and he has the nerve. God has sent our instrument of deliverance."

A telegraph message from George! Brought all the way from Charleston. In San Francisco, after a short confinement, Billy and Brett's child was born, Dec. 2. A son, named George William. It is a happy gift of the season.

Another is the peace that prevails in the district. We remain unmolested, indeed even unnoticed. Prudence now instructs two adult women and one man, along with six children. Those who hate the school must know we can summon Bureau soldiers at will.

I feel we are out of danger. I am thankful; I am tired and want to be left alone to pursue my dream . . .

THE SALARY OF THE PRESIDENT.

The Secretary of the Treasury to-day signed a warrant in favor of Mrs. LINCOLN for the sum of $25,000, less the amount Mr. LINCOLN had drawn for his salary in March last. . . .

News report eight months after the assassination

Strong legal counsel more often than not, and thus it was more than sufficient to offset Baker's known dislike of the fellow. Strength of wit to lose a case, and the lawyer, a suave, smug, tight-mouthed man — a sheaf of deadly personality — left Bent alone. A dimwit cousin who persistently sent brainless, always-blamed first-person failures on others. Bent's old suspicion in their court case — the ties of a Washington lodestar suited Bent, who had absorbed his invisible sponsor. On the broad river he came from a large comptroller — at the comptroller, it salvaged reasons why Baker's dismissal descends. On the close then had even copied the fund to Washington, although he had managed to control matters during every one of other situations had occurred.

Jasper Dills, Esquire, turned seventy-four on Friday, the twenty-second of December, four days after Secretary of State Seward announced that the Thirteenth Amendment had been ratified. Childless and a widower for fifteen years, Dills had no relatives with whom he could celebrate the birthday or the Christmas season. He didn't care. Very little mattered to him any more except his law practice, his position as Washington representative of certain large New York financial interests, and the ceaseless, endlessly fascinating battle for power in the nation's political cockpit.

In the autumn after Appomattox, however, he'd found his practice diminishing. Some of the New York clients shifted their work to younger men; other cases brought to his book-lined office on Seventh Street seemed of an increasingly trivial nature. Fortunately, to offset this, he continued to receive the Bent stipend. It helped pay for memberships in his clubs and the odd bottle of Mumm's with his hotel suppers.

Dills had long ago stopped letting his conscience bother him about the stipend. Two or three times a year he wrote a letter assuring Elkanah Bent's mother that her illegitimate son was alive. According to Dills's latest epistolary fiction, Bent was prospering from cotton acreage in Texas.

The woman never asked Dills for proof of such statements. He'd built up a reservoir of trust since he saw her last, years ago, and he dipped into it now because he simply didn't know what had happened to Bent after Colonel Lafayette Baker, head of the government's secret police force, dismissed Bent for excessive brutality in the course of an arrest. Bent had vanished into Virginia, presumably a deserter to the Southern side.

Should Bent's mother discover that, or any other part of the truth, the stipend would end. The yearly total was substantial, so the mere thought of its loss alarmed the lawyer. At the same time, it didn't grieve him one bit to be shed of dealing personally with Elkanah Bent. An obese malcontent with persecution fantasies, Bent always blamed his career failures on others. Hardly any surprise in that: Bent's late father, a Washington lobbyist named Starkwether, had chosen an unstable woman for his brood mare. She came from a large border-state family that included several persons with histories of mental disorder. One of them had even carried the taint to Washington, although she had managed to control or hide it during years of public scrutiny and personal tragedy.

Bent's mother had never acknowledged her son. He took his name from a farm couple who had raised him in Ohio. He'd gone from Ohio to West Point, and then to failure after failure. By now, his mother was ancient (in the way of the elderly, Dills still thought of himself as middle-aged), but the woman's age didn't matter. Nothing mattered so long as she accepted his lies and wrote bank drafts regularly.

To maintain his high living standard, Dills had recently taken on certain other work. He was a conduit through which five hundred or one thousand dollars could travel to this or that senator willing to use his influence to obtain an Army commission for the applicant. Dills skimmed a percentage for making it unnecessary for such a politician to meet personally and perhaps be seen with a former brevet colonel or brigadier desperately hunting reemployment. Dills fancied that he sanitized the bribe money as it passed from hand to hand.

Dills was also a pardon broker. All sorts of Washingtonians had rushed into that work, including women with no asset other than their sexual favors. A legal background had put Dills in the forefront of brokers. His connections with a few notable Democrats and many powerful Republicans helped too. At the moment he had thirty-nine pardon applications on his desk.

Earlier in the year he'd taken President Johnson an application from Charleston that bore an intriguing name: Main. That was the last name of one of the men Bent held responsible for his various difficulties, starting with his dismissal from West Point. Although the applicant's first name was Cooper and that of Bent's enemy was Orry, they were both South Carolinians, so

Dills assumed a connection. He'd never been south of Richmond, but he envisioned the lower part of Dixie as one great heaving sea of cousins, all related and inbred by marriage.

Nature arranged a wet snowfall for Dills's birthday, a further guarantee of an empty office. He locked up and walked three blocks to the hushed rooms of his favorite club, the Concourse. He wandered through the club until he found someone he knew fairly well, a Republican member of the House.

"Wadsworth. Good morning. Join me in a whiskey?"

"Bit early for me, Jasper. But do sit down." Representative Wadsworth of Kentucky laid aside a copy of the *Star* and signaled a waiter to move a chair. Dills was a tiny man, with tiny hands and feet. Seated in the huge chair, he resembled a child.

The whiskey arrived. Dills saluted his fellow member before he sipped. "What kind of session do you think it will be?" His question referred to the Thirty-ninth Congress, reconvened early in the month.

"Stormy," Wadsworth said. "Issues that go all the way back to Wade-Davis remain unresolved, and the leadership of our party is dedicated to settling them." Wade-Davis, a bill drafted in response to Lincoln's moderate plan for Reconstruction, set much tougher requirements for readmission of the Confederate states. Lincoln had let the bill die with a pocket veto, thereby goading Congressmen Wade and Davis to restate their case in their so-called Manifesto, a blistering document asserting the right of the Congress to control postwar reunification. The Manifesto, published in Greeley's ferociously Republican *New York Tribune,* marked out the lines of the battle to which Wadsworth referred.

"Stormy, eh?" Dills mused. "Rather a dramatic word." He was thinking *melodramatic.*

"But entirely appropriate," the congressman said. "Look at the forces already in motion." He ticked them on his fingers. "In both the House and the Senate we have successfully denied seats to the elected representatives from the traitor states. Compliance by those states with the President's few requirements is not enough reparation for the crime of rebellion. Not nearly enough. Two, we have formed the Joint Committee on Reconstruction—"

"The Committee of Fifteen. A direct affront to Mr. Johnson. Really, though, do you construe it entirely as a radical apparatus?

Most of the members are moderates or conservatives. Senator Fessenden, the chairman, is far from radical."

"Oh, come, Jasper. With both Thad Stevens and Sam Stout on the committee, do you have any doubt of its direction? To continue"—he folded another finger down—"Lyman Trumbull is already drafting a Senate bill to extend the life of the Freedmen's Bureau. If that doesn't provoke His Accidency, I'm Marse Bob Lee."

"I'll grant you that one," Dills said, nodding. Johnson's opposition to the Bureau, on grounds that it interfered with the rights of the separate states, was one of the great running fights of his administration. Dills was reasonably familiar with the Bureau, because of a client, a rich political hack named Stanley Hazard. He was a member of the Pennsylvania family that included George Hazard, the second of Elkanah Bent's declared enemies. Stanley had hired Dills for secret legal work involving ownership of some highly controversial property.

"A friend of mine," Dills continued, "close to the Bureau says they're hearing all sorts of horror stories from the South. Stories of Negroes tricked into signing work contracts that are virtually slave labor agreements."

"Yes, precisely," Wadsworth said. "Mississippi enacted its Black Codes in November. Among other things, they stipulate that a Negro can be arrested, even beaten, if he's accused of vagrancy. Who's to say what that is? Is it occupying the same sidewalk as a white man? Merely passing through a town? It now appears that each of the erring sisters will enact similar codes, to guarantee a docile work force. They're fools down there, Jasper, arrogant fools. Apparently the war taught them nothing. Those of us in the Congress must take over their instruction."

"Johnson will continue to resist."

"Of course. And when you speak of him, you raise the great central issue to which all the others are related. Where does political sovereignty rest? Not with the President or his army, in my opinion. Military conquests made by the United States, whether foreign or domestic, can be policed only by the Congress. I believe that, Thad Stevens believes that, Ben Wade believes that. And we have a three to one majority in Congress to make our view prevail. Over the corpse of Mr. Johnson's political future, if need be," Wadsworth concluded with a smug smile.

"Perhaps your word *stormy* hardly covers it, then. Should we say *cataclysmic*?"

Wadsworth shrugged. "Label it however you wish. Andrew Johnson is headed for disaster."

That subject exhausted, Wadsworth remarked that he had just returned from New York, where he'd seen Joe Jefferson starring in his own adaptation of *Rip Van Winkle*. "Friends saw it in September at the Adelphi in London. They said it was a huge hit, not to be missed. I concur. You must see it, Jasper."

Dills replied that the theater didn't interest him.

"Literature, then? Have you read that amusing story about the California jumping frog? It's being reprinted everywhere. It's by some young sprout of a writer named Clemens."

Dills said he didn't like fiction. He didn't deem it immoral, as many clerics did; he only thought it inconsequential, unrelated to the real world.

Wadsworth rose and consulted his pocket watch. "My dear Jasper," he said wryly, "does anything in the world interest you?"

Seated in the plush chair, his tiny feet inches above the carpet, Dill said, "Power interests me. Who has it? Who is losing it? Who is scheming to regain it?"

"Then you've certainly spent your life in the right town. And you've got a damn good show ahead of you. If you're a gambler, bet on my side—to win. Oh, by the way, I saw the announcement on the members' board. Happy birthday, Jasper."

Wadsworth left, his final words serving as the only celebration for Jasper Dills this year. No matter; Dills was content with his clubs, his whiskey, his stipend from Bent's mother—and his choice seat for the coming struggle.

"Cataclysmic" might not be an exaggeration, he thought. As Wadsworth said, one merely had to consider the forces involved, and the stakes. They were enormous. Nothing less than political control of Southern legislatures and Southern votes, which in turn meant control of Southern land and Southern wealth. In the course of Dills's recent work for Stanley Hazard, his oafish client had shown some figures that vividly illustrated just how rich the pickings were.

His imagination liberated by a second drink, Dills tried to foresee events. Certainly the issue of the Freedmen's Bureau would touch off a new civil war. But the poor clod from Tennessee would be outgeneraled by a Stevens, a Wade, a Stout, a Sumner. Johnson merely wanted to be fair and constitutionally correct; they wanted to turn a minority party into the ruling party, with Negro votes tipping the balance. Johnson fought for principle, as did a few of the radicals. But the radicals as a group fought for a more inspiring cause: their own craving for power.

Suddenly, pleased and smiling, Dills murmured, "A circus. That's a better metaphor than weather, or war." He immediately refined it to a Roman circus. With Mr. Johnson the Christian surrounded by ravening lions.

There was no doubt how the contest would end. But it would certainly be worth watching. He must step up his pardon work, his influence peddling in connection with Army commissions, and even the number of letters perpetuating the fictions about Elkanah Bent. All of it would help him hold on to his box seat for the bloody spectacle soon to be enacted in the Washington arena.

———————

Congress passed a bill; the President refuses to approve it, and then by proclamation puts as much of it in force as he sees fit. . . . A more studied outrage on the legislative authority of the people has never been perpetrated. . . . The authority of Congress is paramount and must be respected.

From the Wade-Davis Manifesto
AUGUST 1864

19

The voice reached the remote corners of the House floor and every seat in the packed gallery, including Virgilia Hazard's in the front row. It was the morning of January 8, 1866.

Virgilia had listened to the speaker many times. Even so, he still had the power to send a shiver down her spine. Those who heard Representative Sam Stout, Republican of Indiana, for the first time always marveled that such a magnificent voice issued from such an unlikely body. Stout was round-shouldered and pale as a girl kept out of the sun. His thick brows and wavy, oil-dressed hair looked all the blacker by contrast.

Congressman Stout was Virgilia's lover. For some time he'd kept her in a four-room cottage on Thirteenth Street, up in the Northern Liberties. He refused to do more than that, refused to be seen in public with her, because he was married to a flat-chested drab named Emily, and because he had enormous ambition. This morning he was on the threshold of a great step upward. His speech was intended to remove any doubt about his qualifications.

During the first ten minutes, he had reiterated the familiar Radical positions. The South had in fact seceded, and Lincoln had been wrong to call the act constitutionally impossible. By seceding, the Confederate states had "committed suicide" and so were subject to regulation as "conquered provinces." Virgilia knew the argument, and the key phrases, by heart.

Knuckles white on the podium, Stout built to his climax. "And so, a philosophic chasm separates this deliberative body from the chief executive. It is a chasm so broad and deep, it cannot, perhaps should not, be bridged. Our opponent's view of the Constitution and the attendant political process epitomizes all that we reject—most especially a leniency toward the very people who nearly destroyed this republic."

He expected reaction there, and got it. Below, in special seats on the House floor, several senators led the applause. Among them Virgilia recognized the aristocratic Charles Sumner of Massachusetts, caned by a South Carolina hotspur at his Senate desk before the war; he'd almost died of the injury. So different from Sumner and Thad Stevens in some respects, Sam Stout was like them in one essential way: he believed in the moral rightness of Negro equality, not merely in the political exploitation of it.

"I have a vision for this nation," he said after the applause subsided. "A vision I fear the chief executive does not share. It is a vision in which I see a willful and arrogant people humbled and rendered powerless, their corrupt society overturned, while another people, an entire race, is lifted from enforced inequality to a new and rightful position of full citizenship. It is a vision the leadership of this Congress must and will fulfill, while casting into ignoble disgrace and ruin any group or individual daring to oppose it."

His dark eyes raked the audience. "The chief executive has employed time and the calendar to circumvent the elected representatives of the people. While Congress was in recess, he implemented his own illicit program. So let there be no misunderstanding. His actions cannot go unnoticed. Nor can they be forgiven. The gauntlet is hereby thrown down. God bless and promote the noble crusade of this Congress. He will surely bring us victory. Thank you."

Virgilia rose for the standing ovation. Warm and not a little aroused by the rhetoric, she couldn't wait to speak to Sam and praise him. The speech had become more openly hostile to Johnson since he'd read her the draft last Saturday. She clapped so hard her hands hurt.

George's sister was forty-one now, and had the sort of mature, full-bosomed figure that a majority of men considered the ideal. Her monthly allowance from her lover enabled her to dress well, though she was careful never to attract attention with gaudiness. Today her dress and Eton were a deep maroon. Her fur-trimmed winter bonnet, cape, and gloves were a complimentary dark gray. She had learned to use cosmetics to minimize facial scars left by childhood pox.

A tide of frock-coated admirers threatened to engulf Stout on the House floor. Watching, Virgilia was touched with a familiar longing. She loved Sam and still wanted to marry him and bear children for him, even though her age, and his ambition, made the dream hopeless. Worse, she'd lately heard gossip about his seeing another woman. By not speaking to him about it, not confronting him, she was trying to deny the existence of the rumor. Trying and failing.

The Speaker gaveled for a recess. Virgilia fought her way downstairs, where she exchanged enthusiastic words with Senator Sumner. "Brilliant," he declared. "Exactly on the mark." As usual, his tone prohibited disagreement.

Stout came through the doors, colleagues behind him, journalists and well-wishers converging in front. Virgilia joined the rush but suddenly pulled up short, her heart plummeting. Stout's eyes met hers and immediately shifted away, without recognition. She knotted her gloved hands together and watched her lover vanish in the crowd.

A voice startled her. "Wasn't that a tocsin, Virgilia? Wasn't that a call to war?"

She turned, struggling to smile. "It surely was, Thad. How are you?"

"Much better since I heard Sam speak. The schism with Congress is entirely in the open now. Johnson will soon be on the run."

Virgilia had met Thad Stevens at a government function in the spring. He knew her family, and their shared ideals had quickly drawn them together. He had soon become her confidant; he was the only person she had told about her relationship with Stout, and her earlier one with the escaped slave, Grady. There was a new word for mixed marriage, "miscegenation," but it didn't apply to her. She and Grady had lived together out of wedlock. Stevens was understanding because of his principles and his great affection for his mulatto housekeeper, Lydia Smith.

He guided her outside to the cool, pale sunshine washing over the Hill. At the other end of the muddy mall stood the unfinished monument to George Washington. Stevens said, "Governor Morton is a wise man to entrust Sam with the appointment."

Joy animated Virgilia's face. "You mean it's definite?"

"By this evening it will be. Sam must leave the Committee of

Fifteen because we require nine House members, but he'll continue to guide our work behind the scenes."

"I can't wait to see him and congratulate him." Stout had promised to take supper with her that evening.

"Yes, well—" Stevens coughed, a curious uneasiness in his eyes. "It would be wise not to expect too much of Sam for a while. He'll be overwhelmed with the details of the new appointment."

Virgilia heard the warning but she was too excited, and too ardent about her lover, to pay serious attention.

When the war broke out, Virgilia Hazard had been adrift and emotionally exhausted. The grief of loss coupled with almost twenty years of abolitionist activity had drained her.

During those two decades she'd quarreled often with others in the Hazard family, especially George, over his friendship with the Mains, a clan of slave-owning Southerners. Her strong views had eventually driven her away from the family and into her relationship with Grady, who had been the property of Ashton Main's husband before Virgilia helped him escape. She and Grady had joined John Brown's small band of militant abolitionists, and had taken part in his raid on Harpers Ferry in '59. Army bullets had ended Grady's life there.

Soon after the start of the war, Virgilia had joined the Union nurse corps. In a field hospital, driven by a need to avenge Grady, she'd let a wounded Confederate soldier bleed to death. Only Sam Stout's covert intervention had spared her arrest and almost certain imprisonment. After that, they had become lovers.

At the time, Virgilia had thought that what she'd done was entirely right and justified. She had seen herself as a soldier at war, not a murderess. Lately, though, exhausted by regret and a strengthening wish to call back the deed—restore the soldier's life —she had found a new idealism; an idealism purified by the guilt she expected to live with for the rest of her life.

She no longer despised her brother George for liking Orry Main, or her brother Billy for marrying Brett. She had no wish to punish the South, as Sam and other Republicans did. Merely putting some of the key Republican tenets into law would be punishment enough. That was evident from the so-called Black Codes the various states were enacting to thwart the Freedmen's Bureau.

Virgilia meditated on all this as she stirred the juice of a pot roast on the cast-iron stove in her little cottage. A light, cold rain had begun to fall at dusk, when her mantel clock chimed half after five. Now it rang half past six. Still no sign—

Wait. Above the pattering rain she heard wheels creak and a horse plopping through mud. She ran to the back door, pushed aside the curtain and watched Sam's covered buggy pull into the little shed at the rear, safe from discovery by anyone passing on Thirteenth Street. A moment later, the congressman appeared, striding toward the house. Virgilia's smile faded. He hadn't unhitched the horse.

She opened the door while he was fishing for his key. "Come in, darling. Here, give me your hat. What a wretched night."

He walked in without looking at her. She closed the door and brushed water from the brim of his tall stovepipe hat. "Take off your cape. I'll have supper ready in—"

"Never mind," he said, still avoiding her eyes. He moved through the small dining room to the front of the cottage. Water oozed from his high-topped shoes and glistened on the polished floor. "I have an urgent meeting with Ben Butler."

"Tonight? What can possibly be so pressing?"

His annoyance showed as he warmed his hands at the fire in the parlor hearth. "My new responsibilities." He turned as she approached, and she was caught short by what she saw in his dark eyes. More exactly, by what she didn't see. She might have been merely another constituent, and not a very familiar one.

"Since Senator Ivey can't serve out his term because of ill health," Stout said, "Governor Morton has announced my appointment as Ivey's replacement. In two years I'll ask the state organization to nominate me for a full term. In the meantime, I'll be able to push our program through and bring that damned Tennessee tailor to heel."

She took hold of his shoulders, exclaiming, "Senator Stout! Thad said it might happen. Oh, Sam, I'm so proud of you."

"It's a very great honor. And a great responsibility."

Virgilia pressed against him, relishing the feel of his hard body squeezing her breasts. When she slipped her arms around his waist, she felt him stiffen.

The magnificent voice dropped lower. "It will call for certain adjustments in my life."

She withdrew her hands slowly. "What kind of adjustments?" He cleared his throat and watched the fire. "At least have the courage to look me in the eye, Sam."

He did, and in the fire-flecked irises she saw rising anger. "An end to these meetings, for one. People have gotten wind of them, don't ask me how. It was probably inevitable. Gossip is the grist of this town. You can't even keep a toothache private. In any case, looking beyond the Senate to higher office—an ambition, I remind you, that I have never concealed—"

In the silence, Virgilia whispered, "Go on, Sam. Finish."

"For the sake of that future, I must shore up the public side of my life. Be seen more often with Emily, distasteful as that—"

"Is it Emily?" Virgilia broke in. "Or someone else? I've heard gossip, too."

"That remark's unworthy of you."

"Perhaps. I can't help how I feel."

Emotion hardened his voice. "I am not required to explain myself or any of my actions to you. That was part of our agreement. It still is. Therefore I don't choose to reply to your question."

From the iron stove she heard the hiss of the pot roast boiling dry. She smelled the burning meat and paid no attention. Stout laid down the curt, cold syllables one after another:

"I almost expected this kind of reaction from you. That's why I decided to make short work of parting. I will deposit the equivalent of six months of support in your bank account. After that it will be necessary for you to take care of yourself."

He walked away. A moment later she shook herself out of stunned immobility. "And that's how it ends? With a few sentences, and dismissal?"

He kept walking, through the smoke clouding off the stove where the scorching smell thickened. Virgilia's fingers raked her dark hair, loosening pins. The hair spilled over her left shoulder. She didn't notice.

"Is this how you treat someone who's helped and advised you, Sam? Someone who's cared for you?"

At the back door, hat in hand, he turned again. She saw open hostility.

"I am a United States senator now. Other people have a greater claim on me."

"Who? That variety hall slut people talk about? Is that who you're off to see, that Miss Canary? Tell me, Sam." Screaming it, she ran at him. Her fist flew up. Stout caught her wrist and forced her arm down.

"You're shouting loud enough for them to hear you at Willard's. I don't know this person you're talking about—" She sneered at him; the lie showed in his eyes. "And although it's none of your affair, I am spending the evening, as I told you, with Butler and several other gentlemen. The topic is how to thwart Mr. Johnson."

He pulled the door open. The rain, falling harder, almost hid the shed at the back of the yard. "And now, Virgilia, if I have offered you sufficient explanation, perhaps you'll grant me leave to go. I didn't want to part on these terms. Unfortunately you forced it."

He thumped his hat on his head and stalked down the steps.

"Sam," she cried, and again, "Sam!" when he raced the buggy down the lane beside the house. The flying hooves of the horse flung up mud. Specks of it struck her cheek as she clung to the post supporting the porch canopy.

The buggy swerved to the right and disappeared.

"Sam . . ." The word dissolved into sobbing. She flung both arms around the post, trying to hold it as if it were a living creature. The slanting rain soaked her hair and streaked her face, dissolving the mud so that it ran like dark tears.

Early the next afternoon, at her bank, Virgilia inquired about the balance in her account. She found it increased by the exact amount of six months' support.

Numb, stumbling once, she returned to the chilly winter sunshine and walked all the way home, carrying the burden of her certainty. She had seen the last of Senator Samuel G. Stout, Republican of Indiana. Unless, of course, she joined crowd when he spoke and listened like any other commoner.

VALENTINES! VALENTINES!
Send for an assortment of Valentines
from our new stock. New mottoes,
new cupids . . .

M A D E L I N E ' S   J O U R N A L

February, 1866. Another packet of old Couriers *today. This is
Judith's kindness—and my sole link to the world. I am not
sure but that I prefer it broken, the news is so bad—nothing
but quarreling and vindictiveness, even in the highest office in
the land. A crowd serenaded the White House a few nights
ago. Mr. Johnson went out to thank them and on impulse
spoke extempore, a dangerous habit for him. He called Stevens, Sumner, and the abolitionist Wendell Phillips his sworn
enemies. Can such rashness do anything but inspire more enmity? . . .*

*March, 1866. Still much unrest in the district; and crowds on
the roads, esp. the first Monday of the month, which has become "sale day," when condemned lands are auctioned, and
"draw day," when freedmen journey for miles to Charleston
and other centers, hoping the Bureau will distribute clothes,
shoes, rations of corn. The hopeful return empty-handed if the
officer in charge is short of supplies, or considers the crowd too
large or "unworthy."*

   *Three classes of people travel on draw day, the first com-
posed mostly of elderly colored men too feeble to work and*

*support themselves. Uncle Katanga is a good example from
close by; he hobbles on two canes and is something of a figure
because he can boast that he was born in Africa. A proud
man, but he is starving. Black women with children, their
men gone for whatever reason, form the second group. The
third, the ones responsible for some Bureau officers saying
"no" so often, are the kind called "low-downs" or "poor
buckras"—whites, usually trashy, inevitably embittered about
emancipation of the Negro, and too worthless or lazy to find
honest ways to support themselves. We have one such tribe in
the district, a sorry lot named Jolly. I have seen their ragged
tents and campfires in the woods near Summerton a few times
when desperate necessity has driven me to Gettys's store . . .*

Captain Jack Jolly and his family settled in a grove of live
oaks near the Dixie Store. The family consisted of its patriarch,
young Jack, and his two married brothers, twenty and twenty-
one years old but already greatly experienced in the ways of surviving without working. The wife of the older had been a whore
in Macon; the wife of the younger, fifteen years older than her
husband, came from Bohemia, couldn't speak English, and had
arms as massive as a coal miner's. Three dirt-caked infants lived
with the Jollys—none of the adults was quite sure which man had
fathered which youngster—and several wild dogs hung around
their trash-strewn encampment.

Their tents were made of blankets stolen at gunpoint from
the homes of freedmen. They also owned a mule and mule cart
gotten the same way. Supplies were obtained by the simple expe-
dient of a trip to Gettys's store.

On his way there in the dim March twilight, Captain Jolly
stepped aside and tipped his old campaign hat as a handsome,
big-breasted woman driving a wagon went by, heading in the
direction of Charleston. Much taken with the tightness of the
woman's dress, Jolly bowed toward the wagon's tailgate and
called out, inviting her in explicit language to stop and let him
pleasure her. The woman flung him a look and drove on. Jolly
was amused by her spunk, infuriated by the rejection.

At Gettys's store, he found what he wanted, a shiny new oil
lantern. "This suits me," he said, starting out.

"Jolly, you're going to send me to bankruptcy," Randall
Gettys exclaimed. "The price is four dollars."

"Not to me." He drew one of his Leech and Rigdon revolvers. "Ain't that so?"

Gettys darted behind the counter. He'd been a fool to invite Jolly and his tatty kinfolk to settle along the Ashley. The man was as dangerous as a rabid dog, and about as sensible. He and his family survived by thieving or taking corn rations on draw day in Charleston. One of the women told fortunes, and the Bohemian lady sold herself, he'd heard.

"All right," Gettys said, sweat steaming his spectacles. "But I'm keeping an account, because my friend Des and I, we're going to want you to do that little service we discussed."

Jolly grinned, showing brown stumps of teeth. "Wish you'd say when. I'm gettin' impatient. Hell, I don't even know who I'm s'posed to get rid of."

"She was just here, driving her wagon. Maybe you passed her on the road."

"That handsome black-haired woman? Why, my God, Gettys, I'll do her for free, no pay expected. Provided you let me have an hour with her, private, before I blow out her lamps."

Gettys mopped his damp face with the inevitable pocket handkerchief. "Des insists we wait for a pretext. A good, safe one. We don't want those infernal Bureau soldiers investigating and going to Washington to testify, the way they're doing with Tom's murder."

"I don't know a damn thing about no murder," Jolly said, no longer smiling. "If you bring it up once more, acting like I do, your lamps will go out prompt."

He scratched his crotch. "As to the other matter, you all just let me know. I'll do it clean, without a trace. And have a fine time while I'm at it."

Andrew J. used his veto power to reject what Congress calls its "civil rights act." As I understand it, the act gives freedmen equal access to the law and allows federal courts to hear cases of interference with all such rights. Read some of the President's objections in a Courier. *He sounds as fierce about the sanctity of "states' rights" as Jas. Huntoon before the rebellion. . . .*

And still the roads are crowded. Men and women, sold away from spouses years ago, rove the state in hopes of finding a loved one. Sundered families seek reunions with brothers, sisters, cousins. The black river flows day and night.

It flooded M. R. in an unexpected and tragic way. A man named Foote appeared yesterday. He, not Nemo, is Cassandra's husband. Foote was sold to Squire Revelle, of Greenville, in '58, and Cassandra gave up hope of ever seeing him again.

But her little boy is Nemo's. When Foote discovered this, he drew a knife and tried to slash her. Andy threw him down and summoned me. I told them to settle it peaceably. This morning, Nemo is gone, Foote has established himself, and Cassandra is wretchedly upset. Is there no end to the misery caused by "the peculiar institution"?

April, 1866. History made in Washington, the papers say. President J.'s veto of the rights bill overridden by the Congress. Never before has major legislation been passed in this way, or a sitting President thus humiliated.

. . . We are reaping the harvest of white against black. Town of Memphis devastated by three days of rioting touched off by confrontations between federal troops—colored men— and angry white police. At least 40 dead, many more injured, and riot not yet under control. . . .

. . . Rioting over at last. Am sure the Committee of 15 will investigate. Col. Munro gone to Washington with a local black man to testify before the committee. . . .

"I know this is difficult for you," Thaddeus Stevens said. "Please collect yourself and continue only when you're completely ready."

Representative Elihu Washburne of Illinois groaned to protest Stevens's emotional tone. The congressman from Pennsylvania could manipulate a hearing until it began to resemble a tear-laden melodrama, which was exactly what he was doing with the poorly dressed black man seated at the table facing the committee members. Sitting behind the committee in one of the chairs for observers, Senator Sam Stout made a note to speak to the leadership about Washburne's unseemly display.

The witness wiped his cheeks with pale palms and finally struggled on with his testimony:

"Ain't much more to tell, sirs. My little brother Tom, he

said no to Mr. Woodville's contrack. He was scared when he done it, but down in Charleston, Colonel Munro, he tol' him it was a bad contrack. The contrack say Tom mustn't ever go off the farm without old Woodville sayin' he could. And he got to be respeckful an' polite all the time or he get no pay. An' he couldn't keep dogs—Tom loved to hunt. He kep' two fine hounds."

A heavy despair pressed down on Stout as he listened. Witness after witness had reported on outrageous work contracts drawn up by Southern farmers who still wanted to be called master. Stout put some of the blame on ignorance, promoted by the South's insularity. Men such as the one who had tried to contract with the deceased had grown up with an agricultural system based on intimidation, fear, and bondage. They probably couldn't imagine any other kind. So they kept writing these damned sinful contracts.

The witness was watching Stevens. "Go on, sir, if you're able," Stevens prompted gently.

"Well, like I say, the Colonel, he tol' Tom not to sign the contrack. So next day Tom went back and tol' old Mr. Woodville. Tom come over to take supper that night, which was the last time I saw him. He said Woodville got pretty mad with him. Two days later they found Tom lyin' "—the voice of the witness broke—"lyin' dead."

From the adjacent chair, Orpha Munro put his arm around the weeping black man. To the clerk Stevens said, "Let the record clearly show that the murder occurred as a consequence of the man Tom's refusal to work under terms amounting to slavery."

"I must beg the pardon of my colleague." Snappish, Senator Reverdy Johnson of Maryland waved his pen. "I am in sympathy with this gentleman's loss. But he has brought forth no evidence to demonstrate conclusively a relationship between the unfortunate slaying and the events preceding it."

Stout glared at the Democrat, a politician of distinguished background who was nevertheless proving an obstructionist on the committee. Stevens too looked choleric. "Do you wish the record to so state, Senator?"

"I do, sir."

"Let it be done," Stevens said.

"I thank the gentleman from Pennsylvania," Johnson said, satisfied and not the least grateful.

No matter, Stout thought, controlling his anger. He and Ste-

vens and the core group of Republican idealists in the Congress
were very happy with the bulk of the testimony the committee
had received. Black witnesses and Bureau officers from state after
state had told stories of physical and legal abuse of freedmen—
while the President kept asserting that Congress had no right to
intervene.

But the Tennessee tailor was on the run, while the Republican cause was blessed by accidents like the Memphis rioting.
Further, to counter a possible court decision declaring the civil
rights bill unconstitutional, there was already in preparation a
Fourteenth Amendment, which would re-state the bill's essential
guarantees: full citizenship for all blacks and denial of representation to any state withholding the franchise from eligible males
over twenty-one.

The Joint Committee on Reconstruction would soon be
ready to write its report, which no doubt would focus on the
South's effort to abridge freedom by illegal means, especially by
enforcement of the Black Codes. The report would offer massive
evidence of this activity and once again affirm the supremacy of
the Congress in setting matters right. And if *that* didn't finish
Johnson with the public, Stout and his fellow Radicals would
write a second freedmen's bill to extend the Bureau's life. Johnson would veto it again, and be overridden again. Freedom's
army was on the march, and Sam Stout was one of its commanding officers.

The elderly witness had once more broken down. He sobbed
into his hands despite Munro's efforts to calm him. Stevens left
the table. Stout rose. He and Stevens exchanged glances as the
latter moved down to put a sympathetic hand on the shoulder of
the witness.

Senator Johnson showed disapproval of Steven's behavior.
Reporters in the back of the hearing room scribbled swiftly.
Good, Stout thought as he slipped to the door. Tomorrow morning they could look forward to some favorable copy in friendly
papers, commending Stevens, and hence all Republicans, for continuing to comfort the oppressed.

*July, 1866. More rioting. New Orleans this time. Courier says
at least 200 dead.*

    Andrew J. vetoed bill to continue Freedmen's Bureau.

They say the veto will not stand, and so J. will seek a means to retaliate.

. . . He has found it. J. denounced the Fourteenth Amendment, urging our state and all of Dixie not to ratify it. Tennessee immediately ratified it, and Gov. Brownlow—the "Parson"—notified Washington with the words, "Give my respects to the dead dog in the White House."

What next?

KILLING OF A NEGRO BY GEN. FORREST.

A letter from Sunflower County, Miss., says a negro employed on Gen. FORREST'S plantation, while assaulting his (the negro's) sick wife yesterday, was remonstrated with by FORREST.

The negro drew a knife and attempted to kill FORREST who, after receiving a wound in the hand, seized an axe and killed the negro. Gen. FORREST then gave himself up to the Sheriff. The negroes on the plantation justify the homicide. . . .

20

On the winter count, Wooden Foot painted the Jackson Trading Company inside a tipi under a tiny Buffalo Hat. Outside he added two stick figures waving hatchets and a third with stick hands covering the fork of his stick legs. Whenever Boy saw that part of the picture he put his hands over his mouth, Indian fashion, and giggled.

As the snowdrifts began to melt, a white visitor rode into the Cheyenne village where the traders had wintered. Broad smiles and shouting greeted him. Mothers raised their babes to touch the black cassock visible under a buffalo robe. Wooden Foot presented Charles to the weathered, gray-haired Jesuit missionary.

Father Pierre-Jean DeSmet was sixty-five now, a legendary figure. Born in Belgium, he'd emigrated to America as a young man. In 1823, he'd left the Catholic novitiate near St. Louis to begin his remarkable career on the Plains. He not only proselytized the Indians, he also became their partisan. Some of his journeys took him as far as the Willamette Valley. To the Sioux, the Blackfeet, the Cheyennes, and other tribes he was "Blackrobe," a confessor, a mediator, a spokesman in councils of the white men, a friend.

Over the evening fire, DeSmet displayed good humor and a broad knowledge of Indian affairs. There was no doubt of his loyalty:

"Mr. Main, I say to you that if the Indians sin against the whites, it is only because the whites have greatly sinned against them. If they become angry, it is because the whites provoked them. I accept no other explanation. Only when Washington abandons truculence as an official policy will peace prevail on these plains."

"What do you think the chances are that it will happen, Father?"

"Poor," DeSmet said. "Greed too often conquers a godly impulse. But that does not defeat me or discourage me. I will strive to bring a peaceable kingdom till God calls me home."

Three roads carried most of the traffic west of the Missouri. The old Overland Trail to Oregon followed the valley of the Platte, with a newer branch, Bozeman's Trail, veering off to the Montana gold fields. The Santa Fe Trail ran southwest to New Mexico. Lying between the northern and southern routes, the Smoky Hill Road followed the river along a generally westerly route to the Colorado mines.

In May of '66 the Jackson Trading Company met another white man while still thirty miles south of the Smoky Hill. The man drove a covered wagon, wore braids, and had cut the hair over his forehead in bangs, then greased it so that it stood up. He was fat, with a face that reminded Charles of a Father Christmas who'd just come off a week's binge. He greeted the traders cordially and invited them to camp the night with him.

"No thanks. We're in a hurry, Glyn," Wooden Foot said, not smiling. He signaled his companions to ride on. Once past the wagon, Charles looked over his shoulder and reacted with surprise at the sight of an Indian girl, fourteen or fifteen, peeking at them from the back of it. He had an impression of prettiness ruined by too much eating; the girl had the multiple chins of a woman of middle age.

"Surely was obvious you didn't like that man," Charles said. "Competition, is he?"

"Not for us. He peddles spirits and guns. Name's Septimus Glyn. Worked for the Upper Arkansas Agency a while. Even the Indian Bureau couldn't stomach him. He sneaks around sellin' what he shouldn't, and every season or so he picks out some young girl, honeys her up with promises, gives her the jug till she grows fond of it, then takes her away with him. When she's no good for anything but whorin', he sells her."

"I saw a girl in the wagon."

"Don't doubt it." Disgusted, Wooden Foot didn't turn around to verify it. "Must be a Crow. He's cut his hair Crow style. They're a handsome people, but he'll ruin her looks 'fore he's done, the no-good whoremaster."

Charles watched the wagon receding on the rim of the gray plain and was glad he hadn't been forced to socialize with Septimus Glyn. When he saw Willa Parker, he must tell her that not all whites exploited the Indians. Jackson didn't. Neither did the Jesuit priest. He hoped that little bit of information would be pleasing. He found himself wanting to please her.

They reached the Smoky Hill route with their forty-six ponies; all their trading goods were gone. Wooden Foot repeatedly said his new partner brought him luck.

They'd seen no white men other than Glyn south of the Smoky Hill. Once on the trail, though, they fought eastward against a tide of galloping cavalry troops, Overland coaches, emigrant wagons. One party of wagons, driven two and three abreast, refused to allow them any clearance, and so the traders had to halloo their pack mules and ponies between the wagons, eating dust. Twice, oxen nearly trampled Fen. Two valuable ponies ran away.

After the traders got through the wagons, they reined up. They looked as though they'd coated their faces in yellow flour. The dust made their eyes all the larger and whiter.

"Swear to God, Charlie, I never seen so many greenhorn wagons this early in the season."

"And the traffic's bound to make the Sioux and Cheyennes mad, isn't it?"

"You're right," Wooden Foot said.

Charles watched the canvas tops lurching west. "I had a strange reaction when those wagons wouldn't give us room. All of a sudden I understood how the Indians feel."

Thirty miles outside Fort Riley, Kansas, they saw the first stakes marking the route of the oncoming railroad. Every mile or so thereafter, they passed piles of telegraph poles waiting to be planted. One pile was nothing but ashes and charred wood. "The tribes are 'bout as partial to the talkin' wires as they are to settlers," Wooden Foot remarked.

They rode on. Weather-burned and toughened by his return to a life outdoors, Charles felt fit and very much in harmony with his surroundings. His burned-out feeling was disappearing, replaced by renewed energy and a zest for living. If he was not yet healed, healing had begun.

The morning was warm. He cast off his gypsy robe, pushed up the sleeves of his long johns, and lit a cigar, noticing eight more vehicles coming toward them over the prairie. These turned out to be high-wheeled canvas-covered U.S. Army ambulances, each pulled by two horses. Mounted soldiers formed a moving defense ring around the vehicles. "Who the hell's this?" Wooden Foot said.

They ran their mules and ponies in a circle and waited. The ambulances stopped. A colonel jumped down and greeted them. A second officer hopped out of the lead wagon, a stringy fellow with a hawk face and bristly red hair mixed with gray. His face startled Charles more than his three stars did.

"Morning," said the general. "Where have you gentlemen come from?"

"The Indian Territory," Wooden Foot said.

"We wintered with the Cheyennes," Charles said.

"I am on an inspection tour. What's their state of mind?"

"Well," Wooden Foot said, cautious, "considerin' that no one chief or village represents the whole shebang, I guess I'd say the tribe's mood is distrustful. Black Kettle, the peace chief, he told us he didn't know how long he could hold his young men back."

"Oh yes?" said the general, bristling. "Then I'd better talk to that redskin. If one more white man is scalped out here, I won't be able to hold my men back, either."

After that he calmed down. Charles puffed on his cigar and exhaled blue smoke. The general gave him a keen look. "Did I detect a trace of Southern speech, sir?"

"More than a trace, General. I rode for Wade Hampton."

"An able soldier. You like cigars, sir." Charles nodded. "I do, too. You're welcome to a fresh one of mine while we cook up some food."

"No thanks, General. I'm anxious to head on east and visit my son."

"Safe journey, then." The stringy officer gave them a casual salute and he and the colonel returned to their ambulance.

As soon as they got the horses moving, Wooden Foot said, "You know that shoulder-straps?"

"Sure. That is, I've seen pictures. His bummers burned a whole lot of my home state."

"Lord God, you don't mean that's Uncle Billy Sherman?"

"Yes, I do. Wonder what he's doing out here?"

At Riley, they learned the answer. Sherman had commanded the Division of the Mississippi since shortly after Charles passed through Chicago. He'd shifted his headquarters to St. Louis, and then, in March, had persuaded Grant to create a Department of the Platte, to shrink the unwieldy Department of the Missouri and promote better management of both within the Division. This displeased John Pope, the commander of the Missouri Department.

There were inevitable Army rumors to go with the facts. The larger administrative unit would soon be renamed Division of the Missouri. Sherman thought the Department of the Platte's commander, St. George Cooke, too old at fifty-six. He wanted Winfield Hancock, "Superb" Hancock of Gettysburg, to replace Pope. He wanted Congress to authorize new infantry and cavalry regiments, assigning some of them to Plains duty, although it couldn't be done in time to help the 1866 travel season.

Charles got the idea that Sherman had strong, largely negative views about Indians, yet did not want to become involved in making policy that affected them. "Sheriffs of the nation," that was Sherman's definition of the Army's role. Pope was more of an activist. He had insisted that emigrant trains organize before leaving jumping-off points such as Leavenworth. Otherwise, he said, his regiments wouldn't be responsible for them.

At the sutler's, Charles picked up a letter from Duncan. "Why, he's a whole lot closer than when I left. They transferred him to Fort Leavenworth in January. Let's hurry up and sell those horses."

By the first of June all the animals were gone, having fetched just over two thousand dollars for the company. The traders rode east and, at Topeka, banked their money, each man keeping fifty dollars for personal expenses. On the winter count Wooden Foot painted three sacks bearing dollar signs. He and Charles shook hands, Charles hugged Boy, and they agreed to rendezvous on the first of September.

With a sly look, Wooden Foot said, "Bound anyplace 'sides Leavenworth? Case I need you, understand."

"Oh"—Charles settled in Satan's saddle—"maybe St. Louis. Have a barber work me over." His beard had grown long and thick. "Take in a show. I met that actress, remember."

"Mmm, that's right. Nearly slipped my mind." Charles smiled. "The saucy freethinker who doesn't give a snap if people scorn her for invitin' a gent to supper."

"That's the one."

"You been so impatient, I figured you had somethin' in mind. So it's that there Augusta."

Suddenly bleak, Charles said, "Augusta was my son's mother. She's dead. I've never mentioned her name."

"Not woke up you haven't. You talk in your sleep, Charlie. I figured it was a happy dream. I'm sorry."

"That's all right."

"I want you to feel good. You're my friend. It was damn lucky we met up at Jefferson Barracks."

"I feel the same."

"Say hello to your youngster and don't get yourself kilt in no tavern fights."

"Not me," Charles said, and rode away.

A road ran due north from Leavenworth City to the military reservation. Charles cantered along this two-mile stretch, passing neat farm plots and the headquarters of Russell, Majors and Waddell, a huge enclave of parked wagons, piled-up freight, penned oxen, noisy and profane teamsters. The river flowed along out of sight under the high bluff on his right.

The ten-square-mile post contained department headquarters, barracks and support facilities for six companies, and the large quartermaster's depot serving the forts to the west. Colonel Henry Leavenworth had established the original cantonment in 1827, on the Missouri's right bank near its confluence with the Kaw.

Jack Duncan's quarters were typical of Western military posts. Spartan rooms furnished with an old sheet-iron stove and whatever furniture the occupant brought, bought, or built from crates and lumber. Normally, the brigadier would have lived in smaller space—"Old Bedlam," the bachelor officers' quarters— but he'd ranked a married captain and thus moved him, his wife, and baby out of married quarters, so that he and Maureen and Gus could move in. This happened frequently to junior officers; the term for it was "the bricks falling in."

Charles couldn't believe how much his son had grown since last autumn. Little Gus walked around Duncan's parlor so fast, swaying, that Charles was constantly starting to dive for the boy, to catch him if he fell. It amused Duncan.

"No need for that. He's damn steady."

Charles quickly saw this was so. "He doesn't know me, Jack."

"Of course not." Duncan held out his hands. "Gus, come to Uncle." The boy clambered to his lap without hesitation. Duncan pointed to the visitor. "That's your father. Want to go to your father?"

Charles reached out to take him. Gus screamed.

"I think it's your beard," Duncan said.

Charles saw no humor in it. He struggled for over an hour to tempt Gus onto his lap. But after he finally did, he soon had him clinging to his thumbs and laughing as he bounced him up and down on his knee. Maureen appeared from the kitchen and expressed disapproval. Charles didn't stop.

Duncan leaned back and lit a pipe. "You look good, Charles. The life agrees with you."

"I miss Augusta and always will. Apart from that, I've never been happier."

"This Adolphus Jackson must be a fine fellow."

"The best." Charles cleared his throat. "Jack, I need to say something else about Augusta. Well, actually, about a woman I met in St. Louis. An actress in one of the theaters there. I'd like to pay her a call. But I don't want to dishonor Gus's memory."

Soberly, Duncan said, "You're a decent and considerate man. There are many who wouldn't even worry. I don't expect you to live like an anchorite the rest of your life. Augusta wouldn't expect it either. A man needs a woman, that's a fact of life. Go to St. Louis as soon as you want."

"Thank you, Jack." He beamed at Maureen, still hovering near and frowning over his rag-bag wardrobe, his tangled beard, his way of handling his son. Charles just ignored it.

"Life's too good to be believed," he said, gazing at his son, whose features had begun to favor his mother.

Duncan smiled. "I'm glad. We all went long enough feeling the other way in the late unpleasantness."

Up went the curtain. The players joined hands and stepped to the apron, Trump pulling the others along and then snatching off his woodcutter's cap. He waved the cap to acknowledge the applause, thus drawing attention from the others in the company. He unpinned his good-luck chrysanthemum from his coarse tunic and tossed the wilted flower, more brown than white, into the audience. An obese man caught it, examined it, threw it away.

The company bowed again. Then Trump took a third, solo, bow. The woman playing his wife exchanged long-suffering looks with Willa, who was prettily dressed in a high-waisted gown for her role as one of the young lovers. The play was Molière's *Physician in Spite of Himself,* which had been "amplified and emended by Mr. Trump," according to posters outside. It seemed to Charles, standing up and clapping hard in the front box at stage left, that the unraveling of the farcical plot about a woodcutter pretending to be a famous doctor had stopped completely at least four times while Sam Trump performed comic monologues that didn't sound like the rest of the play; one described hotels with peculiar French names. The largely male audience roared, apparently understanding some local references.

Charles really didn't care how much Trump had rewritten Molière. Like most of those out front, he was taken with Willa Parker's stage presence. From her first entrance, she'd captured everyone. Not with conventional beauty but with some intangible power that drew the eye and held it when she was on stage. Maybe all great performers had that quality.

He extended his hands over the rail, still clapping. The movement drew Willa's attention to the box. Charles had paid for a bath and beard trim and had bought an inexpensive brown frock coat and matching trousers. Willa saw him, recognized him, and reacted with what he perceived as surprise, then pleasure.

Charles nodded and smiled. Suddenly Willa's glance shifted to a box on the opposite side. An empty box, though the curtain still moved, stirred by someone leaving.

The stage curtain rolled down, revealing painted messages about restaurants and shops. The applause died. The audience of men and a very few ladies with escorts began to file out. Charles wondered what, or who, had brought that flash of anxiety to Willa's face.

Eager and surprisingly nervous, he hurried around to the stage entrance, where he'd stopped the teamster from beating his horse last year. He handed the doorkeeper half a dollar, being pushed from behind by other gentlemen equally intent on going inside. Because of his height, Charles could look over most of the well-wishers, stagehands, and performers backstage.

He saw Sam Trump at the entrance to a corridor leading to dressing rooms. In order to visit anyone, people had to pass Trump and compliment him.

Charles did so enthusiastically. Eyes glassy with joy, Trump said, "Thank you, dear boy, thank you." Brown dye trickled from behind his ears. "Yours is a familiar face. Was it Boston? I have it! Cincinnati."

"St. Louis. I have a beard now." He extended his hand. "Charles Main."

"Of course. I remember it clearly." He didn't. "Frightfully glad you caught us tonight. I'm anticipating sold-out houses starting tomorrow." His eyes had already hopped over Charles's shoulder, hunting the next admirer. Charles slipped by, smelling sweat on Trump but no spirits. Willa must have succeeded in drying him out.

All the dressing-room doors were open except the last on the right. He suspected that was hers, since a short, neatly dressed man was already waiting outside.

As Charles approached, the man turned. Instantly, Charles recognized the unnaturally stiff posture, the trimmed goatee and waxy mustache points, the shoes with a high polish, the clothes without a wrinkle.

Willa's admirer was the man who'd kept him out of the Army. Captain Harry Venable.

21

Charles's nerves wound tight as he walked up to Harry Venable. The dapper officer apparently didn't recognize him, though he understood Charles's intent. Charles read the lettering painted on the door. MRS. PARKER. He stepped forward to knock and Venable slipped in front of him.

"Excuse me. Mrs. Parker's engaged."

Charles looked down into the glacial eyes, tilting his head to exaggerate the height difference. "Fine. Shall we let her tell me that?" He reached over Venable's shoulder and knocked.

Venable turned scarlet. Willa called out, asking him to be patient a moment. Venable said, "What the hell are you smiling about?"

"Handsome Harry Venable"—Charles began rubbing the knuckles of his left hand—"West Point class of '59."

Flustered, Venable tried to identify the bearded stranger. Charles continued, "Last time we met, you had some helpers. I see you haven't any now. If there's some sort of dispute, perhaps we can settle it fairly this time." His teeth gleamed in his beard but the smile wasn't friendly. He kept rubbing his knuckles. Venable recognized him.

Then the door opened. All in a rush, Willa seized him and hugged him. "Charles! I couldn't believe it when I saw you in the box—" She stepped back, gripping his arms while she studied him. She wore a pastel wrapper, an outer layer of gauzy material with opaque satin beneath. Delicate transparent butterflies decorated the gauze. Although tightly belted, the gown didn't quite hide her cleavage. A spot of cold cream glistened on her nose. With strands of her silver-blond hair hanging free, she looked unkempt and absolutely lovely.

"Here, do come in while I take off the rest of this make-up." As she tugged him into the dressing room she dabbed a cloth behind her ear; it came away orange.

Through this, Venable stood rigid, shoulders back, unable to conceal his fury. Good actress that she was, Willa smiled and spoke to him graciously. "Colonel, I'm so sorry to refuse again. Mr. Main and I have a long-standing engagement. I'm sure you understand."

She closed the door.

"I have a long-standing engagement to beat the hell out of that little toad. He's the one who recognized me at Jefferson Barracks."

"Well, he's still stationed there." Willa snatched pins from the dressing table and began pinning up her hair. The small room was a confusion of costumes, personal clothing, make-up pots and brushes, playscripts, all the clutter increased by its reflection in the table mirror. "He saw the play four nights ago and he's been hounding me ever since. Oh, Charles, you've been gone so long."

"It's a long way to the Indian Territory." He found himself gazing into her blue eyes with more intensity than he planned.

"I know. And I thought you'd never get back. When I saw you, halfway through the first act, I nearly walked into that bench."

"I didn't think you saw me until the curtain call."

"Oh, long before that. I kept dropping lines."

"I didn't notice."

"You aren't supposed to notice." On tiptoe, she kissed his cheek, then hugged him again. Her body felt very soft and ripe beneath the butterfly gauze. "May we have supper?"

"Absolutely." He grinned. "No snails this time."

"All right. Wait for me in the hall. I'll be ready in two minutes." She couldn't keep the excitement out of her voice.

In the hall, he saw no sign of Venable. It was a relief. He felt too grand to interrupt the evening with a brawl. He knew that, one to one, he could easily beat the small man, so a fight would mean an inevitable load of guilt afterward.

Just before Charles and Willa left the theater, she waved to Sam Trump standing in the wings with Prosperity, the theater cat, in his arms. Trump broke off his conversation with a stage-hand and nodded to acknowledge them. He gave Charles a peculiar stare, then watched them as they vanished through the Olive Street door.

On the sidewalk, something made Charles stop. She said, "What is it? Oh." She saw him too, across the street in the shadow cast by the wooden Indian chief in front of the tobacconist's. Discovered, Venable executed a right face and hurried around the corner.

Willa shivered. "What a strange man."

"Maybe he won't show up again, now that I'm here."

"Back at the dressing room there was a moment when he looked ready to murder you, Charles."

"He tried it once. Didn't get away with it." He reached over to pat the mittened hand on his right arm. "I'm for supper. The New Planter's House?"

"Why not? It's convenient. I've moved there. Yes, out of the scene loft." They began walking arm in arm through the night streets. "The playhouse has been in the black since February. Not by much, but in the black. The company has established a local following, so the hotel management offered me rooms at a reduced rate. Evidently Mr. Trump and Mrs. Parker are now welcome all over town."

He chuckled; the faint cynicism he heard reminded him of her maturity. He remarked on it as they sat in the familiar dining room, both of them with juicy venison steaks. This time, he'd ordered.

"You're flattering me," she began.

"No. Telling the truth. Not only are you very—well—worldly for someone your age, but you're brighter than most men I know."

A little gesture deprecated the praise. "If it's at all true, and I'm not sure it is, maybe it's because I grew up in the theater. Knowing plays made me hungry for other kinds of books. And my father was liberal about education for girls. He believed in it."

They fell to discussing what had happened to her since their last meeting. Trump's St. Louis Playhouse had assembled its permanent company. "Actors are now willing to sign contracts for a season, because I've convinced them Sam won't drink up the profits." The company had four plays in repertory and was starting to think about touring. "Do you know there isn't a decent theater between here and Salt Lake City? I should imagine that all those new towns going up along the railroad would be ideal for a traveling company with its own tent."

"And the Army posts, too," he said. A waiter poured rich dark coffee from a silver pot. "You do love the life, don't you?"

"Yes, I do. But—here I go, brazen again." Her cheeks colored as she gazed at him. "I thought about you often during the winter."

That gaze ignited something in him. He knew he should retreat; could not.

"I thought about you, Willa."

She drew her hands into her lap. Very quietly, she said, "I don't know what you do to me. I'm shaking like an ingénue making her first entrance. I can't drink this coffee. I don't want anything more." A long pause. "Would you escort me up to my rooms?"

"Yes. Gladly."

And so, much sooner than he'd ever anticipated, it happened to them, in the small bedroom dimly lit by gaslight from the adjoining sitting room. She moaned a little, expectant, as their hands worked, strewing clothes everywhere. While she unpinned her silver-and-gold hair and shook it out, Charles gently, carefully touched one small, firm breast, then the other. "Oh, I'm so glad there's you in this world, Charles," she said, moving beneath him, drawing him down. She ran her palm round and round on his chest, kissed his throat, sought his mouth. He felt tears of happiness on her cheeks.

"I'm not altogether a scarlet woman," she whispered. "There's been but one other man, and that only twice, from curiosity. Each time was a botch, so I'm not experienced. I hope this—"

"Hush," he said, kissing her. "Hush."

She was soft and thick and golden where he entered her. She arched high as they found the rhythm together. Her heels and calves held him, and he lost every worry about entanglements and their consequences. He thought of nothing but the ardent, open warmth of this singular and passionate young woman who inspired him to love with all of his body and mind.

Abruptly, wakefulness returned. He didn't know where he was. He thrashed; turned; saw the gaslit sitting room through the half-open door. His movement roused her.

"Are you all right?"

"I was caught in a dream."

Tenderly, she brought her naked warmth against his side. Kissed his shoulder. "Was it bad?"

"I think so. It's slipped away already."

After a pause she said, "You called out several times. A name." Another pause. "Not mine."

Upset, he struggled up on his elbow. "No, no," she said. "It's all right, Charles. You need to talk about it. There's something I need to talk about, too. Tomorrow," she murmured, drawing his back against her bare breasts, reaching over to close and softly stroke his eyes.

In the early morning hours, for the sake of propriety, he dressed and left the hotel. He walked boldly, even noisily, from the staircase to the lobby doors. The clerk, leaning on his palm, opened one eye. Because Charles acted as though he had nothing to hide, the clerk immediately went back to dozing.

Charles took a room at a cheaper hotel and next morning called for Willa with a rented buggy. She'd packed a lunch hamper. They drove into the country upriver, settling down to picnic in a pretty grove of elms and sycamores, many with wild bittersweet twined around their trunks. The grove smelled of the mint growing there. In the sunlit field just to the north, wild asters and bloodroot and jack-in-the-pulpit grew amid stands of nettle and poison ivy.

"An embarrassing question," Charles said as he helped unpack the hamper: thick summer sausage rounds between pumpernickel fresh from one of the local German bakeries, a corked jug of foamy ginger beer. "Last night, was my beard—? That is—"

"Yes, rough as those nettles over there," she said, teasing. "Notice all this extra face powder? You left indelible evidence of our scandalous behavior."

She leaned close, kissed him lightly. "Which I thoroughly enjoyed and do not in the least regret. Now—" She spread a checked cloth in the shade. The buggy horse switched his tail to drive off flies. A stately stern wheeler appeared in the north, bound for St. Louis. "I want to tell you something, so that we have no secrets. I didn't come to Sam's theater entirely by choice, though now I'm very glad that I did. I was running away from a man named Claudius Wood."

She told the story of New York, the *Macbeth* dagger, Edwin Booth's kindness. It put him sufficiently at ease so that he could tell her about Augusta Barclay, that they were lovers but never married. He did hedge the ending a bit, merely saying the war separated them before she died. He didn't reveal that he'd initiated the separation, to spare her loss and emotional pain if he were killed. Ironically, he was the one left grieving, and wary of another involvement.

And yet here he was—

While they finished their picnic the sun's angle changed. The Mississippi flowed quietly again, the stern wheeler's wake completely gone. The grove grew warm. Sweat ran down the neck of Charles's open shirt.

Willa invited him to put his head in her lap and rest. He asked her permission to smoke a cigar, lit it, then said, "Tell me who you really are, Willa. Tell me what you like and what you don't."

She thought a bit, gently caressing his beard. "I like early mornings. I like the way my face feels after I scrub it. I like the sight of children sleeping, and I like the taste of wild berries. I like Edgar Poe's verse and Shakespeare's comedians. Parades. The sea. And I'm shamelessly in love with standing on a stage while people applaud." She bent to kiss his brow. "I've just discovered I like sleeping with my arms around a man, though not just any man. As for things I don't like—well, stupidity. Needless unkindness in a world already hard enough. Pomposity. People with money who think that money alone makes a person worthy. But most of all"—another soft kiss—"I like you. I think I love you. There, I've let down the mask Pa taught me to keep in place so there'd be fewer wounds from life. I think I loved you the moment I saw you."

His eyes on the river, he said nothing. He felt as if he teetered on the edge of a vast abyss, about to fall.

They kissed, murmured things, fondled one another, till her

sweet breath grew warm as the brilliant summer day. "Love me, Charles," she said, mouth on his ear. "This place, this moment."

"Willa, once is fairly safe, but—what if I got you with child?"

"What a strange man you are. So many wouldn't even worry. There are far worse things. I'd not trap you with a baby." She saw his reaction. "That bothers you."

"Scares me. I couldn't stand to lose someone else I cared about. Once was enough."

"So better not to care?"

"I didn't say that."

"Well, no guilt feelings. Whatever happens, happens just for the moment." Again she kissed him.

Even as he bore her gently backward to the soft mat of browned grass and fallen sycamore leaves, he knew that they had gone too far for either of them to escape without hurt.

Except when she was rehearsing or performing, they spent every hour of the next four days together.

He related his experiences with the Jackson Trading Company; what he'd learned of the ways of the Southern Cheyennes; how he'd grown to respect them, and to admire leaders such as Black Kettle. She was pleased he'd moved away from the typical white man's truculence, an attitude born of greed, mistrust, and, she suspected, general ignorance of the Indians and their concerns.

"We always fear what we don't understand," she said.

They found a photographer's gallery and sat for a portrait. Willa giggled when the fussy man tightened her head clamp behind the velvet settee. "Look pleasant—pleasant!" the man cried from underneath the black camera drape. Standing at her side, Charles rested his hand on her shoulder and adopted a severe expression. Willa kept giggling, from nervousness and joy, and the photographer waited ten minutes until she calmed down.

She wanted to know what sort of man he was, what he liked. Lying in bed with her after the Saturday night performance of *Richard III*, he thought a while and said:

"I like horses, good cigars, sunset with a glass of whiskey. The blue of the sky in South Carolina—no painter ever put such a blue on canvas. I like the clear air in Texas after a hard rain. In fact I like all of the West that I've seen.

"I like the strength you find in most black people. They're survivors, fighters. Yankees wouldn't believe a Southerner saying that.

"I love my family. I love my son. I love my best friend, Billy, who's gone to California with his wife, my cousin.

"I hated the last two years of the war and what they did to people, me included. I hate the politicians and the parlor patriots who thumped the tub until the fighting started. They never had to live through days and nights of battle—the grimmest, most draining work I've ever done. They never had to advance through an open meadow toward enemy entrenchments, watching their friends fall around them, and pissing their pants with fear—excuse me," he said, his voice all at once low and harsh.

She kissed the corner of his mouth. "It's all right. I'd like to meet your son. Would you let me visit Fort Leavenworth? I could come on a Missouri steamer, perhaps in August. August is a theater's worst month. I'm sure Sam would let an understudy replace me."

Fearing the entanglement, he still said, "I'd like that."

The day after, he hugged and kissed her at the stage door, and then mounted Satan. America's Ace of Players appeared suddenly, shooing Willa inside so he could speak privately.

Trump stepped close to the frisky piebald. "What I have to say is quite simple, sir. You may have the idea that because I am a play actor, I am an effete weakling. To the contrary. I am but fifty, in my prime, and strong."

He raised his fist and forearm at a right angle. Charles might have laughed but for the severity of the actor's expression. Trump grasped Satan's headstall and jutted his jaw.

"Willa fancies you, Mr. Main. A marble statue could see that. Well and good. She's a splendid girl—and like my own daughter. So if you trifle with her—if you should in any way hurt her—as God is my witness"—he exhibited his fist again—"I will grind you down, sir. I will find you and grind you down."

"I don't intend to hurt her, Mr. Trump."

The actor released the headstall. "Then a safe journey to you. With my blessing."

But he would have to hurt her in some way, Charles realized as he cantered west from the city. He was in love with her, and confused about it; vaguely angry that he'd let it go so far, *wanted* it to go that far. But he had. So he had to undo it, and soon.

22

When Charles reached Fort Leavenworth, Duncan told him that in late July, Johnson had signed a bill increasing the number of infantry regiments from ninteen to forty-five and, of more pertinence on the Plains, where distances were vast, the number of cavalry regiments from six to ten.

The brigadier, who now wore the olive-green trim of the divisional paymaster's department, was excited about the news. "It means that by next year we'll be able to demonstrate in force against the hostiles."

Charles chewed an unlit cigar and said nothing. Like Sherman, Jack Duncan believed the tribes must inevitably be driven onto reservations if the West was to be made safe for white settlers and commerce. Duncan saw nothing improper in this appropriation of Indian land, and Charles knew he couldn't change Duncan's mind, so he didn't try. Instead, he announced Willa's forthcoming visit.

"Ah," Duncan said, smiling.

"What does that mean—ah? She isn't coming just to see me. She wants to look over halls that the company could rent for a tour."

"Oh, of course," Duncan said soberly. He was delighted to see Charles react to teasing. Perhaps the young man was recovering from the despondency that had haunted him for so long.

Willa arrived in late August. She had already visited City of Kansas—some were calling it Kansas City—on the opposite shore of the Missouri, and Leavenworth on the near side. She said Frank's Hall in City of Kansas was an ideal auditorium.

Duncan's frame residence on officers' row, on the north side of the parade ground, contained an extra room Maureen used. She kept little Gus there in a homemade rocker-crib. She invited Willa to share her bed and the young actress accepted without hesitation. Maureen approved of Willa's adaptability, and in fact she did fit in well. She chatted easily about Sam Trump and the playhouse, and listened attentively to talk of Army life and the Indian problem. She didn't conceal that she stood with the Indians against the great majority of settlers and Army professionals. It didn't nettle Duncan as badly as Charles had expected. The brigadier argued with Willa, but clearly respected her as an intelligent adversary.

The first evening, after the women retired, Duncan poured two whiskeys in the parlor. The open window brought in strong, sweet yeast fumes from the post bakery nearby. For a few minutes, Duncan complained about the paymaster's department. It was thankless work; the officers who rode from fort to fort with soldiers' wages could never travel fast enough to please the men.

Presently he said, "That's a fine young woman. A bit free-thinking, to be sure. But she'd make a splendid—"

"Friend," Charles said, and bit down on his cigar.

"Exactly." Duncan decided not to push Willa's cause further at the moment. Charles looked fierce. He might not be as ready to resume normal life as Duncan had thought.

Where oaks and cottonwoods shaded the bluff above the fort's steamboat landing, Charles and Willa went walking on the last day of her visit. Gus rode on his father's shoulder, happily surveying the world from his perch. Pleasant sounds drifted through the Sunday air: yells and cheers of soldiers playing baseball; the chug of the post steam engine pumping water.

Willa was nervous and a little unhappy. Here at the fort, Charles was less demonstrative than he'd been in St. Louis. She was in love with him—there was no escaping that—but she knew she'd better not say it too often. The bleak, exhausted look that showed in his eyes occasionally said he wasn't ready for an emotional commitment.

Still, she couldn't bring herself to pretend disinterest. So amid the dapple of sun and the shadows of reddening leaves stirring in the breeze, she took Charles's son in her arms. There he rested contentedly, gazing over her shoulder at squirrels racing along tree limbs or picking up decaying green hickory nuts that had fallen in midsummer.

"Gus is a wonderful boy," she said. "You and his mother brought a fine son into the world."

"Thank you." Hands in pockets, Charles stared at the glinting river a hundred and fifty feet below them. Common sense told Willa she shouldn't press. But she loved him so much—

"This has been a grand visit. I hope I'll be invited again."

"Certainly, if it's convenient for you."

Gus laid his head on Willa's shoulder and put his thumb in his mouth. His eyes closed and his face softened, blissful. Willa touched Charles's sleeve. "You're treating me as though we just met."

He frowned. "I don't mean to, Willa. It's just that I get the feeling Jack and Maureen are both—well—pushing us together. That's no good. Week after next, I'm going out to meet Wooden Foot at Fort Riley. I've said it before: trading isn't the safest work, even though most of the Southern Cheyennes are my partner's friends. I don't want to get involved. Suppose we went out one season and never came back. It wouldn't be fair to you."

Her blue eyes snapped. "Oh, come, Charles. Life's always full of risks like that. Who are you really sparing, me or yourself?"

He faced her. "All right. Myself. I don't want to go through what I went through before."

"You think I'm delicate? Sickly? That I'm going to collapse tomorrow, and you'll lose me? By the way, I'm not pregnant." Her use of that generally unmentionable word startled him. "I'll be around for a good long while yet. Your excuse won't wash."

"I can't help it."

"And I thought women were the fickle sex."

He turned away, staring upriver again. The cool breeze fluttered his beard. The low-slanting sun lit Willa's hair till it shone like fine white gold. "Charles, what in God's name did the war do to you?"

He didn't answer.

Undone by his stoniness, she found herself irked again. "We can be friends—casual lovers—but nothing else?"

He looked at her. "Yes."

"I'm not sure how I feel about that. I'm not sure I like it. I'll tell you when you come back from this next trip. Now, if you don't mind, I'd like to go back to the brigadier's quarters. It's gotten chilly." She lifted Gus and handed him to his father, and walked away.

She knew that a display of temper would probably drive him off. Yet she couldn't do anything about it. She was angry at her untouchable enemy—the pain left in him by the death of the boy's mother. Reason, even affection, might never overcome something so deeply wounding. How could she fight it? Only by hanging on. By demonstrating that Charles could love her without risk, though not without commitment.

She hated for the visit to end on a dismal note, but it did. When they parted at the steamer landing, he kissed her cheek, well away from her mouth. He said nothing about visiting St. Louis in the spring, only thanked her for coming. As she went aboard the stern wheeler, little Gus waved and waved.

The steamer churned into the current and Willa watched man and boy grow smaller. Charles looked unhappy and confused. That was exactly how she felt.

But she couldn't deny that she was in love. So she wouldn't give up.

It was going to be a long winter.

As August dwindled away, Charles grew impatient to be moving. He left a day early, and no regrets about it, except for Gus. The boy now called him Fa, and readily came to him for hugs or sympathy. Charles was sad that the whole process of getting reacquainted would have to be repeated next spring. As for Willa, he tried to suppress his feelings for her, hopeful that he'd made it clear that any closer involvement was impossible.

He said goodbye to the brigadier and Maureen on a sunny afternoon. Maureen's final word was a tart, "You ought to marry that girl, sir. She said there's no longer a Mr. Parker, and she's a grand person."

Rather abruptly, Charles said, "Traders don't make good family men."

He didn't get as far as he'd planned the first day. In midafternoon, passing through the Salt Creek Valley, Kickapoo Township, Satan threw a shoe. By the time a local blacksmith replaced it the sun was going down. Charles put up at the Golden Rule House, a place Duncan had talked about with enthusiasm:

"It's only been open a short time but it's already famous up and down the river. The proprietor's a generous young fellow. He'll cut the price of your meal and pour whiskey free if he's had a few himself. If he keeps on, he'll go bankrupt. But it's wonderful while it lasts."

So it proved. The atmosphere in the converted house was noisy and convivial. The owner, though just twenty, was one of those authentic characters who gave the West its flavor. Already well under the influence by six o'clock, the young Kansan regaled his guests with a long story about driving an Overland coach and suddenly being attacked by a huge band of Sioux. He claimed he drove them off with a combination of shouted threats and rifle fire, saving coach and passengers.

Charles shared a table with a huge, amiable man about his own age, who introduced himself as Henry Griffenstein. He said he hailed from one of the German settlements in the upland section of Missouri known as the Little Rhineland.

"That's why I'm Dutch Henry to my friends. Right now I'm bullwhacking wagons to Santa Fe. Who knows what I'll be doing next year?"

Charles chewed a chunk of buffalo steak, then pointed his fork at the talkative young man tending bar. "I don't think I believe that story. Especially the number of Sioux he got rid of. But he's a damn fine storyteller."

"Damn fine stage driver, too," Dutch Henry said. "Besides that, he's handled freight wagons and scouted for the Army. He rode Pony Express at fourteen—he says."

"How'd he get in the hotel business?"

"He and Louisa opened the place after they got hitched in January. I don't think he can last cooped up like this. He's too full of ginger. Not to mention the gift of gab."

"Gather 'round, boys," the young man shouted, waving his customers in. "I want to tell you about riding with the Seventh Kansas Cavalry in the war. Jennison's Jayhawkers. Real hard cases. We—wait, let's all have a refill first."

He poured generous drinks for his listeners, wobbling noticeably as he did so. From the way he knocked back his whiskey, Charles judged him to be something of a hard case himself.

"What'd you say his name was?" he asked Dutch Henry.

"Cody. Will F. Cody."

On horseback with their pack mules in single file, the Jackson Trading Company rode over the autumn prairie, bound for the land beyond the hazy blue horizon to the south. They rode beside the same trampled buffalo trail they'd followed to Indian Territory the year before. In the northwest, dark gray clouds raced toward the apex of the sky. Every half minute or so the clouds lit up, white within.

Above the traders a hawk rode the air currents. Red-tailed and dusky gray of body, she sank and soared in great spirals, her heavy wings spread to their full fifty inches.

Charles alternately watched the hawk and the storm clouds. Wooden Foot said the hawk was looking for mice and gophers, either of which she could see from high above. Suddenly the hawk turned, flexed her wings hard and flew straight away into the rough air beginning to blow out of the north. Charles wondered if something had alarmed her.

The land here undulated, so that the prospect ahead was that of a series of continual rises, none higher than six feet. It was late afternoon. At about the same hour two days ago, they'd crossed the Smoky Hill Road, on which wagons still creaked west with as much speed as their drivers could manage, smelling winter in the crisp September air. At Fort Riley, an officer had told Charles that something like a hundred thousand emigrant wagons had traveled through during the summer.

You wouldn't know it here. They'd ridden past an isolated farm at sunset yesterday. Two youngsters had waved at them from the feed lot, and Boy had laughed and gurgled long after the children were left behind. They'd seen no human beings since. In an old *Harper's Weekly* picked up at Riley, Charles had read an amazing article about the great mountain chain of Asia, the Himalayas. "Special from New Delhi by Our Roving Correspondent." He was fascinated by the description of that remote region, which surely couldn't be emptier than this prairie under the brow of the approaching storm.

The wind picked up. High as Satan's knees, the dry, brittle grama grass seethed. It struck Charles that the piebald was nervous. The other animals were too including Fen. The border collie kept running in circles ahead of them, barking.

The dog loped away down the other side of the next rise and disappeared. Only the disturbed motion of the grass marked his

ail. Charles studied the sky again. "I wonder why that hawk all
f a sudden—"

He stopped, noticing more agitation in the grass. It rippled
s though an invisible man was rushing toward them, creating a
ath but remaining unseen.

"It's Fen," Wooden Foot said above the whistling wind.
Wonder what the devil's biting him?" He reached for his rifle
cabbard. "Boy, stick close."

Boy nudged his horse toward the trader's. "I'll have a look,"
harles said, touching Satan with his boot heels.

The piebald trotted about fifty feet to the summit of the rise.
rit and bits of windblown grass flew into Charles's eyes. He
quinted and shielded his eyes with his hand as he topped the
se.

At the bottom, a line of nine men sat on ponies, waiting.

From the center of the line Scar gazed up at him. He and the
thers wore leggings painted with red stripes, and red paint on
eir faces, arms, and bare chests. Each wore the Dog Society
ap, with a narrow beaded band and feathers from a golden eagle
id a raven; the feathers were gathered and tied so they stood up
raight. Each man had an eagle-bone whistle on a thong around
is neck and carried bow and arrow plus a trade rifle or musket.
was full war regalia.

Scar saw that register on Charles's face. He grinned and
umped his rifle up and down. The others barked and howled.

Wooden Foot and Boy came riding up behind Charles. "Oh
y God, Charlie, this is it. This ain't no accident. I shouldn't of
re that clout off him. He's been waitin' all summer. He knew
e'd prob'ly come back this way."

Charles started to ask whether they should signal for a par-
y. The fiery spurt and bang of an Indian rifle made the very idea
olish.

THE PRESIDENT'S TOUR.

On the Way from Buffalo
to Cleveland.

A Joyful Good-Speed by the
Buffalonians.

————

Enthusiastic Demonstrations at
Silver Creek and Erie.

————

A Party Among the Western
Reserve Radicals.

————

Special dispatch to the New York Times
CLEVELAND, OHIO, Monday, Sept. 3

The enthusiasm of the people in-
creases as the Presidential party pro-
gresses on its tour. . . .

————

MADELINE'S JOURNAL

September, 1865. Sim's boy Pride brought me another
those foul-smelling rocks, this one from his own land. Tol
him I did not know what they were. Must ask Cooper if h
ever deigns to visit again . . .

Judith and Marie-Louise here today. How dear M-
blooms and blossoms! She is already more ample than he
mother. Judith says she is smitten with some Charleston bo
but C. deems her too young, won't permit the boy to call
send small gifts. When M-L is a bit older, and assertive, sl
and C. may fall out over the issue of suitors.

Judith said C. is praising the President ever since he d
cided to retaliate for his legislative defeats by taking his ca.
to the people. Johnson presently making what he calls "
swing around the circle," with Grant and other generals an
dignitaries in tow.

Andrew Johnson and his entourage invaded Ohio, the hom
state of Ben Wade, Stanley's powerful friend and sometime ben
factor. At Cleveland, a major stop, a large and friendly crow
greeted the presidential party at the depot. Outside, a speci

decorative arch over the street expressed support for the visit. THE CONSTITUTION, it said. WASHINGTON ESTABLISHED IT. LINCOLN DEFENDED IT. JOHNSON WILL PRESERVE IT.

Johnson was pleased. From that point, matters began to deteriorate.

At dusk, the Boy General strode down the corridor of Cleveland's Kennard Hotel with Secretary of State Seward. The Secretary's neck still bore red scars from the knife attack of one of John Wilkes Booth's fellow conspirators, who had struck at Seward on the same night that Lincoln was shot.

The Boy General was nervous. This was Ben Wade's fiefdom; Radical country. The President had taken to the rails for the avowed purpose of laying the cornerstone of a Stephen Douglas memorial in Chicago. Actually he was stopping along the way to attack the Republicans.

The strategy might have worked had not a large press contingent, including Mr. Gobright of the Associated Press, decided to accompany the President. The reporters wanted to file a new dispatch at every stop, so it was impossible for Johnson to deliver one prepared speech time after time. He was forced to do what he did so badly—extemporize.

The Boy General's tension was reflected in his bouncing stride and darting blue eyes. Lean, with an aura of high energy, George Armstrong Custer wore a trim civilian suit that showed his slimness to advantage. Small gold spurs jingled on his polished boots. Libbie urged him to wear spurs to remind people of his war exploits.

For a while, because of those exploits, he'd been the talk of the country—an audacious cavalry general with a remarkable talent for victory. Custer's luck, someone had christened it. Like some magic dust, it had covered him all during the war, bringing him success in the field and fame in the press.

Then came peace, the shrinking Army, and obscurity again. When he mustered out in Texas some months ago, he'd held the rank of captain.

Now he was beginning a slow and deliberate journey back to prominence. In a crucial meeting with Secretary of War Stanton he'd secured a captaincy for his loyal brother Tom, and for himself a lieutenant colonelcy in one of the new Plains regiments. He would soon return to active duty with the Seventh Cavalry.

He considered it a fine opportunity because the Seventh's commander, General Andrew Jackson Smith, was a thirty-year veteran—an old, tired, and exceedingly vain man. Smith also had responsibility for the entire district of the Upper Arkansas, so Custer assumed that day-to-day command of the Seventh would fall to him. That was ideal for making the regiment his own, in spirit if not in fact.

He didn't regard the Seventh as a final stopping point, however. Politicians were already promoting Grant as a candidate for President, and Libbie Custer had focused her husband's eye on that same high office. He was fascinated, but he and Libbie agreed that he needed some spectacular military achievement to propel him to eminence again. Meantime, he could polish his reputation by making this swing with Johnson. Or so he'd thought at the beginning; now the trip was turning out quite badly.

Custer's long wavy curls bounced on his shoulders and his glance leaped ahead to the open doors of a parlor. He spied Secretary Welles, Admiral Farragut, and other dignitaries. Grant had hurried on to Detroit, pleading indisposition. Privately Custer believed the indisposition came from a bottle—or possibly from rumors of trouble in Cleveland.

The twenty-seven-year-old soldier hoped the rumors were false. Ohio was his native state, and he'd gotten behind Johnson because he always liked Southerners, even when he fought them. He'd flatly refused a command in one of the new colored regiments, the Ninth, and he believed that if the Republican Party could thrive only with the votes of ex-slaves, it should die.

Nearing the parlor doors, Custer said to Seward, "Do you think the President should be cautioned again, Mr. Secretary? Reminded of Senator Doolittle's warning?" In a confidential memo, Doolittle had said that Johnson's enemies never gained advantage from his written opinions, only from his spontaneous answers to questions or heckling.

"I do, George. I'll take care of it," Seward said.

They entered the parlor. Fashionably dressed men and women surrounded the President and a young woman who resembled him—Mrs. Martha Patterson, his daughter. She traveled as Johnson's hostess because his wife, Eliza, was an invalid.

While Seward slipped in close to the President, Custer circled to the French windows. He studied the crowd below. About three hundred and growing, he estimated. He listened to its communal voice. Noisy, but not particularly cheerful. People at the depot had laughed a lot.

He stepped into the center of the balcony doorway. As he expected, it got a reaction.

"There's Custer!"

That produced some whistles and applause. He started to wave, but checked when he heard booing. His normally ruddy face darkened and he quickly stepped back into the parlor. Perhaps he ought to leave town, as Grant had.

Libbie swooped into the room, drawing attention as she always did. What a lovely creature he'd married, he thought, going to her. Vivid dark eyes, full bosom, the kind of tiny waist other women envied.

She took his arm and whispered, "How is the crowd, Autie?"

"Not friendly. If he does anything more than thank them, he's a fool."

Smiling, he led his wife to the large group. "Mr. President," he said, with warmth. "Good evening."

The crowd in St. Clair Street was growing impatient. Chinese lanterns across the front of the Kennard Hotel cast a sickly pale light on the upturned faces. Ugly faces, many of them, revealing the ugly tempers beneath.

A man at the back of the crowd observed the people carefully. He wore a shabby overcoat and a Union campaign hat with the crossed metal cannon of the artillery. Another man slipped up beside him. "Everyone's in place," the second man said.

"Good. I trust they know what to do."

"I went over it 'fore I paid them."

Secretary Seward appeared on the balcony and introduced the President. The stocky, swarthy Andrew Johnson walked out and raised his hands to acknowledge the scanty applause.

"My friends and constituents, thank you for your generous welcome to Cleveland. It is not my intention to make a speech—"

The man in the campaign hat smirked. The idiot nearly always said that, throwing his audiences an obvious cue. One of the hired men took it. *"Then don't."*

Laughter. Clapping. Johnson gripped the balcony rail. "You

hecklers seem to follow me everywhere. At least have the courtesy—"

"Where's Grant?"

"I regret that General Grant is unable to appear with me. He—" Groans covered the rest.

"Why don't you want colored men to vote in Dixie?" someone yelled.

Seward touched Johnson's sleeve to caution him. The President pulled his arm away. "Cast the mote from your own eye before you worry about your neighbor's," he cried. "Let your own Negroes vote here in Ohio before you campaign to extend the franchise down South."

The voices began a crescendo from various points in the crowd:

"You're spineless."

"Prison's too good for Jeff Davis!"

"Hang him. *Hang him!*"

Johnson exploded. "Why don't you hang Ben Wade?" Loud booing, which only goaded the President. "Why don't you hang Wendell Phillips and Thad Stevens while you're at it? I tell you this. I have been fighting traitors in the South and I am prepared to fight them in the North."

"You're the traitor," someone cried over the booing and hissing. "You and your National Union Party. Traitors!"

The taunt enraged the President. He shook a finger at the mob. "Show yourself, whoever said that. No, of course you won't. If ever you shoot someone, you'll do it in the dark, from behind."

A tumult of oaths and boos greeted that. Johnson roared over it, his temper irrevocably lost:

"The Congress has done this. The Congress has poisoned your minds against me while failing to do anything of its own to restore the Union. Instead, they divide the American people, conqueror against conquered, Republican against Democrat, white against black. Had Abraham Lincoln lived, he too would be suffering the vicious enmity of the power-crazed Radical clique—" Frantic, Seward kept trying to pull him inside. "—the merchants of hatred who now control our House and Senate, and seek to intimidate and control me."

"Liar!" someone screamed. Johnson's jaw worked, but no

one could hear him over the mounting roar. He shook a fist. "Liar, liar," the chant began, louder at each utterance.

At the back of the crowd, the man in the Union campaign hat, who had hired and planted people on instructions from an intermediary, allowed himself a smile. The plan had worked perfectly. Johnson was in a fury, and the reporters would have every word of the debacle on the telegraph wire by midnight. Johnson foolishly thought he could attack Wade with impunity. The man in the campaign hat was sure the senator had arranged and paid for the disruption, though of course there was no provable link. That was the reason for intermediaries.

"Liar! Liar! Liar! Liar!"

The roar was a sweet sound. It meant a generous bonus. The man in the campaign hat walked rapidly away from the chanting mob. At the telegraph window of the railway station, he picked up a blank and a stubby pencil and began to block out the message announcing his success to the intermediary who had hired him. On the first line he printed MR. S. HAZARD, WASHINGTON, D.C.

> . . . *It appears Mr. Johnson's "swing around the circle" is ending in disaster. How sad and strange that this prostrate land is being fought over, savagely, as a great prize. One war has only yielded to another.*
>
> . . . *Another attempt on the school last night. In bad weather its windows are covered by shutters. We cannot afford glass. Whoever did the deed was careless about noise while tearing shutters off. The evening was still, and the sound carried to Andy's cottage. He ran there and laid hands on the malefactor in the dark. The man felled him with hard blows and fled. Andy never saw his face.*
>
> *Do not know who to suspect. The white-trash squatters near Summerton? Mr. Gettys, the man of genteel poverty? That dancing master who fancies himself an aristocrat? Among possible suspects, we seem to have all the white classes represented* . . .

From the pines of South Carolina came turpentine, shipped out of Charleston in kegs. Most of the black stevedores carried but one at a time up the plank to whatever steamer they were loading. Des LaMotte, reduced to their level because there were still no fine families to employ him, carried two.

He worked in gentleman's linen breeches, soiled and torn. He balanced a keg on each shoulder. When he first tried it, the rims left red welts that later bled. Now a ridge of scar tissue had toughened both shoulders.

He detested the work, and all those nameless, faceless Negrophiles in the North who had forced him into it. Yet he took a certain crazed pride in doing more, carrying more, than the strongest buck. He soon became a figure of note on the Charleston docks, an immense white man with bulging arm muscles and the neatly tended chin beard of a rich planter.

He refused to speak to any of the black stevedores unless some circumstance of the job required it. On his second day, he'd almost knocked down a darky who approached him about joining a new Longshoremen's Protective Association. The man opened his appeal with remarks about a burial aid fund, so much contributed each week to guarantee that funeral expenses would be met when necessary.

When Des heard that, his mind flashed white. He quelled his murderous impulses but couldn't banish them. How could the ignorant African understand the depth and subtlety of Des's affection for his wife, Sally Sue, or his commander, Ferris Brixham? Those were the only funerals Des cared about, funerals enshrined in memory.

The incident left him shaken, because he'd come close to killing the stevedore. How long until he really turned on one of them? He realized that by working among freed Negroes, he was playing a dangerous game with his own life. Somehow he didn't care.

In the hot sunshine of a Carolina autumn that was more like summer, he sweated rivers of salt sweat as he labored up the plank of the coastal steamer *Sequoiah* again and yet again, muscles twisting like ropes under his raw-burned skin. He allowed none of his pain to show on his face.

More than pain and the tiny Low Country gnats deviled him this morning. He'd received a note from Gettys. It said that Captain Jolly, the trash they planned to employ to pull the trigger on Madeline Main, had filled himself with stolen corn whiskey, then gone off to try to wreck the school.

Idiot, Des thought, simmering. He heaved a keg to his right shoulder, and then another to his left. His knees buckled a little as he absorbed the weight.

He was as impatient as ever to see the Mains brought down, starting with Colonel Orry Main's widow. He didn't want to hang for the crime, though. And Mr. Cooper Main of Tradd Street, while having no truck with the occupying soldiers, had quite enough influence to turn the soldiers in pursuit of Des if he grew suspicious.

So he had been lying low all these weeks, awaiting a suitable pretext. He believed a nigger uprising inevitable. Some hot night, inflamed by spiritous liquors and the agents of the Yankee government, the freedmen would go wild. There would be arson, rapine, hell to pay for any man with white skin. Such an outbreak was the sort of screen he needed.

And now Jolly had drawn attention to himself, and to Mont Royal. Jolly was accustomed to doing whatever he pleased, terrorizing both whites and niggers in the Ashley district. Well, he wouldn't do as he pleased with the Main woman. Des had already sent off a reply to Gettys demanding that Jolly be restrained until ordered to act.

Groaning and sweating, Des bent his back and struggled up the plank step by painful step. A trio of elegant young ladies, one of whom, Miss Leamington of Leamington Hall, had been a pupil, came promenading along the crowded quay under their parasols. Threadbare dresses told of their poverty, but the easy arrogance of their class—something understood by Des, and even shared—showed in their amused looks at the stevedores and their lively chat.

Miss Leamington stopped suddenly. "Dear me. Is that—?" Des hunched to hide his head behind a cask. "No, it couldn't be."

"What, Felicity? What couldn't be?"

"You see that white man carrying kegs like a nigger? For a moment I thought he was my old dancing master, Mr. LaMotte. But Mr. LaMotte's a white man through and through. He would never demean himself that way."

The young ladies passed on without glancing back. Who cared to waste a second look on dirt?

That was Friday. All night the memory of Miss Leamington's scorn kept Des awake. He drifted to sleep on his sodden pallet around four, waking several hours late for work. He dressed without eating and hurried toward the docks, hearing the blare of a small band on Meeting Street.

When he reached Meeting, he was prevented from crossing by a parade. He saw niggers marching in formation, each man wearing a frock coat of white flannel with dark-blue facings and matching white trousers. They were festive, waving and chatting with people in the mixed crowd that had turned out to watch. At the head of the parade, two men carried a banner.

CHARLESTOWNE VOL. FIRE CO.
Number 2
"BLACK OPAL"

Des stood in the third row of the crowd, glaring as the firemen passed. Behind the marchers, horses decorated with flowers pulled two pumping units. Small American flags were tied to the burnished brass rails of the pumpers. Des's hands knotted at his sides. All that black skin, those Yankee flags—it was almost more than he could tolerate.

A shiny-cheeked, strapping buck waved to someone at Des's left. "How'd you do, Miss Sally? Fine morning."

Des turned to look. The name Sally resonated in his head with sharp echoes. He saw a fat, trashy girl waving a hanky at the fireman, who grinned at her as if he wanted to stroll right over and lift her skirts.

Miss Sally was a white girl. She waved and waved her hanky, taking notice of the nigger, demeaning herself, her race. Des felt as if the blood would burst his temples.

A small five-piece marching band, part of the fire company, had been counting cadence with drumsticks clacked together. Now the brasses struck up "Hail, Columbia!" and the white slut beamed so broadly at the fireman, he blew her a kiss.

Which she returned.

Des's huge hands flew up, one fastening on a shoulder at his left, one at his right. He parted the human wall. Someone protested, hurt, as he lunged into the street.

Then his mind turned to flame, and he remembered nothing.

Col. Munro here, inspecting the school and complaining about duplicate and triplicate reports he must file over "out-

rages." He left two young corporals, charming and friendly Maine boys, to guard the school for a few days. One said he wants to settle in Carolina, he finds the climate and people so winning.

Before Munro marched back to town, he issued a gloomy warning, which I quote as best I can recall it. "I have now been in the Palmetto State long enough to understand something of Southern feelings. So far as my observation goes, I do not find the white people hostile to the Negro as a Negro. They like him in most instances. But when he threatens them as a possible office holder, juror, voter, political and social equal, he goes too far. Freedom's not the issue, but equality. Any persons or institutions promoting that are the enemy."

"Perhaps so," I said. "But Prudence and I will keep the school open."

"Then I predict you will keep having trouble," he said. "Someday it will be of a magnitude that neither luck nor courage will overcome."

. . . Cooper writes that D. LaMotte is jailed. On Saturday he attacked a colored vol. fireman with no apparent provocation, and the authorities arrested him. C. said he has lately been skeptical of LaMotte's willingness to carry out his threats. He is no longer skeptical. For some while, however, we are, to use C.'s word, "reprieved."

23

The Cheyenne's rifle shot blew out the left eye of Wooden Foot's horse. Amid blood and animal bellowing, the trader tumbled into the wind-whipped grass. Charles was already dismounted. He grabbed his Spencer and slapped Satan to send him trotting away. Boy, upset by the sudden attack, vainly tried to control the pack mules from horseback.

"Get down, get off your horse," Charles shouted. The Cheyennes rushed their ponies up the rise. A bullet snapped Charles's hat brim; the hat sailed away. He yelled at Boy again but the howls of the Indians and the bray of the mules competed. But after a few seconds, Boy understood the look on Charles's face and slipped clumsily to the ground.

Wooden Foot knelt and shot at the Cheyennes nearing the top of the rise. He missed. Charles fired as the brave next to Scar flung a feathered lance. Charles dodged it. The Indian took Charles's bullet, blasted off his pony.

Everything was noise and confusion. A few miles west, lightning sizzled down from approaching storm clouds and struck the dry prairie. The grass smoked and sparked. Boiling, tumbling, the black clouds sped on toward the Cheyennes and the embattled traders.

Boy cried out. Charles saw him stagger, clutching a reddened sleeve. A lance had grazed him. Tears of pain and bewilderment rolled down his face.

Wooden Foot shouted, "Behind you, Charlie," and fired his long gun almost simultaneously. Charles pivoted and saw a mounted Cheyenne about to hammer him with a stone-headed war club. Charles shot at the red-painted face, but not soon enough to stop the blow. The club pounded his shoulder with an impact that drove him sideways. The Cheyenne sagged from his pony, his face a sheet of blood.

The storm clouds passed over like a lid closing on the world. Thunder rolled. Lightning glittered. On the wind from the west, Charles smelled smoke. He saw Scar jabbing at Wooden Foot with his lance, from horseback.

The Cheyennes crowded their ponies in close, though with less zeal since a couple of their own had fallen. Wooden Foot dodged back; Scar's thrust missed. He thrust again. The trader gripped his rifle with both hands and used it like a staff to deflect the lance. His face was flushed.

Charles levered a round into the Spencer, aimed at Scar, and pulled the trigger. The rifle jammed.

Another Cheyenne rode by and lanced Charles's right arm. A rush of blood followed the hot pain. He dropped the Spencer, yanked out his Bowie, and drove the blade into the Indian's side. The Indian screamed and jerked forward over his pony's neck. The pony raced away, taking the Indian and the protruding steel too.

Determined to finish Wooden Foot, Scar worked his pony in again. Wooden Foot blocked his thrusts expertly with his rifle. Scar's face showed his frustration. The struggle was taking a toll on Wooden Foot, though. His cheeks were dark as plums.

Charles found himself momentarily free of adversaries. Then he saw why. Three Cheyennes were riding down on the mules and Boy. Weeping, the youngster struck at them feebly, as if swatting flies. One brave jumped down and grabbed Boy. Fen leaped from concealment in the grass as if sprung. The collie's jaws closed on the Cheyenne's forearm. Another Indian beat at the dog with the butt of his trade rifle.

Amid the buffeting of the gale wind, the white flashing of the lightning, Wooden Foot uttered a strange choked cry. Drawing his Colt and dodging as a Cheyenne shot at him, Charles saw his partner lurch sideways in the high grass. Wooden Foot gasped, as if he couldn't get air. He plucked the front of his beaded shirt as if to tear something out.

Charles remembered seeing Wooden Foot's face flushed the same way before. *"It ain't nothing—"* But it was: a heart seizure, brought on by the enormous strain of the attack.

Scar had his hatchet in hand, raised high. Charles fired. The prancing of Scar's pony caused the bullet to miss the target and

ping the hatchet blade. Charles jumped in front of Wooden Foot
to shoot again. Scar quickly trotted away down the rise, bent low
over his pony.

Blood leaked from Charles's wound. He yelled in frustration, a wordless raw cry of rage, because two things demanded
attention at once: Wooden Foot, kneading his shirt with both
hands and trying to get air in his lungs, and three dismounted
Cheyennes who were dragging Boy out of sight beyond another
part of the rise. Fen chased after them, foam flying from his jaws.
Wooden Foot's fingers clawed beads loose from his shirt. They
sparkled and winked in the lightning glare.

Charles couldn't help both of them. He chose the one visibly
near and in peril of instant death.

Wooden Foot swayed backward. Charles caught him with
his left hand while firing at the nearest Cheyenne with his right.
Because of his wound, his gun arm throbbed and shook. His
bullet sped yards wide of the target.

The Cheyennes were going to finish them, so all Charles
could do was go out fighting. He knelt and worked his knee
under his partner's sagging back. The trader braced there, his
eyes wide, his limp hands falling away from his shirt. Helpless,
Charles watched the color leach from his face.

Wooden Foot recognized his partner. He tried to touch
Charles but couldn't lift his hand. Beyond the rise, Fen abruptly
stopped barking, then yelped once.

Charles put his ear near Wooden Foot's mouth. He thought
he heard, "Thanks for all—" Bright lightning whited out everything. When he recovered his sight he almost cried. Wooden
Foot's eyes were still open but nothing lived behind them.

From over the rise the three Cheyennes appeared and recap-
tured their ponies. They trotted down toward Scar, who was
waiting at the spot where Charles had first seen the Indians.

Charles raced toward the place where Boy had disappeared.
As he ran, the storm threw bits of grass and particles of dirt into
his eyes. When Scar saw Charles move away from Wooden Foot's
body, he signaled his remaining cohorts to ride toward it.

Charles passed two fallen pack mules bleeding to death from
bullet wounds. Lightning blazed. The ground rocked under him.
He sensed rather than saw a fence of fire spring up behind him,
where lightning had struck again. "Boy?" he shouted, struggling
up the rise on legs shaking with weakness. "Boy, answer me."

The lightning answered, a scorching sizzling swordstroke straight down into the hollow between rises, the place the three dismounted Cheyennes had just quitted. Grass smoked, glowed orange, then burst into flame. Godamighty, the end of the world, Charles thought as he stumbled down the slope toward a dry stream bed. On the near side, trampled grass glistened wet and black. Amidst that blood lay something as shapeless as a potato sack.

Over the rise behind him, flames six feet high burned in a rampart of scarlet, orange, white. The rampart spread forward and backward and sideways simultaneously. Once in Texas he'd seen a similar prairie fire. It destroyed forty square miles.

He reached the shapeless thing and gazed down, driven past feeling by shock. Boy lay with his sadly swollen head resting in the dry stream bed. A blade had split him open from throat to groin. From the chest cavity already swarming with flies protruded the remains of Fen. A leg, the bone visible in bloody fur; part of the collie's snout and skull, including an eye. Other pieces were strewn on the glistening grass.

Charles stared at the butchery no more than five seconds, but it might as well have been a century. Finally he turned and started back up the rise and the fire rampart behind it. Wooden Foot's dead, Boy's dead, he thought. I'll go next but I've got to take that scarred bastard with me.

From the rise he saw Scar and five others sitting their ponies some distance away, appearing and disappearing behind the blowing smoke. The Cheyennes had shifted slightly to the south of their original position and despite the smoke, Charles recognized something new on their faces: apprehension; or at least doubt. The fire had advanced nearly halfway up the rise where the Jackson Trading Company had made its futile stand.

Sweat dripping from his face, he stumbled back to the place he'd left Wooden Foot. It's Sharpsburg all over again, he thought. It's Northern Virginia all over again.

Behind fuming smoke, Scar smiled. Charles wondered about that as he staggered to Wooden Foot's corpse. Looking down, he choked.

His partner's pale body lay denuded of clothing. A red hole between the legs crawled with flies. Bloody genitals had been forced into Wooden Foot's mouth. On his eyes the Cheyennes had poured little mounds of diamond and triangle pony beads.

The fire made them sparkle. Scar had a fine touch when it came to barbarity.

"You bastards," Charles screamed. "You filthy, inhuman bastards."

Scar stopped smiling. Charles pointed his Colt at the Cheyenne leader, steadying it with bloody hands. Smoke thickened, hiding Scar and the others. Charles squeezed off a round. Another. Another. Until the cylinder emptied.

By then the wall of smoke and fire completely hid the Cheyennes. To reach Charles they'd have to ride through or very wide around one of the ends that kept extending north and south. Gusty wind blew his hair. The fire roaring on the slope lit his wild face as if it were noonday.

The smoke parted again. The Cheyennes were still there. Every one of Charles's shots had missed. Scar signaled the others to advance.

One Cheyenne shook his head, then another. They had no more stomach for the shouting madman on the rise protected by a wall of fire and smoke. Though they didn't understand his words, they understood the meaning of his yelling. "Come on, show me how brave you are! You killed an old man and a boy and a dog. Let's see what you can do with me!"

One of the reluctant Cheyennes shook his head again, emphatically. That displeased Scar. He grabbed the last man to shake his head. The Cheyenne knocked Scar's hand away, turned his mount, and rode off into the stormy darkness.

Four others followed in single file. Left alone, Scar gave Charles a scornful look before he joined the retreat.

"Come back, goddamn it. You yellow sons of bitches!"

The starch went out of him as the fire once more leaped high and hid them. Charles kept yelling at Scar. "You deserve to be wiped off the earth, you and your whole tribe. I'll find a way, you can count on that."

Count on that . . . count on that . . .

He turned and moved from the heat and glare. Using his wounded arm, he tried to jam his Colt into the holster. He kept missing. The gunsight ripped his pants and dug his leg so that it bled. He neither saw nor felt it. From his left hand dangled Wooden Foot's personal parfleche, which he didn't remember snatching off his partner's dead horse.

The storm front flew on eastward, miles away now. A light

rain started, not strong enough to put out the fire. Charles staggered among the dead mules to see what else he might salvage from the disaster. Two mules were still alive, unhurt. With their reins gathered in his left hand he started back toward the rise.

The fire stopped him. The great white-and-scarlet wall now curved across the main rise and around to his right, behind the continuation of the rise shielding the creek bed where Boy and Fen had died. As he watched, the fire completely engulfed the rise where Wooden Foot's body lay.

I can't even bury them.

At that, he wept tears of wrath.

By a lucky chance—his only luck of the day—Charles found his piebald about two miles northeast of the fire site. He was riding one of the two mules and leading the other. A wide strip of cloth torn from his trousers and twisted with a stick had stopped the bleeding of his right arm. The wound hurt and needed attention, but it was far from fatal.

When he came on Satan, standing head down, still as marble except for the movement of his eye, Charles changed mounts and headed on into the north, his emotions a raw mass of sorrow and outrage. At dusk he stopped to rest and camp. He built a buffalo-chip fire, then chewed some pemmican from his own parfleche. Two bites and his belly ached. Four bites, it all came up.

After the storm the sky cleared, leaving him huddled in a cold breeze under brilliant stars. Shivering, he opened Wooden Foot's parfleche. He found the paint pots and the rolled-up winter count. He untied the thong and spread it at his feet.

Although he couldn't explain the reason, something compelled him to try to finish it. He opened the pot of black, moistened the brush, dipped it in, and poised it over the pictograph history of the Jackson Trading Company's final year.

He studied the various figures Wooden Foot had painted, including the three of them in the sanctuary of the Buffalo Hat tipi. How he had misunderstood that incident. It had fooled him into believing the Cheyennes were capable of compassion. They weren't. Only the sanctity of the object, the hat, had saved the traders. The Cheyennes hated all whites, and never mind if they had reasons. They had no reasons good enough to justify the barbarity he had seen. They simply hated whites. The same way he now hated every last one of them.

His bleak face reflecting the campfire, he laboriously painted three exceedingly crude stick figures, a dog and two men. The second figure was to the right and slightly above the first, and the third similarly elevated above the second, as though all stood on an invisible stair.

Trying to conceive a way to picture the Hanging Road above the figures, he faltered. Should he paint wavy lines for the Milky Way? No. Five-pointed stars. He did one, corrected two of the points, then two others, and found himself with a solid blob instead of an open star figure.

He flung the brush into the fire, then the paints. He held the edges of the pictograph and studied each image in turn, finally purged of any impulse to cry. He still grieved, but the grief had hardened. His own life, which he'd tried so hard to reconstruct over the past winter, had been destroyed as quickly and surely as the grass in the path of the prairie fire.

Sharpsburg all over again—

Northern Virginia all over again—

Nothing changes.

Christ!

He laid the winter count on the fire and watched it burn. They want killing, I'll give them killing, he thought. I know more about it than they do. I had five hundred thousand expert teachers.

The figures on the pictograph blackened and burned while he watched, seeking to remember every fiery image.

BOOK THREE

BANDITTI

I have just returned from Fort Wallace, over the line of the
Union Pacific Railway, E.D. The Indians along the whole line
are engaged in their savage warfare. On Saturday three of our
men were killed and scalped within twenty miles of Fort
Harker . . . What can be done to end these atrocities?

JOHN D. PERRY, President of the U.P.E.D.,
to the Governor of Kansas, 1867

The Chiefs have signed it merely as a matter of form. Not
one word of the treaty was read to them . . . If war is . . .
thus commenced, who are to blame? The commissioners.

HENRY M. STANLEY, New York Tribune,
after Medicine Lodge Creek, 1867

The people of the frontier universally declare the Indians to
be at war, and the Indian commissioners and agents
pronounce them at peace, leaving us in the gap to be abused
by both parties.

Annual Report of
GENERAL WILLIAM T. SHERMAN, 1867

24

A thunderstorm swept the sky and shook the earth. On the flooded road from Leavenworth City, a horseman galloped out of the dark.

The weary sentry stepped into the rain, forcing the rider to halt. A lightning bolt etched the horseman in white. His mustache drooped and his full, tangled beard needed trimming. A poncho-style garment resembling a patchwork quilt hung from his shoulders. He clenched a cold cigar stub in his teeth.

Rain dripped from the bill of the boyish sentry's cap. "State your name and business on the post."

"Get out of my way."

"Mister, I order you to state your name and—"

Seemingly in an eyeblink, the man's hand filled with an Army Colt. With a single flowing motion he cocked and aimed it at the sentry's forehead. Another glitter of lightning revealed the man's eyes under his hat brim. The sentry saw hell in them.

Terrified, the sentry retreated against the guard box. The crotch of his long underwear felt damp suddenly. He waved. "Pass on."

The horseman was already beyond him, at the gallop.

The rain beat on the roof. Jack Duncan poured brandy. Charles accepted his drink without a word. The brigadier didn't like that, or the surprise visitor's filthy appearance, or the haunted fatigue shadows ringing his eyes. Charles had stunned Duncan first by arriving at half past one in the morning, second by announcing that he wanted to join the Army.

"I thought you'd had enough."

"No." Charles flung his head back and swallowed all the brandy.

"Well, Charles Main can't enlist. Neither can Charles May, late of Jefferson Barracks."

"I'll use another name."

"Charles, calm down. You're almost raving. What brought this on?"

He slammed his empty glass on a packing box that served as a table. "Adolphus Jackson pulled me through one of the worst years of my life. He taught me more plains craft than I could quote to you in a week. I'm going to punish the bastards who butchered him."

Duncan's face, puffy with tiredness, showed his disapproval. He pulled his old dressing gown together and retied the sash, pacing past the sheet-iron stove, cold now. "I don't blame you for bearing a grudge for what the Cheyennes did. But I don't think it's an ideal motive for—"

"It's how I feel," Charles interrupted. "Just tell me if I have a chance."

His loud voice roused Maureen. From behind the door of her room she made a sleepy inquiry. With the gentleness of an attentive spouse, the brigadier said, "Go to sleep. Nothing's wrong." Charles stared at the closed door, reminded of Willa's staying here.

"A slim chance, no more," Duncan said in answer to his question. "Do you know the name Grierson?"

"I know Grierson's Sixth Illinois Cavalry. They rode six hundred miles in sixteen days inside the Confederacy to pull Pemberton away while Grant crossed the Mississippi below Vicksburg. That ride was worthy of Jeb Stuart or Wade Hampton. If it's the same Grierson, he was good enough to be on our side."

It pleased Duncan to see Charles show a trace of sardonic humor. "It's the same Grierson. He turned into a damn fine cavalryman for a small-town music teacher scared of horses."

"Scared of—?" Charles couldn't believe it.

"True. A pony kicked him when he was eight. He still bears the scar." Duncan touched his right cheek. "Grierson arrived day before yesterday, to await his recruits for his new regiment. It's one of those that Congress authorized in July. Grierson's desperate for good officers who can teach and lead, but nobody wants to serve in the Tenth Cavalry. The men are being recruited in New York, Philadelphia, Boston—the dregs of the urban poor. Mostly illiterate."

"The Army's full of illiterates."

"Not like these. Grierson's men will all be black."

That gave Charles pause. He helped himself to more brandy, thinking hard.

Duncan explained that a Ninth Cavalry Regiment was being raised in Phil Sheridan's Division of the Gulf; Sherman's division would get the Tenth. "Grierson told me the recruiters have been able to sign up only one private so far. The War Department insists on white officers, well qualified, but Union veterans who want a commission don't want one in the Tenth. You know George Custer?"

"I do. I went against him for a minute at Brandy Station. They say he's a glory-seeking peacock, but he surely won battles."

"Custer is anxious to get back into uniform but even so, he wouldn't touch a commission in the Ninth. He's typical. The soldiers on the Union side fought for the colored man, I suppose, but by and large they don't like him or want anything more to do with him. Grierson's an exception. Quite an idealist."

"What would it take for me to get into the Tenth?"

"More than just the desire. Wartime experience. Examination by a special review board. And you'd need a Presidential pardon. Not as Charles Main, either. Charles Main graduated from the Military Academy. But I wouldn't expect someone like you to be willing to command Negroes."

"If they're any good, why not? I know black people a hell of a lot better than most Yankees do."

"These will be Northern black men. They'll hear your accent first thing. They won't like it."

"I can deal with that."

"Think carefully before you say that. Go forward now and you're off the precipice. No changing your mind—"

"God damn it, I'll command men whose skins are blue if they can kill Indians. What are my chances?"

Duncan thought about it, staring through the flawed glass of his parlor window at the dismal rain. "About even. If Grierson would take you, he could help smooth your way with General Hancock at Division. So could I."

"Could I get a pardon?"

"If you lie about your rank as a scout for Hampton. Scale it down. Say you were an irregular. Are there records to dispute that?"

"Probably not. Most burned up in Richmond, they say."

"Then you should be all right. A pardon will require a different name, and the services of a broker. That'll cost five hundred dollars or so."

Charles uttered a defeated obscenity and sat back, his stark face lighted on one side by the guttering flame of a lamp almost out of oil.

"I'll put up the money," the brigadier said. "I know of a top pardon broker, too. Washington lawyer named Dills. He hand-carries applications to the Clerk of Pardons and the President." A pause. "I still have reservations, Charles. I know you're a fine soldier. But you're going back for the wrong reason."

"When can I see Grierson?"

"Tomorrow, I suppose." Duncan cleared his throat, then sniffed with unmistakable meaning. "After you bathe."

Far away, the storm rumbled. Charles smiled. It reminded Duncan of the grimace of a fleshless skull.

The Tenth Cavalry had temporary offices in one of the frame buildings housing Department of the Missouri headquarters, on the east side of the parade ground. A middle-aged captain hunched behind the desk with the wary air of a man defending a fortification. Over a wide down-curving mouth drooped a large pointed dragoon's mustache, mostly white.

"May I see him, Ike?"

"Think so, General Duncan." The captain knocked and stepped into the inner office.

Tilting his head toward the closed door, Duncan said to Charles, "Ike's been in the regulars twenty years. Tough bird. Down at Sabine Crossroads in '64, he helped clear a wagon train blocking the retreat road when Dick Taylor turned back Nate Banks. He was decorated. Couple of months later he was riding for A. J. Smith when old Smitty repulsed Forrest at Tupelo. That action earned him a field commission."

The captain returned, leaving the door open. The brigadier said, "This is my son-in-law, Charles." They'd already decided he should keep that part of his name. "Captain Isaac Newton Barnes. Regimental adjutant."

"Acting adjutant," Barnes said in a pointed way.

While Duncan went in and shut the door, Charles said, "Pleasure, sir." It paid to be respectful to an adjutant; he usually exercised more power than the commanding officer.

Ike Barnes scowled at the litter of orders, files and reports on his desk. In profile he resembled an S—round shoulders, concave lower back, sizable paunch. His right eye cocked slightly.

"I hate this job," he said, sitting. "I'm a horse soldier, not a damn clerk. I'll get C Company as soon as the colonel finds somebody else stupid enough to get stuck shuffling all these damn papers."

A breathless sergeant dashed in. "Captain! Two colored boys on the steamboat landing. They're yours."

"Damn it to hell, Sergeant, you know better than to say colored within a mile of this office. The colonel will not tolerate his regiment being designated the way they were in the war. This is not the Tenth Colored Cavalry, it's the Tenth Cavalry. Excuse me," he snapped at Charles as he followed the noncom out. His formidable paunch seemed to advance separately, like some kind of honor guard. Charles actually managed a smile.

In ten minutes Duncan came out. "He's interested. This time tell the truth, and see if you can work things out." He punched Charles's shoulder. "Luck."

Duncan marched toward the outer door and Charles moved to the inner one. As he passed through, Duncan's image of a man stepping off a precipice flashed through his head.

Colonel Benjamin F. Grierson's huge beard and bold nose lent him a piratical air, enhanced by the facial scar. After inviting Charles to sit, he placed a fresh sheet of paper on his desk near a small gold case holding an ambrotype in an oval matte. Charles presumed the woman to be Grierson's wife.

"I'll be straightforward, Mr. Main. Your interest in the Tenth raises more than one problem. Before we go into them, I'd like to know why you're here. Jack told you that scores of capable officers in this army detest the idea of Negro regiments."

"He did, sir. I'm here because I'm a soldier, and that's all I am. The Southern Cheyennes killed my partner and his nephew a couple of months ago—"

"So Jack said. I'm sorry."

"Thank you. I want to make up for what the Cheyennes did—"

"Not in my regiment, sir," Grierson said, with a touch of ire. "The Tenth won't formulate policy, just carry it out. Our mission from General Sherman is to bolster the military presence on the Plains. It is defensive only. We're to protect the settlers, the travel routes, the railroad construction crews. We are not to attack unless attacked first."

"Sir, I'm sorry if I said—"

"Hear me out, sir. Before we can carry out our mission, we must teach city men to march, ride, shoot, and behave in a military manner. I'm talking about unlettered men, Mr. Main—porters, waiters, teamsters. Black men who've never before had a chance at a decent career. I fully intend to turn such men into superior soldiers that any commander would be proud to lead. I will do it the way I taught the scales to my beginning music pupils in Illinois. With rigid discipline and constant and relentless drill. That will be the responsibility of my officers. They will have no time for personal vendettas."

"I apologize for my remark, sir. I understand what you're saying."

"Good," Grierson said. "Otherwise I'd not waste time on you." Eyeing Charles in a speculative way, he added, "No, that's dishonest. I am not interviewing you completely by choice, but rather, because of the dire need I already mentioned. I confess, however, to being somewhat reluctant to recruit a Southerner."

Despite a spurt of resentment, Charles kept still.

"You see, Mr. Main, I have a peculiar vision of this country. Peculiar in that it is apparently not shared by the thousands of brevet colonels and generals chasing after a very few low-rank line commissions. I believe in the exact words of Mr. Jefferson's declaration that all men are created equal, if not in mind and body and circumstance, then most assuredly in opportunity. I believe we fought the war, whether we realize it or not, in order to extend that vision to the black race. I do know it isn't a popular idea. Many of my fellow officers accuse me of—their words—

niggering them to death. So be it. I believe the vision must prevail first of all in this new regiment. If the regiment won't work, then the Army doesn't work, America doesn't work, nothing works. So my officers must cheerfully bear the extra burden of standing between their men and the extreme hostility and prejudice rampant in the Army."

His stare was unwavering. "You're from South Carolina. I don't care about that *unless* it means you can't live by my rules. If you can't, I don't want you."

Tense now, fearing rejection, Charles said, "I can, sir."

"You can deal honestly, squarely, with Negro soldiers?"

"I got along well with blacks on the plantation where I was raised."

The wrong tack again. Grierson waved with bitter scorn. "Bondsmen, Mr. Main. Slaves. Immaterial here."

Charles's voice hardened a little. "Let me put it another way, sir. No, I won't get along with every last man." Grierson started to retort, but Charles kept on. "I didn't get along with all of the white men in the Wade Hampton Legion or the Second Cavalry in Texas. Every outfit has its share of idiots and berrypickers. I always warned that kind of man once, but only once. If he kept on, I locked him up. If he still kept on, I got him discharged. I'd behave the same way in the Tenth." He locked his gaze with Grierson's. "Like a professional."

Silence. Grierson stared. Suddenly, between the bushy mustache and luxuriant beard, he flashed a smile.

"A good answer. A soldier's answer. I accept it. Men of the Tenth will be judged on merit, nothing else."

"Yes, sir," Charles said, though his prompt answer made him a little uneasy. He was quick to speak because he wanted to join a regiment, any regiment, and this one was desperate for officers. But he had reservations about the ability of city blacks to become good soldiers—exactly the same reservations he'd had about the white flotsam he'd found at Jefferson Barracks. The bias probably came from his West Point training, but there it was.

Grierson leaned forward. "Mr. Main, I detest liars and cheats and am about to qualify myself as both. You will be required to do the same when the special review board examines you. At least one member, Captain Krug, will bore in hard. He hates every man who wore Confederate gray. His younger brother perished in Andersonville prison."

Charles nodded, filing the name away.

"Now. Particulars." Grierson inked his pen. "You've applied for pardon?"

"The letter will be written today."

"I know about your experience at Jefferson Barracks. What name shall we try this time?"

"I thought it should be something familiar again, so I could answer to it naturally. Charles August. The name August has some family connections."

"August. Good." The pen scratched. "What was your highest rank in Hampton's scouts?"

"Major."

Grierson wrote, *None—irregular status (scout)*.

"It's best that we forget you ever saw West Point. How many Academy men would recognize you now, do you think?"

"Any of them who were there when I was, I suppose. That's how I was discovered at Jefferson Barracks."

"Who identified you?"

"A Captain Venable."

"Harry Venable? I know him. Excellent cavalryman but a pompous little monster. Well, in regard to former classmates you might encounter, we'll just have to chance it. Next point. My officers are supposed to have two years of field experience."

"I do. With the Second Cavalry in Texas."

Dryly, Grierson said, "That was before you changed sides. Let's forget about Texas. The subject might lead someone back to the Academy." Charles watched the scratchy pen move. *Prev. exp. — 4 yrs. vols.*

They talked for another hour. At the end Grierson knew a lot about Charles's personal life. He knew about Orry, the surrogate father; about Charles's trouble with Elkanah Bent; about the horrifying impact of Sharpsburg, the loss of Augusta Barclay, the frantic search for their son. Finally, Grierson put his notes away and shook Charles's hand. It struck Charles as more ceremonial than friendly. The colonel was still reserving judgment.

"My adjutant will tell you how to prepare for the written test. You should have no trouble with it. The review board is another matter." Grierson walked him to the door, smoothing his beard. "Do something about your appearance. It works against you. Either trim the beard or get rid of it."

"Yes, sir." He stressed the second word, the old West Point way, then snapped his right hand outward in his best cadet salute. Grierson returned it and dismissed him.

After the door closed, Grierson went back to the desk. He gazed at the ambrotype for a moment or so, then started a letter.

Dearest Alice,

I may have got a good one today. A former reb who wants to exterminate the hostiles. If I get him past the examiners, and harness his wrathful impulses, the regiment may benefit, for I have yet to meet a quality officer who did not have some demon driving him . . .

In front of the pocket mirror Duncan loaned him, Charles gazed at his soaped face. He hadn't shaved in months. The dangerous edge he'd honed on Duncan's razor pulled and tore when he attacked his beard.

He thought of Grierson's warning about the review board as he pulled the razor down with reckless haste. The edge bit through his beard to rasp the skin. As he stroked, sections of his beard fell around the basin. A new, almost unfamiliar face appeared. More lines. More of time's markings.

"Ahh!" He grabbed a towel and pressed it to his bleeding jaw. When the gash clotted a little, he flung the towel down and attacked the other side of his face. Thinking of Wooden Foot, Boy, Fen, he cut himself deeply a second time, but scarcely felt it.

In general, the relation of the Anglo-Saxon race with inferior races, all the world over, is a most unpleasant matter to contemplate. Whether it is with the Hindoos, or the Australians, or Jamaicans, or on this side with California Chinese, or Negroes, or Indians, the uniform habit and tendency of this "imperial race" is to crush the weak. . . .The dealings of this nation toward the Indians form one of the most disgraceful chapters in modern history. We first drive them from their land, and then suffer them to be poisoned with our diseases and debauched by our vices. They are steadily driven back to the region of the buffalo, and now even in the wild mountains bordering on that region, the miners are destroying the game and breaking up the solitude on which their support as hunters depends. . . .

Editorial comment,
The New York Times

25

Brigadier Duncan telegraphed the pardon request to the attorney, Dills, and transferred funds to a Washington bank. He dispatched a carefully worded letter to General Sherman at Division, stressing Grierson's need for qualified officers and the outstanding ability of one Charles August. Charles wondered how Sherman would react if he knew "August" was the unkempt trader he'd met on the prairie.

Charles took a room in Leavenworth City but returned to the post every day, trying to get reacquainted with little Gus. The boy would be two in December. He was walking, talking in rudimentary sentences, and still had a certain reserve in the presence of the tall, gaunt man who took him for walks and called himself Pa.

Maureen usually went along on the walks. She continued to disapprove of Charles as a parent—he was, among other things, merely a man—but since his return, he had shown her a new and unpleasant side of his personality. He showed it again as the three of them came back from a stroll along the river one sparkling afternoon. Hand in hand, Charles and little Gus were marching like soldiers. The boy loved the reviews and evening retreats at Leavenworth, and he liked to imitate them. Charles obliged. The two of them moved briskly down the path ahead of Duncan's housekeeper.

A certain number of Indian men always congregated at frontier posts. These hang-around-the-forts subsisted on handouts and menial work. They spent their money for whiskey and let the whites bestow contemptuous names on them, like Sausage Nose, Lazy Man, Fat Woman.

Fat Woman, an obese Sioux in filthy old uniform pants and

blouse, appeared on the path, coming toward Charles and his son. Fat Woman stopped, blinked, and reached out to tickle the chin of the smiling boy. Charles whipped up his fist and knocked him down.

Fat Woman yelped and crawled away. Gus hung on to his father's hand, but gave him a wary, scared look. Maureen couldn't keep silent. "That poor defenseless man meant no harm, Mr. Main."

"I don't want red scum like that touching my boy."

"Fa, Fa—" Gus tugged his hand. "March."

"No." Charles yanked his hand away, then seized Gus's shoulder, forcing him along the path. "No more marching."

Later, when Charles had ridden back to Leavenworth, the housekeeper confided to Duncan as he sat soaking in his zinc bathtub. "His moods are as changeable as the weather. Some kind of demon's in him."

"He went through a hideous ordeal. Would you scrub a little lower, my dear? Ah, yes—"

"I realize he did, General." Even in bed she addressed him formally. "But if he doesn't get over it his son will despise him. Augustus is nearly terrified of him now."

"I've noticed." Duncan sighed. "I don't know what to do."

The room at Department headquarters looked west over the parade ground. Charles's table faced the undraped windows. No accident, he decided. Nor was the hour. Half past five by the loudly ticking wall clock. Blinding light streamed into his eyes, making it almost impossible to see the five men facing him at their table in front of the windows.

General Winfield Scott Hancock, U.S.M.A. 1844 and commander of the Department of the Missouri, chaired the examining board. Tall, handsome, composed, he'd greeted Charles cordially at the door and wished him well. How strange, Charles thought, to shake hands with a man who probably had shaken hands with Cousin Orry.

On Hancock's left sat General William Hoffman, commander of the Third Infantry, and of Fort Leavenworth as well. Duncan had said Hoffman loathed the idea of Negro regiments.

To the left of Hoffman sat the officer Charles feared: Captain Waldo Krug, slight, severe-looking, and bald, although he was not much older than Charles. Attached to Hoffman's staff, Krug wore the silver star of a brevet brigadier and was addressed as general. He watched Charles with unconcealed hostility.

To Hancock's right, Captain I. N. Barnes, and, completing the panel, a major named Coulter, a schoolmasterish man wearing oval spectacles. Directly to the left of Charles, a row of chairs was set up for spectators. Only Duncan and Grierson had chosen to attend.

Hancock's glance to the right and left signaled for quiet. "Gentlemen, this is the application hearing of officer candidate Charles August, who has successfully passed the written examination. With nearly perfect marks, I might add."

Krug immediately said, "General Hancock, I move to adjourn the hearing. The candidate is unfit by reason of previous service with the Confederacy."

Grumpily, Hoffman said, "Second that." He was U.S.M.A. 1829—Lee's class—an old campaigner from the Seminole and Mexican wars.

Hancock set the motion aside, saying that the candidate had shown good faith by signing the oath and applying for a pardon, as General Lee had. That made Krug explode.

"Robert Lee will *never* be pardoned, no matter how many times he applies. That's fitting for any man who betrayed his country, and I include the candidate."

The scholarly Coulter pushed his glasses down his nose. "I had the impression that hostilities stopped over a year ago, and we were all Americans again. I think we should put the war behind us and—"

"No, sir, I will not put my brother's death by starvation behind me for one moment," Krug said.

Hancock rapped the table to restore order. "Warden Wirz paid for his war crimes on the gallows. He was, and probably will be, the only Confederate officer so punished."

"I'd hang a lot more of them," Krug said, with his eye on Charles.

"Captain," Hancock said, "you will have to desist or disqualify yourself. This hearing will go forward on the basis of the candidate's qualifications."

Krug muttered something unintelligible. Hancock cleared his throat and opened Charles's file. Although it was autumn, the light beating in Charles's eyes felt fiery. He was as nervous as he'd ever been on the eve of battle; certain he'd trip up somehow.

He forced himself to think of Wooden Foot, glittering beads heaped on his eyes. His pulse slowed a little. He sat up straight, straining until his back ached.

"State your name," Hancock said.

"Charles August."

"I have before me the statement of Colonel Grierson which says you served four years with the army of the Confederacy. Please state your unit and rank."

"Scout corps, Wade Hampton Legion. That was later absorbed into larger cavalry divisions during several army reorganizations. But the scouts remained irregulars, without rank." The lie came out smoothly.

"Are there records to prove that?" Barnes asked.

"Yes, I presume, in Richmond."

"Oh, for God's sake," Krug said. "Richmond! Everybody knows the rebs didn't leave a single piece of paper in Richmond. They burned everything. We don't even know how many traitors mustered under their colors, and we never will."

Sharply, Hancock said, "Captain."

"I'm sorry, sir. I am against this. Completely and utterly against it."

Hoffman raised his hand and Hancock gave him leave to speak. Bitingly, Hoffman said to the panel, "If we can't examine the gentleman's records, he will have to supply information. I would like to know his political affiliation."

Charles was unprepared. Grierson and Duncan watched him anxiously. "Why—Democrat, sir."

"Democrat." Hoffman smiled. "Of course. Every unregenerate rebel calls himself a Democrat. Every man who murdered Union prisoners calls himself a Democrat. Every traitor who mixed dangerous compounds to blow up Northern cities or invented hellish schemes to introduce yellow fever to those cities is now merely a *Democrat.*"

Amused, Coulter said, "The general is quite familiar with the campaign oratory of Governor Morton of Indiana, I see. But that election speech you just quoted was meant for civilians, sir. Does it really have a bearing on these proceedings?"

Caught in his plagiarism, Hoffman fumed. Hancock said, "No. I, for one, think that Mr. August is being quite forthcoming. We know there are already hundreds of former Confederates in the United States Army under assumed names." Duncan's start made his wooden chair squeak. Grierson grew interested in the ceiling. "I want to ask the candidate about any military experience prior to the war. I see nothing in the file."

Charles's throat tightened. Was sweat showing on his forehead? Did the sun on his face reveal deceit? Colonel Grierson shifted his scrutiny to the brightly polished toe of his boot. Hancock frowned.

"Mr. August, our time's valuable. Answer promptly, please. What about service prior to the war?"

Charles weighed two murders against another lie and said, "None, sir."

It continued for a half hour, interrupted by an occasional angry objection from Krug or a question from Hoffman that quickly turned to Republican cant. Charles was limp, tired, perspiring heavily when Hancock excused him. He and Duncan and Grierson went out and shut the door.

"They'll approve you," Grierson predicted.

"No, they won't. I botched it."

"To the contrary. You did well. But I must say something that I've already said to Jack. If you're ever found out, I won't be able to help you. I won't compromise the regiment. It comes first. In every other circumstance you can count on me to go to the wall for you."

"Thank you, Colonel. I don't think it'll be necessary for you to worry about—"

The door to the hearing room opened. Ike Barnes, the junior man, stepped out.

"Three to two in favor of commissioning. It's conditional on War Department approval and a pardon." Beaming, Barnes stuck out his hand. "Welcome to the Tenth, Mr. August."

Charles crossed the Missouri on the ferry and rode to St. Louis in leisurely stages, savoring the tangy air and the crimson and gold of the leaves. The calendar kept Willa from making the reunion a physical one, but they slept warm in each other's arms in her bed at the New Planter's House.

When morning came, they kissed and murmured words of affection. Before he dressed, he lathered his face to shave away yesterday's stubble. He whistled while he plied the razor.

"That's very pretty," Willa called from her dressing table. "What is it?"

"This?" He whistled five notes. "Just something that came into my head last year. Whenever I think of Mont Royal, of everything that I loved before the war, I hear that tune."

"There's a piano at the theater. Would you hum it when we're there, so I can write it down for you?"

"Why, yes, of course."

And she did.

"That's my tune?" he asked, staring at the notes, which made no sense to him. She nodded. "Well, if you say so. It'll be a keepsake." He folded the paper carefully. "Maybe I can stop thinking about the past. I've found something better to take its place."

He leaned over and kissed her forehead. She closed her eyes and held his arm.

While she attended to theater business for a couple of hours, he strolled through the bustling streets. Today he wasn't at all troubled by the risk in the strengthening attachment; he was too full of excitement about the commission—an excitement Willa shared until they walked along the levee later, and he told her the reason he'd rejoined the Army. Although he spared her the obscene details, he described the demise of the Jackson Trading Company, and the hatred it had generated.

Willa had a strong reaction. But she kept it to herself, putting her feelings for him above her conscience. She'd never done that before, at least not so far as she could remember.

In her rooms that night, she showed him what she called her prize. It was the large framed photograph of the two of them taken the year before, Willa on the velvet settee with her head in the invisible clamp, Charles with his hand on her shoulder. Amused, he said they looked like figures in a waxworks. She swatted him and said she would retaliate for that by forcing a copy of the picture on him. He said he'd be glad to have it, and halfway meant it.

Over breakfast he learned something else about her. Her birthday was December 25. "Easy to memorize but hard to get anyone to celebrate with so much going on. I'm a horrid cook, but I can do a simple cake and icing. Most years, I even have to buy my own candles." He laughed.

Charles stayed in St. Louis for three more days. He attended a performance each evening. Then Brigadier Duncan summoned him back with a telegraph message. The pardon had been granted.

Willa cried when they said goodbye. She promised that she and Sam would be touring soon, and she'd find him. And love him properly, as she couldn't this time. He was in good spirits as he rode away.

A light drizzle started as Willa walked from the hotel to the theater. She was so preoccupied with Charles, she almost forgot to open her umbrella.

She knew so much about him, yet still knew so little. She sensed a coiled anger within him, an emotion quite different from last year's war-induced malaise. He had an enemy now. That was why she hadn't told him about taking the initiative and starting a local unit of the Indian Friendship Society.

There were six members. A Quaker couple, a Unitarian preacher, an elderly headmistress of a private school patronized by the children of wealthy German merchants, the theater's aging juvenile, Tim Trueblood, and herself. Charles wouldn't have liked to hear about the memorials they had already sent to Congress and the Interior Department.

She reached the theater and found the stage deserted, though she heard Sam's voice somewhere. She closed her umbrella and laid it on the prompter's table. The stage manager shot from behind a flat.

"Not there, not there! If he sees it, he'll go wild."

"That's right, I forgot. No umbrellas on the prompt table. I can't remember all the superstitions. What's he doing?"

"He's behaving a bit strangely. He's been bustling about with Prosperity's feeding dish, and now he's rehearsing in the green room."

"He does insist on doing *Hamlet.*" She and the stage manager exchanged tolerant smiles, and she followed the sound of Trump's resonant voice as it proclaimed Yorick's infinite jest and excellent fancy. She almost stumbled on a crockery bowl of milk. She saw Prosperity curled up nearby, uninterested. She frowned. The bowl smelled peculiar. She picked it up and sniffed it again.

She marched the bowl to the green room, interrupting Sam's rehearsal in front of a long mirror. Despite the lacing of his corset, his black tights couldn't hide his corpulence. He looked silly in that costume, and more so with a wilted yellow chrysanthemum pinned to the front.

"Dear girl—" he began, one thumb hooked in the eye socket of a prop skull. He lost color when Willa extended the bowl at arm's length.

"I'll feed the cat from now on, Sam. You must have mixed up the bowls. She won't touch this one." Willa passed it under her nose with a stagy sniff. "Cats don't like sour mash whiskey."

Trump almost fell in his haste to get the bowl. "It's nothing. A mere nip to brace me up today."

"And every day for a week. I've wondered why you were so excessively cheerful in the morning." She put the bowl on the table, saying sweetly, "Don't touch it."

Trump beat his breast with an aggrieved air. "Yes, my dear." He studied her from under his eyebrows, laid the skull aside, and put a fatherly arm around her. "You look unhappy. Am I the cause?"

"Not really."

"Charles has left, then."

"It's more than his leaving, Sam. He's managed a commission in the Army again."

"The Army's the right place for him. It's what he knows."

"It's the right place for the wrong reason." In a few sentences she described what had happened to Wooden Foot and Boy. By the end, Trump was pale. "He wants retribution. When he talks of it there's a blazing fury in him."

Cautiously, Trump said, "Is it the end for you two, then?"

"Oh, no." A rueful shrug. "It should be, but it's too late. I love him. I know it may bring me grief, and I can't do a thing about it. Mr. Congreve was right about love being a frailty of the mind."

She tried to smile and instead burst out crying. Sam Trump put his arms around her and tugged her in, gently patting her back with both hands while the sobs shook her.

26

Lieutenant August? Come quick."

Charles shot up from the desk. "Someone hurt?"

"Nosir," puffed the recruit. "They taken' down those tents you told us to put up an hour ago. They was ordered to take 'em down."

"What stupid noncom—?"

"It's some general. Krig?"

"Krug. Damn." He grabbed his hat. What a way to start his third day in uniform.

"With all due respect, Captain, what's going on here?"

Krug's gray eyes spiked him. "You'll address me as general."

In a weedy field a half mile outside the main gate, five black recruits, none in uniform yet, struggled to dismantle two A-frames. Tangled canvas hid the fallen poles. Red-faced, Charles pointed at the men. "Why are they striking those tents?"

The raw autumn wind snapped the elbow-length cape of Krug's overcoat. "Because I ordered it. They're to move to the ground immediately west of the steam pump."

"That field is full of standing water."

Krug jutted his jaw. "Change your tone, mister, or I'll have you up on charges. Three quarters of the men on this post would like to see you gone."

Including most of my own, Charles thought. The five recruits watched him as though he were old Salem Jones, Mont Royal's overseer before the war. Through gritted teeth he said, "The barracks assigned us—General—is infested with rats, bats, roaches—it's a damn zoo. While we fumigate it, these men need temporary quarters. Why must they move?"

"Because, August, General Hoffman rode past this morning. He doesn't like to look at nigger soldiers. He wants them out of sight when he travels to and from Leavenworth City. Is that clear enough?"

Charles recalled Grierson's warning about Army bigotry. "Sir, if you insist on this, we'll have to put down lumber to floor the tents. Build walkways—"

"No lumber. They sleep on the ground. They're soldiers, or so we've been led to believe."

"Why the hell are you so angry at me, Krug?"

"Two reasons, mister. One, I still consider you a traitor. Two, the North fought for preservation of the Union, not the glorification of darkies. General Hoffman shares that view. Now move those men."

Krug marched to his horse, mounted, and headed for the gate.

Charles approached the recruits. Slate-colored clouds filled the sky. Dead weeds rattled in the wind, and canvas flapped and snapped. The five black men stared at him with expressions ranging from stoic to sullen.

"Men, I'm sorry. Guess you'll have to move for the time being. I'll try to commandeer some lumber somewhere."

A large walnut-hued man stepped forward. Potiphar Williams, formerly a cook in a Pittsburgh hotel. He could read and write; he'd learned as an adult, in order to understand recipes and prepare menus. Charles had marked him as promising.

Williams said, "We'll hunt the wood. Sir."

"It's my responsibility to—"

"We don't need favors from a white man who rode for the rebs."

Rigid, Charles said, "You get this straight. I didn't go to war to preserve slavery, or the Confederacy, either. I went to fight for my home in South Carolina."

"Oh, yes, sir," Williams said. "My brother and his kin in North Carolina, the only home they had to fight for was the slave cabins they lived in." He turned his back. "All right, boys. Let's pick up and go where the white man tells us."

Ike Barnes, already miserable and in bad temper because of a case of piles, turned the air blue when Charles reported the incident. Grierson went to Hoffman. The general refused to rescind the order. Two of the recruits caught pneumonia from camping on the wet ground. They were sent to the post hospital, causing three white patients to walk out in protest.

The next week, a gaudy troupe of travelers appeared, bound for Fort Riley. The troupe consisted of two white women, a former slave who did the cooking, a little black jockey from Texas, four horses, including a pacer and a racing mare, and dogs: a greyhound, a white pit bull, several hunters.

"Is this a circus or the Army?" Barnes grumbled. "Whatever it is, it's a damn disgrace."

"Agreed," Grierson said. "But you notice we're here, aren't we?"

The two of them and Charles, along with two dozen more of the curious, had gathered to see the elegant young soldier who headed the troupe. As George Custer supervised the loading of his colt Phil Sheridan into a special rail car on the post spur, he shouted boisterously and cracked jokes, playing to the crowd.

Charles remembered Custer vividly from the war. He was still dandified: flowing hair, walrus mustache, bright red scarf, gold spurs. Charles said to Barnes, "I rode against him at Brandy Station. I know he fights to win, but he's too reckless to suit me. I'm thankful I'll never have to serve with him."

The fall produced a smashing Republican victory in the national and state elections. Johnson's catastrophic "Swing Around the Circle" had worked against him and for the Radicals. When Congress eventually convened, the course of Reconstruction would be in Republican hands more surely than ever.

At Fort Leavenworth, meanwhile, in spite of trouble with white men because of their prejudice, and trouble with black men because of his background, Charles again began to savor Army life. He liked the measuring of the days by bugle and trumpet, drum and fife. It had been part of his bone and blood since West Point. In his monastic cubicle in bachelor officers' quarters, some internal clock wakened him every morning at 4:30, fifteen minutes before trumpeters' assembly.

Reveille, guard mount, call for first sergeant's report, mess, fatigue, evening retreat with a formal parade in good weather—he relished every call. His favorite was 4:30 P.M. stable call. At that hour he supervised the new soldiers, many of whom found horses frightening. While trying to correct that and familiarize the men with horse furniture, Charles sneaked in some pleasurable minutes looking after Satan.

Then came some of the day's sweetest music: the gongs and triangles announcing evening mess. The music usually surpassed the fare: hash or slumgullion, baked beans or contractor's beef of dubious color and odor.

Each company of the Tenth was supposed to contain ninety-nine men. But recruits arrived so slowly, Charles wondered if Grierson would ever have a full-strength regiment. The reputation of the Tenth wasn't helped when one recruit ran off, and word reached Leavenworth about trouble in the all-black Ninth Cavalry down in San Antonio. Recruits in the Ninth had clashed with local police and started a riot. Many of them went to jail. "Fine," Grierson snorted when he heard the news. "Just what Hoffman needs to confirm his opinions."

Charles freely admitted responsibility for the desertion. The surly recruit had mistreated one of the horses. Charles had stopped it and assigned extra fatigue duty. "Sure, you *would* take the side of a nag over a nigger, you piece of Southern shit," the recruit said, and punched him.

Charles had to be pulled off the black man; they said later he was on his way to killing the recruit with his fists. Two nights later the recruit ran away. He was recognized over in City of Kansas, captured and quickly processed with a bobtail discharge. When a man got a bobtail, the section of the discharge dealing with character was snipped off. It was a lifetime mark of dishonor.

C Company was formed. Ike Barnes was the commander, and Floyd Hook, a boyish innocent, the first lieutenant. Charles took the third spot. Sometimes Barnes allowed Floyd or Charles to welcome a new man. Charles developed a little speech that was not entirely facetious.

"Welcome to your new home, sometimes called the government workhouse. In addition to learning to be an outstanding cavalryman, you can look forward to carrying bricks, painting walls, and cutting timber. It's called fatigue duty. Sometimes it's called being a brevet architect."

The black recruits never smiled. It wasn't just the word *brevet* that threw them, Charles knew. It was his accent.

Patiently, he showed each greenhorn how to roll a pair of socks and stuff it inside his shirt to save bad shoulder bruises at rifle practice. He watched over first attempts to saddle and mount horses. As soon as the recruits didn't fall off, he started revolver and rifle drill, yelling at the men to take their time, hold their pieces steady as they banged away at piles of hardtack boxes, first with their mounts walking, then trotting, then galloping.

"Steady—steady," he would shout. "The odds are that you'll never see combat more than once in your Army career. But on that day, you could live or die by this drill."

The officers became surrogate parents, protecting the newest as best they could from hazing by the old hands—an old hand being someone who had arrived the week before. One new youngster broke down and wept.

"They tol' me, go get your butter allowance from the mess. Cook'll try to keep it and spend it himself, they said. So watch out. I went to him and said, give me that butter money an' no damn argument." He beat his thighs. "They ain't any butter allowance."

"No. It's an old trick. Look, every new man's hazed. You got through it. You'll be fine."

"But now the others, they call me Butter Head."

"When you get a nickname, it shows they like you."

The recruit wiped his eyes. "That the truth?"

Charles smiled. "The truth." Members of the small officer group in the Tenth were known as Iron Ass and Friendly Floyd.

"What's your nickname, Cap'n?"

The smile grew stiff. "It's lieutenant. I don't have one."

A benefit of duty with the Tenth was the chance to see little Gus often. Charles managed to visit him almost every day for a few minutes. The boy was warming to his father, no longer so intimidated by him, because Charles's demeanor was softening.

Christmas drew near. For gifts, Charles refused to buy any of the handiwork of the hang-around-the-forts, though the quilled and beaded articles were attractive and cheap. Instead, he shopped in Leavenworth City. He bought a set of brushes for

Duncan, perfume for Maureen and Willa, a wooden horse—brightly enameled head and stick with a satin rope rein—for his son. The season brought hops, which he didn't attend, a small candlelit fir tree in Duncan's parlor, and caroling by officers and wives in the cold and starry prairie night.

Then, four days before Christmas—December 21, 1866—the Army got a present it didn't want.

Fort Phil Kearny guarded the Bozeman Trail, which led to the Montana gold fields. The fort's mere existence was provocation to the Sioux and Northern Cheyennes who claimed the land around it. War chiefs with names well known on the Plains—Red Cloud of the Sioux; Roman Nose of the Cheyennes—descended on Kearny with two thousand braves.

Bravado overcoming good sense, one William Fetterman, a captain, said he could smash through the attackers with eighty men. He claimed he could smash through the entire Sioux nation. So he took his men to guard some wagons bringing wood back to the fort, and for Christmas the Army got the Fetterman Massacre. Not one of the eighty survived.

Something unrelenting within Charles took satisfaction from the bad news. Given the massacre, and the resulting outcries for retribution, he believed the Army might move against the Southern tribes. When it did, he'd be there.

For Christmas Willa sent him a small cased ambrotype—their photograph—and a gold-stamped, leatherbound edition of *Macbeth* with a romantic inscription about the bad-luck play becoming her good luck, because it had brought them together. Accompanying the gifts was a letter full of endearments.

> *My dearest Charles,*
> *I shall strive to remember that your new-minted last name is August, and swear a vow never to speak your real one aloud, though it is very dear to me. . . .*

It went on for several paragraphs, pleasing and warming him despite his unaltered concern about entanglement. He had reason for that wariness, he was soon reminded.

> *There is much talk of the Fetterman tragedy. I pray it will not provoke wholesale retaliation. I cannot any longer hide from you that*

I have joined the local chapter of the Indian Friendship Society, which seeks to promote justice for those long victimized by white greed and deception. I enclose a small Society leaflet which I hope you will find—

At that point, he tossed the letter into Duncan's sheet-iron stove, without reading the rest.

On Christmas Day he realized he had forgotten Willa's twenty-first birthday.

27

To remedy his blunder, Charles turned to Ike Barnes's wife, Lovetta, a tiny woman who could make her voice loud as a steam whistle if necessary. Lovetta took some of Charles's pay and promised to find something a young woman would like. Two days later she brought him an Indian pouch with a shoulder thong and an intricately beaded flap. The sight of it angered him. But he thanked her and dispatched the gift to St. Louis with a note of apology.

Soon after New Year's everyone at Leavenworth began talking about General Hancock's taking the field in the spring to demonstrate in force against the Indians, perhaps even punish those responsible for the Fetterman Massacre. Grierson, meanwhile, despaired of getting his regiment to operational strength. So far the Tenth had but eighty men.

Almost all of them had to enroll in Chaplain Grimes's special classes, to learn the three R's. The low level of recruit literacy put extra burdens on the officers. They handled all the paperwork that would normally be picked up by noncoms.

Still, Charles grudgingly admitted that whatever the city boys lacked in education, they more than made up for with their enthusiasm and diligence. With few exceptions, they behaved well. Insubordination, drunkenness and petty thievery, while not altogether absent, occurred with much less frequency than among white soldiers. Charles guessed motivation had a lot to do with it. The men wanted to succeed; they'd picked the Army, not fled to it.

Motivation and performance failed to impress General Hoffman or his staff. Hoffman ordered surprise inspections of the Tenth's barracks, then cited the soldiers for dirt on the floor and

stains on the walls. Dirt blew in because doors and windows
didn't fit. Leaky roofs caused the stains. Hoffman ignored explanations and refused requests for repair materials.

The commandant's campaign against what he called "nigger
dregs" was relentless. If one of Grierson's officers tried to give a
literate recruit some responsibility, the man's reports or memo-
randa came back from headquarters marked *Sloppy* or *Incorrect.*
By Hoffman's order, the Tenth had to stand at least fifteen yards
from white units during inspection formations. When the weather
was mild enough for an evening parade, Hoffman required the
Tenth to remain at parade rest; they couldn't march with the
white troops, because Hoffman refused to review them.

Horses given to the Tenth were blown-out wrecks from the
war, some of them twelve years old. When Grierson protested,
Hoffman shrugged. "The Army's on a tight budget, Colonel. We
are required to use the arms, ammunition, and mounts already on
hand. I'd say those plugs are good enough for niggers."

"General, I respectfully request that my men not be
called—"

"As you were, sir. Your men wouldn't even be here if the
damned Congress wasn't coddling the coons. I don't have to coddle anyone. Dismissed."

To his officers at mess Grierson said, "We have to pull this
regiment together and get off this post. If we don't, something
dire will happen. I am not a violent man. I am not a profane man.
But if we stay much longer, Hoffman's dead. I will kill that bigoted prick personally."

Charles laughed and joined the applause.

Grierson added, "If Alice knew about Hoffman's effect on
my character and vocabulary, she'd divorce me."

Barnes—or the old man as he was commonly called—often
lectured C Company on practical matters not taught in official
Army texts.

"Men," he said one day, striding down the ranks, preceded
by his stomach, "you joined up to be proud of your uniform.
That's fine as long as we hang around the fort." His eyes flicked
across the earnest, attentive faces, tan and amber, mahogany and
ebony. "However, I want each of you to get a new outfit for the
field. I don't care what it looks like so long as it's warm, fairly

loose, and can be peeled off a piece at a time if the sun's broiling you. For the kind of fighting we may do, you don't want to be weighed down with extra gear or heavy duds. So put together a new uniform—shirt, pants, coat, hat. Buy it. Trade for it. If you steal it, don't get caught."

He gave each side of his mustache a short, neat stroke with his index finger to put a period after the whole business, but added: "The less gov'ment blue I see in this outfit, the happier I'll be."

Sometimes when Charles had a spare hour, he rode to Leavenworth City. The Prairie Dog Saloon on Main Street served forty-rod that was much better than the watery stuff in the officers' bar at the sutler's.

Heading for town one sunny Saturday, he heard gunfire. He soon came upon an expensively dressed civilian who'd picketed his horse by the road and stepped away to a safe distance for some target practice. Charles reined in and watched as the stranger blew down a row of twelve bottles with continual fire from a pair of .44-caliber double-action Colts.

As echoes of the shots reverberated, Charles called, "That's fine shooting."

The marksman ambled over. He was about Charles's age and had long hair and a mustache resembling Custer's. A jutting upper lip somewhat marred his appearance. He wore a fawn claw-hammer coat, green silk waistcoat, and costly tooled boots.

"Thanks," he said. "Do I note a trace of the South in your speech, sir?"

The question had an edge. Charles said, "The border."

"Ah, a Union loyalist. Good. I'm from Troy Grove, Illinois. La Salle County. Abolitionist territory." He offered his hand and Charles leaned down to shake it. "Right now I'm earning the handsome sum of sixty a month riding dispatch for the Army. I'm hoping to sign on to scout for General Hancock this spring."

"You practice a lot, do you?"

"Three, four hours a day. There's no magic to killing somebody who's out to kill you first. It's mostly accuracy, plus a few tricks. Always go for the head, never the chest. A man with a fatal wound in the chest can keep firing long enough to finish you."

"I'll remember. Well, keep it up, Mr. —"

"Jim," the stranger said. "Just Jim."

At the Prairie Dog, Charles mentioned the dandified stranger. The barkeep paled. "Oh, God. You didn't insult him, did you? No, I guess not. You wouldn't be here."

"What do you mean? He seemed a polite sort—"

"Call him Duck Bill and see how polite he is. One man called him that and he blew him down. That shootist is J. B. Hickok."

Charles knew the name. Everybody knew the name of the feared killer. "He said he's riding dispatch for the Army."

"Yeh, him and some braggy kid named Will Cody."

Charles let out a low whistle. He had exchanged pleasantries with one of the most dangerous men on the frontier. He was almost as surprised by the mention of Cody. Just as Dutch Henry Griffenstein had predicted, the young Kansan's Golden Rule House hadn't lasted.

In the wet, misty dark, Charles ran toward clustered lanterns, the tail of his nightshirt flapping out of his trousers. Hair in his face, sleep in his eyes, fear drying his mouth, he loped east from the arsenal storehouse to the group of provost's men.

One had pounded on his door to wake him. No one could locate Grierson. The new adjutant, a recommissioned officer named Woodward, wasn't scheduled to arrive till next week. Ike Barnes and Lovetta were taking a short holiday in St. Louis and Floyd Hook was down with winter influenza.

Sweating, his breath clouding, Charles reached the half-dozen men with lanterns standing some distance from the timber piers of the rail bridge over the Missouri. The metal of their revolvers and carbines gleamed.

"Sir, the darky's one of yours," a corporal said after a slovenly salute. "He won't surrender. We'll have to shoot him."

At the dim edge of the light, squatting behind a pier so that only a white eye and a sliver of his black face showed, was one of the new recruits, Shem Wallis.

"Let me talk to him, Corporal."

"Sir, white or nigger, if a sojer takes the Grand Bounce and resists when he's caught, we got orders to—"

"I said I'll talk to him." Charles shoved the corporal's carbine down and walked away from the muttering men.

The closer he got to Wallis, the more he saw of him. That included black fingers tightened around an Allin Conversion, one of the pieces retooled in 1865 by the Springfield Armory and foisted on the Army. An old-fashioned single-shot gun, but its fifty-five-grain charge could still put a man away.

Wallis acted determined, too. "Lieutenant, you stay there. Like I told those white boys, first one who tries to jump me goes to hell."

Charles's gut hurt. So did his head. "Shem, listen. You shouldn't have clubbed that sentry and tried to desert. But it'll be worse if—"

"I joined up to be proud of what I did!" Wallis yelled. "I didn't join up to kneel down again like a nigger slave with a brush in my hand. I spent my whole damn Sat'day whitewashing some officer's picket fence, and then he come out and inspected and said a jackass could do better."

Charles took a step, another. His breath ghosted around him. "That kind of duty's one of the bad things about the Army, Shem. I thought I explained that."

"You did. I just won't do it no more."

Six feet from the pier, still walking, Charles held out his hand. "Give me the piece. I know what's ragging you. Too much winter. Everybody feels it."

The old Springfield steadied, pointed at his chest. "I kill you, Lieutenant."

Charles stopped a yard from the pier. "All right, that will take care of one round. You haven't any more. Those boys behind me will finish you. Give up, Shem. You'll spend a while in the guardhouse, but it's better than going to the cemetery. Then you'll come back where you belong. You've got the makings of a good soldier. I mean it. You're a good man."

Hand held out, he resumed his slow walk forward. Wallis jammed the Springfield against his shoulder. Sighted.

Charles watched the muzzle opening grow larger as he walked.

Larger.

And—

Tension in Wallis's upper body indicated a move. Charles

shifted his weight and crouched, knowing he was too late to dodge the bullet.

The Springfield dropped. With a forlorn moan, Wallis covered both eyes. Then he straightened up, stepped from behind the pier, and raised his hands. Charles saw some whitewash left between his fingers.

Hancock did announce his intention to take the field as soon as the weather improved. One night in the last week of February, he told an assembly of post officers that his soldiers from Leavenworth would be augmented by men from A. J. Smith's Seventh Cavalry. This combined force would strike out from Fort Riley for Indian country.

"Some of you gentlemen will accompany me. Others will remain here. All of you should be clear about the purpose of the expedition, however. I am under orders from General Sherman to overawe the Indians, and meet with the important chiefs to tell them they must stay away from the rail and wagon routes this summer. If their response is defiance, a warlike attitude, then we'll give them war. No insolence will be tolerated. That is now government policy."

In his next letter to Willa, Charles said nothing about government policy. He suspected she'd hear of it soon enough.

"Sit down, Private," Charles said to Potiphar Williams after the exchange of salutes. Suspicious, the ex-cook took the visitor's chair.

"C Company needs a first sergeant. Lieutenant Hook and I have campaigned for you, Captain Barnes agrees, and I'm happy to say Colonel Grierson has accepted our recommendation. You get the job, not only because you can read and write, but because you've proved yourself a good soldier."

Williams's flash of pride was quickly replaced by the old, barely veiled hostility. "Sir, I 'preciate the offer, but I can't take it."

"Don't be so damned stiff-necked. I know you don't like me. It makes no difference. In the war I served with plenty of men I didn't like." Williams cleared his throat. Charles blinked. "Wait. Is it just me, or is there something else?"

"It's—" Williams nearly strangled over it. "Seeing."

"What?"

Williams sagged. "My eyes are bad. I can manage fine in shooting at a rifle target. I can read the letter on the guidon when it's a good way off. Close up, though—well, one reason I left the hotel kitchen was because I couldn't see to carve and chop. Cutting carrots or beans, I had a hell of a time." He showed a long, pale knife scar where his thumb and index finger met. Charles had never noticed it.

"There's an easy remedy, Williams. Let the surgeon test you for spectacles."

Another fidgety silence. "Uh, sir—I can't afford 'em. I send most all my pay to my four brothers and sisters in Pittsburgh."

"I'll loan you the money for God's sake, and don't argue."

After long and careful scrutiny of Charles, Williams asked, "The white officers, they really want me for first sergeant?"

"They do."

"You, too?"

"It was unanimous."

Williams glanced away. "You not so bad as I thought. What you did to help Shem Wallis, that was decent. I'd repay a loan soon as I could."

"Fine. One small warning. You'll be nicknamed Star Gazer or Star Eyes. Every bluebel—uh, trooper with glasses is Star Gazer or Star Eyes."

Williams thought about that. "Well, guess it'd be better than the nickname I got." Charles's eyebrow hooked up. "From Potiphar the boys got Piss Pot."

Charles laughed. So did Williams. "That's a definite improvement. Congratulations." Charles put his hand out. "Sergeant."

Williams pursed his lips. He studied the white palm and fingers, then gave a little nod, and shook.

It was March 1, 1867. Dignified and handsome, General Winfield Scott Hancock left Fort Leavenworth.

It was a wet, bitter morning. Charles stood among cheering soldiers, wives, and camp followers watching the departure. The post band played all the old favorites including that most trite yet most affecting of marches, "The Girl I Left Behind Me."

National and divisional and departmental colors passed. Companies of infantry plodded forward. Horse-drawn gun carriages bore the light and dependable twelve-pound mountain howitzers. The towering canvas tops of supply wagons sailed slowly by like schooners.

The column was not all Army blue. Bland-faced Osage and Delaware trackers mixed with a few civilians, including Mr. Hickok, who was in tight buckskin breeches and garish orange Zouave jacket. His twin ivory-handled revolvers were prominently displayed. Hickok's mare, Black Nell, stepped along smartly; her rider saluted the crowd with sweeps of his hat. When he spied Charles, he hailed him cordially. The troopers of C Company looked at Charles as if he'd suddenly acquired a holy aura.

A lurching ambulance carried Mr. Davis, who wrote for *Harper's Monthly,* and Mr. Henry Stanley, who represented the *New York Herald* and other papers. Generals Hancock and Sherman wanted a good press.

The old man squirted spit between his teeth and said to Charles, "Know what's in some of those wagons? Pontoon boats, for God's sake."

"Pontoon boats? What for?"

"Why, fordin' rivers. If Hancock spies some Indians and there's to be a scrape, y'see, the Indians are supposed to wait half the day so's Hancock can lay down his pontoon boats and cross over and fight." Another squirt of spit. "Shows you how much old Superb knows about war on the Plains. It don't bode well, Charlie."

"I still wish we were going."

"Want some red scalps, do you?"

"Yes."

Ike Barnes studied his lieutenant's face and didn't care for the cold, stark look on it. "You'll get your chance," he said, not hiding his disapproval.

PULASKI CITIZEN
F. O. MCCORD, Local Editor
Pulaski, Tenn.
FRIDAY MORNING, March 29, 1867

WHAT DOES IT MEAN?—The following mysterious "Take Notice" was found under our door early yesterday morning, having doubtless been slipped there the night previous. Will anyone venture to tell us what it means, if it means anything at all? What is a "Kuklux Klan," and who is this "Grand Cyclops" that issues his mysterious and imperative orders? Can any one give us a light on this subject? Here is the order:

"TAKE NOTICE—The Kuklux Klan will assemble at their usual place of rendezvous, 'The Den,' on Tuesday night next, exactly at the hour of midnight, in costume and bearing the arms of the Klan.

"By order of the Grand Cyclops.

"G. T."

First mention of the Klan in the U. S. press

28

Charles was officer of the day when another recruit arrived. He seemed unremarkable at first, a stout, round-faced black man in his late twenties carrying all his belongings tied up in a bandanna. A black silk handkerchief overflowed the breast pocket of his old frock coat, which had a hole in one elbow. The toe of his left shoe lacked a top.

"Stand at attention while I take some information." Charles believed in breaking recruits in quickly. He examined the man's papers. "Your name's Magee?"

"Yes, sir." The recruit grinned, the widest, sunniest mouthful of teeth Charles had ever seen in a human being. The infectious smile tickled him out of the gloom caused by the morning rain. Life might have robbed the man in some other respects, but those teeth were perfect.

"Wendell Phillips Magee," he added. "Mama named me for—"

"I know," Charles interrupted. "The abolitionist." He consulted the papers again. "You enlisted in Chicago." Illinois must be a dull state. People kept leaving; people like Hickok and a couple of other gun artists named Earp and Masterson whom Floyd Hook had mentioned to him. "What did you do in Chicago, Magee?"

"Saloon porter. Swamped floors. Emptied spittoons." He didn't seem bitter, only factual. "Took my share of hard knocks from customers 'cause I'm a nigger. When my Aunt Flomella died—she was Mama's sister, my only kin—a piece in a newspaper caught my eye."

"You read, do you?"

"Yes, sir, General."

"I'm a lieutenant."

"Yes, sir, sorry. I write, too. And I can do sums." The recruit had a jolly, breezy air, undaunted by criticism. His fast talk and bright smile were probably defenses against the abuse he'd mentioned. "The newspaper piece said, young men of color, put on Army blue—" Magee startled Charles by snatching the black hanky from his pocket. He pushed the silk into his left fist with his right index finger. "So I said, Magee, that sounds good, don't it?" Quickly, the silk disappeared. "Change your whole life. Black to blue." He picked at the other side of his fist and pulled out a long twist of silk. Bright blue.

Charles laughed. Delighted, Magee waved the hanky up and down with his right hand while displaying his pale left palm, empty. "Black to blue," he repeated, grinning that wondrous grin. "Whole new life, and glad of it." He pocketed the silk.

"Do you know more tricks like that?"

"Oh, yes, sir, General. I learned my first ones from a barkeep soon after I started work, 'round age nine. Picked up plenty more over the years. Coins, cards, cups, and balls. I read about tricks, too. They had conjurers back when knights rode around in armor, did you know that? The Chinee had 'em a couple thousand years ago. Sort of gives a man a sense of being part of a fine old family." Another grin. "Know what I mean?"

Charles thought of Hickok and his pistols. He said, "You must practice a lot."

"Every day. I get lots of good out of magic. I'd do tricks for some of those mean bast—gents who hung 'round the saloon and they'd tip me a coin or two, 'stead of kickin' the shit out of me 'cause I'm colored." Though the smile stayed fixed, a hurt revealed itself for a moment.

"Can you ride a horse?"

"Afraid not, General. But I'm going to learn. I'm mighty proud to be a U.S. soldier, and I mean to be a good one."

"I expect you will be." Charles extended his hand for the customary greeting. "Welcome to the Tenth Cavalry, Magee."

The regiment found the new man good company, a studious pupil at drill, and unfailingly entertaining. On Magee's third day with the regiment, Grierson showed up for 9:00 P.M. tattoo and roll call at the barracks, solely to watch Magee perform. When the colonel asked for a trick, Magee produced a piece of string.

"Works better with rope, but who can afford rope on a porter's pay?"

"You won't afford it on a private's pay either," Sergeant Star Eyes Williams said. The circle of men laughed.

Magee looped the string in one hand and cut the midpoint of the loop with his pocket knife. He then put the pieces back together and tied the cut ends in a knot. He displayed the string full length, snapping out the ends over his head to show the knot in the middle. He wound the string round and round his left fist, tapped it, then snapped it out again. The string was unbroken, the knot gone.

Grierson applauded. "That's very good, Private. How do you do it?"

"Why, General, if I told you that, they wouldn't be calling me Magic Magee much longer, would they?"

"That's already his nickname?" Floyd Hook whispered to Charles, who whispered back, "What else did you expect?"

Puddles of melted snow and an occasional balmy day promised the end of winter. The Tenth grew and continued to train. Barnes, Hook, and Charles drilled their troopers, broke up fights, staged night raids on barracks gambling games and confiscated the dice or decks of cards, wrote letters for the men, listened to romantic or family problems, and prayed for the day they'd ride west for field duty. C Company was nearly up to strength. Departure couldn't come too soon for Charles.

Couriers brought reports of Hancock's campaign to Department headquarters. Hancock had marched southwest to Fort Larned on the Pawnee Fork of the Arkansas and encamped there with fourteen hundred men from the Seventh Cavalry, Thirty-seventh Infantry, and Fourth Artillery. He sent Lieutenant Colonel Edward Wynkoop, former commander at Fort Lyon and now the Interior Department's man in charge of the Southern Agency, to bring the Indians to hear his warning. These were Cheyennes and some Oglala Sioux living together in a big village thirty-five miles up the Pawnee Fork. The outcome of the parlay would be in the next reports.

Barnes said that since the company would leave soon, Charles should pay a brief visit to St. Louis, if he wished. As April grew warmer, Charles took a Missouri boat. He and Willa made love ardently when he arrived, late one afternoon, before her evening performance as Ophelia.

"I'll never remember my lines now," she said, laughing, as she pinned up the silver-pale hair their lovemaking had undone. "At least I'm sufficiently unstrung to play the mad scene." She kissed his mouth. "And thank you for remembering my birthday. I mean at all."

He spanked her bare bottom lightly and they fell out of bed, laughing and tickling each other.

She promised they'd take supper with some other members of the company after the show. The five acts of *Hamlet* seemed interminable to Charles. Sam Trump ranted and stomped through the Prince's quiet soliloquies and grew so excited in the final duel that he fell down twice, generating hoots.

Rubbing a bruised knee, Trump begged off from supper. That left Charles with Willa, the young prompter-stage manager Finley, and Trueblood, who could be the juvenile only with the help of generous amounts of face powder and rouge. Finley arrived late at the outdoor beer garden; the others were cheerily drinking from mugs of dark German beer. Finley threw a pall on things by showing the day's *Missouri Gazette*.

"Hancock burned an Indian town."

"What?" Willa's pale eyes lost their merriment.

"Right there." Finley tapped the headlined column. "The chiefs wouldn't come in to powwow. Maybe Hancock's threats scared them, because they ran away and took all their women and children with them. Custer took off after them and found a stage station burned, so Hancock burned down the empty lodges —two hundred fifty of them. It's all there," he said, sitting down and signaling the waiter.

"When did it happen?" Trueblood asked, indignant.

Willa smoothed the paper. "On the nineteenth. My God, nearly a thousand robes destroyed, cooking implements, all of the goods they left behind. How heartless. How outrageous!"

Charles said, "Hancock went out to demonstrate to the chiefs that they'd better keep the peace this summer."

"And now he's guaranteed they won't." She thrust the paper at him. "Read for yourself. Absolutely no connection between the village that Hancock destroyed and the burning of the stagecoach station."

"No connection except that it's all part of the same problem. The chiefs should have come in to talk."

"When General Hancock was so imperious beforehand? read his statements, Charles. Bombastic. Belligerent."

"Look, I'm tired of listening to this. You know how I lost my partner to the Cheyennes. A fine man who was their friend who never hurt anyone if they left him alone—"

"And so that's why the Army should be equally brutal? Brutality only begets more of the same, Charles. It lowers the Army to the level of those few Indians who act violently."

"There are more than a few—" he began.

"Well, Washington will hear from the society about this," Trueblood declared. He snatched the paper and snorted as he reread the dispatch.

Charles said, "Every Indian's a potential murderer, Willa. It's their way of life. Like carving up their victims afterward."

Scathingly, she said, "Please." She pushed her plate away. Under the hanging paper lanterns of the beer garden, her eyes flashed with reflected light. The April wind fluttered a wisp of her hair. She stared at Charles with dislike, then stood up. "I'm finished."

They left an embarrassed Finley and a preoccupied Trueblood. Charles took her arm. She drew away. On the walk to the hotel, he repeatedly tried to start a conversation. Each time she shook her head, or said no, or once, "Please don't. I'm sick to death of your bloodthirsty talk."

In bed they neither made love nor touched after a perfunctory goodnight kiss. Charles slept poorly. In the morning both apologized for bad temper, though neither apologized for anything else. He felt resentful about the need to apologize at all.

His river packet left at five. After a late-morning rehearsal, Willa pleaded a headache and wanted to return to the hotel. Charles drew her to a quiet corner backstage. "This might be the last time we meet for a while. Grierson's sending C Company into the field."

Angry tears welling, she said, "I hope you find every ounce of blood you're looking for—though why you're looking at all after four years of war, God knows."

"Willa, I've explained."

"Never mind. Just never mind, Charles. It's probably good

that you're leaving your little boy for a time. He's too young to be taught how to hate."

Charles seized her wrist. "There is very good reason for my—"

"There is never a good reason for barbarity." She backed up, struggling, wrenching, until he released her. "Not for the barbarity of the men who killed your friends, nor for yours either. Goodbye, Charles."

Stunned, he watched her whirl and leave. He heard the loud slam of the door to Olive Street.

Turbulent anger mixed with his remorse. He was raking a match on the sole of his boot when Trump waddled from the dark, a stained towel over his bare, pale shoulder.

"I heard a bit of the quarrel. The Indian question again."

"She absolutely doesn't understand—"

"She understands her own position, and she's very serious about it. You've known that for many months. You pushed her too far and forced a choice. Got the one you didn't expect, eh?" The old actor wiped a dab of powder from his cheek. "At least I'm spared the necessity of knocking you down. You hurt her, but you got your punishment."

"Don't talk like a damn fool, Sam. I love her."

"Is that right? Then why do you drive her away?"

He sent a searching look at Charles, and then he walked off.

Charles leaned on the packet's rail, watching the lamps of St. Louis recede in the spring dusk. Water cascaded noisily over the stern paddles.

He had done what Trump said, hadn't he? Driven her away deliberately.

Why? Was it because he feared a greater hurt if the relationship went on? Or was it really because she hated his obsession with the Cheyennes? Hell, he didn't know. Though they were distinct reasons, he kept mixing them up somehow.

He thought of her eyes and hair. Of her passion and her tenderness. Of her wit and her idealism, so energetic and still unmarred by time and reality. She was as fine in her own way as Augusta Barclay, whom he'd also driven off. He saw himself repeating the pattern, scored himself, then tried to deaden the guilt with memories of Wooden Foot, Boy, Fen.

I'm right, God damn it. She isn't a realist. Never will be.

And yet, gazing at a far sparkling constellation overhead, something in him grieved.

———————

Hancock set a watch on the village. Shortly after nine o'clock . . . it was discovered that the Indians were abandoning it . . . Custer was ordered to take his command—about six hundred men of the Seventh Cavalry—and surround the village, but not to enter it, or attack the Indians. The surrounding was effected with great celerity; no noise whatever could be heard in the village; and closer examination revealed . . . that the Indians had abandoned it and moved northward toward the Smoky Hill . . . Custer was ordered to have his command ready to move at daylight, for the purpose of overtaking the Indians and forcing them to return. He moved with the greatest rapidity, and reached Lookout Station on the Smoky Hill while the station was still burning. There he discovered the half-consumed bodies of the station-men among a pile of ashes. He at once dispatched a messenger to Hancock stating these facts. . . . Upon the receipt of the intelligence, Hancock ordered Smith to burn the Indian village. . . .

Theodore Davis, "A Summer on the Plains"
Harper's Magazine, 1868

———————

29

"Son of a bitch," said Ike Barnes, stomping in.

"Me?" Charles asked, sliding the February *Harper's Monthly* into the desk. It had been passed all over Leavenworth because of a G. W. Nichols article about Hickok. Nichols had chronicled Hickok's exploits as a scout for General Sam Curtis in the Southwest, as a Union soldier at Wilson's Creek and Pea Ridge, and as a pistol artist without peer. He credited "Wild Bill," as he called him, with slaying at least ten men. Although no one seemed to know where Hickok got his nickname, Charles had no doubt after reading the article that it would soon be known all over America.

"No, not you, don't try to be funny," Barnes said. "The son of a bitch I'm referring to is that son of a bitch Hoffman. When we leave for Riley tomorrow, we can't take our laundresses."

That roused Floyd Hook from a doze; he was a fastidious dresser. "Why the hell not, Captain?"

"Hoffman said so, that's why not. The women are ordered not to leave the post in the wagons of C Company."

Charles scratched his chin, reflecting. "Well, if that's the order, let's obey it. Let's ask the ladies to meet us outside the gate."

The old man blinked. "Damn, Charlie, you've been mean as a mad dog since you came back from St. Louis. But I'm glad I kept you around."

Charles spent the evening with Brigadier Duncan and little Gus. He romped and wrestled with his son, who giggled with delight and then gave his father a long hug before he turned over to go to sleep.

Duncan asked about Willa. "You haven't mentioned her once."

"She's fine. Busy with a new cause." There, unexplained, he dropped it.

The next day dawned clear and perfect. The seventy-two men, three officers, and two wives of C Company prepared to leave the Fort Leavenworth reservation. Grierson shook each officer's hand in turn. "I'm proud of this company and this regiment. I just want to last long enough to lead you men in the field. If I don't get out from under Hoffman by autumn, I'll take the Grand Bounce myself."

"Don't do that, sir," Hook said. "We'll send Lieutenant August to shoot Hoffman for you. He's eager to shoot somebody. Anybody."

Feeling mean as a wolf, Charles didn't dispute it.

The company started to move out. Standing with Satan, patting him, Charles watched the troopers walk their horses past in column of fours. They'd heeded the old man's lecture on a field uniform. Charles saw a variety of shirts of faded gray cotton, yellow kersey, green silk. He saw cavalry pants, jeans pants, Indian leggings. He saw kepis, fur hats, straw hats, even a Mexican sombrero. And he saw many new bowie knives and hand guns.

Charles himself was comfortably dressed in yellow-and-black striped trousers and a soft deerskin shirt. He'd jammed his Army blues into his travel trunk along with his gypsy robe and a new sheepskin-lined winter coat. To get the coat and his new flat-crowned black hat with yellow cord, he'd traded away his caped overcoat.

Magic Magee rode by wearing a black derby with a wild turkey feather in the band. He saw Charles and whipped off a smart salute. The second his hand touched his forehead, the queen of diamonds snapped out between his index and middle fingers. He shoved the card under his left arm, where it disappeared. He rode on, flashing that wonderful smile.

A horseman appeared in the dust cloud billowing behind the wagon carrying Lovetta Barnes, Floyd Hook's haggard young wife, Dolores, and the Hooks' small daughter. Charles tensed, slipping his hand to his Spencer in the saddle scabbard.

Waldo Krug reined in. "Where's Barnes?"

"Head of the column. Sir."

"Well, you tell him that his trickery came to my attention. General Hoffman's putting it into the regiment's permanent record."

Charles pretended innocence. "Trickery, sir?"

"Don't give me that goddamn phony tone. You know the laundresses were expressly ordered not to leave the post with C Company."

"They didn't. It's my understanding that they left an hour ago. Do you mean to say the Army would object if we happened to meet them down the road and did the courteous, gentlemanly thing and offered them a ride?"

"All the way to fucking Fort Riley?" Krug's cheeks boiled with color. "You'll answer to me yet, you bastard."

"Look, Krug. I'm a soldier, exactly like—"

"Bullshit. You're a traitor. You're a disgrace to the uniform you refuse to wear. If Grierson didn't coddle you, I'd have you up for that. You and those niggers, too. Look at them—scruffy as a bunch of Sicilian banditti."

Charles stepped up in the stirrup. "Goodbye. General."

In Leavenworth City, C Company took the laundresses into a wagon. Beyond the town they passed through a belt of farms whose rich black soil already showed green shoots. The whitewashed houses and outbuildings had an air of age and permanence, though probably not one was over ten years old.

By choice, the company veered away from the railroad and the parallel line of telegraph poles. A wind rose, whipping the branches of the budding hickories and buttonwoods, willows and elms. Across soft hills hidden by thousands of swaying sunflowers, through gleaming creeks where the wild strawberry grew, sheltered by a cathedral of sky, cleaving an ocean of grass, colors and guidon streaming, C Company rode west.

Charles carried a score of memories of Willa—and a hurt. He hummed the little tune she'd written down for him. He'd packed the music carefully in the folds of his gypsy robe. This morning he found the melody inexplicably sad, so he stopped humming and rode in silence for a while.

The invigorating air and the sunlit country gradually eased his melancholy. In a baritone voice not much better than a monotone, he sang to himself, one of the sweet sad songs he'd first

heard when he lazed outside the Mont Royal praise house, the
slave chapel, of a Sunday when he was small and trouble-prone
and didn't understand the world around him, or the suffering the
song expressed.

> "I'm rollin', I'm rollin',
> I'm a-rollin' through this unfriendly world . . ."

Hook cantered up beside him.

> "I'm rollin', I'm rollin'
> Through this unfriendly world."

"Where'd you learn coon songs, Charlie?"
"It isn't a coon song, it's a hymn. A slave hymn."
"You surely give it a cheerful lilt. Glad to see you feeling
good for a change."
Charles smiled and kept his thoughts to himself.

> The heel of military dictatorship crushes our pros-
> trate state. Its bayonets enforce the new gospel of lust
> and racial mingling. . . . Among us there come the
> blue-clad missionaries of wrath, with vast new powers
> to kindle hate and sow the seeds of damnation. . . .
> Waving their Bible spotted with sin, and their Constitu-
> tion stained with crime and political chicanery, they
> preach but one sermon, Radicalism. . . . Better that
> we should welcome the Anti-Christ himself than these
> emissaries of Hell.
>
> *Editorial in* The Ashley Thunderbolt
> SPRING 1867

MADELINE'S JOURNAL

*April, 1867. The Congress has seized control. Last month's
Reconstruction Act carved the 10 unrepentant states into 5
military districts. The two Carolinas comprise the Second District. Stanton appoints the military governors. Ours at
Charleston is miserable old Gen. Sickles. We shall not be part*

*of the Union again until there is a new convention of black as
well as white voters, a new state gov't. assuring black suffrage,
and passage of the 14th Amend. The Thunderbolt and even
the better Democratic papers are shrill, not to say violent,
denouncing all of it.*

*Such events seem removed from the day-to-day affairs of
Mont Royal. Two sizable rice crops last year brought a slim
profit, almost all of which I paid to Dawkins's bank to reduce
our debt. Bank now absolutely rigid about late payments.
They are not tolerated.*

*. . . Yankee speculators are descending like the Biblical
locusts. They float bond issues for railroad lines that will
never be built, snap up land on sale day at 8 cents on the
dollar, start new businesses in the wreckage of bankrupt ones
that once gave livelihoods to local people. An unexpected letter
from Cooper, very brief and curt, warned me against investing
in such schemes, as he suspects most are crooked. In this case
I will heed what he says. I can't tell the honest Yankee from
the vulture.*

*. . . Today the freedman Steven said that he will leave,
taking his wife and 3 children. Saddening; he is a dependable,
steady worker. But the emigration agent whose wagon is
parked at Gettys's store swayed him with a promise of
$12/mo., guaranteed, plus a cabin, garden plot, and a weekly
ration of a peck of meal, 2 lbs. bacon, one pt. molasses, and
firewood—all this to be delivered to him somewhere in Florida. We have a second plague in these emigration men from
other states. They come here knowing our freedmen have
never gotten over the falsity of the cruel rumor of "40 acres &
a mule" in '65. When I asked Steven to stay, he replied with a
fair question—could I pay him real wages, instead of merely
marking down sums to his credit in my ledger?*

*I wanted to lie; could not. I answered truthfully, so he is
going.*

*. . . Mrs. Annie Weeks in a quarrel with Foote's Cassan-
dra at the Summerton crossing. Annie, who is mixed blood,
very light and delicately featured, attacked and hit Cassandra
because of some fancied slight. Cassandra is full-blooded Negro. I have heard of this kind of animosity before. A mulatto
can sometimes "pass," so will not associate with true blacks.*

*They in turn hate the mulatto's "uppity" ways. I wonder if
there is any end to the rancor caused by the war?*

*. . . The Jolly clan, the squatters, have stayed on. We
occasionally hear of a mule, corn meal, or a woman taken at
gunpoint by "Captain" Jack and his oafish brothers. They do
not discriminate! They prey equally on both races. Am terrified of them, esp. the eldest, who boasts of "slaying niggers for
sport" in the massacre at Ft. Pillow, Tenn.*

*Prudence spoke last night of her unhappiness over the
state of the school. . . .*

"Madeline, I now have fourteen pupils working with al-
phabet and primer, two almost ready to advance to the Second
Reader, and Pride is in the second arithmetic series. I want to
buy a geography for him, and slates for the rest. We have just
three slates for all, not nearly enough."

Head down and pensive, Madeline walked beside the schoolteacher on the shore of the Ashley. The spring twilight was settling, hazy and full of shrill night-bird cries. The familiar vista of
star-specked water with dense forest beyond usually soothed her.
Tonight was different.

"I can't give you any answer but the one you've heard before," she said. "There's no money."

For once the plump teacher seemed to lose her Christian
patience. "Your friend George Hazard has it to spare."

Stopping, Madeline said sharply, "Prudence, I have made it
clear that I won't beg from Orry's best friend. If we can't survive
by our own wits and initiative, we deserve to fail."

"That may be noble, but it does very little to further someone's education."

"I'm sorry you're angry. Perhaps I'm wrong, but those are
my views. I'll do all I can to supply what you need as soon as we
sell the first rice crop."

"Bother. I see nothing wrong in asking a small donation
from a very rich man who—"

"No," Madeline said, though she wondered bitterly how she
could ever fulfill the dream of building a new Mont Royal when
she couldn't buy even the smallest necessities for its school.
"We'll find some other way, I promise."

Prudence gave Madeline a bleak look. The two women returned to the whitewashed house in silence. It was an hour before

they made up. Madeline spoke first, though Prudence was clearly just as eager. Even so, Madeline felt the emptiness of her promise as she lay in bed that night, sleepless with worry.

Who against all hope believed in hope. Prudence might still be that sort of person. She was not.

30

Late on a showery Saturday in that same month, a horse-drawn cab took Virgilia to a small brick house on South B Street, behind the Capitol. She looked matronly, and somber in contrast to the color in the front yard, where snowy blossoms shed by two dogwoods dusted deep yellow daffodils. A mock orange tree sweetened the air in a way that was appropriate to a season of renewed hope.

Virgilia's face was drawn, even severe. She rang the bell and exchanged a warm embrace with Lydia Smith, the housekeeper. She followed Lydia to the parlor, where her friend waited with silver tea things.

"Thad—" She caught her breath. He looked white, far older than when she last saw him, months ago. He rose from his chair with great effort.

Lydia tied back draperies to let in more of the gray light, but that did nothing to improve Stevens's appearance. The housekeeper excused herself. Stevens sat down again. Over the patter of rain, Virgilia heard his labored breathing.

"Sorry to have taken so long to accept your invitation," she said. "I usually work every Saturday. Today Miss Tiverton's nephew drove down from Baltimore for a visit. He excused me for the afternoon."

"How is the old woman? You've been her companion for—how long now?"

"Ten months." Virgilia added cream to her hot tea and sipped. "Her ninetieth birthday falls next Tuesday. Physically, she has tremendous stamina. But her mind—" A shrug said the rest.

"What do you do for her?"

"Sit with her, mostly. Keep her tidy. Clean her up when I must." In response to Stevens's grimace, she said, "It isn't that bad. I had worse duty in the field hospitals during the war."

"You're putting a good face on it. Now tell me how you really feel about it."

A weary sigh. "I hate it. The monotony is terrible. In the nurse corps, I got used to helping people recover, but Miss Tiverton will never recover. I'm nothing more than a caretaker. I suppose I can't be particular. Jobs for single women are scarce. This was all I could find."

"Perhaps we can do something about that." He was about to say more, but his silver teaspoon slipped from his hand. He leaned down to pick it up, and suddenly clutched his back. He straightened slowly. "My God, Virgilia, it's hell growing old."

"You don't look well, Thad."

"The climate in this town aggravates my asthma. I have trouble breathing, and my head hurts most of the time. No doubt some of the headache comes from warring with that fool in the White House." Virgilia followed this struggle in the *Star* but felt far removed from it in Miss Tiverton's vast, silent house out in Georgetown.

The congressman leaned toward her, his wig slightly off center, as usual, and they fell to discussing recent events. She expressed her scorn for Secretary Seward's seven-million-dollar folly, the purchase from Russia of the worthless, icebound Alaskan territory. Stevens couldn't confirm or deny rumors that Jefferson Davis would soon be let out of Fortress Monroe, after payment of enormous bail, to await trial.

They soon came back to the struggle between the Congressional Republicans and the President. To further curb Mr. Johnson's power, bills had been passed prohibiting him from direct command of the Army. Any orders now had to be transmitted by General Grant, who was more sympathetic to the Radicals; some were even saying he'd be their candidate for President a year hence. A second bill, the Tenure of Office Act, challenged the President even more directly. He couldn't remove any cabinet official without consent of the Senate.

"Our most pressing problem remains the South," Stevens went on. "Those damned aristocrats in the Dixie legislatures refuse to call the state conventions demanded by the Reconstruction Act. We've put through a second supplementary bill empowering the district military commanders to set up machinery for registering voters, so we can get on with the job. Johnson balks and argues and tries to thwart us at every step. He doesn't understand the fundamental issue."

"Which is—"

"Equality. Equality! Every man has an equal right to justice, honesty, and fair play with every other man, and the law should secure him those rights. The same law that condemns or acquits an African should condemn or acquit a white man. That's the law of God, and it ought to be of the law of the land, but those Southerners choke on the idea, and Johnson repudiates it. And he is supposed to be on our side! I tell you, Virgilia"—he had grown so agitated he spilled tea from the cup he was holding—"I am pushed to desperation by that man. He is obstructionist to the point of being criminal. There is only one remedy."

"What's that?"

"Depose him."

Her dark eyes widened in the watery gloom. "Do you mean impeach him?"

"Yes."

"On what grounds?"

The hawkish old face at last showed a smile. "Oh, we'll find those. Ben Butler and some others are searching. None too soon, either. Andrew Johnson is the most dangerous president in the history of the republic."

Dangerous, or merely obstinate about yielding power to the Congress? Virgilia didn't ask the question of her friend. She found herself surprisingly unconcerned about the whole matter. Prisoned in the Georgetown mansion caring for Miss Tiverton, she no longer felt any connection with important causes.

"All the key members of the Senate agree about impeachment," Stevens continued. "Sam Stout agrees . . ."

The sentence trailed off. He was probing. Calmly, she said, "I wouldn't know, Thad. I no longer see him."

"So I heard." There was a pause. "Sam feels his voting base is secure now. Consequently, he's announced his intention to divorce Emily and marry some music-hall tart."

"Her last name's Canary." It sounded like unimportant conversation. But her hands trembled; the news had stunned her. "I wish him well." She really wished him in hell.

Stevens studied her. "You aren't at all content with your present situation, are you?"

"No. I'm not the crusader I was ten years ago, but as I said, I feel very isolated, very useless caring for one elderly woman who will never improve."

"Do you have contact with your family?"

Virgilia avoided his eye. "No. I'm afraid they—they wouldn't welcome it." Sometimes, late at night, she longed for it so deeply it brought tears. That too was probably the result of aging, of softening, and growing away from the entrapments of unbridled emotion.

"Well, my dear, I asked you here not only to see you, but also to discuss a possible change of employment. A position you might find more satisfying because you would be helping the most innocent victims of those damned rebels. Children."

For the second time, he'd stunned her. "What children do you mean?"

"Let me show you. Are you busy tomorrow?"

"No. I'm allowed Sundays to myself." A melancholy smile. "I usually have nothing to do."

"Can you be ready at two? Good. My driver and I will call for you in Georgetown."

At the end of a rutted lane off Tenth Street in the ramshackle Negro Hill section, Stevens and Virgilia came to a white house that showed good care. Two or three large rooms at one side looked like a recent addition; not all of the siding was painted as yet.

When the carriage stopped, Stevens didn't immediately open the door. "What you're looking at is an orphanage for homeless Negro children. The children are sheltered and given basic education until they can be placed with foster parents. A man named Scipio Brown founded the orphanage. He ran it personally until he joined a colored regiment. After his discharge he came back and found more waifs than ever before, chiefly the children of contrabands who fled north and somehow got separated from their youngsters. Last month Brown's assistant, a white girl responsible for teaching the children, left him to marry and move to the West—" He broke off. She wanted to speak.

"Thad, I know Scipio Brown."

"Indeed! I thought it a possibility—"

She nodded. "I met him at Belvedere during the war. My brother George and his wife were operating a branch of Brown's orphanage there. They took in all the children he couldn't handle here in Washington."

"Then you're quite familiar with his work. Good. Are you interested in the vacancy?"

"Perhaps."

"Hardly an enthusiastic answer."

"I'm sorry. It's an honest one." How could she explain that because Stout had abandoned her and she was estranged from her family, she felt little enthusiasm for anything?

He opened the carriage door. "Well, a brief visit will do no harm."

Walking slowly with the aid of his cane, he led her inside. He introduced her to the Dentons, a middle-aged black couple who lived at the orphanage, cooking and cleaning for the twenty-two children presently in residence.

Seven of the youngsters, a clamorous, cheerful lot, were adolescents. The others ranged all the way down to four. Stevens knew each name. "Hello, Micah. Hello, Mary Todd—Liberty—Jenny—Joseph." He clucked and fussed among them, touching hands, kissing cheeks, embracing them as if they were his grandchildren. Again Virgilia realized that Thad Stevens was not one of those Radicals who promoted equality for political reasons.

"Here's a handsome friend of mine." Stevens's clubfoot turned awkwardly as he picked up a laughing light brown boy of six. The boy wore a clean, patched shirt and overalls.

"Tad for tadpole. Or Tad Lincoln. Or a tad of trouble. He's a little of each." Stevens hugged and kissed the boy. "Tad, this is my friend Miss Hazard. Can you shake hands?"

Solemn, wary of her, Tad thrust his hand out. Virgilia felt unexpected tears.

"How do you do, Miss Hazard?" Tad said, very properly.

"I—" Dear God, she was stricken silent. The resemblance wasn't exact, yet close enough to bring exquisite pain. He could have been a child of her slain lover, Grady. It took a huge effort to master her shock and say, "I'm very fine, thank you. I hope you are too."

The boy grinned and nodded. Stevens patted him again and put him down. He scurried off. With a sniff, the congressman took note of the pleasing odor drifting from the kitchen. "What's that on the stove, Mrs. Denton?"

"Okra gumbo for supper, Congressman."

They turned at the sound of the front door. A tall, amber-colored man came in, shaking rain off his hat. His shoulders were broad as a stevedore's, his waist small as a girl's. Virgilia guessed him to be around thirty-five now. He immediately gave her his hand.

"How do you do, Miss Hazard? It's very good to see you again."

"Mr. Brown." She smiled, remembering that she'd been attracted by his lean good looks before. He was still handsome, but he'd matured; he charmed her with an easy cordiality:

"I regret we met but once in Lehigh Station. I heard of you often afterward."

"Not in a complimentary way, I imagine."

"Why, I wouldn't say that." He smiled at her. "The congressman told me you might be interested in helping to teach these children."

"Well—"

"Is that gumbo, Mrs. Denton? I missed my noon meal. Will you join me, Miss Hazard? Thad?"

"It's damp outside, and okra gumbo always warms me up," Stevens said. "I'll have a spoonful or two. You, Virgilia?"

She didn't know how to refuse, and she found she didn't want to. They sat down with bowls of the savory soup. While she chatted with Brown and Stevens, her eyes strayed often to the small, merry boy who reminded her so much of Grady. The sight of his innocent face, untouched as yet by the cruelties his color would inspire, pushed her near to tears again. And then to a sudden, startling thought. Sam was gone. Even at the start of their affair, she had known she probably couldn't hold him forever. Perhaps it was time to put the rancor and grief behind her. Time to care for someone who could benefit from love, as old Miss Tiverton could not.

She saw, like an apparition, the dead Southern soldier in the field hospital. She stared at her hands. Others could not see blood on them, but she could. The blood would never wash away. But she might begin to atone for it.

Finishing his soup, Stevens said he had a late afternoon meeting with members of the Committee of Fifteen. Scipio

Brown didn't press Virgilia for an answer, but he expressed his interest in having her at the orphanage and shook her hand strongly to say goodbye. He had a direct way about him, and no small amount of pride in his eyes and his bearing. She liked him.

In the carriage lurching south toward the center of the city, Stevens rested his hands on the knob of his cane. She thought of a lion. An old lion, but one still driven by blood instinct.

"I fall in love anew whenever I visit those waifs, Virgilia."

"I can understand. They're very appealing."

"How do you look on the opportunity there?"

She gazed at passing hovels built of scrap lumber and canvas. From muddy lanes and windows without windowpanes or shutters, dark brown faces turned toward the fine carriage. A woman of seventy or more squatted in the drizzle, smoking a corncob pipe and trying to cook bits of food on the top of a tin can set in smoldering wood chips. Rain dripped from the woman's nose and chin. The smoke from her pipe was thin as thread. She was motionless on her haunches; only her eyes moved with the carriage. Eyes that had probably seen shackles, sun-scorched fields, filthy cabins, loved ones torn away and sold—

"Virgilia? How—"

"Favorably, Thad. Quite favorably."

The old man squeezed her hand. "You would be good for them. I think they would be good for you. I know you cared for Sam. But he belongs to the past, I think."

Weeping at last, Virgilia could only nod and turn away. The old haunted eyes of the squatting woman were lost in the gray murk.

In Georgetown that evening, she gave Miss Tiverton's nephew polite but final notice.

31

Ashton stepped into the June sunshine like a queen emerging from her palace. The building she quitted was not that, but a frame boardinghouse on Jackson Street, right on the edge of one of Chicago's roughest areas, a warren of hovels called Conley's Patch. For months, Ashton had been caged there in a single large, grimy room, together with Will Fenway and his mountains of construction drawings, cost estimates, supplier bids, loan papers. She hated it.

Even more than that, she hated the anonymity Will had imposed on her since leaving Santa Fe. She wanted a photograph of them together; he refused. There must be no pictures of her, ever, he said. What if the señora in Santa Fe still had the authorities hunting for the killer of her brother-in-law? Whenever Will mentioned that, a strange glint came into his watery blue eyes; a look Ashton didn't understand.

This morning, as she stood letting the pleasant sunshine bathe and warm her, she did resemble, if not a queen, then a woman of high station and good income. Her dress and matching hat were bright red silk; there were twelve yards of material in the gored skirt alone. Beneath it, supported by a canvas belt around her waist, a bustle formed by six springlike wires gave a provocative lift to the rear of the skirt. The bustle was a new fashion; very modish. It was hell's torture to put on and wear, but she certainly liked the way it enhanced her sexual appeal.

Unfortunately, on the fringes of Conley's Patch, she appealed to the wrong sorts. A seedy, bleary-eyed roughneck came weaving toward her from a lane between packing-box shanties.

"Hello, lovely." He blocked the plank walk, stinking like a

whiskey works. His bloodshot eyes roved over her breasts. "I reckon from that dress you're a working girl. How much?"

Ashton's lips compressed. One delicate red-gloved hand whipped up her red parasol and laid it hard on his cheek. She shoved her other glove under his nose. The outline of a huge square wedding diamond showed through the fabric.

"You dirty, illiterate wretch. I'm a respectable married woman."

"You look like a whore to me." He reached for her.

Ashton jabbed the point of the parasol into his groin, hard. His eyes practically crossed as he reeled back, clutching himself. A couple of better-dressed gentlemen stepped between Ashton and the derelict.

"Thank you kindly," she said in her sweetest voice. They tipped their derbies while restraining the drunk, and she swept on by, bound for the Van Buren Street bridge. No doubt she was late, and she dared not be late on this important, not to say fateful, day.

Hurrying, she reflected on the clumsy assault. It was at least proof that at age thirty-one, she hadn't lost her looks. If anything, she believed, the passage of time was improving them. It wasn't improving much else. She detested the near-penniless life she led. Often, she couldn't believe how far she and the sometimes curmudgeonly old man had gone as partners. Santa Fe to San Francisco, to Virginia City and then Chicago.

So much scheming, so much struggle. And so much of the future riding on those drawings of a piano that Will had made, and made over, scores of times, strewing their squalid room with tracing paper as his pencil flew, sometimes until three or four in the morning, as he searched his own experience, and obscure German and French books containing manufacturing diagrams, for ways to cut a dime here, another dime there.

It was all culminating today. Everything. The money brought from Virginia City, slightly over one hundred thousand dollars, carried in a satchel. The two loans negotiated locally to pay rent and the wages of Will's four workmen and the salesman he'd hired away from Hochstein's. To get one of the loans, Ashton had been required to spend the night with a banker, a dreadful man with a hog's belly who heaved on top of her for hours and never once managed to get it up.

After his first fifteen minutes of effort she had decided she didn't want one of the banker's trouser buttons for her box. For most of the night she lay staring past his head into the dark. She envisioned herself richly dressed, wealthy and powerful, thanks to Will's success. She saw herself returning to Mont Royal and confronting the arrogant Madeline with any number of choices, each designed to hurt her and drive her from the family land that was Ashton's by right.

Oh, she'd done a lot for Will Fenway and for their scheme, and almost being crushed to death by the fat, sweaty banker was only part of it. First, she'd seduced a records clerk in San Francisco. Not so bad; he was homely but virile. It took her only a week to pry from him a forged certificate of marriage, showing that she had wed Mr. Lamar Powell on February 1, 1864.

Although she now went by the name Mrs. Willard P. Fenway for convenience, she was actually married to a man who was, so far as she knew, still in Virginia City, Nevada. Ezra Leaming was a red-faced, white-haired, sad-eyed widower with no family. He was shy, and a clod around women. Ashton had to arrange a seemingly accidental meeting—a little fainting spell on the street—and pretend to be shy herself, and destitute over the death of Mr. Powell. She did most of the courting, filling Mr. Leaming with one full bottle of Mumm's to induce him to propose.

In bed Leaming proved a reasonably lively husband. Much more lively than good old Will, who had tried just once, in San Francisco, and at the end of a half hour sighed, "That does it. I like to sleep with you to keep warm, if you don't mind, but I reckon I'm too old for the other part. We'll keep it at partners. What do you say?"

From Ezra Leaming she purloined a fly button. He made fairly frequent use of her charms during the eight months of their marriage. He was chief of the local claims office, and naturally happy to assist his own dear wife in establishing her clear title to the Mexican Mine, her late husband's property. She had her marriage certificate, didn't she?

Ashton hired men to reopen the mine, which at first looked highly promising. The silver-bearing ore reduced to the equivalent of one hundred three thousand dollars before the vein ran out. She quietly withdrew the money from her bank account and late one night while Ezra Leaming snored, she decamped on the stage with Will Fenway, who had been hiding out in a cheap room, impatiently sketching pianos.

Oh, yes, a complex, labyrinthine path to Chicago, all right. With many confusions and irritations. She posed as Mrs. Fenway but was still Mrs. Leaming. She dared not show her beauty to posterity by means of a photograph. Will was adamant about that. When he first mentioned it, a day after they arrived in the city, Ashton threw a shoe at him. Next morning, to get back at him, she marched to Field, Leitner and Co., a fine department store on State Street. There, with money from their bank account —money reserved for the piano company—she bought the scarlet outfit, including the bustle.

Will was furious. He cursed her as she'd never heard him curse before. Ashton realized then that she'd met a man whose strength matched hers. Old and stooped and red-eyed as he was from all the worry and night work, he was neither intimidated by her beauty and haughty airs nor upset when she retaliated for his cursing with screams, saying she'd leave him.

Pushed past his limit, he slapped her. Just once, but hard enough to tumble her onto their mussed bed. Then he showed her his fist.

"You go ahead. I've put my whole soul and all your money into this scheme. If you don't care any more, if you don't want to go back to South Carolina the way you're always saying, you just walk out that door. I'll bank all the money we make, and then I'll find myself another woman."

Ashton was thunderstruck. She pleaded, begged, cried, humbled herself until he agreed to make up. She had not crossed him or defied him since.

This was the reason for her haste as she turned west on Van Buren to the wooden bridge over the south branch of the Chicago River. When strangers eyed the tight red silk on her bodice and the provocative bounce of her bustle, she tossed her head and glared. Her heart belonged to Will and what he was about to reveal today. Her heart was wrapped up in him, and so was her money, not to mention her unshakable determination to return to Mont Royal someday and make them pay—Madeline, Little Miss Goody Brett, Charles—every damn one of them.

West of the river, Chicago became an unlovely near-slum crowded with saloons, lumberyards, woodworking mills, boat jetties on the water, and the bleak, cheap residences of a lot of Irish and Swedes and Bohemians. Here, on Canal Street, a dark stairway led up past a crude depiction of a hand pointing to FENWAY'S PIANO COMPANY.

She dashed up, breathless, and into the loft, which was piled with iron frames, spools of different grades of piano wire, unassembled cases from Schoenbaum's in New Jersey, crates of actions from Seaverns's in Massachusetts. Nothing in the piano was Will Fenway's creation except the design.

"Will, do forgive me—" She rushed to him, contrite. The four young men in leather aprons and portly, pie-faced Norvil Watless, the salesman, smiled and offered greetings as she flung her arms around Will's neck and kissed him. "There was all sorts of wagon traffic on the bridge. I couldn't cross for ten whole minutes."

"Well, I waited," he said, sounding edgy as he tapped fingers on the sheeted object that was the center of attention. "Guess we're all here. Let's take a look."

She noticed the tremor of his hand as he grasped the sheet. She also noticed the red rims at the bottom of his eyes; he needed spectacles and wouldn't buy them. But his shoulders squared as he paused for effect, then whipped off the sheet.

The workmen clapped. "Godamighty, what a beauty," Norvil Watless wheezed. Even Ashton gasped.

The piano was an upright, a style made popular because it fit nicely in those small, new-style Parisian dwellings, *appartements,* that were all the rage. The case was a lustrous blackish wood with broad streaks in the grain the color of rust. Centered above the keyboard in a gold-leaf wreath, *Fenway* appeared in Old English script.

"That's a gorgeous rosewood case—" Watless began.

"Brazilian jacaranda," Will corrected. "Cheaper. But call it rosewood anyway."

He stroked the sleek, shiny top, his tiredness seeming to fall away as he explained to Ashton, "I can't build a better one for the money. She's got a full iron frame, overstrung scale—"

"French action," Watless exclaimed. Ashton had learned that a Paris-made upright action was synonymous with fine quality.

"No. I bought the action in the U.S.," Will said. "But the selling sheet says it's French-style, so be sure you get across the idea that it's from Paris. After all, you won't be calling on the most honest customers in the world."

Ashton wanted to say something to please him. "You should be proud, Will."

"I may be proud and bankrupt, too, if she doesn't sell. By the way, it is a she—I named this model the Ashton."

She squealed in surprise, then actually felt touched. She hugged him again, and was aware of the weary sag of his body momentarily resting against hers. He waved. "Try her out, Norvil."

The salesman pulled up a stool, flexed his fingers, then launched a tentative "Camptown Races."

"Louder, Norvil," Will said.

Norvil played louder.

"Faster." Norvil picked up the tempo. The music seemed to push out through the piano's closed front with a clangorous, slightly metallic sound. Norvil segued into "Marching Through Georgia." You could practically hear the bugles and tramping feet.

One of the workmen did a little jig. "By damn, that's an upright!"

"That's right," Will agreed. "You don't give a damn about sweet, mellow tones in a sporting house. You want noise. Noise, Norvil!"

Norvil obligingly gave them Verdi's "Anvil Chorus." Ashton clapped her little red gloves together, delighted. Will gave her a strange, grave, sideways look, then said, "I can make as many as you sell, Norvil, but if you don't sell any, you can visit me at the poor farm, provided the suppliers haven't beat me to death. Well, guess we'd better open the bottle of sour mash, hadn't we?"

Ashton had never seen a celebration announced with such a lack of zest. It made her a little grave too, reminding her of what would happen if the Ashton upright piano failed.

When Norvil and the workmen finished the bottle, Will closed up the loft, giving them the rest of the day free. He dropped the empty bottle in a trash barrel. "The cards are all dealt, Ashton. We might as well spend our last dollar on a venison steak at the café on the corner."

She agreed. Neither said much until they were seated amid

pots of wilting ferns, layers of cigar smoke, and an otherwise all-male clientele, most of whom goggled at her spectacular looks.

Her red-gloved hand clasped his. "Will, what's giving you the glooms?"

He avoided her eye. "You don't want to know."

"Yes, I do." She pouted prettily. "Yes!"

His weary red-rimmed eyes fastened on her. "I've never said this to you, because I was never sure we'd get this far. It eats on me, Ashton."

"What?" Now her pretty pout looked forced, nervous. "What?"

"Santa Fe."

"I beg your pardon?"

"What keeps bothering me is Santa Fe. That man Luis you shot when you needn't have." Anger reddened her face. He gripped her wrist, and she felt the strength hidden in his dilapidated old body. "Let me finish. I have nightmares about that man. Bad ones. God knows I'm no pillar of virtue. And I like you, I really do. I like your pertness, your looks, your grit, the ambition you don't cover up with a lot of mealymouthed lies. But there's a certain streak in you that your daddy should have whipped out of you with a willow wand. A mean streak. It made you shoot down a defenseless man. Whether Fenway pianos are a disaster or the mother lode, either way—" The next came after a rush of breath, as if a burden were lifting. "I've resolved that if you ever do something that low again, we're quits. No, don't argue. No excuses. You murdered him." His voice was quiet, so no one could eavesdrop. But she heard it like a roaring wind, cold as January.

He extricated his hand. "Do anything like that again, we're quits, understand?"

Her immediate reaction was renewed rage. Once, Huntoon had said something similar, and she'd jeered, then tongue-lashed him. Now she opened her moist red mouth to do it to Will—and couldn't.

She shivered. Hastily, she examined her choices. She bowed her head.

"I understand."

He smiled. Tiredly, but he smiled. He patted her hand. "All right. I feel better. Let's order up. In fact, let's ruin the whole blasted day and get drunk. It's either all over or just starting. I gave it everything. So did you."

Their eyes met in a strange, tranquil moment of understanding. Why did she admire this frail old man? Because he had pure steel in him? Because he could deliver an edict and make her take it? Unexpectedly, her eyes misted.

"Yes, we did. Let's drink like lords and then let's go to bed."

"I'll probably do nothin' but fall asleep."

"That's all right. I'll keep you warm."

It perked him up, and he actually showed some jocularity as he snapped his fingers for the waiter. "Well, why not? It's all up to Norvil now. Norvil and the whorehouse owners of these great United States."

32

Someone touched his foot.

Awake instantly, Charles flipped his black hat off his face while his right hand jumped to his Colt. The revolver cleared leather and he recognized Corporal Magee, his dark face patterned by sun falling through parched cottonwood leaves.

Charles's hammering heart slowed. "When I'm asleep, yell, don't grab me. Else you're liable to get a bullet."

"Sorry, sir. We got some smoke."

He pointed away southwest where the Smoky Hill River blazed in the noonday like a cutout of tin. A thin black pillar stood in the white sky. Charles scrambled up and ran to find his tracker.

He and his ten-man detachment were patrolling out of Fort Harker along a twenty-five-mile stretch of the stage line south and west of the post. Here the Smoke Hill branch of the Kaw diverged from the surveyed right-of-way of the Union Pacific, Eastern Division. The soldiers had sought relief from the July heat among the river-bottom trees. They didn't find much. The red bandanna around Charles's throat felt like a wet rag. His bare chest shone with sweat.

He found the tracker seated on the ground and rummaging among the bits of root, flints, arrowheads, spent bullets from his medicine bundle, a small drawstring bag traditionally holding a personal collection of articles selected to promote strength, ward off sickness and enemies, and remind the possessor of important aspects of his religion.

The tracker was a Kiowa named Big Arm, assigned to Charles by the old man. He was a handsome Indian, and an expert horseman, but surly. Barnes said he came from a Kiowa band down in north Texas, and had committed the ultimate mistake on a buffalo hunt some years back. He'd gotten impatient, rushed in ahead of the other hunters, and stampeded the herd. No one got so much as one kill. Big Arm's possessions were taken and broken to pieces and he was shunned. He withstood two winters of that, then spitefully deserted to the service of the whites—in this case a bunch of brunettes, or buffalo soldiers as the Plains Indians called them, reminded of the buffalo's coat by the woolly hair of the black men. The troopers tended to like the term buffalo soldier, because the buffalo was revered.

"What do you make of that?" Charles said to Big Arm, in a tone unconsciously goading. He genuinely disliked the Kiowa, who refused to talk with Charles or his men except when necessary.

Big Arm answered with one of his laconic shrugs, then pulled a bright brass telescope from his belt. He started to snap it open. Charles knocked it down.

"How many times do I have to tell you? That thing shines like a mirror. What's burning? The next stage station?"

Big Arm shook his head, sullen. "Too close for stage. Must be new farm. Not here last time I rode the river." For him, that was practically an oration.

Alarmed, Charles yelled, "Wallis. Boots and saddles."

Having served out his sentence in the guardhouse, Shem Wallis had returned to duty and revealed some talent as a trumpeter. He blew the call with sharp, urgent notes. The black troopers heaved to their feet, complaining; it hadn't taken them long to learn that little Army tradition. Charles detailed two to guard the supply wagon and raced for his picketed piebald.

Despite the intense heat he lit a cigar. Nerves. Sweat poured down his chest and back as he trotted from the trees at the head of eight men in column of twos.

The sod house was still standing. It was the shell of a farm wagon producing the smoke. Charles ordered his men into line, and they approached with rifles and pistols ready. The brim of Charles's black hat threw a sharp shadow diagonally across his face. His eyes darted. Suddenly he smelled something foul. "What in hell's that?"

Evidently Big Arm knew. "Bad," he said.

The line halted at the edge of the trampled dooryard. From

horseback, Charles read sign there and in the beaten-down grass at the edge of the homesteader's small, dying vegetable patch. "I count eight ponies, maybe one more." Big Arm's grunt agreed.

"How's he know that?" one of his men muttered behind him. Charles preferred to keep them in awe of his plains craft; he never explained that Wooden Foot Jackson had taught him everything, and that hardly a day passed when he didn't remember and use one lesson or another. They didn't know it was that simple. When he had them whipped into shape he might take some of the mystery out of it, and begin to teach them. Not yet, though.

He sent three two-man teams, dismounted, to search the ground in different locations. He led Magee, Big Arm, and another trooper around the square house, which was made of mud brick with a sodded roof. Tall grasses jutted from the sod, a weed patch against the hot sky.

The stench grew worse. "Smells like cooked meat," the trooper said. They turned the back corner and saw what remained of the white homesteader, staked out on the ground. Charles wiped his mouth.

"God. They built fires on him."

Magee, not easily impressed by anything, registered a sick astonishment. "The last one on his chest." The other soldier rushed away to tall grass and threw up.

Charles pushed Magee. "All right, let's go back and find a shovel." Both were eager to get away from the body. Around in front, he discovered Big Arm prodding at the sod house door with his telescope. "For Christ's sake, don't go in there until we're sure it's safe—"

While he was in mid-sentence, Big Arm pushed the door open and stepped inside. A roar flung him out again, a foot off the ground. He landed on his back amid drifting smoke. A hole in the bosom of his buckskin shirt welled red.

Charles jumped against the front of the house beside the door and flattened. "We're soldiers. United States Army. Don't shoot again."

He listened. Heard breathing. Then a whimper. A shadow passed by him on the ground. A circling vulture.

"Hold your fire. I'm coming in."

While the others watched, Charles sucked in a breath and stepped into the doorway. "Soldiers," he said, loudly, as he moved forward in almost impenetrable shadow.

The homesteader's wife, a girl with auburn hair, lay in a corner amid broken furniture. Torn pieces of clothing were scattered around. She tried to cover her nakedness while her right hand shook under the weight of her pistol. Charles only glanced at her wet thighs, but it was long enough to humiliate her. He didn't have to ask what they'd done.

Violet eyes filled with tears. "Eulus gave me the gun. I was supposed to save the last bullet for myself. They took the gun away before they—before—is Eulus all right?"

Charles wanted to sink into the ground. "No."

A kind of mad misery glittered in the violet eyes. Her free hand moved across her thighs, as if to rub away the shameful stains. He thought little of it, trying to get hold of his feelings and organize his mind to handle this.

"Look, I'm sorry. Lie back and I'll find a blanket to cover you. Then we'll bring up our wagon to take you—*don't!*"

He lunged too late. His flung-out hand trembled in the air a yard from her as she pulled the trigger of the pistol she'd slipped into her mouth.

Magic Magee touched Big Arm's body with his beaded moccasin. "I'm only a city boy, Lieutenant, but it seems to me this here tracker didn't know his trade too well."

Charles stared at the white horizon and bit on his old cigar. "Fucking fool. Fucking savages. Fucking Hancock." He turned away to hide a typhoon of emotion.

To Shem Wallis, who had tears in his eyes, Magee said, "Going to be a mighty long summer."

Hancock's War, the press called the spring expedition, recently concluded. Hancock's belligerent demonstration-in-force was meant to promote peace; his impulsive burning of the village on the Pawnee Fork insured war. The Plains tribes saw the destruction of tipis, buffalo robes, willow backrests and other personal possessions as a reenactment of Sand Creek and a direct repudiation of the Little Arkansas Treaty.

And they retaliated.

Bands of young Sioux and Cheyennes led by hot-bloods like Pawnee Killer and Scar were pouring into Kansas, attacking homesteads like the one Charles had found, burning stage stations, swooping down on unarmed construction crews of the

U.P.E.D. laying track in the desperate race to be first to the hundredth meridian. Between Fort Harker, the temporary railhead, and Fort Hays, an even more primitive post about sixty miles west, the U.P. crews were refusing to work without armed guards.

Down from Sherman at Division came orders assigning cavalry and infantry units to guard the crews. The railroad's own security force, headed by a former Pinkerton agent named J. O. Hartree, supplemented the Army details. Hartree had a reputation as a killer, but that wasn't enough to stop the raids. The directors of the railroad screamed for more men, more guns.

Governor Crawford of Kansas screamed for protection of his citizens and started to raise a special state cavalry regiment. Sherman wanted the Army turned loose: *"We must not remain on the defensive. We must follow them on all possible occasions. We must clear out the Indians between the Platte and the Arkansas."*

All went well, except for the reaction of the Olive Branchers —these Congressmen, bureaucrats, preachers, journalists who took the Indian side and blamed every Indian outrage on an earlier one by whites. From Boston pulpits and New York editorial rooms, they spoke powerfully and persuasively. They called the Pawnee Fork burning cowardly and provocative. They printed handbills, held rallies and torchlight parades, circulated memorials and more memorials to be sent to President Johnson. One of the strongest constituents of the Olive Branch faction was Willa's Indian Friendship Society—a fact Charles tried not to think about.

Before the incident at the homestead, he had taken his detachment into the field with a good feeling. Patrolling the Smoky Hill and hunting Indians beat living in one of the sorry, rat-infested mud huts that passed for housing at Fort Harker. He'd soon realized, however, that a small detachment lacked the firepower necessary to pursue and destroy large roving war parties. What's more, they didn't have the authority. They were not supposed to act, only react. The more this sank in, the worse Charles's attitude became, so that by midsummer he felt as murderous as he had when he discovered the bodies of Boy and Jackson.

Charles and his men had undertaken the sickening chore of burying the homesteaders and checking through their few belongings in hopes of identifying them. They found a Bible, but there was no inscription in it. All they had was one name. Eulus. Ironically, in the face of this kind of butchery, the Olive Branchers were temporarily taking control. Senator Henderson, of Missouri, a powerful member of the peace lobby, was introducing a bill to establish yet one more commission to negotiate permanent peace with the Plains Indians.

Like so many in uniform, Charles felt beleaguered, held back from winning a war steadily taking its toll of innocents like the man Eulus and his wife. Charles believed the peace faction would not prevail forever, nor succeed if they did prevail for a little while. Ultimately the Army would have to be turned loose, with permission to fight to win. Then he'd have his chance to fulfill his vow of vengeance made over the mutilated bodies of Wooden Foot and Boy.

As he headed back to Fort Harker with Big Arm's body, Charles told himself that he should be thankful. Although his black brunettes were despised by their white brethren, he could have been somewhere a lot worse. With the Seventh Cavalry, for instance.

The Seventh was a regiment already torn by factionalism and racked with trouble. Custer had taken part in Hancock's expedition and, later, had been sent up the Republican River to chase the Indians. A series of forced marches he ordered started wholesale desertions. One night thirty-five men left. In a fury, Custer sent his brother, Tom, an adjutant, and a Major Elliott in pursuit, with orders to shoot any man they caught.

The pursuers recovered five, wounding three. Custer denied them medical treatment for a while. One died at Fort Wallace, and Charles heard that Custer had boasted about his ability to make snowbirds think twice before flying. Not all of Custer's superiors cared for his disciplinary methods.

Just before departing on patrol Charles had heard something else about the Boy General. Apparently he'd left Fort Wallace without permission, dashing through Fort Hays and Fort Harker in order to find his wife, whose health and safety concerned him. There was, in addition to the Indian problem, the threat of a cholera epidemic on the Plains.

Captain Barnes cast his cocked eye at the stout Indian. "Lieutenant August, this here's your new tracker, Gray Owl."

Charles's heart sank. Compared to this hangdog specimen, Big Arm had been a sparkling personality. The Indian was about forty, bundled up in a buffalo robe despite the weather. He had broad, dark cheeks and a nose like a blunt axe blade. Painted buckskin strips bound his braids but beyond that, Charles saw no design or mark to identify his tribe. Certainly the tracker was neither Delaware nor Osage. Some branch of the Sioux, then? Very puzzling. The Sioux were at war.

Noticing Charles's stare, Barnes said, "He's Southern Cheyenne. He's been tracking for the army long as I've been out here."

"I'll be damned. Don't tell me he ran off a buffalo herd too?"

"No, but he doesn't like his people. He won't say why."

Charles saw a swift flicker of pain in the tracker's eyes, or thought he did. He felt peculiar discussing the Indian as if he weren't there. "Well, come on, Gray Owl. I'll introduce you to my men."

"Yes, thank you," Gray Owl said. Charles nearly fell over. The Cheyenne's speech was clear and almost accent-free. He must have spent a lot of time among white people. He turned out to be better than Big Arm in one respect. He'd answer, and with more than a few words, when addressed. He had another problem, however. He wasn't sullen, but he absolutely refused to smile.

"Y'see, Magic," Charles said to his corporal, "I can't make him perform if I can't reach him. To reach him, I have to know something about him. What he wants, what he likes, who he really is. I've asked twice about the reason he turned against his tribe. He refuses to say. We're building a good detachment. I don't want him spoiling it, the way Big Arm did. We've got to break him down. The first step is to crack that stone face. I figure you're the man to do it."

"I want to tell you a little story," Magee said. "But first I have to check on something. The way I understand it, you've hung around the forts a while, is that right?"

Gray Owl nodded. He sat cross-legged, wrapped in his buffalo robe, showing as much emotion as a rock from the bottom of a creek.

The summer evening carried a hint of a break in the weather, a slight cooling in the breeze out of the northwest, where purple clouds helped bring on the night. The wind flared the campfire and strewed sparks above it. Charles and his men had agreed to pitch tents on the prairie, between the post and the river, to avoid sleeping in those dark, rank huts, on old mattresses filled with moldy straw, ants, lice, and God knew what else.

"Then maybe you know what this is?" Magee said, whipping out a worn deck of cards. "You've seen troopers playing with decks like this, right?"

Another nod.

"Are you sure you know what's in a deck, though?" He fanned the cards. "The spots, the picture cards? See, there's four different kinds of kings, four different—"

"I have looked at cards," Gray Owl interrupted, a flicker of his eyes suggesting annoyance.

"Well, good. Good! I just had to find out, so you'd appreciate the full meaning of this story I'm going to tell you. It's a good story, because it shows how far you can go in this man's army if you've got plenty of ambition. In fact that's the name of the story, the Ambitious Noncom."

Magee knelt in front of Gray Owl. "Now this noncom, he was a mighty quick young fellow named Jack." He turned over the top card, the jack of diamonds. Wallis and another trooper drifted up to watch. "Jack was ambitious as the devil. He wanted to be first sergeant and soon received the promotion."

Magee waved the card for the onlookers. Amused, Charles sat smoking and watching the performance.

"Trouble with Jack, though, he had a saucy tongue. He got smart with one of his officers, and they busted him." He held out the cards. "Lieutenant? Facedown. Anywhere you please."

Charles took the jack and slid it in the middle of the deck. Magee squared the deck on his palm. "But old Jack, he was still ambitious. He worked hard. Before long, he made sergeant again."

Magee turned over the top card. The jack of diamonds.

Gray Owl's eyes closed, a single slow, reptilian blink. It spurred Magee on.

"Poor Jack—spite of all that ambition, he had the common problems of us soldiers. He liked his drop of spirits, and one night he had several drops too many, which got him busted the second time."

Responding to a nod from Magee, Wallis took the jack from the top and put it into the deck. After the cards were squared, Magee again revealed the jack as the top card.

"Jack fancied the ladies, too. He made an innocent remark that a general's wife considered fresh, and that got him busted. But he was ambitious."

Again Magee repeated the effect, managing to produce several blinks from the tracker.

"Sergeant Jack, he got busted so often and climbed back up so often, he was sort of a legend on the Plains. Everybody wanted to be able to spring back like Jack." He turned over the top card, by now familiar, and placed it facedown again. "Everybody liked Jack's brand of ambition, which was powerful. And you know what? Pretty soon it rubbed off on the whole Army. Even the trackers."

He gave Gray Owl the deck with the jack facedown on top. He signed for the Indian to take the card and place it back in the deck. Forehead deeply creased, Gray Owl took the card, held it while he thought, and then carefully slid it in very near the bottom of the deck. Magee took the deck, keeping it in plain sight, and snapped the top card over.

Charles clapped. Wallis whistled. Incredulous, Gray Owl took the jack of diamonds and examined both sides. He bit it lightly with his front teeth. He bent it, waved it, flicked it with a nail. Magee waited.

Gray Owl handed the card back.

And smiled.

A trooper brought more buffalo chips to fling on the fire. Gray Owl's reticence seemed to melt in the heat of a fascination with Magee. "The shamans of my people would honor you."

"Shamans?" Magee didn't know the term. "Do you mean there are Indians who practice hocus-pocus?"

Gray Owl didn't know hocus-pocus. "Magic? Yes. They have strong medicine. I have seen them change white feathers to white stones. I have seen a shaman's body travel invisibly from one tipi to another, fifty steps away."

Magee screwed up his face. "Tunnel," he announced. "They got to be using a tunnel somehow—"

"And even chop a man's head off and put it back. Among the Cheyenne who work miracles, you would be a great man. Honored. Feared."

Magee cast a speculative eye on his deck. Charles said to him, "Keep that in mind if you ever need to save your hair."

During the week spent at Harker reprovisioning and repairing horse gear, Charles daily expected—wished, anyway—that the mail would bring a letter from Willa. None came. He started two of them himself, disliked the apologetic tone that crept in and tore them up. He dispatched a note to Brigadier Duncan instead, enclosing an eagle feather for little Gus.

The detachment rode out again. The warrior societies kept roving, attacking. The war spirit on the Plains burned as hot as the July sun.

Gray Owl talked to Charles now. Even smiled once in a while. They got along. The tracker was expert, far superior to Big Arm, and followed orders without question. Still, Charles wasn't any closer to the secret of Gray Owl's abandonment of his people. Until he understood that, he couldn't confidently manage or entirely trust the Cheyenne.

Three wandering Rees crossed their line of march. The bad-tempered trio complained about a new whiskey ranch that had opened up half a day's ride south. The proprietors, half-breed brothers, sold guns and unbranded whiskey. One of the Rees had nearly died from too much of the whiskey.

Charles decided the story was true, so the detachment veered away southward. Whiskey ranchers were simply saloons out in the wilderness, set up by unscrupulous men to make a profit on arming the Indians and getting them drunk. The soldiers found the ranch amid some sand hills, overran it by firing a few rounds and took the owners into custody without difficulty.

The firearms the half-breeds sold from their place of business —perhaps it had been a homestead once—were rusty, short-barrel, big-bore Hawkens, from that family's works in St. Louis. From the condition of the pieces, Charles guessed they might date from the early manufacturing runs of the 1820s. The whiskey for sale was a dark brown fluid, probably grain alcohol laced with red pepper, tobacco juice, and similar hellish ingredients. Even a pilgrim dying of thirst in a desert would think twice about drinking it.

The two ratty traders also sold the favors of a sad, pudgy Comanche woman, who told Gray Owl she'd been abducted from her husband's lodge in Texas.

When Charles said he intended to send the traders back to Fort Harker and let the Indian Bureau deal with them, the older brother suddenly burst out with a harangue about his fear of jails. Abruptly, he thrust his right hand under his coat. Charles put a bullet through each of his legs before the hand reappeared.

Magee knelt, gingerly lifted the man's lapel, and pried something from the limp fingers; the man had fainted. Magee held up a roll of bank notes.

Charles examined them. "A bribe. With Confederate bills, the damn fool." He flung the paper money in the air. The prairie wind shot it upward and whirled it in clouds of worthless wealth. His eye on the bleeding man, he said, "You can never be sure of what a man's carrying under his coat."

Later that night, upset, Wallis whispered to Magee: "He didn't have to shoot that there trader."

"Yes he did," Magee said, not excusing it, just acknowledging it.

Charles released the woman and sent the brothers back to Harker guarded by a two-man detail. The soldiers burned down the whiskey ranch buildings on July 28, the same day the Army arrested George A. Custer for desertion of duty at Fort Wallace.

The war fires on the Southern Plains spread, and ignited the north, too. On August 1, in a hayfield near Fort C. F. Smith on the Bozeman's Trail, thirty-two soldiers and civilians successfully fought off an attack by several hundred Cheyennes. Next day, in a separate incident later called the "Wagon Box Fight," a small group from Fort Phil Kearny drove off a band of Sioux under Red Cloud.

With understandable pride, the Army soon exaggerated the number of Cheyenne attackers to eight hundred, the number of Sioux to a thousand. The incidents inspired a new confidence. The Plains tribes were not invincible. They'd only seemed invincible because rule-book soldiers couldn't adjust to the Indian style of guerrilla war. When the tribes had to stand and face concentrated Army fire power, they were annihilated.

Back at Fort Harker once more, Charles heard all this and cursed his bad luck at being in the wrong outfit at the wrong time.

The day of the Hayfield Fight turned out to be a day of even greater significance for the Tenth. Captain Armes and thirty-two men of F Company had chased some Cheyennes up the Saline, caught them, then had to shoot their way out in a fifteen-mile running fight. Bill Christy, a popular little man who'd once farmed in Pennsylvania, took a fatal round in the head. Lovetta Barnes snipped up a large cloth dyed black, the old man passed out the strips, and each officer and enlisted man in C Company tied one around his left sleeve. Other companies followed suit. The Tenth mourned the first of its own to fall in combat.

Somewhat better news was that of the impending move of Grierson's headquarters at Fort Riley. He and his men would escape the bigoted General Hoffman at last.

Although the raids on the rail line, the stage road, and isolated homesteads continued, Charles soon saw opportunity slipping away. The Olive Branchers had prevailed in Washington: a peace commission had been formed, and a huge treaty expedition was scheduled for the fall. Once again he prepared to lead his detachment out, hungering for his chance.

"Better come back for this," Barnes said on the morning of the detachment's departure. He gave Charles a handbill printed in circus type on lavender paper.

SPECIAL & ONLY WESTERN
TOUR THIS SEASON!

Mr. SAM'L. H. TRUMP, Esq.
"America's Ace of Players"
In a Full Evening's Presentation
of Amusing & Stirring
SCENES FROM SHAKESPEARE
("The Bard at His Best")
ably assisted by Mrs. Parker
& other members of his world-renowned
St. Louis theatrical troupe
—ADMISSION 50¢—
Program Entirely Suitable for Females
& Children

Charles recalled some remarks of Willa's about a tour. And for a moment he was amused. The type in which Sam Trump's name was set was twice the size of Mr. Shakespeare's. A magnifying glass would have helped him read the line containing Mrs. Parker.

"That is her, ain't it?" the old man asked. "The one you talked about a while back?"

"It is," Charles said, his smile fading.

"Well, you got my permission to bring the detachment in the night before, 'less you're in a jam." Inked on the bottom of the handbill were the words *Ft. Harker Nov. 3—Ellsworth City Nov. 4.*

So he rode out that morning with the knowledge that he would see Willa again, and the feeling that he wanted to see her. He wondered what a reunion would be like. Happy? Explosive? Would it give him a worse dose of the pain that had been with him like a toothache ever since he rode away from her in St. Louis?

Come November, he'd certainly find out.

MADELINE'S JOURNAL

August, 1867. Gen. D. Sickles has become the most hated man in the state. He interferes with civil law—puts Negroes on juries and into public conveyances. But worse than that (so runs the argument), he is registering freedmen to vote in the 109 precincts into which S.C. is now divided. Sickles may not last. It's said that Andrew J. feels him too radical.

. . . Another Yankee invader! A man named Klawdell has come to the district to start a Union of Loyal League. In the North during the war, I am told, the Union League was formed for patriotic support of Lincoln and his generals. Patriotism is now replaced by politics. The new leagues are to be clubs to educate the blacks in matters of government, the vote, etc. On the face of it, a worthy purpose—but will freedmen be told about the Democratic as well as the Republic Party? I doubt it.

Andy asked what I thought about his attending a meeting. Reminded him that he did not need my permission, but warned him that the white riffraff will be pushed that much

*closer to renewed violence by this latest instance of Radical
intrusion. . . .*

Randall Gettys's reaction to news of a political organizer in
the district was exactly what Madeline anticipated. Fury. He
could barely concentrate on the monthly report of profits from
his Dixie Store. The report was mailed to an address in Washington, D.C., as were similar reports from all forty-three Dixie
Stores now operating in South Carolina.

The firm to which Gettys sent his reports, his orders for
goods and twice-yearly bank drafts—the store's enormous profits
—was called Mercantile Enterprises. He knew nothing about the
people behind it. Whoever the Yankee owners might be, they
stayed well hidden. On two occasions they'd communicated instructions through an attorney who signed himself J. Dills, Esq.

Gettys finished the report and glanced at a poorly printed
wall calendar bearing the escutcheon of the reorganized Charleston & Savannah Rail-Road. Today was Saturday. He could anticipate a brisk sale of corn whiskey to Captain Jolly and some of
the other whites in the district—perhaps even some lively fun
should a darkly foolish venture to the Summerton crossroads on
this, the recognized day of the week for the white man to enjoy
himself. On the bottom of the calendar Gettys had written *Des
due on Oct. 1.* First thing he'd do when his friend was released
was tell him about this new outrage, the club for niggers. Meanwhile, he had other correspondence accumulated from the past
couple of weeks. There was a pathetic request from a cousin who
needed a loan for an eye operation; Gettys tore it up. Two tatty
circulars from German-run junk shops in Charleston advertised
*the finest goods and the complete libraries of leading Carolina
families at sacrifice prices.* Gettys threw them out.

At the bottom of the pile he found a wallpaper envelope
bearing the address of Sitwell Gettys, another cousin. Sitwell was
a schoolmaster, and a loyal Democrat, up in York County, perhaps the most ardently Southern part of the state. Sitwell had
enclosed a yellowing clipping *from the Pulaski, Tenn. Citizen
which you may find of interest.*

Indeed he did. The brief paragraphs described a white men's
social or sporting club formed some months ago in Pulaski by
several war veterans. What intrigued Gettys was the fact that the
members went roving at night in fantastic costumes that con-

cealed their faces. They visited freedmen considered uppity, claiming to be Confederate dead risen to life, and evidently succeeded in terrifying them.

The club had a curious name. If Randall remembered his schooling in the classics, the word *kuklos* meant circle, and the name of the organization had obviously been derived from that. He re-read the clipping with mounting excitement, then speared it on a nail he used as a wall spindle. When Des got out of jail, he must be told about the new Kuklux Klan. It offered an amazingly simple solution to their very own problem, anonymity. With Des's approval, he would try to get more details.

> *To Charleston. Judith home. Marie-Louise was away for a day and from her studies at Mrs. Allwick's Female Academy, one of dozens of such academies that have opened in the state to offer young ladies and gentlemen a proper Southern education among their (white only) peers. M-L went with her father to inspect the Charleston & Savannah Rail-Road. Cooper is one of a group of investors who have bought the second-mortgage bonds of the insolvent line. Even at $30,000, it is not a bargain. The line remains in ruins, the track runs about 60 mis. down to Coosawhatchie, and at the Charleston end, a ferry crossing is required; the Ashley River trestle is not yet rebuilt.*
>
> *Nor is much of the lovely old city, I discovered. Window-less gutted buildings still abound. Ragged Negroes idle everywhere, and white men loafing outside Hibernian Hall spit tobacco and lewdly accost women. I slapped one's face. Had he known of my "racial status," I would have been in serious trouble.*
>
> *Tradd Street remains an island of cleanliness and calm, though even in Judith's kitchen the ripe stench of the night-soil wagons penetrates. We discussed Sickles, prompting Judith to say that she now utterly despairs of Cooper's political rigidity . . .*

The bell clanged. Under dark gray clouds, in air heavy with dampness, Cooper helped Marie-Louise up the dented metal steps of the single passenger car.

He hated going back in the car. The journey down had been bad enough. Half the car's seats were gone, and every window glass. The car had been almost empty on its slow chugging journey south to Coosawhatchie Station, but now, from the rear of the car, Cooper saw that every seat was filled with civilian or military passengers.

At the car's head end, standing beneath one of several huge holes in the roof, an immense black woman with a bundle in hand timidly studied the seats. That damn Sickles had made it permissible for her to board a car with white passengers. But not one man rose to offer his seat.

A rumble of thunder said the clouds would soon spill their moisture. With a lurch and a squeal of rusty iron wheels, the locomotive jerked the car forward. Dense green undergrowth, the fecund forest of the Low Country, slid slowly past the open windows, into which butterflies and insects flew.

"Here, lean against this part of the wall," Cooper said to his daughter. "It's cleaner than the rest."

Marie-Louise thanked him with her dark eyes and started to change position. Just then a young man, a civilian with a boyish pale face, curling mustache, and the vivid blue eyes and light hair of a German or Scandinavian, vacated his seat. He gestured for the black woman to take it.

Over the squealing of the wheels Cooper heard other passengers mutter. The Negress shook her head. The young man smiled and gestured again, urging her. Clutching her bundle, the woman hesitantly approached the seat. The man sitting beside the window immediately vacated it. The timid black woman sat down.

The man who had left gave the younger man a glare. Another passenger across the aisle reached for a knife in his belt. His stringy wife restrained his hand. The young civilian saluted the couple with a mocking tilt of his hat and walked to the front end of the car, crossing his arms and leaning there, showing no sign of regret over his act of courtesy.

As the young man settled himself, he noticed Marie-Louise at the other end of the car. Cooper saw color rush to his daughter's cheeks. Then he saw the immediate interest on the face of the young civilian.

A thunderclap. Hard rain began to fall through the holes in the roof. "Here, stand closer," Cooper said, opening the umbrella he'd brought along for such an emergency.

With most of the passengers getting soaked, the train of the Charleston & Savannah line labored northward. Cooper stared at the back of the black woman's head. He was outraged. What next, then? Mixed marriage? Sickles and the Radicals were intent on destroying Southern civilization.

He didn't forget the young civilian. Nor did Marie-Louise, though for entirely different reasons.

> *Sickles is to be recalled. Perhaps it is a good thing. We have quite enough excuses for violence already.*

> . . . Since the treaty of '65 the Cheyennes have made war against the people of the United States, and having confederated with them the Apaches and Arrapahoes have in part become involved in the troubles which resulted from this course.
>
> Their annuities have been withheld, and they were gradually sinking to their former wild and barbarous ways when they heard that a great Peace Commission was on the way to their country to settle all difficulties, and restore general harmony . . .

"From Our Own Correspondent"
The New York Times
FRIDAY, OCT. 25, 1867

33

It was the season of changes. The prairie grass yellowed, and leaves of the elm and persimmon trees began to flame with color.

There were changes in command. Johnson, through General Grant, ordered Generals Hancock and Sheridan to exchange posts. Hancock was being disciplined for his adventure on the Pawnee Fork, Sheridan for his too-strict enforcement of Reconstruction in the Fifth Military District in New Orleans; he was a favorite of the Radicals, but of few others in Washington.

Sheridan came to the Plains for a swift inspection, though he was due for extended leave and wouldn't assume full command until sometime in late winter. Charles knew a few things about the Yankee, Academy class of '53. He was small, Irish, ceaselessly and inventively foulmouthed. He was accustomed to waging war and whining. Charles wondered how the command change would fit with this autumn's peace initiative, what many in the Army sneered at as "the Quaker Policy."

There were changes in the fates of great enterprises. It was clear that the Union Pacific in Nebraska would reach the one hundredth meridian first, probably in October. The U.P.E.D. had lost the contest, and Charles heard that as many as twelve hundred might be put out of work. This didn't include the gun-happy security men of J. O. Hartree, some of whom rode every passenger train. Charles also heard the line might change its name to something more individual. Kansas Pacific was mentioned.

There were fundamental changes in the proud but strife-torn Seventh Cavalry. Custer was remanded to Leavenworth, and was there facing court-martial on charges preferred by one of his disgruntled captains, Bob West, and his own commandant, A. J. Smith. The charges were numerous, but the serious ones were the abandonment of his command at Fort Wallace, the dash east to find Libbie, and shooting the deserters. Charles heard that the Boy General was confident of the outcome and talked a lot about his deeply religious nature. Charles was cynical; when caught, scoundrels often mantled themselves in the flag or proclaimed their Christian conversion.

It was, most of all, a season fraught with the possibility of change for the Plains Army. They were held in confined patrol duty while the great Peace Commission, which had already failed to achieve even one successful meeting with the Northern Sioux, turned south through autumnal Kansas to try again with the Southern tribes.

The sky was the color of blued metal the day the cavalcade left Harker. Drums and fifes played one hundred fifty troopers of the Seventh off the post to the melody of their signature march, "Garry Owen." A detachment of infantry followed, then Battery B of the Fourth Artillery, hauling two of the new Gatling guns. Charles wondered if a Gatling really could fire one hundred fifty rounds a minute from its ten hopper-fed revolving barrels. Ike Barnes said Gatlings overheated quickly, and jammed. The Seventh had not tested a Gatling; Custer called them worthless toys, and A. J. Smith refused to authorize ammunition for test firing, afraid the War Department would dock his pay for it.

High-wheeled canvas-topped Army ambulances conveyed the Commissioners and their retinue of civilians. The commission numbered seven: Senator J. B. Henderson of Missouri who had sponsored the bill establishing it; Indian Affairs Commissioner N. G. Taylor; Colonel Sam Tappan, the first Army man to fight vigorously for a Sand Creek investigation; General John Sanborn, one of the authors of the Little Arkansas Treaty; fastidious General Alfred Terry, in command of the Department of the Dakotas; and General C. C. Augur, Department of the Platte, who had replaced Sherman after the latter made some intemperate criticisms of the commission and got yanked to Washington to answer to Grant. The man in charge was General William Harney, a massive white-bearded soldier with a considerable reputation as an Indian fighter. Certainly, a fine, martial lot to be responsible for damping fires on the Plains, Charles thought as he watched the caravan depart southward toward Fort Larned.

Governor Crawford was with the expedition, and Senator

Ross as well. Eleven reporters and a photographer trailed along in the ambulances and supply wagons, which numbered sixty-five. The wagons were loaded with crates of trade goods, including knives and glass beads, surplus Army dress uniforms, campaign hats, and boots, and thirty-four hundred old bugles—a brilliantly stupid inspiration of General Sanborn's.

The wagons carried less pacific gifts as well: barrels of black powder; boxes of trade rifles, percussion caps, paper cartridges. Civilians and Army men were already at odds over distributing these presents. Olive Branchers said they would only arm the tribes for more war. Others, notably General Terry, said no present was more meaningful or necessary to nomadic people who hunted their food. It was the classic debate, which Charles had heard before, and of which he was contemptuous. The only sure instrument of peace was a gun in the hands of a U.S. soldier.

He watched the caravan disappear, wondering what kind of insolent Indians they would confront. Bands of Cheyenne military society men were still roaming Kansas, destroying the stage stations and attacking trains and work crews. Charles didn't doubt Scar and his friends were among them. Who would be left to lie to the Commissioners, saying that their few voices spoke for hundreds of others?

His name was Stone Dreamer. He was frail; eighty winters. All his teeth were gone, and his hair resembled a few thin strands of gray wool. Yet he had proud eyes, and his wits hadn't deserted him, as old men's wits so often did.

He was called Stone Dreamer because of his youthful vision-seeking. When he went apart, fasting and praying to the One Who Made All Things, his eyes blurred briefly, and then the various-sized stones on the ground rose into the air, hovered before him, and spoke in turn about deep, important matters.

Stones, like so many natural objects, were holy to the Cheyennes. Stones symbolized permanence, the unchanging verities of life, the everlasting earth, and the One who shaped it from nothing. Stone Dreamer's vision taught him that, compared to these things, the ambitions, loves, hatreds of a mortal were blades of grass tossed by a windstorm. They were as nothing.

When he returned from the wilderness, he told the council of his vision. The elders were impressed. Here was a young man clearly meant for a special life. He was instructed to become a

Bowstring, a member of the society of the brave, the pure, and the celibate, who could be equally comfortable slaying enemies in battle or philosophizing on issues of peace and tribal life.

So he joined and rose through the ranks. Bowstring, Bowstring Society leader, village chief when he grew too old for fighting, peace chief when he grew older still. In October of 1867, he put up his tipi with two hundred fifty others sheltering about fifteen hundred Cheyennes at the western end of the natural basin of the Medicine Lodge Valley. This was three days' ride from the sun-dance ground to be used by the great caravan of white chiefs with guns who were moving down from the north to make peace with the five Southern tribes.

About three thousand Comanches, Kiowas, Kiowa-Apaches and Arapahoes encamped within twenty miles of the treaty site. They were eager for the gifts of soap and brass bills, tin cups and iron pans, blankets and calico, as well as the weapons described to them by Murphy, the Indian superintendent, who had ranged lower Kansas ahead of the great caravan, urging the tribes to come in. The Cheyennes would not go as close as the other tribes because they had certain memories uniquely their own. Chivington. Sand Creek. The Pawnee Fork.

The peace parley began at the site not far above the demarcation line between Kansas and the Indian Territory. A special emissary rode all the way to the Cheyenne encampment to ask that they, too, meet with the white chiefs. In due course, all the elders were consulted. "What do you think, Stone Dreamer?" he was asked.

"We should go," he said. "But not for the gifts. We should go because it is folly to wage a war that cannot be won. The white men are too many. We are too few. If we do not live in harmony with them, they will trample us to nothing."

He hated to say such bitter words, but he believed them. A renegade whiskey peddler, Glyn, had once showed Stone Dreamer a picture of a white man's town; it was an engraving of Fifth Avenue in New York, from *Leslie's,* though Stone Dreamer didn't know any of those specifics. He merely covered his mouth and popped his eyes at the inexpressible wonders he saw on the page.

He saw rows of solid structures he presumed were forts, lining both sides of a broad way. Along this way, scores of horse-drawn vehicles traveled in both directions, surrounded by hundreds of people on foot. This was but one tiny part of one white man's village, the trader said, and there were hundreds of such villages.

So Stone Dreamer, who wanted to pass his final winters sensibly, at peace, spoke for accommodation. Some others, among them his friend the peace chief Black Kettle, agreed. Other war chiefs including the unquestionably brave Roman Nose did not. Nor for the most part did the younger men, especially those rising to leadership in the soldier societies. When Stone Dreamer considered the headstrong behavior of this group, he sadly concluded that age no longer generated respect, and traditional tribal discipline was breaking down. One of the most feared and admired young men, also undeniably brave but needlessly cruel in Stone Dreamer's opinion, ranted and swore that he'd never submit to the white chiefs while he could draw breath.

These words of Man-Ready-for-War carried special weight, for it was almost certain that he would be chosen a Dog-String Wearer next spring at the annual reorganization of his society. The Dog-String was a wide hide sash, about nine feet long and decorated with paint, quills, and eagle feathers. Four Dog Society men were awarded the sash each year. Those so honored for bravery wore the sash in battle, slipping it over the head by means of a long center slit.

The bottom of the Dog-String bore either a red-painted wood peg or a shorter slit to accommodate the point of a lance. If a battle went badly, it was the privilege of the Dog-Strings to peg or pin their sashes to the ground, signaling their intent to stand and give their lives, so the others might escape. A Dog-String Wearer's death was special, heroic, and was described in song and tale long after his bones went to dust and blew away.

Man-Ready-for-War and young men like him spoke more persuasively than old men like Stone Dreamer. So the Cheyennes remained apart in the valley of the Medicine Lodge, while other great Indian chiefs—frail Satank, who proudly wore a medal graven with the head of James Buchanan; bearlike Santana, another feared Kiowa, who favored a U.S. Artillery officer's coat—led their deputations to the conference ground, listened to the soothing words of the white chiefs, made their marks on a treaty paper that gave away still more of their tribal land, and then, rewarded, reveled in the distribution of the trade goods and guns.

Still the Cheyennes remained apart, though contrary pressure began to grow because of the gifts. Man-Ready-for-War sneered at the idea of a birthright sold for a few bolts of cheap cloth or pistols he had heard were defective. Sadly, Stone Dreamer decided that his wish to live out his last winters peaceably was to be denied.

The shadows of October lengthened and grew cooler. Then, almost on the day when the white chiefs were to pull down their great canvas marquees and ride away, a last emissary came riding among the heavily armed Cheyennes, bringing a last plea for them to come in. Stone Dreamer argued for it almost all of one night. Finally, about four hundred who were willing to face the scorn and wrath of the rest agreed to go in, since about fifteen hundred Arapahoes were also going. Stone Dreamer took heart.

He rode to the conference ground as part of a mounted band, careful to stay near his wise and good friend Black Kettle, and away from a party of Dog Society men who decided to go at the last minute. For what purpose Stone Dreamer wasn't sure, unless it was to replenish their arms or, more likely, make trouble. At one point some of these heavily armed Dog Soldiers rode near him, and he overheard jocular talk of a fierce demonstration for the whites.

Stone Dreamer wore his finest tribal raiment, while Black Kettle wore a long blue robe and the tall hat of a U.S. dragoon. This was not so offensive, in Stone Dreamer's view, as the Army coats some of the Dog men wore in lieu of traditional shirts. The plundered coats bore holes torn by lead balls or lance points that had killed the original wearers. Some of the young men made it even worse by pinning on stolen medals, or hanging Christian crosses around their necks.

In the failing light, the pale and melancholy light of a dying day, the Cheyennes reached the creek and saw on the far side the marquees and Army tents, the wagons and horses and massed blue uniforms of the Commission party. The Dog Soldiers immediately began to wave lances and rifles, howl and hoot and sing. Several charged straight across the creek in a threatening way. The white-bearded chief in charge of the Commission held up his hand to signal restraint to his men. Stone Dreamer saw many Army rifles gleaming as the howling braves splashed through the creek. At the last moment they checked, and rocked with laughter at the expense of the anxious whites.

The white-bearded general lowered his arm. There beneath the marquee, he had not changed his position even slightly during the charge. A brave warrior, Stone Dreamer decided.

After an evening's feast the Cheyennes encamped near the much larger band of Arapahoes. In the morning the Cheyenne and Arapahoe chiefs seated themselves in a wide semicircle just in front of the Commission's main marquee. Stone Dreamer and his fellow chiefs faced the white chiefs, who were attended by strange men scribbling on tablets, and surrounded by a much larger body of soldiers whose brass buttons winked as brightly as their carbines and revolvers.

Through an interpreter the white chiefs presented their message: a very reasonable message, Stone Dreamer thought:

"We have among us wicked men who wish to profit by the calamities of both sides, and these bad men continually seek war. We now think these bad men told wicked lies to General Hancock last spring."

The smooth words of the white chiefs held bitter truths:

"Perhaps some of your young braves with more blood than brains will oppose your making peace with us. Such men must be cast away. Their councils are death. A war long continued will only end in the total destruction of the Indian because his numbers are less."

Stone Dreamer remembered the picture of the white village, which to this day burned in his nightmares, and he nodded to Black Kettle, who nodded back.

The white chiefs wisely addressed the most galling issue:

"As long as the buffalo ranges on the Plains, we are willing that you should hunt him provided you keep the treaties made at the Little Arkansas. But the herds of buffalo are becoming fewer and thinner every year . . ."

Angered, Stone Dreamer interrupted. "I ask the white chiefs who is to blame for that? Our young men say the buffalo are now hunted for sport, not merely to sustain life. You do not need the buffalo to sustain life, as we do. What are we to do if you rob us of them?"

The white chiefs had a saddening answer:

"In lieu of buffalo you must have herds of oxen, flocks of sheep, droves of hogs, like the white man."

Buffalo Chief of the Cheyennes arose with a hot reply:

"We are not farmers. We spring from the prairie. We live by it. You think that you are doing a great deal for us by giving presents, yet I say if you gave us all the goods you could give, we would still prefer our own life, to live as free as we have always done."

And when the white chiefs raised the issue of raids on homesteads and the rail line, Little Raven of the Arapahoe was prepared.

"It is you who should instruct your young men at the forts as to their duty. They are mostly children. You must stop them from running wild. That provokes war."

The blue-coated soldiers disliked the speech, and some made menacing motions with their weapons. The white chiefs calmed them, and as the day wore on the pugnacity of the Indians wore away, while the hunger for the gifts and guns increased. To tempt them, the white chiefs put forth their terms:

The Arapahoes and the Cheyennes must withdraw from Kansas, and settle with the other three Southern tribes on a special reserve of forty-eight thousand square miles to be set aside in the Indian Territory. On this land, with special Indian agents to mediate for them, the five tribes would live. Buildings would be put up to house a doctor, an agriculturist, a miller, a schoolteacher, a blacksmith, and any other white persons necessary for converting a race of nomads to farmers. There would be an annual dole from the White Father besides.

In return, the Indians must promise to stop their war on the wagon and rail traffic on the Santa Fe, Smoky Hill, and Platte River routes. They must promise to stay out of Kansas, although they would be permitted to hunt buffalo on open land below the Arkansas for as long as the herds lasted. When hunting, they were never to venture nearer than ten miles to any road or fort.

Again Stone Dreamer sighed. How could so few agree to such sweeping terms on behalf of so many? Many important chiefs—Tall Bull, Medicine Arrows, Big Head, Roman Nose—and hundreds of the People were not here.

Yet ultimately it was done, agreed to by a few chiefs who

mingled their regret with a sad realism. They touched the pen to a document never read and translated for them.

Not all of the signers of the treaty paper were cheerful about it. Bull Bear roared. "Well, as you are so earnest, so shall I be." Instead of merely touching the pen, he drove it down on the document so hard the point snapped.

The day-long conference was nearly over, and Stone Dreamer was starting to hear an excited buzzing about the gifts. Suddenly, the white chief Terry leaped up and pointed.

A dust trail in the west signaled a rider speeding to the encampment beside the creek. Soon they saw him. A lone man, at the gallop. Stone Dreamer's heart fell. He recognized Man-Ready-for-War.

He came in full regalia, in one hand his eight-foot lance with its glittering head of trade steel, in the other his snake rattle with clicking antelope dewclaws. He had painted his face with red pigment mixed with buffalo fat, leaving only the long hooking scar uncolored.

While blue-garbed soldiers raised their weapons around the central marquee, Scar leaped from his pony and marched to the treaty table. Stone Dreamer clasped his hands. His hair blew like a gray curtain across his anxious eyes. The sunset wind seemed cold as deep winter.

Scar gazed with contempt at the other men from his society, who huddled together, shame-faced. Then he flung a look at the seated Cheyenne chiefs. It was clear what he thought of them.

He surveyed the spread-out parchments, the assortment of fine quills and silver inkstands. Through the interpreter, he spoke swiftly and with passion:

"This paper is the work of devils who betray the People. What good is the white man's promise? The only promise he keeps is the promise to steal our land. And what good are the marks of toothless old weaklings such as those seated here? How can they presume to give away land the Spirit gave to all the People? They can't, and we Dog Men won't allow it. We will carry on the war until all of you white devils and your white women and your white infants are dead."

The commissioners leaped up and exclaimed. Scar laughed, exuberant over the reaction. Before they could stop him, he shot the tip of his lance beneath the treaty table and heaved upward.

Parchment flew. Pens dropped. Ink spilled. Someone fired a

shot, and an elderly Arapahoe cringed. Laughing heartily, Man-Ready-for-War walked back to his pony with a slow, haughty stride. He scrambled up, flung the commissioners another look scorning them for lacking the courage to retaliate, and rode away into the nimbus of light on the western hills.

Black Kettle brought both hands over his face, shamed and angry. Stone Dreamer felt tears he didn't bother to hide. Their brother chiefs looked unhappy, anxious. One of the white chiefs, Taylor, snarled at the men scribbling on tablets.

"Strike that speech from your notes," he told them. "Any man whose paper prints it will no longer have credentials west of the Mississippi. This is a successful conference. Report it that way."

It was a season of changes. The Southern Cheyennes withdrew to their villages on the Cimarron, there to winter peacefully with their trade goods and guns while awaiting removal to their new reservation. Charles heard about Scar's oration when the contingent of the Seventh returned to Fort Harker. He also heard that a mere four hundred or five hundred Cheyennes had represented three thousand members of the tribe. That almost amounted to no representation. "Well," he said, tiny glints showing in his eyes, bright like the point of a polished knife. His mouth lifted slightly at the corners.

All the handbills for the forthcoming visit of Trump's players showed a change. The performance at Fort Harker had been stricken out.

"I hear your lady friend's responsible," Barnes told Charles. "She found out the brass wouldn't let any colored boys into the same hall with whites. Our men, y'understand. Your friend sent a letter saying that she and Trump had talked it over, and the Army at Fort Harker could go fry. You want to see her, you'll have to traipse on over to Ellsworth."

Just like Willa, he thought. Crusading was an unchangeable part of her nature. It was one reason, though not the main reason, that he continually warned himself to stay away from her. Then he would remember the silver-gold glint of her hair, and her vivid merry eyes, and the feel of her in his arms—

He knew he'd traipse to Ellsworth, no matter what the consequences.

ST. LOUIS, MO., FRIDAY, NOV. 1

HON. O. H. BROWNING, *Secretary of the Interior:*

*Please congratulate the President and the country upon the en-
tire success of the Indian Peace Commission thus far. It concluded a
treaty with the Cheyennes of the South on the 28th, this being the only
tribe that has been at war in that quarter. More than 2,000 Cheyennes were present . . .*

[Signed] N. G. TAYLOR
*Commissioner of Indian Affairs
and President of Peace Commission*

34

Trump's players performed in Frank's Hall, City of Kansas, then ferried over the river to repeat their show at the Leavenworth post hall the following night. The troupe consisted of Sam, Willa, Tim Trueblood, and a stout character actress, Miss Suplee. A large trunk held their few simple props and costume pieces. Willa had argued Sam out of such encumbrances as a stock of "genuine" diamond rings, the sort of trinket given away on Saturday night by many touring companies.

Brigadier Duncan attended the Shakespearean evening. He'd invited Willa to stay with Maureen until her train left for Fort Riley the next afternoon at five. "I imagine you're anxious to see my grand-nephew," he said. Willa said she was.

"Why, he's grown remarkably," she said next day. Duncan had just returned for the noon meal, instead of taking it in the officers' mess. Little Gus kept scrambling off his chair. Duncan ordered him back, good-natured but firm about it.

"He'll be three come the end of this year." The brigadier spooned into the hot turtle soup Maureen had prepared. The boy, sturdy and towheaded, jumped off his chair and seized Willa's hand.

"She's all thumbs," he said to Duncan, and broke into a shrieking laugh. "All thumbs, all thumbs! Thumbs on her head, thumbs on her arms." He was red-faced, convulsed.

"What is he talking about, Willa?"

"After you left this morning, I brought a bowl of corn-meal mush to the table. I was careless and dropped the bowl. It cracked. I was annoyed with myself and said I was all thumbs. He sees the picture in his imagination."

"All thumbs," Gus cried, jumping up and down until

Duncan shushed him. The boy obeyed but he couldn't be repressed for long. He tugged her hand again. "Another walk, Aunt Willa?"

She noticed Duncan's keen look, turned pink. "After your nap, but not until."

Maureen scooped him up and carried him to bed. His legs kicked and his arms waved in uninhibited merriment. "All thumbs!" He was giggling as the door closed.

Duncan said, "Aunt Willa." He tilted his head with an approving smile.

"I didn't prompt him. It was his idea."

Over the noise of a troop of mounted men riding by on the parade ground, Duncan said, "You'd like to be more than his aunt. That would be good for him. And for his father."

"Well—" A bit nervous about it, she shrugged. "I would. But I'm not sure how Charles would feel. He's a wonderful man, but there's a strange, distant streak in him."

"The war." Willa gazed at the brigadier, her pale eyes as quizzical as his had been a few moments ago. "The war did that to a lot of soldiers. On top of it, Charles lived through the massacre of a man who befriended him."

"I understand. I just don't know how long someone can use the past to excuse present behavior."

Duncan frowned. "Until the patience of others is exhausted, I suppose. Patience, and affection too."

She concentrated on folding her napkin. "Never the latter. But the former—I don't know. My patience grows very thin sometimes. I refuse to deny everything I believe just to please Charles."

"Charles is strong, like you. Right or wrong, he won't abandon this vendetta against the Indians."

"And I hate it. I hate it for what it is, and for what it does to him." She paused. "I'm almost afraid to see him at Ellsworth."

The old soldier reached out and closed his thick-knuckled hand over hers. She turned away, overcome with embarrassing tears. The squeeze of his powerful fingers said he understood her fear. His eyes said she had some cause for it.

Charles's detachment came in the night before the performance. He found Ike Barnes with Floyd Hook, discussing details of a C Company club modeled after the International Order of

Good Templars, a society to promote temperance. There were chapters at many Western posts. As the old man explained, the epidemic Army problem of drunkenness hadn't spread into his troop, and the club would help insure that it wouldn't. First Sergeant Star Eyes Williams would be responsible for calling the initial meeting.

Tense about seeing Willa again, yet eager too, Charles shaved and spruced up in a clean uniform with big yellow bandanna and regulation hat. Since he'd stabled Satan to rest him, he took another company horse for the five-mile ride along the north bank of the Smoky Hill to what was officially called the Addition to Ellsworth. As he rode, he whistled the music Willa had written out. His Carolina music, he called it.

Much of the original site platted by the Ellsworth Town Company had been destroyed in June when the normally placid Smoky Hill overflowed its banks and washed away flimsy cottages and stores. Scarcely had they disappeared when the town promoters bought new land, on higher ground to the northwest. They filed a new plat in Salina to create the Addition, which showed every sign of becoming the real town of Ellsworth. It already had its own depot to supplement the one at Fort Harker; the first passenger train had rolled in from the east July 1.

The town also had cattle pens and chutes, testifying to the developers' faith that Ellsworth could become a shipping point for the trail herds pushing up Chisholm's Trail from Texas. Ellsworth boosters derided Abilene, about sixty miles east, and its promoter, Joe McCoy, even though McCoy had received his first big herd in September.

The November evening was clear and bitter. Charles was bundled in his thigh-length double-breasted buffalo coat. Weaving through wagon and horse traffic on the Addition's rutted main street, he saw half a dozen wagons approaching in a line. Red-stained tarpaulins mounded over the bed of each. Broad swipes of dried blood marked the wagon sides. Riding ahead of the wagons was a young man Charles recognized. The horseman next to the young man recognized Charles.

"Howdy. You're Main. We met at the Golden Rule House."

Charles wasn't accustomed to hearing his right name, but he didn't let on. "I remember. You're Griffenstein." He peeled off his gauntlet and leaned over to shake hands.

"This here's my boss, Mr. Cody."

Charles shook hands with the young man too. "Griffenstein said you wouldn't stay in the hotel business. Are you two hunters for the railroad?" He'd recognized the blood smell pervading the air.

Cody said, "For Goddard Brothers, the railroad's meat contractor. They pay five hundred a month, and me and my boys guarantee them all the buffalo meat they need to feed their crews. We knock 'em down fast, which makes it a profitable trade."

Charles studied the wagons, their reeking cargoes silhouetted against twilight stars in a rosy sky shading up to deep blue. Dutch Henry Griffenstein was amused by something. "You don't know the meanin' of fast till you watch Buffalo Bill work. He knocks down eleven, twelve bison in the time it takes most of us to load a Winchester."

"Mighty boring, though," Cody said. "Wouldn't mind scouting again. We'd better hustle, boys. It's almost dark."

He waved the wagons ahead and rode on. Dutch Henry grinned inside his huge chest-length beard. "You ever get tired of soldiering, Main, look us up. We can always use another good shot."

After Dutch Henry trotted off, Charles looked at both sides of the street, to see if there was anyone who might have overheard his name.

"Our revels now are ended. These our actors are melted into air, into thin air."

With flamboyant gestures, Sam Trump boomed Prospero's farewell to the audience. This portion had been purloined from the end of the Act IV masque. Trump was confident no one would detect the theft.

A half circle of chimneyed lamps lit the improvised stage. Blankets hung on rope served as side curtains. The theater was the dining room of the unfinished Drovertown Hotel, a room heavy with the smell of new pine lumber.

Charles had arrived too late for a seat on the benches brought in for the evening. He stood at the back, among some other bachelor officers from the fort. Seated in front of him were officers, their wives, and plainly dressed townspeople, but not a single black soldier.

Over the heads of the audience, Willa spied him only moments after he came in. She immediately fumbled one of Juliet's lines from the balcony scene. She was playing against Trump's giggle-inducing Romeo. Not only was Trump paunchy and too old, but he slapped his heart with both hands at any reference pertaining to romance.

The audience, however, starved for entertainment, clearly loved the Shakespearean excerpts, and listened attentively for two hours. During that time only one tipsy teamster had to be removed.

"We are such stuff as dreams are made on . . . and our little life is ended with a sleep." With but a breath between, he jumped to the epilogue of *The Tempest,* squeezing every syllable of the text for its juice. *". . . or else my project fails, which was to please . . ."* Charles fidgeted from foot to foot, while the actor fairly begged the audience for applause. *"As you from crimes would pardoned be . . . let your indulgence set me free."*

Trump's last line was spoken as he swooped into a low bow, anticipating his ovation. He got it. Willa, Trueblood, and the stocky character woman dashed from behind the blankets. All linked hands and bowed. Ike Barnes's wife jumped up and yelled, "Bravo, bravo," which prompted Trump to step forward for a solo bow. He knocked over a lamp. A soldier in the front row stamped on the leaking oil as it flamed, preventing a disaster. Trump paid no attention.

Each time Willa bowed, her eyes remained on Charles. He held his hands high so she could see him clapping. Lord, how pretty she was, and how he warmed at the sight of her. For a moment he felt peaceful; free of spite, the past—all his pain.

As the audience broke up, he joined others moving forward to congratulate the company. "Dear boy," Trump cried, spying Charles and lunging out to have his hand shaken. "How splendid to have you here. I'm glad you saw us this evening. This tour is a triumph. I'm sure they're already hearing of it in the East. When they send for us, I'll have to cancel the rest of the itinerary." And off he went to another admirer.

Charles strode to Willa, took hold of her arms, and kissed her forehead. "You were wonderful."

She slipped a hand behind his back and hugged him. "And you're very bad for my acting. Will you take me out of here?"

"Right now," he said, clasping her hand.

"I'd like to walk," she said. He reminded her about the cold. "I have an old wool coat, very heavy, and a muff."

So they set out, walking away from the unfinished two-story Drovertown Hotel. Suddenly they were facing a rolling black prairie with white and yellow stars sparkling above it.

"Don't you want supper?" he asked. "Aren't you starved after all that work?"

"Later. I want to hear about you." She fairly blushed. "Are you all right?"

"I'm all right." She linked arms with him. He commended her for refusing to play Fort Harker. "Sam told me the tour's been a triumph. You can tell me the truth."

She laughed. "Fort Riley was fair. The audience was off somehow, or we were. I caught Sam trying to sneak to the sutler's just before curtain."

"Did you play Leavenworth?"

"Yes. The audience there was fine."

"Did you have a chance to see my boy?"

"I did. He's wonderful, Charles. Very smart. The brigadier said he'd trained himself with the chamber pot before he was eighteen months old." Charles cleared his throat. She laughed a second time. "Oh, that's right, proper females don't mention such things to gentlemen. The looseness of my profession is showing again."

Amused, he said, "I knew about the chamber pot."

"I should have guessed. The brigadier did say it's difficult for him to handle Gus, because he adores the boy, and spoils him even though he doesn't intend it. He shows him your photograph constantly. Gus knows who you are. He missed you." Another squeeze of his arm. "I miss you, too. Buy me supper and ply me with a little wine and I'll show you how much."

She turned, directly in his path. She flung up an arm, hand around his neck, and pulled him into a kiss. He put both arms around her waist and felt her cold mouth warm quickly. They held one another in silence. Then something in Charles began to push away, distancing him from her.

"Oh, I *have* missed you. I love you, Charles. I can't help it." She didn't pause, the conventional signal that she expected him to say it in reply. She didn't want to push him. "Perhaps you'll get to see more of Gus now. There seems to be peace on the Plains."

They resumed their walk, going up a small round hill on

crackling frost-killed grass. At the summit they stopped, awed by the gigantic canopy of stars.

At length he answered her. "It's always peaceful in the winter."

"Yes. But what I mean is, now there's the Medicine Lodge Treaty. That should promote—"

"Willa, let's not start. You know that the subject of Indians always causes a muss between us." Did he want that? Was that why he put a certain testiness into his tone?

She heard it; it irked her. "Why should we not discuss it, Charles? It's a meaningful treaty."

"Come on. No treaty is meaningful, and Medicine Lodge was worse because only a few chiefs touched the pen. Did you read the dispatches Mr. Stanley wrote for the *New York Tribune*? The stupid commissioners didn't even read the entire treaty to Black Kettle and the rest. The chiefs wanted to accommodate the commissioners, they wanted the goods and guns, so they signed." By this point she'd separated her arm from his. "As soon as they realize what they gave away, they'll repudiate the treaty. If the Dog Society men don't kill them first."

"And that's what you want, I suppose?" She faced him, her face dim in the starlight. Her breath was a white cloud that spread and disappeared.

"I want the men who killed my friends. I wish you wouldn't bring it up."

"I bring it up because I care about you."

"Oh, hell." He pivoted away.

"You want the treaty to fail." She was losing control, something unusual for her; he heard it in the unsteadiness of her voice.

"Willa, I told you what I want. As for the rest of it, you're still on stage. Dreaming! The Cheyennes won't quit until they're penned up or killed. That may not be pretty, that may not please you or your Quaker friends who bleed their hearts out for a bunch of savages they never have to deal with, but that's how it is, and you ought to wake up."

"I'm awake, thank you. I thought you might have changed a little. You won't give the treaty a chance."

"Because that's useless, goddamn it. Henry Stanley said it. General Sherman has been saying it for two years."

"And what all of you prophesy eventually comes true? Why don't you prophesy peace for a change?"

"By God, you're the most blind, unrealistic—"

"You're the one who's blind, Charles. Blind to what you're becoming. Some sort of—of hate-filled creature who lives to kill. I don't want a man like that."

"Don't worry, you haven't got one—even though you chase damn hard."

He was shouting. She cried out, "Bastard!" and struck at him with her open hand. He deflected it and stepped back. He was altogether stunned when he realized that even as she cursed him, she was crying.

He stood like a dolt under the autumn stars, watching her flying figure race back toward the lamps of the Addition. "Willa, wait. It isn't safe for a woman to be by herself—"

"You be quiet!" she yelled over her shoulder. She stopped and faced him. "You don't know how to behave like a decent human being. You drive everyone away. The war did it, Duncan says. The war, the war—I'm sick of the war and I'm sick of you."

She turned and ran on. He heard her weeping. The sound faded slowly, and then he lost her running figure against the black shapes of the flimsy buildings of the new town.

He walked slowly along the side of the Drovertown Hotel to the rail in front where he'd tied his mount. He was lifting his boot to the stirrup when someone lurched out of the heavy shadow. The man had been concealed there, waiting. Charles jumped back, panicky because he'd left his sidearm at the fort. The moment the attacker stepped into the light from a saloon next door, Charles saw the chrysanthemum on his lapel, and smelled the gin.

"You damned, base cad!" Sam Trump's face was blotched by anger. His temples were stained by hair dye that had run. He raised his fist, intending to strike Charles's head. Charles took hold of his forearm and with no trouble kept it away. Trump twisted and struggled.

"Let go, damn you, Main. I'm going to give you what I promised you for hurting that fine young woman."

"I didn't hurt her. We just had an argument."

"You did more than argue. She ran in sobbing. She has iron courage, and I have never seen her so devastated." He tried to lift a knee and kick Charles's groin through the furry overcoat. Charles easily threw him off balance. The actor cried out and landed on his rump.

Trump's breathing was strident. He moved tentatively on the ground, as if he'd twisted something. "It must give you satisfaction to injure persons weaker than yourself. You're no better than those savages you purport to hate. Take yourself out of my sight."

Charles hauled his boot back, ready to kick the old fool. Then reason took hold. He mounted the troop horse and quickly trotted away up the street, shaking with anger and self-loathing. If there had been anything at all left between him and Willa Parker, it was gone now.

M A D E L I N E ' S   J O U R N A L

November, 1867. Impossible to do business at the Gettys store. His rates remain a usurious 70%, and a share of the crop. Those are his terms for whites. Black men are turned away.

. . . People somewhat mollified by appointment of Gen. Edw. Canby to command the military district. A Kentuckian; not as harsh as old Sickles. Gen. Scott, in charge of the state Bureau, is said to have ambitions to be the next gov. Very odd for a man who first arrived in Carolina as a war prisoner. Opinion of him is divided. Some say he is a trimmer. Does he want to govern the state in order to loot it? . . .

We continue to flirt with ruin. A late-season storm brought salt tides flooding far up the Ashley. Our rice crop was killed. The old stream-driven saw I saved so hard to buy for the mill broke during the second day of operation. Repairs are dear. To pay, I will have to short Dawkins's next bank installment. He will not be happy.

But there are crumbs of good news. Brett wrote at last. Her little boy, G. W., grows and thrives in the San Francisco climate. After a year's hardship, Billy's engineering firm has won a contract for the water, gas, and elevator systems in a new hotel.

Hearing of successes like theirs, I am sometimes tempted to abandon this place and start over myself. Only what I promised you, Orry—the dream of rebuilding—keeps me here. But every day seems to push the realization of the dream further into the distance . . .

. . . Special election soon, to decide whether we shall

*have a constitutional convention. The Army continues to regis-
ter males to vote. If they are black, the new U. L. club instructs them on how to exercise that right . . .*

In the autumn dusk, Andy Sherman hurried through the
hamlet of Summerton. A soldier, one of the registrars, was hauling down the American flag hung outside the abandoned cabin
taken over by the military. Nearby, a corporal chatted with a
barefoot white girl winding a strand of her hair round and round
her finger. Andy marveled. In some ways, the war might never
have happened at all.

In other ways it remained a hard reality. On the dark porch
of the store, someone in a rocker watched him go by, following
his progress by turning his head. Dying light flashed off the glass
ovals of spectacles. Andy could fairly smell the hostility.

After walking a mile more, he turned off the river road onto
a narrow track fringed by palmetto and prickly pear. The moon
hung above the trees now, a brilliant white circle. A black boy
with bad teeth guarded the road with an old squirrel rifle. Andy
nodded and started by. The boy barred him with the rifle, sheep-
ishly. "Passwords, Sherman."

Passwords, a secret grip—Andy found it childish and insulting. Unfortunately most of the club members enjoyed such
things.

"Liberty," he said. "Lincoln. League."

"God bless General Grant. Pass on, brother."

He entered the cabin after being inspected by Wesley, a
bullet-headed black man with a pistol in his belt. Wesley assisted
the club's organizer and was suited to the task; he was a bully.

A look of dislike passed between them. Andy slipped to a
back bench, noting about twenty others present, young and old.
The organizer nodded a greeting from the end of the cabin where
he stood before a framed portrait of Lincoln swagged with a piece
of dirty bunting.

Nothing about Lyman Klawdell impressed Andy. Not his
shabby clothes and jutting teeth, not his whining Yankee voice or
tied-down Colt revolver. Klawdell called for a lantern to be
blown out, which left a single candle burning on a crate near the
portrait. The candle lighted Klawdell's chin and long nose from
beneath. His eyes gleamed in the black hollows of the sockets.
The eerie effect produced some nervous shivers and grins.

Klawdell rapped a gavel on the crate. "Meeting of the Union League Club, Ashley River District, now in session. Praise God, praise freedom, praise the Republican Party."

"Amen," the listeners responded in unison. Andy remained silent. To be a free man did you have to recite on cue?

"Boys—" If any of the others took Klawdell's word as an insult, Andy saw no sign. "We are approaching a momentous day for South Carolina. I refer to the special election to call the constitutional convention that will set this state on the right path at last. We must have a convention in order to thwart His Accidency, Mr. Johnson"—groans, jeers—"who has proved no friend of the colored man. He continues to work against the Congress as it seeks to guarantee your rights—"

Andy saw bewilderment on many faces, the result of Klawdell's two-dollar words. To impress men, did you have to confuse them?

"—and lately has perpetrated an even greater outrage, suspending the powers of one of your best friends, the Honorable E. M. Stanton, Secretary of War and loyal supporter of our beloved President Lincoln. Johnson wants to keep Stanton from doing his job because he's doing it so well. It's Mr. Stanton who sent the soldiers to protect you. Johnson also wants to test a fine law which the Congress passed to prevent exactly this sort of interference. Do you know what's going to happen to Johnson?"

The men answered, "No." Andy grimaced. Klawdell thumped his gave.

"Your Republican friends are going to twist Johnson's tail. They may even throw him out of office."

That produced a lot of applause and foot-stomping. "All right, settle down," Klawdell snapped. "We have important business here at home too. How many of you boys have gone to Summerton and signed up to vote in favor of the convention?"

Hands were raised, all but Andy's and that of an old man. Klawdell didn't like Andy and singled him out, pointing with the gavel. "Explain yourself, Sherman."

Affronted, Andy leaped to his feet. "I work all day just to stay alive. They won't sign you up at night, which is the only time I've got free."

"Come on, tell the truth," Klawdell said. "That woman who runs Mont Royal won't let you register. She pretends to be a friend of the colored but she isn't. Why don't you speak out and denounce her the way you should?"

"Because she *is* a friend, and I won't lie about her."

Klawdell licked his lips. "Sherman, some of these boys felt the same way about their masters for a while. Do you know what happened to them?"

"I do." He pointed to Rafe Hicks, a tan youth with a dirty bandage tied around his head. "Some of 'em jumped after dark, and got the hell beat out of them."

"Then take a lesson. Denounce her."

"I will not. You want that, I'm out of this club."

He walked quickly to the door, tight inside. Wesley blocked his way, just itching to pull his pistol. Andy stopped, fisted his hands, and stared Wesley down. In a low voice he said, "You try to stop me, Wesley, you're going to have broken bones. Or worse."

Wesley cursed and started to draw. Klawdell whipped out his revolver and used the butt for a gavel. "All right, all right, everybody calm down. We need your vote more than we need a fight in here, Sherman. If you're willing to register—"

"I am. I just have to find time."

"Then we'll forget about the rest."

Andy gave him the same kind of hard stare he'd given Wesley. Then he returned to his bench. A couple of the men he had to step over to reach his seat leaned far back, afraid that even a touch might anger him. Andy felt some small satisfaction, but bitterness too. The League men were pouring into the South—to help educate the freedmen, they said. Why did that education have to include sowing distrust, even hatred, of good white friends? Andy could never think of Madeline as anything but white.

Klawdell resumed. "The special convention will be a great thing, boys. But it will never be convened unless a majority of South Carolina voters approve. Sherman and Newton have got until November 19 to sign up."

The old man, Newton, said, "But we got to do that in Summerton, Captain. Gettys and his friends, like that Captain Jolly, they say, don't stop in Summerton, nigger. Move right on through."

"Why do you think there are two soldiers at the crossroads, Newton? Not just to sign you up. To make sure no one interferes with you when you do it. You tell Gettys and his pals to lean down and kiss your ass."

As the clapping and laughter burst out, Andy winced again. Somehow the tone here was all wrong. His black friends and neighbors were being treated like children. He almost stood and walked out for good. Only the club's larger purpose, more important than Klawdell's behavior, kept him from it.

Klawdell saw Andy's resentment and took a more moderate tone. "I'll say it again, Sherman—we need you and Newton both. Every vote counts. Sign up. Please."

Well, that was better. "Don't worry. I will."

"Praise God," Klawdell exclaimed. He put his revolver away and grabbed the gavel. "All right, let's hear it." *Whack* went the gavel. "What's the party for the colored man?"

All but Andy said, "Union Republican."

Whack. "Who are your enemies?"

"Johnson. Democrats."

Whack, whack. "Who'd steal away the rights we fought and bled to give you, the rights Abe Lincoln died to give you?"

"Democrats!"

"Now tell me the name of your true friends."

They stomped for each word. "Union—Republicans."

"Who's going to take over this state?" Now Klawdell was shouting. "Who's going to take over this whole country and run it right?"

"Union Republicans! Union Republicans!" The stomping shook the cabin. Andy kept his mouth shut, his hands laced together, his work shoes tight against each other on the floor. He scowled as the others swayed and clapped and filled the cabin with their din. "Union Republicans! *Union Republicans!*" Some of the men glared at Andy. He glared right back, damned if he'd act like someone's trained dog. He continued to sit straight as a rod, in silent protest.

The next day, about an hour before sunset, Andy appeared at the Summerton crossroads. Walking swiftly, he approached the flag-decorated cabin. The corporal stepped out, shook his hand, and escorted him inside.

Through the window of the Dixie Store, Randall Gettys watched. When Andy reappeared in ten minutes and started home, looking pleased, Gettys immediately penned a letter to Des in Charleston.

> *She now has registered every one of her niggers. I have urged caution but we cannot wait much longer. You had better come down and talk about it.*

He then wrote his cousin Sitwell, up in York County.

> *The mephitic Republican League is inflaming all the local colored men. They outnumber us and will out-vote us this month. We are desperate for some safe means of thwarting them. Have you heard anything further of that secret in Tennessee?*

> *The vote to call a convention passed overwhelmingly. I suppose there was never a doubt. As many as 80,000 freedmen registered, and only about half that number of whites.*
>
> *The military persuaded Andy to declare himself a delegate candidate, and he did. He will go to Charleston in January.*
>
> *It is our only good news. Two bad crops this year—the stream saw still not repaired—Dawkins demanding the quarterly money—we are even closer to ruin. On the very edge. Again last night Prudence and I argued over appealing to George H. I prevailed, but wonder if I am right. Wouldn't it be better to beg than to lose everything? How I wish you were here to guide me.*

35

Charles, Gray Owl, and the ten-man detachment returned to the field, patrolling the railroad east of Fort Harker. On that segment of the line Indian attacks weren't as frequent as they were between Harker and Fort Hays to the west, but neither were they unknown.

They experienced a spell of unusually hot weather. Warm air shimmered over the plains, creating silver lakes in the distance; lakes that vanished long before a man reached them. On a sunny morning, the soldiers were walking their horses in columns of twos just to the north of a line of low rolling hills. On the other side, parallel with the hills, ran the railroad and the telegraph.

Charles was thankful to be moving again. It helped ease his feelings of sadness and anger about Willa. Except for that, he felt good about things. He had a fine horse; Satan ran strongly, wasn't nervous about gunfire, and had exceptionally good wind. He had ridden the piebald long enough so that horse and man could almost sense one another's thoughts.

He was equally satisfied with his men. He dropped back toward Gray Owl at the rear and inspected them. They all rode competently, and a few, such as Magee, had a real flair for it. Those who'd kept their regulation trousers had reinforced them with canvas patches on the seat and thigh. Brims of straw hats and bills of chasseur kepis shaded their eyes. A bedroll with extra clothing hung over the front of each man's McClellan saddle. The saddle also carried lariat, picket pin, canteen, and a tin plate. A saddle sheath by the right knee held the rifle; at Charles's suggestion, his men had left their generally useless bayonets behind.

They passed him two by two, each with sheath knife on the

left hip, holster with pistol butt forward on the right. Only one man had retained a regulation cartridge box on his belt. The rest kept their metal in bandoliers or belts they'd sewn themselves. For former city boys they were a fierce-looking lot; they really did resemble roving bandits ready for any eventuality.

Shem Wallis rode by. Charles heard him say to Corporal Magic Magee, "Lord, it's hot. I can't believe it's November. When we gonna noon?"

"Pretty soon," Magee said. "Here, watch this coin."

Charles called out to Wallis, "We'll stop there." He pointed to a grove of bare trees some distance ahead and to the left. Since trees usually grew in the damp bottomland, they might find a stream, and cottonwood bark for the horses to forage on.

Charles dropped all the way back beside Gray Owl. The men liked the tracker, but Magee had really taken to him because Gray Owl was always such a fine audience for his sleights. Charles still hadn't learned a thing about his past, especially why he'd abandoned his people. The tracker seemed to be relaxed and in a good mood, so Charles decided to try again.

"Gray Owl, if you're going to track for me, I'd like to know some things about you. Tell me about your family."

The Indian hunched inside his buffalo robe. Despite the heat, no perspiration showed on his lined face. He thought for a while before he answered. "My father was a great chief named Crooked Back. My mother was a white woman he captured. They say she was fair and light-haired. She has been dead a long time."

This surprising information was a wedge. "Any other family?"

"No. Eight winters past, my sister traveled the Hanging Road. Five winters past, my only brother followed. Both were carried off by the same sickness. The one your people brought to us that we had never suffered before."

"Smallpox?"

"Yes." Gray Owl gave Charles a long look, and he felt a stab of guilt. The Indian gazed ahead at the heat devils.

Charles cleared his throat. "What I'd really like to know is why you're willing to track for the Army."

"When I was a young man, I went to seek my vision in order to become a warrior and find the purpose of my life. In the sweat lodge I burned out the poisons of doubt and hate and headstrong selfishness. I painted my face white to purify it and went apart, as seekers must, to a dangerous place. A lonely place, with grass so tall and dry, the smallest spark could ignite a great fire to consume me."

Charles held his breath. He was getting somewhere.

"Three days and nights I lay hidden in tall grass, crying out for my vision. I ate nothing. I drank nothing. I was rewarded. The Wise One Above, the holy spirit you white men call God, began to speak from the clouds, and from pebbles in a stream, and from a snake passing by. I saw myself hollow and smooth as a dry reed, ready to be filled.

"God moved then. All the grasses bent, each blade pointing north toward the ancient Sacred Mountain. In the empty sky, an eagle appeared. It swooped low over my head and flew west. Then, from the center of the sun, a great owl descended. The owl spoke a while. Then the sun blinded me."

"Did the owl become your helper bird?"

Gray Owl was startled; Charles knew more of the tribe's ways than he'd suspected. "Yes. I keep a great owl's claw with me always." He tapped his medicine bundle, a drawstring bag tied to his belt. "And always, if I ask, a great owl will appear and guide me when I am lost or confused. I learned my purpose from the owl and from the eagle."

"What is your purpose?"

"It was to help the People find the way. To lead them to winter camps and to ceremony grounds for the great summer festivals. To track the buffalo south with the snows and north with the green grass. When I returned from seeking my vision I donned a warrior's regalia, but thereafter always followed my purpose."

"To lead the People. But now you're leading us. Why?"

Gray Owl's face turned stony. "The People strayed so far from the right way that not even God could lead them back. It is time to rest. Shall I search those trees ahead?"

It was as if a curtain had fallen in Trump's theater. Frustrated, Charles nodded. The Cheyenne dug in his moccasins and raced his pony away toward the distant grove.

Ten miles east, a westbound passenger train left the hamlet of Solomon and crossed the line into Saline County. In the freight car, two men polished their guns while two others played cards.

In the second-class passenger car, a young woman on her way to join her husband at Fort Harker gazed through the window at the stark landscape. She'd never been west of the Mississippi before. Her husband was a sergeant recently transferred to the Seventh Cavalry.

In the seat ahead of her, a cavalry officer wearing a silver oak leaf intently studied a book on tactics. At the end of the car the conductor counted ticket stubs. The other passengers talked or dozed, and no one happened to glance toward the south side of the train. There, about a mile from the right-of-way, a line of twenty mounted men started down a low hill and, at the bottom, began to ride rapidly toward the train.

While they waited for Gray Owl, Magee pulled out his piece of practice rope. He handed the rope to another trooper, Private George Jubilee, then crossed his wrists and asked Jubilee to tie him. Jubilee's father, a fugitive slave, had chosen the last name after he found sanctuary in Boston.

"Good and tight," Magee said. Sliding his horse closer, Jubilee concentrated on looping the rope around Magee's wrists several times. He didn't notice the momentary stiffening of Magee's spine, the slight shudder of his forearms, the sudden appearance of veins on the dark brown backs of his fisted hands. Charles saw it from his vantage point, though; he'd seen Magee's escapes and was alert to the trick. Magee was almost undetectably putting tension on the rope while Jubilee finished his loops and tied two knots.

Jubilee sat back on his saddle, smug about his handiwork. Magee began to twist his hands in opposite directions, his nostrils flaring. He grunted once and suddenly, faster than Charles could follow, his hands were apart. The rope was still knotted around his left wrist. He'd created just enough slack to allow him to work a hand free.

Magee smiled lazily and picked at the knots while Private Jubilee stared, dumbfounded. He was relatively new to the troop and to Magee's tricks.

Gray Owl returned in ten minutes. He was paler than Charles had ever seen him.

"Whites have passed here," he said with suppressed fury. "There are dead men and dead horses among the trees. The bodies have been despoiled."

Charles took the head of the column, ordered his buffalo soldiers to the trot, and led them toward the grove. Well before they reached it, he saw the meandering stream he expected, a narrow ribbon of yellow water along the grove's north perimeter.

A rank smell floated from the leafless trees. Charles recognized it. He's smelled the same stench at Sharpsburg and Brandy Station and other places where the dead lay a long time after the firing stopped. One of his younger men leaned to the right and shuddered with the dry heaves.

Charles unsheathed his saber and raised it to signal a halt. The saber was a useless weapon in the field, except where it would serve as a standard, something bright and visible to rally around. "I'll go in first. The rest of you water your horses."

He dismounted, shifted the saber to his left hand, and drew his Colt. He approached the grove with caution. Gray Owl followed without permission; Charles was conscious of him as a shadow flicking over the sere grass to his left.

From the edge of the grove he saw a dead horse, then two more. Warriors' horses, usually left alive so that their owners would have fine mounts in paradise. This probably meant that someone other than Indians had shot them.

He swallowed, took a few more steps, and spied the three decomposing bodies. Stripped of raiment, they lay amid broken sections of wooden platforms. Upright timbers that had supported the platforms still stood in the center of the grove. Forcing himself, Charles moved closer to inspect the naked corpses. Near them he found the splintered shafts of several brightly painted arrows. Everything else had been looted.

He heard the anger in Gray Owl's voice. "Do you know what has happened?"

"I do. It's the custom of your people to put their dead on these burial platforms if the winter ground is too hard to dig. These were special men—war chiefs, camp chiefs, maybe society leaders—because they were buried this way when the ground isn't frozen."

Nearer to the sky on the platforms, the dead thus passed more quickly along the Hanging Road to paradise. It was also customary for the Cheyennes to deposit personal treasures, weapons, and a favorite mount, so the dead man wouldn't lack for anything in the afterlife. Oddly, despite his hatred of the Cheyennes, Charles found himself sickened by the desecration.

"Look more closely," Gray Owl said to him. The tracker was almost stammering with rage. "Go. *Look!*"

Charles stepped forward but soon halted again, pale. Not only were the funeral garments gone, but also chunks of flesh, hacked from arms, legs, and torsos. In the fist-sized cavities, maggots swarmed.

"Jesus Christ. *What for?*" This was something entirely new.

Gray Owl shouted, "Bait." He waved wildly at the stream. "Fishing bait. I saw this once before. A soldier of the Seventh bragged that he had done it." Tears ran from Gray Owl's eyes. For a moment Charles thought the Cheyenne might pull his knife and stab him. "The white man is filth. He counts coup on the dead."

"Your own people sometimes—" he began, thinking of Wooden Foot and Boy, the violet-eyed girl in the sod house. He stopped, because those atrocities couldn't cancel this one.

A long wail in the east broke the silence. A westbound train.

Gray Owl turned and left the grove. At that moment he clearly hated Charles and every other white man. Then why in hell did he track for them?

Distantly, again from the east, he heard faint crackling. He dashed out of the grove, glad to do so. He waved his saber and his revolver. "Mount. There's gunfire."

Three troopers at the stream raised dripping faces as he shouted again, *"Mount!"* He wigwagged the saber over his head and ran toward Satan, the horror in the grove and the complexity of the resulting emotions mercifully banished by the sudden, urgent need to act.

The twenty Indians divided, half of them charging around the rear of the chugging U.P.E.D. passenger local. The parallel columns dashed ahead, to attack the train from both sides.

In the second-class coach, the sergeant's wife looked through a window across the aisle and saw brown horsemen riding bareback, their black hair streaming. Some brandished guns, some their hunting bows. At the head of the coach an older woman jumped up, then fainted. "My God, Lester, Cheyennes," a man cried to his traveling companion.

"Arapahoes," said the cavalry officer in the seat ahead of the woman. "You can tell by the unbound hair." He snatched out his service revolver, broke the window with three blows of his elbow, and fired a round. He missed.

The sergeant's wife stared with disbelief at a fierce painted face hovering not three feet from her. It wasn't a man, she realized, but a boy, no more than seventeen or eighteen. He jammed a trade musket to his cheek while he gripped his racing pony with his knees. The boy and the white woman stared at each other for a protracted moment, nothing save the glass and the shining barrel between them.

"Down," the russet-bearded officer yelled at her. He stood and took aim at the Indian. The young brave saw him and shot first. The colonel's body jerked, his eyes rolled up in his head, and he sank to the floor.

A man screamed, "We're all gonna die here!"

"The hell we are," the conductor shouted. "There's railroad men hiding aboard this train."

Concealed in the freight car, J. O. Hartree smiled at his three companions when he heard the hoofbeats, the shrill yells, the first shots. He was a plump, relatively young man, with soft good looks, wavy hair, and a long drooping mustache waxed to points. He had a piously insincere smile and mean eyes.

"Turk, you stand beside me," he said, quickly pulling on shiny leather gloves. He rolled up the sleeves of his white silk shirt and flexed his knees to be sure he had the feel of the moving train. He couldn't use his hands for support once they went into action.

Hartree and his hired shootists had been riding the line for weeks, hoping for this sort of opportunity. All summer the tribes had raided the line's construction sites, terrorized the workers, and butchered a few who foolishly strayed off by themselves. Hartree was under orders to convince the damned red men that they couldn't strike the line with impunity. It was a mission he enjoyed.

He smoothed the front of his green satin waistcoat embroidered with two rearing antelope, majestic pronghorns. "Red, when I give the word, slide the door open. Then help Wingo load the guns." On the floor lay eight powerful .45-caliber Sharps buffalo rifles, four for each shooter. J. O. Hartree planned carefully.

Two bullets thumped outside of the car. Over other noise,

Hartree heard windows breaking. The passengers were under attack. Well, he'd give this red filth a real surprise.

"Let's have the first two rifles, Red. Cock the hammers and rear triggers. Turk, if you fire before I say so, I'll put the first bullet in you."

Charles and his detachment came over the nearby rise in line formation, charging. Billowy smoke streamed out above the train. Howling Indians with unbound hair galloped alongside. The Indians saw the troopers and reacted with surprise and confusion.

The train was about a quarter mile to the soldiers' left, chugging along with many of its coach windows blown out. Charles gripped Satan with his knees and steadied his Spencer, knowing he had only a small chance of a hit with the piebald bouncing under him.

An Indian swung his bow up and aimed at Magic Magee, riding on Charles's left. Charles leaned that way and struck Magee's shoulder with his palm. Magee lurched over and for a moment hung down close to his horse's neck. That was the moment the arrow hissed through the space where his throat had been a few seconds earlier.

Magee dragged himself upright and flung Charles a look of appreciation. Shem Wallis took aim and blew the bowman off his pony. The Indians were slowing their pace now, outnumbering the soldiers but inferior in fire power. Charles yelled orders and half the troopers peeled away to circle the end of the train and go after the Indians glimpsed on the other side.

Drawing near the train, with the wind beating in his face, Charles raised the Spencer again. Then something happened for which the soldiers were altogether unprepared.

J. O. Hartree ran his hand along the barrel of the Sharps, silently starting a ten-count. *Snick! Whump!* He heard arrows striking the car. He took a firmer stance beside Turk and finished the count.

"Open it."

The door squealed as it rolled. Morning light flashed on the double-triggered Sharps held by the two shootists. An Arapahoe goggled at the sudden appearance of the railroad men. Hartree's brown eyes sparkled and his pious smile broadened. "Blow them down, Turk."

Because the rear triggers had been cocked, each front trigger was a hair trigger, needing merely a touch to fire the piece. Smoke and noise erupted from the door of the freight car. The Indian rifleman flipped off the bare back of his pony was instantly trampled by the horses of two other Arapahoes, unable to avoid him.

Incredibly, beyond the racing Indians, Hartree saw a bunch of those black nigger cavalrymen, raffish as bandits. The soldiers and their white officer, likewise racing beside the train, shouted for the railroad men to stop shooting; they were directly in the line of fire. Hartree ignored them, passed the hot buffalo gun behind him, and received another. His next shot missed, but it blew off the straw hat of a nigger, who immediately crouched down over his horse.

"You got my marker now," Magee shouted as he galloped beside Charles. "That red bastard almost had me."

Charles shouted back, "Those idiots on the train are going to kill us." He pumped his Spencer up and down over his head. "Hold your fire! That's an order! Hold—"

The shootist in the green embroidered vest snapped off a round to show how much he cared about the order. The Arapahoes, caught between the railroad men and the galloping soldiers, recalculated the odds; the leader motioned for them to drop back. Soon all of them were behind the train, dodging bullets from the troopers on the far side. They returned fire briefly with arrows and guns. One Indian flung his arms up and slid off his pony, blood running down his chest. The others immediately sheared away south, out of danger.

All of it happened in less than two minutes. Charles was furious. His first good chance at avenging Wooden Foot was nearly gone and he hadn't dropped a single Indian. Not one.

"You want us to chase 'em, Lieutenant August?" one of his men yelled.

Charles wanted to answer in the affirmative. But he was required to take charge of the damaged train and any wounded. He presumed there were some. He saw not a single human face in the shot-out windows of the coach.

"No, God damn it, I don't."

Angry that the soldiers might spoil the show, J. O. Hartree said, "Someone yank the cord. Stop the train. I want prisoners." As quickly as it began, all firing stopped, and the train jerked and slowed and jerked again as the brakes took hold.

Charles and his men brought their horses alongside the train, which bristled with painted arrow shafts. As the Rogers locomotive came to a stop, clouds of steam drifted up, mingling with settling dust. Charles watched the green-vested man jump from the freight car and strut forward. One close look at the man's face and Charles knew there'd be trouble.

36

Charles slid his Spencer back in the scabbard and trotted to the freight car. Three more civilians jumped down; a ratty lot. The plump man in the shiny gloves and green satin waistcoat was obviously in charge, and as the moments passed Charles liked his pushy swagger less and less.

"J. O. Hartree," the man said, as though the name should mean something. In the shot-up car, the excited voices of people in shock could be heard. Displeased by the lack of recognition, Hartree added, "Chief of railroad security."

"Lieutenant August, Tenth Cavalry. You beat us to it. We hardly fired a shot." His regret was evident.

"We've been riding the line and laying for the red bastards. You saw what cowards they are."

"You've got that wrong, Mr. Hartree. An old friend once said you have to turn your notions upside down on the Plains. If my detachment loses a man the Army will send another in a month. If the Indians lose a man it takes five or ten years for a boy to grow up to replace him. They're not cowards, just damn careful."

Putting the man down bled off some of Charles's anger. But Hartree didn't like it. "I don't need a lecture from you," he said. A disheveled woman raised herself into one of the broken windows, saw the black soldiers, and sank out of sight with a horrified look on her face. Hartree shielded his eyes against the sun and squinted eastward, through the dust still drifting behind the train.

"Boys, I see at least one of them alive back there. Bring him in. We'll make an example of him."

"What are you talking about?" Charles asked. Hartree ignored him. Magee scowled and punched a dent out of his derby.

The conductor appeared on the coach platform. "We've got a wounded man in here."

Charles said, "Hurt bad?"

"Flesh wound. He's awake."

"Let me check my own first." He'd no sooner said it than Wallis rode into sight at the rear of the train, waving his kepi. "Lieutenant? Toby's down. Arrow in his leg." Charles swore. "One Indian down over here, too."

Hartree said to the redheaded shootist, "Get him." He and the others hurried off.

Charles handed his rein to one of his troopers and stepped up close to Hartree. Hartree's men, meantime, reached an Arapahoe who had fallen near the caboose. The redhead kicked the body, rolled it over, shook his head, and proceeded on toward another Arapahoe, who was crawling on hands and knees, bleeding from a shoulder wound.

The Indian staggered up and tried to run. Redhead caught him and dragged him back. The other two shootists vanished behind the train in search of the other brave.

A couple of men appeared at the blown-out windows. Charles heard some slapping sounds, and an anxious voice. "Wake up, May Belle. You're all right. Don't take on so. Those are just nigger soldiers."

The wounded Arapahoe came lurching toward Charles, pushed by the redhead. Blood poured down the Indian's arm and dripped from his fingers. Dismounted and hurt, the brave looked harmless and ordinary. One of Hartree's men emerged from behind the train carrying an Indian in his arms. "Hurt leg," the man shouted. "Can't walk."

"Drop him right there," Hartree called back. "You're not his goddamn nurse." The man let go, and the Indian screamed when he hit the ground.

"Listen, Hartree," Charles said, "I think we'd better clear up one matter. It's the Army's responsibility to convey prisoners to Fort Harker."

"You don't have a thing to do with it, mister. The scum attacked railroad property." He grabbed the shiny shoulder-length hair of the Arapahoe prisoner and twisted. "The railroad will deal with them." He squatted and wiped his glove on yellowed grass at trackside. "Greasy damn bastards."

Hartree's eyes flicked back and forth between the bleeding prisoner and the Indian lying on his back at the rear of the train. Stroking his mandarin mustache, he suddenly made up his mind.

"This one's in better shape. He goes free after we take care of his friend. I want this boy to see what we do to red men who threaten railroad property. I want him to tell the others. Turk, fetch those picket pins from my valise."

The shootist named Turk scrambled back into the freight car. Charles was beginning to have a very bad feeling. Turk jumped down again with two of the sharp metal pins used to picket horses. Slowly, hoping to attract no attention, Charles wandered back to Magee, who had dismounted.

Hartree took the picket pins. He tossed them up and caught them in front of the wounded Arapahoe. Charles leaned close to Magee and muttered in his ear. Magee said, "Yessir, I'll see if anybody up front is hurt." He walked toward the locomotive carrying his Springfield rifle.

More passengers were peering from the coach. Hartree addressed them. "Gentlemen—and you ladies especially—I respectfully ask that you stay in there while I deal with these savages. I intend to punish one of them in a way consistent with their treatment of white captives. The lesson will benefit every white man and woman in Kansas."

"Back off, Hartree," Charles said. "I told you this is the Army's responsibility."

Two of Hartree's shootists raised their buffalo rifles. Hartree said, "No, sir, this is railroad business. Don't interfere unless you want several dead niggers to explain to your commanding officer."

A trooper grabbed his sidearm. Gray Owl reached out to stay his hand. "We're on the same side. Or we're supposed to be."

Charles glanced toward the engine cab. Magee had vanished. Hartree tossed the picket pins to Turk. "Go back to that other man and tie him down. Spread-eagle him. Nail those two pins through his private parts."

Charles turned white. The conductor gripped the platform stair rail and said, "Mr. Hartree, that's pretty extreme."

Hartree yelled, "Shut your damn mouth or we'll save a pin for you. Turk?" The man trotting toward the rear of the train turned back. "Be sure you rip off his clout first. Red, take this dirty scum back there to watch."

The Arapahoe whose arm dripped blood was dragged away. He looked sick. Charles swallowed sour saliva.

Gray Owl was gazing at the train. Suddenly his mouth dropped open. Charles warned him with a look, holding motionless while he watched a wild turkey feather, then a black derby, rise above the roof line of the freight car. Magic Magee climbed into sight, unseen by Hartree or the passengers below.

Charles felt sweat gather and drip from his nose. Slowly, Magee lifted his Springfield to his shoulder. He aimed at the back of the green satin waistcoat. At the rear of the train, one of Hartree's men spied Magee and yelled, just as Charles spoke.

"Turn around, Mr. Hartree. If you crucify that Indian, it'll cost your life."

Hartree spun, saw Magee, clenched his fists. "Shit." He flung a look at his men, who were too far away to do him much good. Charles drew his Army Colt and cocked it. Hartree pivoted back, his face scarlet.

"You interfering bastard, the railroad'll have your ass."

Charles said to his troopers, "Collect those three and put them in the freight car. The Indians can travel in the caboose."

Hartree let out a stream of accusations and foul language, until the men in the coach protested. Magee signaled Gray Owl. The tracker ran forward and caught Magee's Springfield when he tossed it down. Magee hung from the roof of the car, and dropped.

"Well done," Charles said to him. "You can tear up the marker."

"Oh, no, sir. This wasn't anything. The marker's a big one. Anytime you need some help, you ask."

Emotion welled in Charles. Until now he hadn't quite realized what good soldiers these men had become. They were able to respond quickly, obey orders, and generally do a lot more than just shoot an enemy. He felt a rush of pride.

Magee took charge of putting Hartree and his shootists in the freight car, which he then closed, posting two guards outside. The security chief could be heard stomping and swearing.

The conductor again appealed to Charles for help with the wounded man.

"Is he bad?"

"No, not bad, but—"

"Then I want to see to my own first." He was testy, because he was doing things he didn't want to do: controlling gun-crazy civilians; saving wounded Indians. Every damn thing but the one thing he'd joined up to do.

He climbed up and over the platform of the passenger coach, completely missing the intense look Gray Owl gave him; a look that carried new respect and regard.

Private Washington Toby, a lanky mulatto boy from Philadelphia, lay next to the caboose with blood all over his fine buckskin pants. A broken arrow jutted from his leg. Toby clutched his leg while he swore and wept from pain.

"Lie back, Toby." Charles tried not to let his anxiety show. "Let go of your leg."

Reluctantly, Toby did so. Charles knelt and pulled out his Bowie knife. He lengthened the slip in the buckskin to more than a foot. Ever since the tribes had replaced stone arrowheads with ones of strap or sheet iron, arrow wounds were terrible. If the iron hit bone, it often crimped around it, making extrication an agony. Of course if the arrow cut a muscle, or nicked a blood vessel—

To one of the worried troopers standing there, Charles said, "Run back to Satan and open my right saddlebag. Bring me the tobacco plug you'll find inside. Easy now, Toby. You're lucky," he lied. "An arrow in the leg is nothing. If you get one in your belly or chest, they play the funeral march before you fall down."

Toby's mouth wrenched, a sad attempt at a smile. Sweat popped out on his face. Charles pulled the buckskin away from the wound and studied the arrow. "Take hold of my left arm. Hang on tight."

The trooper rushed back with the tobacco plug. Charles opened his mouth and the trooper dropped it in. Charles started chewing vigorously while he grasped the painted shaft and gently worked it from side to side.

It felt crimped in there. He exerted more pressure. Toby's eyes bulged. His nails almost dug through Charles's shirt.

"Easy, easy," Charles kept saying, the words sounding squishy because of the chewing tobacco. Toby grunted in reaction to the pain, then rolled his shoulders off the ground. "Keep him down," Charles exclaimed. Two troopers restrained the wounded man.

Blood was pouring from the wound now. Charles tried to imagine his hands were a woman's, with a woman's light touch. He continued to work the shaft one way, then the other, back and forth, back and—

He felt it loosed. A lump formed in his throat, big as a rock. "All right, Toby, we'll be done in just a couple of minutes." He talked to divert the man's attention. "Just hang on for a couple of more—" He yanked. Washington Toby screamed and fainted.

Charles sagged. He rocked back on his haunches, holding in his right hand the shaft, its bloody head only slightly bent. In a moment Toby opened his eyes. Groggy, he started to weep.

"Go ahead and cry," Charles said. "I know it hurts. What I'm going to do now will help some, until we get you to the fort. Tobacco's an old Plains medicine for wounds."

He spat several times, filling the wound with brown juice. He kneaded the edges to mix blood and tobacco thoroughly. There was no spurting; no darker blood showed. The arrow had done no serious damage.

He wound on a tourniquet and ordered his men to wrap Washington Toby in blankets and let him rest aboard the train. One of the troopers, a shy boy named Collet, gave Charles a look of admiration.

"You a good officer, Mist' August."

When he reached the other side of the train, Gray Owl said to him, "There is one Arapahoe dead. Shall we leave him?"

Charles wiped his mouth. On the point of saying yes, he changed his mind. "If you can repair one of those platforms in the trees, put him on it. Since he's already dead, I guess we can give him that much. I'll hold the train."

Gray Owl gazed at him steadily, then turned and left.

"Lieutenant," the conductor said, his voice carrying a note of complaint now, "you've got to take time to look at the wounded man in here. I think he's all right, but I'm no doctor."

Charles nodded and wearily climbed the metal steps. The civilians moved back to allow him through. From between facing seats, boots and yellow-striped cavalry trousers jutted into the aisle. The wounded man leaned against the wall, his right arm limp.

For a moment Charles saw nothing but the wound, a wet red hole in the upper sleeve. Then he took notice of the man. Saw a fine-featured face with glacial blue eyes and russet-colored mustache and beard. Because so much had happened, recognition was a second slow. It hit him as he started to kneel.

"Main," said the officer. "Or is it May?"

"My name is—" He stopped. What was the use?

In the aisle the conductor said, "This man's name is Lieutenant August."

"Hell it is."

"I'll have a look at your wound—" Charles began.

"Don't touch me," said Captain Harry Venable. "You're under arrest."

37

Major General Philip Henry Sheridan, Department of the Missouri, summoned Grierson to Leavenworth. The two met on the day of Sheridan's departure on extended leave.

Grierson walked in while Sheridan was still conferring with his aide, Colonel Crosby. Sheridan was thirty-six, single, with a Black Irish swarthiness and a tough air enhanced by a Mongol mustache and soap-locked hair. He intimidated Grierson; it was more than rank, or the traditional tension between officers who'd graduated from West Point and those who hadn't. Sheridan was famous for being opinionated and ruthless.

"Just finishing with the report on the train fight," he said after returning Grierson's salute. "Have a chair." He shoved a sheaf of papers at his aide. "Telegraph the railroad and tell them to get this dog-fucking idiot Hartree out of Kansas. I won't have vigilantes interfering with the United States Army."

Colonel Crosby cleared his throat. "Yes, General. It's delicate, though. The railroad stockholders are still very upset about the Indian threat."

"Goddamn it, Sam Grant and Crump Sherman put me here to take care of the whore-kissing Indians, and I'll do it. I have no sympathy for them. The only good Indians I ever saw were dead. Follow my instructions. Hartree goes."

The aide saluted and retired. When the door closed, Sheridan went to warm his hands at the iron stove. It was late November, gray and bleak.

"Grierson, there is absolutely nothing I can do for Charles Main. Harry Venable came over to Departmental staff to serve with Winnie Hancock last spring. I don't like the little shit, but he's a competent soldier."

"Main is an outstanding one."

"Yes, but he's also an unpardoned reb who lied about his war record and the Academy. Twice."

"I encouraged him the second time, General. I thought he looked first-rate and I wanted him for the regiment. I'm as much to blame as—"

"Don't say another fucking word. I didn't hear those last ones, either. I'm well aware of Main's ability. He came to summer camp just before I graduated. A year or so later I was told that Bob Lee, who was the supe, thought him the finest horseman in the cadet corps. But he's got to go."

"They're only suspending Custer from duty for a year, and look at all the charges brought against—"

"Colonel, I don't want to hear any more," the little commander said, leaning on his desk. His black eyes bored into the unhappy cavalryman. "Curly Custer fought for the Union. I'll tell you something else. He's a goddamn magnet for men. They'll slit each other's throats to serve with him."

"Some of them. Not the men who testified against him. Not his own commanding officer—"

"Will you for Jesus Christ's sake shut up? I can't save Main's balls on the basis of what happened to Custer. Furthermore, I'm going to drag Curly's ass back here as soon as I can. I want him in my department, because that pissant treaty will never hold. Now you go back to Main and you tell him I'm sorry but he ought to be grateful that I was able to slide him out with just a bobtail discharge instead of three years' hard labor with a ball and chain to keep him company."

Grierson rose, his face showing strain. "Yes, General. Is that all?"

Sheridan's expression softened as he rolled a cigar between his palms. "It is. Isn't it enough? Dismissed."

At Harker next day, Grierson delivered the verdict to Charles, who stood before him in stoic silence. Ever since he'd come upon Harry Venable in the passenger coach, he'd known this moment was inevitable.

"I told you early that I couldn't save you if someone caught you, Charles. I tried. I tried damn hard. You're the only one-hundred-percent cast-iron rebel in the regiment, yet you're the strongest partisan of those Negroes."

"I don't do them any special favors, sir. With a couple of exceptions, they're fine soldiers. They try harder than most."

"That's true. During our first year we've had the lowest desertion rate in the entire Army, and the lowest rate of disciplinary infractions. I told you I had a vision for the Tenth, and you helped make it work. I'm just sorry as hell things didn't work out right for you."

"I guess a man can be forgiven almost anything these days except being a Southerner."

"Your bitterness is understandable." He was silent a moment. Charles watched night settling on the post outside Grierson's window. The office was freezing. Snowflakes were starting to fall. "What will you do?"

"I don't know. Get drunk. Find work. Kill some Cheyennes."

"You're not over that yet?"

"I'll never be over that."

"But you saved the Arapahoe prisoners." One had died the day after being locked in the Fort Harker guardhouse. The other was comatose in the dispensary, refusing to eat.

"I said kill, sir. I didn't say torture. There's a difference."

Grierson studied the tall, faintly menacing soldier with the furious eyes. In Charles's case, he thought, the difference was slight. He didn't say it, however. Stroking his immense beard, he asked, "What about your son?"

"He'll have to live on Jack Duncan's charity a while longer."

"Well, keep in touch with him. A man can stand to lose a lot of things, but not his loved ones."

Charles shrugged. "Maybe it's already too late. God knows I've lost everything else."

Another silence. Grierson could barely stand it. He avoided Charles's eyes as he said, "You're to be off the post by morning. But no one will protest if it takes you a little longer to say goodbye."

"It won't, Colonel. A quick and clean cut's always the best kind."

"Charles—"

"Do I have the colonel's permission to go?"

Grierson nodded. He returned the salute and watched

Charles pivot, leave, and shut the door. Then he slumped in his chair and looked at the cased photograph of his wife.

"Alice, I hate this goddamned world sometimes."

The snow fell harder. Charles collected his few belongings and went on his round of farewells. The sentries on duty in the icy dark still snapped to with salutes; indeed, they seemed more respectful than ever.

In the bachelor officers' quarters he said goodbye to Floyd Hook. Floyd was unkempt, unshaven. He'd returned from a patrol a week ahead of Charles to discover that his wife had run off with a driver for the Butterfield Overland Despatch line. She'd taken their three-year-old daughter, too. Charles had heard that Dolores Hook had tried to kill herself by swallowing something last year. Some Army wives just buckled under the worry and loneliness. Floyd looked like he was starting to buckle, too. He reeked of beer. Charles spent ten minutes trying to cheer him up and failed.

In the married officers' quarters he said goodbye to Ike Barnes and little Lovetta, who wept and hugged him like a mother. The old man, always less than loquacious and ever fearful of showing sentiment, nevertheless squeezed Charles's arm repeatedly and kept his head turned away, unwilling or unable to speak.

Charles found Gray Owl sitting cross-legged, asleep in the dark under the eave at the back of the sutler's. The tracker was wrapped in several blankets and buffalo robes; one covered his head like a monk's cowl. "You'll die of exposure," Charles warned after he woke Gray Owl from his doze.

"No. I can stand any weather but a blizzard. I taught myself long ago." Gray Owl stood up, shedding the robes and blankets. He gripped Charles's shoulder and stared into his eyes. "I will miss you. You are a good man. What you did, sparing the captives in spite of your hatred, that was good."

Charles had no reply except another tired shrug. Gray Owl asked the same question that Grierson had, to which Charles answered, "I don't know what I'll do or where I'll go. Off by myself, more than likely. The colonel let me keep my Spencer, and Satan."

"I think we are much alike," the tracker said. "Outcasts. I went apart from the People when they lost their way."

Gray Owl watched the slanting snow driven on the wind. "Like my father, I took a captured white woman for my wife. I treated her well and loved her very much. Three winters past, while I led the society men and the young warriors to the herd for the final hunt of the year, some jealous squaws tormented my wife with sharp sticks. She bled her life away, and no one would punish the women for their cruelty. The brother of the woman who led the others, a hate-filled man named Scar, praised them and told their story many times. When I returned and saw all this, I knew the People had strayed too far for me to lead them back. So I turned from them, forever. But if you are ever lost, Charles, and I can lead you to safety, I will."

"Thanks," Charles said, almost inaudibly. He was anxious to hurry through the rest of his goodbyes. It was beginning to hurt too much.

He embraced Gray Owl and left the Cheyenne resettling himself against the log wall of the sutler's. From a few steps away, he looked back. In the lamp-lit dark he saw Gray Owl's shoulders and blanket cowl dusted with white, like some strange stunted shrub that had died in the winter.

In this weather the men of the Tenth had no choice but to hole up in the foul, cramped huts that served as Fort Harker barracks. Charles stepped around the corner of the hut in which most of his detachment was bunking. Through the plank door, above the keening night wind, he heard Magic Magee's voice.

He shifted his buffalo overcoat and muskrat cap with ear-flaps to his left arm and eased the door open a couple of inches. By the light of oil lamps, he saw Magee kneeling on the dirt floor. "Now boys, you will observe that in this hand I have a stack of three ordinary tin cups, like we drink from every day. Say, would you slide back, Sergeant Williams? I need more space."

Charles smiled for the first time in quite a while. He watched Magee pluck one cup from the stack and invert it on the floor with a swift, sweeping motion. Magee placed the other cups similarly, in a line.

"What I am about to show you, boys, is one of the incredible mysteries of the ages. Back in Chicago, somebody told me that way over in some old tombs in Egypt, there are pictures of a magician doing this same cups and balls trick. Here's the ball. An ordinary little sphere of cork."

He showed it between the index and middle finger of his right hand, then pushed it into his left, or appeared to push it, making it vanish.

"Shem, where's the ball?"

"Gone," Wallis said.

"Gone where?"

"Don't know."

"Why, come on. It's gone traveling." With zest, Magee raised the first cup to reveal the cork ball.

He took the ball, made it vanish in his hand, and revealed it under the second cup. Charles had watched him often enough to know the secret: four balls, one loaded in each cup beforehand and kept from falling out by Magee's skill in inverting the cups and snapping them down fast on the hard ground.

Magee started his patter again, but Williams felt the doorway draft, raised a hand, and reached for his sidearm. "Somebody out there?"

Charles opened the door wide and went in. "Only me, watching the show. I'm off, boys. I brought this coat and cap. Sell them to whoever you can and put the money in the company fund."

A couple of muttered thank-yous followed, but that was it. Charles felt self-conscious. So did the men. The smiles they tried were thin and sad. He stood there above the ring of black faces, his black hat slanted forward over his eyes. Snow was melting and dripping from the brim. The corners of his gypsy robe scraped the dirt.

He cleared his throat. He felt as awkward and nervous as he had the first time he was called to a West Point blackboard to recite. "I just want to say—you men are good soldiers. Any officer would be—" The words caught. He cleared his throat again. "Proud to lead you."

"We proud to have you lead us, too," Shem Wallis said. "They give you a bad deal, those generals."

"Yes, well, sometimes that's all there is to life. A hell of a bad deal." He shook his right arm gently. In the crook lay his rifle. "At least Colonel Grierson let me keep my Spencer and my horse."

Star Eyes got to his feet, rubbing his knuckles back and forth over his mouth. Charles noticed the scar from the man's hotel days. Haltingly, Williams said, "Since I was about the first man to speak against you, I guess I should be the one to take it all back. For a Southerner, you're a real white man."

The soldiers laughed at the unconscious racism in the remark. Charles smiled. Flustered, Williams put out his hand.

"We'll miss you, C. C."

Charles's hand stopped in midair. "What?"

"He said C. C.," Washington Toby answered. His leg was still bandaged, but he was able to get around.

"It means Cheyenne Charlie," Magee said. "Cheyenne 'cause you're so fond of them."

"Well, Cheyenne Charlie. I guess that nickname fits. I like it. Many thanks."

He turned and started out. "Sir? I clean forgot," Williams said, reaching inside his plaid flannel outer shirt, one of two worn over his regular blouse and long underwear. "This was stuck in my desk for a week. Guess they put it there while we was riding the railroad."

Charles took the pale gray envelope, inscribed in a familiar hand. He held it between thumb and fingertips, tapping it thoughtfully while his eyes froze again.

"Thanks. Night," he said, and left. The last thing he heard as he shut the door was Magic Magee calling out:

"Don't forget about the marker."

At the sentry post nearest the stable, a fire had been lighted against the freezing cold. Charles walked toward the tatters of flame driven horizontally by the prairie wind.

He'd put on gauntlets and he was carrying his Spencer in his left hand, the stock leaning against his shoulder, the blued barrel jutting up behind him. His boots crunched the accumulating snow as he quickened his step, anxious to be away.

As he passed the sentry's fire, he tossed Willa's unopened letter into the flames. He was quickly hidden by the dark inside the stable. Ten minutes later the sentry heard hooves in the snow, receding fast, the only sign of the rider's passing into the vast winter night.

1 8 6 7.

FALL FASHIONS.

DUPLEX SKIRTS.

J. W. BRADLEY'S CELEBRATED PATENTED DUPLEX
ELLIPTIC (or Double Spring) SKIRTS are the most
DURABLE and ECONOMICAL SKIRT made, each hoop
being composed of two finely tempered STEEL
SPRINGS, ingeniously braided firmly together, edge to
edge, and while they are very flexible and easy to the
wearer, they are also the STRONGEST and MOST
SERVICEABLE SKIRT WORN. They are made in the
MOST FASHIONABLE and ELEGANT SHAPES for
RECEPTION, PROMENADE, OPERA, CARRIAGE,
CHURCH, HOUSE and STREET DRESS . . .

MADELINE'S JOURNAL

*December, 1867. Christmas nearly here and we are as close to
starvation as we have ever been. Soon I will have to tell everyone—Prudence, the Shermans, the other loyal freedmen. For
every cent we earn, I pay out two. Unless I go crawling to
George H., I see no alternative but to admit failure and inform Cooper that I lack the ability to manage Mont Royal
successfully. The prospect of leaving this place, with my
dream of rebuilding it a ruin, is exquisitely painful. Yet abdi-
cation, if that is the right term, seems my only course.*

*If I choose to follow it, Andy, of all those here, will take
it hardest, I think. He is proud and excited about going to
Charleston as a convention delegate. Talks about it constantly . . .*

Des LaMotte talked about it, too, with Gettys and Captain
Jolly, in Jolly's shanty.

It was two weeks before Christmas; dark, drizzly weather.
Des was worn to emaciation by his months in prison. Jolly in
contrast looked fit, was sporting a new linen duster he'd stolen
from a traveler. He was busy with a greasy rag that he slid back

and forth on the barrel of one of his Leech and Rigdons, burnishing it.

"We have got to do something besides talk," Des declared. There was a wounded quality in his friend's eyes, Getty's observed. Des would say almost nothing about his time behind bars, but it was evident that it had been a harrowing experience.

Jolly spat on the barrel and caressed it with the rag. "Shit, that's all we ever do, sit around and talk. She's sending her darky to the convention. Why don't I just hunt him up and blow him down?"

"Because then it'll be something else, some other issue or outrage, until she turns the whole district into high niggerdom."

"LaMotte, I'm tired of this," Jolly said. "Do you want to get rid of her or don't you?"

"You know I do."

"Then let's do it. Otherwise you're just a dog with a bark and no teeth."

The tall dancing master reached for Jolly's throat. The captain quickly set the muzzle of his revolver against Des's palm. He grinned. "Go on. Try to choke me. I'll put a ball through your hand into your skull."

Red-faced, Des lowered his hand. "You just don't understand, do you? I want her dead but I don't want to go to prison for it. I've been there, in prison"—he was sweating—"terrible things can happen to a man of intelligence and sensibility. Vile things not even physical strength can prevent."

Gettys decided it was time to relieve Des's misery. He drew a packet from his old velvet coat. "If you all can stop your spatting, I think we've got the answer. My cousin Sitwell traveled all the way to Nashville for a secret conclave—" He saw Jolly's puzzlement and took pleasure in saying with a superior air, "Convention, Captain. Meeting. He brought this back."

He showed a wrinkled broadsheet with a big, bold heading. TENNESSEE TIGER. The tiger, a steel engraving, crouched ferociously in front of a Stars and Bars. "Read the poem," Gettys said, pointing it out.

Des read it aloud. *"Niggers and Leaguers, get out of the way. We are born of the night—"* Captain Jolly's interest perked up. Des said, "You mean they allow publication of this sort of thing in Tennessee?"

"And similar things in a lot of other places, Sitwell informed me. You don't see any names, do you? Read on."

"Born of the night, and we vanish by day. No rations have we but the flesh of man. And love niggers best . . . the Kuklux Klan."

Des stared at the others with slowly dawning understanding. Loftily, Gettys explained to Jolly, "The Kuklux is that club for skylarking and scaring darkies. Sitwell says it's turned into something more. A white man's defense league. Klaverns are springing up all over the South."

"What's that?" Jolly said.

"Klavern? It means a Klan den, a local chapter. They have a regular constitution, called the Prescript, and a whole lot of fancy titles and rituals. And robes, Jolly. Robes that hide a man's face." Grinning, he tapped the captain's sleeve with the broadsheet. "Know who's going 'round the South helping to set up the klaverns? The head man of the Klan. The Imperial Wizard. Your old friend Forrest."

"Bedford himself?" Jolly's tone was reverential. Service with Forrest's cavalry remained the high point of his life, and for a moment he was in the past, remembering how they had campaigned. In the worst rainstorms, through winter sleet, riding with the blood up, faced always with the possibility of death and never turning from it, because they rode for the cause of the white race.

As Jolly thought of his great leader, he kept losing track of his surroundings, the shanty that smelled of stale food, discarded coffee grounds, urine. He kept seeing the general on his great war-horse, King Philip. And the niggers. The wailing, terrified niggers of Fort Pillow—

It was in '64 that Jolly had helped Forrest invest the garrison forty miles north of Memphis. After capturing Fort Pillow, Forrest had busied himself elsewhere, allowing his men to deal with the prisoners. They dealt with them with gun, sword, torch. Jolly had personally driven six nigger privates into a tent at gunpoint, then ordered his first sergeant to set fire to it. He could hear the niggers screaming now. The memory made him smile.

After Fort Pillow, the North howled "atrocity" and "massacre." Forrest insisted that he hadn't ordered the killings, and had been elsewhere when they took place. But neither had he restrained his men.

Lowering his voice, Gettys said, "Cousin Sitwell's friends in York County have invited Forrest there to help start a klavern. I'd say we need one on the Ashley, too."

Des's carroty hair glowed in the light of the kerosene lamp behind him. "Can we get Forrest here? Send him a telegraph message?"

"Yes, and I'll pay for it from store profits," Gettys said with enthusiasm. "Got plenty to spare. Where do we send it?"

Jolly stroked his close-shaven face with the gunsight, raking the disfiguring scar because it itched like the devil. A nigger corporal at Fort Pillow had given him that with a skinning knife, a moment before Jolly put one of his Leech and Rigdons against the buck's eye and fired.

"Mississip," Jolly said. "Sunflower Landing. That's the general's plantation in Coahoma County. Last I heard, he was trying to farm again. You sign my name to the message, Gettys—no, shut up. Do like I tell you. Sign Captain Jackson Jerome Jolly. The general will come here for one of his officers, I promise you."

He leaned back, pleased. Again he dragged the metal sight back and forth over the Fort Pillow scar.

"Things is finally movin', boys. We're about ready to declare open season on uppity nigger women."

> Have resolved to break the news of Mont Royal's plight no later than a week before Christmas. Meanwhile, there is some startling geologic discovery at Lambs, a short distance down the river. It has the entire district excited. Must find out why.

38

The night local chugged up the Lehigh Valley in a thunderstorm. Near Bethlehem, George's attorney, Jupiter Smith, fell asleep, leaving his client to stare out the window at the rainy dark.

The men rode in a private car at the back of the train. Built to George's specifications, the car had furniture upholstered in red plush, fine wood paneling, and etched glass dividers to screen the dining table. Years ago, Stanley had bought a similar car for the Hazards; a rail accident had destroyed it. George had scorned the wasteful expenditure until a year ago, when he began to see a certain sense in it. Pittsburgh was fast becoming the state's iron and steel center. George wanted Hazard's to have an important part in that expansion, and he expected to travel there often. He decided he'd worked hard and deserved to travel comfortably.

The train was almost an hour late. Yawning, he rested his forehead against the window and watched raindrops on the other side. He wished the engineer would speed up. He'd been away four nights. He knew men who could leave their wives for weeks and enjoy it. He couldn't. He imagined Constance in their warm bed at Belvedere. He'd be there soon, his body curled around hers, holding her as they slept.

Constance heard a strange sound.

She put down her hairbrush, rose, and walked to the dormer nearest the canopied double bed. She wondered about the noise, because both the children were away at school and the house was empty except for the servants in a remote wing.

Frowning, she pushed the window open six inches. Lightning glittered behind the laurel-covered mountains. The misty night sky was reddened by light leaching up from Hazard's furnaces. Rain blew in, dampening her face and her powdered cleavage. She'd chosen the Chinese silk bed gown because George was coming home tonight. He was late.

She stared into the storm, trying to recall the sound. But it was difficult. She assumed some piece of debris had been lifted by the wind and flung against the dormer. It was two and a half stories above the lawn, but the wind was strong.

Constance was tired, but happily so. She'd spent the evening in the kitchen, helping to bake pastries for the holiday. Every cranny of Belvedere was awash in pleasant scents that spoke of Christmas: the yeasty smell of bread dough; the tang of the huge blue spruce tree down in the parlor; the smoky sweetness of perfumed candles that burned throughout the mansions until very late in the evening. She looked forward to the warmth and festivity of Christmas—to the children being home from their schools, to the family being together.

Over the noise of the rain, she heard a distant whistle. She smiled. That was his train. She closed the window, leaving it unlatched as she always did. Seated again, she gave her gleaming red hair twenty more strokes, then performed her customary evening inspection of the woman in the mirror.

A woman not unattractive for her age, Constance believed. But definitely overweight, by at least thirty pounds. Most days she ate sparingly, inspired by the previous evening's mirror inspection. And yet she gained weight. Who would have thought that a happy life could include that kind of struggle?

Smiling drowsily again, she stretched. George should be home and in bed within a half hour. Thoughts of him drew her attention to a small velvet box lying amid her pins and cosmetic pots and brushes. He was such a dear, generous man. He liked giving her presents, even when there was no special occasion. The velvet box held the latest—earrings.

She took them out. Two large pearls were clasped in tapered mountings of filigreed gold. The effect was that of teardrops. She held one up beside her earlobe, pleased with the effect. She thought of how much she loved her husband, how good their life was after four years of war and separation.

Gazing at the mirror, she didn't see the dormer window slowly begin to open.

Taking the full brunt of the storm, a contorted figure had clung to the roofpeak of the dormer when Constance opened the window in response to the strange sound. Presently she had closed it, but the figure had remained still as a gargoyle on a cathedral.

Down among the misted town lights at the foot of the mountain, an arriving train whistled into the depot. The man on the roof had paid no attention, caught up in what was about to happen. Tonight was the culmination of years of waiting. Months of wandering and planning. Days of skulking about the town asking questions. Then more waiting, until nature provided the cover of this thunderstorm. Tonight, the guilty would begin to pay for thwarting and hurting him.

The climb to the dormer, using slippery gutters, ornamentation, windowsills, had taken a half hour. The wetness, the slickness of everything increased the difficulty. So did his own memories of the fall into the James, the ghastly pain lancing his body as it caromed from rock to rock. He was proud, very proud of himself for overcoming those memories and the accompanying fright, and for making the climb successfully.

He had waited a few moments, then reached down from the roof of the dormer. He worked grimy fingers into the thin space between the frame and the upper edge of the window. A wind gust tore the stolen top hat from his head. He grabbed for it, causing his right foot to slip and scrape the roof. The hat sailed away. He clenched his teeth, cursing silently. Just such a noisy slip had brought Hazard's wife to the window the first time.

He hung in a strained position, waiting. Nothing happened. Evidently she hadn't heard the second scrape. Slowly, he crept down the side of the dormer and with great care pried the window open.

Squinting through the narrow opening, he saw a gaslit room, handsomely furnished. Beyond a canopied bed a woman sat at a dressing table, holding earrings to her ears to study the effect.

He pulled the window open, stretched a crippled leg over the sill, and jumped into the room.

Switchmen with lanterns uncoupled the private car. Above the dim lights of town George saw the shining windows of Belvedere on its terraced peak. To his left the sky shimmered red; the night crews at Hazard's were at work.

Preparing to leave the car, he enjoyed a rare moment of tranquillity. In Pittsburgh he and Jupe Smith had negotiated the purchase of McNeely's Foundry. McNeely, a premier Pennsylvania ironmaster, had died in late summer, and George had stepped in to try to buy the foundry from the heirs. McNeely's was ideal for conversion to the new Bessemer process.

Tonight he was coming home on the crest of success. He had McNeely's in his pocket, and here in Lehigh Station, Hazard's was operating day and night, turning out everything from rails and architectural wrought iron to iron frames for a growing Chicago piano manufacturer, Fenway's. George felt very good about all of it, and in that way he reflected the prevailing mood of the North. The North was enjoying almost unprecedented growth and prosperity. In the wake of four years of carnage and deprivation—years that had clearly shown war of any kind to be unthinkable—Americans of all classes exhibited a fierce dedication to turning a profit. Out of ashes, the industrial phoenix was rising triumphantly.

No credit was due the politicians. George thanked God that he'd gotten out of Washington before the war ended. He couldn't stand to be there now, enduring the sordid intrigues and partisan schisms. Indeed, some conversations he'd had in Pittsburgh suggested that a great many citizens were growing tired of the political war. They were tired of Johnson's harangues about constitutional principle, tired of the Radicals' maneuvering to impeach him, and, sadly, they were tired of the issue of Negro rights.

As always, the politicians failed to recognize a changing mood, or chose to ignore it. But the signals were clear. In the fall elections, the Republicans had been turned out in New York and Pennsylvania and their majorities whittled away in Ohio, Maine, and Massachusetts. Referenda on black suffrage had been defeated in Kansas, Minnesota, and Ohio, states thought to be enlightened.

Despite a weakening hold on the electorate, the Radicals continued on their narrow course. Johnson remained the Arch-Apostate, or the "arch-demon," as Mr. Boutwell, of the House Judiciary Committee, called him. The committee had brought in a 5–4 vote to impeach, although some moderate Republicans with whom George agreed—Wilson of Iowa who wrote the committee's minority report was one—refused to take part in the blood sport. So did the House as a whole. On December 7, it had rejected impeachment, 108–57.

Unfortunately the Radicals remained undeterred. They would find grounds. Stanley's crony and patron, Wade, was already in place as president of the Senate. The Congress might well name him President of the United States if Johnson could be removed.

Virgilia's friend Thad Stevens wanted him gone. Some said nothing else kept the old Radical alive. Stevens and his crowd wanted Johnson on trial for "monstrous usurpations of power," and one defeat in the House wouldn't spell the end of it. God, how vicious some men became when dogma drove them.

"Finally," Jupe Smith groaned. He pressed his upper dentures with his thumb and collected his carpetbag and umbrella. The men said good night to the Welsh porter and the black chef who traveled with the car. It was only a few feet from the covered platform to the waiting Lehigh Station hackney.

"Sorry we're late, Bud," George said, shaking water off his hat as he climbed in. "A fallen tree blocked the track for an hour. Thanks for waiting."

"Glad to," Bud said through the roof slot. "By the way, Mr. Hazard. Been a man askin' for you in town the last day or so."

George moved to give the grumbling lawyer more room. "Who?"

"Didn't say his name. Queer lookin' bird, though. Looks like he was crippled in the war. Leon at the Station House Hotel told him you was away for a while. I s'pose it's just some fella wantin' to sell you something."

"I get my share of those, God knows."

"If this fascinating conversation is over," Jupe said, "I'd like to get to bed. I'm an old man."

"You don't have a corner on that, Jupe." George's bones ached; was he coming down with influenza? He signaled Bud and the hackney lurched off through the almost deserted streets.

One moment the mirror was empty, then his image filled it. She pushed away from the dressing table. She was so stunned and terrified that she didn't notice the earring as it dropped from her left hand. The other pearl-and-gold teardrop bobbed on her right earlobe.

He leaped at her, clapped his left hand over her mouth, and pushed his right knee into her back. "You be quiet. One sound and I'll kill you." He pulled her back harder against his knee to demonstrate his intent. Her back bowed painfully.

Terror crippled her mind. Her eyes flew over the image in the glass, trying to make some sense of it. Who was this stubbled, paunchy hobgoblin in rain-soaked clothes? His eyes were dark and disturbed. The nails of the hand on her mouth were black underneath; he smelled of dirt.

"Don't know who I am, do you? I'm an old friend." He chuckled. A little rope of spit descended from his lip, broke, struck, and made a dark spot on the shoulder of her gown. "An old, old friend of your husband's. Down in Mexico, he and his lickspittle crony Main, they called me Butcher. Butcher Bent."

Under his hand, Constance screamed—or tried to. She knew the name. George thought Elkanah Bent had died, or at least disappeared. But there he was, in the glass, chortling as his right hand dipped into his soiled coat, which was missing all its buttons. He drew something into the light.

"Butchers kill cows. You'd better be careful."

He shook the straight razor's blade open. It glittered in the gaslight. Constance thought she'd faint. Her mind cried out: *George! Children!*

No. They weren't here. They couldn't help.

Slowly, tantalizingly, Bent lowered the razor past her eyes to her throat. Suddenly he jerked it inward.

Another muffled scream. Only then did Constance realize he'd turned the razor at the last moment. It was the dull top edge pressing her neck.

"Now I'm going to let you go, you dirty cow. I want to ask you some questions. If you yell, you're finished. Do you understand about keeping quiet? Blink your eyes if you do."

Her eyes reflected in the mirror, huge. She blinked four times instead of once. Gaslight flashed on the razor's blade as he lifted it away and then, slowly, his foul-smelling hand.

Constance nearly collapsed. "Please, oh, God, please don't hurt me."

"Tell me what I want to know and I won't." He stepped back, almost affable. "I promise you I won't."

Ashamed of her fear, yet unable to overcome it, she turned on the padded seat to face him. "Can I—can I trust you?"

He giggled. "What choice do you have? But, yes, you can. I only want information. About the people who ruined me. About their families. Start with your husband's bosom friend, Orry Main. Did he really die at Petersburg?"

"Yes." Constance held her hands between her knees, digging nails into her palms. She neither felt the pain nor saw the small seep of blood onto her gown. "Yes, he did."

"He had a wife—"

How could she endanger Madeline, or any of them? Struck silent by conscience, she stared at him, her mouth open. Bent yanked her hair. "We made a bargain. No answers"—he waggled the flashing razor inches from her eyes—"it's all over."

"All right, all right."

He withdrew the razor. "Better. I really don't want to harm an innocent woman. Tell me about Main's widow. Where is she?"

"Mont Royal Plantation. Near Charleston."

He grunted. "And your own husband?"

On the way up to Belvedere this moment, Constance remembered. She must hold Bent in conversation, detain him until George arrived. The train was in; it couldn't take long. Oh, but what if he'd missed the train? *Dear God, what if—?*

"Mrs. Hazard, I don't have infinite patience." The man's left shoulder hung below his right one, giving him a look of vulnerability. Strange, then, that she'd never seen a more commanding, terrifying figure.

"George—" She licked dry lips. "George is in Pittsburgh on business."

"You have children."

New, cold terror. She hadn't imagined he would—

"Children," he snarled.

"Away at school, both of them."

"I think your husband had a brother."

Which one did he mean? Better to name the most distant. "In California. With his wife and son."

It worked. The man acted disappointed. He didn't ask for specifics. "And there was a relative of Orry Main's. A soldier I met in Texas. His names was Charles. Where is he?"

"So far as I know, he's in the Army again, out in Kansas." she was so frightened, so desperate to please him and save her life, she quite abandoned caution. "He went out there after the war, with his little boy."

The man smiled suddenly. "Oh, he has a child, too. What branch of the Army is Charles serving with?"

"The U.S. Cavalry. I don't know exactly where."

"Kansas will do. So many children. I hadn't thought of children. That's interesting."

Constance was again on the verge of uncontrollable trembling. Just then, to her amazement, the filthy, rain-soaked man stepped back. "Thank you. I believe you've told me all I need to know. You've been very helpful."

She sagged, close to hysteria. "Thank you. Oh, God, thank you."

"You may stand up if you like."

"Thank you, thank you so very much." She pushed both palms against the padded seat and swayed to her feet, the tears bursting forth, tears of relief that he was going to spare her life. He smiled and stepped forward.

"Here, careful. You're unsteady." His free hand grasped her elbow. Rotten breath gusted from his mouth. The smile on his face grew huge, and his eyes luminous, all in an instant.

"Cow bitch." One cool, silver, feather-light stroke cut her throat.

He stood over her, watching the blood gout and clutching the immense hardness between his legs. He flung down the razor, spied the teardrop earring she's dropped, plucked it up, dipped it in her blood, held it in front of his eyes, and smiled at the red on the gold. He finished his work in less than a minute and climbed out the way he'd come in.

George unlocked his front door. The hackney clattered away down the hill.

He climbed the great staircase two steps at a time, humming. His anticipation and a blissful euphoria made him hum louder as he strode along the upstairs hall, pooled by low-trimmed gaslights. Hard rain pelted the mansion. He turned the bedroom doorknob, saying as he stepped through, "Constance, I'm—"

The unbelievable sight silenced him. He dropped his carpetbag, running forward. He reached down to lift her, certain she was only unconscious. He couldn't recognize the significance of the blood sopping the carpet, the great throat wound.

He saw the open dormer window, the rain driving in to soak

the carpet. He saw one of the teardrop earrings he'd given her, but not the other.

The mirror caught his attention. He moved toward it, choking on the stench of the wet wool rug. On the mirror, in blood, were four letters.

B E N T

He looked from the mirror to the open window to his motionless wife. The bottom of the T on the mirror grew, swelled, blood accumulating in a fat drop that finally burst. The blood trickled down from the upright of the T, making it longer and longer.

"I thought he was dead," George said, not aware that he was screaming.

BOOK FOUR

THE YEAR OF THE LOCUST

*Intelligence, virtue, and patriotism are to give place, in all elections, to ignorance, stupidity, and vice. The superior race is to be made subservient to the inferior. . . . They who own no property are to levy taxes and make all appropriations.
. . . The appropriations to support free schools for the education of the negro children, for the support of old negroes in the poor-houses, and the vicious in jails and penitentiary, together with a standing army of negro soldiers will be crushing and utterly ruinous. . . . The white people of our State will never quietly submit.*

A South Carolina protest to Congress, 1868

ALL LOOKS WELL. THE CONSTITUTION WILL BE VINDICATED AND THE ARCH-APOSTATE PUT OUT OF THE WHITE HOUSE BEFORE THE END OF THE WEEK.

*Telegram to the
New Hampshire Republican Convention,* 1868

BOOK FOUR

THE YEAR OF THE LOCUST

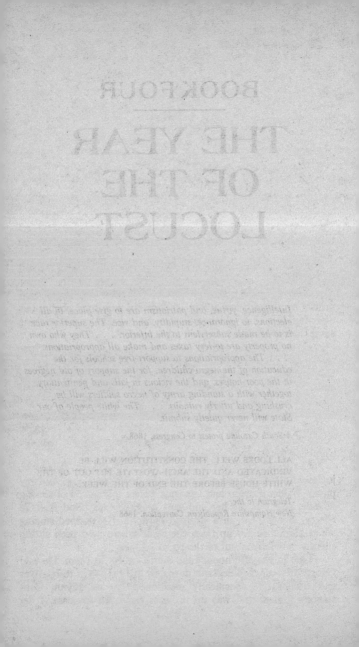

Intelligence, virtue and patriotism are to give place in all elections to ignorance, stupidity, and vice. The superior race is to be made subservient to the inferior. . . . They who own no property are to levy taxes and make all appropriations. . . . The appropriations to support free schools for the education of the negro children, for the support of old negroes in the poor houses, and the vicious in jail, and generally, together with a standing army of negro soldiers will be crushing and utterly ruinous. . . . The white people of no State will never quietly submit.

— Ulysses S. Grant, speech to Congress, 1868

ALL LOOKS WELL! THE CONSTITUTION WILL BE
REINSTATED AND THE ARCH-APOSTLE BIGOT OF THE
WHITE HOUSE BEFORE THE END OF THE WEEK.

Delegate to the
New Hampshire Republican Convention, 1868

39

That night the rain changed to sleet. In the morning the temperature plummeted. Iron cold gripped the valley. Bleak skies hid the sun.

Jupiter Smith handled arrangements for the funeral; George was incapable. Even in the worst days of the war, he had never experienced anything like this. He had no appetite. When he tried a little broth he threw it up. He was stricken with continuous diarrhea, like that which killed so many men in the wartime camps on both sides.

He swung back and forth between not believing that Constance was gone and outbursts of grief that became so noisy he had to lock himself in a bedroom—not the one they'd shared; he couldn't stand to enter it—until the violent emotion worked itself out.

The homes and churches of Lehigh Station prepared to celebrate Christmas, though with less exuberance than usual because of the dreadful event at the mansion on the mountain. George thought the pieties of the season an abominable joke.

Christmas Day was somber and misty and, at Belvedere, joyless. Patricia played a carol on the great gleaming Steinway piano. William, ruddy and vigorous from a fall season of rowing at Yale, stood beside her and sang one verse of "God Rest Ye Merry, Gentlemen" in a strained baritone. He stopped singing when his father got up from the chair where he'd been sitting silently and walked out of the room.

Late in the afternoon, Jupe Smith called on them. He told George that all the telegraph messages had been sent to relatives and friends. He specifically mentioned Patrick Flynn, Constance's father, who was up in years now. "In his case, I described the cause of death as heart seizure. I saw no point in telling an old man that his daughter was, ah—"

"Butchered?"

Jupe stared at the floor. George waved, condoning the falsehood, and with a listless air walked back to the sideboard. He rummaged among cut glass decanters, accidentally overturning one. He was trying to get drunk on bourbon. His stomach had rejected it all afternoon.

He righted the decanter, dripping sour mash on the polished floor. "Where did you send the message to Charles Main?"

"Care of General Duncan at Fort Leavenworth."

"And Billy? Virgilia? Madeline? Did you—?"

"Yes. I warned every one of them, exactly as you instructed, George. I said that anyone in either family might be a target of this Bent, though I wonder if that's really likely."

"Likely or not, it's possible. What about the earring?"

"I described it for each of them. Pearl, with a gold mount forming a teardrop. I don't quite see why—"

"I want them to know everything. Bent's description as I remember it—everything."

"Well, I took care of it."

George poured a drink. His linen stank, his speech was full of long pauses and unfinished thoughts, and his usually calm dark eyes had a wild glint. Jupe decided to leave.

"He's sick, Mr. Smith," Patricia whispered as she ushered the lawyer through the door. "I've never seen him act so strangely."

George had recovered slightly by the day of the funeral, which was held two days before the New Year.

Madeline was present, all the way from South Carolina. She was self-conscious, oddly shy. She was forty-two now, her hair heavily streaked with gray, which she refused to touch up with coloring. Her coat and mourning dress of black silk were old and shabby. When George first saw her, he greeted her with forced warmth and held his damp cheek against hers a moment. She didn't think he noticed her impoverished appearance. She was thankful.

Virgilia came from Washington. She was neatly though not expensively dressed. In her presence, George felt weak and small, very much the younger brother, even though there was only a year's difference between them. Much of Virgilia's old rage had been purged by her new life. She was able to embrace George with real feeling, and express her sorrow and mean it. The change confounded some of the townspeople who remembered the radical harridan of years past.

About three hundred men and women from Hazard's and the town joined the family for the funeral mass at St. Margaret's-in-the-Vale, then drove or walked in the freezing air to the hillside burying ground maintained by the church. Father Toone, Constance's priest, intoned his Latin beside the open grave, then traced the sign of the cross. Gravediggers began to lower the ornate silvered coffin on its straps. On the other side, red-faced and uncomfortable, Stanley and Isabel stared everywhere but at the grieving husband. Fortunately for everyone's peace of mind, they had not brought their obnoxious twins. Although it was not quite two in the afternoon, Stanley was noticeably drunk.

From behind George a gloved hand touched his arm. He reached across to take the hand without looking. Virgilia held tightly to her brother's fingers. The crowd broke up.

The bitter wind whipped the hem of Father Toone's surplice as he approached George and the two crying children. "I know this is a grievous day, George. Yet we must be confident in God. He has His purpose for the world and each of His creatures, no matter how hidden by clouds of evil that purpose may be."

George stared at the priest. Pale and hollow-cheeked, he bore a strong resemblance to photographs of the demented Poe in the last months of his life, Madeline thought. Stonily he said, "Please excuse me, Father."

It was the obligation of the Hazards to open the doors of Belvedere that afternoon and offer food and drink to the mourners. All of the rich breads and cakes, cloved hams and juicy beef rounds and oyster pies that normally would have been prepared for Christmas Day were served instead at the wake. Alcohol loosened tongues, and, before long, groups of guests were chatting noisily, even laughing, throughout the downstairs.

George couldn't tolerate it. He hid himself in the library. He'd been there about twenty minutes when the doors rolled back and Virgilia and Madeline came in.

"Are you all right?" Virgilia asked, hurrying to him. Madeline closed the doors, then fiddled with a black handkerchief tucked into her sleeve. His cravat undone, George sat staring at the women.

"I don't know, Jilly," he said. Virgilia was startled; he hadn't called her by that childish nickname since they were very small. Suddenly, he got to his feet. "What happened to her defies all reason. My God, it defies sanity."

Virgilia sighed. She looked matronly, and neat and well groomed in contrast to Madeline's obvious poverty. She said, "So does the world. Every day of our lives, I've discovered, we live with stupid mischance and clumsy melodrama, cupidity, greed, unnecessary suffering. We forget it, we mask it, we try to order it with our arts and philosophies, numb ourselves to it with diversions—or with drink, like poor Stanley. We try to explain and compensate for it with our religions. But it's always there, very close, like some poor deformed beast hiding behind the thinnest of curtains. Once in a while the curtain is torn down and we're forced to look. You know that. You went to war."

"Twice. I thought I'd seen my share"

"But life's not so logical as that, George. Some never see the beast at all. Some see it again and again, and there seems no sense to any of it. But when we look, something happens. It happened to me with Grady, and it took me years to understand it. What happens is that childhood comes to an end. Parents call it growing up, and they use the phrase much too casually. Growing up is looking at the beast and knowing it's immortal and you are not. It's dealing with that."

Head down, George stood by the library table. Near the fragment of star iron and a sprig of mountain laurel sat a soiled old beaver hat. It had been found on the lawn below the dormer Bent had entered. George's hand swept out, knocking the hat off the table and, inadvertently, the laurel. He put his foot on the laurel and crushed it.

"I can't deal with that, Jilly. I can't do it."

Madeline's heart broke. She wanted to take him in her arms, draw him close, comfort him. She was surprised and a little embarrassed by the strength of her feeling for the man who was her late husband's best friend. Color in her cheeks gave her away, but the others didn't notice. She quickly brought the emotion under control by turning away and putting her handkerchief to her eyes.

"Jilly—" He was calmer now. "Would you or Madeline

please ask Christopher Wotherspoon to step in? I'd like to start on the arrangements for my trip."

Virgilia couldn't believe it. "This afternoon?"

"Why not this afternoon? You don't think I'm going out there and drink and crack jokes, do you?"

"George, these people are your friends. They're behaving in a perfectly appropriate way for a wake."

"Damn it, don't lecture." The brief communion, begun when he first called her Jilly, was over. "Wotherspoon has a lot to do to oversee Hazard's in my absence. He and Jupe Smith must also start up the Pittsburgh plant."

"I hadn't heard you were going away," Madeline said.

A listless nod. "I have business in Washington. After that— well, I'm not sure. I'll go to Europe, perhaps."

"What about the children?"

"They can finish the school year and join me."

"Where?" Virgilia asked.

"Wherever I happen to be."

Madeline and Virgilia exchanged anxious looks while George picked up the broken sprig of laurel. Contemptuously, he flung it in the cold hearth.

That night, very late, George woke. He felt like a child, frightened and angry. "Why did you do this to me, Constance?" he said in the dark. "Why did you leave me alone?"

He struck the pillow and kept striking it until he started to cry. He felt ashamed; ashamed and lost. He put his head down on the pillow. From the heavy starched cloth crept a scent, her scent, the imprint of someone who had shared the bed and the pillow for years. She was gone but she lingered. He tried to stop crying and couldn't. He cried until the gray light broke.

Every sheriff and metropolitan detective in Pennsylvania searched for Elkanah Bent. When he wasn't found by New Year's Day, George suspected he would not be found soon, if at all.

On the second day of the new year, 1868, George called on Jupe Smith and instructed him to put the new rail car up for sale. He then packed one valise and bid the servants and Patricia and young William goodbye. The children felt cast adrift. Could this cold, empty-eyed man be their father? William put his arm around his sister. In a moment, he felt years older.

George boarded the noon train to Philadelphia, speaking to no one.

At the War Department, a captain named Malcolm went through the ritual of sympathy. He asked, "There's no sign of this madman?"

"None. He's disappeared. I'd have caught him if the goddamn train hadn't been late—"

George stopped. He tried to relax the hand gripping the chair arm in Malcolm's office. Color returned slowly to his fingers and wrist. He wished he could tear the barbed *if's* from his mind. It was impossible. He wished he could be man enough to do what Virgilia talked about: grow up; look at the beast. He'd looked, but it was destroying him.

Captain Malcolm saw his visitor's state and remained silent. Malcolm himself was under great strain, along with every other staff officer unlucky enough to be posted to Washington. The whole department had been in turmoil for months, following Johnson's suspension of Stanton as Secretary of War last August. Since a suspension was expressly prohibited by the Tenure of Office Act, Mr. Stanton, both a Radical and a clever lawyer, denied the validity of the suspension. Grant, nevertheless, was rather reluctantly serving as interim secretary.

The President had suspended Stanton to test the Tenure Act and defy the Radicals, and they were after him for it. Early in December they had introduced an impeachment bill in the House. It had failed, but Malcom was assured the question would not be dropped. He understood the Senate was preparing to formalize its rejection of the suspension, and that might well provoke another attempt to oust Stanton. All of this made life difficult; Malcolm didn't know which of his departmental colleagues could be trusted with any remark beyond a pleasantry. At least this tragic man seated on the other side of the desk was not a part of the conflict.

Presently George said, "I've hired the Pinkerton agency. I want to give them all available information."

"I have a man searching the Adjutant General's personnel records now. Let me see how he's coming."

Malcolm was gone twenty minutes. He returned with a slim file, which he laid on the cluttered desk. "There isn't much, I'm afraid. Bent was charged with cowardice at Shiloh while temporarily commanding a unit other than his own. Lacking conclusive evidence in the matter, General Sherman nevertheless ordered a notation in his record and exiled him to New Orleans. He remained there until the end of General Butler's tenure."

"Anything else?"

Malcolm went through it. "Created a disturbance at a sporting house owned by one Madam Conti. Apprehended stealing a painting that was her property. Before Bent could again be brought up on charges, he deserted.

"There is one final entry, a year later. A man answering Bent's description worked briefly for Colonel Baker's detective unit."

George knew the work of Colonel Lafayette Baker. He recalled newspaper editors thrown into Old Capitol Prison for dissent about the war or criticism of Lincoln's policies and cabinet officers. "You're referring to the secret police employed by Mr. Stanton."

Malcolm lost his cordiality. "Mr. Stanton? I have no information, sir. I can't comment on that allegation."

George had seen enough bureaucrats to recognize the self-protective mode. Bitterly, he said, "Of course. Is that everything in the file?"

"Almost. Bent was seen last at Port Tobacco, where it's presumed he was arranging illegal entry into the Confederacy. There the trail runs out."

"Thank you, Captain. I'll convey the information to Pinkerton's." He added a polite lie. "You've been very helpful."

He shook Malcolm's hand and left. He felt his gut boiling, and barely reached Willard's Hotel before he was again stricken with violent intestinal trouble.

Virgilia found a doctor for him. The man sent to a chemist's for an opium compound that tightened up his gut but did nothing to stem the sudden fits of weeping that struck him at highly inopportune moments. One such attack took place when he was escorting Virgilia to Willard's dining room for a farewell supper.

With an exertion of will, he recovered his composure. His sister talked throughout the meal, trying to divert him with information about her work at Scipio Brown's home for black waifs, and the mounting Radical frenzy to remove the President by impeachment. George heard little of it, then nothing when he put his face in his hands and wept again. He was mortally ashamed, but he couldn't stop.

In his suite, Virgilia held him close before they parted. Her arms felt strong, while he felt weak, sick, worthless. She kissed his cheek gently. "Let us know where you are, George. And please take care of yourself."

He held the door open, pale in the feeble light of low-trimmed gas.

"Why?" he said.

She went away without answering.

In New York he booked a first-class stateroom on the *Grand Turk* for Southampton. He was carrying the name of a London estate agent with good contacts in Europe, particularly Switzerland. The estate agent recommended Lausanne, on the north shore of Lake Geneva, saying that any number of American millionaires suffering from ill health had found benefit there. George had indicated that he needed a restful haven.

In cold and damp January twilight, he stood at the rail among first-class passengers who were waving, chattering, and celebrating. A steward handed him a glass of champagne. He muttered something but didn't drink. Soul-numbing despair still gripped him. He had lost twenty pounds, and, because he was a short man, the loss seemed severe, lending him a wasted look.

Trailing smoke, her whistle blasting, the great steamer left the dock and moved down the Hudson past the Jersey piers and the shanties surrounding them. George's hand hung over the rail. A slight pitch of the vessel spilled the champagne. It dispersed in the air, the droplets not visible by the time they reached the oily black water.

How like the life of poor Constance, and that of his dead friend Orry, was the spilled champagne. A moment's sparkle, an accident, and nothing.

He walked to the stern, the fur collar of his overcoat turned up against the chill. With dead eyes he watched America vanish behind him. He expected he would never see it again.

MADELINE'S JOURNAL

January, 1868. Back from Lehigh Station. A sorrowful trip. George not himself. Virgilia, reunited with the family after

*long estrangement—she is much softened in temperament—
said privately that she fears for G.'s mental stability. G.'s lawyer, Smith, warned us that the murderer, Bent, might strike
any one of us. It is too monstrous to be believed. Yet the fate of
poor Constance warns us not to dismiss it.*

*Surprised to find that the C'ston Courier carried a para-
graph about the murder—Judith sent it to Prudence in my
absence. I assume the story traveled widely because of its sen-
sational nature. Bent is named as the culprit.*

*Also found a letter from a Beaufort attorney who pro-
poses to visit soon. The discovery at Lambs, still creating furor, will prove our salvation, he claims. . . .*

*Written on the 12th. Andy leaves tomorrow to walk to C'ston
for the "Great Convention of the People of South Carolina"—
the same gathering Gettys's wretched sheet calls "the black
and tan meeting." Though I can ill afford it, I spent a dollar
at the new Summerton junk shop for trousers and a worn but
serviceable frock coat, dusty orange, that was once the pride of
some white gentlemen. These I gave to A. Jane has sewn other
garments for her husband, so he needn't be ashamed of his
clothes.*

*Prudence found and presented Andy with an old four-
volume set of Kent's* Commentaries on American Law,
which law students now use in place of Blackstone's. *A. longs
to study and understand the law. He reveres its power to protect his race. He will study solely for personal satisfaction,
since he knows that even under the most liberal of regimes, it
is likely that no man of his color would be able to practice
profitably in Carolina. Indeed, his very presence at the convention with others of his race is an affront to men like Gettys.*
. . .

After midnight on January thirteenth, Judith carried a taper
to her husband's study at Tradd Street. She found him amid a
litter of newspapers, his reading spectacles on his nose and a book
in his lap. It was a book she hadn't seen him open for years.

"The Bible, Cooper?"

His long white fingers tapped the rice-paper page. "Exodus.
I was reading about the plagues. An appropriate study for these
times, don't you think? After the plague of frogs and the plague

of lice, the swarms of flies and the boils and the killing hail, Moses brandished his rod again, an east wind rose and blew all night, and in the morning it brought a plague of locusts."

Dismayed and alarmed by his fervency, Judith put down the taper and crossed her arms over her bed gown. Cooper picked up the Bible and read in a low voice. *"Very grievous they were. Before them there were no such locusts as they . . . they did eat every herb of the land, and all the fruit of the trees which the hail had left: and there remained not any green thing in the trees, or in the herbs of the field, through all the land of Egypt."*

He took off his spectacles. "We have a north wind instead. Blowing in a plague of Carolina turncoats, Yankee adventurers, illiterate colored men—and they're all going to sit down in that convention tomorrow. What a prospect! Ethiopian minstrelsy. Ham Radicalism in all its glory!"

"Cooper, the convention must meet. A new constitution's the price for readmission to the Union."

"And a new social order—is that another price we must pay?" He picked up a *Daily News* and read, *"The demagogue is to rule the mass, and vice and ignorance control the vast interests at stake. The delegates may well create a Negro bedlam."* He tossed the paper down. "I concur."

"But if I remember my Bible, soon after the locusts came, there was a west wind to cast them back in the Red Sea."

"And you remember what followed next, don't you? The plague of darkness. Then the plague of death."

Judith wanted to weep. She couldn't believe that this spent, embittered man was the same person she'd married. Only by immense will did she keep emotion from her face. "Are you planning to observe any of the proceedings?" she asked.

"I'd sooner watch wild animals. I'd sooner be hung."

In the morning, he left early for the offices of the Carolina Shipping Company. Judith felt sad and helpless. Cooper was indeed becoming a stranger to her. He no longer had anything at all to do with Madeline.

Marie-Louise wasn't much better company for her, though the reasons were different. Judith found her daughter at the sunny dining table, her chin on her hands, her breakfast untouched, her eyes fixed dreamily on some far unseen vista. She was neglecting her studies and she talked of scarcely anything but boys. Marie-Louise especially admired some of General Canby's occupying soldiers. Whatever the other consequences of military Reconstruction, it was quite literally robbing Judith of a family.

Of the one hundred twenty-four delegates who convened on January 14, seventy-six were black. Only twenty-three of the white delegates were Carolina-born, but of those a fair number were former hotspurs. Joe Crews had traded in slaves. J. M. Rutland had collected money for a new cane when Preston Brooks broke his over the head of Charles Sumner, almost killing him. Franklin Moses had helped pull down the American flag after Sumter surrendered.

Andy sat among the delegates in his dusty orange frock coat, the first volume of James Kent's *Commentaries* on his knee. He was very erect, proud to be at the convention, but overawed, too; many of the Negro delegates were far better educated than he was. Alonzo Ransier, a native-born freedman, had chatted with him at length about the sweeping social changes the convention would produce. The most intimidating Negro was a handsome, tall, portly chap named Francis Cardozo. Although his skin was the color of old ivory, Cardozo, a free-born mulatto, proudly seated himself among the black delegates. He was an example of what a man could make of himself if he had unlimited opportunity, Andy thought. Cardozo had graduated from the University of Glasgow and formerly held a Presbyterian pulpit in New Haven, Connecticut.

To overcome feelings of inferiority, Andy frequently recalled some earnest words that Jane spoke when she said goodbye to him at the river road. "You're just as good as any of them if you prove you are. You all start out equal in the eyes of God. Mr. Jefferson said so, and that's what the war was really about. Whether you end up ahead of where you started is up to you."

She'd hugged him then, kissed him, and whispered, "Make us all proud." Remembering it, he sat a little straighter.

There was none of the predicted "Negro bedlam" on the convention floor, though enthusiastic black spectators in the gallery had to be gaveled to silence by the temporary chairman, T. J. Robertson, a well-respected businessman of moderate views. The noisiest part of the hall was that occupied by members of the press, most of them Yankees. Many were dressed in plaid suits and gaudy cravats. Andy saw one reporter spit a stream of tobacco juice on the floor. He felt smugly superior. Earlier, Cardozo had remarked to him and some other black delegates, "The reporters have come down here to measure this convention against Northern morality. They'll measure our utterances and our behavior as well. Take heed and act accordingly, gentlemen."

Robertson's gavel brought the hall to order. "Before I turn the chair over to our great and good friend Dr. Mackey"—he was another respected local man—"I should like to remind those assembled of our high purpose. We are gathered to frame a just and liberal constitution for the Palmetto State, one which will guarantee equal rights to all, and gain us readmission to the Union."

The spectators demonstrated their approval. Again Robertson gaveled them down before continuing.

"We do not claim any preeminence of wisdom or virtue. We do claim, however, that we are following the progressive spirit of the age . . . and that we shall be bold enough, honest enough, wise enough to trample obsolete and unworthy laws and customs underfoot, to initiate a new order of justice in South Carolina. Let every delegate turn his thoughts, and his utterances, solely to that purpose."

He means my thoughts, Andy said to himself. All right, he'd speak up. If he was wrong about something, he'd learn. Without making a few mistakes, how could you lift yourself from what you were to what you wanted to become?

He straightened in his seat, hand firmly on the law text. A rush of pride renewed his courage and restored his confidence.

"Now, ma'am," said Mr. Edisto Topper of Beaufort, "this is why I urgently requested a meeting." Standing beside Madeline in the pale January sunshine drenching the fallow rice square, the small, dapper attorney broke open the blue-gray lump of clay.

Madeline stepped back from the familiar stench. "I've always called that our poisoned earth."

Topper dropped the clay lumps, laughing. "Poisoned with riches, Mrs. Main." He turned to his young and servile clerk. "Gather several of those nodules and put them in the bag. We'll want an assay."

Madeline's forehead glistened with perspiration. When Topper's carriage had come rattling up the lane, she was busy brushing a new coat of whitewash on the pine house. Specks of it stippled her hands and the bosom of her faded dress.

"I can hardly believe you, Mr. Topper, though I'd certainly like to do so."

"Do, my good woman, do. The rumors are true. There is mineral treasure hidden along the Ashley and Stono rivers, and in the riverbeds as well. Your so-called poisoned earth is phosphate-bearing."

"But it's been here for years."

"And not a soul realized its worth until Dr. Ravenel of Charleston assayed samples from Lambs last fall." Topper swept the vista of rice fields with a flamboyant gesture. "Mont Royal could run as high as six or eight hundred tons of marl per acre. High-grade marl, sixty percent tricalcic phosphate, ten percent carbonate of lime—far richer than the marls of Virginia."

"It's very welcome news. But a little overwhelming."

He laughed again, and dry-washed his hands. "Understandable, dear lady. After years of defeat and privation, we are quite literally standing upon the economic rebirth of this section of the state. It's there in those foul-smelling nodules. That's the smell of money. That's the smell of fertilizer!"

They returned to homemade chairs on the lawn in front of the whitewashed house. From his valise, lawyer Topper produced reports, assays, surveys which he thrust at Madeline, urging her to read every word.

"Already there's a positive stampede to buy mineral rights from property owners. I represent a group of investors organized as the Beaufort Phosphate Company. All fine Southern gentlemen; Carolina natives, like myself. I'm sure you'll feel more comfortable knowing that when we do business."

Madeline brushed back a stray strand of graying hair. "If, Mr. Topper. If."

"But you have the complete advantage in the matter! It's our capital what will be at risk, whereas all you give up is temporary use of your land. We handle everything. Dig the pits, build a tram road for horse carts, install steam-driven washers to separate out the sand and clay. We assume full responsibility for freighting or barging the washed rock to drying yards. Then we negotiate a favorable sale price. Mr. Lewis and Mr. Klett have already capitalized one processing firm to crush the rock and convert it to commercial fertilizer. Competing companies are sure to spring up soon. We'll be in a splendid position."

It was all too perfect. She kept searching for flaws. "What about men to dig the rock?"

"Likewise our responsibility. We'll hire every available nig— ah, freedman. Pay them twenty-five cents per foot dug, rock removal included."

She shook her head. Topper looked puzzled. "Something wrong?"

"Very definitely, Mr. Topper. There are black families starving all along this river, and I don't exclude Mont Royal. If you're going to mine my land, you'll have to create jobs that are worthwhile. Shall we say fifty cents per foot dug?"

Topper blanched. "Fifty? I'm not certain—"

"Then perhaps I should negotiate with someone else. You did mention competition."

The lawyer began to squirm. "We can work something out, dear lady. I'm certain we can work something out. Here, I've brought the option paper. I'd like to obtain your signature this morning, in advance of a full contract satisfactory to both sides." He took the folded document from his clerk. It was thick and wrapped with green ribbon. He flourished it as if it were a road map to El Dorado.

Trying to hide her excitement, Madeline scanned the finely written pages of tortured language made even more obscure by occasional Latin. She thought she understood the general sense of it.

"Ask your clerk to add a sentence about the agreed mining wage and I'll sign."

"We understand that a second signature will be needed."

"No. I have the authority to sign for Cooper Main."

With a trembling hand, she did.

Orry, Orry—joy beyond belief. We are reprieved! To celebrate, I called everyone to the house tonight for saffroned rice. Jane brought a jar of sweet berry wine she was saving, and while the full moon rose, we laughed and sang Gullah hymns and danced like pagans. Sim's music, blown from the neck of an empty jug, outsang the greatest orchestra. We only wished Andy were here, but he is in the midst of his important work. I longed for you.

The river is shining like white fire as I write this. I have seldom felt it so warm in January. Perhaps our winter of despair is finally over. Best of all, if there are indeed riches in the ground of Mont Royal, then I can make the dream live. I can build the house again.

She was wakened by the sound of a horse coming up the lane from the river road. She wrapped her old gown around herself and rushed out to identify the visitor. Unbelievably, it was Cooper, jumping down from a lathered bay. A foot-thick carpet of mist lay all about them.

"It was all over Charleston by ten last night, Madeline. We're laughingstocks."

Sleepily, she muttered, "What are you talking about?"

"Your damned contract with Beaufort Phosphate. Apparently you're the last person in the district to find out who's behind the company."

"Local men, the lawyer said."

"The scalawag lied. He's the only South Carolinian involved. The principal share owner is a goddamned Radical senator, Samuel Stout. You've sold us out to a man who flogs with one hand and bleeds us with the other."

. . . I could do nothing to appease him. He rained invective on me, refused my offer of food, treated Prudence rudely, and ordered me to withhold my signature from the formal contract, legal consequences notwithstanding. I said I would sign a pact with the Devil if he would save the Main lands and give our freedmen food. He cursed me and leaped on his weary horse and rode away. Although he stands to profit by my error, I fear he now hates me more than ever.

February, 1868. Convention expected to last nearly 60 days. Andy S. sends all but $1 of his $11 delegate per diem to his wife. He works nights at the Mills House and pays token rent to a black family for sleeping space in their shanty. Jane showed me his latest letter, simply phrased but a model of clear English. What a wondrous thing is a human mind when it is free to grow. . . .

Andy Sherman felt he had never stretched his mind, or learned so much, except for the time during the war when Jane was his teacher. Every morning as he dressed for his delegate work, he ached from hours spent on his knees polishing hotel floors or carrying jars of night soil out to the carts. Somehow a few hours of sleep sustained him, as did the one full meal a day that he allowed himself. He was nourished by the convention and the work he was doing there.

When he didn't understand a word, a phrase, an idea, he asked questions of the chair or fellow subcommittee members. When something was explained and he grasped it, he felt like a carefree boy waking on a summer morning.

Certain delegates, acting from timidity or expedience, tried to modify the great cornerstone of the emerging constitution, suffrage. They tried to add a qualifying poll tax of one dollar, and a literacy provision: any man coming of age after 1875 without the ability to read and write would be denied the vote.

In hot arguments against the amendments, Andy heard Union League doctrine recited by some of the black delegates. Some, but not many; a majority of the blacks were still too overawed by their white counterparts, or simply too shy and uncertain to speak up. He tried to persuade a couple of them to take part. He was answered with apologetic evasions.

He discussed the problem with Cardozo, whose quick mind and impressive oratorical skills he continued to admire. "You're right, Sherman. As a race we are too reticent. Only education will alleviate that. Given the history of this state, however, I don't believe an adequate public school system can be in operation by 1875. I will vote against the amendment."

Andy spoke against it—his first time on his feet in the convention. Nervously, but with conviction, he read the little statement he'd phrased and rephrased on scraps of paper until it satisfied him. *"Gentlemen, I believe the right to vote must belong to the wise and the ignorant alike, to the vicious as well as the virtuous, else universal suffrage as an idea means nothing."*

Ransier was the first on his feet to applaud.

The provision was rejected, 107–2. The poll tax, which Cardozo scathingly branded the first step to returning power to the "aristocratic element," went down 81–21.

Work has begun! The whole Ashley district is swarming with laborers, promoters, men from the new processing plants that have sprung up. After nearly three years of chaos and poverty the district is once again energetic and hopeful. Our improved prospects dictate a visit to Charleston soon—in preparation for relieving the burden of our debt. . . .

The blacks of Mont Royal were as protective of Madeline as if she were a child. They continued to insist that someone drive her to the city. She relented, and chose Fred.

On a crisp February morning, they stopped the wagon shortly after turning onto the river road. In the cleared field behind the fence a gang of thirty black men swung shovels. Flagged stakes outlined a trench six hundred yards wide by one thousand yards long, to be dug around the field to drain it.

Six men were dragging a huge timber with ropes to smooth a path down the center of the field. On that path, horse carts would eventually haul away mined rock. Edisto Topper had informed Madeline that most of Mont Royal would soon be covered by similar fields.

Here was the first. She was studying it proudly when a bright flash, as from a reflecting mirror, caught her attention. She turned and saw a mounted man about a quarter-mile down the road in the direction of Summerton. From his pudginess, and the light flashing from his spectacles, she recognized Gettys.

For a moment or so the storekeeper sat very still, as if watching her. Then, with a contemptuous flick of his rein, he turned and trotted away toward Summerton.

Madeline shivered. Somehow the day was spoiled.

It got worse. At the Palmetto Bank on Broad Street, a bald clerk, Mr. Crow, informed her that Mr. Dawkins would be unavailable all day.

"But I wrote him that I was coming. It's important that I speak to him," she said.

Crow remained cool. "In what regard?"

"I want to arrange to pay off my mortgage sooner than the bank requires. Mont Royal's being mined for phosphates. We should be receiving substantial income. I wrote Leverett all about this."

"Mr. Dawkins received your letter." Crow emphasized the

mister, implicit criticism of her familiarity. "I was instructed to tell you that the directors of this bank are not disposed to prepayment. It's our prerogative under terms of the mortgage to insist that you continue regular quarterly payments."

"For how long."

"The full term."

"That's years. If it's a matter of the interest, I'll gladly pay that, too."

Crow stepped back a pace, disdainful. "It's a matter of policy, Mrs. Main."

"What policy? To keep me on a leash you can cut any time you choose?"

"Are you referring to foreclosure?"

"Yes. Is that a matter of policy, too?"

"Kindly lower your voice. Why should the Palmetto Bank wish to foreclose on Mont Royal? It's valuable land, with dramatically improved prospects for generating income. You're raising an extraneous issue." He thought a moment, then added, "Of course it's true that foreclosure remains an option of the bank, should you default. But in that event, the person to suffer would be the owner, Mr. Main. I'm sure you wouldn't want to be responsible for putting your relative in such a position—"

The point—the threat—was made. But how clumsy they were, how obvious in their passion to control her. Was the whole state, the whole South, still insane on the subject of *Africanization*? Surely, surely they no longer feared unlikely conspiracies, uprisings, arson plots against property, the raping of white women—

Then, abruptly, intuition pointed to the real cause, less dramatic but nevertheless lethal: the convention. It was meddling with the vote, and with taxes; it threatened to touch white money. Did Leverett Dawkins know of her connection with a black delegate? He must.

Crow stood behind a gleaming oak rail with a gate in it. Provoked by his rebuff, and by snide looks from a couple of tellers, she reached for the gate. "I'm a good customer of this bank, Mr. Crow. I'm not satisfied with your explanations, or happy about your rudeness. I'm going to take this up with Leverett whether he's busy or not."

"Madam, you will not." Crow seized and held the gate shut.

"Please leave. Mr. Dawkins reminds you that colored are not welcome on these premises."

He walked off. Her eyes brimming with tears of rage, she fled.

> *. . . Some of the shock of the bank experience is leaving. But not the humiliation—or the anger.*

> *March, 1868. What confusion and melodrama! Two months ago the Senate in executive session refused to concur in the matter of the suspension of Mr. Stanton, whereupon Gen. Grant resigned and permitted Stanton to return to his War Dept. offices. Johnson immediately appointed Gen. Lorenzo Thomas in Grant's place, and Thomas boasted that he'd remove Stanton by force if need be—whereupon Stanton quite literally barricaded himself in his rooms and had a warrant drawn for the arrest of Thomas! The warrant was delivered at a masked ball!!—it would all be perfect for a comic opera libretto if the passions behind it were not deep and deadly.*

> *But they are, and the wolves pursuing Johnson have at last cornered him. On the 24th instant, a vote to impeach for "high crimes and misdemeanors" passed in the U.S. House by substantial margin. It is an event without precedent in the nation's history, and those on both sides are rabid about it. Stout and his crowd call J. "the arch-apostate," insisting that he has betrayed Lincoln, the Constitution, the nation, etc. The President's supporters claim that he, deeming the Tenure of Office Act unconstitutional, had no choice but to test it by direct action. The Radicals are bent on bringing him to trial. I cannot believe a chief executive will be so humiliated. Yet many are rejoicing at the prospect. . . .*

> *Andy home last night. The convention adjourned after 53 days, having called special elections for April to ratify the new constitution and elect state and national representatives. . . .*

> *Topper here with assay results. I confronted him with the deceit about Stout's ownership of his firm. With a cool arrogance I have noted in some short men, and many lawyers, he turned aside my accusation by showing a profit projection based on the assay. The sums are staggering. . . .*

> *. . . Much activity in the district. Horsemen on the*

*road at all hours, lanterns glimmering in the marshes long
into the night. I suspect either the election campaign or the
influx of surveyors, mining experts, etc. But neither can altogether explain a curious change among the freedmen. Few are
smiling, and they seem easily alarmed. I hear many conversations kept private by the use of the swift Gullah tongue, which
must be clearly overheard to be understood. . . .*

*. . . I am convinced now—they are frightened. Pru-
dence has noticed it. Why?*

The Imperial Wizard came by night.

In a lonely grove of great oaks a mile from Summerton, they
planted and lit a ring of torches. Wives and sweethearts had sewn
the regalia according to instructions sent earlier by letter. The
Invisible Empire prescribed no color for regalia. At Des's urging,
the initiates chose red. Gettys had paid for the expensive yard
goods out of his handsome earnings from the Dixie Store.

Standing six feet two inches and powerfully built, General
Nathan Bedford Forrest had a swarthy complexion and gray-blue
eyes. Streaks of white showed in his wavy black hair and neat
chin beard. He impressed the initiates as a man it would be un-
wise to challenge. When he presented them with an official copy
of the Prescript, the national constitution, and told them the fee
was ten dollars, no one objected.

The initiates stood in a line. The torches smoked and hissed
around them. Erect and clear-eyed, Forrest moved from man to
man, inspecting them. Des was almost dizzy with excitement.
Jack Jolly carried himself with a certain smugness; this was his
old leader, after all. Gettys sweated, though not nearly so much
as Father Lovewell, who kept shooting glances into the insect-
murmurous dark beyond the torches. One of the two farmers
who completed the group recognized the priest, whom he saw in
church every Sunday.

Forrest began his instruction.

"This is an institution of humanity, mercy, and patriotism.
Its genesis and organizing principles embody all that is chivalric
in conduct, noble in sentiment, heroic in spirit. Knowing of your
previous declaration of loyalty to these principles, I shall, by order of the Grand Dragon of the Realm of Carolina, ask you ten
questions."

His stern eyes raked them. "Have you ever belonged to or

subscribed to the principles of the Radical Republican Party, the Union League, or the Grand Army of the Republic?"

As one, *"No."*

"Do you righteously oppose Negro equality, both social and political?"

"Yes."

"Do you advocate a white man's government?"

"Yes."

"Do you favor constitutional liberty, and a government of equitable laws instead of a government of violence and oppression?"

"Yes!"

So it went, for nearly an hour. The lessons:

"We protect the weak, the innocent, the defenseless, against the lawlessness and lust of the violent, the brutal, the deranged. . . .We serve the injured, the suffering, the unfortunate, giving first priority and highest allegiance to widows and orphans of the Confederate dead."

The rules:

"Any ritual, hand grip, code or pass word, as well as the origins, designs, mysteries, and other proprietary secrets of this organization shall not be knowingly betrayed. If any are so betrayed, the perpetrator shall incur the full and extreme penalty of our law. Never shall the name of the organization be written by any member. For purposes of printed announcement it shall be identified always and only by one, two, or three asterisks."

The investiture:

From the ground, Forrest plucked up a robe and sacklike hood of shiny sateen-weave cotton. Solemnly, he handed these to Des.

"I endow you with the title, rights, and privileges of Grand Cyclops of the klavern and, additionally, the title, rights, and responsibilities of Grand Titan of this district."

To Jolly: "I endow you with the title, rights, and privileges of Grand Turk, charging you to assist the Cyclops in all regards, and serve as his loyal adjutant."

"Yes, sir, General." Jolly accepted the regalia, his eyes brimming with anticipatory pleasure.

Grand Sentinel, Grand Ensign, Grand Scribe, Grand Exchequer—each man had a responsibility. With great solemnity and a high sense of patriotism absent from his life since he'd mustered out of the Palmetto Rifles, Des donned the shimmering red robe and hood. So did the others.

The torches fumed and smoked. General Forrest surveyed the hooded den. Well pleased, he smiled.

"You are the newest knights of our great crusade. Begin your purge here, on your home soil, where the face of the enemy is known to you. Joined klavern to klavern throughout our great Invisible Empire, together we will sweep the debased government of certain evil men from this land we love."

Des licked his lips and exhaled, rippling the mask that hung below his chin. Again he felt the weight of his boon companion, Ferris Brixham, sagging dead in his arms.

Jolly felt the rolling gait of a war-horse, and heard the screams of the dying at Fort Pillow.

And Gettys grew stiff under his robe, thinking of Orry Main's widow, denied her sudden new wealth, abducted and brought to a remote clearing like this, stripped bare for whatever punishment, or pleasure, they chose.

Eerily, Des sensed his thoughts. "Certain white men, Randall," he whispered. "A certain white woman, too."

> *Slavery and imprisonment for debt are permanently barred.*
>
> *Duelling is outlawed.*
>
> *Divorce is made legal. The property of a married woman is no longer subject to sale or levy for a husband's debts.*
>
> *Henceforth judicial districts are to be called counties.*
>
> *A system of public schools shall be established, open to all and financed by uniform taxes on real and personal property.*
>
> *Railroads and poorhouses shall likewise be built with tax monies, collection of which by municipalities, townships, counties and school districts is hereby authorized.*
>
> *There shall be no segregation by race in the state militia.*
>
> *Universal manhood suffrage is granted to all regardless of race or previous condition.*
>
> *No person shall be disfranchised for crimes committed while he was enslaved.*
>
> *Distinction on account of race or color in any case whatever shall be prohibited, and all classes of citizens shall enjoy equally all common, public, legal and political privileges.*

Some provisions of the forty-one sections of the
South Carolina Constitution of 1868

40

Marie-Louise Main came into the springtime of her fifteenth year bothered by a number of things.

She was bothered at night by vivid dreams in which she waltzed with a succession of handsome young men. Each young man held her waist firmly and flirted in a Yankee accent she found wickedly attractive. Every face was different, but all the young men were officers in blue uniforms with bright gold buttons. The ending of each dream was similar, too. The young officer whirled her away to some dim balcony or garden path and there bent to kiss her in a highly forward way—

Whereupon she invariably awoke. She knew why. She was ignorant of what came after a kiss.

Oh, she had a general idea. She'd seen animals, and, well, she knew. But she hadn't the faintest idea of how it felt, or how she should behave. Mama had provided basic facts, but to questions about response she said, "Time enough to talk about that when you become engaged. That will be some years yet." Of course Marie-Louise never mentioned the subject with Papa.

She was bothered by what she perceived as her inadequacy when she compared herself with her peers, the five other young ladies in her class at Mrs. Allwick's Female Academy. While she worked at her translation of selected passages from Horace or the *Aeneid,* the other girls passed notes and whispered about their beaux. Each had several, or claimed they did. Marie-Louise had none. Papa was so grim and preoccupied all the time, he wouldn't give her the slightest encouragement about boys. Not that it really mattered. She didn't know even one boy who might want to begin the courtship ritual with the customary small gifts and parlor visits.

She wondered if her looks contributed to this unhappy situation. She had to accept her height, and a slim figure; both parents were built that way. She'd inherited Mama's dark blond curls and a large mouth with good teeth. Her small bosom came in some mysterious way from Papa's side, she decided; Mama was flat.

When she felt good, she thought herself passably pretty. When something got her down—usually the lack of boys in her life—she was sure she was a homely horse. Objectively, she was considered an attractive young woman, with a pretty face suited to smiling and a natural warmth that invited friendliness, although it was true that she was a little too tall and thin ever to be deemed a beauty.

Marie-Louise was bothered by her father. He was stern and unsmiling, and although she had once been comfortable in his presence, she was no longer. Nor was Mama. Mama liked to entertain Aunt Madeline whenever she was in Charleston, but it could only be during the day, when Marie-Louise was at school; Papa refused to allow Uncle Orry's widow to eat supper at Tradd Street or call when he was at home. He never explained this intolerant behavior, but it wounded Marie-Louise, who was fond of her aunt by marriage. Mama said Aunt Madeline needed the affection and support of her family. Uncle Orry's best friend Mr. Hazard, the brother of Aunt Brett's husband, had lost his wife in some terrible accident. Aunt Madeline had gone to the funeral and was still upset about it, Mama said.

Papa didn't care. Papa was not himself; not the man Marie-Louise remembered from her early childhood. He was busy with all sorts of personal causes. For instance, twice a month he traveled on horseback to Columbia. He was one of thirty-eight trustees of the old South Carolina College, now reopened as a state university with twenty-two students. "If the Radicals and General Canby will leave us alone, we might make something of the institution." Exactly what he wanted to make of it, Marie-Louise couldn't fathom, but he was fiercely protective of the university, and of his position as trustee.

Papa was always delivering angry little sermons at meals. Marie-Louise knew there was turmoil in the state because of the new constitution that had something to do with public schools, one of the topics that most often prompted Papa's sermons. One evening he flourished a letter from General Wade Hampton. "He's chairing our special committee to write a protest to Congress about that damnable constitution." The next evening he waved some cheap inky sheet and declared, *"The Thunderbolt* is a trashy paper but in this case the editor's right. A property tax rate of nine mills per dollar would be thievery. The school scheme is nothing but a pauper's cause, engineered by approximately sixty Negroes, most of whom are ignorant, and fifty white men who are Northern outcasts or Southern renegades. Their tinkering with the social order will destroy this state morally and financially."

The new schools, to be attended by black as well as white pupils, were not the only issue that incensed Papa. He ranted about charges of treason brought against Mr. Davis after a long imprisonment. "Our caged eagle," Papa called him. As for the President of the United States, Mr. Johnson, Papa said he was "high-principled" and "the friend of Southerners," but he was apparently about to be driven out of office by a scheme Marie-Louise didn't understand at all. She only knew the fiendish Republicans were behind it.

Papa hated Republicans. He frequently rushed off to evening meetings of the Democratic party, which he supported with his effort as well as his money. Marie-Louise wished he'd spend more time with the family and less attending meetings and writing letters to newspapers castigating the Republicans. He had no time for his daughter when she tried to plead that she needed a beau, if not several. She decided she would have to acquire one of her own or be forever humiliated in front of her classmates at Mrs. Allwick's.

Finally, Marie-Louise was bothered by a competition at the female academy where she studied Latin and Greek (a bore), algebra (a mystery), and social deportment (useful with beaux; at least so she was told). To conclude the spring term, Mrs. Allwick planned an evening of dance demonstrations under the supervision of Mr. LaMotte, the academy's part-time dancing master. LaMotte was a peculiar man with a huge body, almost feminine grace, and eyes that Marie-Louise found unsettling; they always seemed to be focused on someone other than those he was teaching.

LaMotte frequently harangued the young ladies about "Southern womanhood." He said they represented its finest flowering and must protect themselves against men who would degrade it. Marie-Louise knew that "degrading" had something to do with men and women together physically, but when she mentally ventured beyond that, she was soon in the fogs of ignorance again. Two of her classmates giggled at such references; they understood everything, or pretended they did. It made her so mad she wanted to spit.

To open the program for parents, there would be a grand tableau. One of the six girls in Marie-Louise's class was to be chosen to represent this self-same Southern Womanhood. Mrs. Allwick would make the selection. Marie-Louise had decided that being picked was the most important matter in her life, next to beaux. She also feared the prize would go to a sow named Sara Jane Oberdorf, who said she had seven beaux. Marie-Louise had seen three. One was an undertaker's boy who liked to discuss and compare funerals. One was the shy son of a local magistrate; he never answered anyone who said hello, merely grunted. The third was a lout so overweight that his neck bulged like those of certain old women afflicted with a condition Mama called "the goiter." But at least the three boys were alive and breathing, not creatures of some scarlet dream. Botheration!

One afternoon in early April, Marie-Louise left school at half past four, only to discover, when she stepped on the porch, that it was raining hard. She couldn't see Fort Sumter in the harbor.

Her chattering friends skipped off to parents or servants waiting in carriages. Marie-Louise clutched her Virgil and her algebra text and prepared for a soaking walk to Tradd Street. Then a familiar two-passenger buggy rounded the corner from the South Battery, and there was Papa, driving and waving his gold-knobbed stick.

"I was at a committee meeting at Ravenel's house. I saw it start to rain and thought I'd save you a drenching. Climb in. I must stop at the Mills House to drop off some papers. Then we'll drive home."

Marie-Louise's side curls bobbed as she jumped up beside him, sheltered by the buggy's top. With adoring eyes she gazed at her pale, tired-looking father. This was the most attention he'd paid to her for months.

A great many carriages and saddle horses were tied along the Meeting Street frontage of the hotel. Cooper found a space and told her to wait. He was gone more than the ten minutes he'd promised.

The rain diminished, swift-flying dark clouds moved on out to sea, and a steamy sunshine pierced through while she waited. She noticed a small crowd of men and women listening to a speaker on the steps of Hibernian Hall. Nearby, other men held placards. One said, REPUBLICANS FOR FREE SCHOOLS.

Bored, Marie-Louise left the carriage and strolled toward the crowd. The hoarse-voiced speaker, who might or might not have been a mulatto, was urging his listeners to vote in favor of the new state constitution. Marie-Louise paused at the back of the crowd. The two men just in front of her were unshaven farmer types. They gave her suspicious looks.

Suddenly she noticed a young man not far from her on her left. He wore a fawn coat and breeches and a billowing brown cravat. He was staring.

She almost sank through the ground. She recognized the pale face, light hair and curling mustache, and those brilliant blue eyes. It was the young civilian who'd given his seat to the Negress on the train from Coosawhatchie.

He smiled and tipped his hat. Marie-Louise smiled, feeling she must be red as fire. She clutched her textbooks to her bosom. Was she acting like a perfect fool?

"—and it behooves every citizen of good conscience to support free schools for South Carolina by voting aye on the constitution one week from—"

"Just a moment."

Heads turned. Marie-Louise pirouetted. Her legs wobbled from shock. Where had Papa come from so silently? Well, obviously from the Mills House, while she was all wrapped up in wondering about the young man.

Cooper pushed through the crowd. "I'm a citizen with a conscience. I'd like to ask a question."

"Yes, sir, Mr. Main. I recognize you," said the speaker, defensive and a bit sardonic. Marie-Louise flashed a look at the young man, trying to say that Cooper was her father, but of course the young man didn't understand. To the crowd, the speaker said, "This gentleman is a factor and shipping agent. A Democrat."

Predictably, the people growled. When someone said, "Hell

with him," Marie-Louise reacted with a wrathful expression. How dare they be so rude to Papa?

Cooper elbowed his way to the steps of Hibernian Hall. Marie-Louise could tell that he was in one of his angry moods. "I listened to the fine platitudes this gentleman purveys as part of his Republican cant. I wonder if any of you know their true cost?"

"Shut him up," yelled one of the rough men standing in front of Marie-Louise.

"No," said Cooper, "I'm sure you don't. So I'll remind all you tenderhearted idealists that before the late unpleasantness, when South Carolina had some claim to prosperity, only seventy-five thousand dollars a year could be raised from property taxes to support public schools. Most of that money came from the tax on black bondsmen—"

"Get him down," shouted the rough man. Marie-Louise wanted to hike up her skirts and kick him with her pointed shoe. The speaker signaled to a couple of ragged musicians, who began to play "The Battle Hymn of the Republic" on fifes.

"Damn you, I'll have my say." Cooper was flushed. Marie-Louise grew alarmed. She didn't see the young man drop back and circle the crowd, coming toward her.

Over the music Cooper shouted, "The stupendous and ill-conceived school scheme is estimated to cost nearly a million dollars a year. It can only come from taxes. If you vote for the Republican-inspired constitution, you'll be placing an intolerable burden on the state. South Carolina is on her knees, struggling to rise. This school plan will keep her down forever."

A woman shook her parasol at him. "It isn't taxes you hate. It's the colored people."

The rough man yelled, "Either step down or we'll pull you down."

Marie-Louise didn't pause to consider her next action. She just beat the man's shoulder twice, hard, with her Virgil. "Let him alone. He has as much right to speak as you do."

The man turned, and so did his companion. Marie-Louise looked at them closely and grew petrified with fright. The one doing the yelling had a milky eye and wore a gold ring in his left ear. He glanced at Marie-Louise's bosom and smirked. "They take their concubines young in Charleston, don't they?" He said it in a hard Yankee accent.

"Watch your mouth, sir," said a low voice at her elbow. She turned to see the blue-eyed stranger. He confronted the two older men without apparent worry. "I believe the gentleman speaking is related to the young lady. You owe her an apology."

"Damn if I'll apologize to some mush-mouthed Southron. Why you taking her part, sonny? You sound like a Northern man."

"Chicago," he said with a nod. "I'm taking her part because you have the manners of a hog, and the South has no corner on respect for womanhood."

"Smart-mouthed little shit." The milky-eyed man drew his fist back. A woman shrieked. Suddenly, whistling down, Cooper's stick smashed the raised forearm. He struck a second time with the heavy gold knob, while the young man took hold of Marie-Louise's waist, lifted her, and set her out toward the curb, away from the press of people.

Breathing fast, the young man raised his fists defensively. It was an overly dramatic pose, but it thrilled Marie-Louise. Milk-Eye was groping for Cooper, who kept jabbing him with the ferrule of his stick. The rest of the crowd, though Republican, quickly turned against the uncouth pair. Hands restrained them. The speaker as well as several others offered exaggerated apologies.

Cooper pushed Milk-Eye aside with his cane. The young man lowered his fists. "Thank you, sir," Cooper said to him, brushing off his lapel. All at once he seemed to focus on the young man's face. He frowned. "We've met before."

"Not formally, sir. We saw one another on the railroad from Coosawhatchie some time back."

"Yes." Cooper froze him with that word. The crowd began to disperse. The speaker and the musicians blowing their fifes tramped away down Meeting Street in an impromptu parade. A few others joined them. Milk-Eye stood watching Marie-Louise and her two protectors until his companion convinced him to leave.

Cooper bowed.

"Cooper Main, sir. Your servant."

"Theo German, sir. Yours. I find it a pity that freedom to disagree was not tolerated here today."

Cooper shrugged, very cool toward him. Marie-Louise recalled how Papa had fumed when the young Northerner gave his seat to the black woman. "The new constitution is a ferocious issue, Mr. German. Our survival hinges upon its defeat."

"I am nevertheless in favor, sir."

"So I gather, sir, you not being a Carolinian."

"No, sir, I am only here temporarily, due to my, ah, job. I have rooms with Mrs. Petrie in Chalmers Street."

Marie-Louise looked past Papa's shoulder to the blue eyes of Theo German. She understood why he'd stated his address. Cooper suspected the reason, too.

"Papa, you haven't introduced me."

Icy, Cooper said, "My daughter, Marie-Louise Main, whom you so thoughtfully protected. I am in your debt." Cooper took her elbow. "Shall we go?"

Clouds above Meeting Street let through shafts of sunshine, one of which bathed the street near Hibernian Hall. Theo German's face shone like that of some golden statue. Marie-Louise felt faint.

The young man stepped forward abruptly. "Sir, I wonder if I might ask your permission—"

Oh, yes, she thought, dizzy with happiness. Before he could finish, Cooper literally pushed her toward the Mills House, interrupting. "Good afternoon, Mr. German."

In the carriage, aflame with resentment, she beat her gloved hands on her skirt. "Papa, how could you? He was about to ask permission to call."

"So I sensed. I don't believe we want any Yankee adventurers polluting Tradd Street. He's probably a Union League organizer, or something just as bad. He was a gentleman, I'll grant you that. But not enough of one to pay court to my daughter. When it's time for beaux, I'll inform you."

"Papa," she said, nearly weeping. He ignored her. He snapped the reins and swung the horse south toward Tradd Street. They rolled right by young Theo German, still standing outside Hibernian Hall with the golden light falling on him.

Chalmers Street, Chalmers Street, she thought, wanting to wave to him and not daring. I'm a grown woman. I'll not be told who to love. Mrs. Petrie, Chalmers Street.

Unknowingly, Cooper had just fueled a revolt.

Marie-Louise spent two days composing her note, on lavender paper. In it, she thanked Theo German effusively for guarding her honor, as she put it. Then, having weighed the worst consequences and pictured herself dealing with them, she added a final paragraph inviting him to attend the spring program at Mrs. Allwick's. *Please address me here at the school if you care to reply,* the note concluded. She signed her name, folded the paper, and wrote the school address on the outside. She moistened the note with a heavy floral perfume before waxing it shut.

The freedman who did odd jobs at the school took the note for delivery, asking no questions. The next day, a note came back, briefly and boldly inscribed:

> *I should be honored and privileged to accept your invitation.*
> *Yours obediently,*
> *Brvt. Capt. Theo. German*

"Captain!" she exclaimed, hiding the letter against her bosom. Then he was indeed a Yankee adventurer. Probably one of those ex-soldiers who'd come down to plunder and pillage, as Papa put it. She hoped he hadn't been with Sherman. Papa would go insane.

She counted the days until the spring program, which fell a week after the elections. General Canby dispatched soldiers to watch polling places throughout the state and prevent interference with black voters. The new constitution was approved by some seventy thousand votes to twenty thousand. You might have thought a hurricane had struck Tradd Street. "Only six Democrats elected for thirty-one state Senate seats! And only fourteen Democratic representatives! The other one hundred ten are damned Black Republicans!"

"Cooper, please don't curse in front of your daughter," Judith said.

"We're ruined. We'll be bankrupt in a year." He remained in a rage up through the Tuesday night of the program.

Mrs. Allwick's on Legare was ablaze with lamps and tapers. Chairs were set around the fusty parlor, and a double curtain of white gauze and calico hung at the end adjoining the dining room. Behind the curtain, giggling girls in ivy wreaths and bedsheet togas rushed to position themselves around Sara Jane Oberdorf, who had been chosen for the role of Southern Womanhood.

Marie-Louise no longer cared. She was tingling with expectancy. If this wasn't love, then it was something just as dizzying and delicious. She barely managed to stop chattering when Mrs. Allwick hissed for silence.

The curtain was pulled. Stiffly posed with the other girls, who represented Womanhood's handmaidens, Marie-Louise searched the audience. She almost fainted again. What a precious little dummy she was! Overlooking the obvious, assuming something totally incorrect.

All the chairs were filled by parents and relatives in their finery. He'd been forced to stand at the back, by the window bay overlooking the street. Thanks to all the lamps moved in for the program, he fairly glittered in his Army blue and bright metal buttons. He wasn't an ex-captain. He was a captain *now*.

And there in the second row sat her family, Papa visibly upset. His expression told her he knew he'd been defied. And over a Union Army officer. How would she ever explain?

She lost her balance, knocking Sara Jane off the box on which she stood. Southern Womanhood crashed into her handmaidens and spilled them like a bunch of circus tumblers. Children in the audience screamed with laughter, the tableau ended in chaos . . . and the night was only starting.

The program concluded with the young ladies performing an elaborate quadrille. At the conclusion, a few parents immediately jumped up to applaud. Soon they were all standing. The curtain opened again, and Mrs. Allwick's pupils bowed to acknowledge the ovation. A couple of the girls giggled; because of her girth, Sara Jane had trouble bowing from the waist. While she attempted it, she shot murderous sideways looks at Marie-Louise. Cooper's daughter saw only the young officer, who was applauding wildly.

As the audience broke up, Judith took hold of Cooper's arm to get his attention. At the side of the parlor, wearing a white cravat and stockings and a dark green coatee and knee breeches, Des LaMotte stared at Cooper while mouthing thank-yous to the parents pushing up to congratulate him.

"Cooper, is that dancing master the one who—"

"Same," he snapped. "Empty threats, I've decided."

"I don't know. He looks as though he'd like to crucify you."

Cooper shot him a glance. LaMotte held it a moment, unintimidated. Then he switched his attention to his admirers, bowing and kissing hands.

"We're leaving," Cooper called to his daughter, who was struggling through a crowd of pupils and parents near the curtain. "Get your bonnet and shawl."

"Please, Papa, I have to speak to someone."

"I saw him. We'll have nothing to do with any of Canby's mercenaries."

Judith said, "I think it's unfair to refuse her a few minutes of harmless conversation."

"I'll decide what's harmless and what isn't." Cooper seized his daughter's wrist. "Where are your things?"

Marie-Louise turned red. She wanted to perish on the spot. Captain German was moving toward them. Through welling tears, she saw him stop suddenly. She pulled, but her father wouldn't let go.

Judith gave up and hurried to find her daughter's things. Moments later, Cooper pushed Marie-Louise out a side door to a passage that led to Legare Street. She was crying loudly.

41

A man of seventy-six is too old for this, Jasper Dills thought. His journey on the Baltimore & Ohio had been a sleepless nightmare of jerks, bumps, cinders, and filth. Even in a first-class car, he found himself packed in with the canaille. Sweaty peddlers, pushy mothers with weepy children, flash gentlemen hunting victims to fleece at cards. Horrible, not to be borne.

But he was bearing it, was he not? He'd obeyed the imperious summons the moment it arrived by telegraph. He'd purchased his ticket and packed his carpetbag, because he was fearful of the consequences if he didn't.

The train arrived at the depot at dusk. A mild spring dusk, with flowers and trees blooming all along his route to the east side of town. God, it was horrible to be pulled away from Washington at this moment, when the curtain was about to rise on the last act of the high drama of Johnson and the Radicals—the Senate trial of the chief executive on the eleven articles of impeachment. Never before in the history of the republic had there been an opportunity to witness the dethroning of a sitting president.

Still, that drama was remote, while this one, if you cared to call it a drama, was immediate, touching his life and livelihood. All the way across the mountainous darkness of West Virginia, he had tried to imagine other reasons for the summons besides the one he feared.

The sweet scents of Ohio springtime did little to mask the city's noxious odors. Even here, in a quiet east-side district of fiercely steep streets and huge old houses, many decaying, the air smelled of the river, and the German breweries and slaughterhouses. Detraining at the depot, Dills had nearly choked on the odor of hogs and more hogs. A European traveler had called Cincinnati "a monster piggery," and nicknamed it Porkopolis. In the *Tribune,* old Greeley hailed it as "the queen city of the West." Which only confirmed that Greeley was unbalanced. When Mr. Dickens made his American tour in 1842, what could he possibly have found here that was worth seeing?

The hackney labored to the crest of a hill and turned into a circular cul-de-sac, where it stopped. Dominating the sullen sky between the cul-de-sac and the river was an immense Gothic Revival house, forbidding as a castle, which it resembled because of three adjoining octagonal towers on the river side. The rough stonework was dirtied by time and overgrown with untended ivy, much of it dead. Many of the ground-floor windows were planked over; others showed numerous breaks in small panes of stained glass.

Behind a rusting iron fence, the weedy yard sloped up to a recessed entrance. There Dills discerned a figure hovering in the shadows. Not the same damned caretaker after twenty-five years, he wondered, climbing out with his carpetbag. He paid the driver, adding a handsome tip with well-concealed regret.

"Come back for me in an hour and I'll double that," he said. It was outrageous to spend so much, but he was terrified by the thought of being isolated out here without transportation. He heard bird song in the distance, but near the great Gothic house not a bird warbled or flew. He couldn't help thinking he was in a place of the dead.

"Right, sir," the driver said. "Didn't know anybody still lived in this old dump." And away the hackney went down the hill, its side lamps dwindling and dimming, leaving him by the rusted fence in the lowering dark.

He heard the shuffling step of the old man coming down the walk. It was indeed the same caretaker, still fetching and doing for the resident of the house. He was crudely dressed, stooped, his age impossible to guess because he was albino, with red-tinged eyes and skin nearly as white as his hair.

His broken nails showed as he reached to open the gate. Rusty hinges squealed. From under a soiled cap, his red eyes watched the visitor as he pulled the gate wide. Dills stepped through, and then the caretaker slammed the gate again, a sound like a chord of wrong notes.

Halfway up the walk—roots and weeds had broken through

the stairstep blocks, shattering them—Dills started violently when the caretaker spoke from behind him:

"She found you out."

He felt frail and vulnerable then. His heart fluttered and raced. He tried to summon the resentment he'd felt during most of the long, dirty journey. He needed every bit of it to endure what was to come.

Her room was at the very top of the tallest octagonal tower. Dills reached it by struggling up a creaky stair and stepping through a doorway with the shape of a classic Gothic arch. He was out of breath and feeling more unclean every moment. At least there was some air stirring up here. He could feel it, damp and fetid, as he shuffled across the stone floor toward the figure seated in a huge high-backed carved chair.

The chair was the only piece of furniture aside from a broken spinning wheel lying on its side amid skeins of yarn that had long ago rotted. In bowls and saucers set around the floor, fat homemade candles burned, a dozen of them, relieving some of the gloom and enabling him to see the chair's occupant. Behind her, two smashed-out windows afforded a commanding view of the Ohio River and the hilly dark blue shore of Kentucky. In the river, like boats on the Styx, barges moved slowly, their lanterns gleaming.

"I do not have a chair for you, Mr. Dills." Her tone suggested it was punishment.

"That's perfectly all right. I came as soon as I received your message."

"I shouldn't wonder. I shouldn't wonder you came—to protect your ill-gotten stipend."

She reached under the chair. He heard glass clink. Then something rattled. "You deceived me. Now and again my houseman fetches a local paper. He discovered this. You deceived me, Mr. Dills."

"Relative to that, please let me say—"

"You said Elkanah was in Texas. You said he was a wealthy and respected cotton farmer. I have paid you, trusted you for years on the basis of such information. And this is your gratitude? All those letters concealing the truth?"

Blinking, feeling the frail heart in his breast racing faster, Dills dropped his carpetbag. "Might I see that?"

"You already know what it says." Thick blue veins bulged from the back of the hand she extended. He took the paper. There, in the general news column on the front page, he saw a paragraph under the heading BIZARRE PENNSYLVANIA MURDER.

He scanned the paragraph until, without surprise, he came upon the name Elkanah Bent. He stopped reading and returned the paper with a trembling hand.

The woman held it a moment, then flung it away. Rationally, Dills knew he had little to fear from someone so old. And yet he was frightened.

It was partly the room—the candles in greasy pools of hot melted tallow—and partly the woman. Scarcely a hundred pounds, if that, and so ravaged by age and the unguessable emotions that had rioted in her sick mind all these years, she hardly looked human. She was more like a wax figure, a ghastly museum exhibit with a queer resemblance to her albino caretaker. She powdered her face, she powdered her hair, she powdered her hands, a thick layer of white dust. It formed a kind of crust beneath her livid old yellow eyes.

Time had worn away her eyebrows. The bony ridges pressed against her almost transparent skin, as if the skull sought a way into the light. Her hair, turned gray years ago, was whitened by the powder, which sifted down from her high-piled coiffure whenever she moved suddenly, as when she discarded the paper.

Far down on the river, a boat's bell tolled. Dills's attempt to summon resentment had altogether failed. The yellow eyes, unblinking, like the eyes of some armored lizard, reminded him of her mental condition. That he knew the history of nervous disorder running through her family did not make her any less intimidating. He wanted to flee.

"My son committed a hideous murder. Why?"

"I don't know," Dills lied. "I don't know his connection with the victim. Probably an accidental choice." What was the point of trying to explain the vendetta against Hazard and Main? Dills had never been able to explain it to himself in any reasonable terms.

He licked his parched lips. A breeze passed over twisted lead strips that had once held stained glass and fluttered the candles. Somewhere under his feet, Dills heard the scurry of rats.

"You told me Elkanah was in Texas. I have letter after letter—"

"Madam, I wanted to spare you the painful truth."

Dry lips parted to reveal yellowed teeth. "You wanted to spare yourself loss of the stipend."

"No, no, that was not—" Dills gave it up. The mad old eyes, inquisitor's eyes, saw through his attempted deception. "Yes. I did."

She sighed, seeming to grow even smaller inside her heavy gray-silver dress. Patches of green mold showed on the lace hem, much of which had crumbled from rot. The low bodice hung out from her emaciated, heavily powdered breastbone.

With a quiver of her lips and a lift of one hairless brow, she said, "That is perhaps your first honest statement of the evening. You have cruelly deceived me, Dills. It was a condition of the stipend that you watch over Elkanah with utmost care."

The resentment burst out at last. "Which I did, until he made it impossible with his—" He choked back the word *crazy*. "His erratic behavior."

"But it was a primary condition of our arrangement."

"I would appreciate it if you would speak a little less unkindly," he said, testy. "I responded to your telegraph message out of consideration for you, and—"

"Out of fear," she spat. "Out of some imbecilic hope that you might keep the stipend." He stepped back; her yellow teeth were fully visible, like an enraged dog's. "Well, it's gone. The news article said my poor Elkanah killed some wretched woman, but no one knows why, or where he might be found, because he disappeared years ago. You knew that."

Somehow, though still frightened of her, Dills was experiencing a relief. Perhaps his nerves had been strained too far, could bear no more. "I did. I understand your anger."

"I loved him. I loved my son. I loved my poor Elkanah. Even when he was hundreds of miles from me, even when he was grown, and I had no idea of what he looked like, how his voice might sound—" She passed a hand in front of her face. Her fingers were almost hidden by dirt-encrusted rings of silver and gold, some with stones missing. It was a curious brushing motion, as if she were bothered by a cobweb he couldn't see. There were cobwebs in plenty elsewhere. All over the smashed spinning wheel, and in a gauzy weave under her chair.

"Well," the woman said, less rancorously, "I am glad of the truth at last. My son did not prosper in Texas, then."

"No. Never."

"Where is he hiding, Dills?"

Ah, a chance to wound her. Forcefully, he said, "I have not the slightest idea."

"How long have you not known?"

"Since shortly before the end of the war. He left the Union Army in disgrace." She flung back against the tall chair. "He deserted."

"Oh, God. My poor boy. My poor Elkanah."

She groped beneath her chair again, stirring cobwebs, which became attached to her fingers and hand. She drew into the light an old green wine bottle and a fine lead-glass goblet with a crack and a patina of dirt so thick that the goblet looked translucent. Into the glass she splashed some dark fluid, a port or sherry, perhaps, brown as coffee. He smelled only the rancid odor of spoiled wine.

She sipped without offering him any. Not that he would have touched the filthy stuff. "I should like to retire, madam. It was an exhausting trip."

The yellow eyes slipped across his face, and beyond. The dark brown fluid in the glass leaked from a corner of her mouth, running down her chin like a muddy river through snow. "You have no idea how I cared for him. How badly I wanted a decent life for him. All the more because he had such a terrible start."

What was she saying? The eyes sought his, almost pitiable in their sudden plea for understanding. "You know about my family, Mr. Dills."

"A little. By reputation only."

"There is a strain of mental instability. It runs back many generations, and has spread widely."

Even to the Executive Mansion, he thought.

"It tainted my father. After my mother's death, when Heyward Starkwether began to pay court to me, my father grew jealous. I was his favorite child. Heyward proposed. When I told my father that I wanted to accept, it drove him to incredible rage. He had been drinking heavily. He was very powerful physically—"

Dills felt he was about to peer into some buried place, a place where something had been hidden, putrefying, for decades. He was gripped, perversely fascinated. Somewhere the rats shrieked, and there was another, lower sound, as of prey caught and hurt.

"Allow me to guess the rest, madam. Marriage was by then a necessity? You were already carrying Starkwether's child, later named Bent after the farm people who raised him. You revealed your condition to your father, and he beat you."

A vacant smile. Her right hand lolled over the carved chair arm. The filthy goblet slipped, fell, broke. She paid no attention. "Ah—ah. If it were only that simple. My father did use force the night I told him I wanted to marry. The rest of your chronology is out of order." He didn't understand. "Later, I wanted to do away with the unborn child. My father in one of his rages said he would kill me if I did. I was too terrified of him to attempt it. Together—his was the hand forcing mine, you see—we summoned Starkwether and convinced him of his responsibility. His guilt, if you will. I suspect he carried it until he died, poor wretched man."

Dills's hair crawled. Light was shining into the putrefying burial place.

"Are you saying you deceived Heyward Starkwether, madam?"

"Yes."

"My late client—Elkanah Bent's patron and declared father —had no connection with the boy?"

"Heyward supposed he was Elkanah's father. We convinced him of it."

"But he was not?"

"No."

"In other words, all those years, my client was coerced into helping and supporting—?"

"Not coerced, Mr. Dills. Once he was convinced that Elkanah was his child, he helped him gladly, as any father would."

"Who was Bent's father, madam?"

The yellow eyes, moist and mad, reflected the candles around the tower.

"Why, Mr. Dills"—she giggled, a hideous coquetry— "surely you know. I said he used physical force."

"Sweet Christ! Elkanah's father was—"

"Mine, Mr. Dills. Mine."

The straw-littered stones of the floor seemed to tilt and

shiver beneath Jasper Dills. The rational underpinning of his world threatened to collapse. "Goodbye," he said, snatching his carpetbag and rushing toward the door. "Goodbye, Miss Todd."

In the cul-de-sac, shivering, he waited and waited for the hackney to return. Now he understood the cause, and the extent, of Elkanah Bent's insanity. He no longer cared about the stipend. He wanted no more of it, or the woman he'd deceived, or Bent. Especially Bent, wherever he might be.

Dills finally understood much that he'd never understood before. Bent's unreasonable grudge against the Mains and the Hazards, a preoccupation since his cadet days; the brutality of the Lehigh Station slaying—Bent had inherited a capacity for evil.

Chilly sweat broke out on Dills's face as he recalled the times he'd criticized Bent, reproved him, ordered him out of his office. If he'd known the sort of man Bent really was, and if he'd known why, he'd never have done such things. He'd probably have cowered instead.

The hackney never came. Dills picked up his carpetbag and stumbled downhill, all the way to the lodging house he'd previously telegraphed for a room. There, at a late hour, he paid exorbitantly for a zinc tub of heated water.

Feeling filthy down to his bones, he sat in the tub with a cake of homemade soap as yellow as her eyes, scrubbing and scrubbing at his wrinkled, mottled skin and thinking of Elkanah Bent, his brain, his blood, his very being poisoned before his birth.

Dills slumped back in the tub, inexplicably sorrowful. God pity poor Bent, whom he surely would never see again. God pity even more the next person to incur Bent's wrath.

42

North of Washington on the Seventh Street Road, Maryland farmers once a week set up stalls and wagons for an open-air market. On the last Saturday in March, two days before the President's trial was to begin in the Senate, Virgilia and Scipio Brown went to the market to buy food for the orphanage. Brown drove the buggy and carried the money, amusing Virgilia by this insistence on handling all the male duties. He didn't seem upset by the looks they drew because she was white and he was not.

They moved through the crowded lanes of the market, among hens squawking in crates and piglets squealing in improvised pens. They argued about the subject most of Washington was arguing about these days.

"He's usurped power, Virgilia. To make it worse, he's the elect of an assassin, not the people."

"You have to be more specific than that to convict him."

"Good Lord, they've drawn up eleven charges."

"The first nine are all related to the Tenure of Office issue. Ben Butler's tenth article condemns Johnson for speeches criticizing Congress. Is free speech now a high crime or misdemeanor? The eleventh article is just a grab bag."

"Authored by your good friend Mr. Stevens."

"Even so—" They reached a cross lane. A cart approached, piled with crates of rabbits. "I stand by my opinion on it."

He saw the cartwheel lurch into a rut, tilting the vehicle sideways. Cordage snapped, freeing the crates. The huge stack toppled toward Virgilia and Scipio. He seized her waist and swung her away from the spot where the crates crashed down. Several broke; rabbits escaped in every direction. The driver ran off in pursuit.

Virgilia was abruptly aware of the mulatto's strong hands on her waist. And of a curious intensity in his dark eyes. She'd noticed similar looks several times lately. "Perhaps we'd better search for eggs and forget politics, Scipio. I wouldn't want it to ruin our friendship."

"Nor I." He smiled and released her. She tingled from the touch of his hands, and was more than a little startled by that reaction.

With arms grown strong from hard work, Virgilia pushed the wood paddle around the steaming kettle of thick pea soup. It was noon the next day. Across the kitchen, Thad Stevens sat with a tawny little boy dozing in his lap, thumb in his mouth. Virgilia's friend looked pale and weary.

"You will be there tomorrow for the opening of the trial?" he asked.

"Yes, and for as much thereafter as I can manage without falling behind here."

"You want him convicted, I assume."

Reluctantly, she said, "I don't think so. He denies any crime."

"His denial is estopped by his previous behavior. He sent Thomas to remove Stanton."

"Thomas failed, so it was only an attempt, not a removal."

"You're becoming legalistic, my dear." He didn't sound happy about it, although the whole Stanton mess was nothing if not a lawyer's delight.

Even Grant had been caught in the tangle. Grant's withdrawal as interim Secretary of War had precipitated a series of bitter exchanges with Andrew Johnson; a final letter from Grant charged the President with trying to "destroy my character before the country." That letter completely alienated Johnson, and persuaded many people that Grant was at heart a Radical. No one had been quite sure before. Grant's detractors immediately called him an opportunist, a political chameleon, and—the old canard—a drunkard. Never mind. Grant had purified himself in the eyes of the Radical leadership. In late May the Republicans would convene in Chicago to nominate a presidential candidate. Cynics said the general would there be "confirmed as a new member of the Radical church," and be chosen to run.

"Legalistic, Thad?" she said. "No. I'm only trying to look at matters fairly."

"The devil with fair. I want Johnson out. I will hound him till he's gone."

She let the paddle rest against the rim of the kettle. In the yard, where a mild March sun fell through the bare branches of two unbudded cherry trees, Scipio laughed and romped with several of the children. "Whether he's guilty or not?"

In his glare, she saw the answer before he gave it. "We are purging the man, but we are also purging what he represents, Virgilia. Leniency toward an entire class of people. Unrepentant people who still conspire to return this nation to what it was thirty years ago, when an entire black population was in chains and Mr. Calhoun arrogantly threatened secession if anyone dared object. There are seven impeachment managers. Do you have any idea of the enormous pressure already being brought against us? Letters. Cowardly threats—"

Disturbing the boy nestled in his lap, he pulled a wrinkled yellow flimsy from his pocket. "This came from Louisiana, that's all I know for certain."

She unfolded it and read. STEVENS, PREPARE TO MEET YOUR GOD. THE AVENGER IS UPON YOUR TRACK. HELL IS YOUR PORTION. K.K.K.

Shaking her head, she handed it back. For a moment Stevens's waxy cheeks showed some color. "The avenger is upon Mr. Johnson's track, too. His portion is a guilty verdict."

Scipio ran in the sunshine, whooping. The joyful sound seemed chillingly at odds with the congressman's angry eyes. His dogma had carried him down a road Virgilia had abandoned. There was no longer much hatred in her, but in him the war raged on.

On Monday, March 30, she arrived an hour before the doors to the Senate gallery opened. When they did, she fought her way upward among people hurrying and pushing. By the time Chief Justice Salmon P. Chase took the chair and opened the trial, there wasn't an empty seat or vacant stair step in the gallery.

Days ago, Chase had organized and sworn the Senate as a court. Today, all fifty-four legislators representing the twenty-seven states were present on the floor. Among them Virgilia saw Sam Stout, calm and smiling. He'd been quoted widely about his confidence in the outcome. He believed there would be no problem in obtaining the thirty-six votes necessary to convict Johnson on one or more of the articles.

The gallery was noisy, demonstrative, divided by partisanship. Some spectators whistled and waved handkerchiefs when the impeachment managers, seven men from the House, including old Thad with wig askew, took their places amid piles of books and briefs at a table to the left of the chair. President Johnson's five eminent attorneys faced them on the other side of the chair. All of the senators were squeezed into the first two rows of desks, with the desks behind packed with members of the House. Reporters filled the back aisles, lined the wall, and blocked the doors.

The trial opened with a three-hour oration by the chief manager, Representative Ben Butler of Massachusetts. Spoons Butler, the Beast of New Orleans, was a skilled and abrasive lawyer. He generated cheers and a blizzard of waving handkerchiefs when he declared that Johnson was patently guilty for removing Stanton in defiance of Congress and while Congress was in session.

Seated in the restless, noisy crowd, Virgilia gazed down on Sam Stout and felt no great hurt, only a melancholy emptiness. Time was indeed changing and mellowing her. To her surprise, her attention wandered several times from the scene below. In its place she saw Scipio Brown's eyes after he'd saved her from injury when the market cart overturned. She remembered how his hands had felt on her waist, pressing tightly. She liked the memory.

By the ninth of April, the managers had rested their case. Perhaps the high point of the prosecution's presentation had come when Butler whipped out a red-stained garment and flourished it. He said it was the shirt of an Ohioan from the Freedmen's Bureau whom Klansmen in Mississippi had flogged. Next morning Washington had a new phrase for its political lexicon; you whipped up anti-Southern sentiment by "waving the bloody shirt."

Johnson's lawyers presented the arguments for acquittal. Because of an epidemic of measles at the orphanage, Virgilia missed many of those sessions in April. When she read about them in the papers, she didn't regret it. The legalisms, the hair-splitting over the language of the Constitution, and the all-day orations sounded boring.

She wondered why long speeches were necessary. The issue seemed clear enough. Johnson's authority had been challenged by the various Reconstruction bills, including the provocative Tenure of Office Act, which effectively denied the Chief Executive the power to remove cabinet officers whom the Senate had confirmed. On this issue Johnson had dug in, to force a test.

Virgilia thought that that was not only valid but also necessary. Further, Edwin Stanton was Lincoln's appointee, not Johnson's, and it was in Lincoln's term, not Johnson's, that the Senate had consented to the appointment. She thought there was a strong argument that Stanton was actually outside the Tenure of Office jurisdiction.

Lengthy summations began. She heard the one by William S. Groesbeck, an eloquent Cincinnati attorney. He spoke to the subject of Johnson's character.

"He is a patriot. He may be full of error, but he loves his country. I have often said that those who lived in the North, safely distant from the war, knew little of it. We who lived on the border knew more . . . our horizon was always red with its flames, and it sometimes burned so near we could feel its heat on our outstretched hands. Andrew Johnson of Tennessee lived in the heart of the conflagration . . . in the very furnace of war . . . and his tempered strength kept him steadfastly loyal to the Union . . . impervious to treason. How can he then be suddenly transformed, in the words of the gentleman from Massachusetts, Mr. Boutwell, to the arch-demon? It is ludicrous."

At the managers' table, George S. Boutwell glared.

On and on they went, accusing, defending, interpreting, theorizing. Occasionally fist fights broke out in the gallery, and the trial would be stopped while ushers removed the combatants. The atmosphere in the gilt-and-marble chamber grew more and more charged with emotion, until Virgilia began to feel she was no longer in the United States, but in some Roman arena. The difference was that the victim to be sacrificed had not made even a single appearance. Johnson had organized a staff of runners to report each new development.

The Roman analogy proved especially apt the day the Honorable Mr. Williams, manager from Pennsylvania, attacked the accused:

"If you acquit him you affirm all his imperial pretensions and decide that no amount of usurpation will ever be enough to bring a chief magistrate to justice. That will be a victory over all of you here assembled. A victory to celebrate the exultant ascent of Andrew Johnson to the Capitol, dragging not captive kings but a captive Senate at his chariot wheels."

Men jumped up in the gallery, some cheering, some protesting. Chief Justice Chase needed four minutes to restore order. Virgilia saw faces red with indignation, and she saw others that made her think of predators—predators who fed on every accusation, no matter how outrageous.

Suddenly, on the far side of the gallery, she was startled to spy two other faces overlooked before. Her brother Stanley and his wife Isabel.

Virgilia no longer had contact with them; no invitations to dine at I Street, no birthday greetings, nothing. She often heard Stanley's name in the city, sometimes not in a flattering way.

Isabel glanced at Virgilia with no recognition. Stanley was absorbed in matters on the floor. How puffy he looked, Virgilia thought. Older than his forty-five years. His skin had an unhealthy, jaundiced coloration.

Williams eyed the quieting gallery. He raised his voice:

"If indeed the miscreant returns like a conqueror in Roman triumph, I can predict what will follow. A return of the Rebel office-holders whom he favors, and a general convulsion of their states, casting loose your reconstruction laws, and delivering over the whole theater of past conflict into anarchy, injustice, and ruin."

Again members of the crowd surged up, yelling and waving handkerchiefs. Virgilia sat in sad silence. In her view the managers had proved nothing, except that they wanted Johnson's blood before he ever came to trial, and would have it whether he was guilty or not.

The session recessed. On the packed staircase, Virgilia came upon Stanley leaning against the wall and mopping his yellowish face with a large kerchief. She stopped on the step above, trying to shield him from the buffeting crowd.

"Stanley?" she said over the noise. She tugged his sleeve. "I saw you earlier. Are you all right?"

"Virgilia. Oh—yes, perfectly fine." He seemed remote, eyeing the people pushing past her down the stairs. "And you?"

"Well enough. But I'm worried about you, Stanley. You look ill. It's been so long since we talked, and there are so many unkind stories afloat."

"Stories?" He jerked back like a felon threatened with handcuffs. "What sort of stories?"

She smelled the clove he'd chewed. To hide what other odor? "Stories about the things you do to hurt yourself. Great long drinking sprees—"

"Lies." He leaned his sweaty forehead against the marble, gasping. "Damn lies."

Grieving for him, and for his own lie, she touched his sleeve. "I hope so. You're a prominent man, enormously wealthy and successful. You have everything now."

"Perhaps I don't deserve it. Perhaps I'm not proud of what I am. Did you ever think of that?"

The blurted words stunned her. Stanley guilt-ridden? Why?

From behind, someone seized her shoulder. Virgilia was nearly toppled off balance; if she'd fallen, those pouring from the gallery might have trampled her.

Not four inches from Virgilia's nose, Isabel's long, horselike face seemed to inflate with rage. "Leave him alone, you mongrel slut. Stanley is tired, that's all. We have nothing to say to you. Stand aside."

Like an officer disciplining a private, she took hold of her husband's arm and thrust him down the stairs. She elbowed and pushed to open a path. Stanley was unsteady. He glanced back at his sister with a swift look of apology. At the landing, he and Isabel disappeared.

Virgilia thought she'd never seen her brother look so bad, so tormented. Why should great success cost him so dearly? she wondered again.

The summations concluded in the first week in May. By then all of Washington was charged, and changed, by the trial. Some called it the majestic working of justice. Others called it a saturnalia, a circus. Police routinely broke up fights that erupted over the trial. Gamblers poured into the city on every train, crowding the hotels and taking wagers on the verdict. When Chief Justice Chase closed the doors on Monday, May 11, and the court went into private session, the odds favored acquittal.

In the *Star* and other papers, Sam Stout had announced that the gamblers were wrong. Thirty-one votes for conviction on at least one article were firm, he said. Six more would tilt in favor of conviction by the end of the week.

On Thursday, Stevens sought refuge at the orphanage. "The damned press won't let me alone. My own constituents won't either." He looked even more tired than he had the last time he'd come.

"How is the vote?" she asked, pouring him hot herb tea. His veined, age-spotted hands shook as he tried to lift the cup. He gave up.

"Thirty-five certain. It hinges upon one man."

"Who?"

"Senator Ross."

"Edmund Ross of Kansas? He's a strong abolitionist."

"Was," Stevens corrected, with distaste. "Ross insists he'll vote his conscience, even though people in Kansas are deluging him with telegrams saying he's finished if he votes acquittal. Senator Pomeroy's hammering him. So is the Union Congressional Committee." That body of Radical senators and representatives had been organized to send messages to local party organizations urging them to pressure undecided senators. "Ross has even received threats against his life," Stevens added. "He isn't alone."

With exhausted eyes, he stared at Virgilia. "We must sway Ross. We must, or it's all been for nothing, and the Bourbons will recapture the South."

"You mustn't take the verdict quite so seriously, Thad. Your life doesn't depend on it."

"But it does, Virgilia. If we fail, I'm through. I don't have the heart or the strength to fight such a battle again."

On Saturday, the sixteenth of May, four days before the Republican convention, Virgilia awoke well before dawn, unable to sleep. She dressed and left the cottage in which Stout had once kept her; she'd thought of moving, to rid herself of memories the place aroused. But it was hers, it was comfortable, and she was able to afford it on her orphanage wage.

She walked through a silent section where the homes grew smaller and poorer. Soon she reached the orphanage. Surprisingly, she found the front door unlocked. She smelled coffee as she walked to the kitchen. He was seated at the table.

"Scipio. Why are you up?"

"Couldn't sleep. I'm glad you're here. We must talk. I'm supposed to deliver Lewis to his new foster parents in Hagerstown this morning."

"I remember." She accepted a mug of coffee from the enameled pot. His amber hand brushed hers. He reacted as if burned.

"I'd feel better if you didn't go to the Capitol," he said.

"I must. I want to hear the verdict."

"It could be dangerous. Huge crowds. Possibly a riot."

"It's good of you to be concerned, but I'll be fine. You mustn't worry."

He walked around the table and stood gazing down at her. The words seemed to tear from him. "But I do. Far more than you know."

Their eyes held. Shaken, feeling a torrent of response, she slammed the coffee mug on the wooden table and dashed out. She was unable to deal with the emotions revealed so unexpectedly in him, and in her own heart.

"That's thirty-four," whispered the stranger on Virgilia's left. "I mark Waitman Willey of West Virginia probable. So it's up to Ross."

Hisses from those nearby silenced the man, who went on scribbling and rechecking his tally on a scrap of paper. Before the roll call, George Williams of Oregon had moved that the first vote be taken on the final article, the omnibus, because if that passed, so would the others. The change in order was approved.

Chief Justice Chase spoke. "Mr. Senator Ross, how say you? Is the respondent, Andrew Johnson, President of the United States, guilty or not guilty of a high misdemeanor as charged in this article?"

He stood there a moment, the unprepossessing man from Kansas. Union veteran and old-line abolitionist, he was currently campaigning for removal of the Indian tribes by force. Virgilia watched Thad Stevens sit forward at the managers' table, white with strain.

Ross cleared his throat.

"How say you?" Chase repeated.

"Not guilty."

A roar in the gallery. Then wild applause, loud booing, handkerchiefs waved, a sea of whipping white. Stevens slumped back, eyes shut. One arm lolled limply over the arm of his chair.

Virgilia knew the vote was a watershed. The Congress had tried to exert its primacy over the executive and, a moment ago, the effort failed. No matter what else transpired, Radical Reconstruction was over. Thad Stevens had predicted it would be so if the vote went against impeachment. Stevens's body, slumped in his chair, said it again, unequivocally.

On the Capitol steps, people screamed, danced, hugged one another. A beefy man in a derby caught Virgilia's arm. "Old Andy twisted their tail. That's worth a kiss to celebrate."

His mouth swooped toward her while a hand stole to her breast. Those capering around them paid no attention. Virgilia twisted aside, but she was trapped. "Ain't you for Andy?" the man growled, pulling her.

"You drunken sot, leave her alone."

Virgilia recognized his voice before she saw him. The beefy man shouted, "No damn nigger can tell me—" Then Scipio's hand caught him by the throat, holding him until he gagged.

The revelers kept yelling, pushing, tilting bottles, dancing on the steps. Scipio released the beefy man. He fled as fast as the crowd would allow.

"What about Hagerstown?" Virgilia exclaimed above the noise.

"I postponed it. I couldn't let you risk this mob alone. Thinking about it kept me from sleeping, or eating anything—"

Behind him, people staggered and pushed. He was thrown against her. She raised her hands to arrest his forward motion and found herself holding him. A white woman, a mulatto man. In the tumult, no one cared.

he put his mouth close to her ear. "This is an easy place to tell you I've come to admire you. I've watched you and watched you with the children. You're a gentle, loving woman. Intelligent, principled—"

She wanted to tell him of all the evil things in her past. Something stronger, something live-giving, crushed the impulse. *People can change.*

"Beautiful, too," Scipio Brown said with his lips at her ear. She denied it with a nervous laugh. He was amused. "Does all this really come as such a great surprise?"

"I had some hint." She kept fighting against the buffeting of her back. "I saw the looks you gave me. But there are too many things against it, Scipio, not the least of them color. There's my age." A hand strayed to her graying hair. "I'm ten years older."

"Why should that bother you? It doesn't bother me. I love you, Virgilia. I have the buggy waiting. Come with me."

"Where?"

For a moment he seemed less than his assured adult self. He seemed shy, hesitant. But he managed to say, "I thought—if you weren't unwilling—could we be alone at your house?"

Her eyes grew damp. It was overwhelming, the idea of someone caring for her that much. Yet she knew a similar emotion had been stirring in her, beneath the level of thought, for a long time. She hadn't dared recognize it, or name it, till now.

"Virgilia?"

"Yes. I would love that," she said softly. Because of the tumult he couldn't hear the words, but he understood. She took his arm. "I'll fix breakfast for us afterward."

EMPIRE SIDE-WHEEL LINE.

The fast and favorite steamship

MISSOURI

W. LOVELAND, *Commander*

43

Three weeks after the parents' program at Mrs. Allwick's Academy, the term ended. For the last time until fall, the girls trooped noisily out the front door at 4:30 on a sparkling June afternoon. Several beaux waited on the broad, cool porch, including Sara Jane Oberdorf's apprentice undertaker.

Marie-Louise remained unforgiven for the tableau tragedy. Sweeping past, Sara Jane said sweetly, "Still no one waiting? Well, perhaps when you grow up in a few years." She clutched her young man. "Lyle. How darling of you to be here."

Desolate, Marie-Louise pulled her books against her bosom and walked down the steep wrought-iron steps. Her head was lowered; she saw the shadow fall on her skirt. "Excuse me." She sidestepped, glanced up, and dropped the books.

"Miss Main." Theo German bowed and swept off his straw planter's hat, which had a peacock-feather band. He was again out of uniform. "Allow me." He knelt to pick up the books.

"I thought—" *Get hold of yourself, ninny.* "I imagined you'd never speak to me after that dreadful evening. You must have thought I cut you."

"Of course not. I saw it was your father's doing." He straightened and offered his arm. "Do you have time for a stroll on the Battery?"

If I'm late, Mama will quiz me. And what if Papa should find out?

But Cooper's behavior at the program had lighted the fires of revolt in his daughter, and heightened her attraction to the young officer. "Oh, yes," she said.

Her bosom accidentally touched his coat sleeve. She felt as

though a lightning bolt had struck her. Theo smiled, taking note of the sudden pink in her cheeks. There was some in his as well.

Bedazzling needles of reflected sunlight bobbed on the surface of the harbor. Gulls followed a fish trawler chugging in from the Atlantic. Out at Sumter, above the ruins, the Union flag stood straight in the breeze.

"Do you often go about town without your uniform?" Marie-Louise asked, desperately trying to remember Mrs. Allwick's lessons on social conversation. Her mind was a mass of glue.

"I do," he said. "General Canby doesn't object, and it's easier for me to get people to talk. I get helpful insights about local feelings that way. Of course, there are a few people who refuse to say anything at all after they hear me speak."

"Because of your accent."

He laughed. "I don't have an accent. You do. I find it charming, though."

"Oh, Mr. German—Captain German—"

"How about Theo?" he said, warming her with the friendly innocence of his blue eyes. Marie-Louise was suddenly so in love she could have perished of ecstasy and sunk through the ground to China.

"All right, but you must call me Marie-Louise."

"With pleasure."

The gulls squawked and swooped. The young couple strolled under stately old trees near the water. Theo told her that he was twenty-four—she'd known he was a worldly older man the moment she saw him—and attached to Canby's staff. "That day on the railroad, I was sightseeing. The loveliest sight I saw was in that passenger car."

"Papa was in a perfect fury when you gave the colored woman your seat." She sighed. "He's still fighting the war."

"Your father and half of Charleston. Still, the other half's enchanting. I've never encountered Southerners before, except for great lots of prisoners who naturally weren't in a good mood. I find Southerners are warm, charming people. And Carolina has a grand climate except in the summer."

"What did you mean about prisoners?"

He explained that he'd been commissioned in the last year of the war and posted to Camp Douglas, the huge prison compound south of Chicago. "We had thousands of inmates, but I heard shots fired only once, when a half-dozen attempted an escape. Only once did we feel any real danger. There was a Sunday in November of '64 when Chicago was seething with rumors that Confederate secret agents were going to torch the city and liberate our captives. Nothing came of it. When the prison was closed a year later, I decided to stay in the Army and see some of the country. I had never been out of Illinois until I came here." He smiled again, lightly touching her mittened hand on his arm. "I was lucky to be posted to South Carolina. I'd like to settle here and escape the snow and cold weather forever."

"Will you always be in the Army?"

"I think not. I was a law apprentice when I joined up. I'd like to finish my studies and practice." Marie-Louise feared she'd topple off the esplanade and drown if he kept turning those blue eyes on her.

Other beaux strolling with their sweethearts drifted in and out of the dappled shade cast by the trees. Along one of the oyster-shell paths came an old black man waving a fly whisk and pushing a creaky two-wheeled cart. He advertised his wares with a musical chant. "Buy melon. Sweet winter melon here."

"Would you like a slice of musk melon?" Theo asked. She was too nervous to do more than laugh and nod, but he didn't seem to mind. He bought slices from the vendor, bringing them back to the iron bench where he'd laid her books. Marie-Louise grasped the melon by means of a bit of paper wrapped around the rind. Careful as she was, the juicy melon leaked all over her chin. She was mortified.

Theo whipped out a handkerchief. "Allow me." With gentlemanly dabs, he dried her chin. Her body throbbed at every touch.

"I hope you don't think me too forward, Miss Main."

"Oh, no. But you must think me silly, nattering and giggling all the time. It's just that—" *Did she dare?* Yes, better to risk an explanation than lose him. "I'm not experienced with beaux. I've never really had one."

The melon dripped in his fingers. He bent toward her in the cool and breezy shade. "May I say it's my fervent hope that you'll never need another?"

That declaration brought her near the point of collapse.

Then, astonishing her again, he leaned forward quickly and brushed his lips across the corner of hers.

A great silence enveloped her. The chant of the melon man was gone, and the gull cries, the whistle of a packet putting out to sea, even the frantic lubbing of her heart. Her nervousness dropped away as she stood near him, gazing at him, irrevocably changed. Girlhood was over.

In their hands, the melon slices dripped, pattering the oyster-shell path. Neither of them noticed.

Gradually she forced herself back to reality. She saw the slant of the light falling on the great gabled houses of South Battery. It was late.

"I must be going back to Tradd Street."

"May I escort you?"

"Certainly." This time there was no fumbling as she slipped her arm around his. She felt at ease, womanly. No one paid them any heed as they strolled up Church in the mellow spring light.

"I'd love for you to meet my family," Theo said.

"I'd like that, too."

"I have eleven brothers and sisters."

"Good heavens," she cried.

He grinned. "I love them, but it did make for a crowded household, and skimpy portions at the table. Father's wage wasn't big enough to handle so many mouths. He's a Lutheran minister."

"Oh, dear. Not an abolitionist, too?"

"Yes, he was."

"And a Republican?"

"I'm afraid so. I'm the second youngest child, so I always had to sleep on the floor. We didn't have enough beds. It's the reason I joined the Army. To have a bed of my own and regular meals. Soldiers grouse about the poor food and bad mattresses. For me, it's the life of a prince."

Seeing the Tradd Street intersection but one square away, she said, "Like you, I'm very glad the Army brought you here, Theo." She was shocked by her own boldness.

As they walked on, she told him about the loss of her brother off the North Carolina coast, and the harrowing moments in the sea when she feared they'd all drown. "Papa was much less severe before Judah died. It did something to him, and he's never recovered."

"That's tragic. It does explain the way he reacted to me. I hope it isn't an impossible obstacle." In the shadow of a high brick wall, he faced her and clasped her hand. "I want to pay court to you in the proper way— You're frowning."

"Well, it would be much easier if you were—not what you are."

"As in Mr. Shakespeare's play?"

"What?"

Romeo, Romeo, wherefore art thou Romeo? In other words, why am I Romeo, a Montague? An enemy? Will it truly make a difference?"

Marie-Louise went swirling down into the blue whirlpools of his eyes, abandoning herself to emotions so fierce, she wondered if she could endure them. "No," she declared, all at once very certain of what she wanted. "No, it shall not."

"Your father—"

"No," she repeated confidently.

He left her at the gate of the Tradd Street house, promising to call formally the next afternoon. With a parting clasp of her hand, he was gone, leaving her floating there, several feet above the mundane earth.

"No!" Cooper clattered his spoon against the bowl of lamb stew. "I won't have some Yankee freebooter calling on my daughter."

Marie-Louise started to cry.

Judith reached out to squeeze her daughter's hand. To her husband she said, "It's a perfectly reasonable request."

"If he were a Southerner. One of us."

"Aunt Brett married a Yankee officer—" Marie-Louise began.

"Without causing the collapse of civilization as we know it," Judith remarked.

The irony was lost. "I refuse to have some yellow dog from Canby's staff sniffing around my family."

"You make it sound so crude and nasty," Marie-Louise cried. "It isn't like that."

"Please reconsider, Cooper," Judith began.

He shot his chair back and rose. "Allow my daughter to be courted by a shoulder-straps whose father is a Bible-thumping Republican? I'd sooner have that fellow LaMotte in my house.

The decision is made. I am going to the garden to work while the light lasts."

With quick strides that rapped hard on the polished floor, he left the room. Judith braced for a new flood of tears. Instead, she was surprised by what she saw in her daughter's eyes. A silent rage not at all typical of a girl so young.

Marie-Louise wiped her cheeks. She kept staring at the doorway through which her father had disappeared.

Later, when it was dark, Judith went quickly to the piazza overlooking the garden. Insects circled the oil lamp burning on a wicker table. In a chair beside the table, Cooper had fallen asleep, his waistcoat open, his cravat undone.

Stepping over papers covered with columns of figures, she leaned over to wake him by kissing his forehead. Cooper jerked erect, momentarily unsure of his whereabouts.

"It's almost ten o'clock, Cooper. Marie-Louise ran up to her room right after we ate, and I've scarcely heard a sound since. I think you should go make peace, if that's possible."

"I did nothing wrong. Why must I—?" Judith's look silenced him. Rubbing his eyes, he stood. "All right."

She listened to his slow step ascending the stairs. Heard a faint knock. "Marie-Louise?" She was gazing into the dark garden when he came bolting down again, shouting. "She's gone."

"What are you saying?"

"She must have used the side stairway. Her room's empty, half her clothes are missing. She's gone!"

The specklike insects circled the flickering lamp. Judith allowed herself anger for the first time. "This is your doing. You've driven her out."

"That's impossible. She's a mere girl."

"Of marriageable age, I remind you. Many South Carolina girls are mothers at fourteen. You misjudged her attachment to that young man. Because of him—and you—she's run away."

A muffled pounding broke through the mists of sleep. Trying to interpret the sound, Madeline slowly raised her head. She heard Prudence Chaffee stirring in the other bedroom.

The pounding grew louder. "Please—someone—"

A woman's voice. Madeline thought she should recognize it,

but she didn't. She was still too sleepy. Was it one of the freed-men's wives?

Prudence lighted her lamp and brought it to the door of Madeline's room. Her plain, stout face was alert, her eyes anxious. "Do you think it's trouble with the school?"

"I don't know." Barefoot, Madeline went to the front door. "It's the middle of the night."

It was actually morning, she discovered as soon as she opened the door. Between the great trees she saw jigsaw pieces of orange-tinted sky. The light silhouetted a disheveled figure on the stoop.

"Aunt Madeline—"

She couldn't have been more stunned if Andrew Johnson had come calling. "Marie-Louise! What are you doing here?"

"Please let me come in, and I'll explain. I walked all night."

"You walked all the way from Charleston?" Prudence exclaimed. "Twenty miles, by yourself, on a dark road, and you didn't think twice about it?"

In the space of a heartbeat Madeline knew something dire had happened. A death? Some act of violence? Then she saw the bulging valise. People didn't pack a valise in order to report a tragedy.

"There's this boy. Papa refuses to let him court me. I love him, Aunt Madeline. I love him and Papa hates him."

So that was it. A young girl in love would do many a dangerous or thoughtless deed when her mind was fixed on her own problems. She remembered how it was with Orry; how romantic emotions had swept away many a practicality, and all fear of danger.

"Will you let me stay, Aunt Madeline? I won't go back to Tradd Street."

Then there would surely be trouble with Cooper. But Madeline couldn't turn her away. "Come in," she said, stepping back to welcome the breathless fugitive.

WHITE MEN—TO ARMS!

To-day the mongrel "Legislature" convenes in Columbia. The maddest, most unscrupulous and infamous revolution in our history has snatched the power from the hands of the race which settled the country, and transferred it to its former slaves, an ignorant and corrupt race.

This unlawful and misbegotten assembly will trample the fairest and noblest states of our great sisterhood beneath the unholy hoofs of African savages and shoulder-strapped brigands. The millions of freeborn, high-souled countrymen and countrywomen are surrendered to the rule of gibbering, louse-eaten, devil-worshiping barbarians from the jungles of Dahomey, and peripatetic buccaneers from Cape Cod, Boston, and Hell.

The hour is late; the cause is life itself; our sole recourse is force of arms.

Special issue of
The Ashley Thunderbolt, July 6, 1868

MADELINE'S JOURNAL

June, 1868. Cooper here not 24 hrs. after we took his daughter in. Terrible scene . . .

"Where is she? I demand you produce her."

He confronted Madeline on the lawn in front of the whitewashed house. Down by the river, the steam machinery chuffed at the sawmill. A blade whined, straining to cleave through live oak.

"She's on the plantation, and perfectly safe. She wants to stay with us for a while. She definitely doesn't want the strain of more arguments with you."

"God. First you do business with black Republican carpetbaggers. Now you turn my daughter against me."

"Marie-Louise is in love with the boy, Cooper. I'd look closer to Tradd Street for the cause of her defiance."

"Damn you, produce her!"

"No. The decision to leave will be hers."

"Until she reaches majority, only I have the legal right—"

"The legal right, perhaps. Not a moral one. She's almost sixteen. Many girls are married, and mothers, before that age."

Madeline walked toward him and around him. "Now, if that's all—"

"It is not. Are you aware that there is a Kuklux den in the district?"

"I've heard rumors. I've seen no evidence."

"Well, I have it on good authority. The den keeps what's called the Dead Book. It contains names of those who offend the Klan. Do you know the name at the top of the first page? It's yours."

"It doesn't surprise me." Madeline's forced calm hid any sign of the sudden tight pain in her midsection.

"I warn you, those men are dangerous. If they come here, if they hurt my daughter because of you, I won't let the courts punish you. I'll do it personally."

She tried to plead reason one last time. "Cooper, we ought not to quarrel. Things will smooth out with Marie-Louise. Give it a week or so. Meanwhile, don't forget we all have ties. We're family. My husband was your brother—"

"Don't speak of him. He's gone, and you're what you've always been—an outsider."

She retreated, wincing as if he'd whipped her across the face.

His reckless rage was out of control. "I curse the day I convinced myself you could be trusted. That I owed you the management of this plantation because of Orry. Because he wanted you here. I wish to God I could cancel that moment and tear up the agreement and cast you out, because I would, Madeline. I would! You're not fit to stand in my brother's shadow. Orry was a white man."

Jamming his tall hat on his head, he strode to his horse. His face was hollow-cheeked, the color of gruel, and wrenched by hatred as he rode away.

> *Orry, I can't forget what he said, or overcome the effects of it. I must not write of it at length. I do not want to fall into the slough of self-pity. But he has left a deep wound. . . .*
>
> *. . . The mine is in full operation. A little money at last!*
>
> *. . . Mr. Jacob Lee, Savannah, rode all night to meet with me this morning. He is young, eager, comes well recommended as an architect. Raised in Atlanta, where his parents lost everything to Sherman's fire, he knows little about the*

*Low Country, and nothing of me. Exactly why I hired
him . . .*

Small and energetic, Lee drew swiftly on his pad with a
charcoal stick. She had apologized for her unfamiliarity with architectural terms and sketched Mont Royal's columns as she recalled them. It was enough.

"The Tuscan order. The pilasters relatively freer of ornamentation than the Greek orders. A spare, clean capital and en-
tablature—is this what you remember?"

Hands pressed together, Madeline whispered, "Yes."

"Was the siding like this? White?" He slashed horizontal
lines behind the columns.

She nodded. "Tall windows, Mr. Lee. My height, or slightly
taller."

"Like this?"

"Oh, yes." She couldn't hold back her tears. On his pad,
created by a few expert strokes and her own imagination, she saw
it at last. The second great house. The new Mont Royal . . .

The house in which Cooper says I am an intruder.

*July, 1868. We belong to the Union again! Congress accepted
the new constitution, the state legislature has ratified it, and
we were readmitted on the 9th. A great occasion for public
rejoicing. But there was none. . . .*

*. . . 14th Amend. ratified. Andy very proud. He said,
"I am a citizen now. I will fight any man who tries to deny me
that." . . .*

*. . . Theo German visited last night. What a splendid,
upright young man. He came in full uniform, alone—a brave
act, given the temper of the neighborhood. He spent all morning at the school. M-L is helping there. Unless I can no longer
judge such things, they truly love one another. How they will
make their relationship permanent without alienating C. forever, I do not know. . . .*

*. . . Strange times. The mixture of men controlling
our lives could not be better represented then by our delegates
to Congress. The senators are Mr. Robertson (of the convention, and one of the first prominent state men to join the
Republicans) and Mr. Sawyer of Mass., who came down to
take charge of Charleston's Normal School. Of the four repre-*

*sentatives, Corley and Goss are Carolinians with no strong
detractors, but few speak in their favor, either. Whittemore is
a Methodist Episcopal parson from New England, with a
splendid bass voice; they say his powerful hymn-singing
helped him win over the Negroes. Then there is the remarkable Christopher Columbus Bowen, organizer of the state
Republicans and former faro dealer and gambler. He was
court-martialed from the Confederate Army and, at the time
of the surrender, was in Charleston jail for the alleged murder
of his commander.*

*Gen. Canby says reorganization of the state under the
Reconstruction acts is finished. The government is handed
over from the military to the elected civil authorities. In Columbia we have Gen. Scott of the Bureau as governor, his
ambition realized—the mulatto Mr. Cardozo as sec'y. of state
—and a cold, refined Republican and Union veteran, Mr.
Chamberlain, for att'y. general. Chamberlain brings both
Harvard and Yale degrees to the post, along with a disdain for
all Democrats.*

*What is most remarkable to behold, or most reprehensi-
ble, depending on one's politics, is the new legislature. . . .*

Cooper stood beside Wade Hampton at the rail of the gallery. Democratic Party business had brought him to Columbia to
confer with party leaders. Hampton had suggested they go downtown for a firsthand look at those now running the state. From
the moment Hampton led him inside the still-unfinished statehouse, he was aghast.

Dirt and trash littered the hallways. The doors of the House
were guarded by a shiny-faced Negro who sat in a cane-bottom
chair tilted back against the wall. Ascending to the gallery,
Cooper discovered what looked like a great smear of dried blood
on the marble wall of the staircase.

Now he clutched the rail, stunned again. He knew that seventy-five of the one hundred twenty-four elected representatives
were Negro, but seeing them in the chamber had a far greater
impact. The Speaker was black. So was his clerk. In place of the
decorous white youths who had formerly served as pages, Cooper
saw—"Pickaninnies. Unbelievable."

Some delegates were neatly dressed, but he saw many
secondhand frock coats as well. He saw short jackets and shabby

slouch hats, the uniform of the field hand. He saw torn trousers; heavy plow shoes; woolen comforters and old shawls pinned around their wearers in lieu of a decent coat.

He recognized many of the white legislators. Former owners of slaves and great estates, they were a hushed minority among the blacks they once might have owned. As for the blacks, Cooper suspected their only political education was Union League cant. It would take years for such men to master the subtle arts required to govern. The state could be ruined first.

His face aggrieved, Hampton said, "Seen enough?"

"Yes, General." The two men fled up the steps to the gallery doors. "The old saying's come true, hasn't it? The bottom rail is on the top."

Hampton paused in the corridor to say, "What transpires in there is a travesty and a tragedy. I am persuaded that we must redeem South Carolina from such men or face extinction of everything we value."

"I concur," Cooper said. "Whatever it takes, I'm willing to do."

August, 1868. Old Stevens is dead at 76. A greatly hated man in Carolina—but I cannot share that feeling. He lies in state with an honor guard of Negro Zouaves. There is already furor over his burial place in Pennsylvania. . . .

Virgilia saw her old friend three hours before the end. She sat holding his hand under the watchful eyes of Sister Loretta and Sister Genevieve, two nuns from one of the old man's favorite charities, the Protestant Hospital for Colored People.

She and Scipio took the train to Lancaster to attend the funeral. On the trip they endured the angry stares and insulting remarks of other passengers. When they reached their destination, Virgilia struggled to contain her grief. She succeeded until they got to the graveyard where her friend was to lie.

Stevens had carefully considered his resting place during his last days. Because there were no prominent Lancaster cemeteries that accepted the bodies of blacks, he chose a small and poor Negro burying ground. He ordered that his stone be engraved with the reason:

I HAVE CHOSEN THIS THAT I MIGHT

ILLUSTRATE IN MY DEATH

THE PRINCIPLES WHICH I ADVOCATED

THROUGH A LONG LIFE:

EQUALITY OF MAN BEFORE HIS CREATOR

When she saw that, Virgilia cried, great surging sobs, of the kind that had torn from her long ago when she went along to Grady's grave near Harper's Ferry. Scipio put his arms around her. It comforted her. So did his quiet words:

"Only a very few can say they died as they lived, testifying before the world. He was a great man."

Virgilia pressed against him. His hand clasped tightly on her shoulder, and neither paid attention to the startled looks they drew. She was glad his hand was there. She hoped it would always be.

How brazen they are—the "Klan." Gettys's Thunderbolt *carries a notice saying they will show themselves in a parade Friday night at Summerton. All who oppose them are warned to stay away or risk punishment.*

Andy declared that he would go have a look. I said no. He replied that I was not in charge of his decisions. I said I was concerned for his safety, and begged him to promise me he would remain at M.R. I took his silence for assent.

The humid dark of a Low Country summer sapped strength and shortened tempers. At the old table in their tabby house, Jane pointed to the paper Andy had been reading and smoothing over and over with nervous strokes of his palm while he chewed his lip.

"Andy, it says right there, 'All disloyal white men and Leaguers are warned away.' What's to be gained?"

"I want a look at them. In the war, the generals on both sides always scouted the enemy."

"You gave Madeline your word."

"I kept quiet. That wasn't a promise. I'll be careful. And back soon."

He kissed her and slipped out. She touched her cheek. How

cold his lips felt. She stared at the paper lying beside the candle that was attracting a whirl of tiny gnats. The black-bordered announcement repeated the same pattern of asterisks several times:

* * *

Asterisks were substituted wherever the name of the organization should have appeared. It seemed the only matter about which the Klan members were secretive. Their threats, their hatreds, were fully displayed in Mr. Gettys's copy. *All disloyal white men and Leaguers are warned away.*

Jane clasped her hands together and pressed them hard against her mouth. She closed her eyes. "Andy—Andy." There was dread in her whisper.

He circled toward Summerton in a wide arc, traveling through the marsh, trusting his memory of the usable footpaths. He slipped knee-deep in salty water only once.

It was a cloudless night, with no wind stirring. A thick haze dimmed the moon. The air was full of mosquitoes and tinier insects that flew near his ear with a sound like the steam saw cutting. As he approached Summerton from behind Gettys's store, he heard voices and laughter.

He crouched amid the underbrush growing in heavy woods at the rear of the Dixie Store. At the end of the front porch visible to him, some slatternly white women lounged. One had the front of her dress undone. A scrawny baby suckled at her left nipple. The conversation of the women was loud and profane.

On the other side of the dirt road Andy saw children seated in dust, along with a couple of the poorer sharecroppers from the district. All at once the talking stopped. The white people turned their attention to something out of sight beyond the store.

Sweating, he decided to move closer and observe from behind a huge live oak that stood about ten feet from the porch. To reach it he would have to cross open ground directly in front of him, weaving through a clump of foot-high yucca plants with rigid leaves sharp as spears. The open space was brightly lighted —a row of oil lanterns-glowed on the porch, and a cropper's boy stood nearby with a blazing torch—but the people in the clearing were all looking the other say, up the road. He counted to three and moved.

He dodged among the yuccas, running with barefoot stealth. A woman on the porch heard him, but before she turned around he was crushed against the back of the tree, the bark rough against his shirt. He heard the woman grunt. "Just some animal, I reckon."

After a period of silence, he heard a faint rhythmic thudding. Horses or mules, walking down the dusty river road. In the crossroads clearing, someone cried, "Hurrah! Here they come."

Andy slid his face to the left behind the tree trunk, until one eye cleared the edge, giving him a good view of the crossroads, brilliantly lit now; half of the new arrivals carried smoking torches.

He knew they were men, and only that. Yet the sight of them struck him hard. They wore robes and hoods with eyeholes. The costumes were sewn of some shiny stuff the color of blood. It shimmered with highlights from the torches. He clutched the trunk and watched with his left eye, holding his breath.

In single file they paraded into the crossroads. The right side of the lead rider's robe was pulled up and tucked behind a belt gleaming with metal cartridges. The butt of his holstered pistol hung free. Among the other riders Andy spied old squirrel rifles, an ancient spontoon, even a saber or two.

Dust puffed up where the hooves fell. Round and round the clearing they rode, somehow all the more frightening because of their silence. Even the white slatterns and the croppers looked cowed.

The leader reined his horse in front of the Dixie Store. Andy noticed something he hadn't seen before. The second man carried some kind of wood box on his saddle, partly concealed under his robe. The box appeared to be rectangular, about two feet long, and made of unpainted pine.

The leader raised an old ear trumpet of the kind used by deaf people. He spoke through it. The trumpet made his voice tinny and gravelly, disguising it somewhat.

"The knights of the Invisible Empire gather. Enemies of white chivalry beware. Your days are numbered. Your deaths are certain."

It was trumpery, Andy knew. A childish masquerade. Yet he

also knew the hearts of the hooded men, if not their faces. They were determined, and full of hate.

"Let the word go out," the leader bellowed through the dented trumpet. "Here is the first who will feel our wrath."

The second rider tossed the box on the ground. The lid pooped off. The box held some kind of doll.

The leader motioned and the file of riders moved out. Andy decided he'd seen enough. He started back through the yuccas to the thick woods from which he'd emerged. His mistake was glancing over his shoulder to check on the Klansmen.

He stepped too near one of the yuccas. The point of the long leaf stabbed his leg through his pants, and he exclaimed in pain. Not loudly, but he drew the attention of the night riders. Someone yelled, rifles came up, pistols came out. The leader signaled toward the black man bolting for the trees.

Leaves daggered his legs as two hooded men rode him down, one on each side of the clump of yuccas. Panting, Andy ran faster, out of the yuccas. A musket butt slammed his head and knocked him to his knees.

The men dismounted and dragged him around in front of the porch. One of the white women, the one nursing, leaned over and spat in his hair. Held by his ears and shoulders, he was pushed near the leader's horse.

"Niggers were warned from this gathering," the leader boomed through the trumpet. He was a fearsome, towering figure, looming over Andy in robes that shone as if on fire. "Niggers who defy the Invisible Empire get what they deserve."

Another Klansman pulled out an immense hunting knife. The blade flashed as he turned the knife this way and that. "Drop his pants. You're through, boy. We boil nigger heads and nigger balls for soup."

"No." The leader slashed the air with the trumpet. "Let him carry word of what he saw here. Show him the coffin."

A man yanked Andy's head around so he could see the box open on the ground. A bullet had been fired into the velvet dress of the crude cornhusk doll inside the box. The leader indicated blackened letters burned into the coffin lid. Crooked letters, but legible.

"Someone read him what it says."

"I know this nigger," another Klansman said. "He's a Mont

Royal nigger. He can read it for himself." Though the speaker tried to roughen his voice to disguise it, Andy recognized Gettys.

He was so frightened, his eyes blurred. He had to clamp himself tight with his inside muscles to keep from urinating. The leader roared, "All right, then. You tell that woman what you saw and what you read right there, nigger." He signaled again. Andy was released and kicked toward the woods.

He staggered forward. A pistol boomed four times. Each time, he started violently, expecting to be hit. He kept running, past the yuccas toward the woods. Luckily, he didn't fall. He twisted when he reached the trees and saw gun smoke drifting blue above the robed men. They laughed at him. He ran into the dark.

> *Unable to sleep all night. Andy saw the Klan, and what they had burned into the coffin representing their intended victim. He wrote it out for me, his hand shaking, sweat dripping from his brow to the old brown paper:*

> **"Dead Damned & Delivered"**
> *the nigress*
> **MAIN**

44

On the day of the trouble, Charles woke an hour later than usual —five in the afternoon. He reached under his cot, uncorked the bottle, and took his first drink before getting out of bed. It had become his habit to start the day this way.

It was mid-August. The shanty where he slept, behind the place he worked, was airless and hot. Noisy, too. Texas cowhands shouted and stomped around the dance floor in the main building while Professor played a polka on the establishment's brand-new Fenway upright.

After a second drink, he reluctantly got up. He was already dressed; he usually slept in his clothes. He faced a twelve-hour shift as night bouncer at Trooper Nell's. Nell's was a thriving dance hall with upstairs rooms for the whores and their clients. It was located on Texas Street, between the Applejack and the Pearl, south of the railroad. If he listened carefully, he could hear the horses and hacks bringing paid-off trail hands to this less-than-respectable section of Abilene.

Trooper Nell's never closed. Abilene was booming, quickly becoming the most popular shipping point in Kansas. The gamble of Joe McCoy, an unassuming Illinois farm boy with a keen business sense, had paid off. Last year, in its first season, McCoy's two-hundred-fifty-acre complex of pens and chutes had loaded about thirty-five thousand head of Texas cattle aboard the U.P.E.D. This second season promised to double that. Despite the Indian trouble all summer, herds continued to pour across Humbarger's Ford on the Smoky Hill south of town. Almost every night, Charles had plenty of free-spending, hard-drinking cowpokes to sit on when they got out of hand. The Dickinson

County sheriff did little. He was a grocer by trade, with no talent for handling rowdies.

Charles used his fingers to comb tangles from his long beard. From a chair with a broken leg, he picked up a canvas scabbard he'd sewn together after studying a picture of a fierce Japanese warrior in an old copy of *Leslie's*. The warrior, called a Samurai, carried his long sword in such a scabbard on his back, the hilt jutting above his left shoulder. Charles put on the scabbard and shoved his Spencer into it. That plus his strapped-on Colt usually damped the fighting urge of the cowboys. He'd taken a lesson from Wild Bill, who'd become quite a legend in Kansas. Sometimes Hickok wore as many as five guns, plus a knife. That way, he cowed men instead of having to kill them. Charles hadn't seen Wild Bill in a while; he'd heard he was riding dispatch for the Army.

It was Charles's bad luck that he wasn't employed the same way. In fact, he hadn't put his sights on an Indian since his dismissal from the Tenth. And this was surely the year for it. The tribes had wintered peacefully enough. But then the Washington politicians had been unable to agree on the amount of the annuities to be paid under the terms set at Medicine Lodge Creek. Rations, guns, and ammunition went unissued as well. Last spring the angry Comanches had broken loose and gone on the warpath in Texas. Then the Cheyennes under Tall Bull, Scar, and other war leaders stormed into Kansas, supposedly to attack their old enemies the Pawnee. Before long they turned their hostility on the whites.

The Saline, Solomon, and Republican river settlements soon felt the fury. Fifteen whites were killed, five women raped in just a few weeks. So far August had been the worst month, with a wagon train attacked and almost destroyed at Fort Dodge, three wood choppers slaughtered while they worked near Fort Wallace, a Denver stage caught in a four-hour running fight from which driver and passengers barely escaped.

Agent Wynkoop could control the peace chiefs, but not the young men. Sheridan was in trouble. He had but twenty-six hundred infantry and cavalry with which to stop the raids. He'd sent a couple of experienced scouts, Comstock and Grover, to try to restore peace with the Cheyennes. A group under Turkey Leg welcomed the men, then turned on them with no warning, murdering Comstock and badly wounding Grover before he got away. The treachery didn't surprise Charles.

He hated being trapped so far from the action. But he didn't know any Indian-fighting outfit that would take him, and he wasn't fool enough to set out alone, a solitary executioner. So he worked in Abilene, and drank, while his rage and frustration built inside him.

One more drink and he left the shanty. He trudged across the trash-strewn backyard toward the rambling two-story building. He'd slept hard, but with more nightmares. He usually dreamed the old dream of blazing woods, wounded horses falling, his own slow death from smoky suffocation. Last night it had been different. In his dream, Elkanah Bent dangled a big pearl earring in front of him while he pricked Charles with a huge knife.

Early in the year, a telegraph message sent care of Jack Duncan had informed Charles of the murder of George Hazard's wife. Bent's long vendetta against the two families only strengthened Charles's conviction that the world and most of those in it were worthless. He didn't suppose Bent would ever come after him, though. Charles had frightened him badly in Texas before the war.

Since January, Charles had returned to Leavenworth only twice. Duncan treated him with stiff-necked correctness, but no warmth. He let Charles know that he disapproved of the frequency with which Charles took a drink. Charles had tried to play with his son, talk to him, but the boy didn't like to be alone with him, always wanting to return to Maureen or the brigadier.

There were no letters from Willa waiting at Leavenworth, either. Nor had he written.

He was in his usual sullen, spiteful mood as he yanked the flimsy back door open and stalked down the dim hall to start work.

Professor was hammering the Fenway. Two cowhands were dancing with two of the whores on the plank floor. Three tables held groups of noisy, dusty drinkers. Charles saw some of the cowhands eye him as he strode toward the end of the shiny fifty-foot brass-fitted bar.

"Hit me, Lem." The bartender dutifully poured a double shot of his special-stock bourbon. Charles knocked it back, not noticing a seated cowboy whispering to another, who had curly blond hair. The blond youngster studied Charles with contempt.

The place smelled of spit and sawdust, cigars and trail dust, and of cow chips someone had stepped in. Trade was brisk for half past five, and no more boisterous than usual. Down a staircase opposite the bar came the owner, five-foot-tall Nellie Slingerland. Nellie was somewhere over forty, always wore high-necked gowns, and had the biggest bosom Charles had ever seen on a woman so petite. Her eyes were bright and calculating, her cheeks pitted from some childhood disease. Nellie cost twice as much as any of the other whores, but to Charles she gave herself free. They slept together once or twice a week, usually during the day, and Charles always had to be good and drunk first. "Roll over here, buck," she'd say, and then he'd straddle her and push in and hold himself with straightened arms while he did her. She always yelled and jumped a lot. Because he was so tall, his head stuck out beyond hers. She never saw his closed eyes, or the strange twisted-up expression on his face. He always tried to pretend she was Willa. It never worked.

"How are you, buck?" Nellie's expensive tooled mule-ear boots thumped as she approached. She was called Trooper Nell because she refused to take the boots off for any man, Charles included. Abilene told a lot of tales about her: She was a former schoolteacher; she had poisoned her husband for his money on their farm near Xenia, Ohio; she preferred women.

"I'd be better if this heat would break," Charles said. He hated her term of address, buck, as if he were some field hand. But she paid him, so he put up with it.

"You look mad enough to chew a brick."

"I didn't sleep so well."

"Something new," she said sarcastically, reaching for the glass of lemonade the bartender poured from her private pitcher. She drank no strong spirits. "You're a damn good bouncer, buck, but you make it pretty obvious you don't like it. I'm starting to think you don't belong here."

She helped herself to more lemonade while surveying the customers. She paid special attention to the table where the blond cowhand sat. He was making all the noise.

"Watch that bunch," she said. "The young ones cause the most trouble."

Charles nodded and remained lounging with his back

against the bar, the Spencer stock jutting above his left shoulder. Presently the blond cowboy staggered to the dance floor, rudely pushing Squirrel Tooth Jo and her customer out of his way as he veered toward Professor. He requested something. Professor looked dubious. The cowboy slapped gold pieces on the top of the shiny black upright, looking truculent. Professor shot a look at Nellie and swung into "Dixie."

The blond cowboy whooped and waved his hat. He stepped on his chair and then onto the table where his friends were seated. Nellie bobbed her head at Charles. It meant, *Stop that.*

For the first time since awakening, he felt a pleasant anticipation. A roughly dressed man pushed the street doors open just then, caught Charles's eye, and grinned. The big bearded fellow in quilled pants and a fringed buckskin coat was familiar, but Charles couldn't quite place him. He had other things on his mind.

At the front end of the bar someone had left half a glass of whiskey. Charles gulped it, then reached across his left shoulder, unslinging the Spencer. He walked toward the table where the cowboy was dancing. The other men at the table stopped talking and pushed their chairs away. The cowboy's boot heels kept pounding the table, which sagged now.

"Buying drinks doesn't entitle you to break the furniture," Charles said, forcing a conversational tone.

"I like to dance. I like this music." The cowboy was no Texan. His thick accent said cotton South. Alabama, maybe.

"You can enjoy it sitting down. Get off the table."

"When I'm ready, soldier."

Charles's eyebrows shot up. The cowboy gave him a bleary grin, challenging him. "Soldier, I heard all about you in a place up the street. Hampton's Cavalry, but you went back in the U.S. Army afterward. We'd tar you for that in Mobile."

Out of patience, Charles reached for his leg. "Get down."

The cotton South cowboy hauled back with his boot and kicked Charles, clipping his left shoulder and throwing him off balance. The cowboy jumped down as Charles staggered.

Another cowhand snatched Charles's Spencer. Two more seized his arms. Charles bashed one and temporarily drove him back. Loco drunk, the blond youngster drove two blows into Charles's belly.

The impact knocked Charles away from his captors. He

slipped and skidded, then dropped into a crouch. His Spencer lay six feet away.

"Stop that damned fool," Nellie cried as the cowboy pulled his .44 revolver.

His friends dove out of the way on either side, leaving no one near him. A similar exodus emptied the dance floor. The cowboy fired as Charles rolled to the right. The bullet flung up splinters and dust.

Nellie screamed, "That floor cost three hundred dollars, you son of a bitch!"

The bleary cowboy aimed at Charles again. Something slid along the floor to Charles's right hand. He saw only the boots and quilled pants of the man who'd slid him the Spencer. Before the cowboy could shoot again, Charles shot him in the stomach.

The cowboy flew backward, landing on the table and breaking it. Charles lurched up, favoring his left leg, which he'd twisted badly. One whore shrieked; Squirrel Tooth Jo fainted. In the ensuing silence, Nellie began, "Well, I guess that—" She got no further. Charles put a second bullet in the fallen cowboy. The body jerked and slid a foot. Charles fired a third time. The body kept jerking and sliding.

"Leave off," Nellie said, dragging his arm down.

"Self-defense, Nellie." He was shaking, fury barely under control.

"The first time. Why'd you need the other shots? You're as bad as any damn Indian."

Charles stared at her, trying to summon an answer. His left leg gave out. He hit the floor in a sprawl.

They carried him to the shanty and lowered him to the cot. Nellie shooed the barkeep and the porter out and regarded him soberly.

"The boy's dead, buck."

He said nothing.

"You can rest here till you leg's better, but I'm giving you notice. I know you had to defend yourself but you didn't have to mutilate him. Word gets around. Temper like yours, it's bad for business. I'm sorry."

Stony, he watched her turn and leave. Goddamn her, he was only trying to save himself—

No. That was a lie. Trooper Nell was right. One bullet was enough to finish the foolhardy youngster and he knew it. Why couldn't he get rid of the rage that had prompted him to fire the other shots?

A knock. He lifted his forearm off his eyes.

The shanty door opened. Against the fading August daylight, he recognized the silhouette of the bearded stranger, quilled pants and all.

"Griffenstein," the man in buckskin said.

"I remember. Dutch Henry."

"Had a hell of a time finding you. How's your leg?"

"Hurts. I'll be off it a while, I guess."

"I hate to hear that. I rode a hundred miles. All the way from Hays."

"For what?"

"To recruit you." Griffenstein pulled up an old crate and sat down. "The Cheyennes are running wild and all the cavalry does is chase 'em, so Phil Sheridan's decided to take the offensive. He's ordered one of his aides, Colonel Sandy Forsyth, to hire fifty experienced plainsmen and go into the field and kill all the hostiles they can find. I said we couldn't get a better man than you. You're still the talk of the Tenth Regiment."

Sourly, Charles said, "You mean my bobtail."

"No, sir. They talk about how you whipped those colored men into some of the best cavalry in the Army. They don't call your old troop Barnes's Troop, they call it Main's Troop—your real name—and the old man says amen."

"That a fact." Charles gripped his aching leg. "Here, give me a hand. I know I can get up."

He did, but he fell right back down, tumbling across the cot. "Damn. I wish you'd come one day sooner, Griffenstein."

"So do I. Well, next time. The way the red men are scalping and burning, there'll be a number of next times. You can join up then."

"Count on it," Charles said.

"How will I find you?"

"Telegraph Brigadier Jack Duncan. He's with the Departmental paymaster at Fort Leavenworth."

"A relative, is he?"

The convenient lie: "Father-in-law."

"Nobody said you were married."

"Not any more. She died."

*And you killed every iota of feeling in the only other woman
you ever loved as much.*

The big man said, "Truly sorry to hear that." Charles's curt
nod dismissed it.

They shook hands. Dutch Henry Griffenstein tipped his hat
and left, closing the slat door, leaving Charles to swear with renewed frustration. In the dark he reached for the half-empty
bottle under the cot.

Nellie Slingerland stuck by the firing. Charles was bad for
business. Trooper Nell's was almost empty for the entire seven
days that he lay in the shanty. The grocer turned sheriff dropped
in on the last day to say witnesses had exonerated Charles on the
grounds of self-defense.

Hobbling, he packed his few possessions. Nellie didn't bid
him goodbye personally, just sent ten dollars with the barkeep.
Charles used the money to get Satan from a livery in the respectable part of town. He left Abilene in the summer dusk and rode
east into the dark.

45

When Willa went to pieces and forgot her lines a third time, Sam Trump said, "Ten minutes, ladies and gentlemen."

He drew her aside to the cushion-strewn platform serving as a rehearsal bed. He sat her on the edge, leaving inky prints on the sleeve of her yellow dress. Because of the fierce September heat, his blackamoor makeup ran and smeared.

"My dear, what is it?" He knew. She looked bedraggled; her silvery hair was dull and pinned up carelessly. He sat beside her, his black tights and tunic darkened by sweat. The white chrysanthemum pinned over his heart was wilted. Prosperity jumped in his lap and purred.

When she stayed silent, he prompted her. "Is it the weather? It will surely break soon."

"The weather has nothing to do with it. I just can't keep my mind on my part." She touched his hand. "Will you cancel rehearsals long enough for me to dash to Leavenworth again?"

"You were there not thirty days ago."

"But that poor child needs someone besides a housekeeper to pay attention to him. The brigadier's gone with the pay chest for weeks at a time. Gus might as well be an orphan."

Sam stroked Prosperity's sleek back. It was imperative that he find some way to jolt Willa out of her melancholy. It was deepening day by day, robbing her performances of energy. He nerved himself and said, "Dear girl, is it really the little boy who concerns you? Or his father?"

She gave him a scathing look. "I don't know where his father is. Furthermore, I don't care."

"Ah, no, of course not. 'The poet's food is love and fame,'

Mr. Shelley said, and it's true of actors also. But you are telling me that only half applies to you."

"Don't torment me, Sam. Just say you'll let Grace stand in for me for a few nights. I'll do better with *Othello* once I know Gus is all right."

"I hate to delay rehearsals. I have a premonition that our new production will be the one that propels us to the heights. I have telegraphed several New York managers, inviting them to come—"

"Oh for God's sake, Sam," she said, her face uncharacteristically hostile. "You know all those wonderful triumphs exist only in your imagination. We'll live and die provincial actors."

Trump stood. Leaping off, the theater cat caught claws in his tunic and left a long rip. Trump stared at his partner, wounded. Willa's blue eyes filled with tears.

"I'm sorry, Sam. That was a vile thing to say. Forgive me."

"Forgiven. As to your absence, what choice have I? You are sleepwalking through your roles. If one more trip to Leavenworth will arrest that, by all means go. Since we are being so candid, permit me to continue a moment more. I liked that young man when I first met him. I no longer like him. He's hurt you. Even when he's absent he hurts you. Somehow he reaches out into my theater to poison everything."

Willa gave him a sad half-smile. "It's called love, Sam. You've had affairs of the heart."

"None that destroyed me. I'll not see you destroyed."

"No, Sam. Just a few days, then things will be fine."

"All right," he said, doubting it.

On the train that carried Willa across the state, passengers jumped off at every stop to buy late papers. An unfolding story from eastern Colorado had burst onto the front pages. On the Arikaree Fork of the Republican River, a special detachment of Indian-hunting plainsmen under a Colonel Forsyth had been surprised by a huge band of Cheyennes. The detachment took refuge on a sparsely treed island in the river and forted up to fight.

Incredibly, they repelled charge after charge by the Indians, who numbered as many as six hundred, according to some of the dispatches. In one of the charges a renowned war chief named Bat had ridden in wearing a great war bonnet whose medicine was supposed to turn aside bullets. The medicine failed him. He was blown down, this Bat—Roman Nose, some called him.

Passengers on the train reveled in the reports of the battle of Beecher's Island, named in honor of the young Army officer, second in command, who had taken a fatal wound there. "They're safe," a passenger in the next seat exclaimed to Willa, showing a paper. "The men Forsyth sent to Fort Wallace got through. The relief column found 'em still holed up and carving their horses for meat."

"How many did they kill?" another passenger asked.

"Says here it was hundreds."

"By God, there ought to be fifty more fights like that, to make up for all the poor innocents who got scalped and outraged this summer."

Fuming, Willa spoke across the back of the seat. "You expect the Cheyennes to be peaceful when they aren't even treated with simple fairness and honesty? Almost a year ago, the peace commission promised them rations and weapons for hunting. By the time the weapons were issued, summer was nearly over. Do you expect them not to break faith when we do?"

Her voice trailed away over the clicking of the wheel trucks. The male passengers stared at her as though she carried cholera. The man with the paper said to the others, "Didn't know there was squaws who could pass for white women, did you, boys?"

Willa started to retort, but before she could, the man with the paper leaned forward and spat a large gob of tobacco pulp on the floor.

In times past, that kind of behavior would have challenged her to fight all the harder. Not now. She felt despondent, even foolish, caught in a battle that couldn't be won.

She stared out the window at white barns and cattle grazing in the twilight. She tried to close her ears to the sarcastic jokes the man continued to make about her. She felt miserable. *Somehow he reaches out to poison everything.*

Maybe her often-impractical partner was wiser than she knew. Maybe she should stop chasing doomed dreams. Maybe she ought to make this visit to Leavenworth her last.

"No, the brigadier's not heard from him in weeks," Maureen said when Willa arrived on a gray, gusty morning.

"Is the general here?"

"No. He's riding the pay circuit again."

"Where's Gus?"

"I put him to hoeing the vegetable garden in back. It's entirely the wrong time of year—we've already harvested our squash and potatoes—but the poor thing needs something to fill his hours."

"He needs a normal life." Willa set her valise near the cold iron stove. "He needs schooling, parents, a home of his own."

"No disputing that," Maureen said. She looked older; the harsh prairie weather had wrinkled and aged her skin. "He'll not find those things here, I fear."

A low-pitched howling underlay their conversation. The front door rattled in its frame. Maureen twisted her apron. "Mary and Joseph, I hate this place sometimes. The heat. That infernal wind. It's blown for weeks."

Willa went to the back door. From there she could observe little Gus, a sturdy, strong boy bending over a corner of the garden patch and listlessly poking at the dirt with his hoe. Dust and debris whirled over the garden and the nearby buildings. Gus's little round-crowned hat threatened to blow away at any moment.

Watching from the open door, Willa felt her heart near to breaking. How forlorn he looked. As hunched as a little old man. Digging, chopping—to no purpose.

She stepped outside. "Hello, Gus."

"Aunt Willa!" He dropped the hoe and ran to her. She knelt and hugged him. Charles's son was almost four now. He'd lost his baby pudginess. Although he was outdoors a lot, he tended to fair skin and paleness.

Despite the wind, she took him walking along the bluff above the river. She was asking questions, which he answered with monosyllables, when she heard a hail behind them. She turned.

"Oh good Lord."

Down the path lurched Charles. Over the back of his gypsy robe he wore some sort of canvas sling from which the stock of his rifle jutted. His beard was long again, and unkempt.

Little Gus spied his father, a smile burst onto his face, and he ran toward him. He'd gone but halfway when Charles stumbled over a rock and fell. Only a jarring stop with his hands kept him from slamming face first on the ground.

Gus halted, confused. Willa's expression grew strained. From the way Charles weaved as he stood up, she knew he was drunk.

"Hallo, Gus. Come give your pa a hug."

The boy continued to advance, but cautiously. Charles crouched down, enfolded the boy in his arms. Gus turned his head and Willa saw his eyes close and his mouth purse, as though he feared the man hugging him. The moment of spontaneous exuberance was gone.

Willa held her feathered hat against the gusting wind. That wind brought her a ripe whiskey smell. Drunk, all right. Gus quickly wriggled away from Charles. He looked relieved.

Charles stared at her, almost unfriendly. "Didn't expect to run into you. What're you doing here?" He spoke thickly, slowly.

"I wanted to see Gus. I didn't imagine you'd be around."

"I just rode in. Gus, go on back to Maureen. I need to talk to Willa."

"I want to stay out here and play, Pa."

Charles grabbed his shoulder, spun him, and flung him toward the row of officers' houses. "Don't sass me. Go along."

Little Gus looked ready to cry. Charles yelled, "Go on, goddamn it."

Gus ran. Willa wanted to upbraid Charles, strike him, horsewhip him. The intensity of her emotion upset her, both in its own right and because she knew she wouldn't feel it if she didn't love him.

Somewhere on the post, artillery pieces fired practice rounds. Charles took Willa's elbow and turned her almost as rudely as he'd turned the boy. He all but pushed her down the weed-grown path toward the river. Fighting for control, she said, "Where've you been, Charles?"

"Oh, do I answer to you about that?"

"For God's sake, I'm curious, that's all. Can't you recognize a polite question anymore?"

"Abilene," he muttered. "Been in Abilene. Had a job, but I quit it."

"What kind of job?"

"Nothing you'd care to hear about."

In a clump of willows near the edge of the bluff she stopped, confronting him. The wind stripped yellowing leaves from the weeping branches and flung them into the dusty gray distances.

She hated the whiskey smell on him, the odor of unwashed clothing. Emotion overwhelmed her again.

"Why are you so angry all the time?" She braced her gloved palms on the front of the gypsy robe and, on tiptoe, she kissed him. His beard scratched. She might as well have kissed marble.

"Look, Willa—"

"No, you look, Charles Main." Something warned her not to give rein to her feelings. She couldn't stop. "Do you think I'm here out of charity? I love you. I thought you loved me once." His eyes swept past her, to the dust-hazed river. "I want you to stop this wild life you're living."

"I came to see Gus, not hear lectures."

"Well, that's too bad. You'll hear this one. You don't belong on the Plains. Find a job in Leavenworth. Take care of your son. You've frightened him. You have to win him back. Can't you see that? He needs you, Charles. He needs you the way you were two years ago. I need you that way. Please."

He tugged the brim of his black hat low over his eyes, holding it against the roaring wind. "I'm not ready to come back here. I've got unfinished work."

"Those infernal Cheyennes—" She was nearly in tears.

"For whom your heart bleeds. You go take care of your Friendship Society and your goddamn petitions."

Not an hour here, and it's all going wrong, she thought. "Why are you yelling at me, Charles?"

"Because I don't want you interfering with my son."

"I care about him!"

"So do I. I'm his father."

"Not much of one."

He hit her, open-handed, not hard. But she felt a pain beyond description.

Holding her cheek, she stepped back. Her small feathered hat blew off. He stabbed a hand out automatically but the hat sailed by, lifting on a gust, spinning on through the willows toward the Missouri. "Oh," she said, a small, forlorn sound. Then she looked at him again. Something hard kindled in her blue eyes.

"You've turned into a complete bastard. I used to wonder why it was happening. I used to care. I don't any more. Your boy doesn't either, but you're too stupid and drunk to see that. If you keep on, he'll hate you. Most of the time he's terrified of you."

"Christ, you're superior." He was loud, scornful. "First you had all the answers about the Indians. All the wrong answers. Now you're telling me how to raise my son. I don't need you. Take care of your own problems. Find some other man to drag into your bed."

"Go to hell, Charles Main. You just go to hell! No—" She shook her head, a violent movement. "You're already there, as low as anybody can get."

Enraged, he grabbed for her. She dashed by. "Willa!" A fleeting look back showed Charles her tear-streaked face. "Go ahead, run. *Run!*"

RUNRUNRUNRUN—it went echoing over the river. She was gone in the blowing clouds of leaves and dust.

"Miss Willa, you just got here."

"A mistake, Maureen. A huge mistake. Take care of that poor youngster. His father won't."

She walked all the way into Leavenworth City, the dust caking on her lids and lips and hands. A kindly ticket agent found her a basin of water and a piece of clean rag. She left on the four o'clock steamer for St. Louis.

When she walked back into Trump's Playhouse, filthy from travel, the old actor was astonished at the brightness of her manner. "Call a rehearsal, Sam. I'm eager to get back to work. I'll not be seeing Mr. Main again, if I'm lucky."

So boys! a final bumper
  While we all in chorus chant—
"For our next President we nominate
  Our own Ulysses Grant!"
And if asked what State he hails from
  This our sole reply shall be,
"From near Appomattox Court House,
  With its famous apple tree."
For 'twas there to our Ulysses
  That Lee gave up the fight—
Now boys, "To Grant for President
  And God defend the right!"

Campaign verse in Greeley's
New York Tribune, 1868

MADELINE'S JOURNAL

> *September, 1868. Klan activity much increased in the state with elections less than two months away. York County, up near the N. Carolina border, is a hotbed. The Klan has seized the public fancy in a bizarre, faddish way. Visiting Marie-Louise here, Theo brought and displayed a tin of "Ku Klux Smoking Tobacco." He saw for sale in C'ston sheet music of a song written in the Klan's honor. In Columbia a base-ball team called "Pale-Faces" openly pays homage to the organization.*
>
> *The Summerton "den" remains visible but has not moved against us. Sometimes cannot decide whether to laugh at this blight of pretentiously costumed bigots, or tremble. . . .*

The muscular young black man, Ridley, put his arm around his wife. May was a slight, frail girl. She was in her third month, beginning to show.

Ridley had come home tired from digging and hauling all day in the Mont Royal phosphate fields. But the weather was so agreeable, he'd persuaded May to delay their supper and come enjoy the air with him. He felt good these days. He was earning a decent wage, and starting to build his own two-room house of tabby with help from his friend Andy Sherman and some tools loaned by Mr. Heely, the white foreman of the Mont Royal work force. Ridley was proud to be able to do all these things, and go wherever he wished as a free man. That included Summerton, where he intended to vote for General U. S. Grant for president, as Mr. Klawdell of the League suggested.

The last redness of the day was fading behind the thick woods bordering the river road. Walking together, Ridley and his wife heard a low hooting. May huddled close against him. "Sun's gone. We walked too far."

"Felt so peaceful, I lost all track," Ridley said, all at once aware of the lowering darkness. He gripped her hand and lengthened his stride; he couldn't hurry her too much because of her condition. Suddenly, behind them, they heard horses.

Ridley and May turned to look. They saw glowing lights

floating above the road, and a red shimmer. They heard the jingle of bridles. Robed riders, carrying torches.

"May, we got to run. It's them Klan men."

She turned without a word and sprinted toward Mont Royal, her bare feet flying. He caught up with her and, side by side, they sped away from the trotting horses. Their bare feet thumped the sandy road. Ridley's breathing quickened; soon he was gasping. May let out a groan. The exertion was too much for her.

The four riders broke into a gallop. They quickly overtook the black couple. Ridley and May saw the shadows of the Klansmen appear on the road as they drew up close behind with their torches.

Two of the riders booted their mounts past the fleeing couple. Ridley smelled the animals as they dashed by, raising dust. The horsemen wheeled back in the center of the road. Ridley and May were encircled.

"Nigger, you know you're not s'posed to be out after dark," one of the riders said. All four were robed and hooded in scarlet cloth that rippled and gleamed when they moved. Ridley clutched May's shoulder, angry but not wanting to provoke them; they might hurt her.

"We were just on our way home, gentlemen."

"Gentlemen," another of them guffawed. "We're not gentlemen, we're hell's devils come to haunt rebellious darkies." The speaker dismounted and slouched forward. Ridley saw blue behind the eyeholes of the hood, but he didn't recognize the man by his build or his voice. The man thrust a Leech and Rigdon revolver under Ridley's nose. "Where you from, boy? Answer me respectfully."

"From down the road. From Mont Royal."

"Oh, then you're one of them Union League coons who expects he's going to vote come November. Going to try to put that goddamn Grant in the White House, are you, nigger-boy?"

May's dark eyes flashed with fury. "He is. He's a citizen and just as good as any of—"

"May, stop," Ridley begged.

"We are the devil's agents and we demand respect," the man said, raising his revolver to strike the pregnant girl.

Ridley jumped between them. "Run, May," he shouted. His

hands darted to the throat of the robed man. The man fired a
round. The sound of it was thunderous.

"Jesus, Jack," another of the riders protested. Ridley
dropped to his knees, a wound just above his belt pouring blood
onto his shirt. May screamed and leaped at the man with the
revolver. Instead of shooting her, he drove his elbow into her
round stomach. She cried out and fell on her back in the road,
holding herself and weeping.

Her faded dress was twisted around her hips. She wore clean
cotton drawers that suddenly showed a dot of blood. Jack Jolly
pulled off his mask and gazed at May with repugnance. Another
of the men said, "She's just a girl, Jolly."

Jolly pointed the Leech and Rigdon between the eyeholes of
the man's hood. "You ain't got a goddamn word to say about it,
Gettys." Ridley slowly rolled onto his side, quivered, lay still.
Jolly gave a satisfied grunt, cocked the revolver, aimed at May's
head, and fired another round.

Her body jerked. The sound boomed through the woods,
rousing unseen birds that flapped away in alarm. Jolly laughed
and wiped his damp chin with the hem of his hood.

"That's one nigger vote we'll never have to worry about.
Two if she was carryin' a boy."

"No violence," said Devin Heely, the small, red-bearded
Irishman who had been hired in Charleston by the mine opera-
tors. "The Beaufort Phosphate Company's dead set against violence. It's my job as foreman—"

"They killed two innocent people," Madeline exclaimed.
"How do you propose we deal with mad dogs like that? Invite
them to tea to discuss the issue?"

Silence. Heely chewed on the stem of his cob pipe. It was
dusk, twenty-four hours after the double murder on the road.
Every available lantern was lit outside the whitewashed house,
and every black man employed in the phosphate fields was standing or kneeling there in a great semicircle. They'd brought their
wives, and all their children, too. A baby fretted. The mother
rocked the bundled infant.

Seated together on the stoop, Prudence Chaffee and Marie-
Louise watched Madeline. A woman in the crowd, May's sister,
wept loudly. Heely opened his mouth to say something.

"She's right."

Heely and everyone else turned toward the voice. Andy stepped into the center of the lighted area. "They've left us only one choice. The one printed in the U.S. Constitution."

"What are you talking about, Sherman?" Foote asked.

"I'm talking about what it says in the second amendment. 'The right of the people to keep and bear arms shall not be infringed.' "

"Showin' off his damn lawbook learnin'," someone else muttered. Andy paid no attention:

"I'm talking about starting our own militia company. Right here."

"You're a fool," Heely said. "If there's anything those Klan boys hate worse than the League, it's nigra militia. I am opposed—"

"I'm afraid you have nothing to say about it," Madeline broke in. "I think you're right, Andy. We have to protect ourselves. If those Klansmen come to Mont Royal, we won't have time to send to Charleston for soldiers."

Jane asked, "Where will we get guns?"

"Buy them in the city," Madeline said.

"Won't it be expensive?" Prudence asked.

Madeline gave her a strange, grieving look that neither she nor Marie-Louise nor any of the others understood. "I should imagine. I'll find the money."

Wrote Mr. J. Lee, the architect, asking him to suspend work. The money for his services must be spent another way.

46

Here was the true prairie. Not a tree broke the horizon. It was the last day of October, and the wind scything over the ground foretold winter. Steel-colored skies expanded the vast, bleak space.

A tiny dot appeared, near the cut bank of a meandering creed. It enlarged to a horse and rider—Satan and Charles. Bundled into three shirts layered beneath the gypsy robe, he was still freezing. The hem of the robe whipped and snapped around him. The Spencer stock jutted above his left shoulder.

His eyes searched a large arc ahead, saw nothing. He chewed on a cold cigar, grumpily. Hell of a season to start a war, he thought. But if there was to be war, he wanted to take part. He'd quit his most recent job, loading freight at the wagon depot near Fort Leavenworth, and ridden over two hundred miles in the bitter autumn for that purpose.

In another half hour buildings of stone and adobe appeared on the horizon. Fort Dodge at last. He'd been resting Satan at an easy pace. Now he put him into a fast trot.

He saw a big wagon park, then mounted squads drilling. He heard the crackle of practice fire from beyond the fort. This wasn't a post sunk into routine; there was too much activity. It got his blood up.

The officer of the day cast a wary look at the somewhat sinister stranger and said he might find those he asked about in the sutler's. Charles turned south past the stables to a flat-roofed adobe building with horses tethered outside. He put Satan with them and went in.

Dutch Henry Griffenstein was playing cards at an old round

table in the corner. The largest pile of paper currency lay in front of him. Charles didn't know the three other civilians in the game. One, a nondescript man with tangled hair and a pipe in his teeth, kept spilling the deck as he tried to shuffle. "You're too drunk, Joe," said the player on his left, relieving him of the cards. Joe belched and slouched down on his tailbone, indifferent.

"Charlie," Griffenstein exclaimed, jumping up. "You got the telegram."

"I started the very next day."

"Boys," Dutch Henry said, leading him to the table, "this is Cheyenne Charlie Main. Charlie, this here's Stud Marshall, this is Willow Roberts, and here"—his tone shaded into deference as he presented the unkempt man, who was about ten years older than Charles—"our chief of scouts, California Joe Milner."

California Joe, whose eyes barely focused, shook Charles's hand. It was hard to say whose palm was more callused. Milner wore a filthy Spanish sombrero, his red side whiskers hadn't been trimmed in a while, and he was altogether one of the most slovenly men Charles had ever seen.

"Joe's the man I work for, Charlie," Dutch Henry said. "You, too, now."

California Joe belched. "If the general says so." He had an accent. Nothing cultivated, like fine Southern speech. It was the nasal whine of the mountain border. Tennessee maybe, or Kentucky.

"He means Custer," Dutch Henry said. "We got more than one general. We got General Al Sully, too. Little Phil put him in charge of the Seventh while Curly was still exiled. Sent him south of the Arkansas to chase the Indians. He didn't do so well. That's when Phil asked Sherman to remit Curly's sentence so we'd have a field commander who knows how to fight. They're both lieutenant colonels, Custer and Sully, but Sully's brevet is only lieutenant general, so Custer says he ranks him. They're sniping and fussing all the time."

"No business of ours," California Joe said to Charles. "I report to Custer, and so do you if he hires you. Ever scouted in the Indian Territory?"

"I traveled it for more than a year with a couple of trading partners. I can't say I memorized it."

"That part don't make no difference. All you really need to scout is a pocket compass and balls."

"You'll have to take my word that I qualify."

California Joe laughed. "You said he's all right, Henry. He is all right. Main, you go see Custer. You'll find him drillin' his troops at the new camp down on Bluff Creek. If he okays you, the wage is fifty dollars a month."

"I brought my own horse."

Another belch. "Then it's seventy-five. I'm gonna need another damn snort soon."

Charles wasn't much impressed by Milner's drunken buffoonery. Dutch Henry saw that and tugged his arm.

"I need a drink myself. Come on, Charlie, I'll buy. Deal me out, boys." They walked toward the log bar. California Joe picked up his new hand and dropped three cards in the lap of his greasy trousers.

"That's Custer's famous pet?" Charles said, incredulous.

Dutch Henry grinned. "One of the two-legged ones. Custer also brung two of his staghounds when Sherman fixed it so's he could come back from Michigan. We're getting ready for action here. Phil and Uncle Bill finally convinced Grant we should carry the war to the hostiles. Offense, not defense. The plan is to push 'em back to the Territory, and kill those who won't go peaceably to the reservation and stay put."

Charles drank a tall shot of razor-edged popskull in three swallows. "You mean to say that's the plan with winter coming on?"

"I know it's contrary to sense, but it's really pretty smart of Little Phil. The hostiles will be settled into their villages, and you know as well as I do, their horses will be weak from lack of forage."

"I heard talk at Leavenworth that Sherman wanted Sheridan to move as early as this past August."

"He did, but the damn Interior Department screwed him again. The Olive Branchers made the Army hold off until it set up a safe camp for the hostiles who don't threaten anybody."

Charles scratched the head of a match with his thumbnail. He squinted behind the flame and puffed strong smoke out of the stubby cigar. "Where's the camp?"

"Fort Cobb. Satanta already took his Kiowas in. Ten Bears took his Comanches. Some Cheyennes went there, too, but General Hazen sent them away because we're not at peace with the Cheyennes. The Cheyennes are the ones we're going after. Some of 'em captured another poor white woman, Mrs. Blinn, and her little boy, over by Fort Lyon, first of October—"

"Who were the Cheyenne chiefs who went to Fort Cobb?"

"There was just one. Black Kettle."

Charles took the cigar from his mouth. He rolled it back and forth in his fingers. "And they didn't let him in? Of the whole crowd, Black Kettle's the least likely to harm anybody."

"A Cheyenne's a Cheyenne, that's the way Hazen saw it." Dutch Henry didn't understand why Charles looked troubled. Nor did he care. He slapped his friend's shoulder. "Ay God, Charlie, you missed a fine muss at Beecher's Island. The Solomon Avengers showed plenty of sand and spirit."

"That's what you called yourselves, Solomon Avengers?"

"Yes, sir. We killed a passel of Indians. But there's plenty more waiting. Cheyennes and Arapahoes—"

"The Army should stay away from Black Kettle."

"Hey, I thought you hated the whole bunch."

"Not him," Charles said, uneasy. He saw a vivid image of Willa's blue eyes. Dutch Henry frowned.

"Charlie, I told you, nobody cares which Cheyennes are all right and which aren't. The main idea's to kill 'em. You object to that, maybe you better forget it."

He thought of Boy and Wooden Foot, of their poor slaughtered collie.

"I don't object."

He ordered another drink. The smoke of his cigar drifted up past eyes grown as chill as the autumn sky.

He couldn't understand how a rum-pot like California Joe Milner could win George Custer's favor, but obviously he had, so Charles shook hands with the chief of scouts before he walked out of the adobe building. A snow flurry whirled big flakes around him. The sky was as black as dusk. A caped soldier appeared and handed him something.

"Compliments of the post Grant for President Club, sir."

Charles examined the leaflet and its engraving of the candidate with military collar and epaulets showing. "No, thanks." He handed it back.

"Sir, voting is the civic responsibility of every—"

"I've got other business," Charles said. The boy in the dark blue cape saw his eyes and didn't argue.

Charles curried and fed Satan and slept in the stables at Fort
Dodge overnight. Next morning he reprovisioned and set out for
the Seventh Cavalry encampment on the north bank of the Arkansas, about ten miles south of the fort. Flurries continued to
whip out of the slate sky and he soon felt frozen again. He kept
his spirits up by whistling the little tune that reminded him of
home.

Camp Sandy Forsyth had been named for the commander of
the Solomon Avengers. Charles saw its lights glimmering
through the gloom of an early dusk. The sentry who challenged
him said he was lucky not to have been shot at by some Cheyennes who'd lately been sniping at the camp. Charles shrugged
and said he'd seen no sign of the Indians. He figured he'd had so
much bad luck, he was due for some good.

He bedded in the wagon park with the permission of the
noncom on duty. After chewing a little hardtack, he pulled down
the earflaps of his muskrat cap, secured them by a thong under
his chin, and rolled up in his blankets. He was thirsty; the water
in his canteen had frozen. He felt tired, alone, depressed.

What he saw and heard soon after reveille changed that and
got his blood up again. Rifle fire with the steady rhythm of practice drew him to the far side of the tent camp. He found a dozen
troopers banging away at wood targets. He asked an old three-
striper what was going on.

"When we find the hostiles, old Curly wants to be sure we
can knock 'em down. These boys are some of the forty he picked
out for his *corps day elite.* Sharpshooters. Lieutenant Cooke's in
command."

Charles continued his walking tour. There was an air of
bustle in the encampment, a sure sign of a massive campaign. He
counted twenty supply wagons and forty oxen present already.
He saw evidence of an experienced military mind at work when
he came upon two troops wheeling and maneuvering under the
gray sky. All of one troop rode bays, all of the other chestnuts
and browns. Custer had adopted the Confederate custom of coloring the horses. Putting all the men of one troop on similar
mounts made identification easier in combat, and it had a way of
enhancing pride and discipline, too.

Hammers whanged on hot anvils; Charles saw half a dozen
farriers working to reshoe large numbers of horses. The Seventh's

bandsmen drilled to the strains of "Garry Owen." Their gray mounts reminded him of Sport.

Another half-dozen wagons arrived during the afternoon. Shortly after five o'clock he was able to see Custer in his large A-frame tent.

"Be still, Maida." Custer patted the growling staghound who'd gotten up the moment Charles entered. He'd interrupted the general as he vigorously washed his hands in a basin of water that was still clear when he finished. Custer dried his hands and bounded forward energetically, his smile broad and white beneath his reddish-gold mustache. Blue eyes sparkled above the harsh ridges of his cheekbones. As they shook hands, Charles sniffed oil of cinnamon on Custer's ringlets.

"Mr. Main. Been expecting you. Please, sit right there."

"Yes, sir, General. Thank you." Charles sat on the canvas chair, noticing Eastern newspapers on Custer's crowded field desk. Reading upside down, he noted a headline circled in black ink. It had something to do with Grant's presidential campaign.

Elbows on the desk, Custer scrutinized him. It was hard for Charles to remember that this world-famous soldier was not yet thirty years old.

"We've met before, somewhere," Custer said.

"You're right, General. We were on opposite sides at Brandy Station."

"That's it." Custer laughed. "You gave me one or two hot moments, I recall. What was your unit?"

"Wade Hampton's Legion."

"Fine cavalry officer, Hampton. I've always liked Southerners." Custer opened a file. "You know the general purpose of our expedition, I presume. We're to search out and attack the enemy when they are least prepared, and kill as many of their warriors as practicable. To use the phrase of Senator Ross, we intend to conquer a peace."

Charles nodded. Custer scanned something in the file. "You must have an affinity for the Army. I see you tried to get back in twice, under a different name each time."

"Soldiering is all I know, General. I went to the Point a few years before you did. Class of '57."

"I see that here. I graduated in '61 by the grace of God and the fall of Fort Sumter." He closed the file. "Do you know the Indian Territory?"

"Your man Milner asked that. I was there for over a year, with a couple of trading partners the Cheyennes butchered."

The blue eyes pinned Charles. "So you'd have no hesitation about taking the lives of hostiles?"

"No, none."

Yet he was vaguely troubled by his answer. He decided it was because of the news about Black Kettle being turned away from sanctuary at Fort Cobb. Well, chances were the expedition would miss the tipis of the peace chief. The Indian Territory was vast.

"Griffenstein recommended you for this campaign. You two hunted together."

"Yes, sir. We worked for Buffalo Bill Cody."

"Do you speak Cheyenne?"

"Some."

"I've got a greaser who was raised with the tribe. You can back him up." He wrote a note. "Now let's go back to your experience. How well do you know the Territory?"

"I told Milner the exact truth. I've been over part of it. Any man who claims much more than that is a liar. The whole western part has never been explored in any systematic way. The Salt Fork of the Arkansas, the Canadians—white men have seen pieces of it, that's all."

"Fair enough. I'd rather have candor than lies."

A few cursory questions, and then Custer nodded. "All right, you're on. You take orders from Milner or from me. The first time you don't, you'll be disciplined."

A muscle in Charles's jaw jumped. He knew about Custer's famous discipline. It included such illegal punishments as head-shaving, flogging, imprisonment in a pit in the ground—and then of course there was Custer's order to his subordinates to shoot deserters.

Charles's hesitation annoyed Custer. "Something unclear about what I said, Mr. Main?"

"No, sir. It's clear."

"Good," Custer said, no longer quite as friendly.

Charles took it as dismissal. Standing up, he inadvertently knocked the stack of newspapers onto the frozen ground. Retrieving them, he saw several other articles marked in ink. "You must be interested in politics, General."

Custer gave him a cold look as he stood and drew on fringed

gauntlets. "I make no secret of that. I'm watching General Grant's campaign closely, because some important people in the East have suggested I consider running for office. From a military victory to the presidency isn't such a long step, provided the victory is substantial, and gets headlines." Charles wondered how that might affect tactics on the campaign.

"Good evening, sir," Custer said, lifting the tent flap and following Charles outside. Charles's attention was caught by a man crossing the far side of the lamp-lighted headquarters area. Although his features were indistinct—light snow was falling again—his russet beard and stiff bearing were unmistakable.

The officer ducked into a tent. Custer said, "Do you know that man?"

"Unfortunately, I think so."

"If you have a grievance against him, keep it to yourself. General Sheridan is planning to join us. A number of his aides from Departmental staff are already here. Captain Venable is one of them." Pointedly, he added, "A first-rate officer. Capable and loyal."

Loyal. That word confirmed something Charles had heard before: You were Custer's admirer or you were his enemy. There was nothing between.

"Yes, sir," he said.

"You will excuse me." From the way the general turned his back, Charles knew Custer's final impression of him was poor.

Custer rode away into the dusk. The snow gathered on Charles's shoulders and hat brim. Venable. Good God. He recalled the sentry's remark about luck when he rode in. His had turned bad again.

47

He waited there on the high seat, the wagon parked close to the wall of the granary. Above him on the wall loomed a huge head, the heroic head of a soldier in uniform, bordered in red and blue with a decoration of white stars. LET US HAVE PEACE appeared in large letters in the decorative border above the head. Similarly large, the lower border said GRANT.

Cold rain poured from the night sky. Bent sat glaring at the portrait of the candidate. From time to time a shiver shook him; the November air was as bitter as January. All the residents of the tiny farm community of Grinnell were safely indoors.

From the granary came Drossel, a wad of cash in his fat hands. Drossel was a farmer for whom Bent had worked since drifting into this hamlet in Iowa late in the summer. He was smaller than Bent, an elderly but hardy man. He stepped close to the wagon, counted off bills, and handed them up. "Your wages," he said in his heavily accented English.

"Thank you, Herr Drossel." Herr and Frau Drossel addressed one another that way, with old-world formality, and he'd fallen into the habit.

The Drossels had migrated to America shortly after the political upheavals in Europe in 1848. They had found rich land in Poweshiek County, Iowa, and a promising future. They were Republicans, Lutherans; gentle, industrious people who had unquestioningly accepted Bent's assertion that he was a Union veteran traveling west in search of relatives believed to have gone to Colorado during the war. He wanted to be reunited with his family, he said. The Drossels understood that kind of quest, and the loneliness that fueled it. God had blessed them with everything but children, Frau Drossel had told him at supper on Bent's third day at the farm. Saying it, she wept, her head averted.

"The last of the crop is sold, handsomely. Our cribs are full for the winter. Follow me home, Herr Dayton. I have a special schnapps put by for this festive evening."

"Not very festive weather," Bent said, watching the roll of cash Drossel put away beneath his shabby wool coat. Drossel was portly, wore half-spectacles, and had a neat fringe of white beard running from ear to ear. His boots slopped in the mud as he walked toward a wagon parked ahead of Bent's. His mind racing, planning, Bent pointed at another poster on the granary wall. Grant's had been pasted over it, and all that was visible of it were the letters MOUR.

"I take it the Democratic candidate isn't popular in this part of Iowa?"

"Tcha," Drossel said, a kind of clicking sound. He clamped his round wool hat on his head and climbed the wheel to the seat of the first wagon. "What do we know of that Seymour? A New York governor. He might as well come from the moon. Grant, though, Grant we know. Grant is a national man. That is why he was nominated. That is why he will win."

"On his reputation," Bent said, experiencing the first turn of the awl of pain between his eyes. Pinpoint lights began to wink in his head. Military success could have carried him to the nation's highest office if only his enemies hadn't denied him an Army career.

Calm, he thought. *Stay calm.* Thinking of old wounds only reopened them. They could never be healed. All he could do was continue to extract a blood price from them. He'd done it in Lehigh Station and soon would do it again with his next, thoughtfully chosen victim.

"Herr Dayton, are you asleep?" Drossel was teasing, but with a certain Teutonic sternness. Many times during the weeks of hard labor in the cornfields, Drossel had ordered Bent to do this or do that, and Bent had almost gone for the old man's throat. Only the larger goal, the money he needed to continue his quest, overcame the strong urge to choke Drossel's orders down his throat.

"The rain is very hard. We are wasting time. Frau Drossel is waiting with a special supper."

In Bent's head, a white light-burst shaded into warm pink.

Another flashed scarlet. *That isn't all that's waiting tonight,* he thought, with a sly smile Drossel didn't see. The old man was shaking the reins over his mules, turning the wagon into the dark, away from the lights of the farming community.

The Drossels lived a half hour from Grinnell, on rolling land. There was no neighbor within two miles, and the topography made it hard to catch a glimpse of their neat white house and barns from a distance.

Once in the house, Bent changed to a dry shirt and socks in the cramped garret space up a short stair from the entrance to the Drossels' second-floor bedroom. Frau Drossel, resembling some little girl's button-eyed doll, and always prattling, brought steaming platters of schnitzel and red cabbage to the lace-covered table. Herr Drossel offered his dusty bottle of schnapps as though it were French champagne. Its hot peppermint bite soothed Bent's nerves somewhat; it warmed him and made him forget the tedious sound of the rain. Presently, the rain stopped. Bent was gratified. That would help his plan.

"We are so sorry you will be leaving, Herr Dayton," Frau Drossel said after the meal was over. "It is lonely out here. So hard to fill the long winter nights."

You'll never have to fret about filling another, Bent thought. He was barely able to grunt an answer, because his head hurt so much. When Drossel left the table, Bent noted the bulge of the cash in his pants pocket. The farmer kept the money with him as he busied about the downstairs, checking window latches, locking doors. Bent pleaded tiredness and said good night.

"Good night, Herr Dayton," Frau Drossel said, impulsively standing on tiptoe to kiss his stubbly cheek. He fought to keep from recoiling in disgust. Her weepy old eyes sickened him. "It has been so good, your company for all these weeks."

"I wish I could stay, Frau Drossel. You and your husband are like a family to me." The lights were flashing and bursting behind his eyes. His low-hanging shoulder throbbed from the damp cold. "I shall truly miss you. But life takes each one of us along a different road."

"Yes, what a pity," she exclaimed, while he envisioned the hell-bright glare at the end of her road. He nearly giggled. But he maintained his pious expression as she patted him. "But I understand that you must locate those who are dear to you."

"Yes, and I'm close now. It will be soon."

"Good night, Herr Dayton," Drossel called as Bent climbed the narrow little stair. Closing the garret door, he heard Drossel's parting remark. "You are a good man."

Instead of preparing for bed, he donned his coat again, then wrapped a long wool scarf around his neck. He pulled his valise from under the bed and examined the contents. He did it every night, a kind of superstitious ritual to guarantee success.

The rolled-up painting lay in the bottom under a few dirty garments. He groped down among the clothing until his fingers touched the teardrop earring.

Smiling, he shut the valise and snapped the clasps. From a corner shelf he took the soiled plug hat stolen to replace the one lost in Lehigh Station. He put the hat on, then drew on mittens with most of the fingertips missing. He sat fully dressed on the edge of the bed while the awl of pain bore deeper into his skull, and the imaginary lights burst and dazzled.

Below, he heard the clock in the old couple's bedroom chime half after twelve. Time.

He crept down the stairs and slowly turned the knob of their door. He opened the door, listened to the regular breathing from the two sleepers. He stepped in and shut the door, which clicked faintly. A moment later muffled cries filled the house.

The rain had passed, but a residual damp remained. Bent was shivering as he hobbled out of the dooryard of the farm. He turned left into the westbound road, a rutted mire of standing water and wet brown soil. His boots went in and out of the mud with sucking sounds.

He walked a quarter of a mile before feeling safe enough to stop and look back. He kept his left hand in his pocket, the fingers stroking and caressing the huge lump of cash taken from Herr Drossel. His excited manhood pushed against the lump from the inner side of the pocket.

"Ah—" A beatific sign. The farmhouse was no longer merely a white blur in the night. Rosy light glowed behind smoking curtains in upstairs windows. As he watched, the curtains ignited.

Bent huddled at the roadside, anticipating the delicious

sound that he heard a moment later. The old couple. Bludgeoned unconscious, then securely lashed to their bed with strips of sheet. They were waking up. Feeling the heat of the fire he'd set in the downstairs parlor. Feeling it scorch and cook the floor under their bed—the bed they couldn't escape from.

They had thought him such a *good* man. They should have learned it was dangerous to trust appearances, or take strangers at their word, in this shit-hole world.

An upper window burst, then another. Flames shot out. Behind the roar, he heard screaming.

Bent turned his back on the brilliance and crouched over his valise. From it he took the teardrop earring in its setting of filigreed gold. He passed his fingertips over the pearl several times, each time with an exquisite sexual thrill. The memory of Constance's gashed throat was vivid.

Small foamy bubbled on his lip burst as he screwed the post of the earring into his left lobe. Wearing the memento of his punishment of George Hazard pleased and amused him.

He set the plug hat on his head and hobbled westward. The bobbing pearl caught the light of the burning farmhouse; it was as if an iridescent drop of coagulated blood hung from his left ear.

Slowly the firelight receded to the horizon and he hobbled in darkness, keeping himself warm by squeezing the great lump of cash and imagining his next victim and thinking, Soon. *Soon.*

LESSON XI.

Boys at Play.

Can you fly a kite? See how the boy flies his kite.
He holds the string fast, and the wind blows it up. . . .

Boys love to run and play.

But they must not be rude. Good boys do not play
in a rude way, but take care not to hurt any one.

When boys are at play they must be kind, and not
feel cross. If you are cross, good boys will not like to
play with you.

When you fall down, you must not cry, but get up,
and run again. If you cry, the boys will call you a
baby. . . .

McGuffey's Eclectic
First Readers
1836–1844

MADELINE'S JOURNAL

October, 1868. Civil authorities can find no culprit for the
murders of May and Ridley. Why did I assume they would?
Justice might be done if the military investigated, but they
cannot. S.C. is "reconstructed." . . .

Theo bought an old ship's bell in C'ston. I rubbed off the
tarnish and nailed it up beside the front door to sound an
alarm if it's needed. We now have our own Ashley District
militia—all Negroes, most from M.R.—organized to prevent
interference at the polls. The Klan is seen frequently in the
district. Tensions remain very high. So a man stands guard
over this house each night. In a civilized country, a country at
peace, it seems unimaginable. Yet I hear the watchman pa-
trolling, his bare feet rustling the mat of pine straw on the
ground, and I know the peril is real. . . .

M-L growing listless because of her confinement here.
Her education is neglected. An unsatisfactory situation. Must
do something. . . .

November, 1868. To town, on the second-to-last day of the
campaign. Saw a soldier's parade—marching unit calling
themselves "Boys in Blue for Grant." Posters by Thos. Nast,
the N'York cartoonist, render the Gen'l. with a marble ele-
gance. But Badeau's and Richardson's campaign biographies
go begging in a bookshop.

Seymour, Grant's opponent, poorly regarded here, but
Blair, his running mate, is a darling of white citizens. Blair

calls the Reconstruction gov'ts "bastard and spurious," offers broad promises of restoring the Southern "birthright," and openly declares the white race "the only race that has shown itself capable of maintaining free institutions of a free government." No wonder Yankees say, "Scratch a Democrat and you will find a Rebel under his skin." Judith said she feared to scratch Cooper lest she learn the truth. I saw great anxiety behind the weak jest; C. is rabid for Blair. . . .

. . . All over, with no surprises. Grant is elected. In Dixie, Seymour carried only Louisiana and Georgia. So much for Blair's promises to "disperse the carpet-bag state gov'ts and compel the army to undo its usurpations." Every eligible man at M.R. voted, of which I am very proud. . . .

Theo here for supper. Left just before I sat down to write this. For the first time, he and M-L raised the subject of marriage. I do not oppose it, but she is Cooper's child. How far do I dare go to abet something sure to inflame— Must stop. Noise outside—

In single file, the riders turned into the lane from the river road. A sickle moon set white highlights flashing along the barrels of their weapons.

They proceeded slowly under the arch of trees and rode around the white house quietly. They drew up in a line at the front door. In the moonlight their shimmering robes and hoods had a black cast. The eyeholes reflected no light at all.

The horseman in the center of the line raised his old squirrel rifle. A man on his right saw the signal, scraped a match on the heel of his plow shoe, and touched it to an oil-soaked torch. The light blazed up, illuminating the half-dozen riders.

"Call her out," said the man at the extreme right of the line. He sat his horse near the lowest limbs of a huge gnarled live oak. The upper portion of the oak's trunk was all but hidden by Spanish moss. Some bird or squirrel moved there, a faint rattling. The rider on the end peered upward, saw nothing.

The man at the center of the line raised an old speaking trumpet. Suddenly the front door flew back and Madeline stepped out, her left hand rising toward the rope of the ship's bell.

"Stay," ordered the man with the trumpet and squirrel rifle. Madeline looked pale as she clutched the front of a man's cotton robe worn thin at the elbows. Behind her, the stout schoolteacher peered out, and then Marie-Louise.

"We are the knights of the Invisible Empire assembled," said the man in the center. His nervous horse shied.

Madeline startled them all by laughing. "You're little boys hiding your faces because you're cowards. I recognize your long legs, Mr. LaMotte. At least have the decency to remove that hood and act like a man."

A Klansman at the left of the line hiked up both sides of his robe and put his hands on the matched butts of revolvers. "Let's kill the damn bitch. I ain't here to debate a nigger."

The man in the center raised the squirrel rifle to quiet the speaker. To Madeline he said, "You have twenty-four hours to leave the district." The torch hissed. There was a clicking sound, a lever action putting a cartridge into a chamber, and a voice behind and to the right of the line boomed out:

"No, sir. Not just yet."

They all turned as Madeline's glance flashed to the mossy tree. A burly, round-faced black had crept into sight on a thick limb that bent under his weight. He braced his shoulders against a limb above, freeing both hands for his rifle. Madeline recognized gentle, reticent Foote; she hadn't known who was standing guard tonight.

"I think you gen'men had just better turn 'round and ride off," Foote said.

"Jesus, it's only one nigger," protested the man with twin revolvers.

"One nigger with a repeating rifle," said another of the Klansmen. "I wouldn't be hasty, Jack."

"No names," the man in the center exclaimed. Marie-Louise whispered at Madeline's shoulder:

"It *is* Mrs. Allwick's dancing teacher. I know his voice."

Madeline nodded, her lips compressed. The man in the center of the line began, "Madam—" Madeline leaped forward, shot her hand upward, and tried to snatch his hood.

His horse danced and sidestepped. He batted at Madeline with the squirrel rifle but she wouldn't be driven back. She jumped and clawed at the hood again. This time, she pulled it off. Des LaMotte's face was red with fury.

"Well. At last. The notorious Mr. LaMotte. And I have a souvenir of your visit." She held up the hood.

All of them watched her—the other two women and the Klansmen and Foote on the sagging limb. During the struggle for the hood, the Klansman with the two revolvers had drawn both of them. Still unnoticed, with everyone's attention on Madeline, he bent his right arm, laid the muzzle of his left-hand gun on it, and squeezed the trigger.

The revolver roared. The horses whinnied and bucked. Foote took the bullet in his left thigh, blown back off the limb and out of sight behind the Spanish moss. "Foote," Madeline cried, running past the horses to reach him. Before she could, the rider nearest the tree raced his mount under the lowest branches. Another roar reverberated. Madeline jerked to a halt. *"Foote!"*

"Stop that other one," shouted the Klansman with the twin revolvers. Jack Jolly tore off his hood and aimed at Prudence, who had dashed outside after the second shot. The disfiguring scar showed white on his face.

Jolly was momentarily hesitant about putting a bullet in a white woman. His hesitation allowed Prudence to seize the bell rope. LaMotte's shout went unheard in the clangorous ringing. Another man cried, "That's done it. Let's go."

Eyes glassy with confusion, LaMotte shouted at Madeline: "You have twenty-four hours. Clear out. Everything. This teacher, your nigger militia—"

Something inside Madeline broke. She ran at LaMotte's horse again, caught hold of the headstall, and yelled at him in the voice of a dock hand. "The hell I will. This is my land. My home. You're nothing but a pack of cowards dressed for a music hall. If you want me off Mont Royal, kill me. That's the only way you can get rid of me."

The horse of the Klansman at the left of the line began to stamp. LaMotte threw anxious looks at his men. Jolly was enraged. "If you're scared to kill a nigger woman, I'm not." He pointed both Leech and Rigdon's at Madeline, grinning. "Here's a one-way ticket to Hell Station on the devil's railroad."

The hooded man next to him grabbed and lifted Jolly's arms an instant before the revolvers went off. One bullet tore into the shakes of the roof. The other sped high in the dark. The Klansmen were now in panic, but scarcely more frightened than Madeline, who'd flung herself back against the whitewashed house, certain that one of the bullets would find her.

"I'll not have it," said the man who'd interfered with Jolly.

Hearing him for the first time, Madeline registered astonishment. "Father Lovewell? My God."

"I'll not sink to this," he said. Jolly turned the pistols on him. Undeterred, the hooded priest grabbed his arms again. "Stop it, Jolly. I'll not condone murdering women, even a colored—"

"You pious fucker," Jolly cried, wrenching one arm free. He aimed at Father Lovewell's hood. Again the Episcopal priest struck Jolly's arm before the revolver discharged. The bullet plowed under the belly of Father Lovewell's mare, raising a spurt of dust. Out in the dark, answering the bell, men were shouting.

Father Lovewell snatched a revolver away from Jolly. Jolly aimed his remaining gun. His skittish horse reared, forcing him to delay his shot. With both hands steadying the piece he held, Father Lovewell pulled the trigger.

Jack Jolly stood up in his saddle, then slumped forward. Blood darkened the front of his sateen robe and leaked down his mount's flank. The other Klansmen were totally disorganized; freedmen could be heard running and hallooing.

Des LaMotte looked bilious as he backed his horse and yanked its head toward the end of the house. He raced away. The other Klansmen jostled each other trying to follow. Jolly's horse galloped off last, its dead rider wobbling and bouncing and threatening to fall.

Madeline's legs felt weak. She pressed her hands against the whitewashed wall to support herself. Bitter powder smoke choked her. The torchlight faded as the Klansmen galloped down the lane.

"Are you all right? Who fired shots?" That was Andy, charging in from the road to the slave cabins.

Madeline's nerve collapsed suddenly; shock shook her. Hair straggled in her eyes as she ran toward the darkness under the tree. "Foote. Oh, poor Foote—"

Before she reached him, she had to turn away, violently sick.

At the edge of the dark marsh, by torchlight, they weighted Jack Jolly's body with stones and slid it under the water.

"They shot him, and he fell right by the house. That's the story," LaMotte said, hoarse. "We couldn't bring him out because they were swarming all over us. Don't worry, his kin will never go to Mont Royal to collect the body."

"And we aren't going back either," Father Lovewell said.

"Oh yes we are," LaMotte said. "I take the blame for what happened. I never imagined she'd have a guard posted. But I won't be whipped by a woman. A nigger woman at that. She shamed my cousins. Destroyed them—"

"Des, give it up. Father Lovewell's right." It was the first time Randall Gettys had spoken.

"If that's the kind of Southerner you are, all right," LaMotte said. His face was nearly as red as his hair. He was furious, because months of delay had culminated in a bungled night's work. But he wouldn't quit. "She's not going to stay on the Ashley and flaunt herself. She's going to die. I'll hide out a while. Then I'll go back alone if the rest of you are too yellow."

No one said anything. They threw their hissing torches into the brackish water and dispersed, leaving Jack Jolly submerged, with darting fish and frogs and a three-foot baby alligator for company. The alligator swam close to the body, opened its jaws, and with needle teeth began to feed on the face.

> We buried Foote. Cassandra inconsolable. She lost Nemo when Foote came back. Now this. Nothing I said helped. Late this afternoon, we found her gone. . . .
>
> . . . To C'ston—and not eagerly. With a cold demeanor, Cooper listened to my story, and my assertion that Prudence and his own daughter would corroborate it. He was clearly angered by M-L's proximity to danger, but he contained it—then. As for the Klan visit, he advised me curtly to drop the matter because no Carolina juryman would convict them. Further, Des's family would certainly find witnesses to prove he was elsewhere at the time. Father Lovewell's presence would never be believed, witnesses or no. The authorities can get nothing from Captain Jolly's trashy kinfolk. No doubt hearing of his involvement, they have already left their campground and vanished from the district.
>
> Cooper said he was sure there would be no more incidents. How he could be so certain, I did not know. But his tone permitted no argument. Quite suddenly, he began to harangue me about Marie-Louise. I held fast, saying she would continue to stay at Mont Royal as long as she wished. That incited a burst of ugly recriminations. Before they grew as bad as last time, I fled.

Orry, I don't know what to do. I am sick of fear, and the oppression of fear. . . .

"Yes, I understand," Jane said when Madeline expressed her feelings. "My people lived with that kind of fear for generations. But I don't know that Mr. Cooper's right about the Klan giving up. Do you remember when Mr. Hazard visited, right after the war? I said I thought there would be many more years of battle before a last victory. I still believe it."

"I could go to General Hampton. He promised to help me."

"How can he help? He hasn't any troops, has he?"

Madeline shook her head.

"I think we'd better stay on watch," Jane said. "A man like that LaMotte, he might take defeat from a person of his own class, another man, but a woman? A colored woman? I'll bet he'd lose his mind rather than let that happen."

"I think he's already lost it."

Jane shrugged, not caring to argue the point. "It isn't the last battle. He'll be back."

BOOK FIVE

WASHITA

Let us have peace.

GENERAL ULYSSES S. GRANT,
Election Campaign, 1868

As brave men and as the soldiers of a government which has exhausted its peace efforts, we, in the performance of a most unpleasant duty, accept the war begun by our enemies, and resolve to make its end final.

GENERAL SHERMAN *to*
GENERAL SHERIDAN, 1868

To proceed south, in the direction of the Antelope Hills, thence towards the Washita River, the supposed winter seat of the hostile tribes; to destroy their village and ponies; to kill and hang all warriors, and bring back all women and children . . .

GENERAL SHERIDAN *to*
GENERAL CUSTER, 1868

48

The scouts rode in, chased by four yapping dogs. Griffenstein came in, and the Corbin brothers, and a stout young Mexican interpreter who had been raised by the Cheyennes and spoke the language fluently. His name was Romero, so naturally everyone called him Romeo.

California Joe rode a mule. Observing his arrival, Charles watched him sway from side to side, blithely smiling at nothing. "Drunk as a tick," he said later to Dutch Henry. "How can Custer tolerate such a clown?"

Dutch Henry scratched the head of a terrier with a stubby wagging tail. There were now at least a dozen stray dogs around the camp. "I kinda get the impression that the only strong man Custer likes is Custer. Don't really make any difference, does it? You said you wanted to kill Cheyennes. Curly's going to do it."

November came down, skies like dark slate, winds bitter. In the camp on the north bank of the Arkansas, Custer ordered a double-up of rifle drill. Twice daily, men of the Seventh fired at targets set up at one hundred, two hundred, three hundred yards. Cooke's sharpshooters frequently dropped around to jeer and offer superior comments.

Generals Sully and Custer called a meeting of the officers and scouts to review the strategy Sheridan had conceived and gotten approved by Uncle Billy at Division. To Griffenstein, Charles whispered a question about Harry Venable, who was absent. Griffenstein said Venable was getting over a bad case of influenza.

General Sully, U.S.M.A. '41, was a bit older than Orry would have been had he lived. The general had a famous father,

Thomas Sully of Philadelphia, the painter of portraits and historical scenes; even a man like Charles, unsophisticated about art, knew Sully's heroic depictions of General Washington's passage over the Delaware.

The artist's son was a dignified sort, with the usual chest-length beard. Although he'd recently failed to find and whip any Indians south of the Arkansas, he had a first-class reputation going back to the Mexican War. He was considered an experienced Indian fighter, having chased the Sioux in the Minnesota Rebellion of '63 and driven them to refuge in the Black Hills. Charles watched Custer closely; the Boy General couldn't entirely hide his resentment of Sully. There was not room for both of them on the expedition, Charles decided.

Using maps, Sully explained that three attack columns would thrust into the Indian Territory simultaneously. A mixed infantry and cavalry column was marching east from Fort Bascom, New Mexico Territory. A second column, Fifth Cavalry troops under Brigadier Eugene Carr, would strike southeast from Fort Lyon, Colorado, toward the Antelope Hills, a familiar landmark just below the North Canadian.

The central column was Sully's, or Custer's, depending whose side you took. It was considered the main attack force. It consisted of eleven troops of the Seventh and five infantry companies from the Third, Fifth, and Thirty-eighth regiments. The column would strike due south, establish a supply base to be garrisoned by the infantrymen, then push on to trail and harry any Cheyennes or Arapahoes they found encamped in the Territory. The other two columns were like jungle beaters, Sully said, sweeping the Indians ahead of the main column. Charles discovered that all of this was made possible by some old friends of his.

"Your boys from the Tenth," Dutch Henry said after the meeting. "They're posted all along the Smoky Hill now. Wasn't for them, Custer would still be patrolling up there, 'stead of chasing glory down here. Those darkies got a damn fine reputation. Man for man, they're better soldiers than all the white rum heads and peg legs in this army. Nobody much likes to admit it, but it's true."

That brought memories of Magic Magee and Star Eyes Williams; of Old Man Barnes and Colonel Grierson. It brought a thin, pleased smile to Charles's bearded face, too. The first in some time.

One evening at the scouts' cook fire, Charles was eating a late supper when he glanced up to see a mangy yellow dog standing and watching him. Charles kept chewing his piece of jerky. The yellow dog, a stray he'd noticed before, wagged his tail and whined imploringly.

"What the hell do you want?"

On the other side of the fire, Joe Corbin laughed. "That's Old Bob. He's been roaming all over looking for a supply officer. He thinks he's found one."

"Not me," Charles said. He started to chew the jerky again. Old Bob frisked around him, wagging his tail and mewling more like a kitten than a dog. The mournful yellow-brown eyes stayed fixed on Charles. Finally Charles said, "Oh, hell," took the piece of jerky from his mouth, and threw it to the mongrel.

Old Bob was his from then on.

Charles wanted no part of the continuing schism in the Seventh Cavalry. Unfortunately, a man couldn't avoid it. Custer had plenty of enemies, and most of them talked about their feelings whether or not they were asked. One of the bitterest was a capable brevet colonel, Fred Benteen, who commanded H Troop under his actual rank of captain.

"Don't be fooled by how cool he acts, Charlie," he said once. "Underneath, he's smarting over the court-martial. Of course, the Queen of Sheba"—that was what Custer's detractors called Libbie—"keeps telling him how great he is, and innocent as a lamb. He doesn't quite believe it, though. Watch him and you'll notice he runs off to wash his hands ten, twelve, fifteen times a day. No man with a clear conscience does that. This may be Sheridan's campaign but it's Custer's game. He's playing for his reputation."

Custer had plenty of defenders, too. Cooke, of Cooke's Sharpshooters, was a strong and vocal one. So was Captain Louis Hamilton, grandson of Alexander Hamilton. Not unexpectedly, the man who usually spoke ahead of all the rest was the general's younger brother, Brevet Colonel Tom Custer, first lieutenant of D Troop. Charles listened to all the praise from the apologists and took it with appropriate cynicism.

He found one of Custer's partisans likable in spite of his blind loyalty. The man's name was Joel Elliott. He had an ingenuous manner and a reputation for heroism that no one disputed. In the war, without connections, he'd risen from private to captain. In '64, riding with the Seventh Indiana Volunteer Horse in Mississippi, he'd taken a bullet through the lung. He made a miraculous recovery, and after the surrender jumped back into service by taking the competitive officer examination. He'd scored so high, he won a majority. He was Custer's second in command, and led his own three-troop detachment. Charles formed an immediate impression that Elliott was a good soldier.

No mistaking where Elliott stood, though.

"The general's a man of impeccable character," he said. "He quit drinking and smoking years ago. He swears occasionally, but his heart's never in it."

"He wouldn't command black troops, but I've heard it said that he'll sleep with a black whore."

Elliott froze. "A lie. He's faithful to Libbie."

"Sure. She's pumping him up for president."

"Charlie, he isn't a politician, he's a soldier. The winningest soldier I've ever known. That's because he fights aggressively."

"Oh, yes, I've heard how aggressive he was," Charles said, nodding. "He led the Third Michigan to the highest casualty rate of any cavalry outfit in the Union Army."

"Doesn't that say he's a brave man?"

"Or a reckless one. One of these days he could do himself in with that kind of recklessness. His whole command, too."

"By God it better not happen on this campaign. I'm shooting for a brevet. A brevet or a coffin, nothing in between."

Charles smiled sadly at that. Elliott was so earnest. They got along because they argued without personal animosity. It was hard to remember that Joel Elliott was one of the three who'd chased and brought back the infamous quintet of deserters, three of them shot—on Custer's order.

Well, he liked Elliott in spite of it. The young officer was unpretentious, enthusiastic, and most important, a self-taught professional. You could probably depend on him to carry out orders, even bad ones, to the letter. In a hot fight, that counted for a lot.

The weather grew worse, the days dark with the threat of storms that lurked in billowing black clouds in the north. The drilling continued. Farriers tended to the animals, and issued each man a spare front and rear shoe and extra nails, to be carried in a saddle pouch.

The scouts fretted to be away. They had their own encampment, shared with another group, one Charles didn't care for—eleven Osage trackers, led by chief Hard Rope and Little Beaver. Charles disliked their eyes, hiding God knew what treacherous thoughts and schemes, and their ugly flat-nosed faces, and the way they constantly caressed and fussed over their big bows of hedge-apple wood, or came begging among the white scouts for sugar for their coffee. Indians were insane about sweet coffee. They put so much sugar in a cup that what resulted was a damp brown mound they ate rather than drank.

"Just keep them away from me," Charles said to California Joe Milner, whose real name was Moses, not Joe, he'd discovered. Hard Rope had approached Charles—"Me need sugar" was the best English he could manage—and Charles told him to go to hell. California Joe had called him down.

"You got to ride with 'em, Main."

"I'll ride with them. I don't have to be social."

California Joe was in his cups, and pliable. "Well, if that's how it is, that's how it is, I guess," he said.

Charles tended to his gear, curried Satan and fed him extra forage, scrounged scraps for Old Bob, and waited. At the end of the first week of November, the clouds cleared away. Everyone took it as a sign that they'd march soon.

Charles was ready. He felt fit, missed his son, thought of Willa more than was good for him—remembering her was melancholy and painful—and deemed it wisdom, not cowardice, to avoid Handsome Harry Venable.

Inevitably, running messages for Milner, he saw Venable around the encampment at various times, from a distance. On each occasion he managed to walk or ride away quickly. Of course, he knew a confrontation was certain one of these days.

On November 11, the camp stirred with the excitement of new orders. Next day, they marched.

The huge, noisy advance started at daybreak. It was a spectacle unlike any Charles had seen since the war. The supply train carrying winter clothing, food, and forage had grown to four hundred fifty white-topped wagons, an immense cavalcade split into four columns traveling abreast. Two companies of the Seventh rode in front, two formed a rear guard, and the rest were divided to ride wide and protect the flanks of the train. The infantry was assigned to march near the wagons but everyone expected that the lazy foot soldiers would soon be hitching rides, which proved to be the case.

Sully and some other officers took the south bank of the Arkansas while the first of the wagons lumbered in and splashed across. So many wagons, their teamsters swearing and popping whips, created a colossal din, augmented by trumpet calls and the creak of horse gear and the lowing of the beef cattle pushed along between the wagons and the flanking cavalry.

Spruce and boisterous, Custer rode with his point detachment, avoiding Sully. Charles saw Custer on his prancing horse on the north bank, the Seventh's standard, with its fierce eagle clutching sharp golden arrows, unfurled in the wind behind him. The Seventh's mounted bandsmen played "The Girl I Left Behind Me" as accompaniment for the fording.

The land directly south of the river was a kind Charles had seen with Wooden Foot Jackson: a scoured waste of sand hills cut by dry gulches. Travel for the wagons was slow and difficult. Axles snapped. Coupling poles split. The teamsters whipped their mules and oxen pitilessly but fell behind. The mounted soldiers soon drew away, leaving a great billowing rampart of dust in their wake.

Charles, Dutch Henry, and two of the Osages galloped ahead and sited a camp on Mulberry Creek, barely five miles from their departure point. Sully and Custer jointly decided they would go no farther the first day because the wagons were having so much trouble.

In camp, after Charles ate a supper of beans and hardtack, his luck ran out again.

Stiff from being in the saddle all day, he fed Satan and blanketed him against the night chill. He was walking back toward the scout camp when he saw a familiar figure striding down a low knoll on a path that would intersect his. Captain Harry Venable looked neat and unwrinkled after the day's march. The eternal prairie wind lifted his overcoat cape as he stepped in front of Charles.

"Main," he said curtly. His eyes were even bluer, more glacial than Custer's. "Or should I say May? August, perhaps? Which is it this time?"

"I expect you know."

"I do. I spotted you a week ago. I know you saw me. I thought that in light of past circumstances you might be smart enough to get the hell away from this expedition."

"Why? I'm not in uniform. California Joe hired me."

"You're still under Army jurisdiction."

Old Bob, following Charles as he usually did, went up to Venable to sniff. Venable kicked at him. Bob crouched and growled. Charles whistled the dog back to his side. Old Bob obeyed but kept growling.

"Look, Venable, General Custer knows that I rode for the Confederacy. He doesn't object."

"By Christ *I* do." Venable's russet beard jutted; his face was nasty. Old Bob growled louder. Venable stepped forward. "You reb son of a bitch!"

Charles reacted by shoving his palm hard against Venable's dark blue overcoat. "Take your complaints to the general."

Venable surprised Charles by relaxing, stepping away. A puzzling smile drifted onto his face. "Oh, no. I haven't said a word about our past encounters, and I won't. I want you to myself this time. Pounding your dumb skull at Jefferson Barracks didn't discourage you, and neither did a discharge after you lied your way into the Tenth. I'm going to find something that works. Something permanent."

"Fuck you," Charles said. "Come on, Bob."

Venable ran after him, but Old Bob's growl brought him up short. "It's your job to keep your eyes on the trail ahead," Venable called. "But just remember, I'll be watching your back, every minute."

The threat bothered Charles more than he cared to admit. He wanted to tell someone. He drew Dutch Henry away from the other scouts around the fire and in a few words described the run-in, concluding, "So if you find me shot in the back, get that damn Yankee."

Dutch Henry looked baffled. "Why's he got it in for you?"

"Because of what John Hunt Morgan did to his mother and sister. I'm not responsible for it, for God's sake."

The burly scout gave him a peculiar look, his eyes flecked with points of light from the blazing campfire. "No, and the

Injuns we're chasing probably didn't chop up your partners. But you're going to kill them anyway."

"Henry, that's—"

"Different? Mmmm. if you say so. Come on back to the fire, Charlie. It's too damn cold to stand here palavering."

He stumped off toward the wind-tattered flames, leaving Charles motionless, staring after him with a curious strained look on his face. Almost a look of confusion.

On November 13 they advanced to Bluff Creek, where Custer had rejoined the regiment when he came out of exile in Michigan. They made Bear Creek the following day, and the Cimarron, and the Indian Territory, the day after that. There, a winter norther tore down on them, providing a wicked foretaste of the season to come.

Heading east along the Beaver fork of the North Canadian, they still found no trace of hostiles. A day later that changed. Charles and the Corbins discovered a ford with signs of many ponies having passed, but no travois. A war party. They galloped back toward the main body to report:

"Anywhere from seventy-five to one hundred fifty braves, trailing in a northeasterly direction."

"To attack settlements, Mr. Main?" General Sully asked. He'd gathered officers and scouts in his big headquarters tent. The lanterns illuminated faces beginning to show beard stubble, trail dirt, fatigue. Venable lounged at the back. He folded his arms, a signal he distrusted anything Charles might say.

"I don't know any other reason they'd be headed away from Indian Territory in the winter, General."

Custer stepped forward, almost quivering in anticipation of a fight. Was it accidental that he moved in front of Sully, partially hiding him from the others? "How old is the sign?" he wanted to know.

Jack Corbin said laconically, "Two days, most."

"Then if we strike out in the other direction, where they came from, we might find their village with most of the men gone. We could take them by surprise."

"General Custer," Sully said with weighted irony, "that's absurd. Do you for one moment suppose that a military force as large as ours, accompanied by such an immense train of wagons, could have gotten this far into Indian country and remain undetected? They know we're here."

Instead of arguing, Custer said, "What do you think, Main?"

Charles didn't like the unexpected and unsubtle shift of responsibility, but there was no point in feeding Sully's lies, whether he got offended or not. "I think it's entirely possible no one knows we're here. The Indians don't move much this late in the season. That war party has to be an exception. They assume we wouldn't move either."

"You see?" Custer exclaimed to Sully. "Let me take a detachment—"

"No."

"But look here—"

"Permission denied," Sully said.

Custer shut up, but no one in the tent missed the rush of red in his cheeks, or his glare of resentment. Nor did he intend that they should. Charles figured Sully had blundered in a way he would regret.

"My partner, Jackson, said a white man has to turn his notions upside down out here," Charles remarked to Griffenstein after the conference broke up. "Sully won't do it. Same old Army." He sighed.

Charles and the scouts ranged south, hunting for a suitable location for the supply base. They found one about a mile above the confluence of Wolf and Beaver creeks, which joined to form the North Canadian. There was timber, good water, and abundant game. At noon on the eighteenth of November, the forward detachments of the Seventh reached the site.

Charles, Milner, and the other scouts rode into the woods for game while the infantry fell to chopping trees for a stockade. Additional parties of men began digging wells and latrine trenches, or scything down the frost-killed meadow grass for forage.

Charles flushed a flock of wild turkeys and bagged three with his Spencer. California Joe, temporarily sober, killed a buffalo cow but lost a dozen more that stampeded at the first shot. Most of the scouts brought in a kill of some kind. The expedition would eat better tonight.

Camp Supply rose quickly, a stockade one hundred twenty-six feet on a side, with lunettes at two corners, loopholed block-houses at the other two. Log palisades protected the west and south sides; barrackslike storage buildings served as the north and east walls. The men had pitched their tents outside; the wagons unloaded inside. The expedition had stretched its supply line a distance of one hundred miles from Fort Dodge.

Charles heard that Custer and Sully were arguing almost continuously. Custer was still furious with his rival.

An advance party of white scouts and Kaw trackers appeared in the north, heralding the arrival of General Sheridan and his three-hundred-man escort from the Nineteenth Kansas Volunteer Cavalry. Custer saddled up and galloped out to greet the Departmental commander. By nightfall, Little Phil was stumping around the camp, shaking hands and grousing obscenely about the fierce norther and howling sleet storm that had plagued his rapid march from Fort Hays. Sheridan was squat and thickly built, with black eyes and a pointed Mongol mustache. Charles had never seen a New York Bowery bartender, but Little Phil fit his mental picture.

Later in the evening, reclining by the scout fire with Old Bob curled up against his belly, asleep, Charles heard music. He recognized "Marching Through Georgia."

"What the hell's going on, Henry?"

"Why, I'm told old Curly sent his bandsmen to lighten General Sheridan's evening with a serenade. Don't you recognize that tune?" He smirked. "The title should be 'Farewell, General Sully.'"

That was the sixth day after departure from the camp on the Arkansas. General Sheridan took personal charge of the expedition, and then Sully and his staff left suddenly for his headquarters at Fort Harker. It wasn't hard to tell which commander Little Phil had backed in the dispute over rank.

Quartermasters began issuing overcoats lined with buffalo hide, high canvas leggings, and fur mittens and caps to the men of the Seventh. Sheridan ordered Custer and his eleven troops to prepare to march before daylight on the morning of November 23.

The issuing of rations and ammunition continued all night. Horses were inspected and questionable ones replaced. Custer cut a new one, Dandy, from the remuda. The best teams were matched with the soundest wagons, which were loaded with provisions for thirty days.

After dark, a peculiar stillness settled over Camp Supply. Charles had experienced a similar quiet before Sharpsburg, and several times in Virginia. In these last hours before a campaign began in earnest, a man liked to be alone with himself and his Bible or the pencil he used to write a farewell letter to be left behind, just in case. Charles wrote such a note for Duncan to read to little Gus. He was sealing it when Dutch Henry stomped into the tent they shared.

"Guess what we got outside."

"The usual. The wind."

"More'n that now." He held the flap open. Charles saw a slantwise pattern of white. "She's piling up fast. They said it'd be a winter war. Damned if they were fooling."

Old Bob snored now and then, but Charles couldn't sleep. He was already bundled in his gypsy robe, waiting impatiently, when the trumpeters played reveille at 4:00 A.M.

He made sure his compass was secure in a pocket—not even the Osages knew much about the country south of Camp Supply —and stepped outside while Dutch Henry yawned himself awake. The wind howled. Snow pelted his exposed flesh. A drift in front of the tent measured six inches. Not an auspicious start.

Likewise awake early, General Custer sent for Dandy, and with the staghounds Maida and Blucher loping after him, rode alone over to the headquarters encampment. He was greeted by darkness and silence. Everyone was still sleeping.

Not daunted, he called for General Sheridan. Presently Little Phil emerged from his tent, two blankets clutched over his long underwear. An orderly lighted a lantern while Custer patted his fretful horse. The snow blew almost horizontally. With his sleep-slitted eyes, Sheridan resembled a Chinese.

"What do you think of this storm, General?" Sheridan asked.

"Sir, I think nothing could serve our purpose better. We can move. The Indians will not. If the snow lasts a week, I'll bring you some scalps."

"I'll be waiting," said Little Phil, returning the salute of his eager commander.

The trumpets sounded the advance. As usual, the scouts were first, horses struggling to step through the mounting drifts. The wind screamed. It was hard to hear anything else, and the earflaps of Charles's muskrat cap only made matters worse. He had been astounded to see a journalist who'd arrived with Sheridan, a Mr. DeBenneville Keim, climb aboard one of the supply wagons, now lost in the darkness behind the scouts. Perhaps Custer had persuaded the reporter that the expedition would achieve some noteworthy results.

He thought he heard his name. He lifted the left flap of his cap. "What's that?"

"I said," Dutch Henry yelled, "we got an observer from Sheridan's staff. He's right back yonder with old Curly. Guess who."

In the snow-lashed darkness, Charles imagined Venable's eyes and, despite the temperature, felt a hot prickle down his back.

49

When the day dawned, the world stayed white. Charles tied a scarf around the lower part of his face but needles of snow still broke painfully against his exposed skin. The incessant moaning and crying of the storm wore on his nerves.

Soon a snow crust built up on his eyebrows. Satan snorted and struggled through deepening drifts. Snow on the horse's back would shiver and blow away, only to be thick again in a few minutes. Looking to the rear, Charles could see nothing, though he heard men back there. One of them shouted that the teamsters, already a mile behind with their foundering wagons, were still losing ground.

Griffenstein dropped back to ride beside him. The two tried to exchange comments about the storm. The strain on their throats wasn't worth it. Each man held a mitten near his face, stiffened fingers curled to give some protection to their only reliable guides in the blizzard, the little needles of their pocket compasses. The compasses kept them headed south.

By 2:00 P.M. Custer ordered a halt for the day. The column was strung along the valley of Wolf Creek, which Charles estimated as no more than fifteen miles from their departure point. Horses and men were as blown out as if they'd marched twice that distance. No one knew if they'd see the wagons again.

Stands of timber bordered the frozen creek; around the trunks the drifts were five and six feet high. Among the leafless trees, Charles spied large dark shapes, motionless, very like statues placed in the wilderness by some crazed sculptor. The statues proved to be buffalo standing with their heads down while the storm raged. Only the noise of men wielding axes roused them and started them staggering away. Marksmen brought down three.

Like ants on a white sand beach. Charles and the other scouts moved through a snowy grove. They dug up fallen limbs protruding from drifts, or cut smaller volunteer trees among the bigger ones; they would at least have fires for warmth, even if they got no food from the lost wagons.

Charles and Dutch Henry piled up their wood and went to feed their mounts on the picket line. Satan acted famished; he finished his small ration of oats so greedily, Charles thought the piebald might chew off his fingers.

Next, mostly using their hands, they dug out snow to create their campsite. When they had the snow down to two or three inches, they stomped it to pack it; it was the best floor they were going to get. Of course as soon as they pitched their two-man tent and started a fire outside, the tent floor melted and soaked their blankets.

As the night lowered, Charles heard heavy creakings and poppings—the wagons and their drivers' whips. General Custer went riding past in the storm, Maida and Blucher loping behind.

Custer's cheeks were red as blistered skin.

"*. . . want to see every last one of those damn malingering teamsters in twenty minutes in my . . .*"

The general vanished behind a tossed-up cloud of snow. Charles had never seen him in such a bad temper, or heard him curse.

Old Bob, who'd kept up pretty well all day, seemed to know it was a night of misery. He stayed close to Charles, nuzzling his canvas leggings and whining.

They unpacked their skillets, unfolded the handles, melted some snow, and boiled salt pork. Several pieces of hardtack, softened by sticking them in a drift, went into the pork grease and fried up nicely. That and coffee provided a passable meal, though Charles was still frozen, and chafed raw by the rubbing of his layers of clothing. He kept reminding himself of why he was here. He pictured each member of the Jackson Trading Company as he last saw him.

Captain Fred Benteen stomped by, muttering, "Goddamn idiot."

"Who?" Charles asked.

"The general. Do you know what he just did?"

"What?" Griffenstein asked, in a tone that said a mass execution wouldn't surprise him.

"Arrested all the teamsters for being so slow. Tomorrow they're forbidden to ride in their wagons. They have to walk. We won't have any wagons after that."

He went away into the falling snow. Old Bob whined, and Charles rubbed his muzzle and fed him a morsel of boiled pork. From that moment, a formless uneasiness about the expedition began to trouble him. It had nothing to do with the presence of Harry Venable.

Because of Charles's reb background, he was something of a curiosity. Young Louis Hamilton, the likable captain in command of A Troop, brought the journalist around after dark. He introduced him as a phonographic reporter representing the *New York Herald*.

DeBenneville Keim was eager to talk to Charles. Charles didn't reciprocate, but he poured him a tin cup of coffee to be hospitable. Keim drank some, then pulled a small, worn book from his coat. The title was stamped in gold on the spine. *After the War.*

"I've been reading Whitelaw Reid, Mr. Main. You were in South Carolina when Sumter fell. Tell me what you think of this passage about Sullivan's Island."

He handed Charles the book. Reid was a nationally famous Union correspondent who had written field dispatches under the name "Agate." He'd been one of the first three journalists into Richmond. Charles blinked several times as melting snowflakes dripped water from his eyebrows onto the page and read:

> *Here, four years ago, the first fortifications of the war were thrown up. Here the dashing young cavaliers, the haughty Southrons who scorned the Yankee scum, rushed madly into the war as into a picnic. Here the boats from Charleston landed every day cases of champagne, pâtés innumerable, casks of claret, thousands of Havana cigars, for the use of the luxurious young Captains and Lieutenants. Here, with feasting, and dancing, and love making, with music improvised from the ball room, and enthusiasm fed to madness by well-ripened old Madeira, the free-handed, free-mannered young men who had ruled "society" at Newport and Saratoga, dashed into revolution as they would into a waltz. . . .*

Keim put a red-ruled notebook on his knee. The pages were filled with the squiggles of phonography, a journalist shorthand. "It's a vivid picture. Was that really how it was?"

A vast sadness rose in Charles. He thought of poor Ambrose Pell. "Yes, but not for very long. And it's all gone now. It'll never come back."

He snapped the book shut and thrust it at Keim. Something strange and bleak on his face forestalled any more questions; Keim directed them to Dutch Henry instead. Charles rubbed Old Bob to silence his growling.

Next day the march resumed, the punished teamsters struggling along on foot. The storm abated. The clouds cleared, but that created another difficulty. The glare of sun on the drifted snowfields was unmerciful on the eyes.

They advanced in a southwesterly direction, following the Wolf, which enabled Charles to put his compass away. He rode well in front with several of the Osages, who kept giving him uneasy stares because he sang to himself, in a raspy near-monotone:

> *"The old sheep done know the road,*
> *The old sheep done know the road,*
> *The old sheep done know the road . . .*
> *The young lamb must find the way."*

"Where'd you learn that?" Dutch Henry inquired.

"The nigras on the sea islands back home sing it. Church song."

"You make it sound like we're goin' to a funeral."

"I just have a funny feeling about this, Henry. A bad feeling."

"Well, you wanted to be here."

"That I did." Charles shrugged; maybe he was a damn fool. But the uneasiness stayed.

The route of march was planned to take them upstream to a point where they could strike southward to the Antelope Hills near the North Canadian. The bed of Wolf Creek soon turned in a more westerly direction. Once again exhausted from breaking through so many high drifts, and half blinded by a sun not warm enough to melt the snow significantly, they staggered into another campsite on bluffs above the creek. Charles heard that one of the teamsters had pulled a pistol on Curly, who kicked his balls, disarmed him single-handed, and ordered him flogged with knotted rope. Griffenstein said Custer had summoned the phonographic reporter and ordered him not to write a word about the punishment if he wanted to continue with the expedition.

"Kind of stupid to offend a reporter that way, don't you think, Charlie?"

"Not if you're watching your ass. Not if you want to run for President someday."

In the morning they bore away from their westerly course and advanced due south. Here and there a few dark patches of woodland showed on the horizon, like charcoal smears on a clean sheet of drawing paper. Some topography was apparent despite the great amount of snow. From the Wolf, the prairie sloped upward slightly to a ridge line or divide. By afternoon they were on the downward side. They encamped that night about a mile north of the Canadian.

Charles and California Joe did a sweep along the river, which was still flowing very rapidly, considerably over its banks. Massive ice chunks came swirling down with the current. They located a ford that looked passable. More sober than Charles had ever seen him, Joe Milner cautiously walked his mule across it. Suddenly he sank six inches.

"Quicksand. Well, they ain't any other place to cross. She'll have to do."

After he struggled out, they returned and reported. Custer seemed satisfied. Dutch Henry said Major Elliott had already left with three troops, and no wagons, to range up the valley of the Canadian in search of Indians. The Corbin brothers and several of the Osages had gone with Elliott. Dutch Henry finished his remarks with a reminder that tomorrow, Thursday, would be Thanksgiving.

Charles didn't care very much. It was a Northern holiday, and no Army cooks would be serving the traditional big dinner in this frozen wasteland.

Quicksand, icy water, dangerous ice chunks that smashed wheel spokes and lamed two horses caused the Canadian crossing to take more than three hours early on Thanksgiving Day. Every trooper, civilian, and Indian was soggy and dispirited when it was over, but they perked up at the sight of the Antelope Hills straight ahead. Reaching these familiar formations proved they hadn't wandered aimlessly.

The five clustered hillocks were anywhere from one hundred fifty to three hundred feet high. Two were conical, three oblong, and from the highest there was a magnificent view of the country: the twisty Canadian behind and, ahead, a vista of snowfields that seemed to roll on and on forever.

Early in the afternoon, shouts signaled the approach of a rider coming in from the direction Elliott's column had taken. Trumpeters summoned the officers and scouts to Custer's marquee, where there was a great state of excitement. Maida and Blucher leaped and yapped. Custer struck each dog lightly with a riding crop, and they made no more noise.

"Repeat it for those who just got here, Jack," Custer said.

"Major Elliott's about twelve miles or so up the north bank," Jack Corbin said. "There's a crossing, and sign aplenty. 'Bout one hundred fifty hostiles passed over, going a little east of south. The sign ain't more than a day old."

Charles's fingers started to tingle. Excited murmurs greeted the news, and Custer's blister-red face fairly beamed. Handsome Harry Venable, whose hostile looks didn't faze Charles any longer, stated the obvious:

"If we keep on and they do, they'll cross our trail ahead of us. Maybe today."

"Aye God," California Joe said, reeling slightly from some recent refreshment. "It's Thanksgiving Day, and we got Custer's Luck."

Some of the sycophantic officers went "Hear, hear!" and clapped. The anti-Custer men, including Benteen, glowered. Custer himself looked renewed; he couldn't stand still.

"I want the men ready in twenty minutes for a night march. No tents, no blankets. One hundred rounds per man, a little coffee and hardtack, and that's all. We'll take seven wagons and one ambulance. The rest of the baggage train stays here with one troop and the officer of the day. Where is he?"

"Here, sir." Captain Louis Hamilton stepped forward. He looked unhappy. "I beg the general's permission to go with the detachment. I'll bet those damn Indians are close to their lair, and we're going to find it."

"I commend your enthusiasm, Hamilton. I share it." By now Custer was fairly dancing around the marquee. His blood was up, and so was that of almost everyone else. Charles wondered why, after so many months of yearning for revenge, he didn't share the excitement.

Custer continued: "If you can find a substitute in twenty minutes, you're welcome to ride with us."

"Yes, sir," Hamilton exclaimed, like a boy given a handful of candy. He dashed out without bothering to salute. Everyone laughed.

To Jack Corbin, Custer said: "Can you get back to Major Elliott?"

"With a fresh horse I can, General."

"Tell him to continue the pursuit with all vigor. We should intersect with him about dark. Tell him to expect that."

Corbin hurried away. Custer dismissed the others. There was a huge push to leave the marquee. Dutch Henry fairly exploded with good humor. "I think we're gonna get what we come for, Charlie."

The advance sounded in twenty minutes precisely. The designated force, eleven troops and Cooke's Sharpshooters, struck south again through high drifts. Hamilton was along; an officer suffering partial snow blindness had agreed to take charge of the wagons.

The weather had moderated a little; the drifts were melting. In a couple of hours, Hard Rope and another Osage galloped back past Charles, shouting in pidgin, *"Me find. Me find."* Dutch Henry eyed the trail ahead. Charles nudged Satan to follow the big man's horse. Several of the stray dogs frolicked along too, leaping and barking.

It was a find, all right. Clear sign of the Indian party, as big as Corbin said, with no marks of travois. Braves, then. On a last raid or hunt. The trail continued on through the level, treeless country in a southeasterly direction.

Now there was impromptu singing as they advanced—"Jine the Cavalry" and other Army ditties. Everyone felt warmer, and they had the prospect of an engagement, not just an endless advance through snow. Old Bob kept jumping in the air. He barked almost constantly.

Toward the end of the day the land began to change again. From the level prairie, it sloped slightly downward in a long descent to a horizon-spanning stand of misty timber still miles away. Custer sent Griffenstein ahead with orders to find Elliott and stop his advance until the main column caught up. Elliott was to choose a rendezvous where there was running water and a supply of wood.

Charles judged it to be about five in the afternoon when they reached the edge of the timber. His belly gurgled and contracted painfully. He was sure Satan was just as hungry; none of the horses had eaten anything since 4:00 A.M., hours ago, and Charles had munched only a piece of hardtack, which nearly broke a tooth before he got it softened with spit. He realized that the advance had become one of Custer's ruthless forced marches.

On and on they rode through the mazy timber. Darkness came, and renewed cold. The mushy drifts froze into a hard crust that crackled at each step the horses took; the night seemed alive with a sound like musketry. The dogs barked, sabers clinked, men cursed as the march went on past seven o'clock.

Past eight.

About 9:00 P.M., Charles saw an orange glow ahead. He circled a dark tree trunk and discerned several similar glows. He speeded Satan past the Osages to an expanse of treeless ground. A sentry leaped up to challenge him and Charles shouted, "General Custer's column. Is this Elliott?"

"Yes, we're here."

"We found them," he called over his shoulder. He heard cheering.

Major Elliott's three troops were resting along the steep sides of a stream. Taking advantage of the natural cover the banks afforded, small cooking fires were blazing on the south side. The column prepared to dismount and rest. The air of festivity reminded him of those first blithe days Whitelaw Reid described.

Captain Harry Venable went riding along the line with the good news: "One hour. Saddles and bits off the horses."

The time seemed to fly. Charles dragged the horse furniture off his piebald, dried him as well as he could, and fed him the oats he was carrying. He fed Dutch Henry's mount too, while his friend heated some coffee. That and hardtack was their sumptuous Thanksgiving feast.

At ten sharp, the advance resumed without trumpet calls. Four abreast, the cavalrymen began to move down the steep bank, through the stream and up the other side. The snowfields glittered with a diamond liveliness; a brilliant moon shone.

Little Beaver and another Osage led the column on foot. Because of the noise, the gunshot crackle of the snowcrust, the trackers stayed four hundred yards ahead of the first large group of riders which included the other Osages and the white scouts, all of whom were in single file. Custer rode with this group, surrounded by the noisy dogs.

Charles walked Satan toward what appeared to be a large stump about five feet high. He was startled when the stump moved. Little Beaver had waited for them to catch up.

"Village," he said.

Custer heard. "What's that?" he exclaimed.

"Village near."

"How far?"

"Don't know. But there *is* a village."

There were aspects of Indian tracking so entangled in mystery and second sight that Charles never tried to understand them. Gray Owl had displayed some of the same intuitions, and whites were foolish to disregard them. Custer didn't.

"Very good, Little Beaver. Back to your place. And quietly, quietly." In the dark they heard a couple of troopers laughing and joshing. Custer wheeled out of line, almost trampling a couple of the dogs. Charles saw his blade-nosed profile against the dark moonlit sky. "No talking. From now on, I'll cut down any man who speaks."

Charles had no doubt he'd do it. His nerves tightened up a notch. The uneasy feeling worsened. The advance continued, the black snake of horses and riders crawling over the moonlit snow without the wagons or the ambulance; Custer had left them behind with Quartermaster Lieutenant Bell.

They seemed to be in a region of ridges that ran east and west, parallel to one another, with narrow valleys between. Saddles creaked. The snow crackled. Far away, a wolf howled; another answered. Once Charles looked back and was almost deluded into seeing buffalo sitting upright on the horses. The bulky overcoats of the troopers created the illusion.

Again they came on the two Osages waiting for the main column. "Smell fire," Little Beaver announced.

Custer controlled Dandy after the horse nearly stepped on Blucher. "I don't."

"Fire," the Indian insisted.

"Go see. Griffenstein, Main, go with him. Arm yourselves."

Charles peeled off his mittens. He yanked the scarf from his face so he could lick his lips, stiff as wood and lacerated by painful cracks. He reached over his shoulder and pulled the Spencer from the sling. With Little Beaver striding between them, the two white men walked their horses across another snowy expanse to some widely spaced trees.

"There's something," Charles exclaimed softly. He pointed to an orange smudge, smaller and dimmer than those spied when they found Elliott. Dutch Henry drew both his revolvers and cocked them. Charles held his Spencer ready.

Black wraiths breathing small clouds of transparent mist into the moonlight, the scouts walked their horses into the trees. Charles smelled the smoke distinctly. A fire, all but gone out, built in the lee of some thorny shrubs.

Satan smelled something strange and didn't like it. Charles patted the piebald to quiet him. When he stirred the fire with a stick, the embers billowed; the light helped him see the ground roundabout. It was a churned mess of snow and mud. He stepped in a barely hardened pod of manure. The aroma mingled with that of the fire.

"A pony herd tried to graze here most of the day, Henry. I'd stake my life that this fire was built by the boys tending the ponies."

"So we can't be but two, three miles from the village?"

"That's right. But whose village?"

"Does it make any damn difference?"

The question threw him. The uneasiness returned. Little Beaver began a shuffling dance step, mumbling and chanting under his breath. He sensed engagement soon.

"I'll give the general the good news," Dutch Henry said, turning his horse's head.

Custer sent the two scouts forward again, walking. Charles's mouth felt like a dry gully. His pulsebeat leaped in his throat so hard it almost hurt. Where the trees thinned out, the moon shone on a strip of snowy ground with a sharply defined irregular edge.

"Careful. That looks like a drop-off," Dutch Henry warned.

Belly down, they crept on the edge. A slope sheered away; difficult for horses, though not impossible.

They were gazing out on a shallow river valley. "Got to be the Washita," Dutch Henry said. The river ran right below, silver in the moonlight, chuckling at them. Its course was roughly east and west. About two miles east, to their left, the river looped to the north and disappeared behind a spur of the hills.

Beyond some open ground on the river's far side, a dark mass suggested more heavy timber. Little else could be seen despite the brilliant moon and incredible display of stars in the heavens. Charles sniffed. He and Dutch Henry both smelled the smoke from across the river.

Over in the timber, a dog barked. Charles's hair almost stood on end. A few seconds later he heard the wail of a baby.

"Can't see the lodges from up here," Dutch Henry said. "Maybe if I get lower, I can count 'em against the sky."

He scrambled down the slope, leaving Charles with the thickening smell of smoke in his nostrils. A tinkling bell suddenly showed him the pony herd, a darker mass of shadow that flowed away behind the timber.

Shortly, Griffenstein came scrambling up again. "We got 'em," he whispered. "The tipis are back in those cottonwoods. Right around fifty of 'em. Let's go."

While they stole away Charles thought, *Fifty. But whose are they?*

Custer tilted the face of his pocket watch toward the moon. "About three and a half hours till dawn. We'll go in them. Main, gather the officers on the double."

They were together within minutes. Quickly, Custer revealed that they'd tracked the war party to its base, which the column would attack at first light. Charles could hear the excitement that generated. Venable even forgot about giving him intimidating stares.

With unconcealed enthusiasm, Custer improvised his plan on the spot. He split his seven hundred effectives into four detachments, three to support the main one, which would lead the attack from the bluff where Charles and Griffenstein had observed the village. One of the detachments would advance at the sound of band music. Elliott's and Thompson's detachments were to start toward their positions immediately.

"The men remaining here may dismount until it's time to move forward. They may not speak above a whisper. There is to be no other noise. They may not walk around, and even if they're freezing to death, they're not to stamp their feet. No matches are to be lit for pipes or cigars. Any man who disobeys will answer to me personally. Venable, do me a favor. Take Maida and Blucher to the rear and give them to Sergeant Major Kennedy to hold until we advance."

Venable didn't like this odd, menial duty, but he didn't argue. He whistled softly. The staghounds, well trained, leaped to follow him. Custer's fringed gauntlet swept over the other dogs hanging around near the officers. "Main, you and Griffenstein kill these strays."

Charles felt as though a picket pin had been hammered into his head. "What, sir?"

"You heard me. We want surprise on our side. These dogs could give us away. Get rid of them, and right now."

Charles stared and Custer gave it right back, his eyes like black skull-sockets in the gloom. Dutch Henry laid a mitten on Charles's shoulder, either to soothe him or restrain him. Captain Hamilton got things going, ordering a couple of lieutenants: "Bring up some ropes. We'll muzzle them before we do it."

Charles jumped at Old Bob, intending to pick him up and run him to the rear. Custer snapped, "No. I said every one of them."

"I won't do it."

Custer gave him a long look. "Turning tender-hearted, are we? Get over it before we attack the village." He stalked off, his tiny gold spurs winking in the moonlight.

"Get away from here. Don't watch," Dutch Henry whispered.

The lieutenants rushed up with ropes. The men surrounded the dogs, ten in all, and after some struggle and a couple of chases to catch runaways, got them all muzzled and leashed. Charles, meantime, walked into the woods and leaned his forearm against a tree trunk, his face turned toward the village. Then a frantic yelping, though the muzzles controlled its volume. The yelping continued for a while, and so did the sound of frantic claws tearing the crusted snow. Charles didn't know who cut the throat of Old Bob, but he saw the limp yellow body in the redolent heap with all the others. He walked past it quickly. The air was nearly cold enough to freeze the bitter tears in his eyes.

The flanking detachment began to move out in order to get in position by daylight. Those in the main column had a chance for a little more rest. The moonlit snow resembled a strange park of military statues. Motionless soldiers, stood, sat, or lay by their horses. Every man held a rein. A few wrapped their caped coats around their heads and tried to sleep. Most were too tense.

Some of the officers huddled together, looking stout in their heavy overcoats. They whispered with suppressed excitement. Jack Corbin's pony began to stamp and whinny. Corbin couldn't control him. Charles stepped over and pinched the pony's nostrils shut and held them until the pony quieted down. Another Cheyenne trick Jackson had taught him. Corbin whispered his thanks.

Charles crouched beside Satan, passing the rein from hand to hand. Something in him felt wrong, dangerously explosive. California Joe replenished his liquid courage from his seemingly limitless supply of demijohns. He passed the jug to Dutch Henry, who watched for officers, then drank swiftly. Milner offered the jug to Charles. Charles shook his head.

"You don't seem exactly raring to go," California Joe remarked. "Should be a right lively scrap. 'F we hang on to our edge and surprise 'em, we shouldn't have much trouble, either. I thought that's what you wanted. I thought that's why you signed on. Cheyenne Charlie, just bustin' to kill him some—"

"Shut up," Charles said. "Just leave me alone or I'll ram that jug down your throat."

He stood up, walked away. " 'S got into him?" California Joe asked.

Dutch Henry could only shrug.

As the moon descended behind the timber, a thick ground fog began to boil up and spread, creating an eerie effect. Custer kept opening his pocket watch and snapping it shut. Finally, it was time. He tucked the watch away and pushed down the ivory-handled butts of his Webley Bulldog pistols to snug them in the holsters. He issued his last orders. Haversacks to be dropped. Overcoats and sabers to be left behind. No firing until he gave the signal.

Feeling heavy, filthy, tired, Charles swung his right leg over

Satan. Custer saw that the column was formed, summoned his trumpeter up beside him, and started to walk Dandy forward through the trees. The ground fog stirred and eddied around the animal's knees.

Suddenly a great gasp went up from the men. Charles turned to the east, where Dutch Henry pointed. There above the trees glimmered a golden spot of light.

"Morning star," someone said.

The planet was more like a military rocket, blazing as it ascended slowly and majestically while they watched. Custer's face seemed to pick up a little of that awesome golden light.

"By God," he said in a reverent tone. "By God. This expedition is blessed. That's the sign."

They advanced to the irregular bluff above the river. The muffled thudding of so many shod horses sounded thunderous to Charles. Surely there would be some response from the sleeping village. There was; a dog barked. Within seconds, half a dozen more joined in.

Custer held up his right hand and started down the slope. Dandy slipped and skidded, but reached the river without mishap. Others began to descend, the scouts to the right of the trumpeter, who was leading the bandsmen down.

Charles had his gypsy robe tucked up and his Army Colt ready in his belt. He held the Spencer across his knees with one hand. Slowly, with creakings and jinglings and occasional muffled expletives, the force descended to the Washita. Down at the level of the river, where the water turned the air noticeably colder, Charles had a new perspective on the cottonwoods on the other side. Through them, amid them, against the faintly paled sky, he now saw the crossed poles of many tipis.

Whose?

"Trumpeter—" Custer began.

In the dark woods, someone fired a warning shot. Custer said something wrathful. Then several things happened at once. There was a noise on the open ground across the river; whinnying, as of many ponies suddenly disturbed. They'd probably smelled the white men's horses.

From the background of the dark woods, a man with a rifle broke and ran toward the river. Custer saw the Indian coming and raised one of his pistols. "Trumpeter, sound the charge," he yelled, firing from horseback. The Indian flew backward, his rifle spinning out of his hand.

The trumpeter sounded the call. To the far left and right of Charles, and behind him as well, men shouted and cheered. Before the trumpeter finished, the band burst into "Garry Owen," and the Seventh Cavalry poured over the Washita to strike the village.

50

Satan carried Charles over the Washita with a great leap. He hugged the piebald with his knees, was dashed with icy spray when Satan landed in the shallows on the other side. They galloped up the bank. To one side, he saw Griffenstein, a revolver in each fist, a smile on his bearded face.

The daylight was coming. The bleached hide covers of the tipis showed clearly among the cottonwoods. The pictographs were distinctive; there was no doubt that it was a Cheyenne village. To the left and right of the main force, the support columns were moving in, hallooing and cheering. Charles even heard a rebel yell.

The van of the attack swept toward the tipis across a level areas broken by low knolls. The earth shook from the pounding of the horses. Suddenly the sun cleared the horizon, and streaks of orange shimmered on the great curve of the Washita where it bent away north, just east of the village.

The Cheyennes poured from the tipis as the troopers rode down on them. The men struggled with their bows and rifles. Charles was dismayed by the sight of many woman and young children. Some of the sleepy youngsters were crying. The women wailed in fright. Dogs barked and snapped. The sudden fire from the charging cavalry worsened the bedlam.

Breath plumed from Charles's mouth. He was within fifty yards of the first tipis in the trees, but some troopers had already reached them. One shot a dog snapping at the horses. Another put a bullet in the breast of a gray-haired grandmother. The women screamed louder as their men staggered forward to defend them. Against the mounted blue lines they had no chance at all.

The charge carried Charles into a lane between tipis with smoke curling out of their tops. Griffenstein rode ahead of him, pistols cracking. A spindly old man defending himself with the faded red shield of his youth stared at the troopers with stunned eyes. Dutch Henry put a bullet into his open mouth. A great flying fan of blood spread behind the man. It splattered his tipi like paint.

Charles had to rely on Satan not to fall among the panicked Indians, who were yelling and clubbing at the soldiers, and to avoid the cook fires smoldering in the lane. His mind seemed benumbed. He'd yet to fire the Spencer.

Satan took him on down the lane to the far side of the village. There Charles wheeled back, nearly knocked from his saddle by a collision with two troopers executing the same maneuver. On their faces, in their glinting eyes, he saw an eagerness that didn't distinguish between warrior and woman, society soldier and stripling.

A platoon in double column led by First Lieutenant Godfrey, of K Troop, dashed out of the cottonwoods and away from the village. Waving hats and swinging ropes, the men in the column split right and left, circling the pony herd, which was already beginning to trot away southeast to escape the noise. The troopers managed to turn and surround the ponies. Observing, Charles wondered why General Custer went to the trouble. The ponies were Indian bred and trained; they'd be useless as cavalry remounts.

Powder smoke began to drift in heavy layers. Charles headed Satan back up another lane. He guessed the village to be about the size of their first estimate, fifty tipis. On his left, three troopers pulled one down. Inside the collapsing hide cover, he heard the high-pitched voices of terrified children. The troopers jumped off their horses and riddled the fallen tipi.

The pace of the charge in the lanes slowed now. Men from the detachment that had encircled the village came in, adding to the confusion. Directly ahead of Charles, a woman ran from behind a tipi, a bedraggled woman with unbound hair, holding a small white boy against her shoulder. She clutched the back of his head protectively. Her hands and face were weathered pink; a white woman.

She screamed at the soldiers. "My name is Blinn. Mrs. Blinn." The captive, Charles remembered. "Please don't hurt

Willie or—" A volley of shots jerked her like a marionette. Half
of the little boy's head sheared off as he and his mother crashed
into a tipi, tearing the cover and falling through.

Vomit rose in Charles's throat. He booted Satan past the
torn tipi. The slain boy was no older than his own son.

The lanes filled with troopers excitedly firing despite the
bucking and balking of their horses. Charles saw one corporal
with a bloody sleeve, but no other sign of Army casualties. He
walked Satan forward, peering through the trees to the open
ground they'd crossed in their charge from the river. There,
seated on Dandy on the highest of the knolls, Custer observed the
fighting through binoculars.

Down a short lane between tipis, Charles spied Dutch Henry
kneeling on the bullet-pierced body of a Cheyenne, whose head
he lifted with one hand while he cut quickly around the scalp
with the other. The victim was still alive. He screamed. His face
was seamed and old. Sixty winters, or more. Charles turned
away.

Not all the Cheyennes were so frail and defenseless. Here
and there he saw boys of twelve or thirteen using a knife or lance
in suicidal duels with soldiers. One of these youngsters leaped
from behind a tipi to confront Charles. He was barefoot, wearing
only leggings. From the black braid over his right ear dangled a
battle memento: someone's cross of tarnished brass, pierced and
tied by a thong. The boy had a delicate face. Traces of red showed
on his chest. He was either a young Red Shield initiate, or one
who aspired to that and imitated his elders by painting himself.
All of this registered in the seconds it took for the boy to fit an
arrow to his bowstring.

Charles raised his right hand, using sign to tell the youngster
to run. The boy's face convulsed with rage as he released the
bowstring. Charles flung himself down behind Satan's left side.
The arrow sailed over instead of skewering him.

He kicked his left boot out of the stirrup and dropped to the
ground with the Spencer. Satan trotted away between the tipis. In
the smoky grove, there was now almost constant screaming and
wailing from the women. Charles gestured with the rifle and
yelled in Cheyenne. "Run away. Run before you're killed." He
didn't know why he hazarded his own life this way, except that

he'd never bargained on revenging himself on graybeards and children.

The boy wanted no mercy. He fitted another arrow to the bow. Charles dodged to the right, hoping to dive behind the boy's tipi. The boy pulled the arrow back. Charles was still in the open, running bent over. He saw the bowstring go taut. There was no choice. He fired.

The bullet struck the boy's belly with close-range force, ripping it open and lifting him off the ground. He spun and landed on his back in the coals of a banked fire. His hair began to smoke. Charles ran to him and dragged him out of the fire. The metal cross was already hot, scorching his fingers. Charles's mouth tasted bitter; sweat ran down the bridge of his nose into his eyes. A surge of imagination showed him things the dead boy would never see. Another prairie spring; another prairie winter. The great bison herd migrating and covering the land. The adoring eyes of the first woman he took—

Shaken, he tore the brass cross from the boy's braid and jammed it in his pocket. Something demanded that he keep a reminder of what he'd done.

He went on foot to search for Satan. By now the scene inside the village was totally chaotic. The central part was held by the Seventh. Small isolated groups of Cheyennes had taken cover behind trees and in a shallow ditch and a ravine. Detachments quickly formed to concentrate fire on them, and kill them or drive them out. Women attempted to flee in the midst of the shooting, some clutching babies in cradleboards, some literally kicking their youngsters to hurry them along. Wherever the women ran into a line of troopers, they gave up. Most did, anyway. Charles watched an obese old squaw with a small knife fling herself at three troopers. Rifle fire cut her down.

He caught Satan, who was whinnying loudly, not liking the strange smells and sounds of the melee. Charles mounted and galloped toward the side of the village where they'd attacked first. He thought he recognized pictographs on a large tipi over that way. He knew he was right when he saw two Indians on a single pony racing away from the tipi in the direction of the sun-sparkling river. Even through the dense smoke and at a distance, he knew it was Black Kettle, with Medicine Woman Later riding in front of him.

Their pony reached the bank of the Washita. There, a quartet of troopers caught up with them. Black Kettle raised his hands to plead for mercy. A volley hit him and his wife and hurled them both off the pony and into the stream. The frightened pony trampled Medicine Woman Later before gaining the other bank.

"Christ!" Charles said. Intense revulsion was rising in him. All his past pledges to himself and his boast of wanton vengeance shamed him. Wooden Foot Jackson wouldn't want this—a blood price taken in the lives of children, mothers, the peace chief who had befriended the Jackson Trading Company and shielded it for a season from the wrath of Scar.

He jammed the Spencer in the saddle scabbard, put his head down, and raced for the river.

A flying wedge of eight or ten horsemen came up behind him, broke around him, streamed on eastward, churning up muddy snow. A grinning face looked back at him. "Here goes, Main—a brevet or a coffin." Whooping like boys, Major Elliott and his troopers galloped away. Soon, from the east, Charles heard intermittent gunfire.

He trotted Satan toward the river again. The open ground held fallen Cheyennes, mostly men, nearly all dead. He spied one body in blue. The mouth was open, the eyes fixed on the trampled snow. Louis Hamilton—who'd begged not to be left with the wagons when there was glory waiting.

Satan jumped suddenly, sailing over some obstacle Charles hadn't seen. He wrenched around and looked down. Custer's Blucher lay there, an arrow through his throat.

When Charles reached the Washita, he guessed that about twenty minutes had passed since the attack began. Already the gunfire was diminishing. In the village, many of the tipis were down, and the dismounted troopers running to and fro no longer displayed caution; they had won and they knew it.

He dismounted and waded into the flowing cold water, up to his waist. About halfway across, where there was a sandbar, little threads of red spun off into the current. Black Kettle and Medicine Woman Later had fallen together, her body half resting on his. The back of her head protruded from the water. The peace chief's face was submerged and turned up to the light, every wrinkle visible because of the water's clarity.

Charles felt pain in his gut. For this he'd joined the Tenth, and then the Seventh? To perpetrate the murder of a man who'd done nothing but sue for peace, nothing but try to walk the white man's road? In the clear winter morning on the Washita, the scales were falling from his eyes. He was sick with guilt and shame.

He lifted the body of Medicine Woman Later, which was heavy because of her soaked clothing. He carried her to the bank and there lay her on her back. He sloshed into the water again to get Black Kettle. He was now able to see the chief's five bullet wounds, which the woman's body had hidden before. Tears came to his eyes.

Somehow Black Kettle was lighter. Charles picked him up from the icy shallows and lay him across his forearms, heedless of the water cascading from the body and splashing his leggings and soaking his sleeves. He staggered toward the bank—straight into the shadow of a horse and rider.

Charles looked up. Captain Harry Venable extended his hand and aimed his side arm at Charles. The gun was an 1860 Army Colt with some kind of ivory inlay in the butt.

"Leave those bodies where they fell or take their scalps."

"I won't do either one. These poor old people befriended me once."

"You know them?"

"You're damn right. This is Black Kettle, the peace chief. It's his village. He tried to take the village to sanctuary at Fort Cobb and that damn fool Hazen turned him away. This is his reward." The old Indian now felt heavy and sodden in his arms. "Black Kettle was my friend. I mean to bury him right."

Venable smiled then. He had Charles cold for disobedience. He cocked the Colt. There was hardly another sound save the drip of water from Black Kettle's garments and gray hair.

Then, suddenly, the morning air resounded with the assembly call. Venable turned and glanced toward the village. Mounted troopers and those on foot began to move quickly to answer. Charles stared into the Colt's muzzle and figured he'd bought the farm this morning. He realized he could release Black Kettle, reach his pistol, and rid the world of Venable. He didn't move.

The trumpeting delayed Venable's shot by about fifteen seconds. In that interval a horseman galloped by. It was Griffenstein.

He wheeled and dashed between Charles and Harry Venable.

"You drunk?" he yelled at Venable, knocking the officer's Colt from his hand. "The ones we're killin' got red skins, not white."

Another officer spurring for the trees shouted at Venable, telling him to haul his ass. Not fully understanding the confrontation, Dutch Henry recognized its seriousness. He kept an eye on the little Kentuckian as he dismounted, retrieved the Colt, and warily handed it back. Slowly, Charles lowered Black Kettle to the churned snow and mud. He laid him beside his wife.

Venable rammed the revolver in his holster, threw a look at Charles that promised it wasn't over between them, and quirted his horse with his rein. He went speeding among the knolls and the bodies to the village.

"What'n shit was that all about?" Griffenstein wanted to know. He seemed himself now, his face no longer flushed as it had been when Charles saw him with the scalping knife. The scalp was knotted to the scout's rawhide belt by a strand of bloody hair.

"Venable's got an old grudge," was all Charles would say.

"Well, he better hold his water. This is no place to settle scores." For Charles, the words had a meaning the other scout couldn't appreciate.

"I'm obliged to you, Henry," he said.

"Nothing," the other man said with a wave. "Can't stand by and see a friend taken out by some snotty shoulder-straps." By then, Charles had mounted, reluctantly leaving the chief and his wife where he'd put them. Dutch Henry was in high spirits as they turned their horses toward the assembly point. "Wasn't this a hell of a fine git?"

Charles stared at him. Anger did away with gratitude.

"It was a massacre. Of the wrong people. It's a goddamn disgrace. Look at this." He showed the brass cross with the broken thong. "I took it off a young boy. His whole life ahead of him. I had to shoot him so he wouldn't kill me."

Griffenstein didn't catch on to the depth of Charles's feeling. He reached for the cross. "Got yourself a nice souvenir, anyway."

Charles closed his fist. "Do you think that's why I took it, you dumb ox? This isn't war. It's butchery. Sand Creek all over again."

The burly scout's surprise changed to resentment. "Grow up, Charlie. This here's the way things are."

"Fuck the way things are."

Griffenstein's face changed again. He regarded Charles with the same repugnance a man might show to a carrier of cholera. "I reckon this is where we split. By rights I oughta twist your head off for what you called me. I guess I won't because I guess you've gone crazy. You ride with somebody else from now on."

He moved away. Charles didn't care. Something inside him was dead. Killed here on the Washita.

There was a lot of activity inside the village. A great many soldiers were still riding or bustling around on foot, snatching souvenirs before someone forbade it. Charles saw shirts and trousers stained by scalps hacked from the dead. One young private proudly showed two of them to his friends.

The pony herd, numbering several hundred, had been rounded up by Godfrey's men near the trees on the far side of the village. About fifty women and children had been captured, along with a large quantity of goods. A number of fine saddles, including some Army ones; hatchets and buffalo robes; firearms, bullet molds, and lead; hundreds of pounds of tobacco and flour, and a large winter store of buffalo meat. As Charles jogged in, Custer was detailing Godfrey and his K Troop to gather and inventory the spoils.

Listening to the excited conversations around him, Charles heard claims that several hundred Indians were dead. He doubted it. If each tipi held its usual five or six, that figured to three hundred inhabitants of the village. There were plenty of Indian bodies scattered in the lanes and out on the open ground, but nothing like three hundred. Many of the braves must have escaped. Among the soldiers, only two were known dead: Louis Hamilton and Corporal Cuddy, of B Troop. But then there was Elliott's detachment. No one could say what had become of it.

There was renewed wailing and shrieking. Three of the Osage trackers were gleefully whipping some captive women with switches. "They try to run," an Osage explained. He and the others whipped the women harder, driving them toward a larger group already under guard. From his seasons with Black Kettle's people, Charles thought he recognized more than one of the women. A squaw with thick braids and a bleeding cheek seemed to recognize him, but she was the only one. She said nothing, but her stare was enough to twist knives in his middle.

"General." The sharp voice belonged to Romero, the interpreter. He pushed a bedraggled woman ahead of him. She clasped her hands and bowed her head in front of General Custer, who still looked fresh and energetic. Charles wondered how it was possible; he himself was spent and occasionally dizzy from tiredness and hunger.

"This woman, she say she Mahwissa, sister to Black Kettle," Romero said. Possible, although Charles had never seen the woman before, or heard of a sister during that winter he spent with Jackson. "She say this is not only village on the Washita."

"Where are the others?" Custer asked in the sudden stillness.

Romero found a broken lance shaft and, standing beside the general, drew an upside-down U in the mud. He flared both stems of the U outward, then poked a hole below the left-hand stem. "Here is the village of Black Kettle." Up toward the bend of the U he poked again. "Arapahoes here." Toward the bottom of the other stem of the U, another poke. "More Cheyennes here." Two more pokes near the flared end of that stem. "And more—and Kiowas too. All winter camps. Downstream."

General Custer's ruddiness was gone. He looked pale as the snow on the trees up on the bluffs. Among those trees, Charles thought he detected movement.

"How many in the camps?" Custer asked.

Romero spoke to the woman in Cheyenne. Charles understood enough of her answer to feel a renewed chill.

"To the number of five or six thousand."

The hush befitted a tomb. Somewhere a dog howled. The listening soldiers, so boisterous a little while ago, nervously fingered their side arms.

Somehow the disagreeable news didn't surprise Charles. Custer's impetuous nature was a kind of lightning rod for trouble. He's pushed the pursuit, and the attack, on the unfounded assumption that they were chasing one band of warriors to an isolated village in the valley of the Washita. The night's forced march had left little time for reflection on related questions: Was there only one village? Had the war party actually returned there, or to another village? Even now, they didn't know the answer to the second question. Charles supposed he couldn't score Custer too harshly. He hadn't thought of the questions himself, though they seemed embarrassingly obvious after Romero's revelation.

To his credit, Custer showed no sign of dismay. "We have won a decisive victory over the enemy—" Charles grimaced. He noticed Keim for the first time. The reporter was scribbling in his phonographic notebook. "We will proceed with destruction of this base. We must go about our duties without the slightest indication that we know of the other villages, or care about them. If there are more Indians close by, they won't know our strength.

Someone muttered, "They sure-God know we ain't five thousand."

"Let the coward who made that remark step forward."

No one moved. The general's face flushed again. Charles thought he was more agitated than he let on. Custer opened his mouth, probably to repeat his demand for a confession, but one of the Osages caught his attention with a sudden gesture toward the hoof-torn slopes beyond the river. Three braves with shields and lances rode out of the trees up there. They halted their ponies at the edge, watching. Nearby, other Indians slipped into sight.

Soon the bluffs were crowded with them, and more kept coming. *Custer said this expedition was blessed,* Charles thought. *It's cursed.*

51

The easy victory wasn't turning out to be so easy. By eleven, the bluffs across the Washita held hundreds of armed Arapahoes and Cheyennes. Custer fretted while the work of collecting spoils continued. His colors were planted in an improvised hospital area near the center of the village. From there, he issued orders deploying men in a defense perimeter just inside the cottonwoods in case the Indians attacked.

They did. A band of twenty Cheyennes came galloping in from the river bend two miles northeast. They dashed over the open ground between the low knolls and fired into the trees. Standing beside Romero, Charles returned the fire. Custer strode behind the defense line, bucking up the men.

"Don't show yourselves. They're trying to draw us into the open. Conserve your fire—we're low on ammunition. Stand fast. They'll never ride into these woods."

The jingle of his little gold spurs seemed to linger after he went on. Romero gave Charles a disconsolate look; Custer was right about ammunition. If they remained pinned down for much longer, the Indians would be able to charge in without the danger of return fire.

Charles put his second-to-last magazine into the stock of the Spencer and wiped his eyes. They were smarting and watering from tiredness and the smoke. He felt someone watching him. Several paces to the right he saw Dutch Henry Griffenstein. With a contemptuous smile, Griffenstein said something to the soldier next to him. The trooper turned to stare at Charles, and Charles knew he had to find an opportunity to apologize for calling the scout a dumb ox.

After their last sweep the Cheyennes galloped away again,

out of range. One brave knelt on his pony and thumbed the seat of his breeches. None of the men in the smoky wood thought it funny.

Charles held his place for two hours. During that time a half-dozen attack parties rode down from the heights, though none came close to the trees. Custer was right; the Indians wanted them in the open.

Behind the defense line, other troopers were busy ripping tipis apart and hacking up the poles with axes. California Joe slipped in from the other side of the wood to report that he'd found three to four hundred more Indian ponies. "Must be eight, nine hundred of 'em now, General," Charles heard him say to Custer, who was again prowling the defense perimeter.

One of the Corbins came to relieve Charles. He stumbled away and stepped behind a bullet-scarred tree to relieve his painfully full bladder. It didn't help much. He was in low spirits, remembering how lively and friendly a peaceful Cheyenne village could be, with music, and courting rituals, and storytelling by a fire after a sinfully big feast of buffalo meat. Black Kettle's village was, by contrast, a graveyard, a plundered graveyard. Those troopers not on the defense line continued to pile up goods from the wrecked tipis; dozens of confiscated buffalo robes, painted arrows by the hundreds.

"Pull that one out," Custer said to his orderly. He pointed to a demolished tipi. "If the cover's undamaged, pack it for me. Then move all these separate heaps together and set them afire." Charles listened despondently. What Custer was doing amounted to burning the homes of a civilian population. The owners of the tipis, if they managed to escape, would die of exposure unless they found shelter somewhere else. He thought that driving the Cheyennes out of the village temporarily should have been enough.

Custer thought otherwise. Soon, on open ground out behind the cottonwoods, flames shot up, leaping eight and ten feet in the air as they consumed the great mountain of torn-down tipis. The hide covers produced a bitter dark smoke that trailed across the winter sky like mourning streamers.

The general ordered up a detachment with Joe Corbin and Griffenstein leading it. As the detachment trotted away east, out of the woodland, Charles asked Milner, "Were are they going?"

California Joe eyed him in a suspicious way; maybe Griffenstein had been talking widely about Charles's behavior. "Hunt for Elliott," was all the chief scout said. His speech had a slur again; evidently he still had his supply of alcohol.

"About time the general started worrying about them," Charles said.

California Joe scowled. "You better keep opinions like that to yourself, mister." He walked away.

There was something fierce building inside Charles; something he was powerless to suppress. It was an anger, blind to subtleties, that encompassed every white man in the cottonwoods, including himself. Gnawing on some hardtack, his only food that day, he had an urge to take his Army Colt and shoot Custer. The foolish impulse passed, but not the anger. He hated what was happening here.

Antlike, a file of men moved toward the great fire carrying robes, quivers, bullet molds—every personal article the foragers could find. The flames shot high again, filling the woods with scarlet light and shifting shadow. If the survivors ever came back, they would also have no food or household goods to sustain them through the winter, which was evidently what Sheridan intended.

As the burning continued, men on the defense line raised a shout. "Bell's coming! Here comes Bell!" Charles and the others ran to the edge of the woods on the river side. Careening toward them from a ford somewhere upstream came their seven wagons. Cheyennes and Arapahoes galloped on either side, peppering them with arrows and bullets.

The teamsters returned the fire. One warrior dropped. Up on the bluffs, more war parties were assembling, probably to intercept the wagons. They didn't move quickly enough. With Lieutenant Jim Bell whipping up the lead team, the wagons thundered into the grove. Sparks and flames spurted from overheated axle hubs. Bell's wagon veered to avoid a tree, the mules tore the traces, and the wagon tipped and crashed on its side, dumping its load of ammunition chests. The troopers rushed to them and tore them open.

Sooty, a smoking pistol in his hand, Bell staggered to Custer. "Couldn't wait for orders, General. Bunch of 'em surprised us and we had to dash for the ford upstream."

"It's good you did," Custer said. "Now we have the ammunition we need."

Indeed, the troopers seemed revitalized by the arrival of the wagons, which had reached the cottonwoods without serious injury to any of the drivers. The troopers climbed over the wagons and threw more ammunition chests to the ground. With the bonfire blazing and the mules braying and the teamsters shouting and the Cheyenne women wailing and the children crying and the angry Indians again sniping from horseback, Charles began to think he was in some grotto in hell reserved for the damned of the U.S. Cavalry.

More commotion then. The search detachment was riding in from the east. Pale frightened troopers dismounted and talked excitedly. Custer ran to them, shouting for silence. Charles's eye raked the search party. No Griffenstein.

"How far did you go?" Custer demanded.

"Two or three miles," Joe Corbin said. "We ran into hot fire and turned back. We lost one man. We didn't find Elliott."

"All right. I'm sure you did your best," Custer said. Captain Fred Benteen immediately stepped out to confront him.

"General, we can't let it die there. Elliott may be pinned down somewhere. I'll take another detachment—"

"No!" Custer scanned the bluffs above the river, where bands of Indians walked their ponies back and forth, restless from their failure to draw the soldiers out. Seeing Benteen about to protest again, Custer lashed him with a sharp, "No, you will not. Not now. We are in a predicament, and we must get out."

Charles was in a predicament, too. He needed to patch things up and now it was too late. Griffenstein wasn't coming back. It struck him that although he'd talked with Dutch Henry scores of times, he had never once asked about a family. Nor had Griffenstein said anything. He'd been self-contained; an expert plainsman who carried his whole world with him. If he had kin anywhere, Charles couldn't inform them.

Dumb ox. The memory of his words made him feel just the way he had in the last year of the war. Low, and dirty, and ready to hurt someone.

Three o'clock.

A little earlier, squadrons led by Meyers, Benteen, and Hamilton's replacement, Weir, had advanced from the cottonwoods. Charles wasn't privy to Custer's purpose in ordering the advance. Maybe it was meant to demonstrate that he wasn't intimidated. But neither were the Indians. A large body of them charged the soldiers and, after a brisk but indecisive exchange of fire, retreated eastward again while the soldiers galloped back to the trees. Since then, the Indians had not attacked. The soldiers could hope that they had decided to abandon the fight, but Charles doubted it.

Custer looked haggard when he called all the scouts and officers to the standard again. "We must prepare to get out of here. There are some problems. If we just retreat, those savages will chase us, and I don't want a running fight in the dark. The men are spent. So we'll try a feint. In an hour or so, we'll form up with our prisoners and head in that direction." His gauntlet hand pointed northeast. "In line of battle. Just as if we plan to take out the other villages one by one. We'll give them band music and a big show of confidence. They've seen what we did to this nest of enemies. I think they'll run to protect their own lodges. If I'm right, the moment we have full dark we'll be able to countermarch and slip away north."

No one objected to the plan, or even offered a comment; they were too worn out to raise frivolous questions, and what Custer said sounded reasonable.

The general had ashes in his hair and mustache. One of his high cheekbones was daubed with someone's blood. His gleaming eyes reflected the bonfire still burning. He added, "Before we go we must cripple this village. Cripple it completely. Venable—"

"Sir?"

"Take what men you need and cut enough ponies from the herd to carry the prisoners. The rest of you gentlemen, officers and scouts, may then have your pick of any mount in the herd. Then I want Godfrey—where's Godfrey?—ah. Godfrey, at that point you take charge."

"Yes, sir?" Lieutenant Godfrey wiped grime from the corner of his mouth. Charles heard a high ringing in his ears as his dreadful premonition proved to be right.

"Kill the rest of the horses."

"General—sir—that'll be eight hundred at least."

"So be it, Godfrey. We are not going to leave these damned red murderers any remounts. Kill them all."

Now the gray day had sunk into firelit nightmare. Charles leaned against a cottonwood that had a broken arrow shaft embedded in it and twirled the clicking cylinder of his Army Colt, feeding it loads.

Romero hurried by. "Eh, Señor Charlie, give a hand with the remuda. The quicker we kill them, the quicker we get out of here."

"Leave him alone, Romeo," California Joe called. He was busy brushing dirt from a scalp that had fallen from his belt. "Charlie ain't himself right now."

The ringing in his ears persisted. He walked unsteadily toward the huge fire. The heat brought sweat to his filthy face. He closed his eyes, remembering Sport's last gallop in Virginia. The pristine snow stippled red after the gallant gray passed over it, his heart's blood pumping out as he carried Charles back to the safety of the lines.

Eight hundred horses. Eight *hundred.* He couldn't believe anyone would do that. Not after so much destruction already.

He staggered past the fire, his right cheek scorched by the heat. He stood watching Venable complete his job of cutting out fifty-five mounts for the captive women and children. He and his detail herded the animals to hastily rigged picket lines in the trees. Then they rejoined Godfrey and his four troops of men, who spread out and surrounded the nervous ponies.

On Godfrey's order, men tied ropes into lariats and advanced, intending to catch the horses one at a time. Some of the ponies caught the scent of the soldiers, the white man's scent, and didn't like it. Eyes rolled with fright. Manes tossed.

Lariats sailed through the air. One soldier got a rope over a beautiful sorrel pony. He shouted for someone to come in with a knife and cut the pony's throat. The pony reared and pawed the air. A hoof gashed the soldier's forehead. Blood cascaded into his eyes. He fell on his back and would have been trampled if other troopers hadn't dragged him away.

Godfrey's men tried ropes and knives for fifteen minutes, but the horses hated the soldiers' smell and kicked and bit and reared. "Fetch the general," Godfrey shouted. Charles still stood apart, near the fire, watching.

General Custer came trotting through the trees on Dandy.

"We can't get close enough to slash their throats, General. What shall we do?"

Angered, Custer said, "We have plenty of ammunition now. Use it." He pulled out one of his pistols and shot two ponies through the head. There was a terrible bellowing as they went down. "Do I always have to show you your jobs?" Custer yelled, nearly overrunning Godfrey as he galloped back into the trees.

"Rifles," Godfrey ordered. Men broke away and ran for them. Handsome Harry Venable unbuttoned his dirty overcoat for freer movement, then unholstered his side arm.

"Those with revolvers start using them," Godfrey said. "Otherwise we'll spend the night in this place."

Venable strode right up to a well-built chestnut pony whose eyes shimmered, reflecting the bonfire. The little Kentuckian pressed his lips together like a man about to do a difficult sum. He put his service revolver to the chestnut's eye and fired. Blood and tissue erupted behind the magnificent head.

The shot pealed and reverberated, louder than the loudest prairie thunderstorm. Something went off like a powder charge in Charles's brain. A raw, low sound began in his throat, rising, gaining volume, a long wild cry. He had no memory of starting to move.

52

The horses fell with a strange untormented grace. They fell sideways, the first ones, one into the next. They fell away from the volleying handguns of boyish soldiers, some of whom laughed or shouted, "Well hit." The soldiers knelt and fired round after round into shoulders and ribs, chests and bellies. Blood ran in strong streams, as from coarse sieves, while the horses fell away from their executioners, briefly creating a beautiful orderly pattern much like that of waves flowing outward, outward, on a changing sea tide. Then the pattern lost its beauty and order, because eighty horses had fallen, a hundred had fallen, and there was no more room to die, so some died kneeling. And there was nowhere to flee. Animals that tried to stampede on the far edge of the herd found other boys with carbines there, some with the dirty white pallor of exhaustion, some feebly joshing, some stoic, some patently sick with the loathing of their deed, and from that side, too, the killing began, and soon there was a circle of fire and smoke like a great round ribbon tying up dying animals. As the horses fell and kept falling, the noise grew unbearable, a regular choir of pain. To the smell of pumping blood, which had an appeal for some, there was added the stink of horse bowels emptying in great spasms, and soon the pattern was in complete disorder, full of clashing lines and elements, with here and there a beautiful mute head lifting, the lips peeling back, the long teeth shining, opening to let out a great hopeless cry for mercy that ended when one more good sport of a trooper picked that head to blow apart. In place of the pattern, there grew a mound of shiny, stinking, dying horseflesh; a landmark quite as distinctive as one of the Antelope Hills; a landmark not of nature but of man, there by the Washita.

Charles ran to the perimeter where the young soldiers knelt with revolvers and carbines. He grabbed a blue shoulder. "Put that down. Stop it. Don't kill dumb animals." It sounded perfectly reasoned to him; he had no sense that the words came out in screaming bursts, or that an unfamiliar strength was pumping in him, enabling him to hurl one of the shootists four feet to one side just by gripping his shoulders.

A soldier with eyes as damp and bright as those of the dying horses shied from Charles, warning others near him, "Look out, Cheyenne Charlie's gone crazy."

Charles wondered why the soldier said that. All he wanted was a halt to the killing of the animals, perfectly reasonable.

"Stand aside. I'll deal with him." Charles recognized the voice before he saw Harry Venable, Handsome Harry, small and dapper despite hunger and fatigue and the grime of a forced march.

"Tell them to stop it, Venable."

"You filthy, craven idiot, we are carrying out the general's orders."

Charles formed fists and beat the air and screamed then, really screamed, because it seemed the only way to get through Venable's studied calm. "Let them go. Let them go free. Stop the killing!"

Venable raised his hand. His spotless, lightly oiled Colt with the ivory grips gleamed a foot from Charles's chest. Only a faint tremor of Venable's chin showed he was wary of the threat presented by the screaming, scruffy man. The carbines and pistols volleyed with a sound like stones thrown on a tin roof. The smells ripened. More than one soldier turned away and puked on the churned-up ground, adding a thin pink slime to the brown, the white, the red.

A speck of vomit flew to Venable's right boot, which was already filthy with mud. The speck seemed to excite him. He whipped the revolver across Charles's face, pulling on it so that the sight cut into Charles's cheek like a dull knife.

"Now, Main, leave the field."

Charles stared at him—a mistake, because Venable was ready. "Hold him," Venable yelled to the soldiers as his knee caught Charles between the legs, a clumsy blow but effective. Dizzy with pain, Charles tried to punch Venable. But he was slow. Two troopers seized his arms and jerked them out full length.

Venable's blue eyes danced. In his finest, softest Kentucky voice, he complimented the soldiers. "Very good, sirs. Now hold him fast."

He holstered his side arm and stepped in near Charles. He threw a hard punch into his stomach. For a small man, he was very strong. Charles's head came up slowly. Wild-eyed, he spit at Venable, who wiped it off and punched him low in his groin. Then he pounded Charles's head once from the right. Blood and mucus spewed from Charles's nose. He was going down and he couldn't help it.

A great sense of failure enveloped him. He ought to get up. Fight back. He was unable to. It was Jefferson Barracks again.

Venable stood beside Charles's head, his drawn revolver pointed down. Despite the noise of guns and horses, Charles heard the revolver cock. Venable aimed it at the canal of his ear.

"Sir," a soldier said, "sir, he's out of it. Griffenstein told me he has a thing about seeing horses hurt. That oughtn't to merit killing—" Charles couldn't see which young soldier had spoken, but he saw Venable glare, and heard the boy's assertive tone fade away as he added one more gulping, "Sir."

Charles knew he was going to be murdered right there. He watched Venable glance around at witnesses Charles couldn't see except as pairs of blood-spattered boots. Venable hesitated. He couldn't get away with it.

"Pick up the son of a bitch," he said, jamming the Colt in his holster again. "You—and you. Get him on his feet, the damn traitor. We'll let the general settle this."

53

The two soldiers quickstepped him toward the cottonwoods, where a new fire had been built near the general's standard to provide light and warmth as the afternoon darkened. Almost as fast as it had come, the rage diffused, leaving Charles with pains in his body and a vague awareness of having tried to stop the horse slaughter. A sad finality settled on him; he knew at last what he wanted to do. No, stronger than that. *Had* to do, at all hazards.

General Custer, youthful and somehow rakish and spruce despite his filthy uniform, looked annoyed by Venable's interruption. He had been talking to California Joe, who was saying, "No, sir, I can't find Sergeant Major Kennedy's body no place as yet."

Custer turned from the blazing fire, his right leg slightly bent at the knee, his left hand resting on the hilt of his saber. He always seemed aware of his posture.

"What is it, Captain Venable? Quickly. I intend to march in less than an hour."

"Sir, this man, this damn reb, tried to stop your men from performance of duty." Venable sounded very proper and sententious, although Charles, whose head was clearing and giving him a sense of the enormous trouble he was in, could hear Venable's wrath bubbling underneath. "He attempted to prevent our work with the pony herd."

"Your butchery," Charles said.

"Your tender sensibilities object to that, Mr. Main?" Custer strode over to Charles, addressing him as though Charles did not have an eye swelling shut, a cheek dripping blood, and snot hanging from his nose. "You prefer that we leave healthy horses so the savages can ride them in the spring to commit more atrocities?

General Sheridan charged me with the duty of punishing the Cheyennes and Arapahoes—"

"Black Kettle was a peace chief."

"That's of no consequence. My responsibility is to eradicate the threat to white people—" Why was he talking so much, Charles wondered. To whom was he justifying his actions? He didn't have to do it to a shabby scout of questionable background. Despite his pain, Charles had a sharp sense that Custer was aware that today had damaged him; a sense that he was already on the run. "A duty which I have this day carried out. Only total war will bring peace to these plains."

"May be, but I don't want any more of it."

"What? What's that?" Custer was caught off guard, his blue eyes confused, then angry again.

"I said I don't want any more of your kind of war. I shouldn't have signed on."

"We should not have engaged you," Custer retorted. California Joe looked ready to sink into the ground.

Charles threw everything into the pot and made his last bet. "I'm leaving. If you want to stop me, you'll have to shoot me. Or order someone to do it."

Venable said, "I would be pleased—"

"Be quiet!" Custer shouted. He was breathing fast, his face ruddier than Charles had ever seen it. "You're rash to suggest that, Mr. Main. I can very easily order you shot. Witnesses to your rebellious behavior will testify to the necessity—"

"You've got enough trouble on your hands." Blood in Charles's beard formed a drop that fell and struck a patch of snow between his boots. He tried to shut out the sounds of the steady small-arms fire, the horses dying. "I saw Mrs. Blinn shot. I saw her son shot."

"I have it on reliable authority that the Cheyennes slew the woman."

"Your men shot her, I saw it. So did others."

"We have no evidence the white woman was the Mrs. Blinn who was abducted from—"

"I heard her name and others did, too." Bleeding, glowering, Charles pushed Custer. The Boy General was momentarily panicked; Charles saw that in the bright blue eyes. "They're not going to call this a battle, they're going to call it a massacre. Babies with bullets in their heads. Women scalped by United

States soldiers. A white captive and a peace chief, an old man, murdered. Not a very pretty episode to include in a campaign biography, would you say, General?"

George Custer took one half-step backward; it said everything.

Venable was almost spitting with frustration. "General Custer, no one will believe anything from a man who lied twice to get in the Army."

Charles nodded. "You're right. And I'm really not interested in talking to newspapermen, Mr. Keim or any other. I'm not interested in getting even with anybody. I followed that trail a long time and look where it got me." No one understood what he meant.

His stinging eyes moved over the ruined village, the ashes of the great bonfire, out to the hideous quivering mound of dead and dying horses. "I had to kill a boy this morning. Not a man. A boy. I'll see him in nightmares till I die. I'll see this obscene place, too. I'm sick of this army. I'm sick of soldiers like you who work out their ambitions with human lives. I'm sick of the whole goddamn mess. Now either let me go or shoot me, you miserable excuse for a human being."

Venable stepped in, arm flying back to give Charles a roundhouse blow to the head. "Leave him alone," Custer said. Venable fairly jerked at the sharp order. Custer wiped his mouth. "Let him go. We have enough to explain already."

"General, you can't permit—"

"Damn you to hell, Captain Venable, close your mouth. Mr. Main—" Custer shook a finger under Charles's nose, his teeth gritted together as if he couldn't trust himself to keep control. "I will give you five minutes to cross the Washita. If you are not north of the river in five minutes, I will order a detachment to pursue and shoot you. You are a disgrace to the Army and a disgrace to manhood. Dismissed, sir."

"Yes, sir"—Charles weighted the words, strung them out—"General—Custer."

There was a long, dangerous moment when they stared at one another. Then, like two bears that had clawed and bloodied each other to exhaustion, they simply turned away, both of them, and gave up the fight.

Little Harry Venable wouldn't give up. He followed Charles through the trees, and Charles took some satisfaction from that. Custer's decision had reduced the Kentuckian to something like a small boy who didn't dare use his fists, only taunts:

"It's a long way to Fort Dodge. I hope the hostiles catch you." *They probably will,* Charles thought. "I hope they carve your heart out."

Charles stopped. Venable inhaled loudly. Charles stared at him with a twisted smile. "You hopeless little pile of shit. My war's over."

"What?"

He turned and walked on. He knew Venable would never pull his gun.

He found Satan, untied him, patted him, and mounted. He judged the time to be around four, but the November afternoon was exceptionally cloudy and dark. He rode out of the Cheyenne village at a trot, every movement of the piebald painful to him. The flesh around his left eye was puffy, his vision squeezed to a slit. He could do nothing about the gash on his face except let it bleed until it clotted. He could wash at the stream where the Seventh had found Elliott—if he got that far.

An Indian was approaching on the open ground. Charles reined in, reaching for the Spencer in its scabbard. He saw that the hobbling Indian was one of the Osage trackers. The Indian's leggings were soaked. He proudly showed something in his hand.

"Scalp of Black Kettle. Put him in the deep water. He will be bad meat soon."

"You bastard," Charles said, and rode on.

He crossed the Washita. The water rose to his thighs. Satan strained to keep his head out. Charles was shivering and his teeth were chattering when they emerged. A distant trumpet sounded boots and saddles. Without looking, he could picture the various units of Custer's command forming up to march.

All of the Indians were downstream, or else it had grown so dark that he couldn't see them on the bluffs. Going up over the edge where the attack had started, he heard Custer's band playing. He knew the tune from the war. "Ain't I Glad to Get Out of the Wilderness."

No, he wasn't. A devastating truth had come to him during

the icy river crossing. He didn't belong in South Carolina any more. He didn't belong in Kansas, trying to raise vegetables or dairy cows. And he didn't belong in the U.S. Army, much as he'd liked some of the men he knew in the Tenth Cavalry. What the soldiers had to do was wrong. Maybe they weren't culprits individually, but together they were. He'd thought he could stomach what the Army had to do. He'd convinced himself he could in order to revenge the Jacksons. And he'd marched all the way to the Washita to find out he was wrong.

There was no place for him in all the world.

Smaller and smaller, horse and rider diminished into the snowfields and the dark of the Indian Territory.

———

Headquarters Seventh U.S. Cavalry)
In the Field of the Washita River)
Nov. 28, 1868)

In the excitement of the fight, as well as in self-defence, it so happened that some of the squaws and a few children were killed and wounded. . . .

One white woman was murdered by her captors the moment we attacked. . . .

The desperate character of the combat may be inferred from the fact that after the battle the bodies of thirty-eight dead warriors were found in a small ravine near the village in which they had posted themselves. . . .

I now have to report the loss suffered by my own command.

I regret to mention among the killed, Major Joel H. Elliott and Capt. Louis W. Hamilton, and nineteen enlisted men. . . .

Excerpts from report to
GENERAL SHERIDAN

———

MADELINE'S JOURNAL

December, 1868. Gen. Custer's defeat of the Indians still much in the news. One editor lionizes him, the next scorns him for "warring upon innocents." I dislike him without having met him. I have never liked men who behave like peacocks. . . .

. . . A tedious two days now concluded. Was called upon to smile excessively, explain endlessly about Mont Royal's return from its ruined state of three years ago. Eight members of the Congress here, on a "tour of inspection" (which seems more like a holiday—three brought their wives, nearly as self-important and prolix as their husbands). The man to whom the others defer, Mr. Stout of the Senate, waxes oratorical even in the most incidental conversation. I liked neither his smoothness nor the speed and certainty with which he offered opinions—yes to this, no to that, every remark reflecting Radical policy without thought or question.

As to the reason for the visit, I gather M.R. has acquired something of a reputation as a showplace, for the Washingtonians tiresomely inspected everything: the phosphate fields, sawmill, a drill by our District Militia, which Andy commands. Senator Stout spent an hour seated like a pupil in Prudence Chaffee's class, making sure two journalists from his entourage were present to transcribe his comments. A pox on politicians.

Not comfortable to have the plantation singled out by the Radicals in this way. We are trying to avoid attention, and the trouble which usually attends it. . . .

. . . Another lonely Christmas season. Brett's letter from California expressed similar feelings of melancholy. All is well with Billy's engineering firm, she says. The baby, Clarissa, is four months and thriving. They have had no word from G. in Switzerland since May. It causes them great anxiety. . . .

George dined at half past one, his usual time. The Palace was one of Lausanne's fine hotels and had a splendid kitchen. As a regular, in warm weather he had his own small table by the marble rail of the terrace. Now that winter had swept the tourists out of Switzerland, he had moved inside to a table for one beside a tall window overlooking the same terrace. Through the window he could see across the city's center to Lake Geneva, where one of the trim little steamers berthed at the nearby resort of Ouchy was steaming toward the south shore. He noticed that the sunlight was already pale and slanting.

A few dead leaves whirled across the terrace. He finished his dinner, an excellent terrine of lobster, and his bottle of wine, a delicious Montrachet, and left the table. As he crossed the dining room, he spoke politely to a trio of Swiss, bankers who ate there regularly and had grown aware of him as a regular, too.

They often speculated about the American. They knew he was very rich. They knew he lived without companions, except for servants, in a vast, rather forbidding villa that had a splendid view of the hilly town from the Jorat heights. They wondered among themselves what had marked him.

What they saw was a stout, short man, middle-aged—George had observed his forty-third birthday—with wide streaks of white in his neat dark beard. His posture was very correct, yet he seemed somehow defeated. He smoked a great many strong cigars, with nervous movements; he left most of them half finished. He seemed to possess everything and to have suffered in spite of it. He was, unlike most of his countrymen who visited Lausanne, unapproachable. The tourists prattled endlessly; his warmest greeting was a word or two.

Had his wife left him? Was there some other scandal? Ah, perhaps that was it. He bore a certain resemblance to engraved portraits of the new American President, the general, Grant. Could he be a disgraced relative, exiled?

It would remain his secret. Gentlemen did not pry.

At the dining room door, George said a few words to the headwaiter in French, tipped him, collected his stick, hat, and fur overcoat, and crossed the lobby. An heiress from Athens, a striking olive-skinned woman, expensively dressed, took note of him and caught her breath; she was recently widowed. While a porter sorted her luggage, she tried to catch the eye of the imposing stranger. Nothing forward; merely a recognition. He saw her but strode on. She had the sensation of gazing into a snowbound pool in the heart of a winter wood. Dark waters, and cold.

George walked down a sloping street toward the estate agent's, located just beyond the splendid Gothic cathedral of Notre Dame. There, he found the week's mail delivery, a leather pouch which he tucked under his arm. He walked briskly back up the hills. It took more than an hour to reach the villa, but it was his only activity these days, and he forced himself to do it.

The villa also had a terrace, and a handsomely appointed study overlooking it. A fire was already going in the marble hearth. He pulled a chair close to a bust of Voltaire—Lausanne had been a favorite city of his—and examined the contents of the pouch, starting with the two recent numbers of the *Nation*, the weekly Republican journal started in '65 by Edwin Lawrence Godkin. The publication favored such party causes as honest government and bureaucratic reform. George marked an article for reading later. It dealt with resumption, a return to the gold standard as an antidote to all the inflated paper currency circulated during the war. Hard versus soft money was a passionate issue in his homeland.

Next he unfolded a three-page report from Christopher Wotherspoon. The profits of Hazard's ironworks were up once again. His superintendent recommended substantial political donations to those congressmen and senators who favored strong protective tariffs for the iron and steel industry. He requested approval from George.

There was a rather sad letter from Patricia, written in September, asking what he wanted for Christmas. He could think of nothing. His children had sailed to Europe in the summer, but their visit during the month of July had seemed interminable to him, and, he supposed, to them, since he was uninterested in sightseeing. They had done that for a week, then spent the remainder of the visit playing lawn tennis for hours every day.

Jupiter Smith, who packed the weekly mail pouch, had included three copies of Mr. Greeley's New York *Tribune*, with items of financial news marked. There was also an elaborately inscribed invitation to a Republican fete celebrating Grant's inaugural in March, and another to the inauguration itself. George threw both into the fire.

He clipped one of his Cuban cigars, which cost him nearly seven dollars each to import, though he no longer kept track of such things. He wasn't an extravagant man in most respects, and if money for small creature comforts ever ran out, he would shrug and then decide what to do.

He lit the cigar and stood by the window. Below the charmingly tiered city he saw another steamer, returning in the late afternoon. From the heights of Jorat it was a mere speck, like himself.

He thought of Orry's widow, a handsome and intelligent woman. He hoped Madeline was weathering the political turmoil in the South. He was not moved to write and inquire. He thought of his son, and of William's decision to read law; George continued to have no strong reaction one way or another. He thought of Sam Grant, an acquaintance from cadet days, and wondered whether he would be a good president, since he had no practical experience. He would probably try to run the government like a military headquarters. Could that be done? With a twinge of shame, he realized that when questions arose about the future of his country, he really didn't care about the answers.

On the lake, the steamer was gone. George remained by the window for some time, smoking and staring at the bright water. He had found there was great comfort in saying nothing, doing nothing, reacting to nothing. Or, as little of each as was possible in order to live. That way, though one became a creature of monotony, one never got hurt.

Mr. Lee from Savannah brought the final plans. There is now enough money again. Work will begin after New Year's. Orry, how it breaks my heart that you are not here to see. . . .

. . . Theo back again, out of uniform. There is something nervously distracted about him. About M-L, too. . . .

The lovers embraced in the sharp evening air, safe from observation in the heavy underbrush that had grown up where the formal garden once stood. Marie-Louise almost swooned when Theo's tongue slipped into her mouth. She was frightened but didn't pull away. She locked her hands behind his neck and swayed backward, so that the weight of his heavy wool coat and his body pressed her in a deliciously sinful way. Theo's lips moved over her cheek, her throat. His hand rode up and down on the side of her skirt.

"Marie-Louise, I can't wait any longer. I love you."

"I love you too, Theo. I'm as impatient as you."

"I've found the means. Let's tell her."

"Tonight?"

"Why not? She'll help us."

"I don't know. It's such a big step."

Earnestly, with great affection, he took her right hand between his. "I've cast my lot in South Carolina. And with you. If you're just as sure, there's no reason to wait."

"I'm sure. I'm frightened, though."

"I'll speak for both of us. All you need do is hold fast to my hand."

Marie-Louise felt as if she were dropping through a great dark space toward—what? Something she could only imagine. It would be bliss, or it would be disaster. She swayed and Theo caught her with one hand, a little amused by her girlish romanticism, yet in love with it, too. She whispered, "All right, let's tell her."

He whooped and whirled her around by the waist. A moment later they were hurrying up the dark lawn toward the lighted whitewashed house.

"Resign your commission?" Madeline said, astonished.

"Yes. I notified my superiors yesterday that it was my intention."

While Theo spoke, Marie-Louise stayed half hidden behind him. She held his left hand as though it were a lifeline. The young couple had burst into the house while Madeline was spreading the architect's drawings on the floor to point out details of the new great house to Prudence. In the corner lay some fresh-cut pine boughs intended for Christmas decoration.

"I reached my decision on the basis of two circumstances," Theo continued, with a formality that would have made her smile if his plan was not potentially so disruptive. "First, you said you might find temporary work for me here."

"Yes. I think you'd make an excellent manager for Mont Royal's mill and mining operations. But I never had any intention of precipitating—"

"You didn't," he broke in. "I'm resigning chiefly because of the other circumstance." He stepped forward, blurting, "Last week—"

"Theo." She pointed. "Forgive me, but you're standing on the new Mont Royal."

"Oh, no! I'm so sorry—" He jumped back, let go of Marie-Louise's hand, and knelt to smooth the wrinkle his boot heel had left on the drawing. Prudence smiled. Madeline chided herself for fussiness; it was another sign of age.

"There. Is that all right?"

"Yes. No harm done. You mentioned a second circumstance affecting your decision."

He gulped and leaped: "I've located an Army chaplain in Savannah who is willing to marry us."

Marie-Louise didn't breathe. She grasped Theo's hand again and held it tightly. The four lamps around the room shed an uncompromising light on Madeline's lovely but lined face. "Even though Marie-Louise isn't of legal age?" she asked.

He nodded, tugging at his cravat and then his mustache. "Yes. The chaplain—well, he doesn't like rebs very much. I told him Mr. Main was in the Confederate Navy Department and that's all it took."

Madeline sat back, frowning. "You put me in a very hard position. I can't condone such defiance of Cooper. And Judith."

"We're not asking that you condone it—" Theo began.

"Only that you give us a day or two," Marie-Louise pleaded. "Just don't tell Papa until we're back. Theo will do it then."

"That will still make me a party to deceiving him."

"Say that you knew nothing about it," Theo responded.

"Marie-Louise disappeared and I knew nothing about it?" He blushed, recognizing the foolishness of it. "No. I'd have to be prepared to assume my share of blame." She was silent a moment. "I don't think I want that."

Marie-Louise rushed to her, almost in tears. "If Theo speaks to Papa first, you know Papa will say no. He'll go on saying it till hell freezes."

"Marie-Louise," Theo said, stunned. Refined girls didn't say such things.

"Well, it's true. If you won't let us go, Aunt Madeline, we'll never be able to marry. Never."

Prudence went to comfort her; the young teacher was growing fatter, and tended to waddle. Madeline reflected on the situation, wondering why, now that the Klan seemed to have retreated in silence, and construction was about to start, this new problem had to be brought to her.

She wanted to stand by her refusal and spare herself another scene with Cooper. Then she remembered Orry describing what he'd put Brett and Billy through before the war, when he was uncertain about the wisdom of a Carolina girl marrying a Northern officer. He'd withheld his permission and kept them in torment when hardly anything else could have stopped them.

She studied the lovers. Did she have the right to deny them? Marie-Louise was right; Cooper would be unreasonable. But who was she to judge whether their love was genuine, mature, worthy of the permanent bond of marriage? Had her first burst of love for Orry been mature? No, far from it.

"Well, I'll probably rue it. But I am an incurable sentimentalist. I'll grant you forty-eight hours." Prudence clapped. "You may also have use of my elegant wagon for your bridal carriage," she added, wryly.

> *It's done. How they glowed with anticipation as they drove away! I hope their love will sustain Theo when he goes, as he must, to face his father-in-law. I will ride out the inevitable storm somehow. Cooper's regard for me could sink no lower under any circumstances. . . .*
>
> *. . . Next day. At noon, two of our black men unloaded the first wagons of construction lumber. The lumber sits where I can see it as I pen this, neat stacks of yellow pine, rough-hewn and finished in our own mill. Perhaps we can celebrate next Christmas in the new house.*
>
> *Oh, the world is set right again! . . .*

"I'll not have a Yankee soldier for a son-in-law," Cooper shouted at his wife after the young man spoke his rehearsed speech, took Cooper's abuse, and left, disappointed and noticeably pale. "I'll get the authorities on him. There is some legal way to undo it."

"There's no practical way," Judith said. "Your daughter spent two nights with him in Savannah."

"Madeline's to blame."

"No one's to blame. Young people fall in love."

"Not my only child, not with carpetbagging carrion." Saying that he'd spend the night in his office at the shipping company, he stormed out.

About one in the morning, a knock woke Judith. She found Cooper on the stoop. Two acquaintances had brought him home from the Mills House saloon bar, where he'd drunk bourbon whiskey most of the evening. He had then made insulting remarks to an Army major and probably would have attacked him if all the whiskey hadn't come heaving up suddenly.

The apologetic gentlemen carried Judith's limp and reeking husband upstairs. She followed with the lamp. She saw the gentlemen out, then undressed and washed Cooper, and sat by him until he woke, about half past two. His first words, after a few groans, stunned her:

"Let her lie in that dirty bed she's made with the Yankee. I'll not open the doors to this house to her, ever again."

She burst out crying, angry tears. "Cooper, this is too much. You're carrying your stupid partisanship to ridiculous lengths. I refuse to be separated from my own child. I'll see her whenever I wish."

"Not here," he yelled. "I'll give orders to the servants, and you'd better not defy them. I no longer have a daughter."

He flung the cover off and skidded across the polished floor to be sick in a basin. Judith bent her head in misery.

54

He sat in the chair at the rear of the third box, stage right. He chose the seat to avoid the spill of the stage lights. He didn't want her to see him until the moment he chose.

She lay on a divan upstage. The pillow used to smother her had fallen on the floor. Once he detected an unprofessional flicker of her eyelids. Her silver-blond hair, full to her shoulders, shone with the lovely luster he remembered. He felt no affection for her. His left hand, palm down, worked along his left thigh, as if the motion somehow could restore the severed muscle that had left him unable to leap nimbly in stage duels or perform romantic roles convincingly.

"Then you must speak of one that lov'd not wisely but too well—"

Trump's blackamoor make-up ran from the heat of the stage. It ran in distinct streaks, so that his face resembled zebra skin. Though he ranted to excess, the observer thought he did a generally creditable job. In fact, for a provincial effort, the production was quite good. Good, that is, in every respect but the performance of Trump's Desdemona. She was clearly having an off night.

The man in the box found himself unexpectedly entertaining the thought that Trump's *Othello* might be a passable importation for a three-week slot still open at the New Knickerbocker. With a new leading lady—Mrs. Parker would be in no shape to perform, ever again. He slipped his hand into his left pocket and reassuringly felt what New York toughs called a dock rat's drinking jewelry. Horseshoe nails, bent into finger rings.

"I took by th' throat the circumcised dog, and smote him— thus."

Sam Trump impaled himself on the prop dagger, staggering this way, then the other, his hand clenched aloft to indicate mortal pain. Mr. Trueblood, playing Lodovico, cheated down in order to regain the stage and cried, *"O bloody period!"*

Almost over; four speeches more. Then the important part of the evening's drama would commence.

". . . no way but this," Sam cried, and fell on Willa with unusual vigor. It knocked the breath out of her, hurt her ribs, and almost made her eyes fly open. She shifted under his sweaty weight, hissing through closed lips:

"Sam, your knee—"

"Killing myself, to die upon a kiss." His head and torso rose and slumped a second time. Sam did love to prolong his stage deaths.

She heard Lodovico corner the Spartan dog, Iago, and threaten him with torture for his plotting. *". . . Myself will straight abroad, and, to the state, this heavy act with heavy heart relate."*

The interval before the curtain thumped down seemed endless. Sam inadvertently kneed Willa's stomach as he struggled to his feet, the blackface dripping from his chin. "Are you ill, my dear? It was not good tonight." He jumped away without waiting for her answer. "Places for the call. Places!"

She bowed from her spot in line, again glimpsing the house, scarcely a third full. Very poor, even for the month of January. The curtain fell. Sam looked hopefully toward the curtain puller, anticipating a second call, but the applause was already gone. The actors walked offstage without saying much to each other. Everyone knew they'd been down. Willa simply shook her head at Sam, admitting her guilt, and joined the exodus.

She'd been cross ever since arriving at the theater. Bad temper was an inevitable failing of hers on those rare occasions when illness struck. For three days she'd been suffering from a stomach complaint. She'd felt a chill all evening and a dull ache in her middle; it robbed her performance of energy and conviction.

Sam wiped his embroidered sleeve across his face and chased after her. "Willa, my dearest, we simply must inject more life into—"

"Tomorrow," she broke in, slumping in a dejected way. "I promise, Sam. I know I was bad tonight. I'm sorry. I want to go straight to the hotel. I still feel terrible. Good night."

The burly man with the spongy bulbous nose left the box, turning up the sealskin collar of his overcoat to help hide his face. Not that he knew any of these loud, rude provincials in the audience. Or anyone in the company except the person he'd come to find.

He walked unhurriedly down the stairs and paused for a moment by the gaslit board in the lobby. Photographs of the artists were tacked to it. He studied the one identified as Mrs. Parker. The name had reached him in New York, as a rumor, and he'd next seen it on a crumpled Trump's Playhouse handbill brought back at his request by a traveling acquaintance. He had taken a long rail journey to investigate. His effort had been rewarded.

He slipped away from the lighted lobby, turned the corner, and crossed the street. The severed muscle had left him permanently lamed. It showed in an awkward side-to-side list as he walked.

In a patch of shadow opposite the stage entrance, he settled down to wait. Street lamps paled and their light diffused in a mist rising from the river. A foghorn blared. Chilled, he drew on a pair of yellow-dyed gloves. Then he took a thin silver flask from an inner pocket and drank some brandy. The flask flashed, reflecting a street lamp. The light revealed large initials engraved in the metal: C. W. Claudius Wood.

Willa tied her cape as she hurried out the door to Olive Street. She felt grimy and uncomfortable; she wanted to bathe and sleep. She tucked her hands into her fur muff and turned right, her heels tapping loudly on the planks, like staccato blows of a carpenter's hammer. Usually she waited for one of the actors to escort her. Tonight she was impatient. It had been a truly miserable performance, and a miserable Christmas season as well. Of course she'd joined in the caroling and gift-giving and the company's Yule feast, held on the stage. But whenever she smiled or chatted, she was acting; acting every minute.

President Andrew Johnson's Christmas gift to the nation had been unconditional amnesty for any Confederate still unpardoned. It was a landmark event, second only to the surrender, perhaps, but it had little meaning for her. There was no longer anyone close to her who was touched by the amnesty. Indeed, because it was such a potent reminder of Charles, the only emotion it generated was a bitter sadness.

At the first corner she stopped, having a distinct sense of some—some *presence* nearby. She turned and scanned the shadows across the way. Nothing.

She heard male and female voices as the troupe came out of the Playhouse a block behind her. If she lingered, Sam might catch her and lecture her again. So she hurried on, her breath trailing in a cool misty plume. She was feeling so low, she didn't want to see or speak to another human being.

Wood pursued her steadily, without noise, from a safe distance. When they reached the hotel block, Willa paused and glanced over her shoulder again. Wood held still beside the black rectangle of a bakery window.

As soon as she went on, he moved. He bobbed sideways at every step, a cripple robbed of the agility and panache a leading man needed. Well, the culprit, the thief, would soon be caught and subjected to a fitting justice. In his pocket, through the thin glove leather, the pads of his fingertips indented under the sharp pressure of the filed heads of the horseshoe nails bent into rings.

Warmth, light, the familiar smells of dusty plush and spittoons. Willa was so tired she almost staggered. She crossed the lobby to the marble staircase. A sleepy clerk with an oily forelock like a question mark roused himself. He held up a finger. "Mrs. Parker, there's a gentleman—" Her skirt disappeared around the first landing. Her heels rang sharply on the marble. "—waiting," he finished in the silence.

Wood crossed the lobby with an air of confidence, holding the key to his own room in another hotel so it was visible to the clerk leaning on the marble counter. The clerk studied him, tried to place him, couldn't. A guest who'd signed the ledger before he came on duty? Certainly that must be it. He wouldn't forget a man with such a pronounced limp.

The clerk turned the book so that he could examine the page of flowery signatures. By that time Wood was on the empty stairs. Just above the landing, out of sight of the lobby, he began to climb two steps at a time, pulling himself along by grasping the rail. His limp didn't slow him; it was the engine that powered his rapid ascent through the half-dark.

She turned left down the gaslit corridor, fumbling for her key. She reached her door, inserted the key, and was startled to discover that it didn't turn.

She touched the door. Her blue eyes flew wide. Unlocked?

He slipped the horseshoe-nail rings over the index, middle, and ring fingers of his gloved right hand and adjusted them so the filed heads of the nails were outward. He remembered that he must rake and slash, not punch, because the heads could cut through the dyed leather as easily as they could shred her face.

He stepped from the landing, saw her at the door. Walking rapidly, he said, "Willa."

Willa turned and saw the man limping toward her through widely spaced pools of light cast by the hall fixtures, trimmed low in their frosted mantles. She recognized him, though he was different—heavier, and there was more scarlet in his spongy nose. He bobbed from side to side like some child's toy, something wrong with one leg.

Then it came in a rush. The New Knickerbocker. The *Macbeth* dagger. She hadn't put enough distance between them, and she'd given him a potent motive for hunting her: that limp, ruinous for a leading player. What stunned her most, knotting her aching stomach as he rushed at her with alarming speed, were his eyes. They were pitiless.

"Well," Wood said, stopping. "My dear *Mrs.* Parker. My dear *Desdemona.*"

"Were you in the audience?"

He nodded, licking his lips. "You were wretched, you know. I do fear it's your last leading role. When I finish with you, you'll be fit for nothing but rouged character women. Hags."

She smelled the brandy on him. Her impulse was to bolt. It was the way she usually dealt with unpleasantness. But Wood's mass and height intimidated her. If she moved, he'd be on her instantly. She searched the corridor.

"Go on," Wood said, amused. He raised his yellow glove. He wore what appeared to be rings made of bent nails, the blued heads outward. "Run, yell. Before any of the guests wake and reach us, I'll have your face in tatters. Which is the way I intend to leave it." His left hand started for her throat, there at the door to her room. "The lovely Miss Parker. Lovely no more."

Willa flung herself back against the door. It opened, and she sprawled on the floor in the dark room smelling of furniture too long undusted. A sad little fir tree, totally brown, stood in a corner, its needles and tinsel strewn through the oblong of light cast from the hallway.

Wood swung his fisted right hand, and the sharp nailheads, down toward her face. Some intruder, some stranger who'd been hiding over in the dark window alcove, swept by above her. She saw light reflect from an eye, saw a multicolored cape swirl. Was it possible? Smelling the staleness of a smoked cigar, she knew it was.

"I heard you blustering outside," he said. "What do you want with this young lady?"

"There's a gentleman—" The clerk had tried to tell her. A gentleman *waiting*. He must have talked or bribed his way in with a passkey. *"We're old friends. She won't mind."*

"Stay out of this," Woods blustered, even though the man in the patchwork robe, a man with a ruffian's long beard in which the scab of a healed cut showed, now had him backed all the way across the corridor, to the wall.

"Charles," she called from the room, "that's Claudius Wood."

He turned his head, startled. "The man in New York?"

Wood's damp eyes bulged. Everything had reversed in a moment. He was wild to get away. Struggling up, Willa said, "Yes. He found me somehow and—*watch out.*"

Wood drove his fisted right hand at the stranger's face. Though the bearded man looked worn out, he was agile and strong. He sidestepped the punch, grabbed Wood's extended arm, and pulled it back across the hall full speed. The clenched fist struck hard on the frame of Willa's door. The sharpened nailheads sliced yellow leather, sliced fingers like sausages. Blood spurted. Charles pulled Wood by the front of his overcoat to position him, then punched him once. Wood caromed off the wall and sat down, finished just that quickly.

The night clerk summoned two members of the St. Louis foot police. The police shouted at the guests milling in the corridor, silencing their complaints, ignoring their questions. The younger policeman handcuffed Wood, and Willa led the other into her parlor.

The bearded man gave his name as Charles Main. No local address as yet. He'd ridden in from the west tonight.

"And you're Mrs. Parker. The wife and I, we enjoyed you as Desdemona very much. It's gratifying to have culture in St. Louis," the older of the two policemen said, flustered in the presence of a celebrity. With her statement about Wood's attack and motive, and Charles as a witness, it took but ten minutes for the policemen to satisfy themselves about Wood's guilt. In the hall, Wood alternately mumbled obscenities and raged like an incoherent child, further convincing the policemen that the young woman and her bearded friend were telling the truth.

"You'll have to sign a deposition, Mrs. Parker," the policeman said. "You, too, sir. But I doubt you'll be going anywhere tonight, will you?"

"And no further than the theater tomorrow," she said.

"Present yourselves at the station as soon as convenient. We'll charge the assailant, and lock him up until then."

And so the threat of Wood came to nothing. The policemen hauled him off, his fine overcoat smeared with his own blood, and left Charles and Willa standing in the dusty parlor amid the tinsel and litter of brown needles. Willa was so stunned and so happy to see him, she wanted to cry.

"Oh, Charles," was all she could say as she went to his arms.

She had a little Christmas whiskey left and poured a glass to warm him. She took a little bit herself; it soothed away some of the pain in her stomach. She curled up on a settee and got him talking, because he had a strange, harried look. "Where have you been? What have you been doing?"

"Something that proved you were right and I was wrong."

"I don't understand. Is your son—?"

"Gus is fine. Hardly knows me, I must say. I saw him at Leavenworth for three days, then came to find you." He took her hand. "I went to the Indian Territory, scouting for Custer. I need to tell you about it."

She listened for an hour. It began to rain, the slanting downpour dispelling the mist. Charles had an odd, cold aura, she thought. An aura of the far plains, of deep winter, enhanced by a faintly rank smell that even his malodorous cigars didn't mask.

He needed a bath, and he certainly needed scissors taken to his beard; it was thick as overgrown underbrush.

The whiskey warmed both of them. He interrupted his story at the point where Custer and his men discovered Indians on the bluffs after they took the village. He said he wanted to make love to her.

Reddening, she said of course, but he caught the slight hesitation, and frowned. She told him she'd been ill for the last few days, and wasn't over it. Then love-making could wait, he said. But he was very cold. She led him to the bedroom. He undressed while she put on her flannel gown. They climbed under the covers and he put his arm around her and went on talking.

"I was wrong to chase after the Cheyennes, trying to cancel one death with another. Look what it got me." He held up the tarnished metal cross hanging around his neck on a thong. "The revenge of killing a boy of fourteen or fifteen. Isn't that a fine accomplishment?"

She brushed his lined forehead with her palm. "So you left—"

"For good."

"To go where?"

"I told you, to find my son. Find you."

"And what now?"

"Willa, I don't know. When I crossed the Washita that last time, I said to myself, there isn't a place for me anymore. I can't think of one."

"I'll find one." She leaned close, rubbing her palm on the raw brush of his side-whiskers. "I'll find one for both of us if you'll let me. Will you?"

"I love you, Willa. I want to be with you and my boy. That's all I want. I'm just not sure—" His bleak eyes showed the terrible doubt. "I'm not sure even you can find a place. I don't know if there's any place on this earth that I belong."

55

Two days later, at Fort Leavenworth, Maureen cut biscuit dough with a tin cutter in the kitchen alcove of the brigadier's quarters. During the night the direction of the wind had changed, clearing the clouds and bathing the post in a flow of warm southerly air. The sun sparkled in pools of melted snow in the garden patch below the window. Maureen had propped the door open with her flatiron to let the breeze clean out some of the stale smells of winter.

January thaw usually restored her spirits. This morning she still felt blue. She'd felt that way ever since Mr. Charles swooped out of nowhere almost a week ago, announcing he was through with soldiering. He declared that he wanted to marry that actress in St. Louis, if she'd have him, and settle down to raise little Gus. Maureen heard the boy playing with the building blocks Duncan had sawed and shaped by hand from pieces of birch.

Maureen couldn't deny Charles the raising of his own son, even if she did disapprove of everything about the man, from his raffish dress to his cigars, his temper, and his undependable ways. Here one minute, dashing off the next. He'd stayed three nights and ridden away to see the actress.

No, she couldn't deny Charles; he was the boy's father. On the other hand, ever since the brigadier had brought her from the East, Maureen had hoped, assumed, that the raising and educating of little Gus would fall to her because Charles was too wild and unsettled to manage it. Now he'd come back, saying he wasn't.

Once he took the boy, her dream of the brigadier regularizing their relationship with a marriage proposal would never come to pass. She had almost decided she would have to marry

Jack Ford, a white-haired quartermaster sergeant on the post. Ford, Irish, a widower, loved the cavalry life but claimed he loved her almost as much. She didn't love him, though if she married him, at least her life would have some stability.

Duncan's quarters were quiet except for the sound of Gus playing and the usual drift of noises from the post: trumpet calls, gun caissons rattling, men drilling to shouted cadence. The brigadier was gone again on one of the circuits of the Kansas forts he made every two months with an armed escort. The routine was the same at every post. He would set up a small office while the soldiers queued up outside. The soldiers wore white cotton dress gloves, and each man peeled off the right one when he stepped before the paymaster. After the soldier signed the payroll sheet, Duncan, helped by his orderly, counted the appropriate amount in greenbacks into the soldier's hand. The soldier saluted with his left hand, about-faced, and the next man presented himself. Maureen had watched the procedure at Leavenworth many times.

She expected the brigadier back by nightfall. She was glad. She loved him, though he never uttered the word; probably never thought it in connection with her. She finished cutting the biscuits and laid them in rows on an iron sheet for baking after the sun went down; the stove's heat would take the chill off the shabby rooms.

She thought she heard a wagon somewhere close by. Looking out the window, she saw nothing. On the sill, burnished by sunshine, lay a clumsy six-barrel Allen pepperbox Duncan had bought for her soon after their arrival in Kansas. The Allen dated to the 1840s, but it was dependable for its purpose. In the event of an Indian attack, and impending ravishment, a woman was supposed to use a bullet on herself. The likelihood of Cheyennes or Sioux coming to loot, burn, and rape at a post as civilized as Leavenworth was ridiculous. Nevertheless the custom persisted; most Army women kept a loaded piece handy.

She heard a sound behind her. Gus was there. The sight of him, soon to be denied her, made her all the more blue.

Charles's son was four. A sturdy boy, he didn't resemble his father except for the warm brown eyes. Those were definitely Charles Main's eyes, but the shape of his face was squarer. Gus must have gotten that from his mother, the brigadier's niece, along with his dark blond hair, which formed a cap of tight curls. This morning he wore a gray work shirt and jeans pants with a strap pinned over the shoulder, and quilled moccasins bought from a hang-around-the-fort.

Gus was a smiling boy, but afraid of his father, which made Maureen all the more resentful of Charles's return. He was quick-witted, too. Maureen read to him every night. He knew most of his letters already.

"Reeny—" That was his name for her, a corruption from his first attempts to say Maureen. "I want to go out and play."

"Will you be warm enough?" He nodded. "All right, but stay in the garden where I can see you. Watch out for Indians."

"There aren't any Indians except the old fat ones who sit around."

"You never know, Gus. Just keep your eyes open, because you never know."

He sighed, feeling put upon, and from behind the partially open door fetched the broomstick horse Duncan had made and painted for Christmas a year ago. The horse was a golden color, with a foamy white mane. Duncan had put amazing realism into the painted eyes on the cutout head.

Gus took hold of the rope rein and was soon galloping up and down beside the garden plot, switching the broomstick with an imaginary quirt and then raising the same hand as a pistol fired by the index finger. Watching the boy romping in the sunshine, Maureen grew sadder still. He made her so happy. Why must she lose him?

She went to her room to lie down for five minutes. Perhaps what she was feeling was the onset of the female vapors; she was no longer a young woman. There was gray in her hair. She was very tired. The five minutes lengthened to fifteen.

Gus had slain about three dozen wild Indians when the wagon creaked out from behind the last dwelling in the row of identical houses. The peddler man wrapped the reins on the brake lever, glanced around as if hunting for customers, then climbed down.

Little Gus stood still, watching. He'd been slightly alarmed by the wagon's sudden appearance. Although there was no lettering on the side, he knew the wagon belonged to a peddler because some tin pots were hung on hooks above the driver's seat. Now he was more curious than scared, because the grinning peddler in the plug hat carried a fancy cane with a large gold knob that shone in the sunshine. Something else glittered below the peddler's left ear. Gold and white, it reminded Gus of similar ornaments he'd seen on the ears of officers' wives around the post. He'd never seen a man wearing one.

Assisting himself with his cane, the peddler came down behind the row of houses toward the boy. At each house he glanced at the back window, as if continuing to search for ladies to whom he might sell his tinware. The man's left shoulder was tilted slightly below his right one. From the way the peddler's mouth worked, Gus had the idea that it hurt the man to walk.

"Good morning, my lad. I'm Mr. Dayton, purveyor of kitchen goods and domestics. What's your name?"

"Gus Main."

"Is your mother inside?"

"Don't have a mother. Reeny takes care of me." He ran up the steps and peered in the door. He didn't see Maureen or hear her. "Don't know where she is. She was making biscuits."

He stayed on the bottom step. The peddler had a stale, bad smell, and something in his eyes upset Gus; he didn't know why. The peddler kept staring at him and rubbing the gold knob of his cane. Gus swallowed, trying to think of something to say.

He pointed suddenly. "What's that?"

The peddler stroked the bauble hanging from his ear. "Oh, just a little present from someone who owed me something. Would you like to pet my mule? He's a good old mule. He likes his ears scratched."

Gus shook his head, determined to have nothing more to do with this pestering, vaguely alarming man. "I don't think so."

"Oh, come along, pet him; he's hankering for it." Without warning, the peddler grabbed his hand, so tightly Gus immediately knew something was wrong.

"Gus, who's out there with you?" It was Maureen. The peddler's voice had carried, and brought her from her room. She pulled the door open and confronted a sight that frightened her for reasons she couldn't altogether explain. It was the stranger's eyes, possibly. Bright as those of a rabid dog she'd seen one time. In his greasy old claw-hammer coat, he didn't look respectable. He held Gus's wrist so tightly his fingers were white.

"You'd better let go of that boy, whoever you are," she said, starting down the steps. With a tremendous grunt, the man raised his cane over his head and bashed her skull.

Maureen pitched backward into the kitchen without a sound. The peddler lifted Gus off the ground, pinning him under his arm and covering his mouth with his left hand. The boy was strong and kicked and tried to cry out. The peddler scarcely had time to scratch something in the dirt with the ferrule of his cane.

The peddler lumbered through muddy garden plots back toward the wagon. All at once he was less confident about the outcome of his plan, which he had based on two principles: surprise and terror.

After locating Charles, and then his child, through Department headquarters—he'd been astonished to find the youngster on the same post where he made his inquiry—he'd prepared with some careful observation. For intervals of five minutes to a half hour during the past two days, he'd watched the movements of those living on officers' row.

It wasn't hard to do. Civilians moved about Fort Leavenworth with relative ease. When he first came to the post, he had no trouble convincing the gate sentries that he was a peddler, and that was the also the case when he made his inquiries, and, later, observed the officers' quarters. He *looked* like a peddler, which was just what he intended when he bought and outfitted the wagon with money taken from the dead farm couple in Iowa. Twice, while the wagon was parked near officers' row, people had questioned him, asking if he needed help. He immediately busied himself with one of the mule's hooves and said no, he could handle it, thanks, and that was that.

The one phase of the plan he'd pondered a long time was night versus day. At night, too many of the officers were in their quarters, while at this hour of the morning he had to deal only with women. Of course that was offset by the additional risk of discovery in daylight. But surprise and shock often slowed people's reactions. So he'd chosen daylight, audaciously, considering the stroke entirely worthy of the American Bonaparte.

Now he wasn't so sure. They boy tried to bite his hand. The peddler squeezed harder, until the boy's muffled noise indicated pain. "And you'll get worse, a broken neck, if you don't keep quiet," the peddler whispered.

At the second-to-last house on the row, an older woman's round red face looked out the kitchen window and registered astonishment. The woman ran to her door. "What are you doing with the brigadier's boy?"

By that time the peddler was up on the wagon. He flung the boy into the back and wrapped his head and mouth with a long rag, just tight enough to keep him quiet until they got off the post.

The hardest part was keeping the mule to a steady, ordinary pace while he drove away from officers' row. He heard the woman exclaiming behind him and banked on her running first to Duncan's, to rouse Maureen.

A troop of young cavalry replacements trotted by, going the other way, their drill sergeant cursing them for sloppiness. The peddler heard his captive kick and moan down behind the driver's seat. He snatched up his cane, reached behind him, and brained the boy twice with the gold knob. The second time, the boy went limp.

The peddler watched to be sure the boy was still breathing, then wiped a spot of blood from the knob and perked up the pace of his mule, rolling toward the sentry box at the gate.

Thirty seconds more and he was through, giving the sentry on duty an amiable tip of his old beaver hat. In another minute, the wagon pulled to the left and overtook a line of three oxcarts hauling wood to Leavenworth City. The peddler's wagon passed them smartly and disappeared up ahead.

Charles watched the ticking clock. Half past ten. Willa had promised she'd be back from the Playhouse by eleven-fifteen, so he had a while yet to peruse the *St. Louis Democrat.*

The paper carried an astounding letter, written by Captain Fred Benteen of H Troop. The letter vividly accused Custer of callous abandonment of Major Elliott and his detachment that day in late November. After the one search party had been turned back by hostile fire, Custer had sent out no others, concerning himself only with getting away from the menacing Indians on the bluffs. Exactly as Charles had heard it described, Custer's plan had been carried out. A march downstream with the band playing convinced the Indians that one or more of the remaining villages would be attacked. The Indians scattered to defend them, Custer countermarched, and his command escaped safely in the darkness. Leaving Elliott's body and the bodies of sixteen others where they fell.

No two accounts agreed on the number of Indian dead at the Washita. Custer claimed one hundred forty, all adult males, based on a battlefield count. Charles had seen no such count made while he was there. Later reports credited to "scouts" lowered the total to twenty to forty men, including Black Kettle, and an equal number of women and children. Charles believed the lower numbers; General Sully had recently admitted that Plains commanders usually inflated the number of hostiles killed in order to prove their military ability and satisfy a bloodthirsy public.

In early December, Generals Sheridan and Custer had marched back to the Washita and there discovered the bodies of Elliott and his men. Elliott had fallen facedown with two bullets in his head. The others, all stripped, were mutilated, some with throats cut, some decapitated.

And here was Benteen, mocking Custer's flight with bitter words: Custer, whom the Osage scouts lauded for his stealth by giving him a new name, Creeping Panther; Custer, whom the Olive Branchers were flaying as "another Chivington"—and not without justification, Charles thought. He fingered the brass cross he wore so he wouldn't forget what a man was capable of doing when he lived without pity, humanity, reason.

He couldn't believe Benteen had meant the letter for publication, though. Fred Benteen hated Custer but he was an experienced officer; he knew the rules. Charles was sure the paper had gotten hold of the letter in some unusual way. He was embarrassed by the satisfaction he got from seeing Benteen's accusations in print.

He heard footsteps in the hotel corridor and cocked his head. Ten-forty. Too early for—

She burst in, her face still made up. He tossed the paper aside. "What's wrong, Willa?"

"This came to the theater, for you. Someone slipped it to Sam onstage and he stopped the performance. Rang down the curtain."

"Why?" It puzzled Charles that a telegraph message could cause such consternation.

"Read it," Willa whispered. "Just read it."

YOUR BOY STOLEN BY FORCE YESTERDAY.

ABDUCTOR SEEN BY MAUREEN WHO COULD NOT STOP HIM.

HE LEFT A WORD MARKED ON THE GROUND. B-E-N-T.

IS THIS NOT THE MAN YOU HAVE MENTIONED.

AUTHORITIES IN LEAVENWORTH CITY HAVE NOT
CAUGHT HIM.

COME AT ONCE.

DUNCAN

It took three readings for Charles to believe it. Willa looked
stricken, watching the skepticism crumble from his face, to be
replaced by something frightening.

On the way north from the Washita it had struck Charles
that he was beginning a long and arduous climb back out of the
abyss of hell. Now he knew he'd mistaken the point at which he
started the climb. The Washita wasn't hell, but only hell's doorway; Sharpsburg had been hell's doorstep, and Northern Virginia, hell's approach road—

His mind was a chaos of loss, thoughts of Bent's hatred, Gus
Barclay's death, his failure as a father.

If only I'd been with him—

If only I'd been there—

He looked at the message in his hand. He knew what hell
was. He was there.

BOOK SIX

THE HANGING ROAD

You and I are both going home today by a road that we do not know.

CROW SCOUT *to* GENERAL CUSTER
before the Little Big Horn, 1876

56

Charles snugged Satan's girth. The piebald stamped and tossed his head. He was rested and eager.

"Goodbye, Willa."

Bundled in a shawl and shivering—the January thaw was over—she'd walked with him through the night streets to the stable. A whore and her customer, the latter almost too drunk to stand, were the only human beings they'd seen. A lantern burned on the ground by the stable door. Heavy cold mist from the river coiled and eddied a foot above the ground.

"How long will you be away?" she asked.

"Till I find my boy."

"You said they've already lost track of the man who kidnapped him. It may take a long time."

"I don't care. I'll find him if it takes five years. Or ten."

She almost broke down, seeing him hurting so badly. She rose on tiptoe and kissed him hard, holding his arms through the gypsy robe as if she could lend him strength that way. He was going to need so much. Unspoken between them—she didn't dare utter it, nor could he if he was to keep his sanity—was the possibility that Bent had already done to the boy what he'd done to George Hazard's wife.

"Come back to me, Charles. I'll find a place for us."

He didn't answer. He swung up on Satan and looked at her for a moment in a strange, sad way. His left hand stretched down to touch her cheek. Then he kicked Satan with his heels, and horse and man shot from the stable into the mist and dark, gone.

She blew out the lantern, rolled the doors closed, and walked eight blocks to her hotel, heedless of possible danger. A thought chased around in her head like one of those lines of dialogue an actor thought about endlessly because it was hard to speak or difficult to interpret.

Why didn't he say he would come back?

Guilt and nervous collapse had put Maureen in bed. Tinctured opium kept her drowsy. Charles could see her through the open door as he sat scooping up eggs with a biscuit. Duncan, wearing uniform trousers and suspenders over his long underwear, had scrambled the eggs and cooked them too long, giving them a brown crust. Charles didn't know the difference.

They had gone over it a number of times but Duncan seemed determined to do it again, as if still seeking explanations.

"Only a madman would conceive of stealing a child from a busy military post in broad daylight."

"Well, I told you, that's what he is. Back at Camp Cooper, the other officers in the Second Cavalry joked about Bent fancying himself a new Napoleon. Didn't Napoleon's enemies call him crazy? The devil? An ordinary man wouldn't and couldn't do what he did. I don't underestimate him."

Duncan stretched his suspender with his left thumb. His gray hair straggled over his forehead. He turned toward the bedroom; Maureen had cried out in her sleep. It was a few minutes before midnight.

"You're taking all this very coolly, I must say." Duncan was worn out, and it sharpened his voice. "It's your son, not some hilltop redoubt that was lost."

Charles raked a match on the underside of the table and put it to the cigar stub in his teeth. "What do you want me to do, Jack? Rant? That won't help me find Gus."

"You really intend to track Bent yourself?"

"Do you think I'd sit and wait for him to write a letter saying he's hurt Gus? I think he wants to give pain to as many of the Hazards and Mains as he can. I've got to find him."

"How? He has thousands of square miles to hide in."

"I don't know how I'll do it. I'll do it."

"I think it's just prudence to—to consider the possibility that Bent might already—"

"Shut up, Jack." Charles was white. "I refuse to accept that possibility. I absolutely refuse. Gus is alive."

Duncan's eyes roved away, full of misery, full of doubt.

"Yes, he sold me the wagon and the mule," said Steinfeld, a spry little man in a yarmulke who ran one of the Leavenworth City liveries. "That is to say, we traded even, after some haggling. Two horses, cavalry remounts but strong, for his wagon and the worn-out mule. He threw in the tinware he peddled. I gave it to my wife. He didn't have much, only what hung over the driver's seat."

"I suspect that's all he had to start with," Charles said. "Was the boy with him?" Steinfeld nodded. "What else did you notice?"

"He was polite. An educated man. He seemed to be canted —is that what I want to say?" Steinfeld lowered his left shoulder slightly. "Crippled, like this. A war injury, could it be? I also noticed his good vocabulary, and that pearl earring he wore. Very peculiar for a man to wear such an ornament, wouldn't you say?"

"Not if he wanted you to notice that instead of other things. Thank you, Mr. Steinfeld."

Steinfeld stepped back, away from anger so cold it seemed to burn.

Charles bought a spare horse from Steinfeld, a sorrel mare, three years old. Steinfeld said an itinerating Methodist preacher had owned her before he died of a heart seizure. She had stamina for long rides, he promised.

Charles packed food and ammunition and left Leavenworth in a heavy snowstorm. He tracked in the most logical direction, to the west, along the populated right-of-way of the railroad soon to be renamed Kansas Pacific. He stopped in Secondline, Tiblow, Fall Leaf, Lawrence. He asked questions. Bent had been seen, but no one remembered the earring. For some reason he'd abandoned it, just as he'd abandoned the wagon. Two people remembered a boy with curly dark-blond hair. A café owner in Lawrence who'd served Bent a buffalo steak said the boy looked worn out, and never spoke. He ate nothing. That is, Bent gave him nothing.

Alternately riding Satan and the sorrel, Charles pushed west through the high drifts left by the storm. He passed a plow train throwing huge fans of white to either side of its locomotive. Buck Creek, Grantville, Topeka, Silver Lake, St. Mary's.

Nothing.

Wamego, St. George, Manhattan, Junction City.

Nothing.

But in Junction City he heard that Colonel Grierson was wintering at Fort Riley. Detachments of the Tenth were scattered in the towns and hamlets along the rail line that now stretched more than four hundred miles, to Sheridan, a tiny place near the Colorado border. Work had been stopped at Sheridan in late summer, all hands paid off and discharged until the line received an infusion of cash in the form of a new government subsidy. All the excitement and glamour now belonged to the Union Pacific and the Central Pacific, ready to meet nose to nose somewhere west of Denver after the weather improved.

Charles pushed on. Snow became sleet, then rain. He slept in the open, or in the corner of a stable if the owner didn't charge him for it. Kansas Falls, Chapman Creek, Detroit. Abilene. The cow town was largely closed for the winter, but there he picked up the trail again. A man answering Bent's description had bought flour, bacon, and hardtack at Asher's General Store.

Asher happened to be a part-time deputy. An account of the kidnapping had been telegraphed to every peace officer in the state. When Asher had waited on Elkanah Bent he'd seen no sight of a child, but Bent's description, especially his crippled gait, had registered at once. Asher had pulled a pistol from under the counter and arrested him. Bent raised his hands. As Asher stepped from behind the counter, Bent seized a spade and brained him. The only others in the store, two elderly men playing checkers, failed to react. Bent had run out, and was not seen in Abilene again.

"Near thing," Asher said to Charles.

"Near isn't good enough. No one saw my boy?"

Asher shook his head.

Solomon, Donmeyer, Salina, Bavaria, Brookville, Rockville, Elm Creek. When he grew impatient, Charles had to back off and think of what he had decided before he set out. It was better to go, slowly, methodically, and catch Bent than to hurry and overlook something, thereby losing him.

Even so, he seldom managed to sleep more than two hours a night. Either nerves woke him, or bad dreams, or the simmering fever he'd developed from too much exposure. He was soon shivering and stumbling like someone half dead, his beard down to the middle of his chest and full of hardtack crumbs and tiny

scraps of the green outer leaf of cheap cigars. His eyes seemed to
have sunk into his head, leaving in their place an illusion of two
blurry dark holes. He smelled so bad, and looked so bad with the
Washita gunsight gash healed into a scar above his beard line,
that respectable people avoided him in the towns he visited to ask
his questions.

Which got the same maddening answers.

"No, nobody like that has been through here."

"No, haven't seen him."

"No, sorry."

It was early March when he got to Ellsworth. There he
picked up the trail so strongly, he knew he was meant to do so.

"He rested the night and so did his nephew, a pretty child
but worn out, half sick, the little lamb." She was a huge, hearty
woman with great pink hams for forearms and kind eyes and the
accent of the English Midlands. "I rented them my smallest room
and he ate breakfast with my boarders the next morning. I recall
it because he rudely kept his beaver hat on at the table. He repeated several times that he was going to the Indian Territory.
The boy stayed upstairs. The man said he was too sick to take
food but he didn't look it to me. I had a strange feeling about the
man. A feeling that he hoped to be noticed. I went to see the
town marshal a few hours after he rode away, and the marshal
said the man was wanted for stealing the boy. The bloody villain!
I wish I'd done it sooner."

One more witness, a boy Charles met by the river, corrobo-
rated her story. Charles rode on south twenty miles before he
stopped. He sat on the sorrel in the center of a small creek rushing and overflowing its banks because of a melt. The horses drank
thirstily while rain fell. Four or five miles west, misty shafts of
sunlight pierced down, lighting the land. In the extreme west,
blue showed between the clouds. The rain shower was heaviest in
the south, where it hid the horizon.

Charles pondered the situation. Below the Cimarron Crossing at the Territory line lay thousands of square miles of unex-
plored wilderness. A man hazarded his life if he went in alone.
That Bent would go there with a child was further evidence of his
insanity. Charles really had trouble interpreting and explaining
Bent's behavior in any rational way. He didn't try very hard,

though. Many of the possible explanations led to the same ending. An ending he refused to confront.

The rooming house story might of course be a fabrication. Bent might have doubled back after crossing the Smoky Hill. But somehow Charles didn't think so. Bent could have disappeared right after leaving Leavenworth if that was what he wanted. Instead, he'd strung out just enough of a trail to keep Charles on it. A trail like a thread waved in front of a cat.

Maybe Bent had flaunted his destination back at Ellsworth with the assumption that Charles would tell himself that further pursuit into the Territory was futile as well as dangerous, and give up. Maybe Bent had played out the string only so he could cut it this way, and ride off laughing. If that was what he figured on, he was wrong. Charles was going in.

But not alone.

"Retribution against a child?" Benjamin Grierson said. "That's unspeakable."

"I'd say that describes Bent." Charles sat on a hard chair in the headquarters office of the Tenth Regiment at Fort Riley. He ached deep in his bones. He was too sick to feel much beyond a slight sentimentality over the homecoming.

Colonel Grierson looked gaunter and grayer; the strain of Plains duty showed. But almost as soon as Charles had entered, he'd said that the regiment had fulfilled his expectations, and exceeded them. Now he said:

"What kind of help do you need? Every man in Barnes's troop would like to make up for what happened to you. So would I. We don't have that many fine officers. You were one of the finest."

"Thank you, Colonel."

"You know about President Johnson's Christmas amnesty? He pardoned the last exempted classes. You're not a rebel any longer, Charlie. You could come back—"

"*Never.*"

There was such fierce finality in it that Grierson immediately said, "What kind of help, then?"

"Two men willing to help me track. In fairness, Colonel, I'll be taking them south."

"How far? South of the Arkansas?"

"If that's where Bent goes."

"At Medicine Lodge the government promised to use its best efforts to keep unauthorized white persons out of the Territory. Wildcat surveyors, whiskey peddlers—the Army enforces that promise."

"I know. The ban might be the reason Bent wants to hide in the Territory."

"You'll have to stand on your own if you're caught there."

"Of course."

"Anyone you take, you must tell them first where you're going."

"Agreed."

"You're sure Bent's there?"

"As sure as you can be about a man with crazy impulses. An English landlady fed Bent in Ellsworth. Then a boy trying to fish in the rain along the Smoky Hill saw him riding due south with my son, the direction he told the lady he was going. The boy with the fishing pole thought it was a father and son on one horse, a dapple gray. My guess is, Bent's going down to hide with the Cheyennes and Arapahoes and the renegade traders because none of them will interfere with him, unless it's to kill him."

"Which they may do. Your damn expedition to the Washita stirred everything up. Sheridan's worked all winter to bully and threaten the tribes into surrendering to the government. Now he's got half the Indians starving and ready to come in and the other half ready to drink blood. Carr and Evans are still in the field. Custer, too. He's operating from Camp Wichita."

Charles digested that. The camp was east of the mountains of the same name, deep in the Territory.

"Consequently, no one can be sure where the Dog Soldiers are holed up. They keep moving to avoid the troops. West of the mountains—up on the Sweetwater beyond the north fork of the Red—they've even spilled into Texas, we heard. You won't know where they'll turn up, or the Army either."

"I'll keep that in mind." Charles fingered the brass cross hanging on a thong outside his gypsy robe. The brass was weathered almost black, and he didn't explain the peculiar ornament to Grierson, who wondered about it. Charles didn't act like a man who'd undergone some religious conversion, but he kept fingering the cross. "One thing, though, Colonel. The Washita wasn't my expedition."

"You mean you didn't plan it."

"And I'm sorry I was there. I saw the newspapers. I read what General Sheridan thought of Black Kettle. A worn-out old cipher, he said. The chief of all the murderers and rapers. A stinking lie. I know."

Grierson didn't argue. "Who do you want?"

"Corporal Magee if he'll go. Gray Owl if you can spare him."

"Take them," Grierson said.

Fort Hays remained a primitive post, one of the poorest in Kansas. Ike Barnes's company had wintered there, in the most undesirable quarters, shanties with stone chimneys from which the mortar was crumbling. In Magee's six-man shanty, the sod roof was so weak that he and the others had pegged up a spare canvas to catch falling dirt, melting snow, and the occasional wandering rattlesnake seeking a warm spot to rest.

Magee sat on his narrow cot late one evening after lights out, in the midst of snores and the sounds of flatulence. A lantern burned on the dirt floor between his feet. With a rag he was rubbing rust specks from the barrel of an old .35-caliber flintlock pistol of German manufacture. The rammer fitted underneath the barrel, and there was a blunt hook on the butt for hanging the weapon on a belt or sash.

He'd bought the pistol for three dollars, after a long search for just such a weapon. He'd sewn a powder bag out of scraps of leather; this lay near him on the blanket of his cot, next to five round lead-colored balls of a size to fit snugly in the pistol muzzle.

Polishing and polishing, he didn't pay much attention as the shanty door opened, admitting a gust of windblown rain and First Sergeant Williams in a dripping rubber poncho.

A sleeper sat upright. "Shut the fucking door! Oh, Sarge, 'scuse me." He lay down again.

The low-trimmed lamp set Williams's spectacles to glowing. "S'posed to have that light out, Magee. What're you doing with that old gun?"

"Uh-uh. New gun. Old trick." It was all the explanation he furnished.

"Well, come on outside," Williams said. "You're going to turn the color of a white man when you see who's back."

Magee, shivering in his underwear in the lee of the shanty, found Captain Barnes, wisely protected by a slicker, holding up a lantern to illuminate the visitor. "Popped out of the dark like a ghost, Magic. Ain't he a sight to behold?"

The old man intended a compliment, and Magic Magee's face almost bloomed into that brilliant, one-of-a-kind smile. But he saw Charles's fever-burned eye sockets and his filthy hands, so held the smile back. Charles said, "Hello, Magic."

"Cheyenne Charlie. I'll be switched."

"Get your clothes on, Magic," Barnes said. "I woke Lovetta and she's put the coffeepot on. Charles says he needs some help. He'll tell you about it."

"Sure," Magee said. "You came to the right man, Charlie. You're still holding my marker."

After the men talked, Lovetta Barnes fed Charles amply and made up a pallet for him near the fireplace. He slept sixteen hours straight, undisturbed by the comings and goings of the old man and his wife. Magic Magee hadn't hesitated about traveling to the Indian Territory. Neither had Gray Owl. Both men looked about the same, though each seemed to have more lines, and deeper ones, in his face. Charles supposed he did too.

They provisioned at the sutler's. Charles bought two spare horses, to bring their total to six, and in the ides of March, with bright sunshine returning and a warm wind blowing in from Texas and the Gulf, the trackers rode south over the Smoky Hill. Their first night out, Charles slept hard in the open air, but he dreamed a nightmare of the three of them riding across the sky on a trail of milky stars. They had blood-smeared faces. They were dead on the Hanging Road.

INAUGURATION.

Commencement of the New Era of
Peace and Prosperity.

Ulysses S. Grant Formally
Inducted
Into Office as President.

———

He Delivers a Brief and
Characteristic Address.

———

Economy and Faithful Collection
of the
Revenue Demanded.

———

The Ceremonies Marked
by Unprecedented Display
and Enthusiasm.

———

Special Dispatches to The New York Times
WASHINGTON, Thursday, March 4

The ceremonies attending the inauguration of Gen.
ULYSSES S. GRANT as the eighteenth President of the
United States were to-day carried out with a com-
pleteness and a degree of brilliant success which is a
most auspicious augury for the success of the Government, now transferred to such earnest and patriotic
hands. . . .

———

MADELINE'S JOURNAL

*March, 1869. Grant is president. Hostility to him here is un-
derstandable, but the national mood is one of optimism. Because he organized military campaigns so successfully, and so
often speaks of the need for peace after four bitter years, expectations for his presidency are high. . . .*

The tail of a northeastern snowstorm lashed the capital before dawn on the fourth of March. In the window bay of his
bedroom in the I Street mansion, Stanley Hazard scratched his

considerable paunch and peered at the drizzle, the mud puddles, the creeping mist. What else could go wrong with today's events?

Andrew Johnson would not be present at the swearing-in. Grant had spurned Johnson's discreet peace feelers in the wake of the Stanton dispute, and announced that he would not ride in the same carriage with Mr. Johnson, or even speak to him. The cabinet dithered. Should there be two carriages? Two separate processions? The matter was resolved then Mr. Johnson decided to stay in his office during the ceremony, signing last-minute bills and saying goodbye to members of the cabinet.

Stanley's unhappiness had a more personal side, however. Through the maneuverings of his wife, who was still snoring in bed, he had been appointed to the prestigious Committee of Managers for the inaugural ball. It was a great coup socially, and for a day or two Stanley was blearily pleased. Then he discovered that staging the ball might be akin to building one of the pyramids.

The committee couldn't agree on or even find a site large enough for the expected crowd. Growing desperate, committee members appealed to Congress for permission to use the Capitol rotunda. The House voted favorably but the Senate, after much empty talk of supporting the idea, voted it down. The President-elect sent a note saying it was all right, he didn't mind if no one honored him with a ball. Isabel's reaction was typical:

"He's canaille. Not a social grace to his name. Who does he think he is to deny us the premier evening of the year?"

Charged with bringing off this premier evening, Stanley and his associates spent hours in acrimonious debate. Should it be called a ball or a reception? The latter. Should it be ten dollars per ticket (admitting a gentleman and two female companions to supper and dancing), or a more modest eight dollars? The former. Should Mr. Johnson be invited in view of his estrangement from Grant over the Stanton matter? He was not invited.

Should the "more affluent coloreds" of the community be included, despite broad opposition? This vexing question was resolved when a representative of the group sent a note saying they would not attend if asked. Isabel said, "At long last those people are displaying a primitive intelligence. They know they'll be snubbed if they show their sooty faces."

The site finally found was large enough—it was the north wing of the Treasury building—but it wasn't ideal, because it was unfinished. Stanley had spent most of the past forty-eight hours

on the site. His fine suit covered with plaster dust and specks
paint, he had helped oversee the work of dozens of mechanic
completing the decorating and furnishing of the party rooms.

Now, groggy from exhaustion—he had slept little more tha
two hours—he confronted catastrophic weather. He felt suicida

He staggered to his bureau and picked up the admissic
cards for the ball. They were as big as the pages of a commerci
almanac, gaudily lithographed with a heroic bust supposed
combine the features of President-elect Grant and Vice Presiden
elect Colfax. It looked like neither. "Vile," Isabel called it. Sta
ley had whined for twenty minutes to convince her that he ha
had nothing to do with it. Head down, he stood there wonderir
whether all this travail was worth it merely to provide Isabel wit
one more opportunity to maintain her social contacts and ply h
devious and hypocritical brand of flattery. As usual, he had n
say in the matter.

He swung his head toward the window like a great ox in
yoke. He listened to the drizzle and wished it would grow torren
tial and wash away all of today's events, and his snoring wife to

The procession to the Capitol began at ten minutes befor
eleven. General Grant, a small, compact, retiring man in h
forty-seventh year, wore sturdy, sober American black, like all
the gentlemen attending. He rode in an open carriage. Boisterou
people who eluded the police lines and dashed into the mudd
street reached into the carriage to touch him. He didn't seem t
mind.

His escort consisted of eight divisions of marching units. Th
Washington Grays Artillery of Philadelphia, forty-eight musket
marched. The Philadelphia Fire Zouaves marched with the
twenty-two-man drum corps. The Eagle Zouaves of Buffal
marched, as did the Lincoln Zouaves of Washington, the Butle
Zouaves of Georgetown, and the Lincoln Zouaves (colored) o
Baltimore. These last were brilliant in white leggings and blu
flannel jackets with yellow trim.

The Hibernia Engine Company marched, together with th
Naval Academy Band, the Government Fire Brigade and Hos
Company Number 5 of Reading, Pennsylvania. The Suprem
Court marched. So did the Philadelphia Republican Executiv
Committee, the Lancaster Fencibles, and Ermentrout's Cit
Band, seventeen pieces. The Grant Invincibles of Californi

marched, along with the Montana Territorial Delegation and the Sixth Ward Republican Club, whose horse-drawn car featured a miniature *Constitution* complete with anchors, chains, and cannons manned by youths in sailor suits. This car was the clear hit of the parade, generating riotous applause among the throngs on Pennsylvania Avenue.

President-elect Grant seemed pleased and entertained by the spectacle. President Johnson's reaction was unknown; he was still at the White House, signing bills.

Under skies showing ragged gaps in the clouds and occasional swatches of blue, Stanley deposited his wife in their reserved seats. These were directly in front of the platform built over the steps of the Capitol's east front. The platform was crowded with chairs and festooned with bunting and evergreen boughs.

"Where are you going?" Isabel demanded. She wore a dusty-peach jacket and skirt. Colors were more festive this year.

"Inside, to pay my respects. Perhaps shake hands with the general."

"Take me with you."

"Isabel, it's far too dangerous. Look at this unruly mob. Besides"—it was one of the few points he could score with relative impunity—"these public rites are principally for men."

Her equine face wrinkled. "So was the procession, I noticed."

"You sound like a suffragist."

"God forbid. But don't you forget who made a success of Mercantile Enterprises!" Stanley cringed, hands raised. "*And* watched the books, supervised every expansion, saw to it that our estimable fraud of a lawyer, Dills, didn't rob us of every—"

"Please, Isabel, please," he whispered, his jaundiced complexion fading to paper-white. "Don't say those things, even among strangers. Don't mention that company. We have no connection with it, remember."

Isabel started to reply, realized he was speaking prudently, and said, "All right. But you had better not be gone long."

Clutching his tall hat with one hand, his special ticket with the other, Stanley started through the huge, generally jocular crowd of standees. He wriggled around mounted marshals and passed through a cordon of Capitol Police with heavy batons.

Rumpled, his pearl-gray cravat hanging out of his matching waistcoat, he at last reached the noisy corridor behind the Senate chamber.

He darted onto the Senate floor but saw no sign of his mentor, Ben Wade. The galleries were already packed with a thousand or more spectators. He thought he glimpsed Virgilia but quickly looked away. He wanted no contact.

He roamed among the dignitaries, shaking hands like the important Republican stalwart he was supposed to be. He was somewhat daunted by the rows of gold braid—Sickles, Pleasonton, Dahgren, Farragut, Thomas, and Sherman were already present—and he didn't attempt to greet such famous men. He did congratulate the magisterial Mr. Sumner, about to be sworn in for his fourth Senate term. He greeted Senator Cameron, now returned to power and office; the Boss acted as if he hardly knew Stanton.

He next spoke to Carl Schurz of Missouri, the first German-born citizen to reach the high office of senator. Without preamble, Schurz started to discuss the debt, one of Grant's chief concerns. As a student, Schurz had joined the 1848 revolution, and he was still a political zealot. He talked about greenbacks and specie and fiscal honesty until Stanley excused himself. He found men of conviction such as Schurz intimidating, perhaps because his own convictions were so few and so ordinary. He believed that his wealth would never bring him happiness. He believed his wife was repulsive and his two sons worthless. Levi, whose college career had consisted of one week of study followed by expulsion for knifing a fellow student in a dispute over dice, now owned a half interest in a saloon in New York's Tenderloin, and was also, by his own boast, a successful pimp. Levi's twin, Laban, had managed to get through Yale despite an equally riotous disposition and a bad case of the pox in his second year, and was now establishing himself as a high-status thief, a term Stanley applied to all lawyers.

He went to Wade's office and squeezed up near the closed door. "Sorry, sir," an usher said, "Senator Wade is closeted with General Grant until the ceremonies begin."

"But I am Mr. Stanley Hazard."

"I know," said the usher. "You can't get in."

Smarting, Stanley retired.

Before going outside again, he whisked a slim silver bottle

from an inner pocket and refreshed himself with his fifth drink of the morning. At his seat, he told Isabel he had met the President-elect, theoretically a coup because Grant had done little personal campaigning and had attended few party functions. He promised to introduce Isabel at the ball.

"You'd better."

The crowd stretched away on either hand, with the usual hat-throwing and hip-hip-hurrahing punctuated by screams whenever a tree branch gave way and dropped those whose weight had broken it. At 12:15, approximately the hour Andrew Johnson was to shake hands with his cabinet and depart by carriage from the front portico of the White House, the official platform party emerged from the Capitol.

Grant looked dignified in his black suit and straw-colored gloves. Justice Chase nervously administered the oath. Grant took it, bent to kiss the Bible, then delivered a brief address. Isabel's comment on the entire proceeding was, "Pedestrian."

P E A C E

The great motto burned in the dark high above. Stanley stood admiring the committee's handiwork. The special illumination was created by gas jets across the front of the Treasury Building. It had been expensive to design and erect, but the effect was spectacular. There, for Washington and all the world to see, was the Republican presence, the Republican pledge.

While Stanley gawked, Isabel complained of the delay. They had joined other formally dressed couples hurrying inside.

A string orchestra serenaded from the balcony of the enormous Cash Room. In a stately setting of Siena and Carrara marble, the specially commissioned allegorical painting "Peace" was on display. The easel was surrounded by a good-sized crowd. Stanley and Isabel unexpectedly bumped into Mr. Stout, just returned to the Senate for a full term. On his arm was a hard-looking woman, much younger, with a tiara of sapphires in her hair. Very coolly, Stout said to them:

"I believe you know my wife, Jeannie?"

Isabel was enraged. This was the young woman who had been Stanley's mistress until Isabel discovered it and ended the affair. She was Jeannie Canary then, a variety-hall singer.

"Ah, yes—" Flustered, Stanley straightened his white tie. "I had the pleasure of watching her, ah, perform on many occasions."

Stout didn't immediately catch the inadvertent double meaning. When he did, he reddened, as if ready to call Stanley out for an old-fashioned duel. Jeannie looked equally piqued. Isabel pulled her husband away. Her eyes were misty. Stanley was astonished; his wife never wept.

"You foul-mouthed beast," she whispered, tearfully looking straight ahead. For once he was too thunderstruck to take the slightest pleasure.

Isabel wouldn't speak to him thereafter. She shook her head to offers of food or wine and refused his limp invitation to waltz. She did follow along when President and Mrs. Grant appeared and Stanley, lemminglike, rushed with dozens of others to present himself. Damnably, Stout and his wife were with the Grants.

Eventually Stanley and Isabel got their turn. Stanley mumbled their names, which Stout repeated. Isabel stared at her husband in a hostile way while the President shook Stanley's hand.

"Ah, yes, Mr. Hazard. The Pennsylvania Hazards. I know your brother George. You were a liaison officer with the Freedmen's Bureau, were you not?"

"Yes, Mr. President, until the end of '67. At that time I retired to oversee my business investments. I must say, sir, your program for the economy is very sound."

"Thank you, sir," Grant said, and turned to greet the next couple.

Isabel was even angrier than before. "You lying wretch. You didn't meet him this morning."

"No. They wouldn't let me into Wade's rooms."

"You've humiliated me sufficiently for one evening, Stanley." She had also seen, and been seen by, everyone important. "Take me home."

Stanley was the first of the Committee of Managers to depart.

Grant noticed. To his wife Julia he said, "Very likable, that Hazard fellow. Strikes me as a man of intelligence and substance."

Senator Stout overheard. *If Mr. Grant believes that, we have a naïve dolt in our highest office. God save the republic.*

Marie-Louise and Theo have at last settled in a tiny cottage on Sullivan's Island, found for them by the man who hired Theo for a better job than Mont Royal could offer. The man is another Yankee carpetbagger.

The city is considerably restored, but much more remains to be done. Gullible travelers alighting at the pier are still asked, "Would you like to see Mr. Calhoun's monument?" If they say yes, the cynic points to the city.

Theo's employer has been part of the slow rebuilding process. He arrived in the autumn of '65, saw a need, and set up a firm to construct new sidewalks with sturdy curbs to protect them from vehicle damage. His crews also fill and repair numerous bog holes, and the shell craters left by the Swamp Angel, etc. The glories and excitements of lavish balls, secession conclaves, and romantic farewells have given way to road-mending and other mundane matters.

The Yankee road-mender is prospering. He has developed large city contracts locally, and in Georgetown and Florence. Theo replaced the Yankee's first foreman, who ran off to Brazil with a mulatto girl. Theo works 12–14 hours a day, 6 days per week, supervising black work gangs, and declares that he and M-L are now quite happy. They were not earlier. Upon returning from Sav., and following Cooper's rebuff of them, they lived for some weeks in a poor cabin in the palmetto scrubs here on the plantation. The only thing that made it possible for them to survive was the job I provided. Theo was an excellent supervisor, and I hated to lose him, but I could not refuse his request to leave.

The young couple's relations with C. are not improved, however. C. will not receive them, or in any way recognize their presence in the city. Judith must visit her daughter secretly, the way she visits me. I appreciate that the war damaged many lives. But there is a point where pity yields to impatience. Cooper's new politics, and his treatment of his family, put him beyond sympathy. Beyond mine, anyway. . . .

. . . Sim's boy Grant, a young man now, was caught by the Klan near the crossroads last night. He and two friends were held captive for an hour, forced into what the robed men called a jigging contest. The three danced at gunpoint with

*pails of water balanced on their heads. It all sounds so child-
ish. Yet Grant came home wild-eyed and demoralized. At
least he was not harmed. Last week, Joseph Steptoe was
whipped by some of the same men. Bleeding copiously, he was
wrapped in a sheet smeared with salted lard and left at the
roadside. He and his wife vanished from their cabin near the
Episcopal chapel next day; not seen since. Joseph S. was a
corporal of the district's colored militia. Grant is a member
too.*

*I do not know how a band of men can be ludicrous and
menacing at the same time, but that is the puzzling nature of
this "Klan."*

*To C'ston, to see Theo and M-L, and once more plead
with Dawkins. . . .*

"No," the obese man said. Amid the correspondence and
sheets on his desk, Madeline saw a cheaply printed paperbound
book, *Your Sister Sally.* She had seen a copy before. An import
from Mississippi, the book contained exaggerated descriptions of
the ruin and rapine whites could look forward to under a black-
dominated legislature. Gettys sold copies at his store.

"Leverett," she said with forced composure. "Mont Royal is
earning money. Even rebuilding the house, I have enough to pay
off substantially more of the mortgage every year. I hate to see so
much interest flow out unnecessarily."

The office was dark wood and deep green plush; Dawkins's
special chair was upholstered with the material. "I reiterate the
bank's stated policy. No prepayment." He licked his lips. "If you
refuse to be flexible, so do we."

"Flexible." Madeline gave it a bitter ring. "You mean close
the school. You were a liberal man once. What are you so opposed—?"

"Because these nigger schools are not schools at all. They're
centers for political action. All Conservatives oppose them."
Conservative was the new label of the anti-Republican coalition
of Democrats and former Whigs.

"Wade Hampton's running a school on his plantation. He's
an avowed Conservative."

"Yes, but tainted by certain unfortunate views. There is no
point in discussing General Hampton. He is a unique case."

He means untouchable. Which I am not.

"Leverett, I wish I could understand. Why are you so completely averse to giving people a decent education?"

"Not people. Nigras. The idea is poisoning South Carolina. First we got those Yankee women teaching down at St. Helena. Then your free school. Now we have public ones. As a result, not only do we have vengeful inferiors trying to govern us, but we have a crushing financial burden in the form of obnoxious school taxes."

"So it comes down to money. To greed."

"Justice! Fairness! The provision in the state constitution calling for public schools was none of my doing. None of Mr. Cooper Main's, either, I might say. We dined together at my home only last week, and I know his state of mind. And the various circumstances responsible for it," he added, flashing her a sharp look. She supposed the banker was referring to Marie-Louise's marriage.

"Your brother-in-law and I are in complete agreement about the schools," Dawkins continued. "Since they were forced upon us by the Federal government, let the Federal government pay for them."

"I get no government money, Leverett."

"But I understand you get many visits from Yankee clerics and bureaucrats who think your school is a model of Radical action. I am surprised the Kuklux have not returned. I don't advocate violence, but you will have only yourself to blame when they do."

> . . . *Such remains the prospect for the future. Sometimes I beg God to deliver me from everything connected with* "the Reconstruction!!"

57

"Pretty?" Bent said. "Pretty, Gus?" He reached across to his left ear and shook the teardrop earring.

The small fire crackled and snapped in the March wind. They were camped on a barren slope in the Wichita Mountains, granite peaks that rose abruptly from the plain. Two days earlier, north of the mountains, Bent had sighted a cavalry column moving east to west ahead of him. He identified it as cavalry and not an Indian band because of its orderly march, and the colors and guidons raised above it. He'd dragged little Gus to the ground and forced the dapple gray to lie down until the column passed from view. He hadn't felt safe about building a fire until this evening.

He turned his head slightly, presenting the left side of his face to the boy, extra temptation as he jiggled the earring again. "Isn't it pretty?"

In a face unwashed for days, Gus's eyes shone like polished brown stones. Bent's discipline had left its mark in those eyes. It had also left a scabby welt on Gus's chin, another on his forehead, and a bruise like a splatter of mud around his right eye. Bent had reduced the boy to a state of perpetual fear and total dependence; the four-year-old was grateful for every scrap of stale beef and every swallow of tepid water his captor allowed him. He hardly said a word, afraid of goading Bent to anger. He'd learned quickly that the man's anger could flare without clear cause.

Bent kept jiggling the earring. Gus didn't know what his captor expected of him. Bent smiled and the boy decided he wanted him to touch the earring. He flexed his fingers. Raised his hand. Extended it tentatively—

Bent struck him so hard he fell over. He yanked Gus up by his hair, slapped his face twice. "Bad boy. Mustn't grab. If you're a bad boy, then my friend wakes up."

From the pocket of his filthy claw-hammer coat he took the straight razor. Flicked it open. Gus scooted backward, mouth open. He made no sound; Bent whipped him if he was noisy. But he'd seen the razor before. He'd been cut by it.

The campfire rippled silver flashes along the blade. Gus cringed back another foot or so, scooting on his bottom. Bent smiled again. "You know what my friend does to bad boys, don't you? He hurts them."

Bent got to his knees with great speed and flung his arm out ove the fire. The edge of the razor sped toward Gus's throat. Gus screamed and fell on his side, covering his face. Bent had pulled his thrust at the last moment, stopping the blade six inches from the boy's neck.

Gus's scream was so piercing, it ruined the sport somehow. In his head Bent heard strange echoes of the cry, punctuated by a weird pinging. He dropped the razor, ran around the fire, and shook the boy by the shoulders. "You are a really bad boy. I told you never to make noise. If you make noise again, I'll let my friend bite you. You know how it feels when he bites you."

Gus began to whimper, wet sounds. Bent took off his plug hat and swabbed his shiny forehead with his sleeve, leaving streaks of dirt. "That's better. Pull up your blanket and go to sleep before I ask my friend to punish you for being so bad."

Carefully, silently, Gus hitched across the ground to a filthy saddle blanket. Lice had long ago migrated from the blanket to his body and hair. His eyes showed over the edge of the blanket after he pulled it up. Bent cleaned some dirt from the razor blade with the ball of his thumb. At certain angles the blade caught the firelight, throwing a scarlet-white reflection into Gus's eyes. The third time it happened, the boy hid beneath the blanket.

It was satisfying to hurt the boy. Each time he did, Bent felt he was hurting Charles Main too. Hurting Gus also had a practical benefit. It forestalled attempts to run. Gus was thoroughly cowed; he didn't chatter or display the energy typical of a four-year-old. When he was awake, he was as silent as a sick old man. Bent had broken him like a horse. He surveyed the huddled shape covered by the blanket. "Good," he said under his breath. "Good."

The picketed dapple gray had lain down on the ground for a roll almost half an hour ago and still hadn't gotten up. The horse looked at Bent with eyes that reminded him of the boy's. He was worn out. His ribs showed and he had sores in his mouth. Bent would have to shoot him in a day or two, and then they would have to travel on foot. At least they could eat the meat.

He put his hat on, folded up his razor, and sat with his back against an uncomfortable granite outcrop. He drew his revolver and laid it beside him, then pulled his own blanket over his legs. He listened for a while to the sullen whine of the wind across the treeless slope. Here and there some stunted brush swayed in a strong gust. It was time to give some thought to the future. He needed a refuge for the summer months. Food was running low, and he faced the constant threat of an Army patrol catching him in the Territory, where he wasn't supposed to be.

For a time, chasing across Kansas, deliberately leaving clues to his whereabouts to torment Gus's father, he hadn't worried about personal safety. Then he'd been forced to brain that storekeeper in Abilene, and soon after he'd aroused the suspicion of the fat slut who ran the rooming house in Ellsworth City. At that point he'd decided the game was no longer worth the risk. Charles Main knew he had the boy, which was good enough for the time being. He cut off his trail by turning south to the Territory, where he felt he could hide safely for an indefinite period. Because of the inherent danger, he was convinced Charles would never follow him.

With his shoulders painfully braced against the granite, he stared down at the dark distances of the lightless plain, thinking of Charles as he'd looked when they served in the Second Cavalry before the war. He was a handsome big lout, with the smarmy good manners typical of Southrons. Bent had found him sufficiently attractive to make an advance, which Charles rebuffed. Bent hated him all the more for that. His eyes shifted to the motionless lump of blanket. He wasn't finished with Gus, or his father, either.

Next day he shot the dapple gray and cut him up. When he insisted that Gus eat half-cooked horse meat, the boy resisted. Bent forced meat into his mouth and Gus vomited all over Bent's boots. He had the sharp edge of the razor against Gus's throat before good sense asserted itself. He needed the boy to fulfill his plan later.

Trembling with an excitement much like that produced by sex, he put the razor away and forced the boy to clean the vomit off his boots with small dry branches broken from the shrubs that clung to the slopes.

He left the old stolen saddle with the corpse of the horse, taking only the saddlebags. As he walked in a westerly direction, away from the mountain where they'd camped, little Gus followed one step behind and one step to his left, like a well-trained pet.

Vermillion Creek fed into the Elm Fork, sometimes called the Middle Fork. The creek ran into the river from the north, somewhat west of the Fork's confluence with the North Fork of the Red. It was a lonely region west-northwest of Fort Cobb, and by Bent's reckoning not far from the Texas border.

The barren Wichitas lay behind them in the east. This land was prairie with a lot of shale showing along the waterways, and thick growths of stunted-looking jack oak and post oak to break the horizon. There was abundant wildlife—plump jackrabbits, prairie chickens, even a deer Bent fired at and missed. They didn't starve; generally he was an excellent shot.

Bent began to feel the restorative effect of the spring weather as he and the boy trudged up Vermillion Creek, exploring. An almost constant wind swayed the patches of wild violet and blue indigo, and brought a pink rain of blossoms from a stand of flowering Judas trees. High overhead, wedges of geese flew north.

One moment Bent heard Gus's split-open shoes rattling the shale, and the next moment there was silence. He turned to discipline the boy but he didn't because of the boy's expression. Gus was looking farther along the creek. His eyes were momentarily free of fear and full of curiosity.

Bent turned around again and caught his breath. A fire hidden below the horizon was sending a thin gray column into the clear sky.

Indians? Quite possible. It could also be something like the camp of buffalo hunters. Bent pushed Gus into the ankle-deep water. "Wash your face and hands. We must look presentable in case we meet white men."

Water flowed through Bent's fingers, darkened by dirt. Gus

imitated him, watching him constantly for signs of displeasure. The dirt slowly vanished from the boy's face but the marks of punishment remained.

It was not merely a camp, it was a civilized outpost on the bank of the creek. Completely unexpected, remarkably substantial. The main building, from which the smoke rose, was rectangular, constructed of mud brick with a dirt roof the builder had given a slight pitch for drainage. From concealment in some post oaks, Bent look with astonishment at two Indian ponies tied at the front door, which faced the bright creek. A side door opened into a small corral holding a big chestnut and two mules. A small outbuilding, a primitive stable, was half hidden by the main place.

Gus suddenly cried, "Look," and pointed. Bent slapped a hand over Gus's mouth and twisted the boy's head until he made a hurt sound. Only then did Bent take his hand away.

He was intensely curious about the animal that had excited Gus. It was a raccoon, very well fed. Its furry belly dragged the ground as it loped along the front of the main building. Someone's pet?

Bent slipped the saddlebags off his shoulder and unbuttoned his old coat. He brushed the butt of his tied-down revolver to be sure it was clear, then snapped his fingers. Instantly, Gus grasped his hand.

Man and boy approached the building on the rocky shore of the creek. The raccoon spied them and ran off toward the stable. Bent paused near the front door. He heard voices in conversation. He didn't want to be shot as a prowler and yelled, "Hello in there."

"Hello. Who's that?"

The door squeaked open. First out were the muzzles of a shotgun. Then the man holding it appeared. He was poorly dressed, swag-bellied, and had a face that reminded Bent of a flushed Father Christmas. The man's hair, more gray than white, was center-parted and worn in long braids. A beaded band wrapped the end of each braid. Small trade bells tied in the right braid jingled.

"Captain Dayton's my name. My nephew and I are lost. We're bound west."

"Not through the Indian Territory if you know the law," the man said, implying doubt of Bent's honesty.

"We're not in Texas?"

"Not for a few miles yet." The man searched behind Bent, as if looking for soldiers who might entrap him. He scrutinized Bent again. He decided the tall plug-hatted stranger must be just as close to the edge of the law as he was.

Color returned to the man's hands as he relaxed his hold on the shotgun. "I'm Septimus Glyn. This is my ranch."

Not much of a ranch, Bent thought. "What do you raise, Glyn?"

"Nothing. I sell what the Indian Bureau won't." The man had an assertive manner but he didn't strike Bent as dangerous. A renewed sense of personal importance was energizing him. What if this ignorant trader knew he was speaking to the American Bonaparte? Wouldn't he be amazed?

"I have a little money, Glyn. Do you sell any food?"

Glyn again thought about Bent's surprise appearance in this wilderness. He didn't know what the man was really up to, but he decided a profit merited some risk. "Yes, I do. And whiskey, if you're thirsty. Got something else you might like, too." He stepped aside. "Come in."

Bent strode forward, pulling Gus. "Handsome little boy," Glyn said. "Marked up some."

"Fell off a horse."

Glyn didn't ask questions.

When Bent stepped in, he was startled by the furnishings: two large round pine tables, badly stained; chairs; a wide plank set across nail kegs piled two high with a row of unlabeled bottles on a shelf behind. A red blanket curtained a door, which perhaps led to living quarters.

At one table, two Indians sat with a brown bottle. Both were middle-aged. One was obese. They regarded Bent and the boy with puffy eyes full of suspicion. "They're Caddoes," Glyn said, putting the shotgun on his homemade bar. "Harmless. I run off any Comanches who want whiskey. They're too unpredictable."

So this was one of the illegal whiskey ranches. Bent had heard there were a number of them operating in the Territory. They purveyed weapons, staples, but mostly the whiskey the government didn't want the tribes to have.

The red blanket lifted and Bent saw something else that

stunned him. A light-brown Indian girl stood there, her deerskin dress much soiled by food and drink. He thought at first that she was in her thirties. Her eyes were slitted from sleep and her black hair hung loose in uncombed tangles. She had a sullen air. She moved toward Glyn, barefoot, pushing hair off her right ear and eyeing Bent in a bold way. He in turn noticed the fullness of her breasts under the hide dress. He felt an unexpected quiver. He hadn't had a woman, or wanted one, for over a year.

Glyn poured a clear fluid from a bottle. "This is my wife, Green Grass Woman. She's Cheyenne. I took her from her village a year ago. She wanted to see the world, and I've showed her how it looks from flat on her back. She's but eighteen winters. Got a lively taste for gin, though. I taught her to like it, and certain other things." Glyn cleared his throat. "What I mean to say is—she's for sale too."

Bent bobbed his head. He'd already decided he wanted her. He had no intention of paying.

Septimus Glyn served up some slabs of cold venison and whiskey that tasted like it had been spiked with cayenne. It made Bent's lips burn. "Where do you get this stuff?"

"Over in Texas. Dunn's Station. There's a few Rangers over that way, but I dodge them. Once a month I traipse around to the Indian villages. Not many are left now that the Army's come in. The rest of the time I make a living here. They threw me out of the Bureau but I liked the country, so I stayed. I especially like screwing Indian women. They've got a special musky quality. You can find out for two dollars."

"Maybe later. Gus, eat something." The little boy tore up scraps of venison and forced them into his mouth. Looking bilious, he chewed.

Bent decided he'd found his haven. "We really want to make it to California before the winter. But we can pass the night with you if you've no objection."

Glyn shook his head. "Sleep in the stable, or my wagon, parked in back. Cost you a dollar."

"Fine," said Bent. He found a paper dollar in his coat and smoothed out the wrinkles. He gave it to Glyn, not really concerned, because the transfer was to be temporary.

The old Caddoes, defeated men who drank till they staggered, left before sunset. Bent and little Gus put their blankets in the old covered wagon, which was snugger than the shed that served as a stable. Bent repeatedly touched himself; he'd been stiff with excitement most of the afternoon.

He waited several hours, until he could stand it no longer, then crept from the wagon without awakening Gus. He opened the front door of the whiskey ranch with only a single telltale squeak, which didn't matter since there was already a lot of noise, moanings and gruntings, from behind the red-blanketed doorway. Bent drew his revolver.

He crossed the main room, guided by a glow behind the blanket. The Cheyenne girl was uttering deep, loud moans. Bent peeked past the edge of the blanket. A dim lantern showed him the girl's sweating backside; she was astride the whiskey trader, pumping up and down with her head thrown back, her eyes closed. Glyn was rubbing her breasts. Both hands were in sight, and his shotgun was leaning against the wall, well out of reach. Good. What counted now was speed.

Bent tore the blanket aside and took three strides to the bed. In that interval, Green Grass Woman shrieked and Glyn's eyes popped open. He started to grab for his shotgun but gave up. "What the hell are you doing in here, Dayton?"

"I want this place," he said, smiling.

"Why, you damn fool, it isn't for sale."

Bent reached past the Indian girl's forearm and shot him above the eyes. He dragged the body to the other room, then went back in, unbuttoned his pants, and rolled her on her back. She took him in, too frightened to do otherwise.

So Bent acquired the whiskey ranch. Two days later three other Caddoes appeared. In broken English they asked about Glyn, whom Bent had buried a half-mile away. "Gone. He sold me the place." The Caddoes didn't question that. He made four dollars on whiskey before they left.

Green Grass Woman didn't seem to care who her man was so long as he permitted her to drink gin. The cheapest, sweetest of gin, Bent discovered after one taste, which he spat out. Septimus Glyn must have been a prime seducer of women to corrupt the young girl so completely. One morning Bent refused her the gin to see what would happen. She begged. He continued to re-

fuse. She wept. He still said no. She fell to her knees and tore at
the buttons of his trousers. Astonished, he let her confirm his
belief that all women were depraved whores. While she still held
his legs, he pushed her head back and poured some gin into her
mouth. He didn't see the boy standing at the door, one hand
holding the red blanket aside. His feet were bare, his gray work
shirt stiff with dirt, his eyes huge in his blank face.

At sunset of the seventh day, Bent began to feel at home.
He'd hung up the frayed, cracked oil painting of Madeline Main's
mother, and cleaned up the place. Just before the light went, he
stepped outside with his arm around Green Grass Woman. Her
big soft breast pushed against his side and her lip moved against
his in an arousing way.

Little Gus, left largely to himself, had gotten acquainted
with the tame raccoon. He was chasing it along the creek bank in
the reddening light. The creek shone like flowing blood, and in
the cool evening air Bent heard a sound he hadn't heard in a
while. Little Gus's merry laughter.

Well, why not let him laugh? He'd be deprived of the chance
soon enough. Bent was now set on his plan. He would wait a few
more months; perhaps until the autumn or early winter. By then
Charles Main would be trying to accustom himself to the idea
that his son was lost. At that time, just when he could be expected to be learning to deal with his grief, Bent would move to
renew it. Send him news that Gus had remained alive most of the
year and had only recently been killed. It would be a double-
edged death, guilt compounding the pain. All his days, Charles
Main would be haunted by the thought that his son might have
lived if he hadn't abandoned the search, as Bent was certain he
had by now. Of course he'd have to deliver parts of the boy's
body to prove he was dead. His razor would be helpful.

Little Gus's laughter rang through the sundown. Green
Grass Woman rested her cheek on Bent's right shoulder. He was
happy. The world was good.

58

Charles turned the corner and flattened against the front of the sod house. He held his revolver chest high, cocked. One of the horses whinnied, a faint sound. Gray Owl was holding them about half a mile away in some cottonwoods.

Charles smelled the odor of fireplace ashes. It leaked from the mud chimney, with no trace of smoke. A fire had been banked carelessly, or in haste. Horse droppings in the corral were at least a day old; shod horses had chopped up the ground. No one would farm here, Charles reasoned. They had found the base of some renegade traders.

A muddy boot toe appeared at the far corner of the house. Magic Magee slid around the corner and crept along with his back to the wall. The afternoon light was dimming fast and changing color, to a strange golden-green. Westward, the clouds of a monster storm came toward the house like a carpet unrolling in the sky. Magee watched Charles for a cue. The black man wore his derby with the wild turkey feather, but nothing to identify him as a soldier.

Charles listened at the plank door. The rumbling of the storm would muffle any but the loudest voice. He heard nothing. The wind picked up dust suddenly. Branches of some cottonwoods behind Magee began to toss and clack together. There was going to be a ferocious blow.

The wind dried the sweat gathering in Charles's beard. Magee crept closer, to the opposite side of the door. Charles held up three fingers, then silently mouthed the count. On three, he leaped in front of the door and booted it. Some huge heavy thing hurtled from the darkness straight at his face. He fired twice.

The echoes of the shots sank into the storm's rumble.

Magee's eye followed the bird that had swooped away above Charles's head, almost knocking his hat off. "Gray Owl's helper."

The owl vanished into the dark roiling mass of cloud. With one hand over the other on his Colt, Charles jumped inside the sod house. He smelled the residual odor of tobacco smoke beneath the stronger smell of the ashes. Someone had indeed splashed water on the fire; he saw the bucket. Everything pointed to a quick departure. Who knew the reason?

He put the revolver away. "Tell Gray Owl to bring up the horses. We might as well shelter here until the storm's over."

Magee nodded and left. There was no need to say anything. Charles's discouragement was evident.

The rain fell, hammering torrents of it. They broke up an old chair and relit the fire. It provided some light but didn't do much to relieve the pervasive damp. The horses neighed loudly and often. The lightning was bright, the thunder-peals deafening.

Gray Owl squatted in a corner with his blanket drawn around him. He looked years older. Or perhaps Charles thought so because he felt that way himself. He gnawed on jerky and watched Magee practicing shuffles and cuts with an old deck.

They'd been searching for two and a half weeks. They'd circled southwest to avoid Camp Supply and had found this house on Wolf Creek. Charles had hoped to question the occupants but whoever they were, they had made an abrupt departure, which made him nervous.

The steady rain deepened his discouragement. It fell hour after hour. Coming down so heavily, it would flood away any sign that might have helped them. Not that they had found much so far, beyond the inevitable tracks of Army detachments on patrol. If there were other human beings round about, perhaps white men trading illegally, this house was the first indication.

Charles lay awake long after the fire went out. His mind kept turning to images of his son, and imaginary ones in which Bent, pictured as Charles remembered him, murdered George Hazard's wife and stole her earring. That detail more than any other filled him with enormous dread. Years ago, in Texas, Bent was marginally sane. Not even that could be said now.

They discovered in the morning that two of the horses had snapped their tethers and escaped.

The storm lasted until noon, flooding low spots and carving new gullies. As they prepared to leave the sod house Charles noticed Magee's face. Saddling his horse, the black man looked gloomy, which wasn't like him.

Gray Owl approached with a certain deference. "How much longer do we search?"

"Until I say otherwise."

"There is no trail to follow. The man and boy could have gone anywhere. Or turned back."

"I know that, but I just can't give up. You go back if you want." There was no resentment in his voice.

"No. But Magee, it is not easy for him to be away." Puzzled, Charles waited. "He has a squaw now. A good Delaware woman whose husband died."

"Until he tells me he wants to go back, we're going on. All three of us."

Gray Owl felt pain for his friend. The pursuit was futile. Not even the cleverest tracker could find a man and a child when the trail was so old and the country so huge and full of hiding places.

One misty morning in a stand of pines—on the ninth of April, by Charles's careful count of the days—the three men stood with hands muzzling the fretful horses while, not a hundred feet away, three troops of cavalry trotted by in a shallow creek. They were Kansas state troops, probably some of the Nineteenth Volunteer Cavalry old Crawford had raised and brought in to support Sherman. Gray Owl's pony tossed his head free and whinnied. Charles cursed under his breath. A yellow-haired lieutenant, a pink-faced farmer boy, glanced sharply to the misty pines. He pulled his horse out of the column and sat staring at the trees. Charles prayed a clumsy wordless prayer. The farmer boy on horseback chewed his lip, doubtful about what he'd heard because the horses and men in the column were quite noisy. He tugged his rein and rode on. In five minutes the splashing stopped; the water flowed calmly again; the troopers were gone.

April brought the crows and the redbirds. Any shower brought a profusion of hoptoads afterward. The sweet blooming fecundity of the spring embittered Charles unreasonably. He slept deeply at night, and had many dreams. He had never felt so tired or hopeless. Conversation among the three men had long ago diminished to the minimum necessary to convey a question or the day's plan.

One morning, early, they spied the distant mass of the southern buffalo herd, returning north with the warm weather. They rode hard and reached the herd in two hours. They killed one cow, gorged themselves on fresh roasted meat, and packed all they would be able to eat before spoilage. Buzzards kept them company, awaiting their departure.

The ride to the buffalo reminded Charles again of the vastness of the Territory. A whole army corps could be maneuvering and they might miss it. He'd convinced himself that he could search the Territory as you'd search a room. He was desperate; he had to think that way. Now he saw the foolishness of it. He was thinking more realistically. That befitted a man who'd partnered with the Jackson Trading Company, but it whittled away his hope.

The mood of his companions didn't help. Magee was morose because of the Delaware woman, and Gray Owl because he couldn't guide them with any success. He was failing in his life's purpose.

They rode for hours without speaking, each man sunk into himself. The Wichitas rose in the south like monuments in a flat field. Wending across the lower slopes of the western side, they found abundant sign. A large number of Indians had pitched their tipis about a week ago. So many Indians—several hundred by Charles's estimate—that time and weather had not yet been able to erase all the traces.

After they camped that night, Charles went searching on foot in the sparkling dewy morning. He discovered a rusted trade kettle which he picked up and pressed with his thumb, immediately making a hole in the thin rust. It was an impoverished village that had camped here.

Gray Owl trudged up. "Come see this," he said.

Charles followed him down to the base of the peak to a set of travois pole tracks that had survived. He knelt to study them.

Between the pole tracks he saw the prints of wide moccasined feet. He brushed his fingers lightly over one print, half obliterating it. The print belonged to a woman, and a heavy one; no man would pull a travois.

Charles pushed his black hat back and said what Gray Owl already knew. "There are no more dogs. They've eaten them. They're starving. They didn't move because they wanted to; they're in flight. From here they could logically go south. Or west, to Texas. Maybe all the way into the *llano.*"

Gray Owl knew the *llano*—the staked plains; a scrubby, inhospitable wilderness. "West," he said, nodding.

They rode with a little more energy. Here at last was a large group of people, one or more of whom might have seen a white man and a boy. Charles knew the odds against it but at least it was a crumb. Until now, they'd been starving.

The sign of so large a migration was easy to follow. They tracked the village to the North Fork of the Red, then northwestward along it for a day and a half. Suddenly there was confusing sign. The remains of another encampment and, across the river, trampled hoof-marked earth, which showed that a second large body of Indians had joined the first.

Gray Owl left for a day, scouting north and east. He returned at a gallop. "All moved east from here," he said. His skin was free of sweat despite his blanket and the hot spring day.

Magee used his nail to scratch bird droppings from his derby. "Don't make sense. The forts are east."

"Nevertheless, that is the way."

Charles had a hunch. "Let's go up the river a while. Let's see if all of them rode east."

Next morning they found a campsite where perhaps thirty lodges had stood. The day after that, they found the grandfather.

He was resting in cottonwoods with a few possessions from his medicine bundle—feathers, a claw, a pipe—spread around him. The malevolent odor of a chancred leg seeped from under his buffalo robe. He was old, his skin like wrinkled brown wrapping paper. He knew his death was imminent and showed no fear of the oddly assorted trio. Gray Owl questioned him.

His name was Strong Bird. He told them the reason for the great migration eastward. Some six hundred Cheyennes under chiefs Red Bear, Gray Eyes, and Little Robe had decided to sur-

render to the soldiers at Camp Wichita rather than die of starvation or face the bullets of the soldiers of General Creeping Panther, who was roaming the Territory sweeping up bands of
resisters. The grandfather was part of a group that had bolted
with Red Bear after he changed his mind about surrendering.

"Thirty lodges," he said, his eyes fluttering shut, his voice
reedy. "They are eating their horses now."

"Where, Grandfather?" Gray Owl asked.

"They meant to push up the Sweet Water. Whether they did,
I don't know. I know your face, don't I? You belong to the People."

Gray Owl seemed heavily burdened. "Once long ago."

"Age has rotted my flesh. I could not keep up. I asked them
to leave me, whether or not the soldiers found me. Will you help
me die?"

They hewed down branches and fashioned a burial platform
in one of the strongest cottonwoods. Charles carried the old man
up to it, with Magee bracing him below. He could barely stand
the stench but he got the grandfather settled with his few possessions and left him with warm sun shining on his old face, which
was composed and even showed a drowsy smile.

As they rode out, Gray Owl said, "It was a generous thing
to help him to the Hanging Road. It was not the deed of the man
they named Cheyenne Charlie. The man who wanted to kill
many."

"There's only one I want now," Charles said. "I think our
luck's changed. I think we're going to find him."

That was his blind hope speaking again. But the sunshine
and the springtime buoyed him, and so did the possibility that
Red bear's band of holdouts might have seen a white man. Gray
Owl warned Charles and Magee that Red Bear, now a village
chief, was formerly a fierce Red Shield Society chief, which no
doubt explained why he'd balked at giving up along with the
others.

They found the village far up the Sweet Water's right bank.
The Cheyennes made no effort to hide themselves. Cooking fires
smoked the sky at midday and from a rise, through his spyglass,
Charles saw several men with raggy animal pelts on their heads
shuffling in a great circle around the edge of the encampment.

The wind brought the trackers the faint thumping of hand drums.

Magee used the spyglass. Uncharacteristically sharp, he said, "What they hell have they got to dance about? Aren't they starving to death?"

"Massaum," Gray Owl said.

"Talk English," Magee said.

"That's the name of the ceremony," Charles said. "They put a painted buffalo skull in a trench to represent the day the buffalo came to earth, and the dancers pretend to be deer and elk and wolves and foxes. The ceremony is a plea for food. The old man said they're starving."

Magee rolled his tongue over his upper teeth. "Damn mad about it, too, I guess."

"You don't have to go in with me."

"Oh, sure. I came this far to be a yellow dog, huh? That isn't the kind of soldier somebody trained me to be." Staring at Charles's haggard eyes, at the long pointed beard nearly down to his stomach, Magee suddenly winced. "I'm sorry I sound sore. I just think all this is hopeless. Your boy's gone, Charles."

"No he isn't," Charles said. "Gray Owl? Go in or stay?"

"Go." The tracker eyed the village, but not in a comfortable way. "First, load all the guns."

It was a splendid balmy day. The wrong sort of day for the tragedy of a lost son or a starving belly. The wind floated fluffy clouds overhead and the clouds cast majestic slow-sailing shadows. In and out of the shadows, in single file, the three rode in the Z pattern Jackson had taught Charles.

One of the pelt-clad dancers was first to spy them. He pointed and raised a cry. The drumming stopped. Men and women and children surged toward the side of the camp nearest the strangers. The men were middle-aged or elderly; the warriors were undoubtedly off somewhere searching for food. Well before Charles was within hailing distance, he saw the sun flashing from the metal heads of lances and the blades of knives. He also saw that no dogs frolicked anywhere. The tipis were weathered and torn. There was an air of despair about the village beside the Sweet Water.

The wind still blew in their faces. Charles smelled offal, smoke, and sour bodies. He didn't like all the gaunt angry faces lining up behind the dancers, or the truculent expression of the stout old warrior who strode out to meet them with his eight-foot red lance and his round red buffalo-hide shield. The horns of his headdress were red but faded; he had distinguished himself in war many winters past.

Charles held his hand palm outward and spoke in their language.

"We are peaceful."

"You are hunters?"

"No. We are searching for a small boy, my son." That touched off whispers among some of the grandmothers. Magee caught it too, raising an eyebrow. Those starved old women with their watering eyes acted as if they knew who Charles was talking about. "May we come into the village a while?"

Chief Red Bear thrust his shield out. "No. I know that man beside you. He turned his face from the People to go and help the white devils of the forts. I know you, Gray Owl," he exclaimed, shaking his shield and lance. One of the dancers with a scrap of pelt on his head sank to a half-crouch, his knife moving in a small provocative circle.

"You are soldiers," the chief said.

"We are not, Red Bear—" Gray Owl began.

The chief pointed his lance at the trackers and shouted: "Soldiers. Call Whistling Snake from the Massaum lodge."

Magee brought up his Spencer from the saddle where he'd been resting it. "Don't," Charles said in English. "One shot and they'll tear us up."

" 'Pears they'll do it anyway." There was a slight quaver in Magee's voice; Charles feared that what he said was so. More than a hundred people confronted them. In terms of physical strength each of the Cheyennes was no match. Hunger had shrunk them and age enfeebled them. Numerically, however, they had the fight won before it started.

"Do you know this Whistling Snake?" Charles asked Gray Owl.

"Priest," Gray Owl replied, almost inaudibly. "Ugly face. As a young man he scarred his own flesh with fire to show his magical powers. Even chiefs like Red Bear fear him. This is very bad."

Small boys darted forward to pat the horses. The animals sidestepped nervously, hard to control. Indian mothers chuckled and nudged one another, eyeing the trackers as if they were so much contract beef. Charles didn't know what to do. He had bet on having an ace facedown and turned over a trey.

One last try. "Chief Red Bear, I repeat, we only wish to ask if anyone in your village has seen a white man traveling with a small—"

The crowd parted like a cloven sea. There was a great communal sigh of awe and dread. The old camp chief's gaze was curiously taunting. Along the dirt lane fouled with human waste came the priest, Whistling Snake.

MADELINE'S JOURNAL

April, 1869. The school has a new globe, a world map for the wall, eight student desks to replace the homemade ones. A party of distinguished Connecticut educators plans to visit next month. Prudence insists we must clean and refurbish the place.

The rasp of the mill saws and the rattle of the mining carts I hear amidst the sweet noise of house construction remind me that we can afford windows to replace the schoolhouse shutters. Andy will glaze them. Prudence and I and one or two of the youngsters can do the other tasks at night. It is suitable work for lonely women: demanding, tiring. Prudence, strong as a teamster, grows a little stouter every month. Though she still quotes her favorite passage from Romans, I now detect a sadness in her eyes. I think she knows she will remain a spinster. As I will remain a widow. To work until the body aches is the best medicine for the loneliness that seems to be one of God's great blights on existence.

I share sadness of another kind with Jane. She told me that despite long effort she cannot conceive a child. Prudence, the Shermans, Orry's dying as he did, senselessly—they are all linked somehow. Is it because they all testify that we are never guaranteed a happy life, only life itself? . . .

Encountered a man, young and poorly clothed, riding a white horse on the river road. He gave no greeting, though he stared as if he knew me. Despite his youth there was a cruel aspect to his face. He is no good-hearted Northerner come to inspect our school, I think. . . .

. . . Andy saw him this morning.

> *And again I met him. I hailed him. He charged his white*
> *horse at me as if to trample me down, forcing me to throw*
> *myself aside and take a bad tumble in the weeds. For one*
> *moment his face flashed by above me, a perfect study of ha-*
> *tred. . . .*
>
> *. . . No sign of him for two days. I suspect and hope he*
> *has gone elsewhere, to terrorize others. . . .*

The small Negro cemetery overlooked the Ashley in the
scrubs outside Charleston. The ground around the grave mounds
was a musty carpet of brown decaying leaves. Bunches of wilted
sunflowers and even a few brown dandelions lay on the graves;
the place was poor, and poorly kept.

Des LaMotte knelt and prayed before a wooden marker
from which he'd chiseled a shallow circular depression. Into this
he had wedged a common-looking plate, chipped at many places
on the edge and showing a long crack. On the marker, above the
slave's plate, he had carved an inscription.

J U B A

"thou hast been faithful
over a few things, I will
make thee ruler over many things"
Matt. 25,21

Where the trees opened on the water, a silver-colored sky
shone with a strangely threatening luminescence. The wind, a
rising nor'easter, streamed in from the Atlantic. It was too cold
for spring. Or maybe Des was feeling the effects of time, and
poverty, and his strange inability to come to grips with his enemy. After the travail of war and the passage of years, he no
longer wanted vengeance so ferociously. Honor was less important than bread, or keeping possession of his tiny room in town,
or preserving clothes he couldn't afford to replace. "LaMotte
honor" now had the queer sound of a foreign phrase impossible
to translate.

His old ties to the past were gone. Ferris Brixham, dead.
Sallie Sue, dead. Mrs. Asia LaMotte, dead; a year and a half now,
her insides a feast for a cancer. Now Juba; the last. He had been

so crippled at the end, he couldn't crawl from his pallet. Des had fed him and bathed him and cleaned him as if he were some expensive artifact, the last artifact, from a razed house. Juba had died in his sleep, and Des had stared at the corpse by the light of a candle for nearly an hour. His servant's passing reminded him that the human body was frail enough without deliberately endangering it. The hotblood who'd confronted Cooper Main on the plank bridge seemed like a foolish and very distant relative who didn't understand life's realities and whose ideas no longer had any pertinence. Des was old; he was sick; he had fought long enough.

He got ready to stand up. It required mental preparation because he knew his knees would creak and hurt. Strange that the same arthritic trouble that had tormented Juba had now fallen on him, and at a much younger age. He could no longer do a formal dance step gracefully. That was another part of his life that was over. His face, drawn down into sad lines, reflected the attrition of the years, and so did his carroty hair; the white streak was broader, and forked into a trident.

As he started to stand, he heard a horse walking into the cemetery. A hoof snapped a fallen branch. He groaned as he rose and turned, expecting to see some black sharecropper riding his sway-backed animal to a family grave. He was startled to discover a white man. Behind the man the clouds boiled like black soup in a hot kettle.

The stranger was young, scarcely more than twenty. He wore plow shoes and an old black coat with the collar turned up. He had shaved closely, but his black beard showed. The sun had burned his nose and upper cheeks and hands; they looked raw. When the young man climbed down from his milky horse Des saw the back of his neck. Red, from field work.

While the young man walked toward Des, other details registered. Something was wrong with the stranger's left eye; it had the fixed look of blindness. The horse made Des think of Revelations: *And his name that sat on him was Death.*

"You are Desmond LaMotte?"

"I am, sir."

"I was told I'd find you here."

Des waited. There was a suppressed ferocity about the stranger. Somehow it fit with the rawness of his red face, red hands, red neck, ghastly staring eye; it frightened Des badly.

He saw no sign of a weapon, but his long legs shook when the stranger began reaching into various pockets of his thread-bare coat, saying, "I am Benjamin Ryan Tillman of York County, sir. I have ridden here with instructions to speak to you."

"York County." That was a long way; above Columbia, at the North Carolina border. "I don't know anyone in York County."

"Oh, yes," Tillman said, presenting what he'd found in his pocket. A news clipping already yellowed. The headline startled Des.

THE KUKLUX

DISCOVERY OF THE REMAINS
OF DETECTIVE BARMORE

Des's fear sharpened. The nor'easter snapped the corner of the clipping, which came from some paper in Nashville. "I don't understand this, sir—" he began.

"I'm here to explain it to you. The story says the man's body was found in some woods, along with an empty pocketbook and part of his K.K.K. rig."

"What does that have to do with me?"

"I am here to explain that, too. This white man, Barmore, he failed to carry out an order from the Grand Dragon over there in Tennessee." Tillman plucked the clipping from Des's pale hand. "The Grand Dragon of Carolina wanted to show you that the Invisible Empire won't be disobeyed."

Des felt a keen, hurting urge to make water. The stranger's good eye had a fanatic glitter. The wind, near gale force now, shot leaves past them in swirling clouds. Old tree limbs creaked. One broke off and sailed away.

"I've not disobeyed a single order," Des protested.

"And you won't disobey the one I'm here to give you, either. Your klavern hasn't controlled this district like it should. Everybody in the state knows about that woman at Mont Royal, coining money left and right with her mill and her phosphates while she runs that nigger school."

Des's gut hurt. "We tried to burn the school—"

"Tried," Tillman said, the initial T sending little sprays of spit into Des's face. "Tried is no good. You botched it. Now the damn Yankee politicians and Bible-thumpers are coming down to see it and praise it, and you do nothing. It's a stench in the nostrils of God-fearing white men. You're to get rid of it, La-Motte. You're to get rid of it or you'll go the same way Barmore went in Tennessee."

"Do you know who you're talking to?" Des shouted. "I fought the whole war in the Palmetto Rifles. An elite regiment. What did you do? Stay home with the rest of the redneck farmer boys?"

"You shit-face Charleston snob!" He was spitting again; there was something primitive and utterly dangerous about him. "I lay sick two years, trying to get well enough to join up. I lost the sight of this eye and I lost two brothers to war wounds and another to the camp fever. I'm foursquare for the South and the white race, and I've killed to prove it. I ride for the Klan in York County, and I'm to give you just one warning. The Grand Dragon of Carolina wants some blood down here. Nigger blood. That Main woman. Get your den together, get rid of her school, then get rid of her." Scornful of Des's fright, he held up the clipping. The wind tore the edges. "Understand?"

"I—I do."

"That goes for the rest of your klavern, too."

"Believe me, Tillman, I want what you want. What the Klan wants. But we had opposition last time and we'll have more now. There's nigger militia at Mont Royal—"

"Nobody gives an ounce of rat pee if all the archangels from glory are on guard with their harps and halos," Tillman said. "Either she's gone in thirty days or you're gone. I will return with pleasure to execute the sentence."

He stared at Des until Des looked away. Then, with a snicker, he tucked the clipping into the side pocket of Des's coat. He strode against the wind to his milky horse and mounted nimbly. "Good day, sir," he said, and rode out of the burying ground, his black coat the same color as the sky ahead of him.

Des leaned against a tree, weak. He read the Barmore story, then read it again. He didn't doubt the authenticity of the visitor's credentials, or the seriousness of the warning. The stranger, Benjamin Ryan Tillman of York County, was one of the most daunting human beings he'd ever met. He made Des think of Romans who slew Christians, and of the Inquisitors of Spain.

Carolina would hear from the young redneck if the darkies didn't rise up and kill him to save themselves first.

In the howling wind he rode Juba's mule back to Charleston.

At dusk he set out for the Dixie Store at Summerton. Arriving there, he instructed Gettys to buy explosives. Gettys stuttered that it was too dangerous. Des told him to ride to Savannah, or upriver to Augusta if necessary. He told him it was the Klan's order. He told him the Klan's sentence if they failed. After that Gettys didn't argue.

59

Though Whistling Snake was at least seventy winters, he walked with the vigor of a young man. His neck and forearms had a taut, sinewy look. His pure white hair was simply parted and braided without adornment. He wore a hide smock that long use had buffed to the color of dull gold. A plain rawhide belt gathered the smock at his waist. In his right hand, chest high, he held a fan of matched golden eagle feathers two feet wide from tip to tip.

Charles couldn't remember seeing another old man with such an aura of strength. Or human eyes quite so arrogant and unpleasant. The right iris was only partly visible, hidden by a lip of puckered flesh. Scar's face was smooth by comparison with that of Whistling Snake's, which looked as though his flesh had melted from temple to jaw, then been pushed and twisted into ridges as it hardened. Indentations like large healed nail wounds stippled the ridges of flesh. The man was hideous, which only made him seem stronger.

"They say they search for his son," Red Bear told the priest, with a nod at Charles.

Whistling Snake regarded them, fanning himself with a small rotation of his bony wrist. A toddler, a plump bare girl, started toward him, reaching out. Her mother snatched her back and clutched her, dread in her eyes.

The priest shook the fan at Magee. "Buffalo soldier. Kill them."

"Damn you," Charles said, "there are other black men on the Plains besides buffalo soldiers. This is my friend. He is peaceful. So am I. We are looking for my little boy. He was stolen by another white man. A tall man. He may be wearing a woman's bauble, here."

He pulled his earlobe. An elderly Cheyenne covered his mouth and popped his eyes. Charles heard the excited buzz of the women before Red Bear's glare silenced them. Charles's stomach tightened. They'd seen Bent.

The priest fanned himself. "Kill them." The brown iris shifted in its trench of hard scar tissue. "First that one, the betrayer of the People."

Gray Owl's pony began to prance, as if some invisible power flowed from the priest to unnerve and befuddle his enemies. The pony neighed. Gray Owl kneed him hard to control him. His face showed uncharacteristic emotion. Fear.

Magee spoke from the side of his mouth, in English. "What's that old bastard saying?"

"He told them to kill us."

Magee swallowed, visibly affected. "They better not. I want to get out of here with my wool on my head. I want to see Pretty Eyes again." The squaw, Charles assumed. "I'm not going to cash in here. I been trounced by nigger-hating saloon trash—"

The priest pointed his fan, exclaiming in Cheyenne, "Stop his tongue."

"I been cussed by white soldiers not fit to shine a real man's boots. I won't let some old fan-waving Indian just wave me off this earth, whisssh!" There was a strange, fear-born anger prodding Magee. He shook his derby the way Whistling Snake had shaken his fan. "You tell him he doesn't touch a wizard."

"A—?" Startled, Charles couldn't get the rest out.

"The biggest, the meanest of all the black wizards of the planetary universe. Me!" Magee flung his hands in the air like a preacher; he was back in Chicago, encircled, with only his wits to forestall a beating.

Red Bear retreated from him. A fat grandfather protected his wife with his arm. Magee looked baleful sitting there on his horse, arms upraised, shouting. "I will level this village with wind, hail, and fire if they touch us or don't tell us what we want to know." A moment's silence. Then he yelled at Charles like a topkick. "Tell 'em, Charlie!"

Charles translated. Where he faltered, as with the word for hail, Gray Owl supplied it. Whistling Snake's fanning grew rapid. Red Bear watched the priest for a reaction; Whistling Snake was temporarily in control of things. "He is a great worker of magic?" Whistling Snake asked.

"The greatest I know," Charles said, wondering if he was insane. Well, what was the alternative to this? Probably immediate annihilation.

"I am the greatest of the spell-workers," the priest said. Charles translated. Magee, calmer now, sniffed.

"Cocky old dude."

"No," Charles said, pointing to Magee. "He is the greatest."

For the first time, Whistling Snake smiled. He had but four teeth, widely spaced in his upper gum. They were fanglike, as if he'd filed them that way. "Bring them in," he said to Red Bear. "Feed them. After the sun falls, we will test who is the greatest wizard. Then we will kill them."

He studied Magee over the tips of the fan feathers. His laugh floated out, a dry chuckle. He turned and walked majestically into the village.

Magee looked numb. "My God, I never figured he'd take me up on it."

"Can you show him anything?" Charles whispered.

"I brought a few things, always do. But it's only small stuff. That old Indian, he's got a power about him. Like the devil was singing in his ear."

"He's only a man," Charles said.

Gray Owl shook his head. "He is more than that. He is connected to the mighty spirits."

"Lord," Magee said. "All I got is saloon tricks."

The prairie sunshine had a precious glow then; this morning might be the last they'd be privileged to see.

The Cheyennes put the three of them in a stinking tipi with old men guarding the entrance. A woman brought bowls of cold stew too gamy to eat. Before dark, the villagers lit a huge fire and began their music of flute and hand drum.

An hour of chants and shuffling dances went by. Charles chewed on his only remaining cigar, nursing a superstitious certainty that they wouldn't get out of this if he smoked it. Gray Owl sat in his blanket as if asleep. Magee opened his saddlebags, rummaged in them to take inventory, closed them, then did it all over again ten minutes later. The shadows of dancing, shuffling, stomping men passed over the side of the tipi like magic lantern projections. The drumming grew very loud. Charles reckoned

two hours had passed when Magee jumped up and kicked his
bags. "How long they going to string us out?"

Gray Owl raised his head. His eyes blinked open. "The
priest wants you to feel that way. He can then show a different,
calm face."

Magee puffed his cheeks and blew like a fish, twice. Charles
said, "I wish I hadn't got us into—"

"I did it," Magee said, almost snarling. "I got us here. I'll
get us out. Even if I am just a nigger saloon magician."

A few minutes later, guards escorted them outside. A hush
came over the ring of people around the fire. The men were
seated. The women and children stood behind them.

The evening was windless. The flames pillared straight up,
shooting sparks at the stars. Whistling Snake sat beside Chief
Red Bear. The latter had a bleary smile, as though he'd been
drinking. Whistling Snake was composed, as Gray Owl had predicted. His fan lay in his lap.

A place was made for Charles to sit. Red Bear signed him to
it. Gray Owl was roughly hauled back with the women, further
punishment for his betrayal. The grandfather on Charles's left
drew a trade knife from his belt and tested the edge while looking
straight into Charles's eyes. Charles chewed the cold cigar.

Red Bear said, "Begin."

Magee spread his saddlebags flat on the ground. Charles
thought of the campfire circle as a dial. Magee was at twelve
o'clock, Whistling Snake sat fanning himself at nine o'clock, and
he was seated at three, with Gray Owl behind him at four or five.

Magee cleared his throat, blew on his hands, reached up for
his derby, and tumbled it brim over crown all the way down his
arm to his hand. An old grandfather laughed and clapped.
Whistling Snake's slitted eye darted to him. He stopped clapping.

His face already glistening with sweat, Magee pulled his blue
silk from a saddlebag and stuffed it into his closed fist. He
chanted, "Column left, column right, by the numbers, hocus-
pocus."

Red Bear showed a slight frown of curiosity. Whistling
Snake regarded the distant constellations, fanning himself.
Charles's belly weighed twenty pounds. They were doomed.

Magee pulled a black silk from his fist and popped the fist
open to show it empty. He waved the silk like a bullfighter's cape,

displaying both sides, and sat down. Whistling Snake deigned to glance at Charles. The four filed teeth showed, in supreme contempt.

Whistling Snake handed his fan ceremoniously to Red Bear. He rose. From his robe he produced a wide-mouth bag made of red flannel. He crushed the bag, turned it inside out, displayed both sides, balled it again. Then suddenly he began a singsong chant and started a hopping sidestep dance around the circle. As he danced and chanted, he held the top corners of the bag by the thumb and index finger of each hand.

The heads of two snakes with gleaming eyes suddenly rose from the mouth of the bag, as if the snakes were crawling straight up to the stars. People gasped. Charles was momentarily mystified. Then, as the snakes dropped back into the bag, he noticed their lack of flexibility. Magee, cross-legged by his saddlebags, glanced at him with a disgusted look. He too had identified the snakes as snakeskin glued over wood.

The Cheyennes thought it an impressive trick, however. Chanting and dancing, Whistling Snake went all the way around the fire, revealing the climbing snakes at each quarter. He finished the circuit and crumpled the bag a last time before he sat. He fanned himself with evident satisfaction.

The Cheyenne faces shone in the glow of the fire. The atmosphere of lighthearted sport was gone. Whistling Snake watched the black soldier as if he were game to be cooked and devoured.

Magee produced a quilled bag. From the bag he took three white chicken feathers. He put two in his leather belt and changed the third to a white stone. He held the stone in his mouth as he changed the next two feathers. He took the three stones from his mouth one at a time and with one hand passing over and under the other he changed the stones back to feathers. When he had three feathers in his belt, he concealed them all in one fist and waved over it. He opened his mouth and lifted out three feathers. He showed his empty hands, reached behind the head of a seated man, and produced three white stones.

He eyed the crowd, awaiting some sign of wonder or approval. He saw hard glaring eyes. Charles realized Magee had not offered a word of patter during the trick. The black soldier sat down with a defeated look.

Whistling Snake drew himself up with supreme hauteur.
Again he handed the village chief his fan. He showed his palms to
the crowd; Charles saw the heavy muscles on his forearms. Tilting his head back and chanting, the priest stepped forward close
to the fire and laid his right palm directly into the flame.

He kept it there while slowly lowering his left till they were
parallel. His face showed no sign of pain. No stutter or falter
interrupted his singsong chant. Magee sat stiff as a post, his eyes
brimming with curiosity and admiration. He had momentarily
forgotten that the Cheyenne wanted to kill him and take his wool
and hang it up in his lodge. He was wonderstruck by the magic.

A great rippling sigh—"Ah! Ah!"— ran around the circle,
and there were smiles, grunts, scornful looks at the three interlopers. Slowly, Whistling Snake lifted his left hand from the fire.
Then his right. White hairs on his forearms above his wrists
curled and gave off tiny spurts of smoke. His palms were unblis-
tered; not even discolored.

Charles looked at Gray Owl, who exhibited as much expression as the granite of the Wichitas. Trying to hide what they all
knew, no doubt. Magee flung Charles another look that was almost apologetic. Charles smiled as if to urge him not to worry.
With a defeated air, Magee climbed to his feet. Charles snatched
a faggot from the fire and with the hot end lit his last cigar.

From a saddlebag Magee pulled a leather pouch which he
carefully laid on the ground. He next took out a small hand-
carved wood box which he opened and displayed. The box held
four lead-colored balls of a kind Charles hadn't seen for years.
Magee plucked one out and carefully placed it between his teeth.
Then he closed the box and put it away. With a sudden flourish,
he yanked a pistol from the saddlebag.

Several Cheyennes jumped up, readying their knives or
lances. Magee quickly gave them the peace sign. He balanced the
pistol on his palm and slowly turned in a complete circle, so all
could see it. Where had he found an old flintlock? Charles wondered. The barrel showed no rust. Magee had cleaned it well.

With slow, ceremonious motions, Magee opened the leather
pouch and inverted it, letting powder trickle into the barrel. Suddenly he stamped his right foot twice, as if bitten by an insect.

Along with most of the others, Charles looked down and didn't see anything.

Magee pinched off the flow of powder and tossed the pouch aside. He found a patch in his pocket and wrapped it around the ball he took from his teeth. He slipped ball and patch into the barrel, unsnapped the ramrod underneath, and with careful twisting motions seated the ball. He replaced the ramrod and primed the pan.

Fat sweat drops rolled down Magee's cheeks. He wiped his hands on his jeans pants. He signed for Charles to stand up.

Astonished, Charles did. Magee glanced at Red Bear. The chief's attention was fixed on him. Whistling Snake saw that and frowned. His fan moved rapidly, stirring the hair at the ends of his white braids.

"What I did before was just play," Magee said. "I am going to kill King Death before their eyes. Tell them."

"Magic, I don't understand what—"

"Tell them, Charlie."

He translated. Hands covered mouths. The fire popped and smoked. If silence had weight, this was crushing.

Magee faced about in precise military fashion. He used his hands to make a parting motion. Those in front of him jumped up and shoved one another until a yard-wide lane was cleared. Magee summoned Charles to him with a bent finger. He gave Charles the old flintlock pistol and looked hard and earnestly into his eyes.

"When I say the word, I want you to shoot me."

"What?"

Magee leaned up on tiptoe, his mouth next to Charles's ear. "You want to get out of here? Do it." He made a puckering sound, as if kissing the white man. Several Cheyennes giggled over the strange ways of the interlopers.

Magee snapped the brim of his derby down to snug it; the shadow bisected his nose. In the shadow, his eyes gleamed like discs of ivory. He took ten long strides, rapidly, along the cleared lane, his posture soldier-perfect. He stopped, knocking his heels together, at attention. He about-faced. He was standing a foot from a tipi with a great ragged hole in its side.

"Aim the pistol, Charlie."

Christ, how could he?

"Charlie! Aim for the chest. Dead center."

Charles felt the sweat crawling down into his beard. Whistling Snake leaped up, his fan flicking very fast. Red Bear rose too. Charles drew the hammer back. Magee's shirt was taut over his ribs and belly. Charles's arm trembled as he extended it. He couldn't—he wouldn't—

Magic Magee said, "Now."

He said it loudly, a command. Charles responded to the tone as much as to the word. He fired. Sparks glittered, the priming pan ignited, the pistol banged and kicked upward.

Charles saw a puff of dust, as if something had struck Magee's chest three inches below the breastbone. Magee stepped back one long pace, staggering, closing his eyes, snapping his hands open, fingers shaking as if stiffened by a lightning charge. Then his arms fell to his sides. He opened his eyes. Whistling Snake's fan hung at his side.

"Where is the bullet?" Whistling Snake cried. "Where did it strike?"

In a drill-ground voice, Magee said, "King Death is dead. You will answer our questions and release us without harm or I will bring back King Death, riding the winds of hail and fire, and this village will be finished." He shouted, "Tell them."

Charles translated quickly. Gray Owl's guards had drifted away from him, as awed as he was. While Charles spit the words out, trying to make them as fierce as Magee's, he scanned the trooper's shirt. He saw no sign of a tear. Magee brushed his shirt off as if something had tickled him.

Red Bear listened to the threats and instantly said, "It shall be so."

Whistling Snake screamed in protest. The sound broke the moment. The Cheyennes rushed forward to swarm around Magee, touch him, pat him, feel his black curls. Charles stared at the old flintlock pistol, felt the warm barrel. King Death was dead, and there through rifts in the surging, laughing crowd was the banner of his conqueror. The familiar huge white smile of Magee, the wizard.

Red Bear prepared a pipe while Gray Owl attended to the horses. Charles didn't want the forgiving mood to fade, didn't want to linger and possibly lose their advantage and their lives. Ceremony required that he sit at the fire with Red Bear, however.

Magee sat on his right. The village chief and several of the tribal elders passed the pipe.

Red Bear had forced Whistling Snake to join the group. When his turn came he passed the pipe without smoking. He snatched a handful of ashes from the edge of the fire and flung them at Charles's crossed legs. They covered his pants and the toes of his boots with gray powder. Red Bear exclaimed and berated the priest, who merely dusted his hands and folded his arms. Red Bear looked embarrassed, Gray Owl upset.

Since the ashes did no real damage, Charles forgot about it. Having finished his cigar, he was grateful for a deep lungful of pipe smoke, though as always, the unknown mixture of grasses the Cheyennes smoked left him light-headed and euphoric, not a good thing at a time like this.

Red Bear was not only polite but respectful. After asking Charles to describe again the white man he sought, he said, "Yes, we have seen that man, with a boy. At the whiskey ranch of Glyn the trader, on Vermilion Creek. Glyn is gone and they are staying there. I will tell you the way."

He pointed south. Charles was so dizzy with relief, his eyes watered.

Silently, the People formed a long lane through which the three trotted out. Looking back, believing their luck would break any moment, Charles heard Gray Owl laugh deep in his chest. A single figure remained by the campfire, apart from the others. Charles saw Whistling Snake raise his golden feather fan and disdainfully walk away.

They put miles and all of the rest of the night behind them before Charles permitted a stop. Spent men and spent horses rested on the prairie in the cool dawn. Charles knelt beside his black friend.

"All right, I know you don't tell your secrets, but this is one time you will. How did you do it?"

Magee chuckled and produced the hand-carved wooden box. He removed one of the round gray balls and displayed it sportively, just out of Charles's reach. "An old traveling magician taught me the trick back in Chicago. Always wanted to do it for an audience, but till this winter I couldn't afford the right pistol. Saved my pay for it. First thing I did was to short the powder. You never saw it because everybody looked down for a few seconds when I pretended a bug bit me. A little misdirection. But that's only half of it. The trick won't work without this."

"That's a solid ball of lead."

Magee dug his thumbnail with its great cream-colored half-moon into the pistol ball. The nail easily cracked the surface of the ball. "No, it isn't solid, it's melted lead brushed all over something else."

He caught the ball between his palms and rubbed them hard back and forth. He showed the crushed remains, tawny dust. "The rest is just good old Kansas mud. Hard enough to build a house, but not hardly hard enough to kill a man."

He blew on his palm. The dust scattered against the sun and pattered on the ground. He laughed.

"What d'you say we ride and find your boy?"

An hour later, Charles remembered to ask about the ashes on his boots. Gray Owl immediately lost his air of good humor. With a grieved expression, he rode a few moments before he answered.

"It is a curse. As the ashes touch you, so will failure and death."

60

This time they rode in swiftly from the river road. They were less concerned with noise than with surprise. A dozen blacks who belonged to the district militia lived at Mont Royal, scattered over the acreage in wood shanties or little tabby houses. The less time given them to wake up and come running with their old muskets or rifles, the better. That was the agreed strategy when the Klansmen mustered at the crossroads, and they followed it.

Bits jingled and saddles creaked and hooves rap-rapped the sandy road as they neared the whitewashed house with the beams and rafters of a much larger, two-floor structure rising near it. The roof beams were slanting black lines across the stars and the quarter moon. Passing from under the heavy trees, the Klansmen trotted along the road to the old slave quarters. The silvery light of the sky gave a sheen to their robes and hoods. A short distance ahead, on the right, they saw the lighted windows of the school, and people moving inside. All the better.

Riding beside Gettys at the head of the column, Des La-Motte felt a blessed calm descend. This was like a homecoming; like the docking of a vessel after a long and uncertain sea voyage. This night would finish it.

The other Klansmen were equally confident. One spoke to another, jocular; the listener laughed.

Pistols slipped out from underneath robes. Hammers clicked back. A rifle muzzle shimmered as the metal caught the moon's light. Des kept his hands free. He was in command, and his was the privilege of putting a match to the fuse of the dynamite.

"You ladies about through?" Andy said, yawning rather than speaking it. "Must be close on to eleven." He was sitting on a small desk with iron legs which was pushed into a corner beside others like it. His back was braced against the new blackboard. One of the volumes of his set of Kent's *Commentaries* lay across his lap; he'd been underlining lightly with a pencil.

Fifteen minutes ago, he'd walked over from the cottage to collect Jane. She and Prudence and Madeline and a thin golden-colored eleven-year-old named Esau had spent the evening finishing the cleaning of the school—washing the sparkling new windows Andy had puttied in night before last, scouring the floor. Madeline and Jane used soapy rags but Prudence, as if somehow purifying herself by making the task harder, scrubbed in the old primitive way of the Low Country, with a handful of moss dipped in water.

"It feels later than that." Madeline straightened, stiff and chilly. Her wine-colored skirt was soaked around the hem. She dropped her rag in a wood bucket. The windows gleamed with reflections of two lamps burning on stools. "We're done. We can put the furniture back tomorrow."

"Esau, you were kind to help," Jane said, patting him. "But it's too late for a boy your age to be awake. Andy and I will walk you home."

"I wanted to help," the boy said. "It's my school."

Madeline smiled, twisting a strand of gray hair away from her forehead and tucking it in so it wouldn't fall again. She was spent, but it was not an unpleasant feeling. All evening they'd worked in the relaxed, easy way of good friends, and now the school was freshly whitewashed and cleaned of the eternal mildew of the Low Country—ready for the visitors from Connecticut.

She bent to pick up the bucket. Her glance fell across the front window, bright with reflections of the lamps. Behind them, something red shimmered. Instantly, she knew who was out there.

She had time only to say, "They've come." A shotgun blew out the front window. One of the pellets flicked Madeline's sleeve as she flung herself against the wall by the front door. Flying glass opened a cut in the cheek of the bewildered Esau. Prudence heaved to her feet, the clump of moss dripping water on the floor so carefully scrubbed and dried.

Madeline heard horses, and men shouting the word *nigger*,

and she knew her sense of peace had been false. She heard a man say, "Light the dynamite."

"Oh my God," Jane said.

Andy flung his book aside. "Somebody's got to go wake the militiamen. Miss Madeline, you take the others out the back, and I'll do it."

Her voice cracking, Jane said, "No, you don't dare. They're right outside."

"I'll run in the trees beside the road. Stop talking. Move." He shoved them, first Madeline, then Prudence, who was still breathing hard from the work; she was too stout to run far. Madeline signaled Esau to her side, pulled him against her skirt, and cradled his head with her hand. She could feel him trembling.

"Come on out, niggers. You stay in there, you're going to die."

Madeline recognized the voice of Gettys. Andy flung the globe at the side window, breaking it. The distraction drew a volley of fire on that side of the building. Andy used the cover of the noise to break the back window with his lawbook. He pushed Madeline again. "Hurry up!"

Jane hung behind, tears tracking down her cheeks. She knew what might happen if he ran for help. Her dark eyes begged him silently. His refused her. He gave her a swift kiss on her cheek and said his parting words:

"Don't forget I love you. Now go on."

Madeline climbed through the window. Then Prudence lifted Esau through the jagged opening, and Madeline lowered him to the ground. Andy jumped through the side window and ran into the dark, arms pumping.

A Klansman yelled, "There goes one." Horses whinnied. At least two went pounding in pursuit. The sound of three gunshots rolled back through the night, overlapping, reverberating. Jane had just jumped to the ground after Prudence. She gave one terrible short scream of grief and pain. She knew he was dead.

"The dynamite," someone shouted in front.

"Lit," someone else yelled. Something thumped inside and rolled on the floor. Above the glass sawtooths in the lower window frame, a snaky line of smoke rose.

Madeline pushed Prudence and dragged Esau. "Get away from the building. Run."

"Which way?" Prudence gasped.

"Straight ahead," Madeline said, pulling the boy. Straight ahead lay a heavy belt of water oaks with spiny yucca growing between. If they could break through that, they'd reach the marsh. The path across was solid but narrow; difficult to find and follow even in daylight. It would take luck and the bright moon for a successful escape.

"Hold hands," she said, groping and finding Prudence's pudgy fingers, cold and damp with her fear. With her other hand, Madeline hurried Esau into the darkness that rose like a wall behind the school.

Low-growing yuccas stabbed her legs. Spanish moss caressed her face like threatening hands. She saw nothing ahead, no light-glossed waters of the marsh. She'd forgotten how thick and deep the woods were.

Esau began to cry. Behind them, a fiery cavern opened in the night, spilling red light over them. They felt the concussion as the dynamite blew the school walls outward and the roof upward. Madeline saw half a desk sail up through the fiery glare as if it were the lightest of balloons. They ran on, hearing the triumphant yells and hoots of the Klansmen.

Madeline ran faster. A pain spread outward from the center of her breasts as she breathed with greater and greater difficulty. The school was gone. Andy was gone. Prudence was weeping. "I can't go any faster, I can't."

"If you don't we'll all die." With a surge of effort, Madeline ran through a patch of burrs that ripped her hem and scraped her ankles like tiny spurs. But they were through the trees—through and standing in shallow water with the moonlit salt marsh spread before them.

She pushed a fist into her breast, trying to stop the pain. She scanned the marsh, searching for the path over to Summerton. She'd taken it often, but always in daylight, and now, badly scared, she had trouble remembering where it was. The moon-dazzle on the water and the reed thickets confused her all the more.

"They're coming," Jane whispered. Madeline heard them.

"This way." She started across a muddy space, praying her memory wouldn't mislead her.

Two dismounted Klansmen dragged Andy's body from the dark to the firelight. The back of his head was gone, and his shirt was soaked dark red from collar to waist. Des looked at the body, then snatched off his hood as he ran around the burning ruins of the school.

"I saw them run into the trees." He waved in that direction with his old four-pound Walker Colt.

"I'll come with you," Gettys said from behind his hood. His soft white gentleman's hands looked incongruous clutching a shiny pump gun.

"You stay here and take charge of the others. Some of those nigger militia boys may show up. If you have to retreat, disband and scatter."

"Des"—Gettys whined it like a child denied a toy—"I've waited nearly as long as you to exterminate that mongrel woman. I've just as much right—"

Des jammed the old Walker's muzzle under Gettys's chin, twisting the fabric of his hood. "You have no rights. I'm in charge." He had to hurry; the white was flickering at the borders of his mind. He didn't want another spell to knock him out and cheat him of success. And there was Tillman's warning.

Gettys was stubborn. He started to protest again. Des flung his pistol hand back, then forward, bashing Gettys's hood so hard the storekeeper nearly fell over. Gettys saw the demented glaze of Des's eyes. With that pale trident in his carroty hair, he looked like some sort of devil.

"All right, Des. They're yours."

Madeline sensed the others faltering; so was she. They were in water six inches deep, struggling over a muddy bottom that sucked them down and slowed them. The moon's reflections on the water tricked the eye, and the reeds swaying and rattling in the wind only heightened the visual confusion. Somehow she'd led them off the narrow path. And Prudence was breaking down. She staggered along sobbing and muttering gibberish.

"Oh, Lord Jesus." That was Jane, looking behind them because of a sudden noise. Madeline stopped, holding Esau's hand tightly.

First she heard the splashing of the pursuer. He was making no effort to be quiet. Then she saw him, a great ungainly figure with immense hands. One held a gun.

"I'm coming for you niggers." The strong, clear voice rolled over the marsh. A frightened heron rose from the reeds, flapping away. "You're going to die tonight, all of you."

Prudence moaned. She dropped to her knees in the water, hands clasped, head down, mumbling a prayer.

"Will you get up?" Enraged, Madeline bent over the teacher. Only that saved her when Des fired two shots. Esau was crying again.

Madeline shook Prudence. "If you don't get up, he'll kill us. We've got to keep going."

He was coming again, all elbows and lifting knees, a strange terrible scarecrow dancing across the marsh, brandishing his gun. The three women and the boy started to run. Madeline's grief was almost beyond bearing; clumsily but completely, it was all ending tonight. The school, Andy, their own lives. Those ludicrous hooded men still had the power to destroy.

She found the path. She held to it for ten yards, then stumbled, twisting her ankle badly. Prudence lagged again, out of breath, giving up. Jane jerked Prudence's arm, exactly as if it were the halter of a reluctant mule. The night was peaceful except for the loud breathing of the fugitives and the steady splash of LaMotte. Coming on. Closing the distance.

He fired a third shot. Prudence flung her arms over her head as if in praise, then fell and sank under the water.

Jane crouched, hands rattling the reeds, probing the water. "I can't find her. I can't—wait, I've got her." Groaning, she pulled the teacher's head and shoulders out. Water cascaded from Prudence's nose and eyes and mouth. The eyes were without life. Madeline bit her knuckle; at the last, Prudence's hope had failed her.

Esau sniffled, striving not to cry. Madeline took his hand and started on. She refused to surrender herself to execution even though she knew they were finished. Jane's moonlit face showed that she knew it too. With Esau between them they walked on, their last act of doomed defiance.

Between the pursuer and the place where Prudence fell, the bull alligator swam silently, submerged. He was sixteen feet from snout to tail tip and weighed six hundred pounds. His dark hemispherical eyes broke the surface. There was great commotion in the water, and something threatening just ahead. The alligator's nostrils cleared the water as his jaw opened.

Des knew he had them. They were no longer running, only walking at a pace that would allow him to catch them in another minute or so. He was sopping, scummy with mud, yet strangely buoyant; he seemed to dance through the water, just as he'd danced for so many years on the polished ballroom floors of the great houses the Yankees had destroyed along with everything else that was fine in the South. The white light lanced his head, spikes of it shooting in from both sides to meet behind his eyes. He felt exalted but anxious. He prayed silently to allay the anxiety. "God, let the light hold back until I've caught them. God, if You have ever favored me as a member of Your chosen race, spare me another few moments—"

The white sizzled and fused, consuming the dark in his mind. He smelled cannon smoke. He heard shells whistling in. He ran through the water screaming, not aware that the women were barely fifty feet ahead. His screams were full of zeal, full of joy:

"Forward the Palmetto Rifles! Charge to the guns! Glory to the Confederacy!"

Something like a club struck him: the alligator's huge lashing tail. Des fired a bullet at the moon as he went down. Then, as the alligator closed his jaws on his torso, he felt a sensation like dozens of heavy nails piercing his flesh. The alligator killed him in the customary way, holding him in the vise of its jaws until he drowned.

Only then was the body allowed to rise and float. Amid the blood eddying in the marsh water, the alligator began to feed by biting off Des's left leg at the groin.

Shouts and a burst of gunfire surprised and alarmed the Klansmen waiting for Des where the embers of the school gave off dull light and enormous heat. Gettys heard someone order them to throw down their arms. "To the road," he exclaimed, booting his mount.

Because he fled first, leaving the others momentarily bunched together, one of the blacks had a clear shot with his militia rifle. As Gettys galloped into the turn to the entrance lane, the bullet slammed his shoulder and knocked him sideways. He kicked free of the stirrups, terrified of being dragged. He fell in a vicious clump of yucca as the other Klansmen streamed by, robes flying. Gettys bleated, "Don't leave me," as the last horses galloped away.

Barefoot men approached on the run. A black hand snatched off his scarlet hood. Randall Gettys stared through steamed spectacles at six black faces, and six guns, and fainted.

"It's all right, Esau," Madeline said, trying to calm the crying boy. It was hard, because she was on the verge of tears herself. Andy was gone, Prudence was gone—God, the toll.

Suddenly, clear in the moonlight behind her, she saw the bubbling, roiling water, then a flash of scaly hide. An arm was briefly raised to the sky like some grisly Excalibur. It sank.

Jane leaned her cheek on Madeline's and wept.

With perfect clarity, she saw Des LaMotte's severed hand pop to the surface and float, shiny white as a mackerel. Something snapped it under and the marsh water was smooth and still again.

61

A grove of wind-blasted pecan trees shaded the bend in Vermilion Creek. Magee sat by one, his derby inverted in front of his outstretched legs. With hard snaps of his wrist he sailed card after card into the hat. He didn't miss.

Satan and two other horses were tied to a low limb; Gray Owl had left his pony behind and ridden the rangy bay. Charles hunkered near the trees on the shore of the purling creek. The sun was at the zenith. The spring day was balmy, and he sweated under his shirt and gypsy robe.

Above him, throwing a dark bar across his face, a leafless limb jutted over the creek. He studied the limb, judging its strength. The April wind caressed his eyes and beard. It was too fine a day for matters of fear and death—

"Look sharp, Charlie."

Magee emptied the cards from the derby and put it on as he stood up. They heard hooves splashing in the shallows. Charles drew his Army Colt. Gray Owl trotted from behind a clump of budding willows, hunched in his blanket. The bay was winded and glistening, not used to such a heavy rider.

Charles holstered his revolver and dashed down the bank to meet the tracker. "Did you find it?" Gray Owl nodded. "How far?"

"One mile, no more." The Cheyenne's expression was characteristically glum. "I saw a small boy."

The noonday sun seemed to explode in Charles's eyes. He felt a dizziness. "Is he all right?"

Gray Owl clearly didn't want to answer. He chewed his bottom lip. "I saw him sitting outside the house feeding a raccoon. His face—" Gray Owl touched his left cheek. "There are marks. Someone has hurt him."

Charles wiped his mouth.

Magee scuffed a boot in the shale. "Anyone else around?"

"I saw an old Kiowa-Comanche come out with a whiskey jar, get on his pony, and ride away. Then I saw a Cheyenne woman leave the big house and go to a small one, where I heard hens. She brought back two eggs."

"He has a squaw?" Charles said.

"Yes." The tracker's eyes were full of misery. "She is a young woman. Very dirty and sad."

"Did you see the man Bent?" Gray Owl shook his head. "No one saw you—not the boy or the squaw?" The tracker shook his head again. "You're certain?"

"Yes. There are some post oaks near it. A good hiding place."

Magee rubbed his hands together, trying to treat this as something ordinary, another field exercise. "We can come in from three different sides—"

"I'm going in alone," Charles said.

"Now that's damn foolishness."

"Alone," Charles said, with a look that killed further protest.

He returned to the trees where he pulled off his gypsy robe. He folded it and put it on the ground. He picked up his Spencer, checked the magazine, snugged his black hat down over his eyes, and walked back to Magee and the tracker.

"I'll watch myself, don't worry. If you hear any shooting, come up fast. Otherwise stay here."

He said it with the officer's tone and the officer's challenging stare. Magee fumed. Gray Owl gazed at the bright water, full of foreboding.

He won't know me, Charles thought as he stalked along the creek bank. *Not with this beard down to my belly.* He was thinking of Gus but it applied equally to Elkanah Bent. He couldn't imagine how Bent looked after ten years. It was immaterial. He just wanted to get the boy away safely. That was the most important issue, the boy.

The spring air was gentle as a woman's hand. It reminded him of similar days in Northern Virginia when hundreds of poor boys died in sunny meadows and glades. Those thoughts, and what Gray Owl said about Gus being marked, put a bitter taint on his anxiety.

He saw the post oaks ahead. Beyond them he glimpsed a structure of mud brick. Smoke drifted out of a chimney at one end, like a twist of sea-island cotton pinned to the sky. Charles thought he heard a child's voice. His hand on the Spencer grew white.

He tried to purge himself of fear. Impossible. His heart lubbed so hard it sounded like an Indian drum in his ear. He knew he would probably have one chance, no more.

He crouched and peered from behind a post oak. He almost cried at the sight of his son seated on the ground doling corn kernels to the raccoon one at a time. The raccoon took a kernel in his forepaws and stood on his hind legs like a paunchy little man in a mask while he ate the kernel. Then he wobbled over to Gus for more. The boy fed him with absolutely no trace of pleasure on his sad, gruel-colored face.

Even from a distance Charles saw the scabbed-over cuts and the bruise around Gus's eye. The boy's feet were so filthy Charles almost thought he was wearing gray stockings. Gus sat in the dirt near the front door of the whiskey ranch. The door was closed.

Charles saw a handsome chestnut horse and two mules in the corral at the end of the building. He saw the outbuilding where the squaw had gotten the eggs, and he heard a hen flutter and cluck. The loudest sound was the gurgling of Vermilion Creek.

He almost couldn't move because of his worry that he'd make a mistake. He tried to forget the size of the stakes and look at the situation as some kind of abstract problem. It helped, a little. He counted five, and on the last count stepped from behind the post oaks into the open, where his son could see him.

Gus noticed him. His mouth flew open. Fearing he'd cry out, Charles put a hand to his lips to signal silence.

He could tell the boy didn't recognize him, a stranger popping up in the wilderness, beard and hair matted, eyes sunken. He held perfectly still.

Gus dribbled the remaining kernels on the ground but he made no sound.

The raccoon loped forward and began to feast. Charles kept

every sense tuned for other noises—a voice, a door's creak. He heard nothing but the water. He took three long strides toward his son, raised his hand, and motioned, a great hooking sweep toward his chest. *Come here.*

Gus stared, clearly anxious about the stranger now. Charles wanted to shout, tell him who he was. He didn't dare. He gestured again. And a third time.

Gus stood up.

Charles was jubilant. Then the boy began to back toward the building, keeping his eyes on the stranger.

Oh God, he's scared. He still doesn't know me.

Gus sidestepped toward the closed door, ready to dart inside. Desperate, Charles crouched and laid his Spencer on the ground. He extended and spread his arms. The muscles were so tight he shook from shoulder to wrist.

Somehow the inviting outstretched arms reassured the boy. His face changed, showed a hesitant smile. He cocked his head slightly.

Charles said in a loud whisper, "Gus, it's Pa."

Wonder spread over the boy's face. He started to walk toward Charles.

The front door of the whiskey ranch banged open.

Bent was yawning as he stepped out. He wore an old plug hat and Constance Hazard's teardrop earring on his left ear. His claw-hammer coat shone as though grease had been spread on it with a knife. He was older, paunchier, with seams in his face, and scraggly eyebrows, and thick uncombed hair hiding the back of his neck. His left shoulder was lower than his right.

Bent saw Charles and didn't know him. Charles snatched the Spencer and leveled it at Bent's grimy waistcoat, which was secured by one button. "Hands in the open," he said loudly, standing.

Bent lifted his hands away from his sides, peering and blinking at the wild man with the rifle. Charles started forward—slow, careful steps. Bent's brambly eyebrows shot upward.

"Charles Main?"

"That's right, you bastard."

"Charles Main. I never thought you'd follow me into the Territory."

"Your mistake." Charles halved the distance between the

post oaks and the house, then halted. "I know what you did to George Hazard's wife." Bent reacted, stepping backward, startled. "I can see that you hurt Gus. I don't need much of an excuse to splatter your head all over that house. So don't even breathe hard. Gus, come over to Pa. Now!"

He watched Bent rather than his son. The boy couldn't grasp his sudden release. As if to test it, he looked at Bent and took a step toward his father. Two steps. Three.

An Indian woman in a dirty buckskin shift came out the door carrying a bucket of night slops. She had a sleepy, sullen look. Charles thought she resembled someone he'd met when he rode with Jackson. Then, stunned, he realized it was Green Grass Woman.

She saw him, recognized him, dropped the slops, and screamed. Gus spun around, alarmed. Bent jumped, and in an instant he had the boy.

Charles's head filled with denials of what he saw. Bent was smiling, the old sly smile Charles remembered with such loathing. Bent's begrimed hand clamped on Gus's throat. His other hand came out of his coat pocket with a razor. He shook it open and laid the shimmering flat of it against Gus's cheek.

"Put your guns down, Main." Charles stared, his forehead pounding with pain. Bent turned the blade. The edge indented Gus's cheek. The boy cried out.

Bent held him fast. "Put them down or I'll cut him."

Charles laid the Spencer in the shale in front of him, and his Army Colt beside it. "Now the knife." He added his Bowie to the pile. The sight of Charles unarmed pleased Bent. His smarmy smile broadened, became almost cordial. Failure pressed on Charles like an invisible block of granite.

"Pick up those things, you bitch. Main, step to the side. More—more—"

Green Grass Woman ran toward the weapons in a kind of crablike crouch. As she took them up, she gave Charles a pleading look and spoke in English. "He said it was a trader's boy, a bad trader."

Charles shrugged in a bleak way. "What are you doing here?"

"She used to belong to the owner of this place," Bent said. "I sell her. She'll hump man or beast for gin, but you won't have the pleasure. I have other things in mind." His face wrenched. Charles remembered how crazy he was. "You bitch, hurry up!" The cry echoed away. The wind blew.

Bent eyed Charles and giggled. "Now, Main. Now we're going to enjoy this unexpected reunion. I'm going to give the orders. You'll obey them to the letter unless you want this child to bleed to death before your eyes. When I say forward march, you come this way and take two steps through the door. Not one or three, *two*, keeping your hands raised at all times. Any mistake, any disobedience, I'll slit him."

Bent could barely contain his good humor. "All right. Forward—march."

Hands above his head, Charles walked to the house.

Magee strode away from the pecan trees carrying his rifle in the crook of his arm. The wind fluttered the wild turkey feather in the band of his derby.

Gray Owl called out, "He said wait."

"He's been gone too long." Magee kept walking.

"Wait. That was his order."

Magee broke stride. Stopped, stared across the bright water at a pair of redbirds swooping in the sunshine. With a fretful look down Vermilion Creek, he turned and slowly walked back to the tracker wrapped in his blanket.

62

The room reminded Charles of a sutler's. The dirt floor bore the imprints of boots, moccasins, bare feet. Dark lumps of cold food scummed the tops of two tables. The chair where Bent ordered him to sit creaked and swayed when he put his weight on it.

Then he saw the crookedly hung portrait. He stared at the woman for about ten seconds before recognition went off in his head like a shell.

"That picture—" He had trouble enunciating clearly. Fear for Gus dulled his mind, slowed his reactions. And coming on the portrait here, he felt propelled into some unreal place, some world where anything was possible, and nothing was sane.

With effort he finished the thought. "Where did you get it?"

"Recognize the subject, do you?" Bent laid the knife, the Spencer, and the Army Colt on the plank bar, then carefully positioned the open razor within easy reach.

"My cousin Orry's wife. It's a bad likeness."

"Because it's her mother. A whore in New Orleans. A quadroon." Bent took a coarse, heavy rope from a box beneath his shelf of bottles. "You don't act surprised that she's a nigger."

"I know Madeline has black blood. But I never expected to see a picture like that."

"Nor find me, I venture to say." Bent was all false politeness. "Hands together, raised in front of you."

Charles didn't respond. Bent struck him with his fist. Blood leaked from Charles's right nostril. He raised his hands and Bent looped the rope around his wrists.

Charles's mind was still sluggish, awash with rage against this stubbled, crippled man who moved with obvious discomfort. He raged at himself, too. He'd failed outside. His mistake would cost his life. He saw it in the feverish shine of Elkanah Bent's eyes as Bent looped the rope a third and fourth time.

All right, his life was forfeit. But there was Gus.

Bent's color was high. Constance's teardrop earring swayed like a pendulum gone wild. Bent had pierced his earlobe to hold the post. Green Grass Woman, so soiled and sad, watched Charles with unconcealed pity. It prickled the hair on his neck, that look. She knew what was coming. She clutched Gus to her side, protecting him while she could.

The boy gazed at him with eyes so dull Charles wanted to weep. He had seen the same lack of life in the eyes of wounded young men the night after Sharpsburg. He had seen the same whipped-animal stare in aging black men who feared jubilo, freedom, as much as they feared a master.

But Gus was not yet five years old.

Bent snugged the rope and knotted it. Charles had been exerting pressure against the ropes, but Magee's trick didn't seem to have gained him much slack. Another defeat.

"Do you know how I think of myself?" Bent asked pleasantly.

Charles let the hate pour. "Yes, Orry told me. The new Napoleon." He spat in the dirt.

Bent smashed his fist in Charles's face. Gus hid behind Green Grass Woman's hip.

Breathing noisily, no longer smiling, Bent said, "Did he also explain that he and Hazard ruined me at the Academy, and in Mexico? Destroyed my reputation with lies? Turned my superiors against me? I was born to lead great armies. Like Alexander. Hannibal. Bonaparte. Your tribe and Hazard's kept me from it."

Bent wiped a ribbon of saliva from his lip. Charles heard birds chirping outside the closed door. The cold ashes on the hearth had a familiar woody smell. The world was lunatic.

Bent picked up the razor and lightly passed the blade over the ball of his thumb. His smile returned. Reasonably and persuasively, he said, "I do think of myself as America's Bonaparte, and it's justified. But I'm forced to be watchful because every great general is besieged by little men. Inferior men, jealous of him, who want to pull him down. Tarnish his greatness. The Mains are like that. The Hazards are like that. So I am not only the commander, I'm also the executioner. Rooting out plotters. Betrayers. The enemy. Hazards. Mains. Till they're all gone."

"Let my boy go, Bent. He's too small to harm you."

"Oh, no, my dear Charles. He's a Main. I've always intended that he die." Green Grass Woman uttered a low sound and averted her head. "I planned to wait several months, until you'd given him up for lost. Then, when I killed him—"

"Don't say that in front of him, goddamn you."

Bent snatched Charles's beard, yanked it up, forcing his head back. He laid the razor against Charles's throat. "I say whatever I please. I am in command." He edged the razor deeper. Charles felt pain. Blood oozed. He closed his eyes.

Bent giggled and withdrew the razor. He cleaned the blade in the armpit of his coat.

Charming again, he said, "After I disposed of him, I planned to send you certain—parts, so you would know. Several fingers. Toes. Perhaps something more intimate."

"You fucking madman," Charles said between his teeth, out of control, starting to rise from the chair. Bent grabbed Gus's hair. The boy yelped and pounded small fists against Bent's leg. Bent slapped him, knocked him down, kicked his ribs. Gus rolled on his side and clutched his stomach, whimpering.

"Stand up, boy." Bent boomed like a revival preacher. How many men lived in that perverted body? How many different voices spoke from that one crazed brain? "Stand up. *That's a direct order.*"

"Don't," the Cheyenne girl said. "Oh, don't. He's so little—"

He slammed her in the stomach with his fist. She fell against the wall, clawing at the rough logs, knees scraping the dirt. "You'll be the next for execution if you say another word." He flourished the razor over his head, silver steel death. "Up, boy!"

Whimpering again, not quite crying, Gus tottered up. Bent seized him and pulled him against his legs, turning him at the same time. He put his free hand under Gus's chin and straightened his head with a wrench, so Charles and his son were face-to-face.

"After him, and after you," Bent said, "the next will be the family of Hazard's brother, in California. I'll exterminate the lot of you before I'm done. Think of that, dear Charles."

Gently, caressingly, he drew the razor over Gus's right cheek. Gus screamed. A thread of blood unwound itself on the pale flesh.

"Think of that while the executioner carries out the general's order."

Magic Magee said, "Shit," which stupefied Gray Owl, because the soldier had an inordinately clean vocabulary for someone in his profession. Magee jumped up from beneath the pecan tree with the big branch over Vermilion Creek. "I don't care about his orders, something's wrong."

Gray Owl started to call him back again. Magee was striding fast. Gray Owl hesitated only a moment before hurrying after him.

Tears rolled from Gus's eyes and diluted the blood on his cheek. Charles was consumed with a rage like sickness. He pulled his hands apart between his knees. The rope burned the backs of his wrists. Suddenly the left hand slid a little, slippery. He was bleeding. He pulled his left hand toward him but the largest part, just below the knuckles, held fast against the rope and wouldn't slip through. No use. No use.

Magee laid one hand on the corral rail. The chestnut and the mules smelled him and tossed their heads. "Now, now," he said, "don't take on. I'm friendly."

He slid between two of the rails. The chestnut neighed. "Don't do that," Magee said, wanting to shoot the blasted horse. He nodded sharply to Gray Owl, who clutched his rifle and padded out of sight, going to the front door. Magee had told him to wait until he called him in. Charles had to be inside. He wasn't in the combination stable and henhouse, or in the abandoned trader's wagon.

Magee didn't know what he'd find just inside the corral door but he hoped the door didn't open directly to the main room. He was sweating as if it were August. Just as he reached for the latch string, a fat raccoon shot around the back corner and ran right up and poised by the door.

"Scat," Magee whispered. He kicked the air. The tame raccoon wouldn't budge. He wanted in, probably for food. He'd give Magee away.

Baffled, Magee held still about fifteen seconds. Then, clearly, he heard a small boy cry out. With a glum face he drew his knife.

"I'm sorry, mister." He swooped down and killed the raccoon with one stroke.

Gus bled from the cut on his cheek. Charles wished the boy would faint, but he hadn't.

Bent's head was blessedly free of pain and those queer hurtful lights. The general's orders were just and right, and the executioner's duties were a joy. He couldn't prolong it much longer, though. The cutting, right in front of the boy's straining, terrified, mad-eyed father, had given him a huge painful erection.

He laid the razor on Gus's throat.

Charles saw the blued muzzle push out between the door frame and the red blanket. He'd heard nothing from that part of the house, not a sound. Loudly, Magee said, "Mr. Bent! You better turn around and see this gun."

There was a slow, tortured moment when Charles knew Bent would cut Gus's throat. Instead, like a soldier, he obeyed the commanding voice. He turned. Magee stepped from behind the blanket.

Charles hurled himself out of the chair and flung Gus down. Bent bellowed, realizing his error. Charles leaped away, stumbled over his son, and fell. Green Grass Woman jumped at Bent and began to claw and pummel him. Magee aimed but she was in his line of fire. Bent shoved her and lashed downward with the razor, laying open her skirt and slashing her thigh. She cried out. A second push toppled her. Bent went for Charles, the razor shining.

Magee shot him. The bullet struck the back of his left thigh. He spiraled down and flopped with his hand flung out. Charles rolled over, his wrists still tied. He reached, pulled the razor from Bent's hand, and threw it. Magee shouted something. A rectangle of light fell over Charles and his son. Gray Owl crouched in the door with his rifle.

"Want me to finish him?" Magee asked. Bent stared, realizing he was unarmed, caught.

"Not in front of the boy. Cut me loose."

Magee freed Charles with his knife, which was bloodstained. Charles knelt, trembling.

"Gus, it's Pa. I know I look terrible, but it's Pa. Pa," he

repeated, with an extra puff to the P, as if that word alone could make the link.

The boy drew away, using his hands in the dirt to pull himself. Some frightened witless animal peered from his eyes. Charles extended both arms, hands spread, as he'd done outside. "Pa."

Suddenly the tears broke, racking the boy, great gulps and shudders. He wailed and ran to Charles. Charles enfolded him and held him. He held Gus a long time, until the tiny body stopped shuddering.

Green Grass Woman's gashed leg bled heavily. She had lost consciousness after she fell. Magee raised her skirt and inspected the wound. As dispassionately as a physician, he wiped some blood from her thick pubic hair. "I used to doctor drunks in the saloon when they pulled stickers on each other. I can tie this off. Be painful for her to walk for a while, but I think she'll be all right."

From his pouch Gray Owl took some roots, which he crumbled and mixed with a few drops of creek water, working the material to a paste on a flat stone brought from outside. He searched the smaller room and found a piece of clean cloth. Magee was busy tying Bent's hands with part of the rope that had bound Charles. He was careful to brace Bent's arms behind his back and loop the rope with no possibility of slack. He wasn't gentle.

"How about his leg?" Charles asked.

"Grazed, that's all. I'd say leave it alone. Serve him right if the gangrene got it."

Gray Owl knelt beside the exhausted boy. His brown hands were gentle as he worked some of the gray-green paste into the cheek wound. "He may be scarred, the way Cheyenne boys are scarred from the Sun Dance."

"Sun Dance hooks go in the chest, not the face."

"Yes," the tracker said sadly. "There is nothing to be done. He will heal."

"Even if he heals he'll be scarred," Charles said.

He returned the Army Colt to his holster, bandaged his rope-burned wrist, and went behind the bar. There he found another coil of rope. He slipped his left arm through and carried it on his shoulder. Bent stood by the door, his pant leg bloody. He blinked in the sunshine. He seemed docile.

Charles drank two swallows of the vile bar whiskey in hopes of staving off the shock that was an inevitable consequence of violence. He walked over to Bent. It was all he could do to keep from putting the Colt to Bent's head and firing it.

"Magic, come along, will you? Keep the boy here, Gray Owl."

Bent cringed in the doorway. A lemon-colored butterfly flirted around his head and flew on. "Where am I going?"

The sun struck the gold filigree of Constance's earring and made it shine. Charles felt the impulse coming and couldn't stop it, or didn't want to stop it. He seized the earring and jerked downward. The post tore out most of Bent's earlobe. He howled and crashed against the door. Charles kicked his ass and drove him into the hot bright light.

The soft air did nothing to take the taste of dirt and bad whiskey and corruption from Charles's mouth. He had never felt the burned-out feeling so strongly. It tasted like sand and alum in his mouth. It hurt like salt and vinegar in a wound.

Palm over his bloody ear, Bent was abject. "Please—where?"

"You white trash," Magee said, imperial in his wrath. "You're going to hell."

"Where?"

Charles leaned close, to be sure Bent heard him. "Waterloo."

RAMPAGE OF
THE KUKLUX.

———

A Night of Terror
on the Ashley.

———

The Mont Royal School
Destroyed a Second Time.

———

Two Are Dead.

> President Grant Expresses
> Outrage.
>
> ———
>
> A Wounded Night-Raider
> Unmasked.
>
> *Special from our
> Charleston Correspondent*

———————

MADELINE'S JOURNAL

*May, 1869. Buried Prudence Chaffee and Andy Sherman to-
day. They lie side by side, by my wish, and Jane's. I read the
scripture, John 14. . . .*

*Fr. Lovewell has fled the district. No trace of the body of
Des L. My feeling about him reduces to sadness rather than
hate. I am told he served in the Palmetto Rifles throughout
the whole four years. Afterward he fought for causes more
suspect. The preservation of slavery in different form. The
supremacy of whites. The honor of a cruel and haughty family. Must men always be prey to evil ideas that cloak themselves in a seductive righteousness? . . .*

*Thinking of D.L. again. In death he excites my curiosity
in a way he could not when he threatened us. Like so many
millions of others on both sides, he was changed and ultimately destroyed by the war. That kind of experience may be
the central fact of our lives for a generation or better. Charleston people still discuss the way the war blighted Cooper. I
know how Mexico wounded you, my dear husband. And how
that unknown Yankee whose name you never knew cut short
your precious life at Petersburg. Had it not been for Sumter,
secession, Lee, and all the other great events and persons now
being tinted with the false colors of romance, D.L. might not
have been driven to fight his last doomed war at Mont Royal.*

*But as I have said before, pity is not without limit. I will
have justice in the matter of the Klan. R. Gettys is still semi-
unconscious in the hospital in Charleston, and the authorities
move too slowly. One good friend said I could appeal to him*

*for help at any time. Will travel to Columbia tom'w., taking a
pistol for my companion. . . .*

Nothing was left of Millwood or Sand Hills. All of Wade
Hampton's land was gone in the wake of forced bankruptcy the
previous December. Rising taxes, shrinking crop income, investments worth forty cents on the dollar—it all culminated in a
single tidal wave of disaster. Over a million dollars in debt had
driven him down.

Hampton and his wife, Mary, now lived in sharply reduced
circumstances: a modest cottage on a scrap of land he'd managed
to keep. The Hamptons welcomed Madeline and insisted she stay
the night on an improvised bed in the room the general used for
an office.

Hampton's age showed, but he was still vigorous and ruddy.
While Mary served tea, he left with his pole and creel. He came
back in an hour with four bream for their supper. Mary set to
boning the fish and Hampton invited Madeline into the
office. He cleared a place for his cup on the paper-strewn desk
and in doing so had to move a handsome gold-stamped volume,
which he showed to her.

"Proceedings of the Democratic National Convention in
New York last July."

"I read that you were a delegate."

Without bitterness, he said, "The Republicans named it the
reb convention. Bedford Forrest was a delegate. Peter Sweeney,
the sachem of Tammany, too—very odd bedfellows, but that's
the Democratic party for you."

"It's about General Forrest and his Klan that I've come to
speak to you. I want the culprits punished."

"What have the authorities done?"

"Nothing so far. It's been over two weeks. If too much time
goes by, other things will take precedence and it will all be forgotten. I'll not have that. My teacher and the freedman at least
deserve simple justice for a memorial."

"I concur. I'll tell you a fact about Forrest. He's ready to
deny his connection with the Klan and order it to disband. It has
gone too far even for him."

"No consolation to Andy's wife, or Prudence Chaffee's
brothers and sisters."

"I understand your bitterness. Grant despises the Klan. Permit me to write him. I shall also ask General Lee to do so. We're on good terms. On behalf of all the investors in the little insurance company I organized in Atlanta, I asked him to assume the presidency. He declined. He's happy presiding at the college up in Lexington. But we're friends, and his word will carry weight." She glimpsed his melancholy as he stroked his side-whiskers and mused, "Now and again there is some small benefit in being a war-horse who came through it alive."

She noted the care with which he'd chosen the last word, leaving others—*unhurt; unmarked*—unspoken.

When Randall Gettys began to recognize his surroundings, Colonel Orpha C. Munro called on him. The hospital matron warned him that he couldn't stay long. With an acerbic smile he assured her that he could accomplish his mission quickly. "I am here at the request and on the authority of President Grant."

The matron unfolded a screen for privacy. Munro sat down beside the bed. Gettys resembled an intimidated child, the sheet tucked up to his pale chin and his pudgy fingers nervously playing with it. In the melee at Mont Royal he'd broken the right lens of his spectacles, which he'd had no chance to replace. He watched his visitor from behind a pattern of cracks radiating from the center of the lens.

With deceptive friendliness, Munro said, "It's my duty to inform you that the small hand press kept at your Dixie Store for printing your newspaper has been confiscated. You are no longer in the business of disseminating hatred, Mr. Gettys."

Gettys waited, certain there was worse to come.

"I would take a horsewhip to you if that were permissible. I'd do it despite your wound, because I find you and all your kind richly deserving of it. You're like the doomed Bourbons of France —kings too filled with arrogance to forget the past, and too stupid to learn from it."

Munro drew a long breath, forcing restraint on himself. "However, the recourse I mentioned is denied me. I suppose that's best. Using a horsewhip would pull me down to your level. Let me instead pose a question." Something hard, even a bit sadistic, showed in his eyes. "Do you know of the Dry Tortugas?"

"Small islands, aren't they? Off the Floridas."

"Quite right. The government now sends Carolina prisoners

to the Dry Tortugas. A godforsaken spot, especially in the summer months. Blistering heat. Insects and rats and vermin. Wardens only a little less depraved than the inmate population." Munro smoothed his gauntlets, which he'd laid on his knee. He smiled. "New prisoners are subjected to certain—initiations, while the wardens look the other way. Without steady nerves and a strong constitution, a prisoner sometimes fails to survive the ordeal, which I understand can be savage. After all, when men are penned up together, without women—"

"My God, what has it all to do with me? I'm a gentleman."

"You're nevertheless going to the Dry Tortugas, for the murder of the freedman Sherman and the teacher Prudence Chaffee."

"I didn't kill them," Gettys exclaimed, his voice rising toward shrillness. "You can't send me to some—some bestial place like that."

"We can and we will. If you didn't actually commit the crimes, you belonged to the unlawful combination bearing responsibility."

Gettys's hand shot to the braided sleeve, clutching. "I'll give you the names of those in our klavern. Every last one."

"Well." Munro cleared his throat. "That might put a different coloration on it, being a cooperative witness." He concealed his amusement. He had expected a quick capitulation. He had inquired extensively about the character of Randall Gettys.

Gettys's pink face sweated. "If you keep me out of prison, I'll give you something else useful."

Colonel Munro was nonplussed. Cautiously, he said, "Yes?"

"I'll tell you about the Dixie Stores. People think it's a Southern company. Some old rebs hiding behind a name and committing usury. Well—"

Gettys hitched higher against the pillow, practically babbling in his haste to save himself. "It isn't that at all. The owner, the people bleeding this state, may be some of the very people who pose as high-minded Yankee reformers. My store and all the others like it are owned by a firm called Mercantile Enterprises. I don't send my receipts and reports to Memphis or Atlanta, I send them to a Yankee lawyer in Washington, D.C. I'll give you his name and address. I'll turn over the records. Is that enough to keep me from the Dry Tortugas?"

From the end of the ward a young man's delirious voice called for his Nancy, and water. Colonel Orpha C. Munro recovered his composure. "I think it may be, Mr. Gettys. I do indeed think so."

Munro here briefly. All the remaining den members are arrested. M. hinted that he has also discovered some scandal involving this district and persons from the North. He would not say more. Cannot imagine what he means.

63

Bent said, "You don't understand what you're doing."

Charles and Magee ignored him. Charles held the bridle he'd put on one of the mules from the corral. Magee, astride the frisky chestnut, pulled on the rope to test it. The rope was tied to the branch of the pecan tree hanging over Vermilion Creek. A few brilliant white clouds floated in the blue northwest. The day was sweet and summerlike.

"Lean your head down," Magee said.

Bent refused. Tears rolled down into the stubble on his cheeks. "To do this is criminal."

Charles was weary of the man's ranting. He glanced at Magee, who knocked Bent's plug hat off. It landed in the creek and sat upside down in the purling water. Magee yanked Bent's head down by the hair and slipped the noose over. He snugged the noose with one pull.

Blood still leaked from Bent's torn earlobe. His wound was soaking his left pant leg. He cried now, spewing wrath and self-pity. "You're trash, ignorant trash. You're robbing the nation of its greatest military genius, you and this lowlife nigger."

"God above," Magee said. He was too astounded to be mad.

Bent shook his head violently, as if he could get rid of the rope that way. "You can't do it. You can't deprive the world of the new Bonaparte." His voice was so loud that redbirds along the creek flew up in alarm.

Charles brought his Colt from his hip, cocked it, and held the muzzle an inch from Bent's mouth. "Shut up." He looked in the direction of the whiskey ranch, not wanting the outcries to carry. His son and the Cheyenne girl had had enough. Bent saw the determined eyes behind the revolver and struggled to control himself. He bit his lip; but the tears kept rolling from the corners of his eyes.

The pecan limb cast a dark shadow over Charles's face. He didn't want to go through with this. He was sick of killing. He reminded himself that Bent represented an obligation that was more than personal. He owed this to Orry and George; especially to George, for his wife. He owned it to Green Grass Woman and God knew how many others Bent had wronged over the past twenty-five years.

Charles stepped back from the mule.

"You can't! Military genius is a rare gift—"

Charles slid the Army Colt into the holster and flexed the fingers of his right hand, brushing the tips over his palm in a cleansing motion. A male and female cardinal flew frantically round and round above the creek, frightened by the shouting.

"You're killing Bonaparte!"

He positioned his hand to slap the mule. A final look at Bent, to be sure he was real—then his arm and hand moved in a blur. The sound of the slap was loud. The chestnut tossed his head and Magee reined him hard as the mule bolted. The rope hummed taut and Bent's weight made the pecan limb creak.

Bent seemed to glare down at Charles. But his neck was already broken. The shadow of his body moved slowly back and forth across Charles's face before he turned away, unable to stand the sight.

"I'll catch the mule."

"Let me," Magee said softly. "You go back to your boy."

In the sundown's dusty orange afterglow, Charles sat on a nail keg, watching the creek. He drank the last of some coffee Magee had brewed. The soldier had killed and cleaned and hearth-broiled one of the chickens but Charles had no appetite for it. Instead of the creek, flawed black glass streaked with colored highlights, he kept seeing Bent's eyes just before the rope sang its last low note. Bent's eyes became a mirror of his own life. In the vengeful Bent he recognized himself, a humiliating image. He was no better. He spilled the bitter-tasting coffee on the ground and went inside.

He crossed the main room, lifted the red blanket screening the doorway, saw his boy sleeping on the old straw-filled mattress in the bedroom. He walked to the bed. Even asleep, Gus had a pinched, anxious look. Charles touched the oozing cut on his left cheek. The boy moaned and turned. Pierced by guilt, Charles drew his hand back. He walked out and let the red blanket drop in place.

Gray Owl sat at a table, enveloped in his blanket, his eyes fixed on some infinity beneath the scarred wood. Magee rested in one chair with his boots on another. He munched some hardtack, his practice deck of cards fanned out in front of him. Green Grass Woman sat on a nail keg with hands clasped and eyes downcast. She looked old, worn, full of despair. Coming in from outside, Charles had found her with a bar bottle. He'd taken it out of her hand and emptied it outside, then done the same with the others.

Now he walked over to her. She raised her head and he saw a flickering image of the young, fresh girl who'd listened to Scar's courting flute with a saucy confidence that the world was hers, along with any man in it that she chose. He remembered the lovelorn looks she gave him that winter in Black Kettle's village. Somehow the memory hurt.

He spoke in Cheyenne. "How did you get here?"

She shook her head and started to cry.

"Tell me, Green Grass Woman."

"I listened to promises. A white man's lies and promises. I tasted the strong drink he gave me and I wanted more."

"This was Bent?"

"Mister Glyn. Bent killed him."

He had a dim recollection of a seedy trader named Glyn. He'd met him when he rode with the Jacksons. No doubt it was the same man.

"Let me look at the dressing."

There was an echo of girlish shyness in the way she drew up the deerskin skirt just far enough. The bandage showed staining but it would do until morning. Green Grass Woman could walk on the slashed leg, though probably not without plenty of pain. That focused Charles's mind on a responsibility that became more inevitable the longer he thought about it.

"I need to take you back to the People."

Gray Owl straightened up, alert, anxious. The girl's eyes showed fright. "No. They would scorn me. What I did was too shameful."

Charles shook his head. "There isn't a man or woman on God's earth who isn't in need of forgiveness for something. The nearest village is Red Bear's. I'll take you there and talk to him."

She started to protest, but she didn't. Gray Owl didn't protest either. Evidently the idea was reasonable.

Magee scooped up his deck and squared it. "Glad we're going to get out of here. Something bad about this place."

"Gray Owl and I will take her," Charles said to him. "I want you to put Gus on one of those mules and ride straight through to Brigadier Jack Duncan at Fort Leavenworth. Will you do that?"

Magee frowned. "I dunno, Charlie. I hate to send you back to those Indians without your wizard. That Whistling Snake, he's probably still burning."

"There won't be any more trouble." It was a declaration, not a certainty. The prospect of returning to the Cheyennes did bother him, but the duty seemed unavoidable. "We'll ride in and out in an hour. Now listen. At Leavenworth, I'd like you to send a telegraph message for me. I saw some paper in the other room. I'll write it out."

"All right," Magee said.

The burned-out feeling consumed Charles. He strode to the door, flung it open, stared at thousands of stars gleaming more brightly than usual in the clear air. He thought of the Hanging Road. He'd nearly traveled it this year. He was so tired. "God, I wish I had a cigar," he said.

In the morning he wrote the telegraph message and saw it safely stowed in Magee's saddlebag along with the flintlock pistol, powder bag, and box of fake ammunition. Charles pulled the nails from the corners of the oil portrait and rolled it up. It was dry and brittle. A corner broke off. He tied the painting carefully with a strip of rawhide.

From a blanket he'd washed and hung over the corral rail to dry, he cut a large square which he slit with his knife, making a small poncho for Gus much like his own gypsy robe. He lifted the boy onto the horse blanket he'd tied to the mule with braided rope; there was no spare horse furniture in the stable.

Gus looked like a little old man, scarred and pale. "Hug your pa," Charles said. The boy took a long, deep breath. He was wary. The hurt flickered in his eyes.

Charles hugged him instead. "I'll make it all right, Gus. I'll come to Uncle Jack's soon and it will be all right."

He wasn't sure, though. It would take months, perhaps years, of attention and love. The hidden scars might never heal. He hugged the boy fiercely, arms around his waist.

Gus laid one hand on the top of his father's head. After a moment he drew it away. His face was sober, without emotion. Well, the touch was a start.

To Magee he said, "Take care of him."

"Count on it," he answered.

Charles and Gray Owl watched until the soldier and the boy vanished on the hazy horizon to the northeast.

The tracker helped Charles pull down two corral rails and shorten them with a rusty axe. They rigged a travois for Green Grass Woman. It was another sunny day, with a light breeze. The Cheyenne girl said nothing as the two men carried her to the travois.

Charles had already saddled Satan; they'd brought the horses back late yesterday. Passing Bent's corpse was unavoidable. The buzzards had already feasted on the American Bonaparte, and plucked his clothes to bloody rags.

"This is an evil place," Gray Owl said, seated on his pony. "I am glad to go."

"Take the travois a little way down the creek, to those post oaks. I'll be there in a few minutes."

Gray Owl moved out, leading the mule. Green Grass Woman exclaimed softly as the travois bumped over a sharp stone. Gray Owl looked apologetic. His pony plodded on. The Cheyenne girl held her bandaged leg and watched the sky.

Charles carried the rusty axe inside. He kicked over a nail keg and chopped it apart. Next he demolished a table and two chairs. He struck with hard blows, letting pain jolt through the handle and up his arms.

He piled up the wood and set fire to it with one of his last matches. He left the whiskey ranch burning behind him.

They reached Red Bear's village on the Sweet Water in pouring rain. No one threatened Charles, and those few people who peeked out to watch the arrival hung back, properly awed because they remembered the bearded white man who commanded a black wizard. The black wizard wasn't with him, but surely his medicine was.

Of Whistling Snake they saw nothing. Charles turned Green Grass Woman over to the care of Red Bear's stout and toothless wife. Green Grass Woman was not of Red Bear's village, but the chief knew about her.

"She will go with us to the white fort," Red Bear said in his tipi. Seated by the fire, Charles used a bone spoon to eat some stew. He no longer worried about the origin of the stew meat.

"You're going to give up to the soldiers?"

"Yes. I have decided it after much thought and consultation with others. If we do not give up we will starve or be shot. All in the village have agreed to go except for eight of the Dog Men, who refuse to quit. I said I would not lead grandfathers and infants to death just to preserve the honor of the Dog Men. It wounds my pride to go to the soldiers. I was brave once too. But I have learned that bravery and wisdom sometimes cannot walk together. Life is more precious than pride."

Charles wiped stew from the corner of his mouth. He said nothing.

He hadn't slept in twenty-four hours. But he wanted to be on his way. Red Bear endorsed that. "The Dog Men know you are here. They are angry."

Then the wise thing was to hurry out of the village. Ceremoniously, he thanked Red Bear's kindly wife and the chief for welcoming them. He said he would like to say goodbye to Green Grass Woman. The chief's wife led him to a nearby tipi where she'd made the girl comfortable. Beside a small fire, bundled in a buffalo robe, Green Grass Woman lay with her head and shoulders elevated by a woven backrest. Charles took her hand.

"You'll be all right now."

The puffy eyes welled with new tears. "No man will ever have me. I love you so. I wish you had lain with me once."

"So do I." He leaned down, holding his beard aside as he kissed her mouth lightly. She cried in silence; he could feel her shaking. He caressed her face, then stood and slipped through the oval hole into the slackening rain.

Stars began to shine through translucent clouds blowing across the sky. Red Bear saw them to the edge of the camp, then turned back. The freshening wind tossed Charles's beard. He patted Satan, watched the clearing sky, began to hum the little melody that reminded him of home. Beside him, Gray Owl trotted his pony and observed his friend cautiously. What the Indian saw brought a fleeting smile.

They spied a lone horseman motionless on a low rise ahead and thought nothing of it. Some boy on duty with the horses, Charles assumed. He angled the piebald toward the stream to avoid passing too near the sentinel. The Indian suddenly loped down off the rise to intercept them.

"What's this?" Charles wondered aloud. Then his mouth dried. The Cheyenne was speeding toward them, booting his pony. In one hand he carried a lance, in the other a carbine with long feathers tied to the muzzle. Something about the rider's head and torso reminded him of—

Gray Owl reined in, despair in his eyes.

"Man-Ready-for-War," he said.

And so it was. Older now, but still handsome, though there was a famished, fugitive look about him. He wore his regalia and full paint. Around his neck hung his wing-bone whistle and the stolen silver cross. From shoulder to hip ran a wide sash painted yellow and red and heavily quilled and feathered. When Charles saw the sash he remembered Scar had been chosen a Dog-String Wearer.

In the light of the clearing sky, the huge white scar fish-hooking from the tip of the brow down around the jawbone was quite visible. Satan snorted nervously, smelling the Cheyenne pony as it trotted up.

"Others told me you were here," Scar said.

"We have no quarrel anymore, Scar."

"Yes. We do."

"Damn you, I don't want to fight you."

Wind fluttered the golden eagle feathers tied to the barrel of the carbine. Scar rammed his lance point in the muddy earth. "I have waited for you many winters. I remember how the old one tore away my manhood."

"And I remember how you repaid him. Let it go, Scar."

"No. I will pin my sash to the earth here. You will not pass by unless it is to walk the Hanging Road."

Charles thought a moment. In English, he said to Gray Owl, "We can bolt and outrun him."

Gray Owl's morose old eyes were despairing again. He pointed to the rise. The starlight showed that four warriors had appeared there to insure they would not escape.

Sick at heart, Charles flung off his black hat. He pushed the gypsy robe over his head and laid it across his saddle. He dismounted, handed Satan's rein to Gray Owl and drew his Bowie from his belt, and waited.

64

Scar drove his lance down through the slit at the end of his sash, pinning it. The lance vibrated as he let go. Charles understood what the sash said. *To the death.*

The Dog Society man began to mutter and chant. He untied a thong at his waist to free a wood-handled axe. He raised axe and carbine over his head in some ritual supplication Charles didn't understand. Then he ran the edge of the iron head along the carbine's barrel, back and forth, a whetstone rasp. Sparks spurted.

I've had enough, Charles thought. Texas, Virginia, Sharpsburg, the Washita. Augusta, Constance, Bent's razor—is it endless?

With a grunt, Scar threw the carbine away. The gun tumbled barrel over stock and landed unseen in the dark. Chanting louder, he kicked out of his moccasins. He sidled around to the right, presenting his shoulder and forearm. He showed the axe, then began to swing it clockwise in a small taunting circle. Suddenly he struck out straight toward Charles, the blade horizontal.

The ground was soggy, the grass still brown and scant after the winter freezes. Charles's foot slipped as he raised the Bowie in both hands and blocked the axe blow, edge against edge. Scar's force drove his arm on. The axe head slid off the knife and whistled past Charles's ear. Charles stabbed at the lunging body, a hard target in the starry dark. He missed.

Scar's sash limited his movement, Charles's only advantage. He knew that if he just walked away, out of Scar's reach, the four riders would come down for him. So he had to finish it here, God help him.

Once more Scar came sidling in, rotating the axe in the

clockwise circle. He swung. Charles ducked. He swung again. Charles ducked again, but he felt the iron pluck at his hair. He stabbed upward. Pricked the inside of Scar's left sleeve. The Dog Soldier leaped away nimbly, turning like a dancer to unwind the sash twisted around him.

Charles crouched, both hands high in the traditional stance of the knife fighter. The Bowie twinkled in the starlight. Already the two men had churned their little patch of ground to choppy mud. It sucked at Charles's boots as he sidestepped, awaiting the next feint or slash.

Scar chanted and tossed his axe to his left hand. Charles shifted to counter the move. Turning toward Scar's left hand opened the left side of his body to attack. Without warning, Scar tossed the axe back, laughing deep in his belly as he chopped with his right hand.

Charles's right-to-left parry slashed the inside of Scar's forearm. Scar reacted by jerking the axe upward. Charles reached for it with his left hand and Scar kicked with his right foot. The hard blow struck Charles's groin. He reeled, lost his balance in the mud, fell.

Scar screeched like a boy who'd won a game. He jumped on Charles with both knees, then rolled him from his side to his back. He seized Charles's knife hand and pushed it over his head into the mud. The axe swung high, a black wedge against a familiar milky veil of stars.

The axe came down. Charles wrenched his head the other way; felt the blade scrape his hair before it buried in the mud. He twisted his knife hand and pricked Scar's knuckles. Scar yelled, more surprised than hurt.

Charles tried to jerk his knife hand free. Scar held fast. Charles smelled the rancid grease Scar had used to dress his body before he applied his paint. Scar swung the muddy axe down again, and again Charles twisted away. The wrenching movement freed his knife hand. He spiked the Bowie through the upper part of Scar's left arm.

The Dog Society man dropped the axe. The blunt top of the blade bounced off Charles's temple. Scar was breathing harshly, in pain. Charles clamped the Cheyenne's chin in his left hand, his right hand with the knife well inside Scar's bleeding left arm. He felt the chin clamped in his left hand turn to flaccid weight. The

wound was draining Scar quickly. Charles had only to reach up
and cut his throat.

"Stab him," Gray Owl said from the dark.

Charles's knife hand began to shake. Scar hung over him
like a meal sack someone was filling; it became heavier and
heavier.

Reach up.

He couldn't do it. He pushed with his left hand and rolled
from underneath as Scar tumbled away. He'd whipped him. That
was enough.

He felt a hand snatch at his right thigh before he compre-
hended what it was. Gray Owl ran forward as Scar sat up, cock-
ing the Army Colt he'd plucked from Charles's holster. Despite
the mud coating the piece, the mechanism worked. Gray Owl
stepped in front of Charles to shield him, and the two Cheyennes
exchanged shots. The tracker took the one meant for Charles.

Scar's head flung backward in the mud with a sloppy splash.
He was hit, though Charles couldn't tell where. Up on the rise,
the ponies of the four riders neighed and tossed their heads. Gray
Owl sank to his knees and discharged three more rounds at them.
In Cheyenne, he shouted that Scar was killed. The Indians hastily
formed a file and trotted out of sight.

Gray Owl exhaled, a weary sound. Charles scraped mud out
of his eyes and crawled toward the tracker as he relaxed and
slipped down onto his back. In the village someone raised an
alarm.

Charles lifted Gray Owl in his arms. The tracker's shirt was
slippery with mud and blood. The starlight whitened his face,
which showed a remarkable repose.

"I found the way for us, my good friend. Now I go on."

"Gray Owl, Gray Owl," Charles said in a broken voice.

"I go on as my vision foretold. I go—"

"Gray Owl."

"There." With a tremor in his hand, Gray Owl reached for
the veil of stars. The Hanging Road. His hand fell back to the
bosom of his shirt and Charles heard the rattle and felt the shudder as he died.

He held Gray Owl's body while he studied that of Scar,
motionless with the Army Colt in his hand. He knew there was
something he should do but exhaustion and confusion kept it
from him a few moments. Then he remembered. He envisioned a

platform high in a tree, nearer to heaven. It was his duty to build that for Gray Owl, a good man. He had believed his gods wanted him to lead others, even if that led him to exile, and the white man's path, and death. To the end he was faithful to the vision. Charles wished he had something as strong to believe in.

But he did. He remembered Gus. He remembered Willa.

Gently he laid the body on the muddy grass. He slipped twice gaining his feet. He heard clamorous voices behind him. Red Bear and his people. They would help him build Gray Owl's resting place. He turned around to wait for them.

Dying but not dead, Scar raised himself a few inches and shot Charles in the back.

———

GEO HAZARD

CARE OF HAZARDS

LEHIGH STATION

PENNSYLVANIA

THE CRIMINAL BENT APPREHENDED AND EXECUTED

IN THE INDIAN TERRITORY ON THE 27TH INST.

I HAVE THE EARRING.

CHARLES MAIN

FT LEAVENWORTH KANS

BY TELEGRAPH

———

MADELINE'S JOURNAL

May, 1869. The press has a new hare to chase. Charleston papers are full of revelations from Washington about the Dixie Stores. Cannot believe the name associated with the scandal.

"Unfortunate," said the Boss. "Very unfortunate, Stanley. I thought you'd make an excellent congressman from your district when Muldoon retires at the end of the next term. You're well known, you can afford to campaign, your positions are highly principled."

Stanley knew what that last meant. He was obedient to orders from the state machine, which was under his guest's absolute control.

The two of them were seated near the bust of Socrates at the Concourse, Stanley's favorite club. Stanley's face had a pale and saggy look these days. He was standing fast in the face of daily exposés, principally in the *Star*. Although Stanley was forty-seven and his guest, Simon Cameron, seventy, Stanley felt that the Boss was the more vigorous. He'd stayed slim. His hair showed no sign of thinning and his gray eyes revealed none of the dullness of imminent senility that Stanley noted in some men Cameron's age. The Boss had returned to the Senate in '67, and had never been so powerful. Political intrigue agreed with him.

Reflective, Cameron sipped his Kentucky whiskey. A warm spring twilight gilded the windows near them. "As to circumstances now," he resumed, "I must be candid with you. Usury may not be illegal but it is certainly unpopular. And Northerners have grown tired of flogging the South. The Dixie affair has actually generated a surge of sympathy for the victims of carpetbag profiteers." He raised a hand to placate his host. "That's a newspaper term, my boy, not mine. But it is regrettable that the moment Dills was confronted with that Klansman's confession, he caved in."

Stanley snapped his fingers to summon one of the servile waiters. He called for another round so blithely, Cameron was puzzled. Stanley was under enormous pressure because of the stories linking him to ownership of Mercantile Enterprises, which owned the forty-three Dixie Stores throughout South Carolina. Almost daily Stanley made a public denial of his guilt; he explained nothing, merely professed his innocence with the determination of old Stonewall resisting the enemy at First Bull Run. Given Stanley's past behavior, Cameron expected him to be not only visibly tired, which he was, but also completely unnerved, which he was not. Remarkable.

Stanley said, "I presume Dills cooperated in hopes of keeping what's left of his practice. In the past year or so his circumstances have been greatly reduced. No one's sure about the reason. He had to resign from this club, for example. He couldn't afford it any longer."

"Like our friend Dills, I presume you'd like to keep something, too? Such as your good name?" The lean old Scotsman's face showed a familiar severity. "You have no political future without it."

"I have nothing to do with the Dixie Stores, Simon. Nothing." There; another sign of Stanley's surprising new assertiveness. Until recently he'd been timid about using the Boss's first name. "I have stated and restated that to the press, and I'll continue to say it, because it's true."

Cameron puffed his lips out and moved his tongue behind them as if trying to dislodge an irritating seed. "Well, yes, but to be candid, my boy, in the Republican hierarchy, they don't believe you."

Stanley sighed. The elderly black man in a fusty formal suit offered his silver tray. Stanley took his glass, which contained twice as much whiskey as the one given Cameron. "Then perhaps I had better be somewhat more forthcoming. I do aspire to that House seat. Of course, to clear myself completely would be hard. Emotionally."

Cameron, who could read most men easily, was thrown. "What are you talking about?"

A swift glance showed Stanley there were no members close enough to hear. A magnificent tall clock behind the periodical table chimed, six sweet, deep notes.

"I'm talking about the Dixie Stores. When they were established, I admit that family funds were used. I had no knowledge of it at the time, however. I was too busy overseeing General Howard's programs at the Bureau." His eyes, so like a mournful hound's, actually sparkled now. "Mr. Dills can verify that all of the stock of Mercantile Enterprises is registered in the name of my wife, Isabel."

The senator from Lancaster nearly spilled his drink.

"Are you saying . 'ie operated the stores?"

"Yes, and she started them on her own initiative, after a visit to South Carolina. Of course I discovered it eventually, but I have never had any knowledge of the details."

The older man guffawed. Stanley took offense but quelled his resentment. Cameron shook a long finger. "Are you telling me that you absolutely deny any association with the Dixie scandal?"

"I am. I do."

"You expect the party and the public to believe that?"

"If I keep saying it," Stanley returned calmly, "I expect they will, yes. I knew nothing. Isabel is an intelligent and driven woman. The shares belong to her. I did not know."

Simon Cameron tried to align this bland, imperturbable Stanley with the timid naïve man he had advised to look into some sort of profitable Army contract early in the war. Stanley had grown enormously rich selling shoddy shoes. He had also changed while Cameron's attention was elsewhere. The Boss couldn't find the old Stanley in the new one.

Relaxed in the leather chair, he gave a grudging laugh. "My boy, that congressional seat may not be out of reach after all. You are very convincing."

"Thank you, Simon. I had a master teacher."

Cameron presumed Stanley was referring to him. He took note of the clock. "Will you join me for supper?"

Stanley handed Cameron another surprise when he said, "Thank you, but I can't. I have invited my on here to dine."

Laban Hazard, Esquire, just twenty-three and only two years out of Yale, had already established a Washington practice. It was not prestigious, but it was profitable. The majority of Laban's clients were murderers, perpetrators of stock frauds, and husbands charged with adultery. Laban was a slight, fussy young man whose earlier handsomeness was fast being eroded by too little sunshine and too much Spanish sherry.

In the club dining room, over excellent lamb cutlets, Stanley explained his predicament, and his decision to speak in more detail to prove his innocence. Laban listened with an unreadable expression. Under the gaslight his carefully combed hair resembled the pelt of an otter just out of a creek.

At the end of Stanley's long monologue, his son smiled. "You prepared well, Father. I don't think you'll even need counsel if the shares are registered as you say. I'll be pleased to represent you in any unforeseen circumstances, however."

"Thank you, Laban." A syruplike sentimentality flowed through Stanley. "Your wretched twin brother is unredeemable, but you gladden my heart. I am happy I took the initiative in reuniting us."

"I too," Laban said. He belched. "Sorry." The S sound was prolonged; Laban had already drunk one sherry too many.

"Will you contact the *Star* for me? I'd like a private meeting with their best reporter, as soon as possible." Stanley's voice was pitched low. There was no mistaking what he wanted his son to do.

"I'll take care of it first thing tomorrow." Laban twirled his wineglass. Then, avoiding his father's eye, he said, "You know I have always had difficulty feeling affection for my mother."

It was uttered in a monotone; Laban was in his lawyerly mode. He made the personal confession sound ordinary.

"I know that, my boy," Stanley murmured. He felt triumphant; he would survive, and ascend to new heights. "But we mustn't harbor ill feelings. She will need compassion when the storm breaks."

Three days later, Saturday, Stanley was in the stable behind the I Street mansion. In shirt sleeves and already fortified by two morning whiskeys, he was admiring his matched bay carriage horses. They were the joy of his life; they symbolized the benefits of wealth.

"Stanley."

Her harpy voice brought him around to face the wide doorway. A pale sun was trying to break through the night mist from the Potomac. The stable had a friendly smell—earth, straw, manure. Stanley saw a copy of the *Star* in Isabel's hand.

"Please leave us alone, Peter," he said. The young black groom knuckled his eyebrow and left.

Isabel was ashen. She shook the newspaper at her husband. "You fat vile bastard. When did you do this?"

"Transfer the shares? Some time ago."

"You won't get away with it."

"Why, I think I already have. I had a congratulatory note from Ben Wade yesterday. He commended my honesty and courage in the face of a draconian choice. He lauded my future as a Republican. I understand the White House considers me exonerated."

Isabel detected the spite in his treacly tone. She started to revile him, then thought better of it. She felt the weight of her nearly fifty years, and she was suddenly afraid of this pudgy man in disarrayed linen whom she'd held in contempt for so long. She crossed over to him.

"What are we going to do, Stanley?"

He stepped away from her imploring hand. "I am going to

institute divorce proceedings. Laban has agreed to handle matters. I can't condone the policies of your Carolina stores."

"My—?"

"I have my future to think of," he went on. Isabel's face showed a sick disbelief. "However, I've instructed Laban to arrange for transfer of five hundred thousand dollars to your personal account. Consider it a sort of parting gift, even though you served me ill as a wife."

"How dare you say that? How dare you?"

Suddenly Stanley was quaking. "Because it's true. You constantly humiliated me, belittled me in front of my sons while they were growing up. You deprived me of the one woman who ever cared about me."

"That music hall slut? You simpleton. She wanted your purse, not your privates."

"Isabel. That's revolting." Deep within, some little gnome of spite laughed aloud. Isabel prided herself on refinement. He'd finally broken her.

He continued. "That remark is further proof of my assertions. Even so, I'll still give you the money to tide you through the scandal. All I ask in return is that you stay away from me. Forever."

The blooded bays nuzzled one another from their adjacent stalls. Shafts of brightening sun speared down from the hayloft. Outside, hidden by the mist, Peter whistled a minstrel song. Isabel's astonishment turned to rage.

"I taught you too well. I taught you too much."

"That's true. Growing up, I never thought very highly of myself or my abilities. Neither did Mother. Neither did George. You convinced me I could become successful if I wasn't overly scrupulous about how I did it." Christ, how he hated her. He was openly nasty for the first time. "In your old age you can take pride in that accomplishment."

"I did too much for you," Isabel screamed, charging at him, fists flying. She was slight; no match for him, flabby as he was. Stanley didn't mean to hurl her away so hard. She struck her shoulder against an empty stall and cried out, then sat down. Bewildered, she gazed at her twisted skirt. She'd gotten manure all over it.

The young black groom dashed into the wide doorway and

checked there, a silhouette against the sunlit mist. Stanley was startled by the strength of his own voice:

"Nothing wrong, Peter. Go about your work."

"I was too good to you," Isabel said, leaning her head against the stall and weeping. "Too good."

Blinking, Stanley said, "Yes, I would have to agree, even though I don't imagine it was intentional on your part. And when you were too good to me, you made a grave mistake, Isabel." He smiled. "Please be out of the house in twenty-four hours or I'll be forced to lock you out. I must excuse myself now. I'm thirsty."

He marched away into the mist, leaving her to stare at the filth on her skirt.

65

Richard Morris Hunt designed the mansion. It occupied the entire block between Nineteenth and Twentieth on South State Street. To lure so fashionable an architect to Chicago had been a great feat. As with most everything else, Will Fenway found that overpaying by a third got him what he wanted.

The extravagance didn't concern him. It was impossible to spend his money as fast as he made it. The Fenway factory had expanded three times, the firm was ten months behind with orders, and, late in '68, Will's sales director, LeGrand Villers, had added three more company travelers, based in London, Paris, and Berlin. Will was beginning to think there were more whorehouses in the world by far than decent Christian homes.

Will Fenway was already sixty-eight when he engaged Hunt. He knew he wouldn't live more than a decade or so, and he wanted to enjoy himself. He asked Hunt to build him the largest, most ostentatious house possible. Mr. Hunt had studied at the Ecole des Beaux Arts, and was the foremost apostle of French Second Empire architecture, considered by people of taste to be no mere revival of an old style, but the essence of modernity.

Hunt designed a granite castle of forty-seven rooms with mansard roofs on its three wings, and a spendthrift use of marble columns, marble floors, and marble mantels throughout. Will's billiard room was large enough to hold a small cottage; Ashton's ballroom would have accommodated three. Only one incident marred construction of the house. At the top of each mansard slope was a cast-iron cresting. Ashton one day discovered that Hunt had ordered these manufactured from his design by Hazard's of Pittsburgh. She flew into a rage and sent a letter discharging Hunt. In reply, her husband received an angry telegram from the architect. Will was forced to leave the factory, where he usually worked a minimum of twelve hours Monday through Saturday, and jump on a train for the East. He begged for several hours to get Hunt to overlook the insulting letter.

The crisis passed, and the Fenways moved into the mansion early in the summer. They spent many pleasant hours discussing and selecting a name for the house. Every important residence had a name. He wanted to call it Château Willard; Willard was a miserable man's name, but somehow it had an impressive ring when connected to a house. In choosing the name he suspected that he lacked taste, but he figured his money compensated for it, and people would therefore excuse his lapses, so he might as well go ahead with whatever pleased him. "Château Willard," he declared.

Ashton rebelled. Instead of nestling sexlessly in his arms that night, she moved into her own three-room suite. She stayed four days and nights, until he came tapping at her door to apologize. She let him in on the condition that they modify the name to Château Villard, with the accent on the second syllable. He seemed relieved, and agreed.

The year 1869 brought a riot of prosperity to the owners of Château Villard. Will couldn't believe the sums flowing in, or the number of Fenway uprights shipped out. A magnificent Fenway grand piano was already in the design stage, and there were orders in hand for the unbuilt instrument. Given all this, Ashton realized she was finally in a position to explore ways to revenge herself on her family. As a first step, she asked Will for a personal bank account. After some consultation with the Fenway Piano Company's bookkeepers, he established it with an opening balance of two hundred thousand dollars. In February Ashton decided she'd pay a visit to South Carolina as soon as weather and her schedule permitted. She had no definite idea of how she would proceed against her brother and Orry's widow; she merely wanted to search for possibilities.

The staff of Château Villard expanded from three persons to twelve, including two stable hands, during the first three months of what was to become the 1869 spending spree. Ashton bought paintings, sculpture, and books by the crate. A two-thousand-dollar red morocco set of the works of Dickens excited Will's admiration—he touched and smelled the books reverently when they were delivered—but he remained an unpretentious man, and only read such things as Alger's stories of plucky and enterprising young fellows who succeeded, or the coarse frontier humor of Petroleum B. Nasby, or nickel novels like *Spitfire Saul, King of the Rustlers.* Although Will had seen the reality of the West, he seemed fonder of the falsification of it.

Ashton tried to get acquainted with the occupants of the mansions above and below Château Villard. To the north lived Hiram Buttworthy, a harness millionaire, a Baptist, a man who kept a spittoon in every corner of every room and had a wife so ugly she looked like she belonged in one of his harnesses. Mrs. Buttworthy, a society leader, didn't approve of the flamboyant Southerner who obviously had not married her husband for his youth, his looks, or his prospects for a long life.

To the south of Château Villard, apparently without a spouse, lived a suffragist named Sedgwick, whose outspoken views and tart tongue reminded Ashton of her sister—which was enough to engender permanent dislike at their first, and only, meeting. Ashton wasn't discouraged by her inability to get along with her neighbors. The fault was theirs. Isolation from jealous inferiors, she had long ago decided, was one of the prices of great physical beauty.

Will bought a summer cottage at Long Branch, New Jersey. He bought it sight unseen. If the seaside resort suited President and Mrs. Grant, it was good enough for him. He bought a sixty-foot lake sailer, a splendid gleaming yacht with an auxiliary steam plant, which he anchored in a costly slip near the mouth of the Chicago River. Ashton was asked to name the yacht. She christened it *Euterpe* after finding the muse of music depicted in one of the seldom-opened books in their large library. Reading the book for nearly an hour made her cross and gave her a headache. She was thirty-three, but her interests had changed little since girlhood. She valued her appearance, and men, and power and money, and found everything else both extraneous and annoying.

Will's money gained them certain entrées but not others. A choice table among the palm fronds in the Palmer House dining room was always available, no matter how many people were ahead of them. Yet older women of better background happily accepted Ashton's donations to charities such as the Chicago Foundling Center but they politely ignored her expressions of interest in joining the menu committee for the annual dinner.

Ashton's application for membership in the Colonial Dames was denied.

Her husband had simpler aspirations. He found a convivial group of friends in his lodge, the International Order of Odd Fellows. He hated organizations such as the Knights of Labor and the Patrons of Husbandry, collectives that threatened the capitalist—that is, him.

Ashton's planned visit to South Carolina was delayed by an inspection trip to the furnished cottage at the Jersey shore. She found the parlor walls decorated with gaudy chromos of the Rockies and the California coast. Will greatly admired the cheap art, and said this was his kind of place.

But they were too early for the summer season, so Ashton pouted and wheedled until he took her to New York, where they saw Bryant's Minstrels, Lydia Thompson and her British Blondes, and Mr. Booth's production of *Romeo and Juliet.* Tickets for this last were in such demand, Will had to pay a scalper one hundred twenty-five dollars for each. Then he fell asleep in the second act, and snored.

Ashton bought three trunks of new clothes. City streets were in such deplorable shape, a lady's skirt got soiled and water-stained within a few weeks of the first wearing. Ashton never bothered to have such garments cleaned; she threw them out. Occasionally, she saw them later on her servants, retrieved from the rag bin.

Will didn't mind. He admired his wife's opulent figure and loved to see her smartly dressed. She was welcome to all the cash he would have spent on a large wardrobe for himself. He got by on a few stiff white collars, two pairs of bright checked trousers, a favorite floral waistcoat, and a solid gold watch chain and enormous gold nugget cuff links. In an assembly of these, and without a coat, he felt supremely fashionable. The hell with what anyone thought.

"I'm going to miss you," Villers said, drawing his hand slowly between Ashton's legs.

"I won't be gone that long, darling. A week or two—"

"Forty-eight hours without this has gotten to be too much for me."

She laughed, took his hand, pressed the palm against her left breast, and wiggled pleasurably.

LeGrand Villers was a vigorous man with a thick head of curly dark blond hair. A Northerner, he had once dealt cards for a living on the Mississippi boats, and although he wasn't much in the looks department, he was extremely masculine and had a persuasive way about him. In the two years since he'd wandered into the Fenway offices seeking temporary work to pay some gambling debts, he had risen from supply room clerk to salesman to manager of the sales force, and had seduced Ashton along the way. Villers was unequivocally the best-endowed lover Ashton had ever known. In token of this, he was represented in her Oriental box by two buttons.

Ashton's belly and thighs were splashed with sun spilling through a porthole above the bunk. *Euterpe* swayed gently with the lap of the river in the slip. The main stateroom had a warm, private feel this June morning. The master and the mate never sobered up and came aboard until past noon, which made the yacht an ideal place of assignation.

"Well, I admit you drive me crazy too, LeGrand." Powell had been handsomer, but not quite as virile.

"And you really don't think Will knows about us after all these months?"

"He knows I have lovers, though we don't discuss it. He understands that I'm a young woman with, ah, needs."

"One of which seems to be a need to go to Carolina. I can't imagine why. I visited Georgia once. Just a lot of darkies and air-headed girls and mush-mouthed whelps who mumble 'yes, sir' while thinking up ways to fleece you."

"LeGrand, I ought to throw you out of my bed for that. I'm a Southerner." She'd just demonstrated it with a heavy dose of the accent she had gradually suppressed during her years of residence in the North. She had gotten used to everything in the North but the howling white storms of the Chicago winter, which must be some kind of curse God had placed on Yankees.

"I want to see my family," she added. Her eyes were like blue-black agates. "A friendly visit."

"Friendly?" Villers toyed with her again. "I've never heard you say anything friendly about those people."

She arranged her unbound hair on each shoulder and eyed the ticking clock nearby. Only a quarter to eleven. Fine.

"Why, I've changed, LeGrand. People do change."

He snickered. "Learned to cover up how much you hate 'em, is that what you mean?"

Ashton stroked his blocky jaw. "I knew I liked you for something besides what's in your trousers. Now don't you tell my secret. Come on over here and do your duty."

A dockhand passing on the pier five minutes later noticed *Euterpe* showing a slight roll in the water, which was unusual for such a calm day.

"The hack is here to take you to the depot, madam."

"Load the luggage, Ramsey."

The butler bowed and retired. Despite his clipped British speech—the reason Will had chosen him over other applicants—Ashton considered him just another slave. He was chained by wages instead of shackles, but that didn't entitle him to any better treatment. Part of the joy of servants, and of the vanished peculiar institution, was having other human beings in fear of your every word.

Will strolled out of the billiard room. The gold nugget links were so large his cuffs sagged. Although he'd aged, he looked much healthier and sprier than he had when Ashton met him in Santa Fe. Success sat well on him.

His lively blue eyes admired his wife a moment. Then he patted her cheek, as if she were a favorite cat.

"Behave yourself."

Ashton felt a little jolt. She saw nothing but warmth in his glance, but his remark reminded her of his warning after she shot the señora's brother-in-law without good cause. No one but Will could inspire the same little thrill of fear she enjoyed inspiring in others.

"Yes, sweetheart. Always," she said.

She registered at the Mills House as Mrs. W. P. Fenway, Chicago. The staff naturally took notice of an attractive woman traveling alone with eleven large pieces of luggage. But no one got a very clear look at her features; she was heavily veiled. There was nothing to reveal that she was a Main.

Ashton deplored the condition of lovely Charleston, which still showed many ravages of war. Darkies lounged everywhere with an air of impertinence that would have gotten them horse-whipped when she was a child. There were still some Yankees in blue uniforms to be seen.

She hired a closed carriage for a tour. The Battery brought back memories of the exciting weeks when Sumter lay besieged. She stood by the harbor while her driver waited at a discreet distance. She looked seaward, a splendid figure of a woman with her waist whaleboned to sixteen inches. She wore velvet the color of fine Burgundy, yards and yards of it in her full flaring skirt with bustle. It was hellishly hot, but the effect was worth it. Strollers enjoying the summer air wondered about the expensively dressed, rather melancholy woman gazing across the water to the Atlantic. Were her thoughts romantic? Was she sweetly musing over some lost love?

I hate you, Billy Hazard. Everything might have been different if you'd loved me instead of my prissy little sister.

Ashton blamed not only Billy but also Orry, Cooper, and Madeline for her exile and her ghastly months of whoredom— and never mind that Lamar Powell had enchanted her with his plans for a new Confederacy of which she was to be first lady. As she considered all she'd lost because of the self-righteous behavior of her own family, she felt the old hatred renew itself. She sniffed and dabbed her eyes dry with her glove and returned to the carriage, ordering the driver to proceed slowly along East Bay.

There she surveyed the house where she'd lived with poor Huntoon. She felt no emotion except contempt.

On narrow Tradd Street, passing the gate of Cooper's residence, she recoiled against the carriage cushions as a woman came out. Cooper's plain-as-bread wife, older but still sharp-nosed and flat-bosomed. Ashton averted her face despite the veil. She called for the driver to go faster. There wasn't a shred of doubt—she hated them all.

During the next few days she learned some surprising things. For one, Orry had never made it home from the war. After ordering Ashton and Huntoon out of Richmond for their role in the Powell conspiracy, he'd gone on duty on the Petersburg lines, where some Yankee had shot him.

Ashton briefly examined her reactions to that. She felt neither sorrow nor remorse, only more anger at her gaunt one-armed brother. His death cheated her of an important opportunity for reprisal, and she didn't like it.

Madeline was living alone, prosperous but despised because of her scalawag ways. Ashton heard about the Klan outrage at Mont Royal and the new house under construction, and then, from a tipsy journalist with whom she flirted, she learned something else which truly excited her. Everyone in town knew it. Mont Royal was heavily mortgaged.

"A pleasure to meet you, Mrs. Fenway," said Leverett Dawkins, enthroned in his special office chair. "How might the Palmetto Bank be of service this morning?"

Ashton sat with perfect posture on the edge of his visitor's chair. The careful way she drew her shoulders back emphasized the line of her full bosom, something the banker did not miss. She watched his eyes slide upward to her face—the poor fool obviously thought his attention had gone undetected—and she knew she had the advantage. She was familiar with Dawkins's name but she had never met him; therefore he would never associate her with the Main family.

Outwardly composed but inwardly straining, she said, "I want to inquire about property in the district. I have old family ties in South Carolina. I treasure the Charleston area and I would like to have a home here."

"I see. Go on, please."

"When I was driving on the Ashley River road the day before yesterday, I saw a lovely plantation that captured my heart. I've been back twice since then to observe it, and my feeling remains the same. I hoped you would be able to tell me something about the property."

"To which plantation do you refer, ma'am?"

"I was told the name of it is Mont Royal."

"Ah, the Main plantation," he said, leaning back. "The owner is Mr. Cooper Main of this city."

Hearing her brother's name startled and confused Ashton. Fortunately her heavy black veil hid her momentary disarray. She recovered, saying smoothly, "I thought a woman controlled the place—"

"You're referring to the owner's sister-in-law, Mrs. Orry Main." Ashton noted a certain distaste when he said that. "Yes. She lives there by arrangement with Mr. Main. She's a sort of resident manager, responsible for the operation of Mont Royal. But Mr. Main holds the title."

Carefully: "Might the plantation be available for sale?"

He thought it over. He considered what he knew of Cooper's feelings about the Negro school, and his hatred of Madeline Main's complicity in the marriage of his daughter to the Yankee. Dawkins's visitor raised a new and most interesting possibility, one in which he saw a dual advantage. Profit, and ridding the bank of a relationship that had grown irksome.

"There is a substantial mortgage on Mont Royal," he said. "Held by this institution."

She already knew that, but didn't let on. "Oh, what luck! Do you suppose the owner, this Mister, ah—"

"Main," he prompted.

"Would he sell if the mortgage could be paid off as part of the transaction?"

"Naturally I can't speak for him, but it's always a possibility. If you would be interested in making an offer, the bank would be happy to act as your representative. For a fee, of course."

"Of course. I'd insist on it. And upon some other conditions as well. My husband, Mr. Fenway, is a wealthy man. In fact, he's richer than Midas. Do you know Fenway's Piano Company?"

"Who does not? Is that your husband? Well, well."

"If Mr. Main found out who was trying to buy his plantation, he might inflate the price unreasonably."

"We can make sure that doesn't happen. If we act in your behalf, you can maintain complete anonymity until the sale is consummated." That pleased her, he saw. "You mentioned conditions in the plural—"

Her heart was beating so hard, she almost shook. Here it was—the chance for the perfect reprisal she'd dreamed about for years. Fighting to keep tension from her voice, she said, "I would want the sale to be completed very quickly. Within a matter of a few days. I would want to take title, and possession, before I return to Chicago."

He frowned for the first time. "What you ask is irregular, Mrs. Fenway. And difficult."

She sat back, as if withdrawing her friendliness. "Then I'm sorry—"

"Difficult," he repeated, swiftly raising one hand. "But not impossible. We would bend every effort."

"Excellent," she said, relaxing. "That's just excellent. Perhaps we can move on to specifics? A suggested offering price. Please name the figure. Not unreasonable, mind. But high enough to be irresistible to this Mr. Cooper Main. That's the magic word, Mr. Dawkins."

She lifted the black veil slowly to let him gaze on her sweet poison smile. He was entranced by the wet gleam of her lips and the even white beauty of her teeth as she whispered to him:

"Irresistible."

BOOK SEVEN

CROSSING JORDAN

I do not believe that the whites can now, or will, live under a rule where persons so entirely ignorant, so venal, so corrupt, have the management of their State government. . . . I think they will bear as long as they can but there will be a point beyond which they cannot bear.

GENERAL WADE HAMPTON, 1871

66

"It's from Sam. In New York. My letter was sent on from St. Louis."

"What does he say?"

She scanned the page. "He was surprised to learn I was in South Carolina. He sends you his wishes for a quick recovery. He'll be happy to give the bride away as long as the ceremony doesn't interfere with a regular performance. What performance?" She turned the sheet over. "Oh, my. This is rather hard to take."

"What?"

"Claudius Wood liked Sam's *Othello*. He imported the production to fill a spot in his schedule and it turned into a huge hit. Sam says it's to run indefinitely at the New Knickerbocker. Eddie Booth's seen it twice. Oh, that is ironic. Sam working for the man who almost killed me."

She tossed down Trump's letter; it, too, had been forwarded from St. Louis.

"You sound angry."

"Well, yes. I should be more tolerant. Sam's an actor, which means he's quite like a little child in some ways. Children's wishes are often stronger than their loyalties. Sam constantly wished for this kind of success—which is bad luck in the theater —so naturally it eluded him. Then when he wasn't looking for it, it arrived. It's foolish to expect him to turn his back on it. He's an actor."

"I think you said that."

"I did, but it explains everything. We'll just have to be married on whatever day the Knickerbocker is dark. That is, if you still—"

"I do. Come here."

Yellow light, summer light, painted the ceiling and the whitewashed wall behind the head of his bed. Work on the new house was ending for the day. Someone drove a last nail into a roof beam; the nailhead sang like a bell at each blow.

In the distance he heard the mill saw whining as it cut. He heard the shouts and the cracking whips of the muleteers driving their carts in the phosphate fields. Nearer, in the main room of the whitewashed house, Madeline and Willa were chatting about supper. They'd gotten along wonderfully from the day he and Willa arrived with the portrait of Madeline's mother in their luggage. Madeline wept when she saw the picture.

Warm in a new blue flannel nightshirt Willa had cut and sewn for him, Charles lay staring at the ceiling. The slatted shutters broke the wash of light into a pleasantly regular pattern. A large undefined area of his lower back, the left side, still hurt. But not as badly as before. He was getting better.

Red Bear and four of his Cheyennes had taken him to Camp Supply, unconscious. There a surgeon probed for the bullet without finding it. An Army ambulance delivered him to Duncan at Leavenworth. Gus was safe there, although Charles was too delirious to know it immediately. The brigadier telegraphed the playhouse, and Willa rushed to Kansas by train. During the three weeks in which she tended Charles and shared Maureen's bed, Sam Trump and company closed Trump's St. Louis Playhouse and decamped to New York.

At Leavenworth, a contract surgeon tried to find the bullet. He failed. Day before yesterday, hoping to alleviate Charles's pain, a lanky freedman named Leander had made the third attempt. Leander said he'd been doctoring most of his adult life; he'd been the only source of medical help for fellow slaves on a Savannah River cotton plantation. Charles told him to go ahead, even though he knew the procedure could end in death.

Leander gave Charles a stick wrapped with a whiskey-soaked rag. While Charles bit down, crazy with pain, Leander cut into the wound using a flame-purified knife. Evidently Scar's lump of lead had shifted recently. Leander found it quickly and removed it with a loop of baling wire.

Beyond the half-closed door, a third voice, smaller, thinner, interposed between those of the women. Charles inhaled the musky damp of the marshlands, felt the faint tickle of pine pollen at the back of his throat. Every year, regular as God's wrath, it dusted every surface yellow-green. He was home.

It wasn't the completely happy experience he'd anticipated when he persuaded Willa to accompany him to Mont Royal for the lengthy recuperation. Madeline was rebuilding the great house in Orry's memory, but the plantation had undergone many changes that struck him as foreign and crass. Nothing was gracious any more. It was all steam engines and dug-up rice fields.

Madeline was estranged from Cooper and ostracized by the white families of the district. An organization he knew little about, the Kuklux, had terrorized the district for a while. Klansmen had murdered Andy Sherman, whom he remembered as a slave without a last name. They'd killed a white schoolteacher, too. The sweet lonely melody of home that he had whistled for years was somehow off-key, inappropriate.

And then there was the problem of the boy who no longer knew how to smile.

Gus remained a polite child. Carrying a little round hat with a floppy brim that Willa had bought for him in Leavenworth, he came into the bedroom quietly. His feet, in rope-and-leather sandals, left a trail of water spots. Willa must have insisted that he wash after he came in from playing. But he still had mud between his toes.

Gus stood by his father's bed. "Are you feeling all right, Pa?"

"Much better today. Would you pour me a drink of water?"

The little boy put his hat on the bed and juggled the cup and large china pitcher. The water gurgled into the cup. Gus watched the stream carefully. On the boy's right cheek, Bent's cut was hardening into scar tissue; a dark ridge in a sun-washed landscape.

Gus touched the scar often but never mentioned it, or the whole dark period of the whiskey ranch. Willa, who granted that she was no expert on mental problems, nevertheless thought common sense dictated silence on the matter for a while yet.

Gus handed the cup to his father. The water was tepid. "Guess what I saw down by the sawmill, Pa."

"What?" Charles said.

"A big white bird with legs like sticks. This long. He was standing in the water but he flew away."

"Egret," Charles said.

"Guess what else I saw. I saw some other birds flying in a line. I counted five. The first one would do this"—he waved his arms up and down—"and the others did it, too. When the first one stopped, they stopped. They had funny mouths, big mouths." He stuck out his lips. "They flew that way." He pointed seaward.

"Brown pelicans, maybe. Pretty far upriver. Did you like seeing them?"

"Yes, I liked it." There wasn't a jot of pleasure in the reply, or even the slightest smile on the small, well-formed mouth, which always reminded Charles of Augusta Barclay's. How long would it be until the boy didn't hurt any more? Forever?

"I'm hungry now," Gus said, and left.

Charles turned his head away from the door. Familiar guilt lapped at him, a kind of stomach-sickness. He pictured the scar. *I let it happen.*

He had a lot to do to make up for it. *I have to leave him something better than scars when he grows up.* He knew of nothing so valuable as money. The simple repayments of fatherly affection and attention—of course he'd make those. They were not enough, though. Not nearly enough. Because of the scars—the visible one and the ones hidden within.

After dark, when the pond frogs and chuck-will's-widows tuned up for their nightly concert, Willa came in and sat with him. Charles set the lamp wick higher, to see her better. Her hair shone like white gold.

"I'm still searching for that place for us," she said. "I don't care where it is; I'll go anywhere with you."

"What about being an actress? You don't want to give that up, do you?"

She wiped a smudge of flour from her thumb. "No, but I will." She studied him. "Wait. You're thinking of something—"

He pushed himself back, straightening, shifting the pillow behind his shoulders. His hair showed a lot of gray now. He'd shaved his mustache and beard, and Madeline and Willa both said he looked ten years younger. "I thought of it day before yesterday, just before Leander cut me and I fainted. Texas. I loved Texas. I learned soldiering, so I don't see why I couldn't learn ranching."

"You mean raise cattle?"

"That's right. I could build a house for us, and put together a herd. The beef market's good. More and more cattle are shipped east all the time."

"I've never seen Texas," she said.

"Pretty godforsaken in some parts. But others are beautiful."

"What would we do for money? I haven't saved much."

"I could go to work for someone else till I learn the business and put a hunk aside."

She brought her warm mouth against his and kissed him lightly but firmly. "You'll have to save a lot. I want a huge old house. I want to raise Gus with brothers and sisters."

"I'll do it, Willa." Some liveliness animated his voice at last. "The truth is, I want to be rich." *To pay for the scars.* "We could settle near some town of decent size, so that, when the money comes in, I can build you a theater. An opera house of your very own."

She hugged him. "Charles, that's a lovely dream. I think you'll do it, too."

He watched the shadows of a woman and a boy outside the partly closed door. He heard Gus ask Madeline a question.

"I promise I will," he said.

Early June in the Low Country. Even sweeter and brighter than Ashton remembered. Warm air not yet tainted by the sickening humidity of full summer. A pure blue sky conveying a sense of repose, even languor.

The matched team was the color of milk. Each horse sported a white pompon fitted to the headstall. The carriage was a barouche with gleaming lacquered side panels. Before leaving Charleston, Ashton had insisted that the two black men in threadbare livery fold the top down.

She sat facing forward in the hired rig. Patterns of sun and shadow from the trees passed rhythmically over her face. Her dark eyes had a liquid look. Surrounded by the sights and scents of her childhood, she found herself struggling against a messy sentimentality.

Opposite her, oblivious to the charms of the scene, sat Favor

Herrington, Esquire, a Charleston lawyer recommended to her when she said she wanted someone who put success ahead of professional ethics.

Mr. Herrington's appearance and demeanor were unimpressive. A pale, slight man of thirty-five or so, he had a mustache so small and fine, it resembled an accidental pen stroke. Below his lower lip, which receded, something resembling a lump of dough substituted for a chin. Herrington's thick 'Geechee accent was, in Ashton's opinion, decidedly inferior to her own cultivated Charleston speech. Nevertheless, at their first meeting, the lawyer had fawned and "Yes, ma'amed" her with such juicy extravagance that she immediately recognized one of her own kind. Underneath his airs, he was unscrupulous.

Ashton remembered this part of the road. Something dried her throat. "Slow down, driver. That's the turn ahead."

Herrington fastened the brass latch on the old leather case containing all the papers. He straightened his cravat as the barouche turned up the long lane. Through the cloudy black of the veil Ashton lowered over her eyes, she saw the raw yellow framing of the new Mont Royal.

Why—the house was huge!

All the better.

"I have the honor to present you with these documents," Favor Herrington said. "Bill of sale, closing statement, deed—and this, to which you'll want to pay special attention."

Ashton's lawyer had expected to find the buxom mulatto woman, to whom he was addressing his remarks. But he hadn't anticipated the presence of the man with powerful hands and weathered skin who limped out in his blue nightshirt as Madeline confronted the visitors on the shady lawn. Nor did Herrington know who the pert young woman with pale blond hair was. Perhaps the man's companion.

The barouche stood nearby. The two black men in livery patted and soothed the white horses. Charles warily watched the woman sitting motionless in the rear seat. She wore burgundy velvet and a heavy black veil. There was something forbidding about her. Something that reminded him of—what?

With a stunned expression, Madeline took the blue-covered document Herrington had presented last. "That is an eviction order," the lawyer said pleasantly. "Yesterday, at the Palmetto

Bank, the mortgage on Mont Royal plantation was liquidated and title to the property was sold to my client." He indicated the veiled woman.

Madeline shot Charles a bewildered look. She turned over page after page of finely inscribed clauses. She found a name. "Mrs. W. P. Fenway. I don't know any Mrs. Fenway."

"Why, my dear, you most certainly do," said the woman in the barouche. She wore mauve gloves, and the little finger of each was elevated slightly. Her hands were graceful as floating birds as she lifted the veil.

"I never expected to lay eyes on you, Cousin Charles." Ashton stood on the coarse grass near the whitewashed house. Spite bubbled in her dark eyes. "Wherever have you been all these years? You look ever so much older."

He could say the same about her. Still, her beauty remained undimmed, almost perfect. Not much of a surprise in that. He could remember her long ago, avoiding the sunshine, fussing for hours, alone, before she appeared in a new party dress. Her looks had always counted for a lot. Evidently they still did. It was her eyes that gave away the changes wrought by time. The haughty, hard eyes. Where had she been? What had she seen and done?

"What do you want here?" Madeline asked, still recovering from the moment the rising veil had revealed the visitor's face.

"Mont Royal is all," Ashton said with a vicious flirt of her eyes. "It's my family's land. Main land. It isn't yours. Your husband, my brother, drove me off the property. I always swore I'd come back and do the same. Or worse."

"Ashton, for God's sake—Orry's been dead over four years."

"So I was informed. Pity." She stepped up on the worn pine stoop, peered inside the house. "How primitive. One of the first things I must do is install a Fenway piano in the new house. You find them in all the best parlors."

Willa caught her breath. "That's what I was trying to remember. Fenway pianos. Sam bought a Fenway for the theater last Christmas."

"Yes, that's my husband's company. And it's expanding ever so fast. Success breeds success, don't you agree?"

Madeline looked dazed. As Charles took the blue-covered document from her, she said, "God, what is happening?"

"Why, it couldn't be simpler, dear," Ashton trilled. "I have bought this entire place."

"From Cooper?" Madeline asked, disbelieving.

"Yes indeed, and you needn't sound so surprised, either. It's true that I made the purchase anonymously. I mean, I didn't appear for the closing, or at any other time, so my dear brother doesn't know that Mrs. Willard Fenway is also his not-so-loving sister. I suppose he'll be a mite exercised about the deception when he finds out. But I don't imagine he'll regret the sale. He got a fine price, and besides, I understand he's been very unhappy about your stewardship here—and your politics. You refused to behave like a respectable white woman. Instead, you flaunted your nigger school. Well, the only way Cooper could get out of his bargain with you was to sell. I'm told he also had another good reason for doing it. You helped his daughter run away and marry some carpetbagger. But then you and Orry always were a crazy, self-righteous pair. Mr. Dawkins says Charleston can't wait to see you gone. Neither can I."

In the silence, the hatred was almost palpable. Ashton swept her eyes across the exposed beams of the new house. "Willard and I have discussed a winter residence in a climate gentler than Chicago's. This should be ideal."

Willa unthinkingly dug her fingers into Charles's arm. She didn't understand all the circumstances behind the confrontation but she recognized its dire nature. There was noise from the foot of the slope leading down to the Ashley: Gus, chasing half a dozen geese kept by a freedman's wife.

Madeline took a long breath. "Ashton, I don't have any home but this one. I beg you—"

"Beg? How charming. How very quaint. It must be a new experience for you."

Rage colored Madeline's face suddenly. "You don't know what you've taken on, buying this plantation. Mont Royal isn't what it was when you lived here—a lazy, sheltered domain. It's a complex business. Part of a hard, complex world. We don't grow any more rice than we can eat. We're entirely dependent on the sawmill, and on the developers of the phosphate fields. Almost forty men live here. Free men, with families. They work so they can have homes, and schooling for their children. You don't want the responsibility for them—"

"Madeline, sweet, I've already bought Mont Royal. So all of this is just chatter."

"No. You've got to take care of those people."

"A bunch of niggers? Oh, fie," Ashton said, shrugging. "The black Republicans just stirred them up so they want what they aren't fit to have. My poor first husband James wasn't much, but he was right about the worthlessness of niggers. They'll get no special favors from me. They'll work all day for a cup and a crust or they can hike down the road and take their trashy litters of young with them."

"Ashton—*please*. Show a little humanity."

"Humanity?" she shrilled, no longer smiling. "Oh, I'm afraid not. My *humanity* went flying away the day your damn husband banished me from my birthplace. I swore I'd come back, and I have. Now it's you who's banished—and damned good riddance, too."

Silence again. Madeline stared at Charles, who raised the blue-covered eviction order, which he'd examined for the proper signatures of court officials. They were all there.

"There's no date on this," he said. "How long have we got?"

Sweet-eyed, Ashton purred, "Why, let's see. I do want to take possession before I return to Chicago, which I must do soon. My husband Willard's an older gentleman, you see. He counts on me for companionship. Of course I don't want to be uncharitable. I do consider myself a sensitive Christian person. Today is—" She sighed. "Mr. Herrington?"

"It's Friday, Mrs. Fenway. All day. Yes, ma'am."

"Then shall we say this same hour next Friday? I'll expect you and all your, ah, boarders to be packed for departure at that time, Madeline. 'Less, of course, you choose to stay and work for me like any other nigger."

Madeline's head tilted down fiercely. Charles stepped over to restrain her. Ashton's flawless smile stunned him again. He wondered why evil left some of its best disciples so unmarked.

"Friday," Ashton said.

In the act of returning to the barouche, she noticed Gus, who had come loping up the lawn, curious about the visitors. The boy stood beside a great live oak whose shadow darkened his scarred cheek.

"My, what an ugly little boy. Yours, Cousin Charles?"

She didn't wait for an answer.

Madeline gazed at the unfinished house. Tears of defeat welled and glistened in her eyes. "Orry, I'm sorry. I'm so sorry that I've destroyed everything."

She stood there quite a long time, lost in pain and self-recrimination. Charles spoke her name. She didn't seem to hear. He spoke again. Again there was no response. He raised his voice, and that way managed to penetrate her tearful state of shock.

When she heard what he proposed, she asked why. "We don't even know where he is. If we did, how could he help us? The documents look completely legal. The sale can't be undone."

Harshly, he said, "Madeline, I don't think you understand. You are going to be turned out one week from today. How much money do you have in your bank account?"

"Only a few dollars. I've had to pay the builders and Mr. Lee, the architect, a sizable monthly draw. It's taken almost all my income—"

"And there'll be no more now that Ashton holds title to the plantation. I'm going to send the message. To ask for a place where you can stay till you recover from this. I've no place to offer you. Cooper's house is closed to you—"

"My God, do you think I'd ask him for anything, after what he's done to us?"

"Granted, granted. All I'm saying is, at a time like this you've no choice but to call on friends."

"Charles, I won't beg!"

"Yes, that's exactly what we must do. I have a feeling that if you'd done it long ago, things might be different. Now there's no other choice."

She thought his idea was too humiliating to be borne. But she was emotionally drained, and she didn't argue any further. An hour later Grant rode out on a mule, leaving a dust trail. In his ragged pants he carried money and the draft of a telegraph message addressed to George Hazard in Lehigh Station, Pennsylvania.

67

There came a day when everything was different. He knew it the moment he woke.

The enormous bedroom was no different. The nymphs and cherubs frolicking on the ceiling were no different. The villa was no different, nor the morning fragrances of hot coffee, a pan of brioches baked before dawn, the fresh-cut flowers in the hallway vases. What was different was George himself. He didn't feel good, exactly. Physically, he was about the same: the usual touch of morning stomach from the red wine he loved and refused to give up. No, it was a subtler thing, but nevertheless quite real. He felt healed.

Lying there, he remembered a time of annoying discomfort before the war. Six or seven months of aggravation he thought would last forever. He'd broken a tooth, later extracted. Before the extraction, the tooth sat in his lower jaw like a forbidden love, one particular edge constantly tempting his tongue. He couldn't keep his tongue from that edge, so his tongue always hurt, and occasionally bled. Constance repeatedly urged him to have the tooth taken out. He was busy, or simply bull-headed, and didn't. His tongue hurt on the Fourth of July, and it still hurt on Christmas Day. That day, his disgust got the better of habit. He paid attention to keeping his tongue away from the tooth until he had it taken out in the first week of the new year. Then one morning in the winter—it was around the time Lincoln was attempting to reprovision Fort Sumter, where Billy was besieged as part of Bob Anderson's small engineer garrison—he woke up and everything was different. A healing lump remained on his tongue, but it didn't hurt any longer.

He tugged the bell rope and remained in bed until his valet

knocked and entered with the silver coffee service and a brioche. He felt relaxed, comfortable, and full of memories of his two children, whom he hadn't seen since the preceding summer. Painted on the canvas of his imagination there appeared a great sweep of mountains above Lehigh Station, where the laurel bloomed. He longed to walk those green heights again. To survey the town, Belvedere, and Hazard's: the proud sum of what he had made of his life.

A pang of guilt troubled him. He didn't want to be too carefree, and thereby disloyal to the memory of Constance, and the ghastly death she'd suffered because of him. The telegraph message about Bent's execution, forwarded in a pouch by Wotherspoon, didn't relieve him of his obligation to mourn her. Still, this morning there was—well, a shifted emphasis. He didn't want to live in isolation in Switzerland forever. That was a clear, new thought.

His valet said in elegant French, "Mr. Hazard, I remind you that the gentleman who sent his card last week arrives this morning. Ten o'clock."

"Thank you," George said. The black coffee in the bone china cup tasted fine; the cook made it strong. He was curious about the man who'd sent his card, a journalist from Paris whom he'd never met. What did the man want? He found himself looking forward to finding out.

He climbed from bed and padded barefoot to the small writing desk. He let down the front. There, pigeonholed, lay the flimsy yellow sheet carrying Charles's message sent from Leavenworth. He knew the text by heart. It had gratified him when he first read it; even inspired a certain vicious thrill as he imagined Bent's last hours. He was past that now. He walked to the small hearth of green marble where his valet always laid a fire on cool mornings like this. He dropped the yellow flimsy into the flames.

Everything was different.

His visitor, a man of about sixty, made a poor first impression because of his untidiness. Dried mud covered his cavalry boots. He wore a military overcoat with a high collar from which the identifying insignia had been torn off. He'd cut the fingers out of both his mittens. His hair was long, hiding his ears and tangling into a chest-length beard. He had a portmanteau full of books and sheets of paper covered with notes written horizontally, vertically, obliquely, and continuously along the edges. The man's card had previously introduced him as M. Marcel Levie, Paris, political correspondent for *La Liberté*.

George quickly saw that his guest was neither crazy nor as careless as he looked. His appearance was a pose, probably to give him an aura of liberated intelligence. He was quick to respond when George asked about refreshment. Although it was only five past ten, Levie said he would have a cognac.

They sat on the sunny terrace above the lake in the blue softness of the morning. George sipped his second and last coffee. M. Levie said, "It came to the attention of our group in Paris that the wealthy American steelmaker Georges Hazard was on holiday in Switzerland."

"Not exactly a holiday," George said, explaining no further.

"I was delegated to approach you and, if possible, develop your enthusiasm for a scheme."

"Monsieur Levie, I am not actively managing my company right now. Therefore I'm not in a position to make business investments. I'm sorry you made the trip for nothing."

"Oh, but I didn't. This has nothing to do with business except in the broadest sense. I am here at the behest of our chairman, Professor Edouard-René Lefebvre de Laboulaye." George frowned, prompting the journalist to repeat the name. It teased George with a sense of familiarity, but he didn't know where he'd heard it before.

"Among his many accomplishments, the professor chaired the French Anti-Slave Society for many years. He is a great admirer of American liberty. On the night a few years ago when he conceived the scheme at his home in Glatingy, I recall his zestful conversation, his enthusiasm, because we had just been informed that Lee was defeated."

"Fine," George said. "Please go on."

"My friend the professor believes, as I do, that America and France are sisters in freedom. General Lafayette helped win your independence. Now America stands as an important beacon of liberty and human rights at a time when"—Levie squinted along the terrace like a conspirator—"France is grievously troubled."

At last George had a political orientation. His visitor was a liberal, and probably not a partisan of Emperor Napoleon III.

Levie rushed on. "What my friend proposes, and our group seconds, is a symbolic gift to your country. A monument or statue of some kind, representing mutual friendship and faith in freedom."

"Ah," George said. "Who would finance such a gift?"

"The French people. Through a public subscription, perhaps. The details are hazy as yet. But our goal is clear. We want to complete and present the monument in time for your country's one hundredth anniversary. Several years away, I grant you, but a project of this magnitude will not be brought to completion quickly."

"Are you talking about some kind of statue for a park, Monsieur Levie?"

"Oh, grander, much grander. On the night the idea was conceived, a young sculptor was present for another purpose entirely. An Alsatian. Bartholdi. Talented fellow. The conception of the monument will be his."

"Then what do you want from me?"

"The same things we request from any important American we hear of and contact on the Continent. An endorsement of the idea. A pledge of future support."

George was in such a fine mood because of the direction the new day had taken that he said, "I should think I could give you that without qualification."

"Splendid! That would be a noteworthy coup for us. What we are also trying to gauge, less successfully, is whether such a gift would be welcomed by the American government and the American people."

George lit a cigar and strolled to the balustrade. "You're very shrewd to ask the question, Monsieur Levie. Right off, you would expect that it would be welcome, but Americans can be a contrary lot. I receive newspapers from home regularly. What I glean from them is this. All that's foreign is suspect." He rolled the cigar between his fingers, thoughtful. "That would be especially true of a gift proposed by a country torn by strife between the right and the left, and ready to plunge into war with Prussia." He took a puff. "Such is my guess, anyway."

Downcast, the journalist said, "It confirms what Edouard has been told by members of the Philadelphia Union League."

George pointed with the cigar. "That's where I've heard his name. He's on our roster."

"That is so, although he has never been privileged to visit your country."

They discussed the European political climate for a while. Levie was vituperative about the Prussian premier, Otto von Bismarck, and his chief of the general staff, Moltke. "They are clearly bent on exacerbating tensions to the point of war. Bismarck dreams of reunification of the Germanic states—a new empire, if you will. Unfortunately our own so-called emperor is lulled by his conceits. He thinks he has built an invincible army. He has not. Further, Moltke has powerful breech-loading field guns, a superb spy system, and Bismarck to goad him. It will come out badly for France. I hope it will not come out badly for our scheme too."

"I'm familiar with General von Moltke," George said. "Two of his staff officers called here last month. They want to negotiate with my company for certain ordnance castings. Back in Pennsylvania, my general manager is working up figures. I've reached no decision on it yet."

Levie became less friendly. "You are saying the possibility exists that you might work for France on the one hand and against her on the other?"

"Unfortunately that's the iron trade, Monsieur Levie. Men in my profession are inevitably represented on both sides of battles."

Levie's hostility moderated. He squinted at his host. "You are forthright, anyway."

"And I'll say just as forthrightly that I'll do everything I can to support and promote your scheme if it develops along the lines you suggest. You can consider me one of your group, if you wish."

It was said before he quite knew he was going to. A gull swooped by and dove down toward the lake. A steamer whistle hooted. The sensations delighted his eye and heart. Everything was different.

After a moment, the journalist said, "Most certainly. You can be an important conduit for estimates of American reaction and opinion. Professor Laboulaye will be overjoyed."

He didn't say he was overjoyed, but they shook hands nonetheless. That evening, over a light supper at home of veal medallions and new beans—no pastries or heavy wines at night; his weight was becoming a visible problem, especially at the waist— George realized he had a new cause. Something not connected with the past, but instead, something that looked forward to the great celebration planned for 1876.

He finished his meal quickly, called his staff together, and announced that he was going home.

George sent a message to Jupiter Smith by the transatlantic cable and sailed from Liverpool on the Cunarder *Persia*. She was larger and more lavish than Mr. Cunard's earlier oceangoing vessels, whose austere cabins had earned the scorn of Charles Dickens. *Persia* advertised "Oriental luxury" and promised a quick ten-day crossing by means of her great forty-foot side paddles, assisted by sails when necessary.

The first night out, George drank too much champagne, waltzed with a young Polish countess, and surprised himself by spending the night with her. She was a charming, ardent companion, interested in the moment, not the future. He was pleased to discover his manhood had not atrophied. Yet the very detachment with which the young woman welcomed him to her stateroom and her bed only renewed his sense of love for Constance, and the attendant loss.

His mood was imperiled even more on the third day, when the huge steamship encountered heavy weather and began to roll and pitch like a toy. Though warned by the purser's men to stay off the decks, George wouldn't. He was drawn to the vistas of impenetrable gray murk with great fans of white water rising up to smash the funnels and sway the lifeboats and swirl around his feet as he gripped the teak rail. It was noon, and nearly as dark as night. Images of Constance, Orry, Bent flickered in his thoughts. The past ten years seemed to trail across his memory like a ribbon of mourning crepe. He lost the feeling of renewal from Lausanne and plunged backward again.

Something in him rebelled, and he sought to escape the bleakness by discovering its cause, by answering, if he could, certain questions that haunted him. Why was there so much pan? Where did it come from? The answers always eluded him.

In the storm's murk, he glimpsed Constance again. He saw his best friend Orry. A set of conclusions came neatly out of the box of his mind.

The pain comes from more than the facts of circumstance, or the deeds of others. It comes from within. From understanding what we've lost.

It comes from knowing how foolish we were—vain, arrogant children—when we thought ourselves happy.

It comes from knowing how fragile and doomed the old ways were, just when we thought them, and ourselves, secure.

The pain comes from knowing we have never been safe, and therefore will never be safe again. It comes from knowing we can never be so ignorant again. It comes from knowing we can never be children again.

Losing innocence. Remembering heaven.

That was the essence of hell.

The liner's whistle bellowed. Members of the deck staff rushed in every direction. George felt the engines reverse. A white-coated steward told him two small children of an Italian olive oil millionaire had been washed into the sea from the stern. A search was conducted until dark, with great difficulty; two of the ship's boats capsized. The children were not found. Sometime during the night, curiously awake and tense beside the sleeping countess, George heard the engines throbbing differently. *Persia* was resuming her journey because there was nothing else to do.

68

On Sunday, at his home in Lehigh Station, Jupiter Smith received Charles's telegraph message. He told his wife to keep supper warm and walked rapidly down the hill to the depot. The operator was just lowering the shutter behind the wicket. "Send this before you go, Hiram," Smith said as he reached for a blank. He penciled quickly, in block letters.

MR HAZARD EN ROUTE HOME ON CUNARD LINE.

IMPOSSIBLE TO REACH HIM BUT AM CERTAIN

HE WILL GLADLY WELCOME

MRS MAIN FOR AN INDEFINITE STAY.

REGRET CIRCUMSTANCES WHICH MAKE THIS NECESSARY.

J. SMITH ESQ.

Charles's message had conveyed the essence of the situation at Mont Royal. How Madeline Main's sister-in-law could be so harsh on a relative escaped Jupe Smith. He'd never met Ashton Main, though Constance had mentioned her several times, never in a complimentary way.

Hiram's key began to click. Smith stood silent in the dusty waiting room, feeling a familiar keen disappointment in the behavior of a majority of human beings Just no explaining it—

As he opened the door to leave the depot, it occurred to him that perhaps someone else in the family should be informed of the appeal, in case help and encouragement of a more personal sort were needed. Self-centered Stanley couldn't be counted on to speak compassionately for the family, but another member could, now that she was reconciled with her brother, and considerably softened.

"Hiram, before you quit, send one more, will you? This one's going to Washington."

On Sunday, in the quiet of early morning, Sam Stout unlocked his Senate office. It was a lovely summer day; the office was already warm.

At his desk Stout arranged a small stack of foolscap sheets and began to answer correspondence from his constituents, most of them dull-witted farm people he held in contempt. A couple from his old House district in Muncie had sent eight Spencerian pages describing their son's qualifications for a Military Academy appointment. Stout knew nothing about the status of appointments from his home state, but he wrote "None available" and tossed the reply in a wire basket for his clerk to expand and send.

He started to read another letter but gave up almost at once. He threw his pen on the blotter and surrendered to the misery he'd been fighting through a long, wakeful night. When he'd divorced Emily to marry Jeannie, he and the young woman had agreed Sam was too old, and too busy with his career, to start a new family. Fine. He'd trusted the little bitch to keep the bargain. Last night, after a champagne supper, she'd announced that she would deliver a child seven months from now. Stout went to a separate bedroom for the night.

Not merely his personal life, but everything seemed to be failing. While giving speeches during his last swing into Indiana, he had sensed that his audience were sick of him and Republicans like him who waved the bloody shirt. Though it was just four years since Appomattox, the public was tired of divisive politics, tired of radical social programs. There were even some indications of disenchantment with the Grant administration, which had just taken office. Grant was a popular man but pitifully innocent. Stout's more cynical acquaintances said it wouldn't be long before the President's cronies were thieving and pillaging right under his nose.

It worried Stout. He'd backed Grant, though out of expediency, not principle. Now he feared he'd bet on a losing horse.

His own shallow convictions reminded him of Virgilia Hazard's stronger and more honest ones. That in turn reminded him of the physical side of their relationship. Virgilia seemed more alluring now that his wife had revealed her deceit. Perhaps he'd been wrong to toss Virgilia aside so hastily.

He snatched a sheet of foolscap and began to write. If he could pull this off, he sensed that everything else would right itself in due course. He poured passion into the phrases, and loneliness—even a difficult admission of his mistakes in the course of their relationship. He felt as cheerful as a twenty-year-old bachelor when he posted the letter early in the afternoon.

On Monday, Virgilia pulled her gray glove over the diamond ring on her left hand and picked up her portmanteau. A hack waited outside the Thirteenth Street cottage to take her to the railway station. She glanced around to be sure everything was in order. On the writing desk she noticed the insulting letter from Sam Stout. She'd forgotten it in the excitement of receiving Smith's message and her preparation to respond to it.

Virgilia's mouth set. She put the portmanteau on a chair and worked quickly with a match and wax to reseal Stout's letter. She inked lines through her own address and wrote his above it. Then she turned the envelope over and on the blank side printed NO.

She mailed it before she caught the night express for Richmond and Charleston.

On Tuesday, Willa again offered to help with the packing. Madeline had thus far put it off, as if anticipating some miracle. There would be no miracles.

"All right, we'll pack," she said, defeated. "There isn't a lot worth taking, but if we don't move it out, she'll destroy it."

She was wrapping pages from the *Courier* around the portrait of her mother; the brittle painting was now protected by glass and a frame. She heard the sound of a carriage and went to the door. It was Theo and his wife. The young Northerner pressed Madeline's hand in his and said he was sorry. Marie-Louise, pink-faced and healthy in her third month of pregnancy, gave freer rein to her emotions. She cried in Madeline's arms, and uttered sobbing condemnations of her father. Madeline patted her. It seemed she was always taking care of someone. She wished someone would take care of her.

Charles came in with a wooden packing box he'd hammered together to protect the portrait. He hadn't seen Marie-Louise in years, and there was a brief period of reintroduction. Charles's manner was brusque.

"Does your father know who really bought the plantation?"

Marie-Louise nodded. "The news was all over Charleston by Saturday noon. Mama said Papa spoke of it at supper that evening."

"And what did he have to say?"

She answered reluctantly. "That—that he liked his sister about as much as he liked everyone else in the family, which—" Red-faced, she blurted the rest: "Which wasn't very much any more."

Charles chewed his cigar so hard he nearly bit it in half. "Fine, Splendid."

"Mama was so mad when she told me, she said a curse word. I've never heard her curse Papa before. She said he's making so much money at the company now, he doesn't need Mont Royal, and he hasn't any feeling for the place. That's the reason he sold it." Madeline and Charles exchanged glances she didn't see. "Mama's just miserable over the whole business. I am too. Oh, Madeline, what are you going to do?"

"Pack. Wait until Friday. Leave when Ashton arrives. What else can we do?"

Willa took Charles's hand. No one answered the question.

On Wednesday, at dusk, Willa ran in from the lawn where she'd been teaching Gus a card game. "There's a carriage in the lane. A woman I've never seen before."

"Damnation." Madeline threw an old Spode saucer into the barrel, breaking off part of the edge. "I don't need strangers coming here to peer at us and cluck over our misery."

She heard the carriage grind to a halt. A few moments later, the woman in the gray traveling dress with matching hat and gloves stepped into the doorway. Madeline's exhausted face drained of color.

"My God, Virgilia."

"Hello, Madeline." The two women stared at one another, Virgilia uncertain of her reception. Charles clumped in from the bedroom, where he'd taken down a framed lithograph of the Plain at West Point. He nearly dropped it when he saw the visitor. Of course he remembered her, principally from her visit to Mont Royal with George and others in her family.

She was a fire-spitting abolitionist in those days. She flaunted
a superior morality, and a hatred of all things Southern. He recalled Virgilia outraging her host, Tillet Main, the day James
Huntoon came to accuse her of aiding the escape of Huntoon's
slave Grady. She'd later lived with the runaway in the North.

Charles particularly recalled her proud, insulting admission
of guilt that day. He had trouble reconciling the old Virgilia with
this one. He remembered a vicious tongue; now she was soft-
spoken. He remembered a slimmer girl; now she was stout. He
remembered a careless wardrobe; now she was conservatively
fashionable, and tidy despite her long journey. He remembered
her with one chin, not two, and it was all a keen reminder of
time's passage. In her case, time had dealt kindly.

"How have you been, Charles?" she said. "The last time we
saw one another, you were a very young man."

Still bewildered, Madeline remembered her manners. "Won't
you sit down, Virgilia?"

"Yes, thank you. I'm rather tired. I sat up on the train all the
way from Washington." She removed her gloves. On the ring
finger of her left hand she wore a diamond in a white gold setting.

Madeline cleared a few stacked books from a chair and gestured the visitor to it. Charles lighted a lamp while introducing
Willa. Madeline seemed nervous, on the verge of crying. He presumed it was because Virgilia's arrival was one unexpected event
too many. Emotions were strained in the whitewashed house.
Pointless arguments had broken out several times during the past
few days.

Virgilia said, "I'd like to stay a day or two, if you'll permit
me. I'm here because George's attorney telegraphed me about
Ashton. We must find some way to undo what she's done."

Madeline knotted her apron in her red-knuckled hands. "We
have no room here, Virgilia. I'm afraid the best we can offer
would be a pallet in the home of one of the freedmen."

"Perfectly adequate," Virgilia said. She radiated a crisp cordiality, and an air of city sophistication. Charles couldn't get over
the change.

"Please don't think me rude"—Madeline cleared her throat
—"but I just don't understand."

Virgilia rescued her from the embarrassing silence. "Why I
am here after all that happened years ago? Very simple. Once I
cared nothing for my family, or my brother's feelings. Now I care

a great deal. I know George's high regard for you and Orry, and this place he enjoyed visiting so much. I had opinions that wouldn't allow me to enjoy Mont Royal. I offer no apology for them. I think they were correct, but that's past. I know George would help you financially if that would resolve matters in your favor. Since it won't, and he's still somewhere on the Atlantic, I'd like to help in some other way if I can. I've changed many of my opinions but not my opinion of Ashton. She always impressed me as a shallow, spiteful creature. Especially unkind to the black men and women her father owned."

"She hasn't changed much," Charles said. He raked a match on his boot sole and then puffed on his cigar. "I'm afraid it doesn't matter a damn what any one of us thinks. This place is hers. Come Friday, we have to get out or she'll have the law on us."

Virgilia's old militancy asserted itself. "That is a defeatist attitude."

"Well, if you've got reason for any other kind, you tell me," he snarled.

Madeline whispered, "Charles."

Virgilia's gentle gesture of dismissal said she wasn't offended. Willa said, "There's a bit of claret left. Perhaps our guest would like a glass while I fix some supper."

None of them seemed to know what to say next. The uncomfortable silence went on and on, until Charles walked out. They heard him calling to his son.

On Thursday, Virgilia asked Charles to stroll down to the river with her. It was a steamy, sunless day, a perfect reflection of their spirits. Charles didn't want to go, but Willa said he must. To what purpose, he didn't know.

The sawmill had stopped work on Tuesday. Its employees awaited the pleasure of the new owner. On the mill dock by the smooth and placid Ashley, Virgilia walked among stacks of rough-cut cypress lumber.

"Charles, I know that for many years I wasn't very popular with the Mains, and justifiably so. I hope you believe I've changed."

Hands on hips, he gazed at the river. He shrugged to say it was a possibility, but only a possibility.

"All right, then. Do you think we might form an alliance?"

He scrutinized her. "We make a pretty unlikely pair."

"Granted."

"What kind of alliance?"

"One dedicated to defeating that vile woman."

"There isn't any way."

"I refuse to believe that, Charles."

Suddenly he laughed and relaxed. "I heard a lot of stories about you years ago, Miss Hazard—"

She touched the full sleeve of his loose cotton shirt. He noticed her hand—blunt-fingered, work-roughened. "Virgilia," she said.

"Well, all right, Virgilia. I guess if you take all the spite out of those stories, what's left is true. You're about as tough as one of my cavalry sergeants." Hastily then: "I mean that as a compliment."

"Of course," she said, with a wry smile. She was pensive a few moments. "We have twenty-four hours."

"I suppose I could shoot her, but I don't want to go to prison, and it wouldn't solve anything. The plantation would just go to this piano merchant she's apparently hitched up with." He sighed. "Wish I could put the calendar back a week or so. Before the sale I might have been able to scare her off. When I was a trader in the Indian Territory, I had a partner who taught me that fear was a powerful weapon."

Virgilia's interest was piqued. "Wait. Perhaps you've hit on something. Tell me about this partner of yours."

He described Wooden Foot Jackson and some of their experiences. Then he remembered the incident involving the false travois sign, which he described.

"Wooden Foot said fear was so powerful that it would trick you into seeing what you expected, instead of what was really there. I proved it. I saw a whole village in those tracks." He shrugged again. He could draw no practical conclusion from the story.

Surprisingly, it excited Virgilia. She whirled around at the edge of the pier. "What you expect instead of what's real—I find that very provocative, Charles. Now tell me more about Ashton. Naturally you've seen her—"

He nodded. "She's older, like all of us. Still dresses like a bird of paradise. I don't know what life's like in Chicago, but she must take good care of herself. She's still a beauty. No change there, either."

He found Virgilia staring with an intensity that puzzled him. She grasped his arm. "Will you go with me to Charleston this afternoon? I must find an apothecary."

He was astonished, but too polite to question her. A half hour later, alone with Willa, he said, "My God, did she fool me. She said she was here to help us. Instead, we have to chase down an apothecary. She's probably got some female complaint. I think she's crazy as ever."

On the drive to Charleston, Virgilia explained what she wanted from the apothecary's, and why she wanted it. At first Charles was speechless. Then, slowly, his desperation turned skepticism to an almost euphoric hope. *Everything on one throw of the dice.*

"It might work," he said when she came out of the shop.

"There is a great likelihood that it will not," she said. "That's why we mustn't tell anyone ahead of time, and raise false hopes. Why are you smiling?"

"Thinking of my partner Wooden Foot. He'd like your grit."

"Thank you. Let's hope it isn't totally wasted."

She settled her skirt over her legs and clasped the reticule that held her purchase. Charles shook the reins over the mules and started the wagon toward home. He had no reason to whistle the little tune, but he did anyway.

69

The barouche raced up the lane much too fast. The top was in place to spare Ashton and Favor Herrington the dust of a swift journey from town. The two liveried black men hung on to the front seat, grinning like hunters closing on a fox. They didn't know much about what was happening at Mont Royal, but they'd quickly grasped that the white woman was haughty as a queen and tough as a general. They liked working for her.

Behind the barouche rattled a second carriage, less opulent. In this carriage rode two clerks employed by Herrington, and a jowly bailiff of the court who'd been bribed to come along.

As the barouche swayed to a standstill. Ashton felt her heartbeat quicken. She'd slept lightly, restlessly, and jumped out of bed while it was still dark to begin combing and arranging her hair. She was nervous as a virgin in the bridal bed; at least she supposed virgins felt this way. She hadn't been a virgin for so many years that it was impossible to recall.

This time Herrington had brought a big carpetbag, whose contents he fussily examined as the driver hopped down to open the door on Ashton's side. Great shinning lances of sun fell between the massive oaks at the head of the lane; the residue of a river mist was burning off. It was half past nine on what promised to be a sweltering June day.

Ashton's upper lip gleamed with perspiration. Her eyes were lively, and despite her state of nerves she could barely keep from smiling. She'd spent half an hour choosing her dress, finally selecting a three-thousand-dollar one from Worth's of Paris. It was rose pink, restrained and elegant. Her gloves and little straw hat were black. The black and rose made her powdered face starkly arresting.

Cousin Charles heard the carriages and walked around from the other side of the house in that lazy cat's way of his. He wore his old cavalry boots, a pair of white linen trousers turned yellow by time, and a shirt with the sleeves rolled above the elbows. His hair was still long as a gypsy's, and as usual he clenched a foul cigar in his teeth. Cousin Charles was no longer young, but exposure to Western weather had given his face the wrinkled toughness of someone much older. Ashton had always found him handsome. She would have found him so today if she didn't hate him worse that a snake because of his family ties.

"Good morning, dear Charles," she trilled. He leaned against one of the studs in the unfinished wall of the new house and stared. If looks were nails, she would be spiked to the barouche.

Insolent bastard, she thought. Herrington summoned his clerks from the second carriage. The bailiff belched and scratched his paunch. He strolled toward the corner of the whitewashed house next door. Charles snatched the cigar out of his mouth.

"Just a minute, you."

Favor Herrington stepped in front of him. "This gentleman can go anywhere he pleases, Mr. Main. He is an officer of the court, and he has the owner's permission. We brought him with us to forestall trouble. We realize this is not a happy day for you all."

The lawyer fairly oozed sympathy. Charles would have smashed him, but there were bigger fish to be hooked. Looking defeated, he said, "You won't need him."

"Good, very sensible," Herrington said, giving a nod to the bailiff. The paunchy man wandered out of sight, pulling at his crotch.

Ashton treated her lawyer to a brilliant smile. "Now, Favor, you know what's to be done. These two gentlemen are to visit every home on the plantation. Tell the niggers that all previous arrangements concerning their land are null and void unless they can show written proof of such arrangements, and can also read the terms aloud."

Herrington nodded crisply. To the pair of pale ciphers accompanying him he said, "Every 'cropper on this place henceforth owes a rental of twenty-five dollars per month, with two months in advance due and payable at five o'clock today. If they can't pay, they can sign one of those employment contracts I drew up. Or they can get out. I'll join you shortly. Get busy."

The clerks fetched portmanteaus from their carriage. Ashton pointed toward the road to the old slave quarters. "You'll find them scattered around down there." Charles folded his arms, high color blotching his dark cheeks.

"Now," Ashton said as the clerks hurried off, "the important business. Where might I find Madeline?"

"Around in front," Charles said with a jerk of his head.

"Thank you, you're so polite," she said with a sneer. She ought to take his sullen behavior as a tribute to her victory. Unfortunately, it just made her mad. She couldn't think when she was mad. She composed herself as best she could and swept down the side of the whitewashed house and stepped around to the lawn overlooking the river, only to be figuratively knocked flat by the sight of three women seated there, stiff as subjects in a photo gallery. One of the women was Virgilia Hazard.

"Virgilia, I'm floored. I'm positively floored."

"Hello, Ashton." Virgilia stood up. She was old, and heavy, and gray as a mouse in her drab dress. Ashton remembered Virgilia's past behavior. Her arrogant pronouncements about Southern ways and Southern people. Her lust for black men. The woman was an abomination; Ashton wanted to spit right in her face. But Mr. Herrington was standing beside her. He wouldn't approve.

"What a charming surprise," Ashton said. "Was your brother too busy to come? Did he send you down here to wring you hands in his behalf?"

The little blond tramp, Cousin Charles's companion, shot her a furious look. Madeline merely looked despondent. Virgilia said, "I regret that George is in Europe."

Ashton pursed her lips. "Oh, too bad."

"For God's sake," Madeline exclaimed, "let's load the wagon and get out of here."

"In a moment," Virgilia said. "There's something Charles and I would like to say to Ashton in private."

That startled the visitors. Down by the ruined dock, Ashton noted, Charles's ugly little boy was chasing geese again. She studied Virgilia, her expression opaque, searching for some sign of a hidden intent. She could detect none.

"I can't imagine we've anything substantial to discuss," she said. "Mont Royal's mine, and that's that."

"Yes, true enough. But we would still like to speak with you."

Ashton tilted her head and blinked prettily. "What do you think, Favor?"

"I see no purpose, but I see no harm in it."

"Well, then, all right."

"While you're busy, I'll join my clerks, if you don't mind."

"Yes, you just go right on ahead," Ashton trilled. Charles threw a swift look at Willa; he seemed to be signaling her in some conspiratorial way. Neither Ashton nor her lawyer paid attention.

Virgilia gathered her dowdy gray skirt in her left hand, which Ashton noticed for the first time. "Let's step inside. We'll only be a moment."

Ashton's sense of triumph puffed her up again. She could afford to be generous to these whipped curs. She was smiling radiantly as she stepped in front of Virgilia without apology and preceded her into the cheap little room that served as Madeline's parlor.

Everything was packed and piled near the door except for one handmade shelf holding a small stoppered apothecary's bottle of dark amber glass. Dim light fell through the curtained window in the stove alcove. Charles followed the women inside. He closed the door and leaned against it, with arms folded. His cigar had gone out but it still reeked.

Ashton's smile wavered and faded away; although there was absolutely no way these people could threaten her any longer, she was nervous. She cleared her throat and said to Virgilia, "My dear, is that an engagement ring?"

"Yes, it is."

"Very handsome. Congratulations. I should like to meet the gentleman." What her tone tried to convey was, *I should like to meet the man desperate enough to marry an ox like you.*

Virgilia seemed to catch that. "I don't really think you would. He's a colored man."

Ashton could have gone all the way through the ground to China. Even Charles looked thunderstruck. Ashton began to feel annoyed and genuinely upset by this queer confrontation in the dark bare room. "Well, that certainly is a piece of news. I wonder, could we just get on with this?"

"Immediately," Virgilia said, "Charles and I would like you to sign something, that's all."

Ashton tittered. "Sign? For mercy's sake, what are you talking about?"

Virgilia picked up the reticule lying on a crate. From it she drew a single sheet of stiff paper, folded twice. She unfolded it. "This. There's a pen in one of these boxes. It will only take a moment."

"What is it? What the hell are you talking about?" She was angry over the mummery.

"A very simple legal document," Virgilia said. "It transfers the title to Mont Royal to Hazard's of Pennsylvania, for a dollar and other considerations."

That was even more shocking than the news about Virgilia's intended. Ashton's mouth opened, and her eyes widened. She gaped at them as if they were crazy people. She abandoned all pretense of politeness:

"You Yankee bitch. You fat whore. What are you thinking? Have you drunk yourself into a state?"

"I suggest you calm down, Cousin," Charles said behind her.

"You shut your mouth, you goddamn good-for-nothing. You're both ready for the asylum. There's no consideration on God's earth that could make me sign that, and you're lint-headed fools even to think it."

"Perhaps this consideration would influence you," Virgilia said. From the shelf she took the amber bottle. She showed it, stoppered, in her open palm.

Ashton's squeal went right up the scale. "Oh, what a fool you are—an idiot! A complete ninny! I always thought you were a crazy woman, now I'm sure. Get that out of my sight, whatever it is. Charles, you open the door."

She stormed toward him, only to stop abruptly when he stayed put, arms still folded. He frightened her.

"Do you think"—Ashton's voice quavered just a little—"do you think some shabby little gift would do anything, anything at all, to influence me? Mont Royal's mine, and I'm taking it."

"Gift?" Virgilia repeated with a puzzled smile. The smile disappeared as though a curtain had come down. "For the likes of you?" Ashton felt a distinct chill. What in God's name were they up to? "Stand fast, Charles. Don't let her out."

Ashton's heaving bodice showed her agitation. She seemed to lose an inch or so of height. Her black-gloved hands fisted at her waist. "What's going on here? What is that bottle?"

Virgilia drew out the stopper. "It's something for your face, but it isn't perfume." She held out the bottle. "Oil of vitriol."

Charles said, "Sulfuric acid."

Ashton screamed.

It didn't disturb Virgilia. "Go ahead, yell. That feeble lawyer of yours has gone off to find his helpers. If he hadn't, Willa was prepared to lure him away. You'll have witnesses to support anything you say about this conversation."

Ashton held still, trembling. From the corner of her eye, she gauged the distance to Charles. A fly buzzed near Virgilia's forehead. Ashton clenched her fists and cried, *"Favor!"*

Silence. Virgilia smiled in a dreamy way. "My dear, it's no use. Even if he were standing right outside and tried to force the door, I'd still have plenty of time to splash this all over you." The smile grew broader. "You know I wouldn't hesitate. I'm a Yankee who hates you and your kind and I'm crazy to boot. So I suggest you sign. There's an old quill and some ink in that box right beside you."

"A paper like that—it's no good," Ashton raved. "I can take it to court. I can take *you* to court. I only have to say that you forced me—"

"Why, there's no duress," Charles said gently. "I'm a witness. There are two of us to testify that you signed voluntarily. Where are your witnesses to say otherwise?"

"Damn you. *Damn you!*"

"Ashton, you're wasting your energy for nothing," Virgilia said. "This paper is perfectly legal, and it will be legal after you sign it. We can hire the best lawyers in the nation to guarantee it. As many lawyers as it takes. My brother George can easily afford that, and a lot more. So be sensible. Sign."

Ashton screamed again.

Virgilia sighed. "Charles, I'm afraid we miscalculated. Her appearance isn't important to her any more."

"Her face, you mean—"

"Yes. Her face."

Virgilia held out the open amber bottle and started walking

toward Ashton. Ashton pressed her wrists to her temples and screamed for a full five seconds. Then she sagged to her knees, rooting in the box. "I'll sign. Don't hurt my face. I'll sign it. Here, I'm signing it—"

She spilled the vial of ink as she dipped the quill in. Huge black spots spread on the rose pink bodice and skirt from Worth's. Spots of ink fell like black tears on the margin of the paper she didn't bother to read. She flung it on top of a stack of books for support, then signed her name.

"There, goddamn you. There." Tears coursed down her face. Her hand was shaking visibly as she thrust the paper at Virgilia.

Virgilia took it and examined the signature. Ashton tottered to her feet, sweaty, pale, breathing noisily. She dropped the quill. It bounced off her skirt, leaving another stain. The vial of ink lay on its side on the floor, gurgling as it emptied itself into a black pool.

Virgilia nodded and raked her cheeks with her nails, screaming like a harpy. "You Yankee bitch!" Her nails drew blood. "You've destroyed me!"

"With a little well water? I hardly think so. Let her out, Charles."

He stood back and opened the door. Sunlight spilled in, lighting the pool of ink. Outside, he saw Madeline and Willa, both anxiously watching the doorway. Farther down the lawn, Gus pointed out something on the river for the paunchy bailiff.

"Goodbye, Ashton," he said.

She screamed as she ran past.

The barouche went down the lane even faster than it had come up, taking Ashton away. The clerks and Favor Herrington, Esquire, showed up an hour later. The bailiff had already taken the other carriage. The bewildered lawyer and his clerks had to walk back to Charleston.

1869

Union Pacific and Central Pacific lines meet in Utah, creating transcontinental railroad.

Samuel Clemens publishes a best-seller, *Innocents Abroad.*

Jay Gould and Jim Fisk manipulate gold market on "Black Friday"; thousands of small investors ruined.

1870

John D. Rockefeller organizes Standard Oil of Ohio.

Congress passes first Force Bill to guarantee civil rights, stop anti-Negro terrorism in the South.

Washington receives first black Senator, Hiram Revels of Mississippi, and first black Representative, Joseph Rainey of South Carolina.

1871

Professional baseball players form the National League.

Chicago fire kills 300, destroys 17,000 buildings.

Indictments returned against William "Boss" Tweed of Tammany for stealing millions from New York City.

1872

Dissident Republicans, unhappy with Grant, nominate crusading journalist Horace Greeley; Vice President Schuyler Colfax accused of accepting bribe from Union Pacific Crédit Mobilier construction company.

Congress refuses to authorize operating funds for Freedmen's Bureau; Bureau closes.

Authorities arrest Susan B. Anthony for attempting to vote; voters return Grant for second term; Greeley dies from mental strain of campaigning.

1873

Presidential proclamation authorizes Centennial Exposition for 1876.

Rumors of corruption in the Grant administration continue to circulate.

Collapse of Jay Cooke banking house touches off panic leading to three-year depression.

1874

Eads' Bridge, world's longest arch, spans the Mississippi at St. Louis.

General Custer confirms discovery of gold in the Dakota Territory.

Cartoonist Thomas Nast draws an elephant to represent Republicans.

1875

Gold prospectors illegally overrun Sioux lands in the Black Hills.

Grant's secretary, Babcock, linked to "Whiskey Ring" scheme to defraud the government of liquor taxes.

Secretary of War W.W. Belknap grants Army trading post licenses in return for cash bribes.

———

THE INTERNATIONAL CENTENNIAL EXHIBITION AT PHILADELPHIA

———

A GLIMPSE OF FAIRMOUNT PARK—THE BUILDINGS
AND THEIR SURROUNDINGS—SIXTY ACRES
ROOFED OVER—THE WORLD'S TROPHIES
AT AMERICA'S FEET—WHAT THERE IS TO SEE
AND HOW TO SEE IT.

———

To-day the grandest spectacle ever witnessed on this continent—and one unlikely to be repeated on our shores for years to come—will begin its six months' existence at Philadelphia. The Nation's hundredth year will be inseparably associated with never-to-be-forgotten memories of the choicest products of every branch of industry and useful and ornamental art. . . .

Charleston *News and Courier*
May 10, 1876

70

"Ladies and gentlemen, the President of the United States."

Rain at dawn yielded to sunlight through the clouds. Special passenger trains from downtown Philadelphia pulled into the new Pennsylvania platform one after another, disgorging crowds.

"My countrymen. It has been thought appropriate upon this Centennial occasion to bring together in Philadelphia, for popular inspection, specimens of our attainments in the industrial and fine arts. . . ."

Spectators, with umbrellas, flowed through the main gates beginning at nine. They found imposing buildings—Machinery Hall and Main Hall side by side—and, beyond, avenues and paths, fountains and monuments, beautiful and colossal. There were halls of agriculture and horticulture; a hall of the U.S. government; and another devoted solely to women's crafts and domestic activities. There were campgrounds for visiting Bedouins and for Army demonstration units. There were massive flower beds, and reflecting pools. There were statues representing Columbus, religious liberty, and Moses striking the rock for water. There were also, by design, many comfort stations, popcorn stands, and restaurants—French, German, Japanese, Tunisian, and more.

"That we may the more thoroughly appreciate the excellencies and deficiencies of our achievements, and also give emphatic expression to our earnest desire to cultivate the

friendship of our fellow-members of this great family of nations. . . ."

Four thousand people quickly filled the special stands in front of Memorial Hall, which was granite and had a great glass dome surmounted by Columbia with arms outstretched. Inside were more than thirty-two hundred paintings, more than six hundred sculptures, and, in a separate building, something completely new: an exhibit of more than twenty-eight hundred photographs.

". . . the enlightened agricultural, commercial, and manufacturing people of the world have been invited to send hither corresponding specimens of their skill. . . ."

A symphony orchestra played anthems of the sixteen nations represented. Since the host country had no official anthem, the orchestra played "Hail, Columbia."

"To this invitation they have generously responded."

At 10:30, drums and cornets announced President and Mrs. Grant and Emperor Dom Pedro II and the Empress Theresa of Brazil. No reigning monarchs had ever before visited the United States. A huge military escort of soldiers, sailors, and marines marched them to the platform.

"The beauty and utility of the contributions will this day be submitted to your inspection by the managers of this Exhibition."

The orchestra played the "Centennial Inauguration March," a new piece composed by Wagner. After a prayer, a hymn, a cantata, and presentation of the buildings, the President spoke:

"While proud of what we have done, we regret that we have not done more."

Grant finished at twelve. Accompanied by an organ, eight hundred choristers sang Handel's "Hallelujah Chorus." Bells began to peal. From a hill overlooking Fairmout Park, artillery fired a hundred-gun salute.

> *"And now, fellow-citizens, I hope a careful examination of what is about to be exhibited to you will not only inspire you with a profound respect of the skill and taste of our friends of other nations . . ."*

Marshals organized the U.S. and foreign dignitaries into a long procession. Rank on rank, the notables proceeded along the walkways to Machinery Hall.

> *". . . but also satisfy you with the attainments made by our own people during the past one hundred years."*

In the Hall, President Grant and Emperor Dom Pedro climbed the iron stairs of the dual-cylinder wonder and showpiece of the exhibition, the Centennial Engine. Twenty boilers in another building powered the fifty-six-ton flywheel and the twenty-seven-foot walking beams of the fourteen-hundred-horsepower engine. George Corliss of Providence demonstrated one of the two silver-plated cranks that would start the engine. Below, among his fellow commissioners, George Hazard gazed blankly at the mammoth machine. He could not quite believe the moment had arrived after so many months of struggle and doubt. He was gratified, exhausted, lonely in the vast crowd. Dom Pedro turned his crank. President Grant turned his. The great walking beams began to shunt up and down. A thrill of response, a wordless exclamation like a rushing wind, rose around George, and then he began to hear the other machines in the hall. Turning, cranking, thumping—all driven by the Corliss engine, by U.S. industrial might.

> *"I declare the International Exhibition now open."*

George wrote:

> *Please be my guests for a week's reunion of the Main and Hazard families at the Centennial Exhibition, Philadelphia. It will be my honor to underwrite all travel expenses, meals, incidentals and lodging commencing Saturday, July 1.*

"When I first saw Los Angeles three years ago," Billy said, "it wasn't much besides unpaved streets and some old adobe houses. Now we're tearing up the whole place and building hotels, warehouses, churches. The town's going to boom. We'll be sixty thousand instead of six thousand soon. I've banked my family's future on it."

His listener, a Unitarian minister from Boston, clutched his hat to keep the sea breeze from snatching it. The little excursion steamer was just putting out from the pier at Santa Monica, bound up the coast to Santa Barbara. It was a perfect morning, with some whitecaps showing on the Pacific.

"You are a civil engineer, you told me—"

"By training." Billy was forty-one now, and as he grew more portly, he resembled his brother George more strongly. His side-whiskers were tipped with gray. He wore an expensive suit. "I actually spend more time developing and selling building lots."

"Many customers yet?"

"No, but it's the future I'm counting on." He leaned on the rail, enthusiasm crinkling the corners of his eyes. "The transcontinental line brought seventy thousand visitors and newcomers last year. It's only the beginning. We have everything, you see. Room for new cities. Magnificent scenery. Healthful air. A temperate climate. I grew up in Pennsylvania. I dream of the snow sometimes, but I don't miss it."

Brett came along the deck, stouter now, holding their youngest, two-year-old Alfred, securely by the hand. Billy introduced Brett to the cleric, who asked, "Is this handsome lad your only child?"

She laughed. "Oh, no. We have four girls and two other boys. Our oldest son's eleven. He's taking care of the others in our cabins."

"And you're all going to Philadelphia by train?" The cleric was amazed.

"Yes," Billy said, "after we travel up the coast and show the children the sights. We'll have one of the Concord coaches all to ourselves, I expect."

"You must be very happy to be going home," the visitor said.

Billy smiled. "I'll be pleased to see my family after so many years. But California's our home."

Brett slipped her arm in his and followed his gaze back past the pier and the shore and up to the bluish mountains. The tiny steamer's whistle momentarily scattered the gulls swooping in her wake over the bright sea.

George read *Scientific American* for a while. He sat in a plush chair in the writing room of the Pennsylvania Building, which faced Fountain Avenue, one of the two main promenades crossing the exhibition grounds. The building, an outrageously ornamented Gothic cottage, was the work of young Schwarzmann, the Bavarian engineer who'd surveyed and platted the grounds and designed several of the major buildings. Since Pennsylvania was the official host, the cottage naturally emerged as the largest of the twenty-four state-sponsored buildings. Objectively, George knew it was a horror. The people of Philadelphia were terrified that it would remain in Fairmout Park permanently. Still, considered as part of the whole exhibition scheme, it was something for a citizen of Lehigh Station to be proud of, and he was.

It had been a busy year for George; a busy three or four years as far as the exhibition was concerned. He was one of the seven vice presidents of the private Centennial Commission, and a member of its Board of Finance. He'd helped raise a million dollars in state funds to underwrite the mammoth exposition. And when funding lagged, he'd spent weeks in Washington lobbying for a congressional appropriation. He'd worked hard on behalf of the Franco-American Union, too, helping to bring part of Bartholdi's planned monument to the exhibition grounds. The statue was to be erected on Bedloe's Island in New York Harbor, if it was ever finished. But as George had predicted to the journalist Levie, the mood of the times was conservative, and even an outright gift from the French was suspect.

George had lately returned from Cincinnati. There he and his friend Carl Schurz and some like-minded Republicans had succeeded in blocking the presidential nomination of Speaker of the House James G. Blaine, who was evidently involved in some insider stock trading that was connected with the Union Pacific. The last thing the Republicans needed after the scandals generated by members of Grant's administration was a tainted presidential candidate. George and his associates had gotten Governor Rutherford B. Hayes of Ohio to be the party's standard-bearer.

He was proud of the Hayes nomination, just as he was proud

of the exhibition—two hundred forty-nine large and small buildings on two hundred eighty-four acres of parkland along the Schuylkill River. He was particularly proud that so many foreign nations had decided to exhibit. It validated the country's claim to be a new industrial giant. He liked to walk the aisle of Machinery Hall where Hazard's displayed locomotive boilers, railroad track, and ornamental iron. In the artillery display outside the government building, Hazard's was represented by two of the smooth-bore coastal defense guns cast by the Rodman method during the war. Though less impressive than Friedrich Krupp's enormous thirteen-incher, dubbed "Krupp's Killing Machine," the Hazard pieces were contributions to the Union war effort in which George took pride.

The words of the *Scientific American* article blurred suddenly. Quite without wanting to, he saw the sham of all his activity. The work he did was worthwhile, he'd never for a minute deny that. But it was a substitute for home and family. He was a lonesome man, and he had been ever since Constance died. He hated the silences at Belvedere. He hated his bed on a cold January night. His children's growing up only aggravated the loneliness. He was a dervish in politics and civic work, so that he wouldn't have to stop and think about what his life had become. But he seemed to remember anyway.

He heard noise in the foyer. Today's exhibit there was yet another Liberty Bell, this one from Harrisburg, a yard high, entirely of sugar. From behind the bell, Stanley stepped into sight.

Stanley would this fall stand for reelection, unopposed, as United States representative from Lehigh Station. It would be his third term. Stanley was quite heavy now, and florid, but he carried himself with the air of power that soon mantled those who went to Washington. With him, munching popcorn from a bag bought at one of the stands on the Avenue, was his ferretlike son Laban.

George laid the tabloid paper aside and strode over to shake his brother's hand. It was half past noon on Friday, the last day of June.

"The train was late," Stanley said, offering no apology.

"They'll hold my reservation," George said, "I haven't seen you in a while, Laban. How are you?"

"Prospering," said the young lawyer with a smirk.

Stanley brushed at his side-whiskers. "Where are we taking dinner?"

"Lauber's," George said as they walked out into the crowds. Far to the left, at the end of Fountain Avenue, a whistle hooted and a train shunted by on the narrow-gauge sightseeing railroad that made a circuit of the grounds every five minutes, for five cents.

As they stepped around a couple of burly Centennial Guards who were hustling a drunk toward the gate, George surveyed the crowds with satisfaction. "We had more than thirty-five thousand paid admission yesterday." For a while, after the crush on opening day, admissions had limped along at little better than twelve thousand each day.

"It will still lose money," Stanley said.

That was true. The commissioners had lost their war with Philadelphia's preachers, who insisted that opening the exhibition on Sundays would desecrate the Sabbath. Although most Americans worked six days a week, they were unable to visit the exhibition on their day off.

"Well, we wouldn't be here at all if the House hadn't passed that million and a half in special appropriations," George said. "I'll always be grateful for your support there."

"Think nothing of it," said Congressman Hazard, who lately had begun to act like what he was, an older brother. George smiled, but Stanley didn't notice.

"When do the others pull in?" Laban asked as he tossed his empty popcorn bag on the ground.

"William and Patricia and their families are already here," George said. "They'll be joining us at the German restaurant. The next group should arrive this evening. Orry's cousin Charles, all the way from Texas."

At that same hour, a train from New York carried Colonel Charles Main, his wife, Willa, and their twelve-year-old son, Augustus, toward Philadelphia. "Colonel" was an honorary title given Charles by his neighbors when they perceived that he was growing rich and therefore becoming important.

Charles still wore his hair long, and he dressed like what he was, a prosperous rancher, in tooled boots, a creamy white hat with broad brim, and a flowing neckerchief instead of a cravat. He owned fifty-five thousand acres a half-day's ride west of Fort

Worth and was negotiating to double that. His cowboys drove a huge herd to Kansas every summer. His ranch was named Main Chance; his horse Satan was enjoying a comfortable retirement there. He also owned several large blocks of Fort Worth real estate, and the opulent Parker Opera House, which was less than a year old.

As the train chugged through the farmlands of New Jersey, Charles read a book with the aid of a pair of spectacles. His son, who still bore a long, thin scar on his right cheek, was a solemn, dark-eyed boy, already growing tall and muscular, like his father. Willa loved him like her own, something of a necessity since she'd never been able to conceive a child, much as they wanted that.

Charles laughed without humor. The book was *My Life on the Plains,* published two years ago. He hadn't had time to read it until now.

"I didn't know it was a humorous book," Willa said. Gus gazed out the sooty window at some rusty-colored cattle in a dairy shed.

"No, it isn't," Charles said. "But it's damn cleverly done. I mean, the bones are there. What's missing is the meat. The bloody meat. For instance, Custer calls one of the Cheyenne children we killed at the Washita a 'dusky little chieftain,' and 'a plucky spirit.' " He put in his leather marker and closed the book. "He's poured on flowing phrases like disinfectant. It was a massacre."

"Which doesn't seem to have harmed the book's popularity."

"Nor the General's reputation, either," Charles said with disgust.

George's son William III and his son's wife, Polly, walked up the steps of Lauber's Restaurant a moment ahead of George and Stanley. William wore good Methodist black. He was twenty-seven now, in the third year of his pastorate at a small church in the town of Xenia, Ohio. Although Constance had raised him a Roman Catholic, he'd met Polly Wharton, whose father was a Methodist bishop, when he was twenty-one, and she had single-handedly won him as a husband and a member of her denomination. She had taught school to support them while he attended a seminary.

They had no children, but Patricia and her husband and their three, all under six years old, more than made up for the lack with noise and chatter at the round restaurant table. Patricia lived in Titusville. Her husband, Fremont Nevin, edited and published the *Titusville Independent.* George liked the tall, thoughtful émigré from Texas, even though he was a Democrat. The couple's children were Constance Anne, who was the youngest, Fremont Junior, and George Hazard Nevin. Growing up among the Titusville derricks, little George Hazard was already saying he wanted to be an oil man.

"Be sure you keep track of how many times you pay fifty cents at the gate, so I can reimburse you," George said to the adults after they were seated.

"What about Grandfather Flynn, Papa?" Patricia asked him.

"I had a very gracious message from him after Filly transmitted the invitation. He's quite old now, and he didn't feel up to making the long trip from Los Angeles. He said he would be with us in spirit. I gather he still handles a few cases that interest him. A remarkable person—like his daughter," he finished with an odd little catch in his throat.

Nevin, whose nickname was Champ, lit a cigarette and said to Stanley: "We're going to whip Hayes in November, you know. Governor Tilden is a strong candidate."

"I came here to eat, not to discuss politics, if you don't mind," Stanley said with ruffled dignity. George signaled the waiter. Laban rearranged his napkin in his lap for the third time. He didn't enter into the conversation. He didn't like any of the others in the family.

"We have a one-bedroom suite reserved," said the clerk at the luxurious Continental Hotel at Chestnut and Ninth Streets. The lobby was bedlam, the noise level heightened by two gentlemen shouting about their nonexistent reservations.

The clerk raised his voice too. "Shall we put a cot in the sitting room for your servant?"

Standing behind Madeline, Jane looked aggrieved, but she was too tired to fight. It had been a long journey from Mont Royal. Madeline was dusty and cross and not inclined to show a similar restraint. "She isn't my servant, she's my friend and traveling companion. She needs a bed like mine."

"We have no other accommodations," the clerk said. Another clerk, to his left, leaped back as one of the men with no reservation took a swing at him. The second clerk yelled for help from the office.

"Then we'll sleep together," Madeline said, almost shouting to make herself heard. "Have our luggage taken upstairs."

"Bellman," the clerk said, snapping his fingers. He looked outraged.

Patricia said, "Fremont, don't play with your knackwurst." Fremont Junior speared it with his fork and flung it on the floor. Patricia smacked his knuckles.

Her husband said to George: "How many of the Mains from South Carolina will be joining us?"

George put down his stein of Centennial Bock Bier and shook his head.

"Only Orry's widow, I regret to say. Orry's niece Marie-Louise is having her second child in August. Her doctor advised her not to travel. As for her father, Orry's brother—" he drew a breath, his face grave. "After a good deal of thought, and despite the slight to his wife, who's a lovely person, I declined to send an invitation to Cooper. He made it clear long ago that he was a Main in name only. Like Ashton. I never had any intention of trying to locate her."

Judge Cork Bledsoe, three years retired from the state circuit, kept a small farm near the seacoast, ten miles south of Charleston. On a hot July morning, seven men riding single file turned into his lane to pay a call. They were not Klansmen; nothing concealed their faces. The only garments they wore in common were heavy red flannel shirts.

No one knew exactly why red had been adopted by loyal Democrats for their mounted rifle clubs; the custom had gotten started a few months ago, up around Aiken and Edgefield and Hamburg, along the Savannah River, where resistance to Republicans and blacks was perhaps the most savage in the state.

Cooper rode third in line. He'd tied a large white kerchief around his scrawny neck to sop up sweat, but it didn't help much. From his saddle scabbard jutted the polished stock of the very latest Winchester big-bore, Model 1876—the "Centennial." It fired a 350-grain bullet heavy enough to stop a stampeding buffalo. Lately Cooper had acquired a taste for firearms, something he'd never had before.

Judith objected to her husband's keeping such a weapon at Tradd Street. She also disliked his new friends, and their activities. It made no difference to him; he no longer cared what she thought. They shared the same house but he displayed little affection toward her; their communication was minimal.

He considered the work of this group and similar ones throughout the state to be crucial. Only a government of dedicated white men could redeem South Carolina and put the social order right.

A dowdy woman with gray hair and bowed shoulders watched the horsemen ride into the dooryard and arrange themselves in a semicircle in front of the house. The woman had been pruning some of her roses; there were dozens of them, pink, dusty red, peach, fuming the air with their sweetness.

The spokesman for the callers, the lawyer Favor Herrington, touched the brim of his planter's hat. "Good day, Leota."

"Good day, Favor." She acknowledged three others by name; Cooper was one. She didn't miss the rifle or shotgun each man carried on his saddle.

Herrington plucked his sticky shirt away from his chest. "Scorcher, isn't it? I wonder if I might have a word with the Judge? Tell him some of his friends from the Calhoun Saber Club are here."

Leota Bledsoe hurried into the house. Moments later, shirt cuffs rolled up and his hot-looking black wool vest hanging open, the judge shuffled out in his carpet slippers. He was a slight man with mild brown eyes. He had shares in several of the larger phosphate processing plants near the city.

"To what do I owe the pleasure of a visit by such a distinguished group from the political opposition?" he said with a certain sarcasm.

Herrington chuckled. "You know we're Democrats, Judge, but I hope you recognize that we're Straightouts, and not damn Co-operationists who want to crawl in bed with the damn Republicans."

"With those red shirts I could hardly make a mistake," the Judge said heavily. All that spring there had been a fierce struggle between those who wanted to keep the Democratic Party pure and those who wanted to strengthen it by means of a coalition

with some of the less obnoxious Republicans, such as Governor
D. H. Chamberlain. Cooper and Straightouts like him were now
resorting to some unusual methods to strengthen the party. Red-
shirt rifle clubs. Visits such as this one. Public meetings; even
some useful, if bloody, rioting. The last day or two, he'd heard,
darkies and white men from both sides of the river had been
knocking heads up in Hamburg.

"We want to discuss the nominating convention in Columbia
next month," Herrington said.

That irritated the Judge. "Blast it, boys, don't you waste my
time. Everyone knows I've voted Republican six years running."

"Yes, Judge, we know," Cooper said. "Perhaps that was in
the best interests of your business." Casually, he laid a hand on
the stock of the Centennial Winchester. "We don't believe that
it's in the best interests of the state."

"See here, I'm not going to discuss my politics with a bunch
of bullies who ride around selling their opinions with rifles."

"These rifles are for defense only," another of the Red Shirts
said.

"Defense!" The Judge snorted. "You use those guns to
frighten honest black men who only want the franchise, which is
their Constitutional right. I know what this is, it's the Mississippi
scheme. It cleaned all the Republicans and nigras out of state
office over there last year, and now you're trying the same plan
here. Well, I'm not interested."

He turned and shuffled back toward his front door.

"Judge, just a minute." Favor Herrington no longer sounded
cordial. In the rose-scented shadows, the Judge blinked at the
armed riders.

"I don't deny what you say," Herrington continued. "Yes,
we are encouraging the niggers either to change their vote or to
stay away from the polls in November. We are going to turn the
Republican majority in this state into a Democratic one. We're
going to nominate a Straightout ticket next month, starting with
General Hampton at the top, and we're going to redeem South
Carolina from the carpetbaggers and mongrel legislators who are
dragging her to shame and ruin. Now"—he swabbed his shiny
face with a blue bandanna—"to make that plan work, we must
also convert erring Republicans to Democrats once again."

"Bulldoze them, that's what you mean," the Judge snapped.
"At gunpoint."

"No, sir, Judge, nothing like that. We ask only that you do what's right for the state. We ask it politely and respectfully."

"Balderdash," the old man said.

Herrington raised his voice. "All your Republican brethren are doing it, Judge. It's a simple thing. Just change over. Cross Jordan."

"Cross Jordan, is that what you call it? I'd sooner cross the Styx into hell."

A couple of the Calhoun Saber Club members started to draw their rifles. In the house, the Judge's wife called a muffled warning. The dooryard grew very still in the heat. One of the horses dropped reeking dung. Herrington cued Cooper with a sideways glance.

Cooper tried to sound reasonable. "We are in earnest, Judge Bledsoe. You mustn't take us lightly. You have a family to think about, many grandchildren. Wouldn't you prefer respectability to ostracism? If not for yourself, then for them?"

"Up in Charleston," Herrington added, "there are a lot of hooligans roaming the streets. Sometimes decent folk aren't safe. Especially girls of a tender age. You have two such granddaughters in Charleston, don't you, sir?"

"By God, sir, are you threatening me?" the Judge cried.

"No, sir," Cooper said with a sober expression. "All we want is your pledge to cross Jordan. To support Governor Hampton when we nominate him in Columbia. To tell others of your decision."

"You boys go to hell, and take your rifles with you," Judge Cork Bledsoe said. "This isn't Mississippi."

"I'm sorry that's your decision," Favor Herrington said with cold fury. "Come on, fellows."

They rode one by one from the sweet-smelling dooryard. Judge Bledsoe stayed on the porch, glaring, until the last rider disappeared up the Charleston pike.

Herrington dropped back to walk his horse beside Cooper's. "You know the next name on the list."

"I know. I'm not going to have anything to do with it. He's my son-in-law."

"We don't expect you to take part, Cooper. You're excused from dealing with Mr. German. But we're going to call on him."

Cooper wiped his sweaty mouth with his long fingers. Softly, he said, "Do what you must."

Two nights later, unknown persons fired three rounds through the window of Bledsoe's house. At church the following Sunday, old friends in the congregation refused to speak to the Judge or his wife. On Tuesday, as their fifteen-year-old granddaughter and her governess strolled home on King Street at dusk, two young white men dashed from an alley, snatched the girl's reticule, and threatened her with knives. One slashed the sleeve of her dress before they ran off. At the end of the week Judge Cork Bledsoe announced his intention to cross Jordan.

1776
THREE MILLIONS OF COLONISTS
ON A STRIP BY THE SEA

1876
FORTY MILLIONS OF FREEMEN
RULING FROM OCEAN TO OCEAN

City of Philadelphia
Centennial poster

"We won't be needing the suite," Virgilia said. "We have a reservation elsewhere."

The clerk at the Continental, the same one who had registered Madeline and Jane, was dubious. "Whatever you say, Mrs. Brown. I hope you're certain of your accommodations. I know of nothing to be had, not even hall space, in any of the good hotels."

"We'll be fine," Virgilia said. She left the noisy lobby and got into the hack waiting at the curb. Elegantly dressed in an overcoat with velvet lapels and pearl-gray gloves, Scipio regarded his wife with mild displeasure.

"Why did you do that?"

She kissed his cheek. "Because it isn't worth the fight, darling. I want to stay where we won't be treated rudely and stared at constantly. We'll have enough of it when we're with the family." She noted his frown and squeezed his hand. "Please. You know I'll always go to the barricades if it's important. This isn't important. Let's enjoy ourselves."

"Where do you want to go now?" the driver called down. He didn't hide his unhappiness about carrying a black man and a white woman, however much he made from it.

"To the Negro district," Virgilia replied. The driver made a face and drove away.

"Bison?"

"Bunk, by God!" Charles whooped and dashed forward to his friend just coming down the marble stairs. People in the lobby stared at the lanky man in frontier costume bear-hugging the proper little fellow in a business suit. Questions and answers tumbled one over another.

"You brought Brett and the youngsters?"

"Yes. They're upstairs. Where's your wife? I'm eager to meet her."

"Conferring with the head porter about train schedules. She wants to go to New York to see an old friend."

They went to the saloon bar. Each studied the other, noting many changes. And although they spoke with enthusiasm and warmth, each felt a little shy of the other; it had been a long time since their postwar reunion at Mont Royal.

Children seemed a bridge over the years. "I'm hoping for an Academy appointment for my oldest son if my brother Stanley can stay in Congress three more terms. Isn't your boy about the same age as G. W.? They could start together, just the way we did."

Soberly, Charles said, "I'm not sure I want Gus to be a soldier."

"He wouldn't have to stay in forever. And it's always been the finest education offered in America."

Charles's eyes seemed to drift away, past the layered smoke and the gaslights, past the noisy regulars and the visitors at the long oak bar, to some distant time, some distant place beside a river in the Indian Territory.

"I'm still not sure," he said.

Willa found America's Ace of Players in a dirty Mulberry Street rooming house that was almost a tenement. She knocked twice, got no answer, opened the door, and saw him seated in a rocker, staring out a grimy rain-washed window. The view was a wall. He didn't turn when she closed the door. He must be going deaf.

The sight of the small room crowded with old trunks, piles of wardrobe items, and clipping books broke her heart. Above the door he'd hung a horseshoe. The chrysanthemum in his lapel was wilted and brown. A black cat in his lap arched and hissed at her. That made him turn.

"Willa, my child. I'd no idea you'd be here today." Her telegram had stated both the exact date and the probable hour of her arrival. "Please, come in."

When he stood, she noticed his swollen, misshapen knuckles. The contrast between his wrinkled skin and ludicrous dyed hair was sad. She hugged him lovingly. "How are you, Sam?"

"Never better. Never better! For a man sixty years old, I am fit as a young bachelor." She knew he was seventy-five. "Come sit down and let me share my exciting news. Any day now, I have it on good authority, none other than Mr. Joe Jefferson is going to ask me to step in for two weeks and play Rip Van Winkle while he enjoys a seaside holiday. The part is around here somewhere. I've been studying."

Under the rocker, next to a glass of water and a bowl of cold oats, he found an old side, from which he blew dust. Willa swallowed, congratulated him, and visited with him for the next two hours. He was dozing in the chair when she stole out. One of Trump's crippled hands rested motionless on the head of his purring cat.

Before she left the building, she located the woman who owned it and paid her fifty dollars, twice the amount she mailed from Texas every month, secretly, for Sam Trump's board and room.

On Monday, they all set out to visit the exhibition. George provided a carriage for each group, two for Billy and Brett's family, and the vehicles took them swiftly and elegantly past crowded horsecars and Pennsylvania short-line trains to the carriage park on the grounds.

They saw exhibits of Pratt and Whitney's metalworking tools, Western Electric's railway signal devices, Ebenezer Butterick's paper dress patterns, Gorham silver, Haviland and Doulton stoneware, LaFrance fire engines, Seth Thomas clocks, McKesson and Robbins medicinal roots and barks, Pfizer chemicals,

Steinway and Chickering and Knabe and Fenway pianos. They saw locomotives, underwater cable equipment, tall glass cylinders containing dirt from various counties in Iowa, giant bottles of Rhine River wine on pedestals, portable boilers, wallpaper printing presses, glass blowers, Gatling guns, Mr. Graham Bell's curious talking device called the "telephone" (George thought it impractical and silly), huge polished reflectors from the Light House Board, fifteen-inch ears of corn and seven-foot stalks of wheat, bentwood furniture, sculptures in butter, Swedish ornamental iron, Russian furs, Japanese lacquered screens, Army, Navy, and Marine uniforms of the last seventy-five years, the innovative new European school for young children called the "Kindergarten," thriving orange, palm, and lemon trees in Horticultural Hall, Tiffany's twenty-seven-diamond necklace worth more than eighty thousand dollars in gold, exhibit cases containing crackers, stuffed birds, blank books, mineral samples, carriage wheels, bolts and nuts, corsets and false teeth, a seventeen-foot-high crystal fountain hung with cut glass prisms and gas-lit for added brilliance, a plaster sculpture of George Washington, legless, perched on a life-size eagle (Madeline covered her mouth and rolled her eyes), and five thousand models of inventions from the Patent Office.

They drank soda water from stands on the avenue and coffee at the Brazilian Coffee House. Stanley liked the French food at Aux Trois Frères Provençaux because it was so expensive. Brett liked the new way all the furniture was exhibited in realistic arrangements called "room settings." Virgilia liked the Women's Pavilion, and especially the newspaper office in the center, where women at desks wrote articles and other women set type and still others printed a newspaper called the *New Century for Women;* she took two copies. The young boys liked Old Abe, the pet bald eagle of a Wisconsin Civil War regiment; Abe was a veteran of more than thirty battles, and for long periods he sat so still on his perch he looked stuffed, but once, after a lengthy wait, he spread his great wings and turned his fierce eye on the boys, who were thrilled. George liked the round four-inch bronze medal with a female figure holding a laurel wreath which Hazard's had received for its ornamental iron; the Centennial judges awarded twelve thousand such medals for outstanding exhibits. Madeline liked the Mississippi state cabin because it was decorated with Santa Cruz Railroad and the mammoth grapevine shipped all the way from California and erected on a great overhead trellis; visitors strolled beneath the living vine. Charles didn't like the display of Indian tipis, pipes, pots, costumes, and other artifacts assembled by the Smithsonian Institution, but he said nothing about his feelings, merely passed quickly through the exhibit with a grave expression. George frequently said things like, "It's the beginning of a new age," or, "And the skeptics say we have nothing worth showing to foreign powers," but everyone was so interested in what they saw, they didn't comment or even hear him most of the time.

Brett's daughters Maude and Luci could hardly be pried away from the Nevins's tiny Constance Anne. Everyone kept mixing up G. W. Hazard and George Hazard Nevin, whom his parents called G. H. Willa, who always spoiled Gus, bought him too much popcorn and he got a bellyache and had to rest an hour at a comfort station. Fremont Junior got lost for ten minutes near the Otis Brothers steam elevator exhibit in Machinery Hall. Brett's youngest girl, Melody, just three and a half, pulled tulips from a bed outside Horticultural Hall before her mother stopped her and spanked her. A couple of oafish white men accosted Virgilia and Scipio, and he started swinging. Centennial Guards swooped in and broke up the clumsy flight. They gave the mixed couple no sympathy. Stanley and Laban, though still in Philadelphia, were nowhere to be seen. Nearly every exhibit that Billy passed inspired some comment about California. Everything was better there, more healthful there, more modern there. To Virgilia, her brother sounded like an abolitionist whose new cause was mammon. Scipio quietly suggested she curb her criticism for the sake of family harmony. George offered his arm to Madeline and with great interest listened to her describe the new house and Mont Royal. He promised everyone that there would be spectacular fireworks the next evening, the fourth.

That same evening, Charles and Willa left Gus with the Billy Hazards. Virgilia and Scipio came to the hotel at half past six—no one was quite sure where they were staying, but no one pressed them—and the two couples took a cab to Maison de Paris, a well-recommended restaurant where Charles had reserved a table. He was the evening's host. Ever since 1869, he'd explained to his wife, he had felt a special indebtedness to Virgilia.

At the restaurant, the suave maître d' drew Charles aside and spoke to him. Charles explained that Scipio Brown was Virgilia's husband.

"I do not care if he is the emperor of Ethiopia," the maître d' whispered in poor English. "We do not seat persons of his color."

Charles smiled and stared at him. "Would you like to review that policy with me out on the curb?"

"Out—"

"You heard me."

"Charles, there's no need—" Virgilia began.

"Yes, there is. Well?"

Red with fury, the maître d' said, "This way."

He gave them a bad table and a surly waiter. It took them forty minutes to get their bottle of wine, an hour and a half to get their dinner; all the plates were served cold. Their laughter soon grew forced, and Virgilia looked sad and miserable under the hostile eyes of other diners in the restaurant.

1776—1876.

BETWEEN THE CENTURIES.

FAREWELLS TO THE OLD.
Greetings to the New.

MONSTER CELEBRATION
IN PHILADELPHIA.

STIRRING CEREMONIES IN
INDEPENDENCE SQUARE.
READING THE ORIGINAL DECLARATION.

ELOQUENT ORATION
BY W. M. EVARTS.

The Pyrotechnic Display in the Park
was. . .

Philadelphia Inquirer

White and red star bursts exploded over the exhibition grounds, each display producing louder cheers than the one before. The dazzling colors played over Bartholdi's huge copper forearm and hand upholding a torch. Appearing to rise from the ground, the section of the Statue of Independence, as it was called, seemed to suggest that a buried giantess was about to break through the earth's crust. A few lucky spectators watched the fireworks display from the observation platform at the base of the upraised torch.

Standing near the statue with Jane, tired from a second day of touring the halls and foreign cottages, Madeline suddenly felt someone's eyes on her. She looked up and saw it was George.

Little Alfred Hazard from California had fallen asleep in George's arm. With disarming friendliness, George gazed at Madeline over his nephew's head. There was nothing improper in his glance, and in a moment he shifted his attention to the sky. A great silvery flower of light bloomed there.

Madeline's throat was curiously dry, however. George had been looking at her differently. She was guilty, pleased, flustered, and a little frightened.

The Carolina Club occupied a large lot in undeveloped land beyond the northern limits of the city. The Chicago fire had not reached that far, but neither had the suburbs as yet. Still, there was always a lot of horse and vehicle traffic on the otherwise deserted road that ran the past the rambling four-story house. The Carolina Club was the city's largest and most fashionable brothel.

The owner called herself Mrs. Brett. On the Fourth of July she awoke at her usual hour, 4:00 P.M. Her black maid was just emptying the last spouted pitcher of gently heated goat's milk into a zinc tub in the next room. She stretched, bathed in the milk for five minutes, then rubbed herself until she was pink. She had no proof that the milk baths promoted youth. Dr. Cosmopoulos, her very prosperous customer who was a phrenologist, professor of electromagnetism, and merchant of healthful tonics, insisted they did, so the baths had become a habit.

She put on a Chinese silk robe and breakfasted on a pint of fresh oysters and coffee. To finish, she lit a small cheroot from the lacquered Oriental box. Her button collection no longer fit in the box. She kept the buttons visible in a large clear-glass apothecary's jar with a heavy stopper. She had over three hundred buttons now.

She dabbed expensive Algerian perfume on her breasts, her throat, and under her arms. Next, with the maid's help, she put on a dress of apple-red silk with a huge bustle. She slipped on ornate finger rings with red, green, and white stones, put on a heavy necklace and bracelets of paste diamonds and a huge tiara as well. At half past six she went down from her third-floor suite to relieve the energetic young Scandinavian who came on duty at 10:00 A.M. to regulate the day trade.

There was already a large crowd of gentlemen mingling with the smartly gowned girls in the four parlors. In addition to the white girls employed in the brothel, there were also a Chinese, three black wenches, and a full-blooded Cherokee Indian who was an accomplished piano player. Princess Lou was at this moment playing "The Yellow Rose of Texas" on the upright in the main parlor. It was a Fenway; she still felt a certain illogical loyalty.

She relieved Knudson, the day man, and was in her office studying his tally of receipts when a customer staggered past the half-opened door. The man lurched back and goggled at her.

"Ashton?"

"Good evening, LeGrand," she said, hiding her surprise. "Come in, won't you? Close the door."

He did; the noise level in the office dropped considerably. Villers gazed at the paintings and marbles decorating the opulent room. With an amazed shake of his head, he lurched to Ashton's private bar and sloppily poured himself a drink. "Don't spill on my carpet, it's imported from Belgium," she said. "And for your information, my name is Mrs. Brett."

"I can't believe this," Villers said, sagging into a chair beside the great teak desk. "I've never been here before. Two of the Fenway peddlers are in town, so I thought we'd go on a spree. How long have you run this place?"

Ashton's face, smoothly and carefully powdered, still showed a slight puffiness. She was forty, and had trouble controlling her weight.

"Since it opened. That was shortly after I left Will. I wasn't exactly prepared to support myself. If you're a proper Southern girl, your education consists of learning to simper and curtsy. At least that was so in my day. Consequently, when you grow up, all you know how to do is be a wife or a whore. In the case of my first husband, who was a spineless no-good, I was the former and felt like the latter. You know, LeGrand, the ladies of Charleston would lynch me for saying this, but lately I've begun to think the suffragists aren't entirely crazy. I've given a local group a very large donation two years in a row." She feigned a demure expression. "Anonymously, of course. I wouldn't want to compromise my reputation."

He laughed. "How'd you get started here?"

"With the help of a patron."

"Yes, you'd have no trouble finding a platoon of patrons. You're as handsome as ever."

"Thank you, LeGrand. How's Will?"

"Making millions, the old son of a bitch. The judges in Philadelphia gave our Ashton model one of their bronze medals. Isn't that something? Now tell me, what happened when you left? One day you're back from Carolina, and the next—whiz. Gone."

"Will and I had a major disagreement." No sense telling him more. No sense in revealing that she'd had the bad luck to be away from Château Villard the day the mail brought Favor Herrington's last bill. Will was at home, recovering from summer influenza. He opened the letter from the unfamiliar law firm and then wanted to know why she had hired an attorney when, according to what she'd told him, all she'd done in South Carolina was visit. She evaded, lied, resisted as long as she could, but he was a stubborn old devil, and success had only strengthened him. When she screamed that she'd roast in hell before she told him anything, he shrugged and said he'd telegraph Favor Herrington and demand an explanation. He would exercise his marital rights and insist that Herrington could not claim confidentiality because Ashton was spending his money. Terrified, Ashton confessed to pledging an enormous sum for Mont Royal by means of a letter of credit on their bank.

She tried to put the best possible face on what she'd done, but she knew she was failing when she saw loathing narrow his eyes and twist his normally relaxed mouth. When it was all out, when she'd admitted she'd almost taken Mont Royal away from her own family, he reminded her of his warning after she murdered the señora's brother-in-law in Santa Fe.

"I said I'd never tolerate meanness like that again. I love you, Ashton, old fool that I am. But I'll be cursed if I'll live with someone so low. I want you packed and out of here by noon tomorrow."

Villers said, "A disagreement, you say. You divorced him, did you?"

Ashton shook her head. She hated the feeling of sentimental longing this conversation was generating. It was a feeling all too familiar. "It's possible he divorced me, though. I don't know."

"He hasn't that I know of," Villers said. "Does he know where you are?"

"No, but I don't expect he cares. I'm perfectly happy," she lied. "If a woman has her health and her beauty and some regular income, what more does she need?" Why had Will been so damned *upright?* Often, in the middle of the night she desperately missed cozying up to his skinny old body under a thick comforter.

Her dark eyes widened in her powder-white face. Villers was studying her in a way she didn't like. "What is it, LeGrand?"

"Just thinking. I appreciate that you and Will must have had a good reason for the split-up. But he was your husband. Maybe he still is. He's going to be mighty sorry to hear what's become of you."

Her heartbeat quickened. "You wouldn't be a snake and tell him about me."

"You care about the old bastard's feelings?"

"Why, no, I—I just want to preserve my privacy."

"I'll preserve it." Villers eyed her. "In exchange for a little taste of the old times."

Ashton's fine bust lifted like a ship's prow heaving from the water. All outraged gentility, she said, "I own the Carolina Club. I am not one of the workers."

He unfolded himself from the chair. "All right, then I can't promise to hold my tongue."

She seized his hand and rubbed the palm with her thumb. "Of course I can always change my policy for an evening."

Villers licked his lips. "No charge?"

She wanted to hit him. She wanted to weep. She smiled, tossing her head back; her elaborately pinned dark hair shimmered.

"Why, of course not. Never a charge for a friend."

Later, while the notes of Princess Lou's "Hail, Columbia" drifted upstairs—aside from some patriotic bunting on the portico, it was the club's sole acknowledgment of Independence Day

—LeGrand Villers finished for the third time, not having roused her once.

As he rolled away, he accidentally touched the soft rounded ridge of fat that kept growing and growing above her mons, no matter how little she ate. The Fenway sales manager wasn't so rude as to say anything, but she felt his fingers hesitate before he drew them from her stomach.

Somehow that touch destroyed her. She was a strong woman, and a successful one, but there was nothing left for her except decay, the slow ruin of her beauty, death. And every once in a while she was forced to confront that.

Soon Villers was snoring. Ashton lay on her side, hands tucked under her chin, knees drawn up to her breasts, wide-eyed and wishing she were a child playing with Brett at Mont Royal once again.

On Thursday night, twenty-nine members of the Main and Hazard families gathered in the private dining room set aside for them by the hotel. At the open end of the horseshoe table, an easel displayed the architect's rendering of the white-columned facade of the new Mont Royal plantation house. Madeline described the house, then invited everyone to come visit whenever they could. She sat down to warm applause.

George rose, proper and polished. The room was quiet except for the rustle of Willa's skirts; she was holding little Alfred and gently bounding him up and down to soothe his fussiness. He began to drowse, thumb in his mouth.

George cleared his throat. Charles lit another of the cigars whose smoke hung heavy in the airless room.

"I am glad we are together on this momentous anniversary. We share so much that is important, though, unfortunately, I cannot include good Republican politics in that statement."

Everyone laughed, Champ Nevin as heartily as anyone. A cigarette balanced on the edge of his coffee cup sent off smoke in an ascending corkscrew. Two places away, Stanley coughed into his napkin, making a show of it and shooting looks at Patricia's husband. Earlier, Stanley and the young newsman had had a row over Grant's 1869 treaty of annexation of Santo Domingo, which the President's emissaries had negotiated without the knowledge or consent of Congress or the cabinet. The Senate had killed the treaty, and the whole affair had started the defection of important

Republicans such as George from the regular wing to a new reform wing of the party. Champ Nevin had nearly given Stanley a seizure when he called Grant's behavior, "criminal."

George continued: "I was trying to organize some appropriate remarks when I thought of the city of Philadelphia's Independence Day poster. Have you seen it?" Several of them nodded. "Allow me to quote from it." He consulted a note, reading the words about 1776 and 1876. He dropped the note beside his water glass.

"That is an expert summation of our country, and our own lives. Since the Mains and the Hazards were first drawn together by a friendship forged at the Military Academy, we have all changed, and so has the nation. We will never again be as we were, be what we were, except in one regard. Our affection, one family for the other, is immutable."

Never again as we were, Madeline thought. *How right he is.* Constance was gone. Cooper had not been invited, though everyone keenly regretted Judith's absence. Ashton was presumably in Chicago with her millionaire husband—no loss. Charles and Billy, whose lives had diverged on such different courses, showed no clear signs of awkwardness with one another, despite their strong ties from West Point and the war period.

Over there, bored and blank, Stanley sat beside his churlish son, no doubt puzzling as to why either of them had agreed to attend George's reunion.

And, most important, her dear Orry was gone. . . .

"That affection has carried us through a time of national crisis and testing," George said. "Through dark days of warfare and political strife, the bond has grown thin but it has never broken. It remains strong to this day.

"My mother believed the mountain laurel has a special strength that enables it to withstand the ravages of the seasons. She said only love and family could generate a similar strength in human beings, and I believe it's true. You are the proof. We have grown from two families into one, and we have survived. That strength and closeness, born of friendship and love, is one of Orry Main's great gifts to us, and the reason he is very much with us tonight. I loved my friend Orry, and I love every one of you. Thank you for coming to Philadelphia to reaffirm—to—"

He cleared his throat again, bowed his head. He quickly rubbed a finger in his right eye.

"Thank you," he said in the silence. "Goodnight."

Charles and Willa were the first to leave the dining room. Charles noticed a peculiar hush in the lobby. Guests conversed in whispers, or stood reading newspapers. He patted Gus's shoulder and strode to the desk.

The clerk put down his copy of the *Inquirer.* "What's wrong?" Charles asked.

Pale, the clerk, said, "General Custer is massacred. And all his men with him."

GREAT INDIAN BATTLE.
SANGUINARY FIGHTING IN THE
WEST.

THE GROUND PILED WITH BODIES.
Over Three Hundred Killed.

THE INDIAN MASSACRE.
Confirmation of the Sad News.
A General Indian War Expected.

LIST OF THE KILLED AND MISSING.

GEN. CUSTER HEADS THE ROLL.
His Brother Slain by His Side.

THE INDIAN WAR.
How Are the Mighty Fallen.
First Rumors All Too True.

FORTY-EIGHT HOURS' FIGHTING.
Rescue Arrives at Last.
Cause of the Catastrophe.

CUSTER UNACCOUNTABLY
PRECIPITATE.

Philadelphia Inquirer
July 6-7-8, 1876

The moon washed the roofs of Philadelphia and the face of the man at the hotel window. He wore his trousers and nothing else. It was half past one. He couldn't sleep. Because of that, neither could Willa. He heard her shifting in the bed behind him.

Musing, he said, "I'm glad Magee's coming down to the ranch to visit when he gets leave. I want to know what he thinks of the massacre."

"It's upset you, hasn't it?"

Charles nodded.

"What do you think about it?" she asked.

"It's hard to decide without all the facts. The dispatches are still pretty muddled. No two agree. I'm sorry for the men who served under Custer, and for his wife, but God help me, I don't feel sadness for him. I don't know, Willa, it's like—like watching a wheel come full circle. A lot of men said Custer took us to the Washita because his reputation had suffered as a result of his discipline and he wanted public favor again. He needed a victory. He got one, but it was dirty. He never quite canceled out the Washita, and this time it sounds like he was after another victory in hopes of doing it. There's some indication that he disobeyed orders and rushed in where he shouldn't."

He let out a long breath. "I keep thinking he was hunting the presidency, not the Sioux. I wish I could say I liked the poor son of a bitch now he's dead."

She heard the confusion in his voice, the echo of bad memories. He saw her outstretched hands glimmer in the light. "I love you, Charles Main. Come here, let me hold you."

He was halfway to the bed when Gus screamed.

Wildly, he crashed the bedroom door back, lunged across the parlor and into the smaller bedroom. Gus was fighting the sheet, rolling to and fro, crying, "Don't do that, don't do that."

"Gus, it's Pa. You're all right. You're all right!" He gathered the boy in his arms and pressed him close. He stroked his hair. It was damp from sweat.

Presently Charles sat back, and Gus stared at him with a bewildered air. The scar looked black in the moonlight. Charles silently cursed all the Bents and Custers of the world.

Gus's huge, terrified eyes focused. "Pa."

Charles's shoulders sagged. The tension left him. "Yes," he said.

Virgilia's was the only white face in the small, plain restaurant. She and Scipio and Jane had come there for a farewell breakfast. Eggs, fried fish, corn bread—all deliciously hot. The other tables held some people who evidently came from the neighborhood, and there was one waiter, the cook's son.

"I'm very glad we had this chance to meet," Virgilia said as she finished.

Jane said, "I am too. I wish my husband could have seen the exhibition." There was no self-pity in the statement, merely a solemn declaration.

"I don't know as I'd wish that," Scipio said.

"Why not?" Virgilia asked.

"I'm not so sure we have much to celebrate." He folded his supple hands together and rested them on the old tablecloth. "The war ended eleven years ago. That isn't a long time, but sometimes I think everything the war accomplished is already gone. Yesterday I saw some signs in a building downtown. Two signs, on different doors. White only. Colored only."

Jane sighed. "We don't have signs like that in South Carolina yet, but we might as well. The Klan keeps screaming 'nigger, nigger,' the white people protest the school taxes, we can't ride the public transportation again, the Hampton Red Shirts are out, the Democrats will win this fall, the last soldiers will leave—the war isn't won at all. You're right. Everything did look bright a few years ago, and now it's almost wiped away. I think we're sinking right back to 1860."

Scipio said, "I agree."

Jane covered her eyes a moment, then shook her head. "Sometimes I get so tired of struggling."

"But we mustn't give up," Virgilia said. "If we don't win in our lifetime, we'll win a hundred years from now. If I didn't believe it, I couldn't live another day."

Outside, Jane and Virgilia embraced, and Jane set off for the downtown hotel she and Madeline would be leaving today. Virgilia linked her arm with her husband's and they walked in an easy, pensive silence toward their rooms three blocks away. A baby cried in a shanty. A yellow dog with sores on his back scratched himself at the edge of a mud hole. It began to rain.

Some white boys, age ten or eleven and probably from a nearby neighborhood of immigrant Irish, skulked after them, and suddenly flung rocks and shouted, "Nigger-loving whore." Scipio ran them off with no trouble. He was startled to see his wife crying when he strode back to her.

He started to ask the reason. She shook her head, smiled at him, and took his arm again. They continued along the lane between the hovels and tilted tenements, and Virgilia thought of living near here with Grady, so many years ago. Like Jane, she was disheartened.

She tightened her hand on Scipio's arm, drawing strength from the contact. They walked on. The rain fell harder.

George had rehearsed the little speech for days. In the confusion of leave-takings at the depot, he found himself as tongue-tied as a boy. The moment he drew Madeline away from Jane, he forgot every word he'd memorized.

Color rose in his cheeks. "I hope you won't think me improper—"

"Yes, George?" She regarded him with genteel calm, waiting. He almost stammered.

"I would loathe myself if I dishonored Orry's memory in any way—"

"I'm sure you would never do that, George."

"I would like to ask—that is, would you ever consider—I mean to say—Madeline, autumn in the Lehigh Valley is a lovely time of year. Would you ever consider visiting me at Belvedere and letting me show you the, ah—" He strangled the next word like a lovesick country swain: "Foliage?"

She was touched and amused.

"Yes, I would certainly consider it. I think I would enjoy it."

He paled from relief. "Wonderful. You must bring Jane if you want a companion. Would coming this fall suit you at all?"

Her eyes warmed. "Yes, George. A visit this fall would be lovely."

71

Autumn wind swept the valley. Sunset spread orange light over the roofs of Lehigh Station, the chimneys of Hazard's, the winding river, the laurel-covered heights. Madeline's dark hair, so carefully arranged before the stroll, tossed back and forth around her shoulders.

George kept his hands in the pockets of his gray trousers. He wore a small white rose in his black lapel, in her honor. She and Jane had arrived on the train that morning.

"I'm very glad you came," he said with obvious difficulty. "I don't find it easy or pleasant to be alone all the time."

"That's exactly how I feel." She could think of nothing less inane than that. His presence, his masculinity, disturbed her in an unexpected way. She liked him and felt guilty about it.

They climbed the worn path. The laurel seethed in the wind. "I remember coming up here with Constance the night before I went to Washington at the start of the war. I thought I'd be home in ninety days." He smiled wryly. "God, we were such innocents. I had no idea what we were really embarking upon."

"No one had any idea."

"It was the most monumental experience of our lives."

"Now things seem a little ordinary by comparison, don't they?"

He avoided her eye. "Yes. They seem unfamiliar, too. Because Constance is gone. And Orry."

She nodded. "I do miss him terribly."

They climbed higher. George's face was red as a truant's when he blurted, "I'm really glad we had the reunion in July."

"Indeed. What you said at that marvelous supper was exactly right. Our families should stay close."

After a long pause:

"I would enjoy seeing your new house, Madeline."

"You're welcome at Mont Royal any time."

The wind rushed over the summits of the mountains. Lamps and gaslights shone down in the town, misty yellow, misty blue. On the western horizon, the light was dimming, as if a hidden foundry was banking its fire. Suddenly George stumbled.

"Oh, good heavens," Madeline exclaimed, clutching his shoulder while he righted himself. She was conscious of his size. He was a full head shorter, but a vigorous figure of a man—although now, again, he had the sheepish look of an adolescent.

She felt none too mature herself. Her stomach felt fluttery. She'd known this moment would come ever since she noticed him watching her in Philadelphia.

"Madeline, I'm a plain-spoken man. I have—great personal regard for you—and not merely because you're the widow of my best friend. I do not—I do not want to press you. But I very much want to ask—would you be outraged if I were to suggest that you and I—in due time, perhaps—"

He couldn't finish. She brushed a windblown strand of hair from her temple. "I would welcome what I believe you have in mind, George. So long as there is no confusion about my past. My parentage."

"None," he said, his voice very strong suddenly. "It doesn't matter a damn."

"Good."

He cleared his throat yet again, lifted himself on tiptoe, and leaned forward. He gave her cheek a chaste kiss.

She touched his arm a moment, then let her hand fall. He understood the assent, and broke out in a great smile.

In near-darkness, they climbed higher. He said he wanted to show her the crater left by the meteorite that fell in the spring of '61, like a harbinger of God's wrath. "I haven't seen it in a year or more. Nothing grows there. The earth's poisoned."

They rounded a bend in the path and saw a deep emerald bowl in the mountain. "This isn't it—" she began.

"Yes, it is," he said, his voice hushed.

"How lovely."

In the crater, on the sloping sides, the concave bottom, a

carpet of summer grass caught the wind and moved gently, gently, as the night came down.

M A D E L I N E ' S   J O U R N A L

November, 1876. Much confusion as to who has won the election, both in S.C. and in the nation. I have little head for it. The bigotry in the state revolts me, and especially when it taints someone named Main. Cooper boasted to Judith that he not only belonged to a Hampton rifle club but was one of those Democrats of extreme view who want all Negroes completely out of the political process. How different he is from the Cooper I first met. . . .

Politics not the real reason for my distraction. George is pressing his suit. Another letter today. . . .

. . . Awake most of night. I will marry him. I hope I am right. . . .

. . . G. coming south for Christmas. Some discussion in his latest letter of an engagement announcement. I do not love him; I like and admire him. I have told him that exactly. He is not put off. It may be that I can come to love him, though not in the same fierce way I loved you, my dearest. . . .

Since I will start a new life with G., and this book is meant for you, I will write only a few more thoughts.

G. and I will divide the year between Mont Royal and Pennsylvania. Inevitably, there will be difficulties. We have both pledged earnestly to work to smooth them out. . . .

George stepped away from the house and across the drive to the place where the lawn began to slope toward the Ashley. He let his gaze rise slowly up the clean white vertical of the column nearest the double doors. Two and a half stories the column soared, blending and mingling with the dazzle of the Christmas morning sky.

Inside the house, Madeline's servants laughed and chattered, preparing the midday feast. The servants were black men and women, all on a regular wage. But it was not that, or the inevitable Spanish moss, or the egret lazily ascending above the tree line that reminded George he was in a different country, so to speak. The windows reminded him: shutters back, sashes raised to let in the mild air. Back home, Belvedere would be closed up against the chill.

Madeline watched his pleased reaction, which in turn brought a smile to her face. George sighed and returned to her where she waited by the tall doors. He took her hand.

"It's a magnificent house. Orry would be proud. But it really does belong to him. I can't live in it, even for part of the year. I just wouldn't feel right."

"I'm sorry, George. I can't say I'm surprised. Well, no harm —I built it in his memory, and there's enough money to keep it in the family. Perhaps when Theo's better established, he and Marie-Louise and their children will move down. In any case, because I thought you might feel as you do, last Thursday I inspected a snug town house in Charleston. I put down a deposit to hold it until the first of the year. If it suits you, it will suit me."

"Oh, I'm confident it will suit me." He stretched to kiss her cheek. "Merry Christmas, my dear."

> *. . . I feel too guilty to write more; must end. Know that you are not forgotten, my dear one. I will love you always.*
>   *Madeline*

72

Madeline closed the journal. She found a length of white satin ribbon and tied the book like a package, finishing it with a small bow. She climbed the right side of the great double staircase that reached down from above like welcoming arms, and then climbed a smaller stair to the entrance to one of the vast spaces beneath the roof beams. She lit a lamp taken from a small tripod table and carried it into the attic. Near one of the wide brick chimneys that bracketed the ends of the house was a small red leather trunk with round brass studs and a brass key in the brass lock plate. She opened the lid. There lay eleven more ribbon-bound copybooks like the one she was carrying. She laid the new one in, regarded the books for a thoughtful moment, then closed the lid and turned the key. She left the attic, extinguished the lamp, carried the key down to her writing desk, and prepared a paper tag. She inscribed the tag in ink, to identify the key, and tied it on with good twine. Then she put the key in a small drawer of the desk, for whatever posterity there might be. It was New Year's morning, 1877.

73

"To carry the election peacefully if we can, forcibly if we must."
That was the published intent of the Mississippi, or Shotgun,
Plan originated in 1874. By forcing all white voters into the Democratic party through social pressure or threats of violence, and
by intimidating blacks to keep them from voting at all, Mississippi had been redeemed.

In 1876, South Carolina sought redemption with the same
methods.

That year, nationally, the Republicans faced a difficult election fight. Many in the party wanted to disassociate it from the
carpetbagger governments still in control in Florida, Louisiana,
and South Carolina. Bayonet rule in the South was perceived as a
failure by a majority of the American public. It had become a
huge liability.

South Carolina's carpetbag governor, Daniel Henry Chamberlain of New England, was a cold, polished man who had previously been state attorney general. Somewhat more honest than
the governor before him, he was nevertheless a Republican. So
the Hampton rifle clubs rode against him, and against his sup-
porters.

The situation in the state was explosive. In July, during the
racial rioting at Hamburg, whites executed five black captives. In
August, Calbraith Butler, Charles Main's old commander in the
Hampton Legion and a militant Straightout Democrat, led
armed men to a Republican rally for Chamberlain in Edgefield.
There he took the platform, demanded time to speak, heaped
abuse on Chamberlain and his party, and left the rally in a sham-
bles.

Violence escalated. Negro Democrats leaving a meeting in

Charleston were attacked by Negro Republicans and fought a pitched battle on King Street. Another race riot convulsed Ellenton, in Aiken County. Roving bands of blacks, disgruntled about low wages in the Combahee River rice fields, burned a mill and gin house near Beaufort and tore up track to derail a train bound for Port Royal.

Because of such incidents, extra troops were poured into South Carolina. Thousands of deputy marshals arrived to watch the polls and keep the elections honest. On October 17, in the wake of further pleas for help, President Grant sent a proclamation through General Thomas H. Ruger, ordering all South Carolina rifle clubs to disband. Most merely changed their names.

November 7. Election Day. Despite the presence of soldiers and marshals, men known to be residents of Georgia and North Carolina were seen at South Carolina polling places near the borders. Bands of horsemen galloped from hamlet to hamlet, voting in each. In notorious Edgefield County, where whites voted at the Court House, blacks with the courage to vote were sent to a tiny schoolhouse that couldn't accommodate them all before the polls closed. A few courageous blacks marched to the Court House to protest and demand their rights. Armed men organized by M. W. Gary, the district's foremost proponent of the Mississippi Plan, turned them back.

The shadow of fraud fell across the state and the country.

Disputed vote tallies in Florida, Louisiana, and South Carolina put the outcome of the presidential election in doubt. Democrat Samuel Tilden needed but one electoral vote to win. Rutherford B. Hayes needed nineteen. In the three disputed states, recounts would be necessary.

At first it seemed that South Carolina had given both parties a victory. Hayes had won his race by a narrow margin, with an equally narrow win going to Governor Hampton and his slate of Democratic legislators.

Then the recount began. South Carolina's Board of Canvassers was Republican, and these officials denied enough Democratic votes to ratify Hayes's election while overturning the victories of Hampton and his slate. Governor Chamberlain was given another term, and the Republicans a majority in the General Assembly. The Democrats shouted fraud.

Chamberlain's hold on the governorship was feeble. Late in

November, Grant ordered troops into the State House to sustain his power.

Democratic legislators arriving at the General Assembly were turned away by Republican speaker E. W. M. Mackey. The Democrats organized in Carolina Hall and elected William Wallace as their speaker.

On December 7, Governor Daniel Chamberlain was inaugurated.

On December 14, in a separate ceremony, Governor Wade Hampton was inaugurated.

Observers didn't know whether they were watching a tragedy or a comedy. There was a four-day period in which both Republican and Democratic legislators met in the General Assembly. Both speakers entertained motions and conducted debates. There were simultaneous roll calls and simultaneous votes. Neither group would recognize the presence of the other. But much like the Union and Confederate soldiers who had confronted one another in the entrenchments at Petersburg, some of the opponents grew friendly. When the Republicans neglected to pay their gas bill and the company turned off the supply to the hall, the Democrats paid what was due.

The strain of operating two legislatures in one chamber, not to speak of the confusion, proved too great. The Wallace assembly returned to Carolina Hall. Then the courts judged Hampton and the Wallace legislature to be the legal claimants, but Chamberlain refused to give up the State House. Armed troops continued to enforce his authority.

Congress created a special election commission—five senators, five representatives, five Supreme Court justices—to arbitrate the disputed national returns. On February 9, 1877, the commission endorsed the official Florida tally favoring Hayes. On February 16, the commission endorsed the Louisiana tally favoring Hayes. On February 28, it endorsed the South Carolina tally favoring Hayes.

Tilden refused to contest the decisions. Southern Democrats immediately began negotiating that a Republican administration would be sympathetic to the Southern viewpoint. In return, the Democrats supported Hayes, who was peacefully inaugurated as President of the United States on March 5.

On March 23, President Hayes invited the gubernatorial claimants Hampton and Chamberlain to Washington for separate private meetings. Hampton was persuasive when pledging to uphold black rights if troops were withdrawn. Governor Chamberlain's weak hold on the State House was broken.

On April 10, following a decision by the Hayes cabinet, the detail of Army infantrymen in the State House in Columbia stacked arms and withdrew. The last occupied state in the South was no longer occupied.

On April 11, at noon, Wade Hampton entered the governor's office.

South Carolina was redeemed.

Reconstruction was finished.

EPILOGUE:
THE PLAIN
1883

"Name's George Hazard. I'm from Pennsylvania. A little town you've never heard of—Lehigh Station."

"Orry Main. From Saint George's Parish, South Carolina."

A conversation in New York City, 1842

In front of the stone barracks, the two met for the first time. The shorter boy, the blunt-featured one, had arrived on the morning steamer; the other, not until afternoon.

The taller boy was eighteen, a year older. He had a small diagonal scar on his right cheek. The scar and his long dark hair and strong facial bones gave him the look of an Indian. He was a gentle boy no bully ever bothered.

He spoke first. "Gus Main. Texas."

The boy with the strong chin and softer cheeks shyly extended his hand. "G. W. Hazard. Los Angeles."

"I remember you from Philadelphia."

"I remember you," G. W. said. "We ate a lot of popcorn together. We watched that eagle for hours."

"Yes, what was his name?"

"Wait a minute. Abe. Old Abe."

Gus grinned. "That's right. Do all you Yankees have a fantastic memory?"

"I'm not a Yankee, I'm a Californian."

An upperclassman marched out of the barracks and began to yell at them.

Across the Plain, on the veranda of the post hotel, the two old friends sat side by side in rockers, listening to the shouts in the June twilight. *"Hats off whenever you address a superior, sir. Until you pass the entrance examination you are a disgusting object, sir. Putrefied matter, sir. Scum!"*

Colonel Charles Main of the 1,500,000-acre Main Chance Ranch lit a cigar. William Hazard, president of Sundown Sea Realty Company and Diamond Acres Estates, rested his laced hands on his paunch.

"I enjoyed Willa's performance last night."

"She's glad to get back at it for a few months."

"Mr. Booth's a personable fellow. Talented, too. It was a great treat to have supper with him. I tell you, though, I couldn't expose my legs in black tights to six hundred strangers."

Charles shrugged. "He's an actor. He couldn't build a pontoon bridge over a flooded creek at night under sniper fire."

At the far edge of the Plain, members of the new United States Military Academy class stumbled into a semblance of a formation while upperclassmen continued to shout and scream. *"You are lower than a plebe, sir! You, sir, are a thing, sir!"*

Billy's round spectacles reflected the sunset. "I do feel guilty about coming up here with G. W. You and I act like a couple of doting mamas. My boy resented it."

"So did mine. Never mind, we're old grads. We're entitled to come back. I wanted to see the place."

"How do you feel about it?"

"Not sure," Charles said. He turned his chair so he could watch the great flag float in the evening breeze. Somewhere on the Hudson, a steamer whistled. "I think this place did some unexpected things to me. It made me into a soldier when I probably wasn't cut out for it."

"You were a good one, though."

Charles didn't comment. "About this place—I feel sort of fond of it now that I'm no longer part of it."

"Except through your boy."

"Well, yes. I had some doubts about letting him enroll. It's a fine education, that's what persuaded me. He can resign after he serves his hitch."

"Certainly. There won't be any more wars to fight."

"That's what everyone says."

"Don't you wonder what will happen to our two boys, Bison?"

"Sure. But I think I know. What will happen to them are the

same things that happened to Orry and George. The same things that happened to us. Things we never expected. Things we couldn't have imagined if we tried for a week. Those are the things that always happen to people. Along with ordinary things."

"Like getting old." Billy rose, yawned. "I get so blasted tired anymore. Ready for supper?"

"Any time you are, Bunk."

Billy watched the ragged formation marching away to evening mess. "I'm proud I was here," he said, hooking his thumbs in the pockets of his gold brocade vest. "I'm glad my brother and your cousin met here. Without that, I wouldn't have Brett or my family. George wouldn't have Madeline. I wouldn't have my best friend."

So many births, Charles thought. So many deaths. So important. So inconsequential.

"Yes, I'm glad they met," he said. "I'd like to have seen them that day in 1842. I'll bet they were a pair. The ironmaster's boy and the rice planter's boy. Oh, I'd like to have seen that."

The West Point sunset gun boomed. The two friends went in to supper.

> *For his anger endureth but a moment:*
> *in his favor is life:*
> *weeping may endure for a night,*
> *but joy cometh in the morning.*
>
> Psalm 30
>
> *I form the light, and create darkness:*
> *I make peace, and create evil:*
> *I the LORD do all these things.*
>
> Isaiah 45

AFTERWORD

He had heard it said that Ned had never got over the war. . . . Plenty of men hadn't.

LARRY McMURTRY,
Lonesome Dove

With these last few paragraphs, the curtain comes down on The North and South Trilogy, a project that has occupied me for a little better than five years.

The first volume, *North and South,* dealt with the antebellum period, and endeavored to illuminate the slow, grinding buildup to conflict, as well as the complex causes of it. *Love and War* dealt with the war itself, four years that forever marked, not to say scarred, our national consciousness, and ultimately seized the imagination of the world. To this day the war exerts a magnetic appeal for millions. It was a rare, even unique combination of the old and the new; pitiless suffering and shining idealism. "War is hell," snapped Uncle Billy Sherman, amply covering the suffering. The idealistic aspect was well characterized in 1884 by Oliver Wendell Holmes. Recalling his war experiences (captain, 20th Massachusetts), he said, "Through our great good fortune, in our youth our hearts were touched with fire. It was given us to learn at the outset that life is a profound and passionate thing."

The change in our country during the four years of war was apocalyptic. As a footnote, it's interesting to me that no one thus far has identified my metaphor for this change in the text of *Love and War,* the horses. Images of horses appear constantly in the novel. The very first image after the Prologue is that of sleek black horses galloping in a sunlit pasture. The last image is that of buzzards feasting on the remains of a black horse lying beside a railroad track. It seems that authors spend time on literary devices at their peril.

In *Heaven and Hell* I shifted the focus westward because I felt the sweep of historical events demanded that. At the same time, I wanted to detail something on the full-fledged civil-rights revolution, usually called Radical Reconstruction, that was won and lost in the years immediately after the Civil War. Historians generally designate 1876 as the end of Reconstruction, coincident with "redemption"—that is, return to a Democratic, all-white state government—in South Carolina, the last of the Southern states to be "redeemed," in this case by the so-called Mississippi or Shotgun Plan. In the state where it all began, with John Calhoun propounding his nullification doctrine, it ended.

I have no quarrel with this use of 1876 as the end point. But while I was engaged in reading and research, I began to see the great wave of Radical idealism and opportunism cresting and breaking eight years earlier, dashed back by the failure of Johnson's impeachment and a general Northern rejection of the civil-rights program of the Radicals. This was reflected in the 1868 elections when, as noted in the book, Republican majorities were sharply diminished, and several supposedly enlightened states in the North refused to pass a referendum on black suffrage—something Thad Stevens and his comrades in Washington were enforcing on the South by military means.

In the 1860s we were just not ready, as a people, to practice democracy without qualification. When Andrew Johnson, during his "Swing Around the Circle," told his Cleveland audience to clean up Ohio's house before attacking the South, he was booed and jeered. Even many avowed Northern Republicans—literary men such as the Freedmen's Bureau officer John William DeForest and the journalist Whitelaw Reid—couldn't keep condescension toward "darkies" out of their prose. Their work is full of racial stereotyping. Reid wrote, "Who has not admired the deep, liquid ox-eye of the Southern negro?" and "The ivories that were displayed would have driven a dentist to distraction." Despite Lincoln, despite the Radicals, despite amendments to the Constitution, white America remained racist after the war. The body politic rejected the new social order briefly implanted by a few visionary social surgeons.

The Reconstruction story is relevant to modern America. In January of this year, while I was putting the final draft through the computer, racial violence racked Forsyth County, Georgia. Peaceful marchers were threatened by a white mob just because they were black. Sometimes the lesson that history teaches is a sad one; that we are unable to learn from our past, and must repeat it endlessly, as Santayana warned.

In writing about Reconstruction, I do not mean to ignore another group that played a pivotal role in the novel. I refer to the original inhabitants of this country, the Native American Indians. During the period covered here, they were forced out of their lands at last, and effectively robbed of any chance to participate in the political process, by means of what we now call "genocide." The Indians are not the main ethnic concern of *Heaven and Hell,* but even so, I do not mean it to seem that I have given them what amounts to a historical shrug. Theirs is a tragedy I would like to deal with more fully, in another book, at a later time.

Of course, like the two novels preceding it, this one is meant first as a story, and only second as history (though as always, I never knowingly change or falsify the record for the sake of a plot). Some of the historical aspects of the novel do need brief comment.

I found the Kuklux (that was the customary spelling) a difficult subject to write about, in this sense. Southern victims of the Klan quite rightly considered its hooded members terrifying. Yet it's hard to look at hundred-year-old photographs of bed-sheeted Klansmen, or read their florid and pretentious handbills and newspaper announcements, without smiling. This duality isn't convenient for storytelling, so I am not certain that I accurately captured Klan activities. I do want to assure readers that the bits of ritual and fragments of printed announcements found in the book were not invented by me; they are authentic. General Nathan Bedford Forrest did not start the Klan, but it's generally conceded that he was Imperial Wizard for a couple of years, until violence got out of hand and he made a public statement ordering the Klan to disband.

If, in the sections set in the South, there seems to be a certain shrillness, almost hysteria, in some characters, I hasten to note that this originated in research, not imagination. The racist statements of fictional characters such as LaMotte and Gettys are based on similar pronouncements from the press of platform. On the matter of this overreaction, I agree with the film historian and biographer Richard Schickel, and the revisionist historian Kenneth M. Stampp. Schickel, commenting on Stampp in the former's fine life of D. W. Griffith (who was the son of a Confederate

officer, a circumstance that contributed to the racist tone of Griffith's epic *The Birth of a Nation)*, says, "The alleged brutalities
suffered by the white southerners are difficult to find in any
records; compared to the lot of almost any defeated nation in
history, their 'punishment' was unprecedentedly mild." True; but
—emotionally—defeat is still defeat. A bitter cup, and, in this
case, a cup poisoned by unreasonable and long-standing fears of
those the South had enslaved. The word *hysteria* fits.

To this day, a firestorm of controversy burns around General George A. Custer. A case can be made for Custer as a fine
soldier, or at least a successful one. He had an amazing record of
wins with the Union Army. He generated tremendous loyalty
among some of his men (in others he aroused fanatic hatred, and
this was a problem in the Seventh Cavalry from the moment he
joined the regiment until he led it to disaster at the Little Big
Horn).

My interpretation of Custer is admittedly personal. I find
too many negatives. His vanity was overwhelming, and so was
that of his wife, which only fed it. He can't be excused for refusing to command black soldiers in the Ninth Calvary. His punishments were harsh, frequently illegal, and many of his adventures
in the field were reckless or personally motivated; the dash to his
wife Libbie that got him court-martialed is a good example. Most
of all, to his discredit, there is the Washita—the battle or the
massacre, depending on which source you consult. To me certain
aspects of the Washita bear an eerie similarity to Vietnam. A
frustrated Army, up against guerrilla fighters whose unconven-
tional tactics it was too cumbersome to match, moved in and
destroyed an entire village—men, women, children—the theory
being that even small boys might wield weapons against their
enemies (some evidently did).

Probably I will be suspected of romanticizing the record and
accomplishments of the soldiers of Grierson's Tenth Cavalry. I
plead not guilty. The Army offered these black troopers their first
formal opportunity to get up and out of their past lives in northeastern cities, and they took splendid advantage of it. Most military scholars agree with author George Walton, who said of the
Tenth: "The soldiers . . . developed an espirit de corps that has
seldom been equaled in the United States Army. . . . The desertion rate, always an index of morale, became the lowest in military history." White officers, initially so reluctant, eventually

commanded in the Tenth with great pride. John Pershing won his nickname, Black Jack, during such a tour of duty.

I should also note that, although there was a C Company in the Tenth Cavalry, the officers and men of C Company in the novel are fictitious. The incidents of white harassment of the new regiment by General William Hoffman and others are not.

Although trumpets and bugles are distinctly different instruments, the Army circa 1865–70 ignored that. General orders of the period refer to various daily calls as "trumpeter assemblies." But no cavalryman that I've ever heard of fingered the valves of a trumpet while galloping on horseback. In other words, in this period, trumpeters played bugles but were nevertheless called trumpeters.

As a final note, Henry Ossian Flipper demands mention. Flipper, of the West Point class of 1877, was the first black graduate of the Military Academy, the first black officer in the Tenth Cavalry, and also the first in the regular Army. He was born in slavery in Georgia in 1856, and he got through West Point despite virtual ostracism. "There was no society for me to enjoy," he wrote. "No friends, male or female, so absolute was my isolation." Yet Flipper persevered in the face of heartbreaking difficulty, and so have many black soldiers since, to their great credit.

Now for appropriate acknowledgments.

Unless otherwise noted, newspaper headlines, dispatches, and advertisements are from *The New York Times*.

"The Confederacy's purple dream," a beautiful phrase that I have incorporated in the text, comes from Samuel Eliot Morison.

An anecdote from historian Robert West Howard led to creation of the Fenway Piano Company.

Colonel John W. DeForest, mentioned above, wrote one of the major memoirs of the period at his post in South Carolina. I have made generous use of *A Union Officer in the Reconstruction* for details contained in Madeline's journal.

In making DeForest and so many other books, periodicals, and newspapers available to me, I must first thank the endlessly helpful staff of the Greenwich Public Library. For years I've been what you might call a heavy user of libraries, and I have never before seen such a splendid one in a town the size of Greenwich.

On Hilton Head Island, the local library was diligent as usual in searching out interlibrary materials; particular thanks here to Ruth Gaul and Sharon Lowery. Librarians in South Carolina are fully as enthusiastic as those in Connecticut, the difference being the poor level of financial support South Carolina libraries receive. A majority of county and state legislators seems to care more about tourism and state-supported football teams than they do about learning, and this attitude shows in the inadequacy of many local collections. The librarians, always of good cheer, make the best of a bad situation.

Robert E. Schnare of the Special Collections Division of the United States Military Academy, West Point, New York, was again helpful in providing special materials. Another important piece of research came from the Tennessee State Library.

Assistance with special research projects was provided by my good friend Ralph Dennler, my son Michael Jakes, my son-in-law Michael Montgomery, and my wife.

I also owe thanks to Bill Conti, to Al Kohn of Warner Bros. Records, and to Mrs. Auriel Sanderson, vice president of the David L. Wolper Organization.

As always, people and institutions lending a hand with preparation of the book must not be held responsible for it in any way; not for a single incident or opinion or anything else. I bear full responsibility.

Since *Heaven and Hell* closes a trilogy undertaken with a brief description and a great deal of faith, I would be remiss if I did not tender my thanks to Bill and Peter Jovanovich and all of the good people I have gotten to know during the course of the project. I think especially of Rubin Pfeffer; Willa Perlman; my magnificent editor, Julian Muller; and his efficient and cheerful right hand, Joan Judge.

Through HBJ I was first introduced to Paul Bacon, whose powerful jackets have lent strength to the books in the trilogy, and to thousands of others as well. Paul stands at the top of his profession, and because of his work on *North and South* and its sequels, we have become friends as well as collaborators on a children's book of our own. That kind of good luck is one of the joyous side benefits of publishing.

Frank R. Curtis, Esq., my able attorney and friend, remains a source of strength and wise counsel. In England, my agent, June Hall, and Ian and Marjory Chapman of Collins Publishers have been steadfast in their interest and encouragement.

Some books are easy to write, some are not. This was one of the latter, because of circumstances that had nothing to do with writing. In the midst of work on the first draft I lost my mother-in-law, Nina, to a cruel disease. She was a lovely, courageous woman, small in size but great in wisdom and spirit. She was born and lived most of her life in a conservative Illinois farm town. There she not only raised a strong family but publicly supported black's and women's rights long before either cause was fashionable. She stood by me at all times, and especially at a difficult time a few years ago when many others did not. I loved her with all my heart, and her death in October of 1986 was a grievous loss for all of us who cared for her. Against that event, both impending and actual, *Heaven and Hell* was written.

Another blow fell while the final draft was coming out of the computer. Last Friday my own mother died. It was a different sort of death, because she had been hospitalized for three years, and unaware of her surroundings for more than a third of that time. She was ninety-one, but that makes the loss no gentler.

Finally, without my wife Rachel there would be nothing, and certainly not this work. I acknowledge my debt of love; I can never repay it.

JOHN JAKES

Greenwich, Connecticut
and
Hilton Head Island, South Carolina
August 7, 1986–March 30, 1987